Copyright © 2023 Haley Rhoades
All rights reserved.

7 Deadly Sins is a work of fiction. Names, characters, and incidents are all products of the authors imagination and are used fictitiously. Any resemblance to actual events or persons, living or dead, is entirely coincidental.

Any trademarks, service marks, product names, or named features are assumed to be the property of their respective owners and are used only for reference. There is no implied endorsement.

Cover design by @Germancreative on Fiverr.

❀ Created with Vellum

DEDICATION

To my best friend, Dawn:

For over 28 years, you knew the exact moment I needed to see your face or hear your voice. You never judged my unkept hair, lack of makeup, or my wearing the same t-shirt for multiple days. You took me as I was and loved me for it. You were the greatest therapist and I'm forever thankful. I was blessed to have you in my life.

ENHANCE YOUR READING:

Enhance Your Reading
Check out the **Trivia Page** at the end of the book
before reading Chapter #1.
No Spoilers—I promise.

Look at my Pinterest Boards for my inspirations for characters,
recipes, and settings. (Link on following pages.)

Prefer your romance on the **sweeter** side?
Look for this story under my **PG-13** author name Brooklyn Bailey.
BrooklynBailey.com

UNBREAKABLE

ENVY

1

QUARTERLY TORTURE

Schuyler

Every three months, I'm forced to endure this torture. Once I check in at the reception counter, I assume an empty seat in the crowded waiting room. Amongst those waiting, I'm the outlier. Though I may not look any different, my appointment is the opposite of all the other patients waiting. Bile coats my throat, and my heart aches with jealousy.

I grind my teeth as I fight back tears. My blood pulses loudly in my ears. I attempt to breathe through my nose, hoping to keep my pain from showing, from spilling out for all to see. I won't rain on their parade and dampen their excitement. I might hate them for having what I cannot, but I'm not evil. I'll keep a tight lid on my pain.

I try to focus on reading my current book on my Kindle app, but my eyes can't help but wander. They want to witness what my heart longs desperately for. Directly across from me, an excited young couple with a toddler coo into a baby carrier while they wait for their six-week checkup. On the beige wall behind them hangs a picture, stretched on canvas, of a newborn in a pink knitted diaper cover. There is a pink bow in her hair, and she's napping on a furry, white blanket. Even in all my emotional pain, I must admit it's a precious portrait.

On my right, a twenty-something woman caresses her large baby bump while smiling at the infant and mother next to her. She's clearly near the end of her pregnancy. To my left, another woman, who appears to be near my age, barely has a pregnancy bump. An older woman sits with her, perhaps her mother. Both talk animatedly with smiles upon their faces. I can't help but overhear their plans to shop for the baby's bed after this appointment.

Everywhere I glance, excited families and pregnant women look forward to their appointments today. Every wall displays newborns in delicate poses. On tables and between sets of chairs, are expecting mother and parenting magazines. Clear, plastic stands hold pamphlets on infant formula while scattered about the room are business cards for pregnancy massages and photographers.

In the far corner of the room, a small bin of toys is available for waiting children. One child carries toy after toy over for his parents to see. They remind him he gets to see the baby at today's visit, but that seems of little interest to him. I avert my eyes downward to control my rising emotions, only to find two discarded Cheerios on the carpet. Everywhere I look, I find women and families ready to embark on a joyful journey.

I will never experience such a journey; for that, I'm jealous. This reminder, while sitting in the waiting room every three months, does nothing to quell my pain. Instead of allowing me to move on, it ensures I revisit my pain over and over.

Fifteen minutes pass before a nurse peeks through the open door, calling my name. Happy to escape the waiting room, I quickly follow her to the scale and down the hallway. She pauses near the end, turning around, her face scrunched. Her fair complexion cannot hide the rising blush in her neck and face.

"I must have walked down the wrong hall," she informs me, shrugging her shoulders. "I apologize; I started this week."

I follow her in the other direction to the correct exam room. I step up to sit on the exam table, and I cringe at the rustling white paper. While the nurse records my vitals, I note her name tag states her name is Lyndon.

"When was your last period?" she asks.

Seriously? Why not just slap me in the face? She clearly did not read my chart.

"I've had a hysterectomy," I state. It takes all my willpower not to growl at her.

Lyndon scrunches her brow as she flips through my chart. Still browsing, she asks, "Then, why are you getting a depo shot?" She stops rustling papers and looks to me for the answer.

"I still have one ovary," I explain, my eyes surveying the tile floor. "The depo helps keep the cysts from growing as they did in the past, and by keeping the ovary, I don't start menopause."

"I see." She nods, looking back at the chart. "That makes sense; I've just never seen such a case."

Rage builds inside my belly, my face burns, my ears are hot, and I'm grinding my teeth. *I will not cry; I will not cry.* I force breath through my nose, hoping to fight back the tears threatening to fall. *I just need my shot. Give me my shot so I can get out of here.*

"Are you sexually active?" the nurse asks, putting on her blue latex gloves.

How should I answer her question? I could say, "I should be; I'm 23 years old." If I say 'no,' will she pity me? I could retort, "Does my vibrator count?"

"No," I reply, and she documents my answer in the chart.

Finally, she takes the syringe in hand. That's my cue to stand and bare my hip to her.

"Left side this time," she prompts, and I comply. "You'll feel a pinch."

And just like that, we're done. With the billing sheet in hand, I walk to the desk to check out. It takes too long to make the next appointment for three months and get out of the office; I can't do it fast enough. Of course, I'm not alone in the elevator; a pregnant couple, wearing wide smiles, joins me. I don't think they realize I'm riding with them. *Will the torture ever cease?* It's a vicious cycle I'm doomed to relive on a loop for the next thirty years, like a slap in the face. *Is God punishing me? Did I do something to deserve this?* The wreck left me with scars and stole any hopes I had of starting a family.

2

A GROWN-ASS WOMAN

Schuyler

During the 10-minute drive through Des Moines back to my parents' house, I release my anger. The flood gates open; rivers of hot tears flow down my cheeks. *Why is it this way?* There should be two waiting rooms, one for obstetrics and another for gynecology. I'm only 23 years old; I'll endure this trauma four times a year for at least thirty years.

It's hard continuing my teacher education studies and planning a future that will surround me with children when I can never have my own. My heart aches when I see others living the life I want. It's inevitable—pregnant women and children are everywhere. While at the grocery store, I see mothers shopping with little ones in the cart. When I drive by parks or walking trails, families are everywhere, some with strollers, and some with children on their shoulders.

As I near my childhood home, I wipe all evidence of tears from my cheeks and take calming breaths to steady myself. In the driveway, I sit for a few minutes before exiting the car and walking to the front door. I draw in a deep breath before I open the door.

I balk when I find Dallas sitting in the living room with my mother. I quickly scan my memory to see if we had planned for her to come over this afternoon; I don't recall any plans. Dallas, my best friend, is a ball of energy, her blonde ponytail swaying as she sits on the sofa cushion. Her wide smile and bouncing knee give away her excitement about something.

"Surprise!" Dallas squeals, throwing her arms into the air above her head.

"What's going on?" I look from my friend to my mother.

"My parents are sending us to Mexico for spring break," Dallas announces, hands clapping in front of her chest.

"Wow. You're a lucky girl," I state, trying to find the energy to be excited for her.

"No, silly," Dallas corrects. "They are sending *both of us* for the week to Puerto Vallarta." Her eyes scan my face for a reaction.

"Really?" I take a seat in the swivel rocker next to the sofa.

"It's an early graduation gift for each of us. They thought we might need to relax before we finish the final weeks of the semester," Dallas continues.

I'm not surprised her parents bought such an extravagant gift for her college graduation. She's their only child, and they dote on her constantly. We became best friends in elementary school when her family moved into the house next door. Surprisingly, they're down-to-earth people. They don't flaunt their money or gifts. In fact, Dallas usually shared her gifts with me.

She pulls out her tablet and shows me photos of the resort. She points out the five swimming pools, the beach, and the inside of the bungalow they've reserved for the two of us. It's beautiful; I have no doubt we'll have a great week.

"I'm ready for a cocktail," my mother announces, rising from her chair. "Can I get you girls anything?"

After my visit to the doctor, a drink might help me relax. We join Mom at the bar in our basement. As we sit on barstools, sipping our drinks, I notice my mother eyeing me. She knows how emotional I get on my shot days. I meet her glance and share a smile with her. I don't want to discuss it but want to put her concerns at ease.

My shoulders relax, and I let out a long sigh when we successfully pass through TSA security. The weight of this hectic day escapes with my exhale. Dallas and I left campus at seven this morning. After our two-and-a-half-hour drive, we enjoyed lunch with our parents before they dropped us off at the airport. As spring break is a busy travel season even at Des Moines International Airport, it takes about an hour to check our bags, pass through security, and check in at our terminal.

Dallas scurries to what looks like the only empty seat, and I follow while scanning the area for another. With nothing available, I sit on the floor near her feet with our carry-on bags in front of us. Checking my phone, I calculate we have 30 minutes until boarding. I can sit on the floor that long.

With the phone still in hand, I see a red three alerting me I have unread text messages. I shoot a text to Mom, letting her know we successfully made it through security. Next, I read the messages from my oldest brother.

> LEVI
> Text/call if u need me
> I'd feel better if 1 of us went with u

Then, I read the text from my youngest brother.
Clint
Text me morning & night or I'll fly down
I groan audibly, drawing Dallas' attention.
"What's wrong?" she asks.
"Levi and Clint texted," I whine.
"I'm glad I don't have three big brothers. How bad is it?"
She knows very well the lengths my brothers go to in "protecting" their baby sister. I hand my phone to her, watching her face as she reads them.
"They had better not fly to Mexico," Dallas states. "No one will ruin this trip for us." She stands in front of me with her hands on her hips, one foot pointed to the side. "And you will not text Clint every morning or night. You're a grown-ass woman, and you deserve a vacation."
"This is why I love you," I say, chuckling.
Dallas is the only female friend of mine that didn't swoon at the sight of my three older brothers. Actually, at my house, she often stood up to them for me. To me, they were bulky, muscular guys that had dated half the girls in Des Moines. Our age differences led them to believe they could boss me around.
Not much has changed–all three of them have too many muscles and spend too much time working out. Levi is married, Dan is engaged, and Clint is with a different girl every week. With me at college, their bossiness has turned into overbearing protectiveness. Their roles as protective big brothers amplified after my car wreck. While I focused on my recovery, I didn't notice.
I've only dated one guy, ever. In my junior year, one of Clint's friends asked me out. My brothers only allowed it, as they knew he would try nothing, or they would kill him. We dated from my junior year of high school through my junior year of college when he broke up with me. Now that I'm away at college, they can't control who I date and what I do, so they threaten me. "Before you go out

with any guy, he has to meet us. We'll drive down." "If a guy even looks at you wrong, we'll come to handle it for you." Their domineering big brother roles know no bounds.

With only a few minutes until boarding, I quickly send them texts back. First, I reply to Levi.

> ME
>
> I'll be fine not leaving resort

Next, I text Clint.

> ME
>
> on vacation won't report to you twice a day

Shutting off my cell phone, I gather my bags as the staff announces it's time to board. I know my replies do nothing to calm my brothers' fears. I'm resigned to the fact they will text and call often this week. Maybe I'll leave my phone in the room.

When the captain turns off the fasten seatbelt sign, Dallas immediately unbuckles and turns to face me. For a moment, I worry she has another surprise for me she kept secret until we were on our way, so I wouldn't back out.

"Okay, we have two goals for this trip," she informs me while flipping her hair over her shoulder. "First and foremost is to have fun." She pauses with a wide smile.

"And the second goal?" I'm almost afraid to ask.

As the attendant approaches to take our drink orders, Dallas announces, "We're gonna get you laid." She doesn't yell, but her voice is loud enough all the surrounding seats could hear.

The attendant blushes at Dallas's words and clears her throat before asking for our drink orders. Dallas orders two vodka cranberries, then the woman moves on to the other passengers.

"Really?" I cock my head at my friend. "Any louder and even the pilots would hear you." I point my index finger towards her. "I'm not ready for sex," I whisper. "My body's still healing, and besides, emotionally, I'm not ready."

Dallas merely shakes her head at me while rolling her eyes. "You're ready, and with me as your wingman, scratch that, wing woman, it'll be easy-peasy."

"Dallas, I just want to relax and have fun this week. I don't need any pressure."

The attendant delivers our drinks and quickly darts away.

"Let's toast." She lifts her glass towards mine. "To senior year, to graduation, to best friends, and to moving on."

Her words and wicked smile inform me she isn't giving up on her second goal. This may be a long week.

3

TOO MUCH OF A COINCIDENCE

Schuyler
Exiting the backseat of the taxi, I immediately fall in love with the green vegetation, bright flowers, and the stone facade of our resort. Dallas tips the cab driver before speaking to the bellhops about our luggage. Soon enough, she joins me on the steps leading into the lobby.

As we stand in line at the front desk, I scan our surroundings. The windows have no glass to keep nature out. Grand archways lead guests to the front doorway or a walkway toward the beach and guest rooms. There are more open windows than flat wall space in the lobby. Green foliage and bright blue sky extend everywhere I look.

"Ladies, I have drinks!" A bartender extends the round tray with two glasses of slushy, red beverage topped with a lime wedge and an umbrella.

Dallas wastes no time taking the two glasses and passing one to me.

"Compliments of the men at the bar." The bartender nods in their direction.

While we turn to look, the bartender returns to his area. Dallas smiles and waves at the four men who are staring at us. She tucks a rogue strand of hair behind her ear while flirting from a distance.

I lean in close and whisper, "All drinks are free at the resort. You're flirting with cheapskates."

Dallas looks at me, sticking out her tongue. "Don't be a spoilsport. Four hot guys were thoughtful enough to send us drinks while we wait in line. Now, get with the program. You need to smile, make eye contact, and flirt all week."

I roll my eyes, and she swats my shoulder. We step forward when prompted, sign a few papers, and receive our wristbands and our keys. As I turn towards the exit, Dallas approaches the guys at the bar. I freeze in my tracks, my back toward them, squeezing my eyes shut tightly. Afraid of what she might say about me and "goal number two," I reluctantly join them.

"We're heading to the beach bar at seven," one of the sun-kissed men states. "We'd love it if you would join us, so Joe's fiancé isn't the only woman in our group."

"Where are our manners?" The guy stands. "My name is Rich, and these are my friends." He sweeps his arm wide. "Joe gets married in two days." He points to a man with raven hair, styled meticulously. "His fiancé will join us tonight at the bar. Over there is Calvin, and here we have Garret." He points to each man, his blonde hair swinging as he gestures.

I take in the group of men, relaxed in the casual seating of the lobby bar. All four guys are handsome, but not the guy-next-door good looks; they're movie-star handsome. Dallas quickly falls for their story, but I reserve my judgment. I need more information before I will trust anything they say. For all we know, these guys are here on spring break and not for a wedding.

Against my better judgment, I agree to accompany Dallas to the beach bar. Although she plans to find herself a guy, I'm just here to have fun. I pull our door shut behind me as a petite blonde exits the bungalow next to ours.

"Hi," she greets, waving at us.

I wave back, and Dallas engages. "Howdy, neighbor."

"Welcome to paradise." The blonde crosses her arms over her chest. "What do you have planned for your first night?"

"We're headed to the beach bar," Dallas shares, leaning against our door frame.

"Me, too. I'm meeting my fiancé and his friends there," she announces.

"Your fiancé's name wouldn't be Joe, would it?" I inquire. If it is, I will have to admit to Dallas that I was wrong.

"Yes! How'd you know?" The blonde moves from her door, motioning for us to walk with her.

"We met him and his friends at the lobby bar when we checked in," I admit.

"They invited us to join you tonight," Dallas adds.

"Awesome! I won't be the only girl." She claps with a wide smile. "My name is Drew."

Unbreakable

"I'm Dallas, and this is Schuyler..."

Drew interrupts Dallas's introduction. "What are we waiting for? Let's go join the guys!"

As we round the corner, the petite Drew bounds over and sits in Joe's lap. "Look who I found." She points in our direction.

"You came!" either Rich or Garret expresses his surprise while rising to stand near Dallas. I can't remember which one is which.

"Thought we'd check out the scene. We can always move on if we need to." Dallas twists a blonde strand around her finger as she looks up through her long lashes at each of them.

Leave it to Dallas to flirt while issuing a challenge. It works; all four guys seem up to her challenge of entertaining us for the evening. Dallas's words prompt the men to instantly sit up straight, smirks on their faces, and nod, accepting her challenge. Garret or Rich, I need to learn who's who, motions for me to take the empty seat between Joe and Calvin. Then he snags a nearby chair, sliding it over for Dallas to sit beside him.

"What a coincidence," Drew shares. "Their room is next to mine." Her eyes sparkle with delight as she looks excitedly around the group.

I don't know that I would call our accommodations a room. Dallas's parents spared no expense. We're staying in what the resort calls bungalows. The front doors all open to a small, round courtyard. Inside, a large, open common area boasts unobstructed views of the ocean and a bar area filled with snacks beverages. The first door in the hall leads to a large tile bathroom with a huge walk-in shower and a jacuzzi tub. The other doors lead to two separate bedrooms, complete with king-size beds and sliding glass doors with views of the beach. A small private pool lies just outside the bedrooms. *I mean, seriously, who needs a private pool in a resort with multiple pools and a large beach?*

What the heck? My hand flies to the spot on my neck where something just hit me. In my lap, I find the offensive object is a pretzel. Dallas's snickers lead me to believe she's the culprit. She raises her eyebrows and tilts her head to the right, signaling towards Calvin at my side. She will not let it go. I discreetly shake my head, hoping she will not embarrass me.

"So, Calvin, what do you do for a living?" Dallas asks, clearly attempting to start a conversation between the two of us.

"I'm finishing my MBA," he states.

"Calvin's crazy," Joe announces. "The rest of us thought four years of college were enough."

The guys all laugh and jeer at Calvin; he takes it well.

"What college?" I pry, trying to move the conversation along.

He swivels in his chair, looking in my direction. "Northwest Missouri State..."

Dallas's loud voice startles him. "No way!" All eyes move to her. "That's where we go!" She gestures between the two of us.

"Really?" Calvin asks, looking only at me.

I nod. This is too much of a coincidence. I wonder if Dallas set all of this up ahead of time. I wouldn't put it past her to have found guys on campus and arranged for them to vacation in Mexico and conveniently bump into us.

"What's your major?" Calvin asks, leaning back in his chair, eyes still on me. His gaze is intense.

"Elementary Education," I answer. "Dallas is studying Marketing."

"We're seniors," Dallas brags.

"I graduated last spring," Rich, I think, states. "I can't believe we never bumped into each other on campus."

"Calvin doesn't engage in campus life," Joe states matter-of-factly.

Calvin seems uncomfortable. From the seat next to him, I'm able to see a hint of sweat speckle his brow; he clenches his hands tight in his lap. I feel the inexplicable need to rescue him.

4

CHOOSE BRAINS OVER LOOKS

Schuyler
"I'm sorry; it's been bugging me." I interrupt their teasing and motion in Dallas's direction to the guys flanking her. "I know your names are Rich and Garret, but I don't know which of you is which."

Laughter fills the air. My diversion works. In my periphery, I notice Calvin looking down, a smirk upon his face.

The blonde stands and extends his hand to me, his blue eyes meeting mine. "I'm Rich; I'm taller and better looking than Garret."

"Dude, you're the same height," Joe jeers from across the group.

"You'll have to excuse Rich; his golden locks are an attempt to make up for his deficit in the brains department. I'm Garret." The man to Dallas's left stands, offering me his hand.

Dallas can't peel her eyes from him which leads me to believe she's choosing him over Rich. It's for the best. Two blondes would be much too perfect together.

"Rich-blonde, Garret-brains," I chant repeatedly after shaking Garret's hand.

"Hey! I'm more than just my brains," Garret protests, pouting and crossing his arms.

"I'll choose brains over looks any day," I confess.

"Then, Calvin is your man," his three friends say almost in unison.

Crud! That backfired. Now, they are picking on Calvin again. I decide if they plan to constantly tease Calvin that I'll jump on the bandwagon.

"I know some women go for the whole tall, blonde hair, blue eyes, Nordic look." I motion to Rich. "Your recessive genes are no match for my dominant ones, though," I state in jest.

"Oh, snap," Joe taunts, laughing.

"How so?" Rich counters.

"Brown eyes beat blue. Dark hair beats blonde," I explain until Dallas interrupts me.

"Schuyler would also annihilate you on the volleyball court," she brags, winking at me.

I glare at my friend. She knows my volleyball days ended with my car wreck. *Please, don't let him challenge me.* Dallas grins proudly back at me, unaffected by my glare.

"So, what are we talking about here?" Garret inquires. "High school volleyball or college?"

"College," Dallas answers on my behalf.

Why can't she keep her mouth shut? She's been with me every step of the way in my recovery. She knows I can't play anymore.

"Really?" Calvin quietly asks by my side.

I give him a faint nod, grinding my teeth and glaring at Dallas.

"You're too much for me," Rich admits, throwing his palms out in front of him and resuming his seat.

"I don't play anymore," I murmur.

All eyes on me, I drop mine toward the sand below our feet. Although they've only just met me, they understand my need to drop the topic.

"What time are the bridesmaids arriving tomorrow?" Rich asks Drew.

"They'll all be here by lunch," Drew answers from her perch on Joe's lap. "We'll eat lunch with you men before we meet with the wedding planner. Then, we'll enjoy our mani-pedis in the spa."

"But, you'll join us for dinner, right?" Joe asks his fiancé.

Drew nods, and Joe places his hands on the back of her head, pulling her in for a slow, passionate kiss. I turn away, not wanting to intrude on their moment, to find Calvin looking my way. His mouth curves up at the corners. I can't help the smile that slides upon my face, too.

Nervous, I decide I should excuse myself to the restroom. I stand, and Calvin follows me–I'm acutely aware of his presence. My skin prickles, and the hairs on the back of my neck stand. At a dead-end, I freeze. Calvin fails to stop in time. His hard body collides with mine, causing me to gasp as a flicker of electricity zings through my body at his touch.

He places his strong hands on my upper arms. "I'm sorry," he murmurs near my ear.

Unbreakable

I stand, frozen—my body won't move as my heart and mind run a mile a minute.

"I thought the restroom was back here," I explain finally as I step away from his grasp, turning to face him. My cheeks burn.

"I needed a break. They can be a bit much at times," Calvin confesses. "I saw a sign for the bathroom on the other side of the bar, though," he adds helpfully.

"Thanks," I whisper, unable to find my voice.

"I'll walk with you," he offers.

"You don't have to."

"I know. I want to," he smirks.

The brown flecks in his hazel eyes seem to dance as the corner of his eyes crinkle. He's handsome, but when he smiles, he's as hot as the sun. I have to look away. His hand lightly touches my forearm as he guides me toward the restrooms.

Though his fingertips barely make contact with my skin, I feel faint pulses of electrical current like my electric blanket makes. It's almost like sticking your tongue to the metal of a 9-volt battery. Only this pulsing zing is everywhere all at once. My every cell is alive and alert, wanting more.

"Here we are," Calvin's voice announces, pulling me from my thoughts.

"Thanks." I pause before entering. When he doesn't walk away, I'm not sure what to do. "You don't need to wait. I can find my way back to the group on my own."

Calvin shakes his head as if he's trying to get rid of the cobwebs in his brain. *Does he feel what I feel? Is he distracted by me like I am by him?*

"I know," he states. "I'm just not ready to return."

As I enter the bathroom, my thoughts are on the man outside. *He seems social and engages with his friends, so why does he need a break? Did something upset him?* Washing my hands, I take in my reflection in the mirror. There's something about Calvin that draws me to him; I just can't put my finger on it.

I find Calvin standing right where I left him. His hands are in the front pockets of his shorts, and he's looking through the window at the sun setting over the waves crashing onto the beach.

"Great view," I state, leaning against the stone wall. "It'd be nice to have this view every evening."

"Sure would," he concurs, joining me. "I'm not sure Rich will recover from your rejection," he adds after a few silent moments. He pulls his eyes to look my way. Aware of his gaze on me, I continue looking at the beach. "It wasn't so much a rejection as it was teasing him for teasing you." I bite my lip; perhaps I revealed too much.

"He's used to girls fawning over him. With your teasing and Dallas directing her attention to Garret, the poor guy's ego is taking a major hit this evening."

I pull my eyes from the peaceful view. His tongue sits on his lower lip, and his eyes map my face. I fidget under his stare.

"We need to get back," I suggest, not wanting to separate from Dallas on our first night at the resort.

"They haven't noticed we're gone, or they'd be hunting for us." As he speaks, he walks beside me.

When we round the corner, all eyes from the group look our way. So much for no one noticing. Dallas beams at me. I'm sure she thinks Calvin and I were making out. This will only fuel her desire to get me laid this week. I roll my eyes at her as I take my seat.

"The next round of drinks will be here soon," Calvin informs the group as he slides back into the seat next to mine. He apparently took a detour to the bar.

"Excuse me," Drew says, rising from her fiancé's lap. "I need to go to the ladies' room."

"It's right over there, around the corner," I offer, in hopes they all believe I was in the bathroom while Calvin was ordering drinks.

The rest of the night flies by, and conversation flows easily. After a long walk along the beach, I'm tired from our travels today and need to relax in my room.

"I think I need to call it a night," I announce to the group as we stand on the beach, just out of reach of the water crawling up the sand.

Dallas leans into Garret before walking to my side. "I'm going to hang for a while longer," she tells me in a hushed tone.

I nod. I'm not surprised; she's been flirting incessantly with him all night. I'm not sure what their room situation is, but even in our spacious bungalow, it's not large enough that I won't hear any interactions happening in her room. I hope she doesn't bring him back tonight; I desperately need sleep.

5
GET A GOOD LOOK

Schuyler

As morning light filters through the open curtains, I roll away from it hoping to catch some more sleep. As my left cheek hits the pillow, pain registers in my brain, and my eyes open wide. I sit up. My fingertips find my cheek swollen and warm. I slide from the bed, padding my way to the bathroom down the hall. I note Dallas's door is no longer open; I assume she made it home.

My eyes squint at the bright vanity lights. Leaning toward the mirror, I instantly notice my swollen cheek is bright red. The heat and redness concern me. Wanting another opinion, I knock on Dallas's door.

"What?" she moans.

"Dallas, something's wrong. I need your help." I try to keep the concern I'm feeling hidden until I get her opinion.

At my words, I hear footsteps on the tile floor, then the door flies open.

"Shit Schuyler! What did you do?" Dallas asks as she turns my chin for a better look.

"I woke up this way," I answer.

She guides me into the bathroom for further examination under the lights.

"It's bad, like need to see a doctor bad." I see worry written all over her face. "And you know I can't..." Her voice softens before her words trail off. I know what she meant to say. Dallas has an adverse reaction to doctors, needles, and blood. As a child, she experienced horrible nightmares after visiting her grandmother in the hospital on hospice care. They lasted for months; her parents had to take her to counseling.

"So, you agree I need to see a doctor?"

She nods.

I move to the living room. By the phone, I find a binder with resort information. While I scan each page, looking for any medical information, I hear Dallas talking to someone in her room. Not finding the information I need; I close the book and walk toward her.

"Calvin and Garret are on their way down," she informs me as she changes from her pajamas. "You should hurry and get dressed."

"Why did you call them?" I'm stunned. I don't need their help.

"I'm not letting you go see a doctor in a foreign country by yourself," she explains. Her tone suggests I shouldn't be surprised by this. "Did you get a bite? It looks like here's where it happened." She pushes on the spot, sending white-hot pain through my cheek.

"Ow!" I scream.

I twist my face this way and that in the mirror, trying to get a better vantage point. "Should I try to open it up or pop it?"

"No!" she screams, backing away. "It's not a zit, and your entire cheek is swollen!" Dallas startles again at the sound of a knock at the door.

"Where's the patient?" a male's voice calls from the front room.

Dallas motions for the men to enter the bathroom while she remains in the hallway, looking on with trepidation.

"Wow." Garret's eyes grow wide when I turn my left cheek towards them.

"We need to take you to the doctor," Calvin states, slowly lifting his hand to touch the edges of my swollen cheek.

"I looked in the binder by the phone and saw nothing about a doctor," I share.

"We'll go to the front desk," Calvin informs me. "If they don't have one on the premises, we will take a cab into town."

I want to refuse. I want to wait a day and see if it gets better on its own. I don't think he'll allow it, though, so I nod.

I nervously sit on the exam table while the physician, a short, stout, Santa-looking man, gathers supplies to treat me. My heart jackhammers against my chest. Doctors don't normally have this effect on me. Trusting a man that barely speaks

English with medical treatment, however, scares me. I know the health industry isn't regulated here like it is in the United States.

I flinch when Calvin's large, hot hand rubs my back. Lost in my worry, I didn't notice him leave his chair, moving to stand by my side.

"It's only a bite," he murmurs near my ear. "I'll monitor everything." He points to his cell phone, showing me it is recording from the pocket of his shirt.

Prepping a table in the corner, the doctor asks, "Allergy?"

"Um," I begin to answer. *How do I explain so he will understand me?* Looking at his back, I try to keep my reply simple. "No allergies."

"You have a bug bite?" he asks, rolling the metal table toward me.

"I didn't feel a bite."

"What are those?" Calvin points to two vials on the table near two syringes.

The doctor hands the vials to him, and he reads the labels. Calvin spins them for me to see the words "Penicilina" and "Prednisone".

"I give you an antibiotic. You make cheek cold. You come to see me, *mañana*." I smile at the physician, who is smiling pleasantly at me.

He looks like Santa in need of a beard trim. I feel I can trust him. I nod.

"In *nalgas*." He motions his finger in a spinning move. "*Inyección*."

I look to Calvin to see if he understands. He simply shrugs. The doctor turns toward me with a syringe, ready for my injection.

"Arm or bottom?" I ask him.

The doctor slaps his butt with his free hand. I guess that means in my bottom. I fight a grin and bite my lips, looking to Calvin as I slide off the table, unsnap my shorts, and bare my cheeks. It doesn't escape me that Calvin moves toward the end of the table to "watch" the doctor. I clear my throat, causing Calvin's eyes to dart to mine. I raise my eyebrows, and he smirks. *Well, get a good look, buddy. It's all you get to see of me.*

"Take a seat," Calvin orders upon entering our cabana.

Everything in me wants to protest, but he just did me a huge favor. So, I comply. I watch as he pulls a beer from the minifridge. I'm not in the mood, and it's a bit early in the day.

"Press this to your cheek," he instructs, leaving no room for argument.

I take the proffered can.

"Don't open it; hold it to your cheek like an ice pack," he explains, guiding my hand toward my swollen face.

Dallas and Garret stand in front of me, anxiously awaiting details on my doctor's visit.

"He thinks…" I mumble.

"I can't understand you," Dallas blurts.

With a swollen, aching cheek and a beer can against it, I find it hard to talk.

"Let me," Calvin offers. "The doctor believes it's an allergic reaction to a bug bite. He gave her penicillin and steroids." He looks at me, motioning for me to put the beer can back on my cheek. "Hold it on for 20 minutes."

I want to roll my eyes and argue, but he's right. Twenty minutes of a cold compress, then twenty minutes without. This will be my new challenge on this Mexican vacation. *Aren't I the lucky one?*

My eyes blink at a sudden burst of light. "What was that for?" I yell.

"We need to document this for your mother," Dallas states.

"You didn't," I growl.

"No, but I called Mom when you went to the doctor, and you know it's only a matter of time before my mom tells your mom; then Theo immediately call you," Dallas smiles, proud of her actions.

She knew by talking to her mom, my mother would immediately get a phone call. This isn't a big deal; she just didn't need to inform the parental units. Now, Mom will worry for no reason. I dread the call I know is bound to come.

"Thanks," I bite, full of sass. "I owe you one," I smirk.

"It's my fault," Garret confesses. "Dallas was pretty worked up when you left. I suggested she talk to her mom. It helped settle her anxiety." He shrugs unashamedly.

My heart warms at his actions. Most guys wouldn't know or care about what to do with a freaked-out girl. It's sweet that he cared enough to stay and help her.

"We're headed down for brunch. Want to join us?" Dallas asks, taking Garret's hand in hers.

"I need to shower and change into my swimsuit," I explain. "I'll find you later."

As the two head for the door, Calvin hangs back. I tilt my head.

"I'll wait for you." He smiles, his eyes crinkling at the corners.

"You don't need to," I argue. "You've already done so much for me this morning."

"I'm staying. It's my job to ensure you follow the doctor's orders."

Now, he's smirking. *Cocky, isn't he?* I shrug, turn on my heel, and enter the bathroom. If he plans to wait, he'll need to entertain himself in the living room without me.

6

IS HE SCREENING YOUR CALLS?

Schuyler

Stepping from my shower, I wrap my hair in a small towel on top of my head and secure another towel under my arms. I'm wiping the moisture from the large vanity mirror with a spare cloth when I hear a knock on the door.

"Schuyler, your mother is on the phone," Calvin calls through the closed door.

"Come in," I call back to him. "Can you put it on speaker on the counter for me?"

He complies then leans against the open doorway.

"Hi, Mom," I greet, tightening the towel covering my chest.

"Calvin seems like a perfect gentleman," my mother swoons, unaware he can hear her.

As a red blush graces his cheeks, I decide to not inform her she is on speakerphone. Knowing my mother, she'll have much to say or, better yet, ask about him.

"Dallas shared all the details this morning," Mom continues. "I'm just calling to see what the diagnosis was."

"The doctor believes it's a bug bite that I'm having an allergic reaction to," I share, acutely aware that Calvin's eyes haven't left my towel-covered body. I raise an eyebrow to him in the mirror before continuing. "I received an antibiotic and steroid shot. I'm to keep ice on it and check back in with the doctor in the morning."

"And this doctor," Mom pauses trying to find the right words, "was he trustworthy?"

"I believe so. Calvin kept a close eye on everything to make sure it was sanitary and even read the labels on the vials."

I turn from the mirror to face Calvin. With my index finger, I motion for him to spin around. I need to get dressed. He rolls his eyes at me but complies with my demand.

"So, Dallas mentioned you met the guys last night, and they're part of a wedding party," Mom's voice continues through the speaker. "I only spoke with Calvin for a minute, but he sounds like a nice young man. It was sweet of him to accompany you to the doctor. I hope you'll find a way to thank him."

I pull the last strap of my bathing suit over my shoulder. At Mom's final statement, I glance in Calvin's direction in the mirror. I swear I catch him turning his head away. *Was he watching me change? Did he see me naked?* He didn't seem like the type of guy to take advantage of the situation. Maybe I imagined his head movement.

"The entire group seems nice. Did Dallas tell her mom that they attend college in Maryville and live in KC?" I tap Calvin on the shoulder to signal he can turn around now.

"Oh, where's the fun in that?" Mom draws out. "I'm glad she did. There's nothing wrong with spending more time with a nice guy. She was only looking out for you. Now, tell me, what does Calvin look like?"

I roll my eyes at Calvin and his smirk as I push him from the room with my cell phone in my hand. I only need to slip on my sandals, and then, we can head out for some sun.

"Mom, I need to let you go," I lie, ignoring her question. "I'm supposed to meet Dallas and the others at brunch."

"Okay, dear," Mom replies. "Thank Calvin for me. I'm glad he was there to take care of my baby girl."

"Bye, Mom." I disconnect the call before she can embarrass me anymore.

I point to Calvin. "Not a word," I warn. I press my finger into his salmon, button-down shirt on his hard, muscular chest. "You did me a favor by going to the doctor with me. You wouldn't want to undo all your good deeds by teasing me about Mom's phone call." I tilt my head, smirking and daring him to do just that.

He raises his arms between us, palms out. "I won't say a thing."

His wide smile encompasses his entire face, and his hazel eyes glow with golden specks. He grabs another cold beer from the mini fridge, lifts it towards my cheek, and we head out for the day.

Time flies as we enjoy cold drinks while lounging in the pool. The guys do a great job of bringing me cans of cold beer to hold to my cheek. Of course, they also find many ways to tease me, and they whisper about me when they think I can't hear them. I've played along and posed for a couple of pictures of my cheek for them. I'm afraid to ask what they plan to do with the photos.

"I'm going to the bathroom," I state, leaning towards Dallas. "I'll grab a round of drinks on my way back."

She nods. I guess she doesn't need to pee or want to keep me company. Oh well. I'm a big girl. At my lounge chair, I pat my body dry with a beach towel before pulling my coverup over my head and tugging it to my thighs. I'm nowhere near dry, but it'll do. I slip on my sandals, wave bye to the gang, and walk away.

While waiting for all our drinks, I peek over my shoulder. Dallas and Calvin stand in the water at the edge of the pool, looking up at a lifeguard as he squats to speak. I wonder what that is about as I turn to face the bartenders once again. They offer me a large round tray to carry the six drinks to our group.

As I approach, I notice Calvin talking animatedly on his cell phone near our chairs. Turning my attention toward the pool, I find Joe splashing his way to my side of the pool, and the others decide to follow.

"Don't spill," Garret taunts.

"What if she drops it?" Joe teases.

"Stop it," I demand. "This isn't as easy as it looks." I slowly bend, balancing the tray on the flat of my hand. As I squat, I pass the drinks to Joe, and he hands them to the correct person.

"Here ya go, honey," Garret says, passing me two wet dollars from his swim trunks.

I glare at him as Dallas swats the back of his head. Calvin's phone conversation grows louder as he walks towards me.

"Dude, take a breath before you have a stroke."

I assume he's teasing until I see his face. His brows draw together, and his jaw clenches.

"Here she is," Calvin states, handing the phone to me. "It's your brother."

I stare at the phone in my hand. It's my phone, not Calvin's.

"I climbed out to help you carry the drinks and noticed your phone was vibrating. The screen showed three missed calls, so I answered it for you." He shrugs then shakes his head.

I place the tray on a nearby lounge chair before lifting the phone to my ear. "Hello?"

"Who's the douche?" Levi growls. His raised voice alerts me that he's not teasing. He's mad. When Levi gets this way, the vein in the center of his forehead pulses visibly, and the veins in his neck pop out as he grows more and more red. "Why is that motherfucker answering your phone?"

"Levi," I begin.

"I feel like I need to fly down there!" Levi continues his tirade. "You've been gone 24 hours, and a guy has already--"

"Levi!" I yell into my phone. I mouth, "I'm sorry," to the guests nearby and walk away from the busy pool area. "I'm an adult. I don't need my big brother butting into my business."

While talking, I turn to find Calvin following me. He places his hand on the small of my back.

"I hope you didn't embarrass me in front of my new friend."

"Is he screening your calls?" Levi's anger causes my hackles to rise. "Schuyler, you're not experienced, and guys like him want to control every aspect of your life. It's my job as your big brother to keep these creeps from getting their hooks in you."

"Levi, Calvin is my friend." I talk over the top of my brother's explanation. "He's not controlling. He's not a jerk. He was coming to help me carry six drinks, heard my phone vibrating, and saw I had missed three calls. He answered for me since my hands were full. There's no hidden meaning behind his actions." I pause, taking in a deep breath.

"It's time that you get it into your thick skull that I am 23 years old," I continue. "I'm not a teenager. I don't need you screening every guy I come into contact with. I'm not like Clint, Dan, and you. I don't sleep with every guy that looks my way. I'm not into one-night stands. At my age, you were married."

"Schuyler, you haven't lived the life that we have–you don't understand." Levi tries to explain the carefree, sexual exploits of all three of my older brothers.

"You need to stop right there," I bark. "I'm on vacation. I'm having fun, and I don't need you calling to ruin it for me."

"This is exactly what I'm talking about," Levi responds. "You don't know what dangers surround you down there. I can't believe Dad and Mom agreed to allow you to fly to Mexico alone. I should be there to protect you."

"Levi Dawes, you hear me and listen good. I'm 23; I don't need you here. I don't want you here, and I'm hanging up. Don't call me again, because I won't answer. I can't believe you want to ruin this for me." Keeping my promise, I disconnect the call. My fingers shake, and my hands tremble.

Calvin slips my phone into his hand before wrapping his strong, sun-kissed arms around me. I lay my head on his chest while fighting the tears that threaten to spill down my cheeks. My body pulses with rage and adrenaline.

7
WHO'S WITH ME?

Schuyler

"I'm sorry I answered your phone," Calvin whispers into my ear. "I should have carried it over to you."

I want to let him know I'm not upset with him; I want to apologize for my ass of a brother, but if I speak, I might lose my paper-thin hold on my control. I nod slightly instead. My cheek rubs against his hard, bare pectoral. I feel his racing heartbeat. His heat soothes me. I tighten my arms around his waist, nuzzling my face against his skin.

Calvin slides one hand into my hair, holding me tight to him, while his other lightly caresses my back. An alarm bell in my head warns me this is too intimate. It feels good, and right now, I need this. I'll worry about the signals I might be sending him later.

"Are you okay?" Calvin murmurs. "I mean, I know you're physically okay, but…"

I pull in a deep breath. His musky scent mingled with the outdoors nearly distracts me. I blink a few times, clearing the fog he created. I place my hands upon his chest and push back, looking up into his warm, hazel eyes, so full of concern.

"I'm sorry," I whisper. "Thank you… for that."

When he opens his mouth to speak, I place two fingers over his lips. "I love my three brothers, but they're too…" I search for the right words to express my frustration with their actions.

"They're big brothers," Calvin states. "It's their job."

"Yes and no," I argue. "The word 'overprotective' isn't precise enough to describe what they are. It's partially my fault, I guess, for letting it get this out of control. They can't help it. Levi was a Navy SEAL, and Dan was an officer in the Marines. Protection is drilled into them."

"Wait," Calvin sputters. "The brother I just spoke to on your phone is a Navy SEAL? He threatened to come down here and…" He runs both hands through his hair as he blows out a long, nervous breath.

I place my hands at his waist. "He's not flying down here. And even if he did, I wouldn't let him anywhere near you." I place one palm to his cheek. "He's a man. You know how you are. Your testosterone screws with your head. I honestly don't know how you're able to function most of the time." I chuckle half-heartedly. "Can we get back to enjoying our vacation?"

"You bet," he laughs, pulling me back toward our friends in the pool.

"There you are," Dallas yells across the pool. "Who was on the phone?"

"It was Levi," I answer.

"Oh." Her eyes grow wide. "I can just imagine his beat-red face with bulging vessels and spittle dripping from his mouth as he yelled at Calvin."

My mouth curls at the corners, and I nod.

"What time is it?" Dallas asks.

It takes me a moment to register her change of subject.

"Ten minutes till eleven," Calvin answers.

I don't miss the look between Dallas and Calvin. My brow furrows.

Calvin

"The lifeguards came around earlier, trying to find enough people for volleyball. We thought we'd join the volleyball game on the beach at 11," I share, smiling.

Schuyler's face pales, her eyes widen, and her arms cross over her chest protectively. I'm suggesting a friendly game of volleyball. She reacts as if I'm suggesting we fight MMA style.

"They said it's just for fun," I explain.

Dallas quickly climbs from the pool, wraps a towel around her waist, and approaches the two of us. "Can we have a minute alone?" she asks, shooing me away. "It's just a pickup game," she states to Schuyler, her voice softer than normal.

If she knew Schuyler would react this way, why did she agree we should all play earlier? She's clearly not surprised by the reaction.

"Let's head on over to the volleyball court," I suggest to my friends. "Dallas and Schuyler will join us in a minute." *At least, I hope they'll join us. I have no desire to play if Schuyler doesn't.*

We volley the ball, warming up, while we wait for other guests to join us. Besides the four of us, there are only two other guys interested so far. It won't be much fun with three people on each side.

"Can everyone play, or is it just for guys?" Dallas asks as she approaches the sand court, a smirk on her face.

My eyes dart to her, and the volleyball bonks me on the head. While the group laughs, I walk toward the two girls. Schuyler's arms still cover her chest, but her face is relaxed now. She no longer looks like she's seen a ghost.

My fingers twitch, wanting to touch her, longing to take her hand, and needing to pull her to me. I fight the urge. Though the pull towards her is strong, we aren't a couple.

"Let's warm-up," Schuyler suggests without conviction. "Maybe more women will join us if they see we're over here."

She pulls off her swimsuit cover-up and tosses it on the nearby picnic table. She reaches her arms over her head, then bends at the waist, wrapping her hands around her ankles. I can't pull my eyes from her long, muscular physique. The hint of muscles I saw at the pool now flex and stretch in clear view in front of me. As she bends, stretching this way and that, it's clear she's an athlete, practiced in preparing her body for action.

"Plan to join us, Calvin?" she asks, stepping over the yellow rope on the sand that marks the court.

On her face, I see a faint smirk. She's struggling with something; she's trying to be brave. I give myself a mental pep talk to focus on the game and not her body as I join her on a side. Dallas points toward two more women headed to join us. Five to a side, three guys and two girls, will make for a good matchup.

"Yellow line is out," the male lifeguard states, standing on the wooden picnic table at the side of the net. "Just have fun. Let's volley for the serve." He tosses the white ball towards the center of the net.

The other team cannot return the volley, so we serve first.

"How do you want us to line up?" Dallas asks, looking in Schuyler's direction.

Schuyler doesn't answer; she just shrugs.

"Come on," Dallas whines. "You're better at this than we are. Help us."

Schuyler looks at our random stances, thinking. "If I switch with Joe, I think it will work."

Dallas nods. Joe and Schuyler swap places while my head reels, trying to process the meaning behind Dallas's statement. Dallas shared last night that Schuyler plays volleyball. *If that's true, why does she look like she's facing a firing squad?*

Dallas announces the score of zero to zero, then serves the ball overhanded. Her serve has power. *Clearly, she's played on a team before.* The bulky, military-looking guy in the back row easily bumps the ball back to our side. Joe sets it to the front row, Schuyler calls for it, then easily taps it over the net. The ball glides down our opponents' side of the net as two front row players stare at each other.

On Dallas's next serve, the same guy in the back row sets it up to the tall, blonde guy in the front row. He spikes the ball forcefully toward Dallas. At first, she makes a move for it but dives away at the last second.

"Hey!" Joe yells, irritated through the net at the other team.

"What happened to 'just playing for fun'?" Garret taunts, puffing his chest out as he glares through the net at the blonde guy.

"C'mon, it wasn't that hard," the tall, blonde guy retorts.

"Game on," Schuyler declares for only our team to hear and points to Dallas.

Dallas nods, accepting the challenge. I'm not about to let either of these girls get hurt trying to return his spikes. I decide to go after the next spike the blonde guy makes.

When they serve, Dallas calls the ball, expertly bumping it to me in the front corner. I easily tap the ball to the other side. I've barely reset before the same guy in the front row spikes another bullet towards Dallas. I'm too far away to help her.

Dallas falls to her knees in the sand, digging out his spike before it hits the ground. "Help!" she yells as she makes contact.

I deftly contact the ball for a second hit, sending it soaring to the back row. When they neglect to return the ball, our team takes turns high-fiving Dallas before we rotate. Garret serves the ball into the net, so we roll the ball to the other team. We volley the next serve many times across the net. Attempting to return the ball, the tall blonde on the other side jumps to hit the ball across the net. Schuyler leaps from the sand, arms straight, hands flat. She blocks the ball, causing it to fall on their side of the net for our point.

We share high-fives and pats on the back, then rotate.

Schuyler hits the ball perfectly to Dallas. Dallas calls to set, and out of nowhere, Schuyler, now in the front row, jumps, spiking the ball at a tall, blonde guy. He's shocked by her power and barely swings his arm out in a circle as the ball bounces two feet from him.

Schuyler wears a humongous smile as she returns to my side in the back row.

After we win the third set in a row, we shake hands with the other team before returning to our sandals and clothes on the picnic table. Everyone talks at once, reliving great plays and congratulating each other for awesome hits.

At the first lull in the noise, I speak up. "So, the two of you have played on a team together for years." I gesture between Dallas and Schuyler, smirking.

"We played together for three years in high school," Dallas admits.

Joe looks to Schuyler. "Must have been one heck of a high school team. You've got skills." He smiles, clearly impressed with her performance today.

Schuyler brushes it off, pulling her cover-up over her suit.

"How good were you?" Garret asks the two girls.

"I played at college," Schuyler states as if it's no big deal.

She doesn't seem comfortable talking about her abilities.

"She's Olympic trials good," Dallas brags, ignoring her friend's attempt at making her keep that news to herself.

"I knew it!" Joe cheers. "You were holding back! I knew it!"

"I'm ready for lunch," Schuyler states, clearly changing the subject. "Who's with me?"

Taking our cue from her, we all agree it's time to eat. I have so many questions. I long to know the reason she struggles to talk about her achievements. *I feel there's a story there, and I want to understand. I want to know all about her.*

8

MEET MO

Calvin

"What are you looking at?" Schuyler asks, pointing to my phone as we enter her bungalow.

"Promise you won't get mad?" I prompt, hiding my screen from her view.

"I'll try to keep an open mind," she states, raising her brow.

"I created an Instagram account for--" I point to her still swollen cheek. "I posted the pictures I took of 'Mo.' The guys added some comments, and believe it or not, @MoDoesMexico now has over 200 followers."

"No way. My bug bite has 200 followers?" She smiles at me before glancing at the feed on my phone. "I should be mad that you created this account." She gives me a small glare, but it's half-hearted. She scrolls to the top of the feed, looks at my posted photos in order and all the comments. "How did you guys come up with all of this? You're creative—you should write fiction or something; you have a genuine talent."

I shake my head. "It all sparked from when I referred to your bite as 'Mo.' After that, we fed off each other's comments. It's crazy, right?"

"Do you know all these followers?"

"At first it was just Joe, Garret, and me," I explain. "Then, some of our friends saw it on our feed and followed, then their friends, and so on. Most of these people I have no idea who or where they are."

"This is why you asked if you could take a photo of 'Mo' with an umbrella from a drink," she smiles. "Here's my phone. Follow 'Mo' for me; I'm going to take a shower. I have sand in places it should never be." She tosses her cell phone at me and continues to the bathroom.

"You were a beast out there," I call after her. "You almost spent as much time diving in the sand as you did standing."

She smiles at me over her shoulder before disappearing down the hall. I open Instagram, type in @MoDoesMexico, and click follow. I nearly drop her phone when it vibrates in my hand, signaling an incoming call. Her screen displays "Mom." I hear the shower running, so I make the executive decision to answer. I've already talked to her mother once; there's no way it can be as bad as when I answered Levi's call earlier today.

"Hello," I greet, hesitation lacing my voice.

"Oh, hello," her mother returns. "Is this Calvin?"

Part of me, a very evil part of me, would like to answer 'no,' playing a prank on her mom. But, I think better of it.

"Yes, it is. How are you, Mrs. Dawes?" I pour on the charm. I suddenly feel the need for Schuyler's mom to like me.

"How is my daughter's cheek this afternoon?"

"The swelling has gone down a lot. Don't get me wrong, her cheek is still noticeably puffy." I pause for a quick breath, noting the shower is still running. "I've taken many pictures, and I posted them on Instagram. Do you have an account?"

"I do, but I'm never on it. Clint set it all up for me a few months ago." She giggles. "I do not know how it works."

"No problem. I'll have Schuyler send them to you when she's out of the shower."

A male voice comes across the line. "Why are you on my sister's phone while she's in the shower? And whose shower is she in? Hers or yours?"

It's not the same deep, gravelly voice Levi had this morning. There's only a hint of anger in its tone.

"We're in her room. She needed to shower to get the sand off her from our volleyball game," I explain. "And I only answered her phone because it said her mom was calling. I definitely wouldn't have answered if I knew it was another one of her brothers." There's a hint of snark in my tone, but I don't mind. I feel I need to defend myself and Schuyler.

He laughs.

"I've already spoken to Levi, so I know you're not the Navy SEAL," I deduce. "Which one are you, the Marine or the football player?"

"I'm Clint, the football player," he says through a chuckle. "I heard all about your conversation this morning with Levi."

"Correction," I interject. "You only heard his side of the story."

"Trust me, I'm all too familiar with Levi when he's angry," Clint chuckles. "I bet he pissed Sky off. Sorry if it ruined your day."

"She's definitely mad at him," I confirm.

"Hold it," he orders. "Did you say she played volleyball?"

"Yes. Our entire group played on the beach," I answer. "She and Dallas put on quite a show."

"Huh." Clint pauses. "Well, I'll be damned."

"She's got mad skills," I brag. "Shocked the heck out of all of us. Well, except for Dallas."

"I wish I could have seen it." He sounds genuine.

"Drew took photos while we played. Her wedding is tomorrow, and she didn't want a *Meet the Parents* reenactment," I chuckle.

"That's smart. A broken nose would ruin her wedding," Clint replies.

"I'll see that your sister gets the pics and sends them to you," I offer.

I hear the shower stop, so I place the call on speaker and walk towards the restroom.

"Calvin, can I call you Calvin?" he asks.

"Sure," I agree. "That is my name."

"Well, Calvin, Levi is still on his tirade. He phoned Dan and then me. He suggested we call to see what Schuyler's up to on vacation," he informs. "He seems to think you're a predator who is now controlling our little sister. I think he would have purchased a plane ticket if he weren't on patrol today."

I rap on the bathroom door. "Clint is on the phone," I call to her.

"You've got to be shitting me," she spits as I hear her feet approaching the door.

"Nice to hear your voice, too," Clint teases his sister, who now stands with a towel under her arms, dripping in the doorway.

"Did Levi put you up to this?" She didn't wait for him to answer. "Well, I'll tell you the same thing I told him. I'm a grown-ass woman. I'm 23, and I don't need the three of you looking over my shoulder every second of the day. I can make friends and do whatever I want to on vacation. Don't call again, because I won't answer."

Her face grows redder with each word she yells into the speaker. I shake my head, hoping she won't hang up on him. Her finger hovers over the screen, ready to end the call.

"We've had a civil conversation," I inform her.

"Sky, I'm just checking in to see if you've recovered from Levi's call." Clint's voice morphs into a soothing, big-brother tone. "Calvin seems like an okay guy. He's not throwing up red flags like Levi claims he did earlier."

Schuyler shakes her head and rolls her eyes. The redness fades a bit in her cheeks and neck. I hand her the cell phone. The action pulls the top of the towel down slightly. It's enough that a bit of cleavage peeks out. My tongue darts out to lick my lower lip at the sight.

"Why does my screen say I'm talking to Mom?" she scolds.

"I figured you wouldn't answer if I called you on my phone," he admits.

"You're right..."

Clint interrupts her, "I'm sorry Levi took it upon himself to call you after Mom mentioned a man answered your phone this morning."

Again, she rolls her eyes at me. I find her frustration cute. I'm glad she has older brothers looking out for her.

"Clint, do you need something? If not, I'd like to get back to my vacation."

"I'm satisfied. Calvin's cool. I'll let Dan know he doesn't need to call like Levi asked him to. I just need Calvin to send me the pictures we talked about."

At Clint's words, she looks to me for an explanation. Her brows twitch, and a smirk adorns her face.

"Check out @MoDoesMexico on Instagram." She smiles, sounding proud of the account I created for her. "It's right up your alley. I'm hanging up now. I have vacation fun calling me."

"I love you," Clint laughs. "Bye, Sky."

Her reaction declares she's not fond of his rhyme. She doesn't return the sentiment; she simply disconnects the call.

"You are so lucky that you are an only child," she says to me while pushing me from the bathroom and shutting the door.

Calvin

"Hey, Mom," I greet as she adjusts the camera for our call.

"You know you don't have to call us every night," Mom harps.

"I wanted to make sure Tyler's okay and not giving you too much trouble," I admit, ashamed that I can't relax for five days without checking in.

"We have everything under control. I'm actually at the store right now. You need to relax and not worry about anything back here. Your father and I can care for Tyler while you are away."

For four years, I've cared for Tyler, never being apart for more than a night or two. Every need I met; I sacrificed my college social life to provide loving care. It's not easy to turn off the need to nurture, to worry, and to call to check in. My mother gets her way tonight. I'll look in on Tyler tomorrow. I hang up the call with the promise to check in the next evening.

The fragrant floral arrangement on the desk of our hotel room reminds me of Schuyler's light, fruity scent. What is it about the elusive woman that calls to every part of me? From the moment my eyes fell upon her, a slow burn has sparked within me. My body hums to life as never before. I avoid most situations that might allow such interactions; I must be there for Tyler.

Last night, Cupid's arrow landed in the bullseye of my heart and heated desire grew with every beat thereafter. No man is powerful enough to fight the feeling the arrow brings. Schuyler haunts my every thought, my every waking moment, and even my dreams.

I appease myself with the belief it's five days in Mexico. We'll have five days together, then go our separate ways. With Tyler far away at my parents' house, I will allow myself to indulge in this one week.

9

NAP TIME

Calvin

The next day, as we approach the volleyball court, I wonder why Schuyler told us to go ahead without her. She claimed she wanted to finish her current chapter. *Now that I think about it, she refrained from joining us in the pool this morning, too.* She contentedly read on her lounger, remaining distant.

With sides chosen, we volley the ball to warm up. As I monitor the location of the white ball hurling from side to side, I also anxiously watch for Schuyler's arrival. *Something's up, it bothers her, and I want to help.*

To my relief, she joins us as we prepare to start the match. Schuyler quickly removes her cover-up and takes an empty spot in the front row. The serve is up, and the match begins.

Our team plays with the same enthusiasm as we did last time. We bump, set, and block while we communicate with each other. I admire Schuyler's long, lean-muscled body in her tiny, navy boy shorts and matching sports bra. *She's distracting.* I struggle to follow the ball with her beauty and bare flesh so near. The front of her spandex top swoops down from the thick straps to reveal a hint of cleavage. I've seen these uniforms when I've watched competitive beach volleyball on television. While providing support for the female athletes, they also reveal womanly figures to attract the eyes of us men.

As Sky approaches Dallas in the back row to high-five after a remarkable play, I note a red discoloration on her right side, stretching from her ribs and disappearing beneath her shorts.

It's a scar. It's a long, nasty scar that branches into two lines. They aren't the straight lines a surgeon would leave. These are jagged and rough, and my stomach roils. I place my hands on my knees, taking a couple of calming breaths. With no idea how it happened, I already dread hearing the story.

As the game continues, I attempt to focus on the ball and not glance at her side and abdomen every chance I get. I struggle; I divert my gaze to her luscious ass and bouncing breasts. My wandering eyes spot one scar on her back that looks puckered. I imagine it's how a bullet wound might look. My overactive imagination plans many scenarios in which all her scars were caused. Every part to me longs to hold her and protect her from her past and future pains. She catches me staring at her scar and attempts to pull her top lower and bottoms higher to cover as much as possible.

Schuyler

As I sit on the edge of the bathtub, I slow my breathing and will my mind to forget about my brothers. *It's my vacation, and I'm going to have fun, dammit!* I'm not sure what this afternoon's plans are, but I want to do something fun. I guess we haven't discussed it. I open the bathroom door, cinch the towel around my chest tighter, and tiptoe to the outer room.

"What are we going to do this afternoon?" I ask, my words slicing into the room.

Calvin's eyes lift from his cell phone. They linger on my towel-clad midsection for a moment before meeting mine.

"I'm not sure," he admits, a smirk upon his lips. "I suppose we will hang at the..." his words taper off as he looks at me.

A large yawn escapes me. I close my eyes for a moment as it passes.

"We could take a nap," Calvin suggests.

"Oh, I don't know." I furrow my brow. "Isn't that what old people do on vacation?"

He laughs at my comment. "I guess they do, but they don't stay up as late as we do or rise as early as us. They don't play a competitive game of volleyball and walk long distances along the beach." He glances for the time on his cell phone. "We could rest for an hour or two and still have plenty of daylight left."

A nap sounds good; I am tired, but I can't tell if he is serious. I stand awkwardly in front of him, still only wearing a towel. I fiddle with it, tightening it around my chest.

"Go put on something comfy," Calvin suggests. "When you open the bedroom door, I'll come in to join you."

I don't argue. Instead, I head for my bedroom. *"I'll come in."* So, is he going to nap with me? A tingle of excitement flows through me at the thought of him lying in bed beside me. I hurry to throw on a t-shirt and a pair of plaid boxers with NWMSU printed across the seat. Then, I open the bedroom door a crack and turn on my cell phone light so I may see. I worry he might not see the door is open, so I open it all the way, then hop into bed. I stifle the giggle that builds inside me as I wait.

"Knock, knock," Calvin greets hesitantly from the open doorway.

I pat the left side of the mattress as an invitation. "Can you please shut the door behind you?" I ask, suddenly very nervous about the logistics of this.

Slowly, he saunters along the left side rail. When he reaches the head of the bed, he lays himself gently over the comforter on the pillow. He rolls on his side to face me, his smile sweet and green eyes bright. I turn my phone light off, bathing the room in darkness.

"Wow! It's dark in here," he comments, settling himself deeper into the pillow. "And chilly."

"I have to have the fan noise to sleep," I confess. "I like it dark and cold, too. You can slide under the covers; I don't mind."

I quickly realize that with him under the covers, the chance of us coming into contact with each other increases. *But I can't have him cold on top of the covers while I sleep soundly below.* I watch the faint shadow of him in the darkness, pulling the covers over himself. *Now what? Do I just close my eyes and act like he's not inches from me?* The silence is painful.

"Do you take trips with your friends often?" I struggle to find a topic of conversation to ease the quiet tension in the room.

"No." Calvin's voice is nearly a whisper. "I've focused on my classes for the past four years and had little time off."

I hear rustling as he repositions himself.

"We took a four-day trip to South Padre Island during my friends' senior spring break. They had to rip the textbooks from my hand, dragging me kicking and screaming, but we had a great time." Calvin clears his throat.

Something in his tone hints there's more to this story than he shares. From the conversations I've heard between the guys, at one time, they traveled often. I wonder what happened four years ago to cause Calvin to focus more on his studies than on his friends.

"How about you?" Calvin reverses the question. "Do Dallas and you travel often?"

"Our families have vacationed together since we were children," I share as fond memories of our childhood adventures replaying in my mind. "Dallas and I have taken short girls' weekend trips in the continental U.S. This is our first trip outside the country without our parents." A yawn distorts my last words.

"Roll over. Let me rub your back," Calvin directs.

My limbs feel heavy and tired, so I comply. Calvin's large hand slowly rubs circles at my shoulders, my spine, then my lower back. My body relaxes, and sleep immediately pulls me under.

10

THE BREAK UP

Calvin

My eyes open in the dark room. It takes a moment for me to remember I'm napping in Schuyler's room. Instantly, I'm acutely aware of her slender arm drapes across my bare chest and her long legs twine with mine. I force my breaths to remain steady so as not to wake her. The longer she sleeps, the longer I can enjoy her body snuggling with mine.

Two days in Mexico have flown by. I fear I will never have my fill of Schuyler. Our relationship differs from any I've ever had. It's deeper than I've experienced with other women, and it's not even sexual. I can't fathom how it might feel if we were to sleep together. I already feel my body gravitate toward her. *I want to know more; I want to know everything about her.*

Her arm tightens around me at the same time she lifts her head from my shoulder. In the sliver of light peeking around the edges of the curtain, I see her wipe at her mouth. It's then that I realize there's a pool of moisture on my shoulder.

"I'm sorry." Her voice is hoarse. "That's embarrassing." She wipes my shoulder with the edge of the sheet.

"It's not the first time I've been slobbered on," I quip.

She flops her head back on her pillow. "Do you have a dog, or do women often slobber on you?"

Shit! How do I undo that comment?

I'm not ready; we're not ready for that part of my life to be revealed.

I can't have her thinking I sleep with lots of drooling women, either.

The dog she asked about, that might work. I can use my parents' dog, so it isn't a lie.

"My parents' dog went through a two-year, excessive drooling phase."

"I love dogs," Schuyler states. "My parents had dogs for years. What kind of dog do your parents have?"

She seems to have accepted my explanation. Wow! I skated around that disaster. Well, maybe it won't be a disaster. It's just too soon to tell.

"They adopted a shelter dog," I reply. "We think it's part Labrador, but we don't know for sure."

Schuyler turns on her side, facing me. With the new position, our noses are only inches apart. Though it's dark, I can see her eyes. Instantly, my body's alert to her nearness. Fantasies run through my mind; my body longs to touch her perfect skin, but I refrain. My mind scrambles for something to say to fill the silence.

"We were a great team on the volleyball court today," I murmur, pausing a moment. "I couldn't help but notice your scars as we played. I want to ask you something."

"Go ahead."

"If it's not too difficult for you, I'd like to hear about your scars." I wait with bated breath for her to refuse or share.

I hear her quick intake of breath. *I shouldn't have pushed it; she doesn't want to share. I should just leave it alone until she tells me about it in her own time.*

She repositions herself onto her back, putting some distance between us. "I was driving home from college. It was dark. I didn't leave early enough, because I dropped my backpack off at the apartment after my late afternoon class." Her voice is a gentle whisper, and I strain to hear her.

The covers rustle as she pulls them closer to her chest. I place my hand on her shoulder for comfort.

"I had just passed Mount Ayr on Highway 169." Schuyler cringes at the memory as she retells her story. "Light snow was falling, and as I followed a large truck hauling what looked like steel rods, I allowed two full car lengths between us. The roads were wet, but as the temperature dropped, I realized it might be slick."

Absentmindedly, my thumb gently caresses her neck while my hand lays upon her shoulder.

"With no warning, the truck swerved into the oncoming lane of traffic, and the steel rods began flying off the truck bed. It all happened so fast. One moment, they were in the truck, and the next, they were hurdling toward my car. I swerved to avoid them, and my car left the pavement, slicing through the tall weeds covered in snow. It was so hard to steer. I can remember praying I'd be able to stop the car.

Then I blacked out." She wipes a tear from her cheek, whispering. "I woke up in the hospital three days later."

This was more than a wreck. She blacked out for days and has large, jagged scars. Dallas and Schuyler have alluded to her giving up parts of her life after the accident. It seems to have harmed her inside and out.

"The rest of the details, my mom told me later."

Every part of me wants to hold her and promise it's over, and she's safe now. My hands turn her away from me, and I pull her snug to me. I wrap my arms tight around her waist. The warmth of her back feels good pressed to my chest, and her hips brush against my pelvis. I think of dogs, trucks, and my grandma to keep my body from reacting to her. I want only to comfort her, yet my body can't help its reaction.

"I texted Mom when I left Maryville, and when I didn't arrive at my parents' house on time, she worried. Mom called my phone several times before someone finally answered. Seems it flew from my car when the vehicle overturned. The highway patrol and sheriff's department wrapped up their investigation, and the ambulance already drove the truck driver to the nearest hospital. They waited on a tow truck to help clear the road before they could leave the scene. They didn't even know there was anyone else involved."

Schuyler looks at me over her shoulder. In the faint light, I see her light-brown eyes full of pain.

"With my cell halfway down the hill, it took a while before the authorities heard it and answered. My mother begged them to find me, stating if my cellphone was there, so was I. Because of the snow, they hadn't seen my tire tracks on the shoulder or down the embankment. The official report states they did not find me until two hours after the wreck."

She spins in my arms, remaining close. When she rests her cheek on my bare chest, I feel her tears. I hold her tight with one arm and stroke her back with my other hand.

"It was a steep embankment. My car flipped over several times before coming to rest on a barbed wire fence." She sniffs, taking a shuddering breath. "The metal fence posts impaled my car. One barely missed the gas tank, and another went through the windshield, angling down into my abdomen."

"The scars," I whisper into the top of her head.

"Yep," her voice grows impossibly softer. "The officers on the scene called for a firetruck, paramedics, and Life Flight as soon as they laid eyes on me. They cut the metal post and transported me by helicopter, with part of it still lodged in my abdomen. I had multiple surgeries. When I finally opened my eyes, I found myself in a hospital room hooked up to machines with my three brothers, Mom, and Dad hovering around me."

When she's quiet for several moments, I ask, "How long were you in the hospital?"

Schuyler places her palms on my chest, pushing herself back to look at me. "I caught an infection, so I spent two weeks in the hospital before heading home. Then, I had physical therapy multiple times a week."

Schuyler's tongue darts out to wet her lower lip. My eyes glue themselves to the motion.

"So, it forced me to take an incomplete for my last semester of college. I withdrew my name from the Olympic volleyball tryouts and, with the help of my family, focused on my recovery." A fake smile graces her face. "And that's not the worst part." She looks away.

My eyes plead for her to continue. I want to know everything about her. I want to understand her pain. I need to know why she's holding back and building walls around herself.

"On my discharge day..." she pauses to pull in two shallow breaths. "I need to back up a little. I started dating one of Clint's friends at the end of my junior year in high school. We'd been together five years at the time of my accident, and the fact that he had only visited me in the hospital once during my stay upset me. On my discharge day, he asked my parents if I could ride with him to our house. On the drive, he broke up with me."

I open my mouth to comment, but she places two fingers over my lips to prevent me from talking.

"Our dream had been for me to teach and him to run his family business. He claimed I could no longer be the wife he needed because of my accident." She wipes several tears from her cheeks. "I still had pain when using my abdominal muscles, and he didn't even assist me out of his car. He left me standing in my parents' driveway, sobbing, and drove away without looking back. My parents had to come out and help me up the front steps into the house."

"What an ass!" I spit, rage filling me. "I hope your brothers taught him a lesson."

She chuckles half-heartedly through her falling tears. "I was too focused on my recovery to ask, but I'm sure they did. They had threatened him within an inch of his life when he asked me out for the first time. He was a perfect gentleman until the day he dumped me in the driveway."

I fight the rage I feel on her behalf. *She doesn't need me to act like her brothers. She needs comfort and understanding.*

"You're a survivor," I state. "It couldn't have been easy, but you bounced back, are finishing your degree, and moving on with your life."

Through her dark lashes, she looks up into my eyes. Moisture from her tears cling to them, framing her caramel eyes. I want to assure her everything will be alright. I need to hold her, comfort her. I lower my head to hers, tilt to the side, and cover her lips with mine.

I keep my kiss soft, slow, and gentle. It takes a moment before she gives in, kissing me back. I wrap her hair in my fist. When a gasp escapes, I take advantage of the opening, slipping my tongue into her mouth. The taste of her overloads my senses. I press my body to hers as our tongues continue to tango. It takes all my willpower to keep my hands in her hair and not explore her body. *I can't rush this; I don't want to scare her.* I put everything into my kiss and take everything she offers through hers.

11

DANCE IN THE SHEETS

Schuyler

I'm happy to see Dallas sunning herself on a lounge chair by the pool as we emerge from our afternoon nap. While Calvin quickly hops in the pool with the rest of his group, I signal for Dallas to follow me.

"What's up?" she whispers as we walk from the pool area to the beach. "And where have the two of you been?" She waggles her eyebrows suggestively.

I cross the hot sand to the shade of a palm tree. When Dallas joins me, I whisper, "He kissed me." I then wait for her wisdom and advice.

"Oh. My. God." she squeals, hopping up and down, clapping. "Give me all the details!" Hands together, her fingertips patter against each other maniacally.

"Stop," I demand. "This isn't good."

Dallas places her hands on my shoulders, looking sternly into my eyes. "This is the best thing to happen to you."

I shake my head. *I came to the wrong person for advice.*

"How?" I'm desperate to understand how this could be a good thing.

"You promised to have fun this week. Calvin kissing you is fun," she states, staring into my eyes. "Now, loosen up and see where this goes."

I close my eyes, drawing in a long breath to keep calm.

"Need I remind you, you've only kissed one guy in your entire life? Well, now two." She laughs at my discomfort. "You're 23. It's not against the law to kiss a guy, especially when he's really into you."

If Dallas had her way, I'd get laid this week. Of course, she's going to be all for me kissing Calvin. My head spins with all the reasons I need to stay away from him.

"I can't kiss him anymore," I state. "I'm not able to be what he wants."

"C'mon," Dallas retorts. "It's kissing, not a wedding proposal. There's nothing wrong with having a great time, kissing, and, if the situation arises, having even more fun with him in bed. Not every encounter leads to marriage and a family." Dallas freezes, scrunching her face at her words. She knows it hurts to think of the family I will never have. I can tell that she feels bad about her blunder. "Be honest," she orders. "Do you like spending time with him?"

I nod.

"When he kissed you, did you enjoy it and kiss him back?"

I nod.

"Then, go for it. We're on vacation in Mexico. We're supposed to relax and have fun. It's clear to everyone that the two of you have fun with each other. It's obvious that he's not just into you for sex. He wants to be near you and talk about anything with you." Dallas pulls her hands from my shoulders. "Don't waste time overthinking it. Have fun and see where it goes. There's no need to worry about divulging everything the first week you meet. You're two adults, and you are allowed to live in the moment, no strings attached."

"He's asked if we could go out when we are back at school," I confess.

"It doesn't change my advice," Dallas smiles smugly. "It's time that you work that creep, Will out of your system, and Calvin is the perfect man for the job."

"Here's what's going to happen," Dallas begins with hands on her hips. "We're going to hang out in the pool for a while. You're going to chat with Calvin like you have been all week. We're going to go to Joe and Drew's wedding. We're going to have fun, and you are going to live in the moment and stop worrying. You'll kiss some more, maybe hold hands, dance, and the good lord willing, dance in the sheets with that hot guy."

I love my friend. If only it were as easy as she makes it out to be.

"I'll bet you my new Kate Spade clutch you don't have the lady balls to walk up to Calvin when we return and kiss him in front of the entire group," Dallas dares. She raises an eyebrow at me.

This is clearly a challenge.

I close my eyes and nod my head. *She'll never stop. She's going to push me this week with Calvin and then next month with someone new.*

She grabs my hand, pulling me from the sandy beach toward the pool. All eyes are on the two of us as we return to the group.

I walk down the steps, lowering my body into the cool water of the pool. I waste no time wading to the side and our friends. As Calvin sits at the edge of the pool with his feet dangling in the water, I stand below him, my body between his bent knees. On tiptoes, I reach my hands up and tug on his hair, lowering his mouth to mine. Calvin doesn't protest; he follows my lead. I slam my lips over his. Rapidly, our kiss heats to a not-appropriate-for-public display of affection. Moments pass before our surroundings interfere. Pulling away, I bite my lower lip, blushing as the guys catcall and the girls smile approvingly.

Dallas's words haunt my thoughts all afternoon and evening. There's one little secret that I kept from my best friend. *I guess it may be a big secret.* If she knew about my lack of experience, I'm sure her advice would be different. She's cavalier about sex and doesn't think the fact that I've had a hysterectomy should keep me from trying to find a long-term boyfriend. I don't see the point in putting off the inevitable. I don't want to string a guy along for months or even years just to divulge that fact when he talks about our future family.

I find my fingers touch my lips often tonight. I can't get our kiss off my mind. I swear my lips still tingle where his fought with mine. Calvin notices my hand on my mouth and smirks knowingly, winking at me.

Cocky little turd.

I'm not sure if I kissed him just to win Dallas's new designer clutch, or if with Dallas's prodding, I gave in and took what I wanted. All I know is I put everything into that kiss. I poured all my repressed attraction into it. The fact that I can't stop thinking about it says a lot about my feelings for this man.

As the sun slowly sinks into the blue ocean waters, we emerge from the pool, towel ourselves off, and return to our rooms to dress for dinner.

"We'll meet at the lobby bar in an hour," Garret instructs the group as we head to our rooms in opposite directions.

Linking her arm with mine, Dallas leans towards me. "I'm so proud of you." Her voice is a light whisper in my ear.

I'm glad she pushed me, but hate the I-was-right smirk upon her face now.

"You should wear the green sundress this evening," she suggests. "Calvin won't be able to keep his eyes and hands off of you in that little number."

I love that sundress, but doubt it will have such an effect on him.

In our room, Dallas and I quickly shower, change, and meet in the bathroom to apply makeup and style our hair. She looks stunning in her black, strapless maxi dress with a much too high slit up the side.

"What do you think, up or down?" I ask, playing with my hair.

"Down," she replies without hesitation. "Calvin sees it up during volleyball and swimming, so having it down will be a nice change."

I nod. In record time, the two of us are out the door, heading to meet the group.

"I'll probably stay with Garret again tonight," Dallas informs me. "So, Calvin and you will have the entire place to yourself." She nudges me and gives me a wink.

I roll my eyes, shaking my head. *We've only kissed twice; I'm not ready to invite him into my bed.* I brush off her suggestion.

We're the first two in the lobby bar. Dallas and I choose the casual sofa area with a view of the beach. It only takes a moment before the bartender takes our drink orders.

Our drinks are nearly empty when the guys join us. Only Joe and Drew are missing. I'm sure the soon-to-be newlyweds are practicing for the honeymoon while their parents sightsee in town.

"What's everyone want? I'll go get us drinks," I offer, rising from my cushioned chair.

I can't help but notice Calvin's face as his eyes scan me from top to toe. My green sundress falls to mid-thigh with a wide, flowing skirt. A fair amount of cleavage shows with the halter top portion. I bite my lips under his gaze and smirk, imagining his reaction when he sees the back of the dress. I'm sure his eyes will bug out at the backless design with a terrifyingly low plunge to the skirt. *Any lower and a plumber's crack would show.*

"I'll help," Calvin offers, snagging my hand in his as I walk by.

I lead him between the sofa and chair, all the while feeling his fiery gaze upon my bare skin. He's reacting to the view from behind. With more floor space opening up as we approach the bar, Calvin releases my hand to place his soft, warm palm on my lower back.

The heat of his hand upon my bare skin sends jolts of electricity up my spine. My body revolts when he removes it to carry the drinks back from the bar. It doesn't escape me he opts to walk behind me as we return to our group. Dallas was right about this green sundress and its effect on him.

12

IT WILL NEVER BE ENOUGH

Schuyler

I intentionally sit opposite Calvin at dinner. The pull towards each other grew exponentially today after our pool-side kiss. Besides, from this side, I can flirt and tease him from a distance. I'm careful not to go too far. I only playfully flirt with him. I'm not so cruel to lead him on or suggest I'm ready for something I'm not. *Perhaps it's the dress giving me confidence and a mojo boost.*

With eyes closed, I groan out loud at the first bite of my appetizer; the crisp calamari with Buckaroo sauce engulfs my mouth.

"You've got to try this," I inform Calvin, extending a bite on my fork across the table for him. When he hesitates, I urge him, "C'mon! Don't be afraid."

Calvin leans forward in his chair and allows me to place my fork in his mouth. I melt into a pool of mush when his full lips close around the tines, pulling back to slide the bite with him.

I hope no one notices the full-body shiver that his action causes. My mind wanders to his mouth, tasting my body in the same manner. My thighs ache to rub together, providing me the friction my core longs for.

When I can't make up my mind on dessert, Calvin suggests I choose one, and he'll order the other for us to share. He claims we will have the best of both worlds. *Sharing dessert feels intimate; I hope I'm just reading too much into it.*

Unbreakable

As our energy levels begin to wane, our group plans to call it a night. I'm not ready to return to my room alone. I contemplate staying at the dance party or watching the late-night magician the resort scheduled.

"Want to head to the lobby bar for another drink?" Calvin murmurs to me.

The skin on my neck prickles at the warmth of his breath. I'd love to spend more time with him this evening, but I need to be clear on what is and isn't on the table for tonight.

"Or, we could sit outside my room, raid my mini-fridge, and talk over the sounds of the waves pummeling the beach," I counter.

Wait!

Why did I do that?

So much for not giving him the wrong idea. Inviting him back to my place is usually code for sex. Now, what do I do?

"Okay," Calvin accepts.

Walking towards my room, I'm both excited and nervous to spend time alone with him. As we walk, Calvin's hand remains on my lower back. With our proximity, my wrist occasionally grazes his thigh. The slight contact and gentle friction cause me to imagine friction at the apex of my thighs. *For someone who's not ready to have sex with a guy, I sure think about it a lot.*

At my bungalow door, I fumble with my keycard, my hands shaking. Having Calvin at my door after our intimate nap earlier gets to me more than I anticipated. Calvin places his hand over mine, assisting me with the lock. When the green light signals, we push open the door.

"I'm gonna change into something comfy. Would you mind opening the patio doors for us?"

I do not wait for his reply, heading into my room. I waste no time, slipping into a shirt and shorts then returning to the outer room. I join Calvin on the patio with a drink waiting for me on the little table between the chairs.

"I'm gonna miss this," I confess, taking the seat next to him. "The waves on my sound machine don't hold a candle to the real thing."

Calvin nods, sipping from his drink. As he stares at the ocean beyond the beach, I attempt to memorize his profile. A light dusting of scruff adorns his relaxed jaw from chin to ear. In the muted light from the front room, the red highlights in his brown hair mix perfectly, preventing the brown from seeming black.

I'm caught staring when he looks my way.

"I'm gonna miss this," he admits, motioning between us. "Promise me we'll meet up back on campus." His eyes plead with mine.

Life will be hectic upon returning to college. Final reports, evaluations, and licensing paperwork will fill my days. During the evenings, I'll be scouring the internet and applying for teaching positions.

"I know we'll be busy preparing for graduation," he states, as if reading my thoughts. "Surely, we can find an evening or an hour to get together each week."

His hazel eyes plead for me to promise. In their moss green depths, I see he wants me; he's serious. He doesn't want this to end when we fly back to the U.S.

"I'd like to see you, too," I confess. "That doesn't mean I want to rush things; I like being with you. It seems natural, and I don't want us to force it."

My heart slams repetitively against my rib cage. *I've shared too much; I'm too honest.* I've never put myself out there before this moment. My throat's tight, my eyes wide, and sweat forms on my brow, armpits, and palms.

Calvin's warm hand wraps around my right wrist. He tugs me onto his lap. Facing him, I straddle him. I place my palms flat on his chest. His large hand cups the back of my neck, pulling my mouth to his. It's not a sweet, slow kiss. His mouth collides with mine, sucking and nipping at my lips. In his kiss, I feel his desperate need to be with me.

Wanting more, I part my lips, allowing my tongue to glide along his lower lip. It's all the invitation he needs. Calvin's powerful tongue massages mine. At times, his mouth sucks my tongue in. My mind swims as my body molds further into his. Calvin feeds upon my mouth as if it were his last feast. His hands on the back of my neck hold me to him; unable to escape him, I join him. I can't get enough—it will never be enough.

I slide my pelvis forward and back. The sweet friction seems to ignite a fire deep within him. When I repeat the motion, he growls. It sounds like a plea, like a warning. With hands on my hips, he lifts me from his loins. In the moment, his strength surprises me.

"I need a minute," he rasps.

Standing in front of him, my eyes focus, and the lusty haze lifts.

"Oh my god. I'm sorry." I look right then left, scouring for an escape.

He laces his fingers with mine, forbidding my flight response. I stare at our joined hands in confusion.

"There's nothing to be sorry for," he explains. "It's just..."

I interrupt him. "Can we forget what happened and return to our separate chairs, our drinks, and our conversation?" I will do anything to ease the embarrassment I'm feeling.

A slow, wide smile grows upon his face. He rises, standing in front of me. He wraps his arms around my waist. Then, he kisses the corner of my mouth before moving his mouth to my ear. "We can go to our separate corners and talk, but I will never, and I mean never, forget how you make me feel."

He stares into my eyes, daring me to argue. As I fight a smile, we take our seats and sip our drinks.

"If you could spend an hour with any person, alive or dead, who would it be and why?" I blurt nervously.

With a head tilt, he smirks. "Hmm, let's see." He gazes up at the night sky, his hand cupping his chin in thought. "I'd choose JFK, because I'd like to ask if he had any knowledge that he might be assassinated. I'd also like to ask him about Marilyn Monroe."

"That's a good answer," I state.

"If you could spend an hour with any person, alive or dead, who would it be and why?" he parrots.

"I'd choose Nichelle Nichols," I state.

"Who?" His face scrunches adorably in confusion.

"She played Nyota Uhura on *Star Trek*. She was a trailblazer for women everywhere," I explain. "She led the way for African-American characters on television. She also worked with NASA to encourage diversity."

Why?

Why do I over share?

I let my nerd flag fly. I'm such an idiot. Hesitantly, I glance at him out of the corner of my eye, nervous for his reaction.

"Wow! Your answer beats mine," he claims.

"Next question. If you could travel to any time in history, where would you go and why?" I challenge, eager to keep our conversation going.

"I'd travel to the Neolithic period to witness how Stonehenge was built." Proud of his answer, he crosses his arms across his chest. "Where would you go?" he counters.

"This is a little more difficult for me to answer," I begin. "As a woman, I have to take in the status and treatment of women in any given period before I could travel there. Throughout history, women have been the most oppressed and mistreated group of people."

"So, let's pass on that question," he suggests. A few moments fly by as we listen to the waves. "I've got it. If you could put together the best concert ever, what artists, alive and dead, would you choose?"

"Oh, this is easy," I preen. "Queen, Michael Jackson, Aerosmith, Prince, Nirvana, Elvis, Ricky Nelson, Chicago with Peter Cetera," I stress, "Warrant, Garth Brooks, Nickelback, Maroon Five, Mötley Crüe, Pink, and George Michael."

"Wow! That would be a long concert," he teases.

"Who would you choose?" I reverse his question.

"Elton John, Buddy Holly, and John Legend."

I can't believe he only chose three. "That's it? Just those three?"

"If I list others that aren't on your massive list, you will judge me," he claims.

"This is a safe circle, a no judgment zone," I promise.

"Justin Timberlake, Imagine Dragons, Run DMC, and Guns N' Roses," he adds.

"I bet you'd like to have a boy band in there," I tease.

"Hey! Where'd the safe circle go?" He pouts.

"I'm sorry," I laugh then signal a cross over my heart with my index finger.

After my third yawn in a couple of minutes, we decide to lay in bed and talk.

"I didn't make the bed after our nap this afternoon. Please, don't judge me," I plead.

"This is a safe circle, a no judgment zone," Calvin parrots my previous words.

13

THE MONSTER UNDER THE BED

Calvin

Climbing back into Schuyler's bed seems as natural as if I do it every night. Being near her is easy and comfortable. I feel like I've found the other half of me, my soul mate.

With my head propped on two pillows, I watch Schuyler turn on the ceiling fan, her fan on the floor, close the blackout curtains tightly, turn the flashlight from her phone on, shut off the overhead light, then dart to the bed, hopping on the mattress with a giggle.

I fight the laugh, trying to escape. In the faint light from her phone, she squints at me.

"What?" Schuyler demands, shutting off her phone light and snuggling under the covers.

"That's quite a routine," I chuckle. "I especially like the sprint after turning off the light and the hop onto the bed." I turn onto my side, facing her in the dark. "It's the monster under the bed, isn't it?"

"Maybe," she murmurs sheepishly.

"I can't sleep with a closet door open," I confess. I'm sure she thinks I'm teasing, but I'm not.

"Who's turn is it?" she asks, repositioning herself closer to me.

"Yours."

Schuyler fires her next question immediately. "What were you like in high school?"

Seems she's had this question ready for a while.

"Garret, Rich, and I became friends in middle school," I begin. "We played football, baseball, basketball, and ran track."

"Um, I asked what you were like, not who your friends were." Schuyler protests my answer. "I assumed you were a jock; what kind of student were you, what clubs did you join, and how many hearts did you break?"

Well, now we get to the interesting portion of getting to know each other. I'm glad she swayed our conversation in this direction. I've several questions I've been looking for the right time to ask.

"I was a jock, but a cool one." I've never had to explain any of this. *I don't want her to think I was a dumb jock that bullied others in my school.* "I did okay in school, had fun, socialized…"

"So, you partied," Schuyler butts in.

"I had fun in and outside of school," I admit. "I'd like to think I got along with everyone."

"Uh-hum," she clears her throat. "And girlfriends…?"

"I didn't worry about girls," I state. "I spent time with the guys or working at Dad's firm."

"I call bullshit." Schuyler raises her voice. In the darkness, she places her palm on my chest and shoves playfully.

"Really," I insist. "I tried to avoid all the distractions and drama. I was close friends with a neighbor girl, Riley. When we attended an event that required a date, we were always each other's plus one." I reach my hand out. Feeling her arm, I trail my hand down, entwining it with hers. "I was Riley's beard."

"So, you want me to believe you didn't date in high school?" She seeks further clarification.

"I made out with a girl here and there at a party," I admit. "But dating? Nope. It was always Riley and me."

"So, this neighbor girl…" she pries. "Were you friends with benefits?"

I smile, knowing she can't see me do it. "When I stated I was her beard, I meant it. She wasn't ready to step out of her closet with the entire student body. She helped me, and I helped her."

Schuyler

. . .

The next day, the tropical sun begins its descent for the evening, and the ocean serves as a backdrop for the ceremony. The staff raked the warm sand into a smooth floor and placed three rows of four white, plastic chairs on each side of the palm prawns that make up the aisle.

Joe, Calvin, and Garret stand handsomely in pale blue, button-down, Cuban-style shirts with light tan shorts and brown, leather topsiders. The bridesmaids' sun-kissed skin glows in the pale blue halter-top sundresses that fall mid-thigh, adorned with a light floral pattern.

The bride, Drew, faces Joe as they exchange vows. All eyes are drawn to her in her white crocheted maxi dress with lace-like scallops at the hem. Her light blonde hair falls in soft, springy curls beneath a wreath of white and blue flowers. Her bouquet contains bright orange, yellow, and green flowers with a simple blue ribbon tied in a bow around the long, green stems. As the waves ebb and flow, the soft, lulling rhythm adds to the perfect setting for the ceremony.

Dallas and I sit in the third row. She holds my hand tight in hers as she *oohs* and *ahhs* at their vows. My body feels electric in reaction to the wink Calvin sent my way before Drew walked down the aisle to meet her man. I failed to completely calm myself after our many kisses this afternoon. I splashed water on my face and stood in front of the fan, but all was in vain. My boiling blood melded into a simmer as we walked the beach before he left me to prepare for the ceremony. One sexy wink from 20 feet away, however, sparked my desire once more. His back to me while he stands beside Joe during the vows, my mind imagines his lips on mine, his hands in my hair, and his strong, muscular body pressed against me. Any hope of maintaining control of my body flies out the window.

Dallas pats my arm. "Hey! Earth to Schuyler!"

My eyes blink, and I look at my friend as I attempt to hide my traitorous thoughts. She smiles knowingly.

"Let's go," she chuckles. "The ceremony's over, so he can…"

"Don't you dare," I warn, covering her mouth with my hand. I know exactly what she plans to suggest we do. It's her goal for me this week, after all.

Calvin stands across the room, carrying on a conversation with the parents of the bride. As if he feels my eyes upon him, he looks my way. I blush, and he smirks, knowing what's on my mind. Tilting his head, a slight jerk invites me to join him.

As I approach Drew's parents, they turn from Calvin to smile at me. *No way did they just happen to turn in my direction. What did he say about me?* I raise my eyebrows, causing him to chuckle. Drew's parents pat his arm before excusing themselves.

"What was that all about?" I prod. "What did you say to them," I point to Drew's parents, "before I made it over here?"

He opens his mouth to speak but closes it before uttering a sound.

"I want the truth," I state, hands-on-hips, acting angry.

"Earlier in our conversation, Drew's mother asked which woman had me swooning. She said my silly smile and twinkling eyes had lust written all over them," he spews quickly. "As you walked over, I told them, 'Here comes the woman you asked about earlier.'" He shrugs.

"Wow." I don't know what to say.

Swooning?

Does he look like he is swooning over me?

I look at his smile and eyes, confirming Drew's mother's astute diagnosis.

"I don't know what I expected you to say, but that was not it."

Calvin's left arm reaches for my right hand. Still reveling in his swooning, I'm unable to move my hand towards his. I relish the warmth of his palm against mine, his fingers entwined with mine. It's only been a few hours since he dropped me off in my room. I shouldn't miss his touch this much this soon.

"I'm ready to get out of here," he whispers, his molten hazel eyes full of desire.

I look around the space. "As the best man, are you allowed to leave the reception early?"

Calvin smirks. "I've given my toast, I've visited with all the guests, I've consumed two drinks, and I've smiled for the camera."

"You've been a busy man," I tease.

His hand releases mine, settling itself at the small of my back, causing my pulse to quicken. I follow his lead as we say our goodbyes to the bride and groom and wave to the others. Exiting the lounge, the cool night breeze prickles my exposed skin, the sensation at odds with the heat building in my core.

"I was thinking..." Calvin murmurs as we pass the outdoor festivities and other guests. "We could enjoy the night from your bungalow patio." He raises an eyebrow at me as he waits for my response.

I turn, placing my mouth close to his ear and whisper, "Sounds perfect."

I don't recognize my breathy voice. I've never been this worked up in the presence of a man before.

I both love it and fear it at the same time.

14

WELCOME THE INVASION

Schuyler

The two drinks I consume on the patio calm my nerves as the ocean waves pound against the sandy beach. I've enjoyed our conversation along with the soft, featherlike motion of Calvin's fingertips on my arms, shoulders, and the back of my neck.

I look up after placing my empty bottle on the cement beside me to find Calvin's hooded eyes and luscious lips moving toward mine. I stifle a moan at the contact. They caress gently, slowly at first. In his kiss, I feel his want, his need, and his desire for me. It's gasoline on the flames low in my belly.

His hot, wet tongue glides along my lower lip suggestively. He's ready for me to open up for him, to let him in. Like him, I want more. I press myself closer to him, my breasts longing to be free from their confinement to find friction against his chest. One large hand cups the back of my neck as the other presses on my lower back. He guides me with him as he stretches out on his lounger. His hands nestle me tight against him from my head to my thighs. I part my lips, a gasp escaping as the length of his hard cock registers in my brain.

His tongue slides along and over mine, and I welcome the invasion. I lean my head farther to the side, opening myself wider for him. To the rhythm of his kiss, I slide my body on his. My breasts ache, and my nipples pebble. The words of my grandmother "brazen hussy" come to mind as I grind my pelvis to him. The friction inflates my desire. I'm light-headed. I can't breathe.

I slide my knees toward his chest as I peel myself from him. I sit straddling him, panting, and my chest heaving. So lost in the moment, I forgot to breathe. His lust-filled eyes speak volumes.

"Wanna go…" I suggest.

"Yes," Calvin interrupts.

As we walk, his hands clutch my hips; his body closely follows mine. When I spin in his arms at the opening to the hallway, he pounces. His lips collide with mine. We're all hands, gasps, pants, and shivers. My breasts are heavy, and my nipples are nearly as rock hard as his erection, straining in his shorts. His fingers trace the neck of my dress, and his thumbs brush over my pert nipples. My hand slides along the length of him. The thought of the pleasure such a beast will cause brings wetness between my legs.

I unbutton, then tug off his shirt. He slips the straps of my dress off my shoulders, his mouth peppering kisses along my collarbone, then the tops of my breasts, peeking from the cups of my bra. We fall onto my bed, the moonlight faintly illuminating the room.

Bam!

My brain turns on to ruin the moment. Everything I've read about post-hysterectomy sex slaps me in the face. Symptoms like dryness, pain during sex, pain after sex, and difficulty climaxing whirl to the front of my thoughts. Instantly, my body stiffens.

"Sky, what's wrong?" Calvin asks. With an ab curl, he presses his forehead to mine.

I attempt to shake my head, eager to brush off his concern.

"Something's wrong. Please talk to me," he pleads. "If you're not ready…"

"I'm ready," I profess. "I want this." I chew on my lower lip as I search for the right words. "It's been a while since I've had…" I can't confess. *Think. Think.* "… a boyfriend…"

Placing his fingers over my lips, Calvin promises, "Okay. So, we'll go slower." A wicked smirk slides upon his mouth. "I'm good at foreplay." He waggles his eyebrows suggestively.

"Only good?" I tease, mustering up more bravado than I own.

"Well, since we're in your bed, you can judge just how good I am."

"I'm nervous," I whisper.

I want to share the reason for my fears, but that would be a cold, wet blanket on the fiery flames between us.

I can do this.

I'm ready to do this. I'm just nervous he might not enjoy my body.

Calvin

We lie naked under the sheet on Schuyler's bed. It takes all my willpower to not hover my body over hers, thrusting balls deep, and making every part of the gorgeous woman mine.

I brush a strand of hair behind her ear. I leave my fingers in her hair, my thumb gently caressing her cheek. She leans into my touch, her eyes closing for a moment.

"I'm ready," she whispers. "Let me judge your 'good' foreplay skills."

Although she teases, she doesn't smile. I sense her fear, but of what, I don't know. I long to prove she has nothing to fear with me.

Schuyler moves away from me, touching her lips gently to the corner of my mouth. She places a peck on each side of my mouth before focusing on the center. I part my lips, and she takes advantage of the opening. I let her lead. She needs to control the situation if I want her walls to come down.

Slowly, her fingertips explore my shoulders and pectorals, then work their way down, gently tugging at the strip of hair at my waist. The slight tug shoots electricity straight into my balls. *I'm glad I chose not to wax away my happy trail.*

With one hand, she gently scrapes her fingernails across my abdomen; with her other hand, she continues tugging. The conflicting sensations are more than I can handle.

Needing to distract her, I cup her breasts. They fit perfectly in my hands. My thumbs graze each nipple, and she moans in response. I lower my mouth, nuzzling her neck, before licking my way toward her hard pebbles. She writhes as my hot, wet mouth licks, sucks, and nips first at one peak, then the other.

I suck in a breath through gritted teeth as her hands grasp my cock. She softly rubs her thumb along my shaft as the weight of me sits in her palm. She wraps her fingers around the base, applying gentle pressure. I moan when she glides the length of my shaft, tickles the head with her fingertips, then moves back toward the base. She repeats the motion over and over. On its own, my pelvis thrusts into her hand. When her thumb spreads the bead of precum over my tip, I place my hands on her hips and lift her body on top of mine.

She throws the sheet behind her. On her knees, she takes my cock in hand, slowly sliding it past her opening and inch by inch into her channel. My hands grip her hips, my fingertips digging into her flesh, seeking to hold her against me.

Fully impaled upon me, she remains motionless, her eyes closed. *I long to know what she's thinking, how this feels for her, and why she's so scared of intimacy.*

When her lids open, her gaze locks on mine. She marginally lifts her hips, then slides down. The slow movement is excruciating. Her lips part as she speeds up.

I struggle to watch her face for a reaction. The delicious friction of her tight, hot core consumes me. It's unlike anything I've ever experienced. When Sky grinds herself against my pelvis on a downward stroke, her head wobbles and eyes close. With one hand, I cup a bouncing breast. I slide the other between us. I place the pad of my thumb on her swollen clit. As I make small circles, her head falls back, and she increases her speed again.

I pinch her nipple while pressing my thumb harder against her tight ball of nerves, eliciting a long groan from her. On the next downward motion, she grinds into me, screaming, "Yes! Yes! Yesss!" Her fingernails bite into my skin while her inner muscles spasm around my shaft.

I'm unable to remain still as she rides the pleasure of her orgasm. With one smooth motion, I flip her onto her back and lift both of her legs over my shoulders. Although I feel the need to drive myself into her, I begin with long, slow thrusts. Her inner walls delectably grip my shaft. I thrust once, twice, then on the third thrust, I erupt. Hot semen flows through me, shooting into her. I quiver above her while I pulse within her. My arms burn as they try to keep me planked above her.

I drag myself from her heat, falling beside her on the bed, one hand playing with her hair. When my free hand lowers to remove the condom, I freeze. My entire body turns to stone. Internally, I'm freaking out.

I've never forgotten to use a condom.
Never.

With great effort, I turn my head to face her. Her face reflects my fear.

15

ALL-CONSUMING ASSAULT

Schuyler
Myth busted.
I lie lifeless on my mattress. *I love the sensation of sated desire. Not only did I have an orgasm post-hysterectomy, but it was a long, magnificent one.*
It feels much better than the releases my vibrators give me.
As I come down from my post-orgasmic high, fear floods me.
Was it as good for Calvin?
Did my body feel different to him?
Could his tip feel that?
Does he know I'm a 23-year-old freak?
Reluctantly, I turn my head in his direction. He confirms my worries when I see the look on his face.
Slowly, his face morphs into a smile. His tongue darts out to wet his lower lip. He rolls onto his side.
"I failed," he murmurs.
My brow furrows.
What does he mean he failed?
Is he blaming himself for my faulty equipment?
"I lost my focus and failed to show my foreplay skills," Calvin apologizes.
"I didn't notice," I confess. "You gave me a…"
His fingers press against my lips, silencing me. "I felt it from the inside." He smiles.

"And for you…?" I let the question hang in the air.

"You couldn't tell?" he asks. His eyebrows pinch together.

I bite my lower lip, unsure how to respond.

"It was amazing. You were amazing. You felt…" he pinches his lips. "I… I forgot to use a condom."

Fear returns to his features.

Did he not notice?

Couldn't he tell my girly parts aren't natural?

The fear on his face pains me.

"I've got us covered," I murmur.

He processes my words for a moment. "I'm clean. I haven't been with anyone in four years, and I have an annual checkup." His eyes beg me to believe him.

I nod. "Me, too." I hope he assumes I am on birth control or have a female condom. I'd really like to save my uncomfortable conversation for later.

His face relaxes, and he breathes a sigh of relief. *It seems his only fear was the lack of a condom.*

"I've never been bareback." He sucks in a deep breath. "You felt phenomenal."

If I don't leave this bed, the day cannot start, and tomorrow will not come. I refuse to look at my cell phone to see what time it is. *If only it was that simple.* The tiny ray of sunlight alerts me the day has started without us.

During our hours of conversation late last night, we vowed to sleep as late as we could this morning. Trying not to disturb Calvin, I slowly roll on my side to face him. I smile when his sleepy eyes look at me.

"Good morning," his gravelly voice greets me. "I don't want this week to end."

"I know, but we'll see each other back on campus," I remind him of our decision to date when we return to school.

"Right, but with classes and graduation preparations, we won't get to spend every day together like we do here in Mexico," he murmurs.

I feel the same way. I like it here in our bubble, away from the real world. I've lowered some of my walls. *I'll need to rebuild them when we return to college and the real world.*

"Let's get some brunch," he suggests, pulling me tight against him. "I need to rebuild my strength," he whispers near my ear.

"I guess you're right; we need to eat," I groan.

"I know what will perk you up," Calvin states, exiting my bed. "Come join me in the shower." He smiles at me, a hint of excitement on his face.

He walks from the room, bare-assed, and doesn't look back. He doesn't need to coax me, and he knows it.

I take my time rolling out of bed and padding to the bathroom. I'm rewarded with the view of Calvin under the shower spray. The water glistens on his bronze skin. I pause in the doorway, taking in the awe-inspiring view.

My body sparks to life, and my blood hums through my veins. Like a flower, I lean toward the sun. Calvin's the center of the universe, his gravity constantly pulling me to him. I step behind him in the tile shower, lightly scraping my fingernails down his back.

He adjusts the shower spray to flow from the rainforest shower head above us and the spouts on both walls. When he turns to face me, his pupils dilate as he rakes his eyes over my wet, naked form. One hand cups the back of my neck, and the other plants firmly at my hip. Slowly, he pulls me to him, eyes glued to mine.

Our bodies meet as water flows down our backs, and our eyes remain locked. Calvin's hand on my neck pulls my mouth to his. This is not a sweet, slow kiss. This is a hungry, all-consuming assault, and I welcome it.

I give as good as I get. My hands quickly find their way south of his waist. His kissing pauses when I take his satin-covered hardness in hand. As I stroke, he moans before his tongue tangles with mine once more.

No longer needing to hold me close, his hands cup my breasts. The pads of his thumbs provide splendid friction when he pinches and flicks my hardening buds while the water caresses me. My breath quickens, and Calvin's forehead presses to mine. We speak no words, yet we know exactly what the other wants and needs.

I spin, nestling my bottom against his growing erection and lifting my arms back to pull his face towards mine. I wiggle my butt, inviting him to take me now.

"Please."

I mew when his finger barely brushes my center. He opens my folds, targeting his ministrations on my swollen clit.

"Yes," I moan, begging him to continue.

I slide my hand behind me, directing his cock between my thighs. Calvin thrusts as he rubs my bundle of nerves faster and faster. The head of his cock caresses my opening, teasing me, winding me tighter and tighter. I'm teetering on the edge of a precipice, ready to fall at the tiniest nudge. I can feel my orgasm hovering close, and I desperately need the release.

When I squeeze my Kegels, I'm rewarded. The coil releases in my belly, molten heat flows throughout my limbs, white light flickers behind my eyelids, and his continued circles on my clit extend my climax. Every muscle flexes and burns with unbridled pleasure. Coming down from my release, my legs tremble. I feel weak and sated.

I place my palms upon the cool tiles, jutting my bottom back into Calvin. The tip of his cock teases at my entrance, coating itself with my wetness. Slowly, achingly so, he slides his length inside. My inner muscles still spasm from my orgasm. When they constrict around his cock, Calvin halts.

"Fuckkk," his feral growl excites me.

I enjoy bringing the animalistic side of him to the surface. I love that my body and my touch can evoke such sensations from this muscular man. I feel powerful and sexy for the first time in my life.

Calvin

I stare at my full plate on the table in front of me. It will be my last breakfast here, maybe my last ever with Schuyler. We've connected in many ways, but she still has walls up. She's not letting me in all the way. I realize I'm a hypocrite for desiring so much openness from her when I keep a secret, too.

Her fork moves the fruit from one side of her plate to the other as she absent-mindedly stares into space.

We plan to see each other back at school, so we shouldn't waste the last day in Mexico pouting.

When I lift a chunk of melon towards her lips, Schuyler looks up through her long lashes, questioning me. I slide the melon across her lower lip, leaving a trail of juice in its wake. I stare at her perfect mouth. She opens for me, and I place the melon on her tongue.

"Mmm," she moans, her smile shining brightly at me.

Next, I offer a large grape. As I slowly lean toward her, she parts her lips. I lay it on her tongue, and she closes her lips tightly around my finger. Her cheeks are hollow as she sucks suggestively. I close my eyes, and my mind imagines her lips tight on my shaft, her tongue caressing my swollen cock. It's all I can do not to make an inappropriate noise at the table.

Schuyler slowly withdraws my index finger. My cock twitches in my trunks; I adjust myself beneath the table. She smirks, proud of her sensual teasing.

She chooses a strawberry, but before she can feed it to me, Dallas and Garret approach.

"Well, it looks like we weren't the only couple sleeping in this morning,"

Dallas coos, assuming the seat beside her friend. "Didn't he let you sleep last night? You look exhausted."

Schuyler swats at her friend, glaring. She lowers her gaze to her plate, avoiding Garret, embarrassed. *I hope it's embarrassment and not regret. She seems to share her body with me without hesitation. I long for her to share her thoughts and secrets with me, too.*

With our meal finished, we excuse ourselves and invite our friends to join us as we hang out at the pool. My hand seeks Schuyler's; our fingers entwine. As we approach the pool, it feels like I'm right where I'm fated to be. *Rather than mere days, it's as if we have dated for years. My body and soul welcome hers as their missing halves. She completes me in every way. My only hesitation is that she's still guarded. She's holding something back, which prevents me from telling her about Tyler. I don't mean to mislead her. I know she will run if I tell her this soon, and I wouldn't blame her. So, I'll enjoy what we have now while I wait for her total trust.*

I squirt sunscreen into my hand while she removes her coverup and tosses it on a nearby lounge chair. Standing behind her, I rub the dollop between my palms to warm it before I apply it to her neck, shoulders, and the exposed sections of her back. I squeeze more into my palm, then both hands massage her outer thighs.

Quickly, Schuyler steps away from me, turning to waggle her finger in my direction while smirking. I only planned to apply the sunscreen to the backs of her legs. Now that she scolds me, I realize the proximity of my fingers to a very sensitive part of her body. I hold my palms out to her in apology, then pass her the sunscreen so she can finish applying it.

"Your turn." She motions for me to spin away from her, and I do as instructed.

Her hands gently massage my neck, shoulders, and rib cage before her finger tips slide beneath the band of my trunks. My cock twitches when I imagine her slickened fingers on my shaft.

Now, I understand her protest to my applying lotion to her thighs.

16

SNOWED IN

Schuyler

We enjoy a couple hours relaxing in the pool, using the swim-up bar, and soaking up our last day in the tropical heat. I relish Calvin's attention and his body, which seems to be constantly in contact with mine.

While in the deeper section of the pool, he loads me onto his back as he walks about. I lean over his shoulders to clasp my hands in front of his chest, and my thighs grip his hips. The sun-warmed skin on his back starkly contrasts the cool water that surrounds me. He lowers me to stand near the pool's edge.

"I saw that," Calvin murmurs into my ear.

"Saw what?"

"Your yawn." He moves to stand directly in front of me. "Let's dry off and head in for a nap."

I open my mouth to protest, but thoughts of playing under the sheets before we nap flood my mind. I attempt to quell the smirk that forms upon my lips, but fail miserably. I nod, and we exit the cool waters of the pool.

Our eyes remain on each other as we try to towel off as best we can. I smooth out a dry towel upon my lounger before laying on my back. I turn toward Calvin's lounger to find him lying on his stomach, with his head turned to face me.

Grinning, he murmurs, "I'm hiding my reaction from your sexy body. I wouldn't want the tent in my shorts to scare the other guests."

I roll my eyes before I look away. I long to hop up and scurry to my bungalow. His constant touch perpetuated my arousal over the past hours.

Unbreakable

The clock near the bar shows it's nearly three. Soon, we'll meet with our friends for our last meal at the resort, then go our separate ways for the final night of our vacations. Although I'm ready for the semester to end and to celebrate my graduation, I don't want to leave our little bubble in paradise.

"Sky," Calvin's voice beckons, so I turn my head in his direction. "Remember our promise today."

Before we left the room this morning, he proposed we focus on our remaining time here and not on what tomorrow brings. It's hard not to let the disappointment hang heavy in the air. Many things will change when our planes touch down on U.S. soil.

"It's written on your face," he informs me.

"I'm sorry," I explain. "Maybe I need you to distract me and cheer me up."

Excitement glimmers in his brown-green eyes, his smile reaching to crinkle their corners.

"I changed my flight from Kansas City to Des Moines. I'm on the same flight as you."

I stand, dumbfounded.

Did he really say that?
Did I hear him correctly?
Why would he do that?

"I needed to spend more time with you," he explains.

My wide smile lets him know I approve. He sits with a towel across his lap while I gather up my swim bag and pull my cover up over my head. I wave to our friends as Calvin follows a step behind, towel still in hand.

On the path toward the private bungalows, I remind him, "You're supposed to leave the towel in the basket at the edge of the pool area."

He pauses, tosses the towel over his shoulder, and glances down at his shorts. My eyes follow.

He was not exaggerating when he mentioned the tent in his swim trunks. As if reaching for me, his erection points to my abdomen.

"I want to bite that lip," his baritone voice growls.

I know I'm chewing on my lower lip as I marvel at the impressive rod he's packing for me. I look up through my lashes, lust igniting every part of me.

"Shall we?" He positions the towel in front of himself again and motions toward my room with his free hand.

I lead the way to my bungalow, thoughts of unwrapping his erection swirling through my brain. All tiredness from drying in the warm sun disappears. Every cell springs to life with desire. *After waiting 23 years for sex, now I can't seem to get enough.* I'm addicted to my desire for Calvin, the anticipation of a building climax, and the blissful oblivion that rocks my body with release.

"This is your captain speaking." A formal male voice intrudes into the cabin, causing all conversation to halt. "The tower has us in a holding pattern while they plow the runway. Des Moines has 19 inches of snow on the ground, and it's forecast to continue for the next 12 hours. They will close the airport after our plane lands. The fasten seatbelt sign will remain on. I've instructed the flight attendants to stay seated until we taxi to the gate."

Dallas and I exchange looks. *I long to be back in Mexico on the beach in the scorching sun.* I expected a let down upon returning to the Midwest, but not a blizzard. I remind myself that it's the first week of March in Iowa, and the weather is very fickle.

The cabin fills with anxious chatter. Those with connecting flights discuss what they will do for the night; others contemplate the hazards ahead for their drive home. With no access to cell towers or the internet, we can make no official plans until we land. *I'm glad they dropped us off at the airport; I'd rather my dad pick us up in the SUV than try to drive home in this weather. I doubt we'd even leave. I'm sure they don't plow the parking lots if they find it difficult to keep the runway clean.*

The longer we fly in circles over the metro area, the more the passengers grow anxious in their conversations.

"Ladies and gentlemen, this is your captain," the authoritative voice begins again. "The tower has given us permission to land. Flight attendants, please secure the cabin for landing."

The three attendants quickly walk through the cabin, ensuring we fasten our lap belts, lock our tray tables, and all seats are in their upright positions before fastening themselves back into their seats. The cabin lights flicker off, and our plane descends.

The moment the wheels stop rolling, passengers connect their phones to cellular service. I watch as those around me frantically scroll and text, hoping to secure new plans. Beside me, Dallas answers a few texts, and I sit quietly, knowing my father will chauffeur us to safety.

Once inside the terminal, Dallas and I stand to the side, waiting on Calvin and Garret to join us. As the four of us make our way to baggage claim, I listen to the conversations at the airport. The buzz is overwhelming; everyone is frantic to get out of the airport. *It's never fun to be stuck in here overnight.*

Unbreakable

"I think you two should stay with us at my parents' house tonight," I state while the guys pull Dallas's luggage off the carousel. "I heard someone say that I-35 has been closed, and law enforcement cautions everyone to not drive. They've even declared a 'no tow' warning, banning the use of tow trucks until the storm passes."

The guys look at each other, concerned.

"We don't want to put your parents out," Garret states, hesitant.

"Sky's parents love to host and have two extra bedrooms," Dallas reassures them. "They'll love having you stay and would be upset if we let you get a hotel room."

"I'll text Mom," I offer, my fingers already dancing on my phone screen.

> **ME**
> can Calvin & Garret stay with us instead of driving to KC?

Her reply immediately lights my screen.

> **MOM**
> of course
> don't let those boys go to hotel
> your father and Clint there to pick you up

> **ME**
> thanks

I extend my cell phone for Calvin and Garret to read. From the looks on their faces, they are apprehensive. *They really only have two options: my house or a hotel. Seeing as they don't have a rental car yet, they would need us to drive them to a hotel anyway. They don't really have a choice.* I open my mouth to share this information.

"Okay," Calvin gives in. "Your brothers won't stay at your mom's, will they?"

Garret and Dallas laugh loudly at Calvin's fear of my three brothers. I pat his shoulder, not divulging the fact that my youngest brother joins my dad to pick us up.

With all our checked luggage collected, we roll our way toward the exit. I'm not sure if my quickening heartbeat comes from a fear of driving in the snow or if it's because of Clint being in the vehicle. *Surely, he will behave with Dad present and leave Calvin alone.*

"Look for a red Suburban," Dallas instructs the guys.

As we peer through the windows, the heavy snow makes it hard to see a vehicle until it is directly in front of us. We wait several long minutes before we spot the red SUV park at the curb, and I lead the group into the storm.

My father climbs from the passenger seat, immediately assisting us to fill the back hatch with suitcases. Wordlessly, the four of us slide into the back seats, grateful for the warmth of the heater. Once Dad buckles in the front, Clint pulls slowly away from the curb. Visibility is nearly zero.

"I thought we were just picking up the two girls," he questions Dad, not taking his eyes off the white sheet of snow in front of him.

"Calvin and Garret planned to get a rental car and drive to KC," Dallas tells Clint. "You wouldn't want us to leave them alone at the airport until tomorrow, would you?"

"Your mother wouldn't be pleased with us if we left them," Dad tells Clint. "She'd make us turn right around and head back to the airport to pick them up. Besides, it's too dangerous for anyone to be stuck in an unfamiliar place. They're better off at home with us."

It's quiet for the rest of the drive. We don't want to distract Clint. It's normally a 10-minute drive from the airport to our house; today, it takes nearly 40 minutes. My muscles are tight, and I'm gripping the door handle with white knuckles when we finally pull into the driveway.

"Here we are! Safe and sound." Clint announces proudly. "Now, let's get inside so I can meet these guys."

17

QUESTION EVERYTHING

Calvin

Though I try, the snow prevents me from taking in the front of the Dawes's home. With luggage in hand, we scurry into the open garage to escape the cold. Schuyler hands my bag to her brother then guides me into the house. Warmth assails us as we pass through the laundry room into a large kitchen with a breakfast nook.

"Oh, thank God! You made it home safely! Now, all my babies are safe and nearby," the woman, I assume is Sky's mom rejoices, her hands pressed together in front of her. She greets Schuyler and Dallas with a hug, commenting on their sun-kissed skin. "Hello, Calvin." She looks at me then at Garret. "You must be Garret." It takes me a moment to remember how she knows me. *I spoke to her on one of Schuyler's FaceTime calls.*

We take turns making introductions with Theo and her husband, Richard Dawes. They instruct Clint to carry our luggage up to the guest rooms, then guide us into the living room to sit. I strain, but I cannot make out what Clint mumbles under his breath at her request.

"I'm so glad you chose to stay with us instead of attempting the drive to Missouri. I couldn't live with myself if something were to happen to either of you." Theo's warm, motherly smile matches her words.

"Thank you for allowing us to stay for the night." I smile at both Mr. and Mrs. Dawes. "You have a lovely home."

"After you relax for a while, I'll have the girls give you a full tour," Theo states. "Can I get you anything to drink or eat?"

Before we can answer, Clint enters the room, hands planted on his hips, chest puffed out. "Calvin, you and I need to have a talk." There's anger in his tone.

"Nonsense. Clint, where are your manners?" Theo reprimands. "You will not intimidate our guests."

The tall, muscular man heels at his mother's orders. We carry on with easy conversation until Theo announces her chili is ready. Dallas and Schuyler excuse themselves to set the table, and Richard offers to help, leaving Garret and me alone with Clint.

He cranes his neck to ensure the others are all out of earshot. "Why are you here?" He gruffly demands answers. "And don't blame it on the blizzard. You changed your flight to be here. Why?" Even though his questions sound like they could be for both of us, he's glaring straight at me.

"We enjoyed the girls' company this week and didn't want it to end yet," I explain.

"What are your intentions with my sister?"

I look at Garret's wide eyes. He's clearly as uncomfortable as I am right now.

"Your sister is an adult. Whether we plan to date or not is not your business unless she wants to tell you." I repeat Schuyler's words from one of her phone conversations with Levi this week.

"She's my business," Clint spits. "I make her my business. She's inexperienced in relationships. If you plan to be fuck buddies, that's not going to work for me or my brothers." He fixes me with a steely gaze.

I rise from the sofa. "Not that it's any of your business, but we plan to date when we return to campus." I turn my back on him and stride to the kitchen.

I will not be intimidated by Schuyler's brothers. While I like that they want to protect their little sister, our relationship is our business. I don't plan to let them interfere.

Theo's chili warms us from the inside out, and we visit around the table for over an hour after we finish eating. It's not until Dallas's parents, who live next door, walk over to join us that we clear the table and load the dishwasher. I help Theo and Schuyler clean the kitchen while the others retire to the family room.

"The boys are here," Richard calls from the front room as the sound of two snowmobiles can be heard.

Fabulous.

This won't be awkward. I can handle Clint. Her three older brothers together will surely cause problems for me.

"Stay close to me," Schuyler whispers as I rinse the stew pot while she dries the other pans.

Nonsense. I don't need her protection. I plan to be in her life, so I need to stand up to her brothers, not cower behind my girl.

As we enter the large family room, a reporter on the television points to a map of power outages in the Des Moines area, shows videos of stranded drivers being rescued, and reads a formal statement about the official closure of the interstates. The weather person explains that the snow will continue to fall for the next eight hours. High winds will cause drifting, making travel more difficult in the area.

"May be snowed in for a couple of days," Richard states, looking to Garret and me.

"Over my dead body," mumbles one of Schuyler's brothers. The three are huddled together, so it's unclear which one spoke the words.

I take a seat near Schuyler and her mother on the sofa while Garret sits on the floor near Dallas.

"Tell us more about this bar you mentioned," Richard prompts.

Garret motions for me to speak.

"Garret and I, along with one other investor, hope to open a restaurant with an attached bar in the back by fall," I begin. It's hard to share much about our business venture when we keep many aspects of our plan a secret. "Guests must go through the restaurant to find the bar. There's a great reason for this, but we're keeping the theme a secret until the official opening."

"I wouldn't like walking through a restaurant to enter the bar," Levi states. He seems pleased with himself for finding a perceived hole in our plan.

"I think we could trust these two families to keep our secret until we open." Garret urges me to share.

"Okay. Our bar," I pause for dramatic effect, "Is a speakeasy."

"Like a prohibition era speakeasy?" Schuyler asks, suddenly more interested in our project.

"Yes," I concur. "We plan to hide a door near the back of the restaurant for club goers to slip through."

"Will your restaurant have the same theme?" Theo asks.

"No. We plan for it to seem like any other place to eat. That will help add to the mystique of the bar in the back." I scan the room, finding all eyes on me, interested in the details. "We'd like the restaurant to be open Thursday through Sunday with the bar open those nights, too. Our menu will be different every weekend with three entrée options to choose from. One weekend might be Mexican dishes, the next weekend Italian, and the next southern comfort foods."

Dallas's father asks, "Won't it be expensive to not use the space three days a week?"

Garret jumps in on this question. "We will allow private luncheons, dinners, and parties to book on Mondays, Tuesdays, and Wednesdays. It's our hope that limiting the time we open will benefit us like supply and demand does the retail industry."

"Are there similar bars in the Kansas City area?" Richard asks.

"There is one similar to a speakeasy, but they don't have a hidden bar, staff in prohibition era clothes, or require a password to get in," I admit.

"A bar like you're describing might do very well in Des Moines." I look towards Schuyler's dad while he speaks. "On Court Avenue, we have three night clubs that cater to the under 30 crowd. Scattered throughout town are bar and grills that allow families with children to dine, but there's nothing of interest to the community encompassing everyone from age 21 to 75."

"Sure, there is," Clint argues. "It's called The Lumberyard." He wiggles his eyebrows suggestively.

Loud laughter erupts from Schuyler's three brothers.

"Clinton Dawes, you behave yourself," Theo chides.

"The Lumberyard is a strip club," Dallas informs Garret and me.

I don't say it out loud, but I bet the strip joint does draw in men of all ages. But that's not what Mr. Dawes meant. I understand the niche he's describing, but I hadn't applied it to our plans. We cater to everyone over 21, unlike the loud night clubs for the 21 to 30 crowd.

"That warehouse near the tracks downtown is on the market and would be perfect for this restaurant and bar layout," Dallas's dad states, and Richard agrees.

With thoughts of our business on my mind, I ignore the next topic of conversation for the group. We have much to accomplish between my graduation in early May and our projected opening in September.

After Schuyler's parents shoo Levi home to be with his wife, Dan and Clint assist the neighbor boy with clearing all the driveways in the cul-de-sac. The rest of us play 10-point pitch at a table for four. After each game, the losers move, and a new team of two tries to defeat the winning team.

Hours later, Dallas's parents walk home and Sky's parents head to bed. We continue to play cards until after midnight. Once settled into the guest room, I'm unable to sleep. Richard's words haunt my thoughts. I contemplate opening our business in Des Moines versus Kansas City, completely rethinking the only plan I've made in the last four years. I now question everything I thought I wanted.

18

NO END IN SIGHT

Schuyler

The weeks after our Mexico trip pass quickly. While my friends attend class, I busy myself with online applications and paperwork. My student-teaching successfully ended, so I apply for my teaching license and graduation. I spend many hours applying for teaching positions in Iowa, Missouri, Nebraska, and Kansas. I also post my resume and paperwork to many of the education sites that districts use to recruit new hires. It's almost a full-time job, but I'm eager to secure a position.

I fear the reason I'm not hearing back on jobs is the two-semester break in my college studies. It's a giant red flag, bringing up questions about my work ethic and follow through. I refuse to explain my absence in my cover letter, though. I worry they will pity me for the accident, and I don't want a pity hire. *I want to earn a position based on my credentials.*

Calvin calls or texts me each day. We've met a couple of times on campus for lunch between his classes. His studies demand most of his time, and he spends every week night working on projects and papers or with a study group.

I don't mind his unavailability during the week; it allows me to place some much-needed distance between us. I allowed several walls to crumble while on vacation, and now I rebuild them.

I love the time I spend with Calvin, but I need to remember there is no happily ever after for the two of us.

He deserves better, more than I can offer him.

At the end of the semester, I'll let him go.

This weekend, Garret drove up from Kansas City to spend four days with Dallas. They are too lovey-dovey for my liking. Their constant smiles, touching, and kissing, remind me of what Calvin and I shared on vacation. Part of me longs to have Calvin to myself this weekend; another part tells me it's better if we're apart.

I'm jealous of my best friend. Dallas can have a future with Garret; together, the two of them can marry and start a perfect little family. Me, on the other hand, I want nothing more than to constantly smile, touch, and kiss Calvin, but I can't allow it. I can't deny him of a future family, so I must look on as others have what I wish for.

I excuse myself, leaving the love birds cuddling on the sofa while I shut myself in my room. I flop on my bed, staring up at the ceiling. Full of angst and unable to focus on anything, I open the top drawer of my nightstand.

I kept this toy busy with plenty of action upon my return from spring break. Quietly, I turn off the lights, click the lock on my doorknob, then crawl back onto my bed. I slip off my pajama pants, slide my tank top up to my neck, and call up visions of Calvin dripping wet in the shower.

My thumb presses the button, and my vibrator hums to life. I imagine Calvin's hands caressing my skin, and his mouth between my thighs. I bump the power up two more notches. Within seconds, I'm coiled tight, ready to explode.

Just. One. More. Minute…

My body turns to stone, and I curse like a sailor when I hear a loud noise.

"Yes! Yes! Yesss!" Dallas wails from the other side of my bedroom wall.

I can't even masturbate in my room with the loving couple here. Calvin wasn't exaggerating when he claimed the couple kept him up all night in Mexico. Now, I'm even more riled up than when I entered the room, and there's no way for me to find release while they loudly have sex in the next room.

My life sucks.

Calvin

My thumb hovers over the send arrow. I've rewritten this text three times and read it even more. I worry I shouldn't send it.

Mexico was heaven. We connected, and I knocked down some of her walls. Now that we are back in the real world, Schuyler has withdrawn a bit. I realize we moved fast on spring break, and I understand her need to slow it down a bit. But I miss her; it's that simple. Finally, I take a deep breath and send the text.

> **ME**
> can't sleep
> nothing on tv
> what r u up to?

I stare at my screen, willing the three little dots to appear, so I know she is responding to me. I find the fact she doesn't have read receipts set up in Messenger frustrating.

If I push her, contact her too often, or seem clingy, she might run. I'm trying my best to keep it cool. I only text her during my lunch breaks or late in the afternoon when my last class ends. Then, the ball is in her court; it's up to her to reach out to me in the evening.

Three dots.

I see the ellipsis. I hold my breath as I will her to send a text.

> **SCHUYLER**
> staring @ bedroom ceiling

> **ME**
> find anything interesting?

> **SCHUYLER**
> No
> Garret's here need noise canceling headphones

> **ME**
> been there
> headphones won't work

> **SCHUYLER**
> here for 3 nights!

ME
yep

called me on drive up

surprise her for weekend

SCHUYLER
heads up would've been nice

ME
dropped the ball

sorry

will warn u next time

SCHUYLER
Thanks

but won't help next 72 hrs

ME
(Sad face emoji)

I'd invite u over, but still working on presentation

I have crap everywhere

SCHUYLER
no prob

wanna get together this weekend?

ME
I'm free either night

Friday's best

SCHUYLER
yay

plan on Friday

ME
it's a date

SCHUYLER
(Thumbs up emoji)

Unbreakable

> get back to project

GOOD NIGHT
ME
> Nighty night

> sweet dreams

I watch my phone for a minute. When no dots appear, I figure she's locked her phone, so I do the same.

I hate lying to Sky, but I can't invite her over while Tyler's here.

I'm not sure how much longer I can use the excuse of writing papers and working on projects to keep Sky away in the evenings.

Dead week is two weeks away; I will need a new excuse by then.

I'm glad she asked for us to get together this weekend. I usually hint and wait for her to make plans. Tonight, she took the lead. I don't feel like I'm hounding her if she initiates it.

If Dallas and Garret are at their apartment, I'll want to find somewhere else for us to be alone. Even if Tyler is out of the house, there are still too many things for her to see and ask about at my place. Perhaps I can persuade Garret to take Dallas out to a movie and dinner. Schuyler and I would then have her place to ourselves.

I know I need to tell her about Tyler; I just don't think our relationship is ready for a big secret like that.

Schuyler

Thursday's here before I know it. My heart rate picks up, knowing what tomorrow brings. *It's inevitable. I know going is much better than the alternative.*

I just can't take the happiness of the staff behind the reception desk or the families in the waiting room. *I desperately want to be in their shoes, living their lives, instead of the one life dealt me.* They don't understand how I must work myself up to even call and make the stupid appointment. Then, it's a waiting game. The appointment is on my calendar, and every day, I move closer to it feels like I move closer to a firing squad. The closer it gets, the more melancholy I feel. I lose sleep about three days prior to the appointment. When I close my eyes, I see myself in the waiting room, surrounded by families living the lives I want. I don't want the pain that comes from not keeping my appointments, but I wonder if the heartache, the longing, the stress, and the pain of these shot appointments every three months is any better. There's no end in sight. I'll be doing this for the rest of my life. Repetition and heartache, that's my future. I've checked out other offices, but it's all the same.

I can't avoid it; this is my new normal.
This is my life.

When I can't sleep, I close my eyes and imagine what life could be like if I had stayed at college that fateful night. If I didn't drive after dark, I would have avoided the accident. The truck wouldn't have been in front of me. I wouldn't have needed to swerve, and I wouldn't have ended up impaled on that farmer's fence. I would wake the next morning and still make it to Mom's before noon. In the night's silence, behind my closed eyelids, so many scenarios play out in which I don't find myself dead inside.

The endless possibilities prevent me from getting any of the sleep that I hope for. Lack of sleep further perpetuates my discomfort at the appointment. Everything's worse when I'm exhausted. And, believe me, I don't need it to be any worse than it already is. Compounding the hurt further breaks my heart.

Before that fateful night, I thought heartbreak could only come from a break up. I thought that all heartbreak was the same. I didn't realize that sometimes, the heart continues to crack and fracture, little pieces falling away with each passing day.

I now know actual pain, genuine fear, and real heartbreak.
I'm dead inside.
I'm useless; I'm unwanted.

19

THE POST

Schuyler

"Go ahead and change into the gown. Wear the opening in the front. The doctor will be in shortly," the nurse states as she exits the exam room.

"Couldn't they make these gowns more feminine, more glamorous?" I mumble, removing all my clothes. "It's bad enough we must have this appointment annually. The least they could do is let us feel pretty while we do it."

With the thin hospital gown over my shoulders, I hold the front closed as I climb onto the exam table. The white paper crinkles annoyingly. The cold, sterile environment causes my skin to crawl.

The doctor whips in with her nurse, and they quickly begin the breast and pelvic exams. I lie on the table, staring up at the fluorescent lights, praying for this to all be over quickly. You'd think after a hysterectomy, pelvic exams would no longer be necessary. I don't question the logic, though; I endure it as every woman does.

With no concerns, my exam ends, and I'm briskly walking toward the door and exiting the lobby. My jaw tightens as I share an elevator with a happy couple and a very pregnant belly. Thank goodness I only have to ride for two floors. I'm ready to find the safety inside my car.

I waste no time hitting the highway and driving back to campus a state away. Using voice commands, I text Mom, "All is well, and I'm headed back to school." I turn up the radio, hoping to drown my thoughts with rock music. I love guitar riffs and drum solos. They help me to clear my head.

An hour into my drive, I'm still angry. *Why don't I deserve a family of my own? I've surrounded myself with children since my early teens. I helped with the nursery and Sunday school at church, I babysat for several neighborhood and church families, and I've always wanted to be a teacher. So, why am I fated to have no children?*

Why me?

I hear stories all the time of parents that neglect and abuse their children. News stories of parents that forgot their child in a locked car in the heat of summer or cold of winter haunt my dreams. Others have left them home unattended. *I'd be a fabulous mom. There's no chance I'd ever forget my child.*

I long to hold every infant I see, cuddle it tight to my breast, and keep it as my own. I'd never steal a child. I'm just angry that another woman is the mother. I deserve to be a mother.

Jealous?

Yes. I'm very jealous.

Why should other women get to be mothers when I can't?

When I near the location of my accident, I pull onto the gravel shoulder. I take my phone from its cradle and shoot a text to Calvin.

> ME
>
> can't come over 2nite
>
> sorry need time to myself

It's time to end it.

He deserves happiness, a family, and a future; I can't give him that. He's amazing, so gentle and attentive. There's no doubt he'd be a terrific dad. I can't place the ball and chain that is my lonely future on him. It's better that it ends today instead of drawing it out any longer. He won't like it, but ripping the bandage off quickly is best.

I place my cell phone back in the holder. I'm parked on the shoulder, looking down the embankment to the spot where my car landed that fateful night. *Here is where my dreams of a family shattered into a million pieces that can't be glued back together.* Like a zombie, I exit my car, not even looking for traffic before I do.

It's a windy spring day, the scent of rain hangs in the air. I can't peel my eyes off the tall grasses and the fence line below. From here, I see no sign of the devastation of that night. The barbed wire and fence posts have been replaced, and a new layer of natural grasses hide the ground where my car lay upside down.

I slip a few times, climbing down the slope from the road to the field. *It would be fitting if I fell head over heels in the same spot my car rolled over and over.* Inches from the fence, I freeze. The green metal fence posts and their white tips catch my eye, proudly standing every ten feet.

Slowly, I approach. I reach my hand out to touch the metal, pausing at the last moment. Flashes of my pain and images of the white gauze I opened my eyes to in the hospital last year cause me to freeze. I shake my thoughts away. *This is not the wire fence that wrapped around my car; this wire hasn't hurt me.*

The metal is cold to my touch. I run my fingertips from one galvanized, steel barb to the next. I place the tip of my forefinger upon the sharp point. I barely press, and the metal pricks, drawing a tiny drop of blood. I quickly pull my finger away, lift it to my mouth, and suck on it.

The sky begins to spit; the moisture chills my bare arms. I take another step along the fence. The metal post is strong. It doesn't move as I place my fingers upon it. It doesn't wiggle as I attempt to shift it to the right then left.

A post, just like this one, pierced my car and impaled my body.

A post like this one took away my future happiness.

A post like this one will forever haunt my nightmares.

As the spitting becomes a cold drizzle, I walk along the fence toward the next pole. To navigate through the tall grasses, I must step high as it hides the uneven ground.

The knots in my stomach from earlier today are anvils now. Bile climbs my throat, and tears stream steadily from my eyes, blurring my surroundings. I slowly walk along the fence line, looking for any remnants to clue me in to the exact location my car landed. On my next step, I find a hard object not the dirt I expect. I gently kick my toe around the hard object. *It's a post.* Bending down, I struggle to remove the thatch of grass that's grown around it. I fall to my bottom, crossing my legs in front of me. I wiggle it side to side. I remove all the grass, starting at the bottom and working my way up the bar.

Finished my dirty hands hold a metal fence post. It's not like the ones securing the three long rows of barbed wire for the fence. Rust corrodes most of the distorted metal. The once six-foot post resembles the number six now. I turn it in my hands, inspecting the scrap. My eyes scan the rust, intermixed with splotches of green, and then I see it. My heart is the size of a bowling ball pounding in my chest. My breathing halts. I'm staring at two spots of blue paint. They stand out like a neon sign. They're from my car. This twisted metal I clutch in my hands with its blue evidence was from my wreck.

This is the post.

The. Post.

This is where they sawed through the metal, leaving the other portion impaled in my abdomen as I flew in the helicopter.

This is the green post that ripped away my happiness.

This post stole my hopes of a family.

This is the post.

The questions from the night before rise in my mind again.

Why?

Why me?

Why did I take my backpack to the dorm instead of leaving campus immediately?

Why didn't I pass the truck in front of me?

Why couldn't my car have landed four inches to the left so that the post would miss me completely?

Why did my car roll four times instead of three?

Why?

It's not fair.

I deserve happiness.

20

HE CHANGES EVERYTHING

Calvin

My presentation is over, and my college classes are officially complete for the week. I pull my cell phone from the side pocket of my backpack, turning it on as I walk through the hallway. I push through the heavy metal doors into the warm spring sun.

Done.

Finally.

It's time to pack up my stuff and move into the next phase of my life. But first, I'll spend the evening with Sky. Since I didn't convince Garret to let me have the girls' apartment tonight, I've invited her to my place, promising to fix her a meal to die for. She's begged me all week to tell her what's on the menu, but I've kept that a secret, just like the big one I plan to reveal to her tonight. I'm nervous, yet ready.

After tonight, she'll know everything. With Sky in my home, there can be no more hiding Tyler. I think I'm finally ready for the secrets to stop.

Finally awake, my cell phone vibrates several times, signaling a missed phone call, many social media updates, and two texts. Since there is no voicemail, I open the texts.

SCHUYLER

can't come over 2nite

> sorry need time to myself

Talk about a blindside. I'm a statue in the middle of the sidewalk, staring at my phone screen like a modern sculpture of a college student, a slave to his smartphone. I reread the texts over and over, trying to comprehend their meaning. Things have been great between Schuyler and me since Mexico. Our text and phone conversations flow easily. As busy as we are finishing our final semester, we've still carved out one night a week to see each other in person.

Desperate, I break the text into chunks. "Can't come over 2nite." *I could totally understand if she's had a long day and might be too tired or will get home too late for dinner. I don't like it, but I can live with it.*

"Need time to myself." *She's had tons of time to herself over the past month and a half. Although I've wanted to see her every night, we've kept it to one date per week. Sure, she is busy with coursework, licensing paperwork, and trying to find a teaching position, but she has down time.* I haven't tried to monopolize her every free minute.

"Sorry" Sorry. Sorry? Sorry for what? Sorry for bailing on me tonight, or sorry for taking time for herself? Or, sorry, I don't want to see you anymore?

An overstuffed backpack slams into me as a group of students brush by on the sidewalk. I don't look up for an apology; I just walk. I walk and walk with no destination in mind. My brain struggles to read into the hidden meanings of her words. I search for clues in our interactions this week that might help me decode the text.

The alarm on my phone reminds me it's time to pick up Tyler. I've walked around campus for over an hour with my mind on Schuyler's text, and I still don't know what they mean. I tuck my phone into my pocket, picking up my pace as I walk toward my car.

I place an afternoon snack in front of Tyler on the breakfast bar and pull out my phone to reach Schuyler. I dial her number, but it goes straight to voicemail. I choose not to leave a message, as I'm not sure I can steady myself to seem less worried. I decide to text.

Unbreakable

> **ME**
> where are you?
> please call me

I rack my brain for what to do now.
I can't let it end like this.
I text Dallas.

> **ME**
> is Sky with you?
>
> **DALLAS**
> supposed 2 be with u 2nite.
>
> **ME**
> she cancelled by text
> said needed time alone & sorry
>
> **DALLAS**
> (shocked emoji)
> let me call her
> don't freak yet

"*Don't freak yet?*" Seriously?

I was at DEFCON 3. Now, after texting Dallas, I'm at DEFCON 1.

My plan backfired. I thought Dallas would know where she was and what was going on. Now, I'm even more concerned.

"Done," Tyler announces, sliding off his kitchen stool.

"Wash your hands, then you can have 30 minutes of screen time," I state, tossing his paper plate and napkin into the trash and his cup into the sink.

Screen time will entertain him for a while, giving me time to think of a new plan. Schuyler had an appointment in Des Moines early this afternoon. She planned to drive back, joining me for dinner tonight. She texted me when she woke at her parents' house this morning.

What happened at the doctor's appointment or on the drive home to change her mind about tonight and seeing me?

> ME
> any news?

> DALLAS
> voicemail & won't text back

> ME
> I'm calling her mom
> maybe stayed there

> DALLAS
> maybe
> keep me posted
> (fingers crossed emoji)

"Theo, this is Calvin," I greet with a shaky voice when I hear her pick up. "Did Schuyler decide to stay at your place instead of coming back to campus today?"

"No." At Theo's sharp intake of breath, I realize I've scared her. "What's going on?"

"I'm not sure. She texted me after her appointment to cancel our dinner, stating she needs time to think and that she's sorry," I explain.

Theo's the second person I've shared this information with. I grow more scared with each retelling.

"Dallas hasn't heard from her all day," I add.

"I'm placing you on speaker," Theo says. "I'm looking her up on our GPS app. Give me a second."

Silence is the enemy.

It seems like an hour before Theo speaks again. "Her phone last pinged at Kellerton. Maybe she stopped for gas or snacks."

I hear a loud beep in my ear. "Theo, Dallas is calling me. Please let me know if you hear from her, and I will do the same."

"Okay. I'm sure she's upset about her appointment today. Give her a day or two, and she'll be back to her old self," Theo soothes before disconnecting.

I switch to Dallas's call, pushing back the confusion I feel at Theo's words. "Hello?"

"I've got nothing," she states, defeated.

"Theo looked her up on a GPS app," I inform. "Her phone last pinged in at Kellerton on Highway 2."

"I know where she is," Dallas confidently announces. "I should've known. These appointments always mess her up."

"Dallas," I interrupt. "Where's Schuyler?"

"At the site of her wreck."

Shit! Clearly, I'm missing some important information here.

"Garret just got back from the store," Dallas informs me. I can hear a muffled voice in the background. Then she informs me, "We'll be over to pick you up in five minutes."

"I'll be ready," I reply.

I spend my wait time coaxing Tyler into a jacket and packing books and the iPad into a backpack to entertain him. He fights me when I insist he go to the bathroom before Uncle Garret gets here. When I ask again, he glares at me; my eyes plead with him to obey. We're opening the front door when Garret's truck pulls into my driveway. Tyler waves excitedly; he loves hanging out with Garret.

With his booster seat in one hand, backpack in the other hand, and Tyler walking beside me, we move toward the large, black truck. At the wide-eyed look on Dallas's face, I realize that, like Schuyler, she doesn't know about my son.

There's no time to get into it now. I'll tell her once we hit the road.

I need to get to Schuyler ASAP.

I place the backpack in the center of the rear seat, then set the booster seat in place. Tyler poses in front of me with his arms in the air, waiting for me to lift him up into the large truck. While I click the buckle and tug it tight across his chest, he smiles shyly at Dallas.

"Uncle Garret, is she your girlfriend?" Tyler asks in his sweet little boy voice.

Garret's eyes meet my son's in the rearview mirror as he backs out of the driveway. "Ty-man, this is Dallas. Dallas, this is the coolest little dude on the planet."

I smile at the use of his nickname. I love my friend takes his relationship with my son seriously and assumes the role of honorary uncle.

"Dallas," Tyler addresses the stranger in the front seat, "Are you Uncle Garret's girlfriend?"

I bite my lip to not laugh while making eye contact with Garret in the mirror. He tried to avoid the question, but Tyler is tenacious when he wants something.

"Would it be okay if I was his girlfriend?" Dallas asks, turning to face my little guy.

"Yes," Tyler replies. "I thought he'd never get one."

Laughter erupts in the cab. I welcome the levity, as I'm unsure what we are driving toward.

"You're very pretty," Tyler approves. "Uncle Garret, you did good."

I cringe, knowing all the adult conversations he's eavesdropped on will now come back to haunt me. *But that's a worry for another day.*

"Dallas, do you have a pretty friend for my dad?" Tyler presses.

I choke on my own breath. Tyler and I have never talked about girlfriends or me dating.

Garret smiles proudly at me in the mirror before his eyes return to the highway.

It's a long car ride. I need to distract Tyler so I can talk to Dallas. "Let's put on your headphones, and you watch a movie on the iPad."

Tyler doesn't complain. He's quickly lost in the cartoon movie. His headset ensures he won't hear our conversation.

"Okay," I sigh, happy to have Tyler distracted. "How long is the drive?" I ask Dallas.

"Uh-uh." She waggles her index finger toward me. She's almost turned completely around in her bucket seat to address me. "You don't get to bring that little cutie along without an explanation. If he's who I think he is, he changes everything."

An anvil drops in my stomach as bile crawls up my throat. As Schuyler's best friend, Dallas knows how Schuyler will react. *"He changes everything." Does she mean Schuyler will definitely leave me when I reveal my secret?*

"Uh, hello?" Dallas snaps her fingers in front of my eyes. "Open your mouth and start explaining."

21

RESCUE THE PRINCESS

Calvin

"Tyler's my son." I don't know what else she needs to know.

If he's a game changer, I don't want to waste my time telling our story.

"Like I didn't already figure that one out. He looks just like you." Dallas looks fondly in his direction. "Why haven't you shared this juicy tidbit with us?"

"It's a long story. I told Schuyler I had something to tell her at dinner tonight. I planned to introduce Tyler to her this evening." I let out a long breath as I rub my hands down my face. "I tried to date twice when he was a baby. College girls weren't interested in my baggage. It's why I gave up dating for over three years. I needed to focus on what was best for him." I attempt to smile at Dallas. "Why does he change everything?"

"Schuyler's kept a big secret from you, too." Dallas can't help but glance toward Tyler, smiling as she speaks. "The reason we are going to her wreck site is because the wreck took a big part of her life away from her. Every three months, she visits a doctor for a shot. It's not the shot that messes with her head. It's that the appointment flaunts the thing she can never have in front of her." Dallas pauses, turning to face the front again. "That's all I can share. It's her story; it's her secret to tell. Just know that Tyler will give her hope and much to think about."

For the rest of our drive, we're silent. With the windshield wipers' steady rhythm, the dreary drizzle, and my unsure thoughts, my chest grows tighter the longer we drive. Taking a breath is exhausting. My heavy stomach roils.

I love her.

I've known for weeks now that I love Schuyler, maybe even since Mexico.

As Garret's truck hurls me towards her, my fear of losing her grows.

I hope I haven't waited too long to open up to her, to tell her I love her, and to share my final secret.

"Are we there yet?" Tyler inquires, removing his headphones.

I'm not sure how to answer him. We're almost there, but it's not a town; it's not a building.

What should I tell him I'm doing?

Dallas jumps in to the rescue. "We are very close. A friend of mine is in trouble, and we are going to save her." With a smile on her face, she watches Tyler for understanding.

"I want to help! Uncle Garret, Daddy, and I can rescue the princess!" Tyler puffs out his chest, closes his fists, and attempts to flex his muscles.

Maybe I've let him watch too many fairy tales. I guess, he is kind of right. Schuyler is my princess. She just doesn't believe it yet.

I'll make her listen; I'll show her how much I care.

I hope that it's enough to save her and us.

"Ty-man, you're gonna sit in the truck with me while your dad tries to help her. If he needs our help, he'll give us a signal, and we'll hurry to help him," Garret offers, and my son nods his head at the plan.

"Daddy, we need a secret sign," Tyler informs me.

"Hmm..." I pretend to contemplate. "I'll touch my nose if I need help."

"That won't work," Tyler scoffs.

"Why not?" I ask.

"Your nose might itch, and we'll think you need help," Tyler states like I should've known.

"Then, what should our secret sign be?" Dallas asks with a wide smile.

"Daddy could wave at us in the truck," Tyler offers proudly. "Like this." He demonstrates how to wave.

"Perfect, Ty-man," Garret commends.

"There's her car!" Dallas's voice is much too loud for the cab of the truck.

Garret pulls his truck up behind her car, parked on the shoulder. We crane our necks to see if Schuyler's inside. As I look across the road for any sign of her, I notice Tyler is lifting himself up to look out his window, even though he doesn't know who he's looking for.

When I glance out my window, I see Schuyler sitting hunched over near the fence line. My heart crumbles. The sight of her physically hurts. Everything inside me hopes to heal her and protect her. As I exit the truck, Dallas urges me to be patient, Garret states I should remain calm, and Tyler ensures that I remember the secret sign for help.

"Daddy, good luck," Tyler offers along with a manly fist bump.

I give my son a reassuring smile, trying to keep my composure until I shut the truck door and turn towards Schuyler. Then, my pulse skyrockets, sweat forms on my palms and brow, and I worry I'll mess up the best thing in my life next to my son. I slowly place one foot in front of the other, descending the hill at a snail's pace. The tall grass, slick with the rain, proves slippery.

The last thing I want to do is slide down this hill on my ass as I attempt to ride in on my white horse to rescue my princess.

The scenarios I worked through on the long ride here evaporate. I have no idea what I plan to say or do. With each step, I stress more and more about how to approach the situation.

I love her. I love her more than I can ever show her.

The text she sent me hurt. There's a hole in my heart only she can repair and fill.

I need her to trust me. I need her to share with me. But I can't ask that of her if I don't trust her, too.

I need to tell her about my son. Then, I need to listen to her.

I fall to my knees in front of Schuyler. It guts me to see her this broken. She sits cross-legged in the tall grass, wet from the steady precipitation. With a blotchy face and red, puffy eyes, her gaze remains glued to a misshapen post in her hands. I'm not sure she knows I'm inches away from her. It scares me to see her this withdrawn. I've known from the day I met her that she had walls up to protect herself, but the girl sitting before me is defenseless.

"Schuyler," I croak weakly. I don't recognize my soft, broken voice. I clear my throat and drum up all the courage I can. "Honey, can we talk?" When she doesn't react to my voice, I place my fingers under her chin and turn her head to look at me. Her bloodshot eyes slice me open; it's a kick in my gut. I can't take the sight of her in pain. "Honey, are you okay? Can you say something to me?"

Several moments pass before the fog seems to clear, and she responds to me. "Why are you here? I need time."

Schuyler doesn't sound like herself. She sounds like a little girl. Her plea for me to leave her alone further pierces my heart. I look towards the truck. The sight of my two friends and son give me the strength to forge on.

"I love you," I murmur. *I'll beg on my knees and pray for more time with her if that's what it takes.* "I'll give you time, but I need to confess something I've neglected to tell you. And, I have to get you out of this weather first."

Her eyes ping pong left and right, looking deep into mine. "I can't be with you," she tells me. She sounds like she's trying to convince me. "I'm dead inside. I'm useless. You deserve a better woman. You deserve a happy future full of love; I can't give you that."

Her sobs spur hiccups. I wipe away as many tears as I can.

"That's crazy talk," I inform her.

"You don't know," she says through her sobs. "I can't... My accident..."

I pull her tight to my chest and wrap my arms around her with the metal post between us. I don't do it to shut her up. I hope, in my arms, she feels safe enough to trust me with her secret.

"The wreck..." she tries again. "Hysto... hysto... hysterectomy." More sobs blur her words. "You deserve a family."

I kiss the top of her head as my hands rub up and down her back. My heart breaks for her. She's centered her career around children, and fate has dealt her a massive heartbreak. Part of me wonders how she ever found the strength to continue on the same career path after the accident. I would choose a different job that didn't remind me of my loss every day. Several long moments pass as I hold her.

"I love you," I whisper near her ear.

She doesn't acknowledge my statement. She doesn't flinch or shift in my arms. I fear she didn't hear me over her sobs.

I suck in a gulp of air, determined to make her hear what I have to say. "Schuyler Dawes, I love you. My heart breaks for you, but it doesn't change my love for you." I lean back to peer into her eyes. I need her to feel the power of my proclamation. "I love you and want to spend the rest of my life loving you. I know you feel broken and useless, but that's just not true. There are many paths to making a family. I haven't told you yet, but I'm adopted. I love my adoptive parents as if they were my only parents, and I've never felt the desire to seek out my birth parents. We could adopt children, foster children in need, find surrogates, or devote our lives volunteering with as many children as we can." I gulp for breath, my emotion weighing heavily in my words. "Your accident doesn't change my love for you. I. Love. You. Schuyler." I speak slowly, hoping my words sink in through the fog of depression that blankets her usually upbeat personality.

Unbreakable

"I love you. I love all of you. I love your smile and your scars. I love your heart and your pain. I want to share everything with you." I take in a deep breath, preparing to share my final secret and trust her in every way. "See the truck up there?" I point, and her gaze follows my finger. "Inside is Garret, Dallas, and my 4-year-old son, Tyler."

22

UP-HIGH TY

Calvin
There it is.
I've laid it all on the line for her.
My heart is in the palm of her hand to do with as she pleases.

She takes a moment to process my words. She turns toward me, wide-eyed, slack-jawed, unable to speak. I brush wet strands of her hair from her face. My thumbs caress her jawline as I stare deep into her caramel eyes, imploring her to love me, to accept my confession, and to allow us to move on together.

She looks back toward the truck. She doesn't crane her neck or stand for a better view. She stares for several long minutes. As she turns back to face me, I'm paralyzed. I can't breathe. I can't move.

"You..." She gulps audibly. "What's his name?" Her brow furrows as her eyes search mine for answers.

"His name is Tyler. He's four," I repeat.

"Tyler Calhoun?" she questions.

I nod. This is not the reaction I expected. I thought she'd ask about his mother, how we hooked up, why she wasn't in the picture, and where he goes while I'm in class. She doesn't seem concerned with any of those facts. All she wants to know is his name.

"Up-High Ty is your son?" Astonishment sweeps over Schuyler's face.

It's my turn to furrow my brow.

Where did she hear that?

Did one of the guys slip and say something in Mexico? If so, why didn't she ask me who Tyler was?

I pinch my lips, contemplating this tidbit of information.

How does she know my son's nickname?

"Before my accident, I worked at the campus preschool for three years," Schuyler explains, a hint of a smile shining at me. "Last year, there were two little boys named Tyler. One boy loved to give us a high-five when he arrived and left for the day, so we named him Up-High Ty." She shakes her head in disbelief. "I'm Miss Sky. He called me Miss Sky, so it rhymed with his name." She stares back at Garret's black truck longingly, chewing on her bottom lip.

My head spins. She's Miss Sky?

Tyler wouldn't shut up about Miss Sky. It was 'Miss Sky this' and 'Miss Sky that.' I close my eyes. *Schuyler already knows my son. Tyler already knows Schuyler.* The apprehension I had about introducing the two of them evaporates. *Now, I just need her to want to be with me and with Tyler.*

I ask Schuyler, "Do you believe in a higher power, in fate or destiny?"

Schuyler

Calvin's words wake me up. They trigger my brain to switch gears. I push down the thoughts of my childless future and its pain. I believe in signs. In fact, I've been hoping for a sign since December. As my Christmas wish, I asked for a sign to guide me, because I felt so lost. As my student teaching progressed and I began applying for teaching positions, I felt more and more out of control. I fear not being hired. As I widened the area in which I applied for positions, I worry I might have to move far from everyone that I know. Every day, I hope for a sign, and I pray for God to give me strength to heal my body and my soul.

This is the sign I hoped, begged, and prayed for. Before my wreck, my work at the preschool was the highlight of my day. I'd hoped it was a sign when Calvin stated we attended the same college. I kept the little flicker alive in my heart until my shot appointment started drawing near. *It's still burning. It must be a sign that I met and fell in love with a guy in Mexico that is the father of my former student.*

"I believe in signs," I whisper to Calvin.

The brown flecks in his hazel eyes morph into gold. At my words, they shimmer with hope. That spurs my heart to warm to the possibilities a future with

Calvin could hold, and the titanium wall around my heart melts. He releases the breath he was holding in relief, and his shoulders relax.

"So," Calvin pauses, looking down at my lap, "are we going to take this scrap metal back with us to campus?"

How can I explain the bond I feel with this bent metal post without sounding like a complete nut job? I mean, more of a nut job than he already thinks I am.

"It's hard to explain," I begin as I turn the metal around. "It's a fence post, like that one and that one," I state, pointing at the proud green posts holding the barbed wire around the field.

"The blue smudges here and here are from my car." I pause in my explanation, chancing a glance up at Calvin. He's listening attentively. "This post didn't disappear after the wreck. It didn't break in two from the impact. Like my body, it's marred and changed from the events of that day. It bent, but it didn't break."

Calvin runs his hand over the weathered, green post. He doesn't speak. I'm dying to know what he thinks of my infatuation with it.

"Sitting here in the cold drizzle, I had an epiphany of sorts. With the support of my family and Dallas, I didn't let my wreck break me." I point at the post then me. "We bent, but we didn't break."

"I love it," Calvin professes, positioning himself on his knees. "Those are words to live by a mantra of sorts. Maybe we should get it as a tattoo."

A tattoo?

I've never really felt the need to permanently decorate my body. Somehow, at Calvin's suggestion, I totally want it tattooed near my abdominal scars. I smile, causing his smile to grow up to his eyes. I love the crinkles it brings.

"It resembles a candy cane. Thus, we shall keep it," he states, shifting the post from my lap to his hands.

I laugh. I think it looks like a shepherd's hook; he thinks it's a candy cane.

Who would've thought I could laugh on a day that started out so crappy?

"Did you just say 'thus'?" I tease. "You're not the type of guy that can pull off a 'thus.'"

"You're seriously critiquing my word choice?" He acts hurt. "We are discussing a deep, philosophical mantra, and you choose to tease me about my words."

Calvin takes my hands in his while we laugh. His eyes tell me everything. In them, I see love, understanding, and maybe a little lust.

"Let's get out of the rain before you catch pneumonia," he suggests.

"Can you really catch pneumonia from a chilly rain?" I challenge.

"C'mon!" He attempts to pull me to my feet, but hours of sitting here, sobbing, have drained every bit of energy from me. My calves and feet tingle with pins and needles as they are asleep.

When my weak body shows signs of protest, he urges me to stay where I am. He turns toward the truck and waves nonchalantly. Immediately, Garret and Dallas emerge from the truck. Dallas gingerly makes her way down the slope. Garret emerges from the driver's side of the truck with a boy at his side.

Dallas wraps me in a much-too-tight hug. "You scared the ever-loving shit out of me. Never do that again." Her tone is serious despite the emotional hug.

I struggle for breath, then vow to never be so dramatic again.

She looks to Calvin, then back at me. "Why did you signal for help?"

"We need help to carry this work of art to the truck," he states, pointing to the bent post. "And I think Schuyler needs help to traverse the steep climb to the truck."

I giggle, and Calvin shoots me a don't-you-dare-make-fun-of-my-word-choice look. I pretend to zip my lips closed and toss the key over my right shoulder.

"Miss Sky!" the little version of Calvin cheers, running to me. "Daddy?" Up-High Ty looks puzzled at the two of us. "Why didn't you tell me the princess is Miss Sky?" He places his hands on his hips, chastising his father.

"Her name is Schuyler. I didn't know. I promise," Calvin vows.

"Princess?" I ask Dallas.

"It's a long story. I'll share later," she promises, grinning.

"Ty-man," Garret looks towards him, "you make sure Dallas doesn't scratch my truck as she places that in the back, and I'll make sure your dad doesn't drop Miss Sky." He winks at Tyler.

Garret and Calvin place me in the passenger seat of my car, buckling me in. While Calvin drives me back, Garret will transport Tyler and Dallas with him in the truck.

My mind floods with a thousand questions about Calvin and Tyler.

23

THOSE ARE MY HANDS

Schuyler

Moments into the drive, I can no longer take the sound of the windshield wipers on the car window. I scramble for anything to discuss.

"Can you tell me about Tyler's mother?" I regret the words as soon as they spill from my mouth. "I mean, you don't have to."

"I don't mind." Calvin peers over at me for a second before turning his attention back on the road. "I think it's important for you to know. My second year of college, a girl I hooked up with one night the spring before showed up on my doorstep. Her name is Daniel, and she was a sophomore photography major."

Calvin shakes his head before continuing. "I was so freaked out about her tracking me down five months after our one-night-stand that I totally missed her pregnant stomach."

Now and then, Calvin looks toward me in the passenger seat to gauge my reaction before sharing more details. "She claimed the baby was her boyfriend's, but he bailed as soon as she told him she was pregnant. Since she came from a large, very Catholic family, she couldn't go home. She let it slip that she only hooked up with two guys that April. Apparently, she pinned the pregnancy on the other guy at first. When he ran, she settled for me. She sobbed nonstop for 15 minutes on my sofa, which, of course, got to me. So, I offered to let her stay in my house."

I don't know this woman, and I already hate her. God gave her a gift, and she threw it away. She had what I desperately wanted and didn't appreciate it. She saw it as an inconvenience.

"I mean, since there was a 50 percent chance the baby might be mine, I felt I needed to help her. Dani's an artsy type. She's self-centered and saw the baby as a shackle that would prevent her from traveling the world with her photography. She never planned to keep the baby. She wanted to dump the child on the father and go on with her life as planned."

"So, she hid at my house from her family, dropped out of college, and hated every second of the pregnancy," Calvin shares. "We planned to get a paternity test when the baby was born; if I wasn't the father, she planned to put it up for adoption. She was adamant that her parents and five older siblings never found out she was pregnant."

"Wow." It's all I can say.

"Dani split as soon as the paternity test showed I was Tyler's father. She signed over all parental rights and never looked back." Calvin sighs. "I text her a photo of Tyler every year on his birthday, but she never replies. She's made quite a name for herself in the photography world, and travels all over the planet."

"If she doesn't reply, how do you know about her career?" I ask.

"When I didn't hear from her after Tyler's fourth birthday, I looked her up on the internet," Calvin admits, embarrassed. "After Dani, I learned my lesson and swore off one-night stands. It was poor judgement for me to ever consider talking to her. I guess I have horrible taste."

I should be appalled at his statement, as it reflects upon me, but I'm not. I, too, made a terrible choice in the dating world.

"I'm right there with you," I state. "My ex ranks right up there with Dani."

"The one that dumped you after your accident," Calvin asks for clarity. I roll my eyes. "Yeah. I prefer to think of Will as a bad dream." Calvin pats my knee comfortingly as he drives. "I think we've both moved on to better choices." I nod and kiss his hand before leaning against the window.

I'm tired from my emotional day.

I wake as Calvin lifts me from my car, carrying me into his house. I've been here a few times, but only in the entryway. I now know why he didn't take me on a tour or invite me to spend more evenings at his place.

He has a son. Up-High Ty is his son.

My heart beats quicker, and butterflies flap in my stomach. Tyler will arrive with Dallas and Garret in mere minutes. I'm sure my hours in the rain, along with my puffy eyes from crying, will make a great impression. I wiggle in Calvin's arms, attempting to walk by myself.

"Easy," his warm voice advises. "You're weak from skipping a meal and being out in the cold. I'm carrying you to the tub. A hot bath will help warm your inner core back to normal."

I look up through my lashes into his hazel eyes. Their amber flecks shimmer in the overhead lights. I want to argue with him, but I know it's futile. Besides, a hot bath sounds divine.

I'm lowered to sit on the lid of the toilet while Calvin starts the bath water. I squeak when he returns to remove my shoes and socks. Next, he raises my t-shirt over my head then allows me to stand while he removes my jeans. I hold on to his shoulders for support. My body buzzes under his gaze. I'm tired and weak, but apparently, my libido doesn't care. I wrap my arms across my chest while he tests the temperature in the bathtub.

"It's ready," Calvin announces, motioning for me to stand again.

I don't miss his seductive gaze or his dilating pupils as they peruse my bare skin, covered only by my pale pink bra and panty set. My skin prickles when he hooks his thumbs into the waistband of my panties, sliding them down my thighs to pool on the floor. Needing the warmth of the bath to hide my body's reaction, I quickly unhook my bra then step into the tub.

The hot water stings my cold, chafed skin. I slide my hands up and down my arms and legs to help them acclimate to the heat. As the warmth seeps in, I close my eyes, leaning my head against the tub.

"I'll grab some dry clothes and put on some dinner." His shaky voice shows he's affected just as I am. "I'll set the timer for 20 minutes."

"Mm-hmm," I answer, my eyes closed.

I soak for a long time while he's fumbling around in the kitchen. My fingers, toes, hands, and feet are already pruney from the rain; they're so wrinkled they hurt.

"Shouldn't I get out before Tyler arrives?" I holler toward the kitchen.

"I'll text Garret when you're dressed," Calvin states as the timer goes off. I hear some banging in the kitchen before he appears in the doorway and hands me his robe. I slip my arms in, then tie the soft fabric around me. I'm wrapped in the smell of him. I openly sniff the collar. With a smirk on his face, he hands me a pair of sweats and a hoodie, then leaves the bathroom.

I'm glad I'm tall, or I would swim in the length of his gray sweats. I roll the waist once, then lift his sweatshirt and inhale through my nose. His chuckle in the doorway alerts me he saw that. I'm not embarrassed; his warm scent hugs me.

Unbreakable

As he walks from the room again, he informs me he's texting Garret to bring Tyler home and for me to join him in the kitchen for pizza.

"Frozen pizza?" I raise an eyebrow. "You're quite the gourmet chef."

"Daddy, I'm home!" Tyler loudly announces from the front doorway. "Did you take Miss Sky home?"

When he sees me, Tyler runs directly to me at the table. He wraps his little arms around my waist. My heart warms with his long hug. Choking up and not wanting to cry again, I lift my hand.

"Up high, Ty," I encourage.

Tyler doesn't miss a beat. He raises his arm above his head to high-five me.

"I missed you so much," he informs, hugging me once more.

"I can't believe that Princess Schuyler is Miss Sky," he chastises Calvin.

"I didn't know," Calvin promises for a second time, making a cross over his heart with one finger.

"We're going to head out," Garret states with Dallas tucked into his side. We didn't even hear them come in, and they hover in the doorway.

"Bye, Tyler." Dallas waves. "I'm glad I got to meet you."

"Bye, Uncle Garret. Bye, Miss Dallas." Tyler waves back, a wide smile on his face.

Calvin pulls out an empty chair, and Tyler climbs up, sitting on his knees. "I'm glad you're the princess Daddy helped today." He grins at me as he grabs a slice of pizza.

I can only smile. I want to apologize for him seeing me cry. I'm sure I looked like a scary mess to him. I busy myself playing with the two slices of frozen pizza on my paper plate. I lift the smaller piece, biting off part of it. For a frozen pizza, it tastes fantastic.

Calvin takes the empty chair on my other side. While we eat, Tyler fills me in on all that's happened at preschool while I was away. Calvin tosses our empty plates into the trash when we finish. I grab the sponge from the sink to wipe down the table.

"I think we should skip your bath tonight," Calvin says to his son. "Go get your pajamas on, then I'll read you a story."

Tyler looks from his father to me. "Can Miss Sky read a story to me tonight?"

Calvin looks for my approval before saying yes, and Tyler runs to his room. I place the sponge back in the sink before following him. After closing the first book, Tyler begs me to read one more story to him. I find a shorter story and ask him to close his eyes before I will read. Half way through it, his breath evens out, and he's asleep.

I slowly slide from his twin bed, hoping to not make a sound. When I stand from replacing the book on his shelf, I notice a shadow box with Tyler's art work inside.

It's a butterfly he made at preschool. Well, we made it together. The staff was to trace around each child's hand two times, cut out the handprints, color them, then glue them together. Tyler insisted we trace both his hands and mine. His smaller hands form the top two wings, and my larger hands are the bottom wings. He decorated the butterfly with glitter, colors, and pipe cleaners.

The fact that it hangs in his bedroom inside a protective box means Calvin thinks it's as special as Tyler does.

I wonder if he realizes those are my hands.

24

FATE IS A FICKLE BITCH

Schuyler

"Hey," Calvin whispers, peeking his head in the bedroom.

I wave at him to shoo him out, and I tiptoe behind him, suddenly nervous about how the rest of this evening will play out.

"I've prepared my bed for you," he states, motioning me towards the back of the house.

"I can't kick you out of your bed," I argue.

"My couch is plenty big enough for me," he promises.

I walk into his room, finding the blankets pulled back and the bedside lamp on.

"Let me know if you need anything," he says, leaning against the door frame.

I climb onto the mattress, pulling the blankets over me. *I don't want to be alone in his bed. I'm afraid his scent and my fantasies of him might keep me awake all night.*

"Can you lay beside me for a little bit?" I ask, patting the other side of his king-sized bed.

He's hesitant as he lies on top of the comforter, an arm's length away from me.

"Um..." I stutter. "Would you... could you hold me for a while?"

Calvin doesn't wait for a reason or argue. He scoots closer to me. Something in his body language tells me he's relieved. I roll to my side, and he pulls my back tight to his front, his long, strong arms wrapping me up.

"Wait," he says, pulling away, then rolling to the other side of the enormous bed.

I overstepped. I shouldn't have asked him to do that.

"I'm setting two alarms," he states, his back to me. "In case I fall asleep, I need to be absolutely certain that I wake up and get out to the sofa before Tyler wakes up in the morning."

Stupid me. I should have remembered that his son is just down the hallway. Calvin's such a great father. He returns to the center of the bed, repositioning me in his arms. I'm wrapped in his warmth and scent, and it's a heady combination. Relaxing, I close my eyes, and quickly enter dreamland.

Calvin

I wake minutes before my first cell phone alarm. Gently, I roll towards the edge of the bed to turn off both alarms. I sit up, glancing at Schuyler sleeping soundly on her side. *I guess yesterday wasn't a dream after all; what an emotional roller coaster ride it turned out to be. This beautiful, amazing woman revealed her biggest fears to me after she tried to end our relationship.*

Fate is a fickle bitch for stealing motherhood from someone so caring. It's not fair when those that can't care for or don't want a baby continue to conceive. My heart breaks for her. *I wish there was some way I could erase her pain.*

I tiptoe past Tyler's bedroom door, noting he still sleeps soundly. Sitting on the sofa, wrapped in a throw blanket, I try to make sense of everything. *She came home with me without a fight. She asked me to hold her until she fell asleep, but I don't know if we are still a couple or not. I plan to remain by her side, making it difficult for her to toss me away. I'm not giving her up without a fight.*

I smile at the sight of Tyler walking towards me, rubbing his sleepy eyes while sporting a raging case of bed head. Without a word, he settles into my lap, wrapping his little arms around my neck.

"I love you," I whisper, holding him tight against my chest.

"Did Miss Sky go home?" he asks, pulling away to look me in the eye.

"She slept in my room," I state. "Should we make her breakfast?"

Tyler nods, a little smile on his innocent face. "Bacon. I want to make her bacon."

"Okay," I agree, placing him on the floor and walking into the kitchen.

We make quick work of washing our hands, pulling out all the ingredients, and setting the table for the three of us. I flip pancakes while Tyler stands on a chair next to me.

"Hey!" Schuyler calls softly to get our attention, having entered the room behind us.

"Miss Sky, you're awake!" Tyler cheers, climbing down from the chair and running to her. "We're making you bacon." His little voice sounds as joyful now as it does on Christmas morning.

"Yum, yum." Schuyler smiles at me before moving to sit in a chair at the table, Tyler glued to her side.

My belly warms at the sight of the two of them. *Schuyler, in our house, in my bed, feels right. We aren't on solid ground yet, but we will be. I plan to remain at her side as she works through her pain. I'm not sure how to help her; I think the smile on her face when she's with Tyler tells me this is a good start.*

Schuyler

While I nibble on crisp bacon and soft pancakes, the boys prepared for me. My mind boggles at how good it feels to be here.

What was I thinking, trying to break up with Calvin?

I might be able to ignore one sign as a coincidence, but I can't ignore all the signs he mentioned yesterday. We met in Mexico, attend the same college, and I've taught his son in preschool. It seems our paths were destined to cross. We might have met on campus or at the preschool; one way or another, we were bound to find one another.

"I washed your clothes and laid them on the dresser in my room," Calvin informs. "Tyler, wanna help me with the dishes?"

Eager to be of help, Tyler quickly agrees.

After I dress, I sit on the end of Calvin's bed and text Dallas.

> ME
> I need to talk to you, ASAP

> DALLAS
> just woke up is this emergency?

> **ME**
> no just need advice

> **DALLAS**
> pick u up in an hr

> **ME**
> (Thumbs up emoji)

"Thank you for picking me up," I greet, opening Dallas's passenger door. "Is Garret at our place?"

"No." Dallas glances at me, then backs from Calvin's driveway. "He's headed over to play with Ty-man."

"Good."

"Start talking," Dallas orders, keeping her eyes on the road.

I'd rather wait until we can sit face to face on our sofa, but this is Dallas. She's not going to waste time.

"Start from the moment Calvin placed you in your car." Dallas gives me a pointed glare, then returns her attention to the city streets.

I close my eyes, letting the memory play in my mind. I was cold and wet, so he cranked the heater up. Essentially, we rode in silence.

"I fell asleep with my heater vents blowing directly on me," I begin. "I asked him to tell me about Tyler's mother before I drifted off."

"Garret shared her information with me last night after we dropped off Tyler." Dallas turns the car onto our street, scanning for an open parking spot.

I save the rest of my story for when we get inside. Dallas fetches us each a glass of ice water, placing mine on the coffee table in front of me as I sit on the sofa. When we're comfortable, I continue my story.

"Nothing exciting happened in the car. After I found out Tyler's mom gave up her rights, I drifted off." I sip my water and return it to the coaster. "At his house, he filled the tub with warm water, insisting I soak for 20 minutes. He even set a timer."

Dallas smiles devilishly at the news I was naked in his tub. *She thinks we hooked up. I was in no shape for sex; I'm still not ready.*

"He made us frozen pizza for supper. I read Tyler a goodnight story, then Calvin insisted I sleep in his bed while he took the sofa." I stare at my water glass on the table. "I didn't want to be alone, so I asked him to lie with me until I fell asleep. He set two alarms in case he fell asleep, so he'd be out in the living room before Tyler woke up. And that's it."

I rub at my wrist for a moment. "Yesterday, I was lost in my pain; I wanted to cut all ties with Calvin. I wanted him to have a chance at a happy future, and I can't give him that." I rub the back of my neck to loosen my tight muscles. "At the wreck site, Calvin pointed out all the signs that we should be together. We met in Mexico, we attend the same college, and I taught his son in preschool. He claims we would meet in one of those three scenarios."

I lift my eyes from my folded hands, looking to Dallas. "I believe in signs. I can't deny it's more than a coincidence that our lives intersect in three ways. Once I shared about my hysterectomy, Calvin told me he was adopted. He reminded me that there are many ways to start a family. He's such a sweet guy. The more I pushed him away, the more stubborn he became. He had a rebuttal to my every reason to break up."

"So," Dallas pauses, moving beside me and taking my hand in hers. "Where does that leave the two of you?"

"We didn't discuss it. I fell asleep last night before we talked. It's clear he plans to not let me go. And... I'm..." I flounder. "I don't know what I want."

Dallas pulls me into a tight hug. Her hand rubs up and down my back for a moment, then she pushes me away, holding me at arm's length.

"You spent the night with Calvin and his son," she reminds me. "I think you not sending me an S.O.S. last night means you know what you want."

My brow furrows as I attempt to understand her meaning.

Did I stay at his place last night because I was exhausted or because I wanted to?
In my weakened state, did I subconsciously make my decision?

"I think I love Calvin," I whisper, needing Dallas's opinion.

She smiles widely and nods. "That's clear."

"Do you think we can really make a relationship work?"

Dallas doesn't answer immediately. She takes a few moments to gather her words. "I've known you love Calvin for a couple of weeks now," she confesses. "I know your shot appointments wig you out, and I totally understand that. Now, you have no reason to let that scare you. I know you'll be a great mother. And Calvin's right; there are many ways to have a family. When I met Tyler, I knew it was meant to be."

"I can't let Tyler be the reason I stay with Calvin," I inform my friend.

25

GREEN-EYED MONSTER

Schuyler

I mull over my statement. *I can't let Tyler be the reason I stay with Calvin.*

"No, you can't," Dallas agrees. "Calvin and you are together because you love each other. Calvin loves you; he loves all parts of you. He doesn't want to lose you. Now that you know he has a son, and he knows about your hysterectomy, there's no reason to hold back."

"I don't know how it'll work." I slump back into the sofa cushion. "How will we date with Tyler around? What will that look like?"

Dallas shakes her head at me. "It's different, that's for sure. The two of you will have normal dates, though. I'm sure you'll occasionally hang out with both of them. You love kids, so this won't be a problem for you."

"Can it be that easy?" I rub my hands down my face. *It seems too good to be true.*

"Do you love Calvin?" Dallas asks firmly.

I nod.

She holds up one finger between us. "Do you love children?"

Again, I nod, and she holds up a second finger.

"Do you like Tyler?"

I nod, fighting a smile as it attempts to grow on my face.

"I know you planned only to have fun with Calvin until graduation," she says. "There's no reason you can't keep seeing him. I'll be in Kansas City; you can live with me. I can help you apply to schools in the area, so you'll also be close to Calvin and Tyler."

I'm not even sure Calvin wants to continue seeing me post-graduation. I mean, I think his actions yesterday mean he's all in for the long haul. But how can I know for sure?

"I've got a plan," Dallas announces animatedly. "Garret and I can keep Tyler this afternoon and evening, so the two of you can talk. And yes, you need to talk. Now that both of your secrets are out in the open, it's time for you to decide where you go from here. You need to tell him you love him. You need to tell him you'll live with me in Kansas City to be closer to him. And you need to talk about dating, being around Tyler, and what the future holds. I believe the two of you have what it takes to go the distance if you can just get out of your own head for a change."

I look at my best friend. She makes it sound so easy. She makes it sound like we will last forever.

Can I do this?

Can I accept my path to starting a family will be nontraditional?

Can I do it all for Calvin?

Can I do it for myself?

Calvin

"Tyler, can you come here for a minute?" I call from the kitchen table. I've poured each of us a glass of milk and piled a small plate full of Oreo cookies.

"What?" Tyler asks, peeking his head out of his room.

"Snack time," I state. "Come sit with me."

Spying the Oreos right away, he happily hops into the chair next to mine and wastes no time dunking his first black cookie into the white milk. He drips all the way to his mouth, causing me to smile. I remember eating Oreos on the kitchen island, as Mom baked when I was young. I'm glad I can enjoy the tradition with my son now.

"I need to talk to you about something," I inform him, sipping from my milk but waiting to eat a cookie until I'm done speaking. "It's about Miss Sky."

"I'm glad we made her happy again," he says through a mouth full of cookie.

"I want to make her happy all the time," I confess. "Would it be okay if I dated her?"

Tyler halts his chewing, black crumbs on his lips and his wide hazel eyes on me.

"Remember the week you stayed with Papa and Nana?" I look for his nod before I continue. "I met Miss Sky in Mexico. She was at the same hotel as Uncle Garret and me."

Swallowing, he smiles, cookie crumbs still in the corners of his mouth.

"Miss Sky went to the wedding, too?" he asks, his little brow furrowed.

"I went for the wedding; Miss Sky was on vacation with Miss Dallas. We met, talked, and swam in the pool." I search for simple words to make my point. "I like her a lot."

Tyler smiles, clapping his hands.

"When we got back from Mexico, we went to lunch with each other. The night Nana played games and watched movies with you, I went to a movie with Miss Sky." *I'm not sure he understands.* "I went on a date with her. Do you know what a date is?"

Tyler giggles, his hand covering his mouth. "You kiss on dates."

"Yes, couples might kiss on dates, but there's more to it," I try to explain.

"Did you kiss Miss Sky?" His little eyes twinkle at the thought. "Do you love her?" He looks delighted at the prospect.

Well, there it is. In his mind, that is all that matters. He likes Miss Sky and loves the thought of me liking her, too.

"Would it be okay if I keep dating Miss Sky?"

Giggling again, he asks, "Will you kiss her?"

I can't answer him, so I nod.

"She makes you smile when you're on the phone with her," he states before dunking his next cookie.

My face scrunches as I try to decipher his meaning.

How would he know? What makes him think dating Miss Sky will make me smile on the phone? I can't see his logic.

"Why do you think she will make me smile on the phone?" I inquire.

"At night, when I'm in bed, you talk on the phone, and you smile." His full mouth muffles his words.

"How do you know that? Why were you out of bed?"

"I had to go potty, and your door was open. I heard you say 'Schuyler,' and you were smiling," he explains, chomping away on a new cookie.

Wow! I always put him down for the night before I call her. *I guess I'm not as sneaky as I think I am. He's perceptive. He listened for her name and paid attention to my smile.*

"I like when you smile," he admits. "She makes you happy."

A fist squeezes around my heart. I want him to not have a care in the world; he doesn't need to be worried about me. *He is my son. It's always just been the two of us.*

I never imagined he would be concerned with me being single. *He's too young to worry about his dad's social life.*

"She makes me smile," I agree. "I enjoy being with her and want to be with her all the time." I take a deep breath. "Is it okay if I keep dating Miss Sky? Sometimes, you'll be with us, and sometimes, you won't."

"Are you gonna marry her?" He pairs his question with another smile.

How do I answer that one?

I can't deny butterflies flutter in my stomach at the thought of making Schuyler my wife.

"I love her," I admit. A little weight lifts from my shoulders. "It's new. So, say nothing for now. We will date for a long time before we decide if we should get married. It's too soon to get married now."

"I love Miss Sky, too," my little man declares proudly. "When can I go on a date with her?"

I laugh. It's a deep belly laugh. *I dreaded this chat because I didn't think he would understand. Instead, he's in love and wants to date Schuyler, too.*

Heaven help me when he becomes a teenager and discovers girls.

Schuyler

"Fill the glass all the way up," I instruct. "We're gonna need it."

"Two laptops, a wine glass filled to the rim… What are we doing?" Dallas asks with a raised eyebrow.

"We're stalking Tyler's birth mom online," I state.

"Are you serious?" Dallas's voice rises excitedly as she claps her hands and hops up and down.

By the time I take my first sip, she's already typed the name from my Post-It note into her search engine. Pointing at results, Dallas reads, "A midwestern photographer, she travels the world documenting nature, cities, and humanity."

My eyes attempt to read as she scrolls quickly down the web page.

"She's elusive, rarely spotted at public and charity events. Many admire her unique view of the world via her lens. Her work hangs in art galleries around the world and appears in periodicals like *Rolling Stone, Time,* and *Newsweek.* Jackpot!" Dallas cheers, finding a photo of Dani.

Dani styles her brown hair with red highlights perfectly, her green eyes pop with her impeccable makeup, and she strikes quite an image in her casual, artsy attire.

"She's gorgeous," I gasp. "How can I ever compete with that?" I point to the screen.

"She's high-maintenance, and she has drama written all over her," Dallas corrects, attempting to ease my worry. She continues her protests. "She abandoned her son within days of giving birth. She signed documents and disappeared. What kind of woman does that?"

Dani is a gorgeous and stylish world traveler. She's famous and rich.

How can I compete?

She can conceive, and I can't. She's Tyler's real mom, his birth mom, and I will never be.

"Stop it!" Dallas orders. She can tell exactly what I'm thinking. "Don't you dare compare yourself to her. She's a talented photographer but a horrible mother. She chose the life she wanted over her infant son. According to Garret, she's never contacted Tyler or Calvin since the day she left."

I hear my friend, but I'm already lost in my head. My eyes move from one touching photo to the next. Children in the Amazon Rainforest, a couple kissing on a bridge, a jet slicing through white puffy clouds. Some photos make me feel as if a fist wraps around my heart; others make me smile or wonder. Each one provokes an emotion from me.

"I think my father has this one in his office at work," Dallas claims, scrolling on her cell phone. "It seems… Dani doesn't have private social media accounts, only accounts to promote her work."

I lean over to glance at Dallas's phone screen. We find nothing of her family or child.

Everything Calvin told me is true. She left Maryville, cutting all ties with her son and family.

Staring at her headshot, my desire to slap her grows with each passing second. *She has a child. She has an adorable son. She's a mother. She has what I want most and will never have. She took it for granted, and I am jealous of her.* Tears form in the corner of my eyes. If only I could wish and pray hard enough to wake up from this nightmare.

For me, it's just not meant to be. I will forever battle my green-eyed monster at the sight of mothers.

26

THE ONE FOR ME

Schuyler

"He's officially asleep," I sigh, flopping on the sofa near Dallas.

"How many books did you end up reading?" she asks.

"Three, but we had a brief discussion in between each one. He asked me questions about dating." I smile at my friend. "He asked about Garret and you, along with Calvin and me."

"Like what?"

"We talked about love, where we go on dates, kissing, whether Garret and you kiss, if you love Garret, who Tyler loves, and so on." I love Dallas looks as uncomfortable about the topics as I was when he asked me the questions.

"Did you answer all of his questions?" Dallas's worried face causes me to smirk.

"Yes. I think it's important to be open and honest with him," I explain. "I didn't go into detail, and I asked him what he thought a few times. He's a perceptive little guy. He likes to see the adults in his life smile and laugh. And he's glad you make his Uncle Garret smile a lot."

"Wow. I'm definitely glad I don't work with kids. There's no way I could handle all the questions that they ask," Dallas admits.

"I wonder if they are out at a bar or in their hotel room." I change the subject to our boyfriends. "What do you think the guys are doing right now?" I ask, knowing Calvin deserves adult time. It's difficult keeping Tyler on his schedule and having a social life.

Dallas looks at the time on her cell phone. "They're not staying at a hotel."

I scrunch my face at her comment. "What do you mean?"

"Didn't Calvin tell you?"

"I didn't ask for any details of their trip. I was more concerned with preparing for Tyler's sleepover." I feel foolish.

"They looked at the property with our dads today," Dallas states.

"What property?" I'm lost. *Clearly, I needed to ask for more details from Calvin. I thought this was a simple business trip.*

"During our snowy sleepover after the spring break trip, your dad mentioned a site in Des Moines that would be perfect for their restaurant and bar. They talked for a long time about the speakeasy being a perfect fit for the Des Moines market." Dallas pauses for a drink. "Didn't Calvin talk to you about it?"

I shake my head, unable to answer as my head fills with questions.

If they open their business in Des Moines, what does that mean?

Did they change cities for us girls?

And if so, why?

"They've officially decided to open in Des Moines, and they want our dads to advise them. I'm sure Calvin just wants to surprise you when he gets back." She tries to calm my nerves. "Garret texted this afternoon, stating your father made them cancel the hotel reservation and stay with your parents tonight instead."

This is too much. My boyfriend is staying at my parents' house without me, and I knew nothing about it. *Switching the location of their restaurant and bar from Kansas City to Des Moines is huge.* I've still been putting in for jobs in Missouri, hoping to be close to Calvin.

What if I get a job offer in KC, and he moves to Des Moines?

That would be just my luck. Why didn't he give me a hint about any of this?

Calvin

I'm a bundle of pent-up energy as Garret pulls into the Dawes' driveway. Today didn't go as planned. It went better. I have the keys to my future business in my pocket. The lease is cheaper than our projection, which means we can use those funds elsewhere. *I need to call Sky and share the exciting news. But that will have to wait until after we eat dinner with Dallas' and Sky's parents.*

"Here they are," Richard Dawes calls from the front porch. "Well, get in here.

Unbreakable

We're excited to hear how it went with the realtor." He hugs his wife tight to his side while we walk up the sidewalk with our suitcases in hand.

Theo tells us the meal is ready, so we gather around the dining table. With a prayer shared and our plates filled, conversation begins.

"How'd it go after we left?" Richard asks.

"Thank you for mentioning the property to us months ago," Garret starts. "Calvin couldn't stop thinking about bringing our idea to Des Moines since the night you mentioned it. And the meeting went great! We signed the lease today, and we have the keys."

"Wow! That was quick," Theo cheers. "When will you begin renovations?"

"Garret plans to give notice at work and find a place up here by the end of the week." I look at my friend, and he nods in agreement. "He'll get the permits and construction started. I'll be up to join him the day after graduation."

"So, you've found housing?" Dallas's mother asks my friend.

"Not yet. I'm not picky, so I'll probably stay in an extended stay hotel until I find a more permanent place," Garret states.

"You're more than welcome to stay with us. We have lots of room and would love the company," Theo offers.

"Thank you," Garret replies. "I'll have to see how everything comes together."

"Might I ask a favor of you?" I direct my question to Richard Dawes. "If we leave a set of keys with you, would you be able to meet our architect at the site on Monday and let him in, so I don't have to miss classes and Garret doesn't miss work?"

"Of course! I'd love to help." The smile on his face shows his excitement at being a part of our endeavor.

Everything is coming together. I need to call Schuyler then my parents to break the news that I will open my business and moving to Des Moines. *I'm sure my parents will be supportive; they always are. I think Schuyler will like my news. At least, I hope she will.*

I'm sitting in Schuyler's parents' front room; Garret went upstairs to phone Dallas. The long drive to Des Moines gave the two of us time to run through scenarios for the surprise I'm planning. I'm so nervous, my palms are sweating. I keep rubbing them on the front of my shorts. I hope her parents will be as excited as my parents were two days ago.

"I want to talk to you about a graduation gift I hope to give Schuyler next weekend," I begin, and her parents are all smiles. I take a deep breath. "I love your daughter with all my heart. I'd like your permission to ask her to marry me."

There I've said it; it's out there. Now for their reactions. Theo fans her face as happy tears flow. Richard rises, extending his hand to shake mine.

"We'd be honored to have you in the family," Richard states before Theo wraps me in a hug.

"Our baby's getting married!" Theo giggles excitedly.

I had hoped Theo would be this excited. I was worried about Richard's reaction. The three of us take our seats once again, and I pull the ring box from my pocket.

"This was my grandmother's ring. Do you think Sky will like it?" I extend the open, red velvet box toward the two of them.

"It's lovely," Theo gasps. "Schuyler will absolutely love it." She gives me a warm smile.

"Do you think she'll say yes?" I ask what terrifies me.

Sky might think it's too soon, or she'll push me away again since she can't have children. None of that matters to me. I love her and need her by my side forever.

"I don't know... she can be stubborn sometimes," Richard states with a grin.

"Oh, please." Theo swats at her husband. "She's head over heels in love with Tyler and you. There's no doubt in my mind; she'll say yes."

"How do you plan to propose?" Theo asks.

"I don't know," I answer honestly. "I may ask Tyler for his help. I haven't figured that detail out yet. I may ask Dallas for ideas, too." I run my fingers through my hair.

She loves me; I know she loves me. She may need convincing, but she wants to say yes.

"I feel it deep in my bones; she's the one for me," I confess.

27

THE HOUSE IS BUGGED

Calvin

As if they bugged the house, one by one, Schuyler's three brothers all somehow happen to drop by. *I don't plan to share my news with them.* I'd rather they learn of our engagement at the graduation party. Theo tries her best, but she can't hide that she's excited about something.

"Mom, what's up? You look like the cat that ate the canary." Levi looks from his mother to his father, then at me with suspicion.

Theo turns to me, zips her lips, and tosses the key over her left shoulder. *Ya, like that won't make them ask more questions.* I feel I'm in front of a firing squad with all three brothers glaring in my direction.

"You know, we can beat it out of you," Levi threatens.

"Levi Dawes," Theo chides. "Where are your manners? That is no way to treat a guest in our house."

"Spill the beans," Dan orders, pointing to his mom.

Theo's much too excited to keep it secret any longer. She buckles, an excited grin growing on her face. "Calvin's going to ask Schuyler to marry him!"

Six angry, brown eyes bore into me. Levi's jaw muscle ticks, Dan's face is beet red, and Clint's fists clench and unclench at this side.

"Moving pretty fast, aren't you?" Levi growls.

"Levi!" Richard shoots a glare in his direction.

"Are your parents still married?" Clint asks, sitting close to me on the sofa.

"Yes," I answer.

"What's your relationship like with your mother?" Dan asks next. "You can tell a lot about a guy by the way he treats his mom."

"I'm close to both my parents," I inform the group. "I'm so close to my mom that I've never felt the need to find my birth mother." At their lost looks, I explain further. "I'm adopted."

"And what are your plans after graduation?" Levi continues the interrogation. "Do you plan to force her to move to Kansas City while you start your bar?"

"Actually, we leased a space in Des Moines today," Garret shares, coming to my defense.

The three brothers stare at me, processing this new bit of information.

Yes, I'm moving Schuyler closer to her family.

"What if your venture takes over five years to turn a profit, or it fails all together?" Levi asks.

"I have many investments. My father owns an investment company with Garret's dad. I've worked at the office and interned there." I take a nervous breath. "I've invested the money I've earned, along with the money I've inherited. It's the reason I'm able to finance this venture. We could live comfortably for several years on my investments alone."

"Calvin, you don't need to prove yourself to us. I'm sure, together, the two of you will make it just fine on your own," Richard imparts, shooting a glare at his sons.

"And what of Tyler's mom? Is she in the picture? How will she treat our sister as the stepmom of her child?" Dan pries.

"Dani signed over all parental rights the day after Tyler was born. She doesn't phone, text, or drop in for a visit. There will be no friction between Sky and Tyler's birth mother," I promise.

"What do you think of Schuyler working full time?" Clint digs further.

It's a wonder Sky ever made it to Mexico with these three in her life.

"I want Sky to do what makes her happy. She loves children, so she should do what she loves."

"What about the holidays?" Levi inquires.

Theo's had it. "That's enough!" She rises and walks to the kitchen, frustrated with her sons.

Of course, the boys keep interrogating me in her absence.

"Sky can't get pregnant. What if, someday, you want another child of your own?" Dan takes his turn.

"I've discussed with Sky many ways for us to have a family. As I'm adopted, I feel that is a great option. We've talked about taking on foster kids and volunteering in the community to create a family unique to us."

I decide to turn the tables on the three overprotective brothers. "Will the three of you loosen the reins to allow Sky and me to be happy? Can you let us be a couple and only give advice when one of us seeks it? Or will you interfere at every step?"

I love the look of shock on their faces. It's clear they didn't expect me to stand up to them. I'm sure they're used to using their large muscles, military experience, and law enforcement careers to intimidate. No one has ever given them a taste of their own medicine.

"We love our baby sister and will do what we need to ensure her safety and happiness." They didn't answer my questions, but I already knew their answers.

"I am concerned about Tyler's position in our new family." My voice quivers a bit at this topic that is often on my mind.

"We love kids," Dan states, almost offended.

"Sky speaks fondly of Tyler every time we talk. What's important to her is important to us," Levi adds. "From what she's told me, he will fit right in as our nephew. I can't wait to play catch with Up-High Ty." A smile flits across his face, something I'm not used to seeing.

I like Sky shares stories of my son with her family. I have no doubt she loves him. I hope Levi's sincere, and the others will, too.

"Is the interrogation over?" I only half tease.

The Dawes men laugh, causing Theo to return.

When the laughter fades, I turn to Theo. "I have something I'd like to run by you."

She motions for me to continue. I hadn't planned to talk in front of the entire family.

"I did a little research and found that Sky can get her Depo shot at her general practitioner instead of going to the OB every three months," I share. "She can avoid seeing the pregnant moms and the tiny babies this way."

"Why didn't we think of that?" Clint asks.

I shrug. "She's tormented enough daily. I wanted to find a way to avoid some pain. As I'm sure you know, the week leading up to the shot and the day she goes to the office torment her. I thought you might bring up this solution with Sky," I say, looking only at Theo. "She might consider it if it came from you."

Schuyler

. . .

I feel like I'm about to puke; I'm so nervous. Graduation is here, but that's not why I'm nervous. It's the fact that I'm meeting Calvin's parents for the first time today at the party Dallas planned for the three of us.

Calvin told me he speaks a lot about me with his parents when they call. He confessed he even talked to his mom about me while we were in Mexico. From all he shares, I think I'll like them and hope I'll get along fine.

I'm worried they might not be happy that Calvin and Garret started their business in Des Moines instead of Kansas City, moving their grandson further away and closer to my parents. He's told me how they dote on their grandson, so the fact that he's moving hours away to another state must be a sore spot.

It's not fair that Calvin's already met my parents. Now he relaxes while I'm anxious. Tyler's excited to meet my family today. He thinks the idea of me having three older brothers is cool. *I can't wait for him to find out he's getting presents from them; he'll be over the moon.*

"I checked in with the caterers," Dallas states, entering my bedroom where I stand at my full-length mirror. "It's all set up, and food will arrive while we are at the ceremony."

Leave it to Dallas to go all out for a college graduation party. She won the tent, tables, chairs, and waitstaff at a fraternity auction. Friends of hers from the frat will be our waiters this afternoon. She spent hours fussing over the menu with the local grocery store catering department to plan a perfect event. *I'd be happy eating at a restaurant; but that's not good enough for her.*

"You look good," Dallas promises. "Let's go! We don't want to be late for the ceremony."

I pose with my parents while Clint takes our photo after the ceremony. I'd like one with all my brothers, but Levi won't arrive until party time as he worked overnight. I glimpse Calvin and Tyler fighting the crowds of families snapping pictures on the lawn to join our group. Tyler waves excitedly while my stomach turns somersaults. *I thought I'd meet Calvin's parents at the party; I wonder if he plans to introduce me now?*

When Calvin releases his hand, Tyler sprints towards me, his hand in the air for his infamous high-five.

After our palms slap, I bend to his level and point. "Tyler, this is my mom and dad, Theo and Richard. That's my brother, Clint, and he's my brother, Dan. Everyone, this is Up-High Ty."

Everyone says hello and takes a turn, offering him a high-five. Clint leaves his hand up too high, causing Tyler to try three times before he jumps high enough to connect with Clint's palm.

Calvin wraps an arm around my waist, pulling me to his side. "We did it," he whispers close to my ear, causing my skin to prickle.

"Yep! Now, we must spread our wings and adult in the real world," I tease.

"Something like that," Clint retorts. I hadn't realized he was eavesdropping.

"Where are your parents?" I ask Calvin, scanning the crowd.

"They are meeting us back at the house," he informs the group before whispering in my ear, "I thought you'd like a more private setting to meet them in."

My heart melts a bit; he's so thoughtful. *Why did I even doubt him for a minute?*

"Let's head back to the house," Calvin suggests to the group. "Everyone has the address?"

I nod as yesterday I texted them all the address and step-by-step directions from the ceremony to his place.

"Hurry," Tyler motions. "I have a present for Miss Sky." A big smile lights up his face.

I smile back at him, then look questioningly to Calvin. *He wasn't supposed to buy me a gift.* Calvin simply shrugs while smirking his sexy smirk. My body longs to celebrate with him in private. *It's going to be a long afternoon and evening with no time alone for the two of us.*

28

US?

Schuyler

Levi waits for us on the front porch of Calvin's house. I leap from my parents' vehicle, eager to see him and celebrate my special day.

"Hanging in there?" Levi asks, wrapping me in a bear hug.

"Too... many... muscles..." I groan as I struggle to breathe. He often forgets the power he packs in his oversized arms. I take a minute to regain my breath. "What do you mean 'hanging in there'? Graduation's over. It's party time!" I announce.

Levi sports a shit-eating grin. *He's up to something. When any of my brothers are up to something, it's usually a terrible day for me. I'm sure they plan to embarrass me.* I grab my father by the arm, pulling him to the side before we enter the house.

"Levi's up to something," I inform him. "I'm meeting Calvin's parents for the first time today; I don't need him to mess that up. Can you intervene on my behalf?" I bat my eyes, hoping to persuade Dad.

"Your brothers will be on their best behavior," he promises. "They have nothing planned to embarrass you, trust me."

I hug him tightly, then we enter the house together. I'm dumbfounded at the amount of food and drink spread about the kitchen. The catering staff directs us toward the backyard, where I pause at the back door to take in the view.

The giant white tent creates a backdrop for green tablecloths spread over rectangular tables, white plastic chairs, yellow floral centerpieces, and an enormous banner with all three of our names on it. *It shouldn't surprise me. Dallas's party planning skills have grown with each event she's planned over the years.*

"Hey, sweetheart," Calvin greets, taking my hands in his.

He pulls me down the steps to stand in front of him. His hazel eyes are nearly brown today as they search mine before he leans in for a kiss. His warm lips seek…something.

What is he looking for?

Reassurance? Understanding? Love?

Too soon, his lips retreat, and his eyes glue to mine. "Ready to meet my parents?"

His sweet smile calms my nerves a bit. I nod, and he giggles, taking my hand in his. Tyler hops out of a man's arms, running towards us.

"Miss Sky! Miss Sky! Come see Nana and Papa!" Tyler encourages, tugging on my free hand.

With two of my favorite people holding my hands, I stride toward the only couple in attendance that I'm not familiar with. Their eyes assess me as I assess them. His mother's petite frame, trendy hairstyle, and impeccably accessorized designer clothes strike a commanding presence. His father is tall, maybe six-two or six-three. His tailored suit with blue pinstripes definitely isn't off the rack. I shouldn't judge them by their clothing, but compared to my parents in their department store attire, they are way out of my league.

With five steps between us, I now worry they might think I'm not good enough for their son. In addition, they're likely to be angry that he's moving to my hometown in another state, taking their grandson with him.

"Mom, Dad," Calvin looks from them to me as he speaks, "this is Schuyler."

The brown flakes in his hazel eyes sparkle, and his smile warms my insides. In that instant, I have faith that his parents will accept me; they'll want to get to know me all because Calvin loves me.

"Hi." My voice is weak as I wave in their direction.

Wave? I waved like an idiot. Way to make a great first impression, Schuyler.

They don't seem to mind my awkwardness. They wrap me in a hug as they greet me, stating they've heard so many things about me.

"Miss Sky, high-five!" Tyler calls when his grandma releases me. I lift my hand to accept his slap.

"Ty," Calvin's voice assumes a soft fatherly tone, "what have I told you about calling her Miss Sky?"

Tyler apologizes to his father, then to me. Over the past week, Calvin has been working on getting Tyler to call me 'Sky' or 'Schuyler' instead of 'Miss Sky' as he did at preschool. I haven't made a big deal about it when he forgets; I know it will take some time.

I carry on easy conversation with Calvin's parents, introducing my parents, my brothers, and Dallas's family as each group makes their way over to us. I'm happy to find that his parents aren't uptight in their expensive clothes. They fit right in with the rest of our family and friends.

The meal Dallas chose is divine, and the fraternity guys do a great job of serving, refilling drinks, and clearing the tables. We continue our conversations as they work. Eventually, Dallas stands in front of the group, commanding our attention. She thanks everyone for joining us to celebrate today, then she gives a thumb up to Tyler. It's some sort of signal for something they've planned. He rises from his seat with his grandparents and skips to the corner of the tent. Then he walks toward me, a wide smile upon his face and his little hands behind his back.

"Here," Tyler says, extending his arms toward me. In his hands, he cradles a rectangular box.

"What's this?" I ask my little friend.

"Open it," he prompts.

My fingers fumble as I attempt to open a small white envelope, pulling the card from it. Tears well in my eyes as I read the card. "Of all the princesses in the world, I'm glad Dad chose you." It's Calvin's script. Below it, in his own handwriting, is "Tyler". Inside the box, I find a gold chain with an infinity symbol. Engraved on it, I read, "Bend don't break."

Tears spill down my cheeks, and my fingers tremble too much to clasp the necklace around my neck. Calvin deftly helps fasten it for me.

"I love it," I whisper, squatting in front of Tyler, opening my arms for a hug.

"I love you," Tyler proclaims, while squeezing me tight.

"I love you, too," I squeak out, trying to control my overwhelming emotions. Calvin and I share those three words; Tyler and I haven't until today.

When I stand, Calvin quickly pulls me to his chest to allow me to gain some composure. Dallas moves the party along by opening her gift from Garret. Standing at Calvin's side, his arm over my shoulder, my fingers keep playing with my new necklace.

Calvin asks me, "Do you see Tyler?"

I look all over the tent, finally spotting him sitting on Levi's lap at the table with my entire family. When Calvin waves at his son, Tyler slides off my brother's lap, gives everyone a high-five, puts his hands behind his back, and walks toward me.

"I have a present for you," Tyler announces sweetly.

"You already gave me a gift," I remind him.

Unbreakable

He shakes his head at me. "I don't have it. Daddy has it." He points behind me.

I spin around, finding Calvin on one knee with a red velvet ring box open in his hand. I fan my face as my cheeks feel aflame. Hot tears sting my eyes and trail down my cheeks. Calvin rises, pulls my hand from my face, and lays the ring box in my palm.

"My world felt complete the week I met you. You center me, you energize me, and you fill a void I didn't know existed." His voice is soft, saying the words meant only for my ears. He scoops Tyler into his arms. "Schuyler…"

In unison, the two ask, "Will you marry us?"

29

WHO DOES THAT?

Schuyler

I open my mouth; I can't form the words. I try a second time with no luck, so I nod. I nod and nod and nod. I wrap my arms around the two guys in front of me. "Yes!" I squeak in their ears. "Yes!"

Our gathered family and friends cheer and applaud around us. Dallas pulls me from Calvin's arms to hug me. She's as excited as me. Holding my hands between us, she speaks of venue, date, color scheme, and so on.

"Excuse me, Dallas," Calvin interrupts, pulling my hands from my best friend's. "She said yes. I need to slide this ring onto my fiancé's finger."

Fiancé.

I'm a fiancé.

I'm engaged to the sweetest man in the world, with an adorable little boy. I'm getting married.

How is this my life?

Amid all the congratulations, servers pour champagne and pass it to the adults while they give Tyler a glass of sparkling cider. Calvin's father toasts. We clink glasses and drink. Unaware of how it happened, I find myself at a long table surrounded by women while the men gather on the other side of the tent. They suggest wedding ideas, and they pass personal contacts of wedding industry businesses to me. It suddenly dawns on me. *They came prepared.*

"Hold it," I demand, sliding my chair back to stand. "How did you all know to bring names and numbers to our graduation party?" I look at each woman around the table.

Some seal their lips while others point at Calvin.

My mother speaks first. "While Calvin was in Des Moines last week, he asked your father for permission to marry you."

It feels as though my eyes might pop right out of their sockets.

Calvin's mother informs me that Calvin spoke to them a few days before my parents, asking for his grandmother's ring.

Grandmother's ring?

I've barely taken my eyes off of the beautiful diamond and intricate band around my finger. As I look at it now, I recognize it's vintage. My fingertips rub over his grandmother's stunning jewel.

"I didn't know," I murmur, looking to my future mother-in-law.

"Of course, you didn't. He hasn't had time to share the story with you yet." Calvin's mother pats my hand.

"Dallas, you knew, too?"

My friend smiles proudly. She struggles to keep secrets. Actually, she really sucks at it. Somehow, she found the strength to keep this one. *And I love her for it.*

"Can I have your attention for a moment?" Calvin's father asks after clanking his knife against his champagne glass. "Schuyler, Tyler, and Calvin, please come forward."

I look at the women sitting near me for answers. They seem as shocked as I am. While I walk to meet the guys, Calvin's mother walks beside me. His parents sit the three of us down at the end of a nearby table.

While she opens a laptop in front of us, Calvin's father speaks. "My wife and I have purchased a house in Des Moines as our engagement gift to the three of you." He pauses, allowing the crowds to react and his wife to open the browser displaying photos of the house. "We want to wish the three of you the best as you begin your new life together in Des Moines. We're certainly going to miss our grandson, but we'll be happy to come and stay with you for a visit." He winks at us when we smile at him in appreciation.

It's too much. This gift is too much.

Who does that?

Who buys a house as a gift?

Well, I guess the Calhouns do. I'm not sure how to react. I sit frozen while Calvin scrolls through the photos, and Tyler points to parts of the new property he likes.

My family stands behind us to glimpse the home and thank Calvin's parents for the wonderful gift. My mind swims with the beauty. Its exterior boasts gray stone and has a three-car garage. It's a ranch home in Urbandale, a suburb of Des

Moines. Growing up in the area, I know it's in an excellent school district and a great community. It's in the same metro area as my parents and three brothers, but far enough away that we won't feel crowded by them. With Calvin starting a business and me earning a measly first-year teacher's salary, it's a much better house than we could afford on our own. I'm not sure how much time passes before the excitement over the house simmers down.

Levi draws my attention back to the party while clinking a knife against his glass. "It's my turn to make an announcement."

I cringe at the thought of my brother making a toast for Calvin and me. I look to my father for his intervention, but he gives me the "don't know" gesture. *Some help he is.*

Levi stands behind his wife, seated at a table with my other brothers. He places his hand on her shoulder. "I'm gonna be a daddy!" A wide smile of triumph spreads across his face.

Wait.

What?

Oh. My. Gosh. Levi's having a baby!

I'm going to be an aunt! I clap excitedly, smiling at my big brother. I'm so excited for the two of them.

Calvin presses himself to my back, wrapping his arms around me. "I love you," he whispers.

"I love you, too." I spin in his embrace. "Can you believe I'm going to be an aunt?"

Although he smiles, I don't miss that his eyes scan my face to assess my sincerity.

"This is the best day ever," I state, then place a kiss on the corner of his mouth. "We graduated, we got engaged, I'm going to be Tyler's stepmom, and I'm going to be an aunt!" I kiss him once more. "I need to go hug my brother."

As I approach, I feel the weight of my parents' eyes on me. I tap Levi on the shoulder, prompting him to turn in my direction, and I wrap my arms around his giant frame.

"Congratulations!" I squeal. "I'm so excited for you."

My whole family stares at me. I avoid their attention, moving toward my sister-in-law. "Congratulations."

"Thank you." She tilts her head. "We were worried…"

I interrupt. "Are you kidding?" I smile, scanning the faces of my entire family. "I get to be an aunt!"

They pause for a moment in shock before all return to celebrating.

30

BLISS

Calvin

"Tyler's down," I announce as I walk into my bedroom. "I didn't even get to read him a book. We talked for a minute, I rubbed his back, he closed his eyes, and that was it."

"It was a long and very exciting day," Sky reminds me. "I'm not sure how long I'll be awake once my head hits the pillow."

Nope! She isn't falling asleep yet. She can't sleep until we privately celebrate our engagement.

I watch as she removes her makeup, applies lotion, and brushes her teeth. Amazingly, she doesn't seem upset about Levi's baby announcement this afternoon. I'm not letting my guard down; she may have a delayed reaction to the news when the excitement of our engagement wears off.

"Dallas told me she turned down the internship in Kansas City," Sky shares as she places her toothbrush in her cosmetic bag. "She's going to stay with her parents until she gets her own place, and she accepted the job offer in Des Moines."

"Garret will flip when she tells him. He's been fretting about it for a couple weeks now," I share. "I bet Dallas simply moves into his new apartment."

Sky agrees, and we move to the bed. She fluffs her pillow for a bit as I lie on my side, watching her. Once settled, she smiles in my direction.

"My parents had another surprise announcement," I share. "They found a condo on some golf course near the airport in Des Moines. Dad plans to work via the internet and golf on the weekends that they come to visit. Mom claims they plan to drive up three weekends a month during the warm months, plus a few weeks for vacation."

"Which course?" Sky asks, not upset by this news.

"I don't know. It's near the airport."

"Is it Wakonda?" She looks at me for an answer, and I shake my head. "Echo Valley?"

"Yep! That's it," I state. "They bought a condo right on the course."

"It's a nice course," she marvels. "It has three courses totaling 27 holes, a tennis court, a pool, and an awesome clubhouse with a restaurant."

How does she know so much about the place?

"Did you work there or something?" I ask.

"Mom and Dad are members. They joined while I was in high school," she states.

I play with her hair for a few minutes, noting her eyelids growing heavy. We chat about the house my parents gifted us. We both agree with four bedrooms and a pool, it's much more than we need.

"Between your new business and me not having found a teaching position yet, we probably couldn't even afford to rent the garage," Schuyler states.

It's at this moment that I realize we are engaged, and I need to discuss my finances with her. I discussed them with her parents and three brothers; I hadn't found the right time to tell her, though. I'm too distracted in her presence to think of anything more than getting her to myself as soon as possible.

"Honey, I've got this," I profess, wanting to ease her concerns. "We need to chat about our finances soon. For now, understand that I have investments that will cover everything. You don't have to worry if you can't find a job right away."

She opens her mouth to ask a question. I halt her words with fingers over her mouth.

"Soon. I promise. Right now, I want to celebrate our engagement." I run my tongue slowly over my lower lip while I gaze at her mouth, then the top of her exposed breasts. When they return to her face, her pupils dilate, and she understands my meaning.

Schuyler

. . .

Unbreakable

My cell phone states it's three a.m. I'm tossing and turning in the bed, trying not to disturb Calvin as he sleeps nearby. As sleep is no longer in my immediate future, I slowly slip from the bed, pull the door closed behind me, and tiptoe to the living room.

I can't turn on the television as it might wake the guys. I scroll through my phone, open my Kindle app, and attempt to read my book. I read and reread the first paragraph of the chapter.

This will not work. I can't focus. I lay my cell phone on the coffee table, then sink into the cushions of the sofa, and I relive the events of the day.

I'm amazed at how happy I am about the engagement. *Happy doesn't describe it. Blissful. Blissfully happy.*

That's it. I've been light and carefree, admiring my ring all evening.

I have a wedding to plan, a job to find, and a family to create.

I'll be Tyler's stepmom.

I'll be a mom and an aunt.

Levi's having a baby, and I'll be an aunt.

Instead of being overwhelmed, I'm lighter.

How can that be?

What am I missing?

What weighed me down until today?

I haven't felt this way since... winter break my junior year of college.

My breath catches, and my heart stops beating. A concrete block sits heavy where my stomach used to live. My body suddenly overheats, and I can't move. The last 14 months play behind my eyelids. The woman I became causes me to cringe.

I wore my jealousy, envy, and pain like a cloak. The shroud festered and grew with each joyful mother I glimpsed. I was hyper-focused on what I couldn't have instead of celebrating what I had.

I coveted other mothers, and that's a sin. I'm not naïve enough to believe I am free of sin, but coveting others... *That's not the real me. I can't believe how my green-eyed monster fed on my despair, and it grew with each passing day.*

I'm lighter today because I let it go. I focused on celebrating our graduation with family, friends, and nothing else. It didn't happen overnight; it started in Mexico. The more I allowed myself to enjoy the time I spent with Calvin, the less I focused on the negative. Slowly, the time I wasted on hate and self-loathing became the time I spent enjoying Calvin.

Lying in bed last night, just before I fell asleep, I feared everything was falling into place too easily. Now, I see it wasn't easy. My walls didn't crumble the first week I spent with Calvin. Calvin's magical love took over two months to help me see the light. He didn't leave when I pushed him away or when I attempted to break up via text. His patience prevailed, and his love opened my eyes. My hysterectomy didn't steal my chances of motherhood; it forced me to seek other paths to my goal. Calvin showed me I have options, and I can be happy.

I was not being punished by the taking away the possibility of having my own children. Instead, I needed to let my body heal for a year, so when I met Calvin, I'd be ready and open to the life planned for me.

As quietly as possible, I pad over to Tyler's door and peek in to watch him sleep. *I'm going to be his mother.*

I get to be his mother.

It's a gift I won't squander.

"Hey," Calvin whispers, his tired body approaching mine. "What's wrong?"

I shake my head. "He's sweet when he sleeps." I smile. "Do you think he'll be okay staying with your parents for two nights while we move?"

"He loves sleeping at Nana and Papa's," he reminds me. "Since I'm moving into our new house instead of Garret's apartment, we may only need one night. We only have the two beds and the sofa to load into the moving van tomorrow, then we'll hit the highway, heading north."

My seven boxes of stuff left with my family after the graduation party. *I'm no longer moving back into my parents' house, and Calvin won't be crashing on Garret's sofa.* It's hard to believe Calvin already has the keys to the new house. It's harder to believe we have a house.

I take his hand, leading him toward the bedroom. "I can't believe this is my life. Thank you for making me so happy."

Calvin pulls me roughly to his chest. His hazel eyes repeatedly scan left to right, looking deep into my soul. "You deserve all the happiness in the world, and I plan to spend the rest of my life making you smile."

31

BOOM!

Schuyler

Weeks later, I flop myself down on a barstool at the kitchen island, laying my head in my hands. I'm grateful Calvin's parents gifted us this house, but it's much too big for the three of us. The ground floor is all we need large enough with two bedrooms, two and a half bathrooms, a large open living room, dining area, and kitchen. I'm exhausted, and I haven't cleaned the bedrooms or bathrooms upstairs nor the family room, game room, and bathroom in the basement.

Despite both our mothers' and Dallas's forced shopping trips, we still haven't furnished every room, so one would think it would be easy to keep clean. *It's not.* More space equals more places for Tyler to string his books and toys out while dust seems to be a constant battle. I don't know how my mom made it so many years cleaning three bathrooms with four guys in the house. I live with two, and I cringe at the mess. I'm ready to claim one bathroom as girls only.

I deserve a tidy bathroom in between cleanings.

Lifting my head, I stare at the dry erase calendar posted on the refrigerator. Every day holds an event; many have three or more. I've attempted to color code the events to easily discern Calvin's activities from Tyler's and mine. The bar keeps Calvin busy from sun up to sun down. As the opening is just over a month away, he's meeting with inspectors and finishing all the licensing paperwork along with interviewing staff. Tyler and I guilt him into remaining home with us on Sundays. He complies but still spends much of his time on his cell phone, answering texts and emails.

Tyler and I take private swimming lessons in our backyard pool three days a week. Calvin demanded that we learn to swim. Tyler thinks it's cool that I never learned how to swim and now need to take lessons with him. We've joined a neighborhood play group that meets two days a week, and Tyler has met two kids that will attend kindergarten with him in the fall.

I took for granted all my mom handled while she worked full time as the four of us grew up. Tyler keeps me busy with haircuts, dental appointments, doctor appointments, lessons, and play groups.

I think I owe Mom a huge thank you.

I'll plan something with my brothers to let her know how much we appreciate her.

Calvin

My feet kill me; I need to buy arch supports or toss these shoes in the trash. I lean my head left, then right, popping my neck. *I could use a chiropractor appointment.* My entire body is out of alignment. *I need a relaxing movie night with my family and a full night's sleep.*

I open my phone calendar. Tomorrow is Friday; I meet with the contractor in the morning for a status update. *Maybe I can slip away for lunch and spend the rest of the day with my family.* I block off the time slot in my calendar and set a reminder to alert me before noon.

"Calvin, your next interview just arrived," Garret mentions as he passes by with boxes of new glasses for the bar.

"I'm impressed with your qualifications, Mr. Adams. We're looking for more than your average bartenders for our club." I've repeated these words many times in the past week. It's hard to let prospective employees know what I want without divulging the true secret theme of our club. "This is a themed bar. Bartenders will sling drinks while wearing a costume and acting a part to add to the mystique of the venue. Would you be willing to play the part while bartending?" I browse the applicant's resume while he takes a moment to reply.

"The costumes aren't in line with the Chippendale's theme, are they?" he asks, crossing his arms across his chest.

"I can assure you the uniform, or costume, includes shirt and slacks," I chuckle.

"Then I think I'd be interested in the position if you'll have me."

I extend my right hand across the tiny pub table. "You've got the job." I shake his hand, then hand him the printed calendar of the training schedule, the uniform fitting, and the soft opening.

"Thank you," he says, then heads for the exit.

I scroll through my phone. My next interview, for a waitress, begins in 15 minutes. So, I take care of tasks on my phone. I listen to a voicemail. Our booking agent secured us two singers and one comedy duo for the opening. She states she'll keep hunting for the best talent that fits our unique themes. She was right when she told us there would be no issues booking talent. She's found three acts since I met with her four days ago.

Garret appears again from the bar in the back. "I'm heading out. I promised Dallas I'd take her out for dinner tonight." He pauses at my table. "Will you be able to get out of here at a good time today?"

"No, I've got several more interviews," I remind him. "I'm going to try to leave at noon tomorrow, though."

"Cool. I don't want you to get burned out before we even open," Garret states.

"Yeah, yeah. Go on; get out of here." I wave him off.

I want nothing more than to leave right now to surprise Sky and Tyler. I'm hoping the contractor's report tomorrow will confirm my long days at work will grow shorter in the weeks leading up to the opening. Garret and I put in extra hours up front, hoping to relax prior to the grand opening.

Schuyler

I'm updating our family calendar for August and September. With my new position as a long-term substitute teacher for first semester, I now have a teacher in-service training to attend before the first day of school. I'll need to arrange a sitter for Tyler on those days, but since I'll be working at his elementary school, he'll ride with me once the school year begins.

My cell phone rings. The screen displays an unknown 515 area code, so I let it go to voicemail. When I'm alerted, I have a voice message, I play it over the speaker.

"Congratulations! You've won a free wedding planning package from The Perfect Day. You'll receive our Fourth of July wedding package. Please call immediately so we may begin planning. It's only weeks away. We're looking forward to your call to The Perfect Day at 515-555-5151. Congratulations!"

I listen to the message again. Then, still confused, I text Dallas at work.

> ME
> Call me ASAP

I return to my task. Once our paper wall calendar is up to date, I add events to the calendar on my phone. Lost in my work, I'm startled when the doorbell rings. Through the peephole, I spot Dallas. I open the door.

"I said to call me…"

Dallas pushes her way past me, heading straight to the kitchen. "They called me after they left you a message," she begins, pouring red wine from the bottle she carried with her into two of my wine glasses. "A week ago, I wrote a letter to The Perfect Day, entering you in a wedding giveaway. I guess I rock at nominations because they picked you as their winner."

"Back up," I order. "What was the contest for?"

While we sip our wine, Dallas pulls up The Perfect Day website and points out the contest page. The Perfect Day is a wedding planning company with a twist. They have 20 pre-packaged themes for brides to choose from. Each package contains everything needed for a wedding. I move through the different themes on each page. They have a country one, a beach theme, a traditional one, and everything in between.

Dallas draws my attention away from the website. "It will be perfect for your busy life, Calvin's, too, but there is one catch."

When she pauses, I widen my eyes, leaning towards her, urging her to explain.

"Your wedding will be on the Fourth of July."

At least she has the decency to scrunch her face like she knows that's too soon.

I run my fingers through my hair with my eyes closed. *I love my friend, and she means well.*

She tries to defend her decision to enter us in the contest. "Calvin's slammed with the bar and will only be busier when it opens in August. Tyler keeps you busy, plus you'll be getting your classroom ready for the upcoming school year."

She refills her wine glass. "You'll be swamped during the school year, so the next thing you know, it's next June. You'll want to relax during the summer and reboot for the next school year. I'm afraid life will get in the way, and the two of you might never have a wedding. And, you know, I'd never forgive you if you eloped." She smiles at me as if it is that simple.

I see part of her point. On the rare times Calvin and I have mentioned the wedding, we aren't able to find a date that works.

"Thank you for thinking of us, but this is only four weeks away," I debate. "It's just too soon and not possible."

"Hear me out," she pleads. "They do all the work. The package includes the location, decorations, food, music, officiant, tux rental, bridesmaids' dresses, flowers, and a choice of ten wedding dresses."

Dallas swivels my stool so that I face her. "You answer a couple of questions, try on the dresses, have a fitting, and boom! The wedding plans itself." She stares at me. "Why don't you call your mother and see what she thinks?"

32

MY BALL AND CHAIN

Schuyler

I look at the clock on the microwave. "Mom will drop Tyler off soon. If you stay, you can tell her all about this, and let her tell you it's not doable."

I open my cell phone to text my man. *He's going to flip out when he hears what Dallas did.*

> ME
>
> Dallas strikes again
>
> need to chat get home ASAP
>
> not emergency

If he's in the middle of something important, I don't want him to rush. Although I need him here to back me up, I realize starting his business is much more important than convincing Dallas she's crazy.

As expected, Mom arrives right at four like we planned. I greet her at the door and listen to Tyler tell me everything they did today while I place a snack in front of him on the table.

"You were supposed to relax today," my mother reminds me. "You look worse now than you did this morning. What's wrong?"

I swing my arm wide to Dallas, prompting her to explain. She tells Mom about the letter and the contest I won before showing her the website. She explains everything in the package I've won, except for one thing.

"Dallas, this is perfect!" Mom wraps Dallas in a hug. "You have the biggest heart; never change."

"Uh-hum," I interrupt, causing my mom to furrow her brow. "Continue," I order Dallas.

"The wedding package from the contest is this one." She opens the page with the Independence Day package. "The wedding must be on the Fourth of July."

"Oh my." Mom places her hand on her chest.

Oh my?

Please. No way is more like it.

It's not possible.

Where is my level-headed mother?

Mom asks Dallas to repeat everything in the wedding package as she writes the details on a nearby notepad. She taps the end of her pen at the bottom of the list for a few moments.

"It's doable." Mom looks at me. "Four weeks seems rushed, but they've already made most of the decisions and arrangements for you. It may not be the wedding you dreamed of as a little girl. As busy as everyone is, the help this planning package offers would be a blessing. I think you should consider it."

I didn't see that coming.

I figured both Calvin and my mom would revel in all the steps to plan our wedding. With three boys, I'm Mom's only chance to be involved in every aspect of wedding planning. Calvin's an only child. This will be his family's only wedding.

Is she serious?

Does she really think it's doable and that I should consider it?

"You should call Calvin's mom for her input," Mom suggests.

I'm waiting for her to answer the phone when Calvin enters from the garage.

"Hi. Do you have a few minutes?" I ask his mother immediately.

When she says yes, I inform her she's on speaker and name everyone in my kitchen. I explain that Calvin just walked in, and I want her to listen as I share some information with him. She agrees. I start at the beginning, share every detail, then announce that we must use it on Independence Day. I ask for their opinion before giving Mom and Dallas's answer. Calvin is quiet, deferring to his mother.

"Schuyler, this is your wedding," she states. "This decision is for the two of you to make. Traditionally, the bride has a vision of what her special day will be. I don't want to ask you to give that up." She pauses, so I look to Calvin for his answer. But she's not done. "Is it doable in four weeks? Yes, but only because they've already planned most of it. Will our family attend if you choose to do this? Yes. We wouldn't miss it. What do you think, Theo?"

My mom agrees with Calvin's mother that it's doable. Dallas shares her opinion and mentions how busy this fall will be for us, as will the rest of the school year. Unable to decide, I look to my fiancé for help.

Eyes fixed on me, Calvin says, "I'd like to speak to Sky alone for a moment if I could."

Dallas and Mom take Tyler up to his room to give us privacy. Calvin's mom asks us to let her know when we've decided before she disconnects.

Calvin sits on a stool and pulls me to stand between his open thighs. He brushes my hair behind my shoulders, resting his fingertips lightly against my jaws. His warm, hazel eyes lock on mine.

"There's no wrong decision here," he states. "I love you, and you love me. We will get married; it's just a matter of when. I want to give you the wedding day you've dreamt of and deserve."

He places a chaste kiss at the corner of my mouth, still holding my face in his hands. "Dallas is right; we are busy now and will be well into the fall. I'd marry you today if I could. I'm ready for the world to know I'm yours, and you are mine. I can't wait to call you my wife, my ball and chain, and my old lady," he teases, hoping to lighten the mood.

I swat his chest. "You will not refer to me as your 'old lady,' or I'll sic my brothers on you."

He lifts his palms between us in surrender, and I instantly long for them to return to my face.

"What are you thinking?" His eyes search my face. "What do you want our wedding to be like?"

"I'm ready to be married," I confess. "I think it's confusing for Tyler to hear we are engaged to be married and have me living here, sleeping in your bed. I'm ready to be a family. Our lives are crazy busy. You'll open the restaurant, word will spread like wildfire, and all Des Moines will want reservations at Brink. The speakeasy will quickly become the hottest bar in the Midwest. Everyone will want to hang out at Fringe for the entertainment, theme, and drinks. Tyler will start kindergarten, and I'll be teaching." I run my fingers through his hair. "We could try to plan a wedding during winter break or for next June, but I don't want to wait. I'm ready."

"So, we'll get married in four weeks," Calvin states, a wide smile on his face.

"You're okay with a red, white, and blue themed wedding?" I tilt my head in question.

"We could be naked at the wedding. I don't care," he states. "Hey, a naked theme would save us some time starting the honeymoon."

I swat his chest again. "Can you be serious for 10 minutes?"

"I am serious. I want to make you my wife, I want to marry you sooner rather than later, and I don't care what the wedding theme is as long as you are happy."

I move my lips to graze his. "I guess I'll install your ball and chain on the Fourth of July, then."

His lips join mine. This kiss is slow and sweet. It conveys everything we feel for each other and hints at the passion we'll share later tonight.

33

CHINOOK

Calvin

The morning flies by. I met with the contractor and am pleased we are running two weeks ahead of our original construction schedule, and he doesn't see any delays in our future. It's the second week of June, and we have nine weeks until the grand opening. Next, I sit down with Garret to plan our first staff meeting, their training, and the soft opening. We update our list of remaining tasks and the dates we need to place final orders by to allow time for delivery before we open.

While I wait for Sky to arrive for lunch and share a wedding update, I email our talent scout for an updated schedule. Then, I email our accountant to see where we stand compared to our targeted budget.

"Hi, babe," Schuyler greets, sliding into the chair opposite me.

I take in her sexy summer dress that compliments her rockin' body. The sight of my girl always revs my engine. Her smile lights up her entire face, so I assume everything is smooth on the wedding front.

"Before I forget," she starts, while pulling a notebook from her purse, "Dallas wanted me to remind you she's meeting the two of you here around two."

I look at my wrist, noting it's almost one now. I open the large paper bag Sky placed on the table, pull out three clamshell containers of food, then lay napkins and plastic utensils in front of each of us.

"I hope you don't mind. I'm craving Chinese." She shrugs, then pulls her cashew chicken in front of her.

She snags the paper bag I placed on an empty chair, pulling out chopsticks. I

Unbreakable

shake my head, causing her to smirk. She loves rubbing it in that she can use chopsticks, and I cannot. I open the crab Rangoon, distributing two to her and two to me.

"Don't keep me in suspense," I prompt before taking my first bite.

"We've got two weeks until the wedding," she states after washing down her first mouthful.

"Sixteen days," I correct, making my fiancé proud.

"Right. I have my final dress fitting and your final tux fitting set for a week from Monday." She pauses as I make a note of that on my work calendar. "Other than that, everything is set. She said about 85 percent of the guests have RSVP'd. She'll send the final count to the caterer at the end of next week. I tried a sample of the cake today. You're going to love it." She closes her notebook and focuses on her lunch, so I assume she is done.

I share details about the meeting with the contractor this morning.

"I'm glad to hear you're ahead of schedule. I hope you can spend more time at home before the opening," she states between bites.

"I'm looking forward to some quality time with my family," I confess. "For the millionth time, thank you for being so patient and understanding of the crazy schedule I've been working."

Dallas arrives at 1:30, interrupting our lunch. As she joins us, she texts Garret. I cringe at the three-ring binder and legal pad she places on the table in front of her. It was my understanding that she had a few ideas for us. I'd hoped to meet with her for an hour and take the rest of the day off to play with Tyler.

I finish my General Tso's Chicken as Garret approaches. Sky closes her container, placing the leftovers next to her purse. Garret kisses Dallas before assuming the empty seat across from her.

"As I mentioned when we set this meeting, I have ideas to promote the restaurant and bar before the grand opening," she starts.

She passes out a printed agenda to each of us. I raise my eyebrows at Sky.

Dallas encourages us to launch the website and social media immediately. She places the open binder in the center of the table and points to printouts as she speaks. She has examples of other businesses that have shared photos of the construction progress, employees, owners, and the decor as teasers leading up to the opening.

She wants us to post the drinks menu right away, but not the food menu. She points around the room at interesting and unique parts of the restaurant that we can post, raising interest in the community.

She asks about the status of our app, and Garret informs her we're currently beta testing it. She urges us to share our app on all social media platforms with a link for both Android and Apple devices. Through the downloaded app, we can send notifications directly to people that show an interest in the place.

Finally, she offers to create graphics for our social media, website, and advertising. She'd like to be in charge of promoting the grand opening for us.

Garret is quiet, looking at me. I assume he wants my answer since Dallas is his girlfriend, and he feels pressure to like her ideas.

"I like it all," I state, smiling at Dallas. "You've really outdone yourself. This is way more than a couple of ideas for us. I'm ignorant when it comes to public relations. Do you have time to set up our social media accounts and help us with posts?"

Dallas looks from me to Garret, then back, astonished. "I'd be happy to help."

"Great. We've hired a company to create our website. When it's ready, I'll have them add you as an administrator, so you can help us keep it up to date."

At my words, Dallas stands, rounds the table, and pulls me into a hug. I've spent a lot of time with her, but we've never hugged before today. Sky proudly smiles at me over Dallas's shoulder. *I'm not letting Dallas help because she's Sky's best friend or because she's Garret's girlfriend. She's truly talented and will be a great asset to us. Not to mention, she'll do it all for free.*

An hour later, I lie in my bed, sated, Sky's head on my bare chest. While our breathing steadies, I smile, thinking of the look on Sky's face when I told her I'd follow her home after meeting with Dallas; it was priceless. When she told me we only had an hour until Levi brought Tyler home, I sprinted to my truck.

"We need to get dressed," Sky says, lifting her head to look at me. "Levi is never late."

No sooner do we have our clothes on straight than Tyler announces he's home. He cheers as I follow Sky down the steps. He's happy I'm home early.

Levi's raised eyebrow and the smirk that follows informs us he knows about the afternoon quickie we indulged in. It doesn't bother me he knows, but it embarrasses Sky.

"Not a word," she warns Levi, her index finger poking his chest. "Are you ready for a snack?" she asks Tyler.

"Um," Tyler stammers, shuffling his weight from one foot to the other. "Uncle Levi and I have a surprise."

"You do?" I bend to Tyler's height. "What is it?"

Unbreakable

My son looks up at Levi. Levi says he'll meet us in the kitchen, then turns to head back to his truck.

"It's in Uncle Levi's truck," Tyler explains as we move to the kitchen. "Promise you won't be mad?"

What could Levi have in his truck?

I look at Sky to see if she looks worried. *It better not be his first BB-gun. I'm not ready to introduce him to weapons and gun safety yet.*

Levi strolls into our kitchen, an animal tucked under his bulky arm. He moves it in front of his chest, using both hands. It quivers nervously. I think it's a dog, but it's hard to tell as they shaved it down to its pale pink skin.

"Can we keep him?" Tyler begs with folded hands. He juts out his lower lip, attempting to flutter his eyes.

Apparently, Levi taught him how to beg and get his way.

"Levi, you should've talked to us before you showed him to Tyler," Sky scolds. "What is it?"

Levi explains they arrested the owner of a puppy mill a couple of weeks ago. They took the dogs to the Animal Rescue League. The staff cleaned them before giving them vaccines and treatment by a veterinarian. When he checked on the status of the puppies, the ARL had found homes for all the animals except this one. They speculated because of the need to shave off all the matted hair, no one could look past it to see the dog. He shares it's a golden retriever, and all its hair will grow back.

"Uncle Levi, show them what he'll look like when he grows hair," Tyler urges.

"We've seen a golden retriever before," I state, looking at Sky for help with how to handle this.

Before we can speak, Levi promises us the puppy is healthy and loves to play and cuddle. He knows this because he's housed it at his place for two days now.

Sky joins Tyler, batting her eyes at me, and I'm a goner. It's hard enough to say no to my son; there's no way I can deny the two of them when they want something.

"What's its name?" I ask Tyler.

That's all Levi needs to hear. He hands the puppy to Sky and fetches the kennel, dishes, and leash from his truck. His years in law enforcement have made him good at reading people.

Tyler tells us we get to choose a name for the puppy, and he wants him to sleep in his room. He lists off the chores Levi told him he'd need to help with in order to keep the dog. Of course, Tyler claims he'll do everything to care for him.

"I think you should consider the names Apache and Chinook," Levi suggests before he leaves.

I grab a piece of notebook paper.

"What are you doing?" Sky asks.

"I think we should all choose three names, discuss them, then each of us will strike one name from the list before we randomly draw one out of a bowl as the name," I explain.

Tyler, enamored with his uncle, suggests Apache, Chinook, and Black Hawk. He enjoys time with his uncles and their military stories, so he now knows several military words and phrases. Sky lists Remi, Buddy, or Rocky. I add Bo, Riley, and Duke. Tyler throws out Buddy, claiming that's an elf name. Sky states we can't have a dog named Black Hawk, and I want to exclude Rocky.

I tear the names apart and place them in a nearby bowl, stir them several times, then ask Tyler to do us the honor of pulling out our dog's name. He closes his eyes, lowers his hand into the bowl, and takes several moments before he pulls out a name. He unfolds the paper and tries to read it.

"It starts with the letter 'C'," he declares. "Look, here is your name." He holds the tiny strip of paper in front of the puppy.

"May I read it?" Sky asks, and he complies. "Our puppy's name is Chinook."

"Uncle Levi will be so happy," Tyler cheers.

34

A TEXT FROM DANI

Calvin

This is the perfect end to a long, hot day. Sky and Tyler play in the pool when I arrive home. As they already ate, I scarf down the leftovers while watching Tyler demonstrate the skills he's acquired in his swimming lessons.

"You're like a little fish," I compliment.

He proudly smiles, hanging on to the edge of the pool in front of me.

"Sky, show Dad what you've learned in lessons," Tyler prompts with one hand still on the edge, the other motioning to her.

"Maybe later," Sky hedges.

She's shared with me she finds it difficult to learn to swim. She's never been comfortable in the water and finds it hard to trust she'll float. *I'm glad she agreed to take lessons with Tyler. If nothing else, she'll feel more comfortable with him in the water.*

I rise from my patio chair, my empty plate and swim trunks in hand. While Tyler swims to the other side of the pool, I crouch down to Sky.

"Maybe you can give me a private demonstration later."

Her light-brown eyes look up at me through her wet lashes as she nibbles on her lower lip. Satisfied she understands my true meaning, I return to the kitchen, then change.

As our hour in the pool passes, Tyler's yawns grow bigger and more frequent. I look at Sky, and she nods.

"Ty," Sky's warm, motherly voice calls for his attention, "it's bedtime."

Tyler immediately slaps his palms against the top of the water, arguing, "I don't need to go to bed."

As Schuyler approaches, he splashes her.

"I thought I'd let you wrap up in towels and lay on a lounge chair until Dad and I are ready to go inside," she barters.

Tyler likes this alternative. He takes Sky's hand, walking up the steps where she quickly wraps him snug in a large beach towel. He lies on the cushion of the chair, and she places another towel over him like a blanket. I glance at the thermometer hanging on the privacy fence; it's still 82 degrees at eight o'clock. He'll be plenty warm. She kisses him on the cheek, wishes him good night, then wades back in the water to me.

I pull her to me, lifting one of her knees. I encourage her legs to wrap around my waist, and she complies.

"I'll keep it PG until he falls asleep," I whisper as a promise into her ear.

"His eyes were closed the minute he laid down," she informs me. "He's probably already asleep."

That's all the invitation I need. I lower my lips to the area just below her ear. She tips her head back, enjoying the sensation. When I nip, she moans, which makes my cock grow harder. As I alternate licking, nipping, and sucking, my eyes look toward Tyler. He hasn't moved; perhaps he's truly asleep.

I slide a strap off her right shoulder, my mouth taking the same path, then repeat it on the left side. Sky pulls her arms through each hole, and her breasts bounce free. My hands on her hips, I lift her slightly, my lips latching on to one nipple, then the other.

Just as I'm about to get lost in my hormonal, lust-filled haze, I hear a phone vibrating at the edge of the pool.

"Is that yours or mine?" I murmur before closing my mouth around her hardening bud.

"Huh?" she moans, lost in pleasure.

Step by step, I walk us through the water toward the buzzing cell phone. I continue winding her up, my mouth never off her amazing body. At the edge of the pool, I try to figure out how I can look at the phone screen without disrupting her pleasure. I decide a quick peek is best. Then I can place all my attention back on her.

At first glance, I note it's my cell phone. I place one hand at the small of Sky's back and tilt my phone towards me with my free hand. I don't believe my eyes, and I freeze, losing contact with her breasts.

"Calvin, what's wrong?" She looks at me with heavy-lidded eyes. "Calvin?"

"Um..." I'm still in shock, unsure what to say.

Unbreakable

Sky wiggles to stand on her own, placing her suit in the proper position before looking over my shoulder at the screen.

"Holy shit," she whispers.

Holy shit is right. The day she signed over all her parental rights, Dani became a ghost to me. Although I send her pictures, she's never replies and never asks how Tyler is. I stare as if my screen will give me answers or at least a clue.

> DANIEL (DANI)
> I need to see you

Baffled, I look to Schuyler.

"You won't get answers if you don't text her back," she states. "I'll text her if you want me to."

My thumbs hover over the keyboard, unsure what my reply should be.

> ME
> Text? Call? IRL?

> DANIEL (DANI)
> IRL

> ME
> I live in Des Moines

> DANIEL (DANI)
> I know I'm here

Sky gasps. My wide eyes meet hers. I'm sure we're thinking the same thing.

How does she know I moved?
Does she stalk me?
This is too weird.

> DANIEL (DANI)
> meet for lunch tomorrow?

> you name place

"What do I say?"

I hope Schuyler has the answers I don't.

"You must see what she wants. Suggest meeting at that barbecue place behind your work. You can walk over." She quirks her mouth to the side.

"Good idea," I agree.

ME
> noon BBQ corner 10th&Cherry

DANIEL (DANI)
> see you then

"Would it be ok…?" Sky clears her throat. "Can I be there, too?"

"Of course."

She's tried to ease into the role of mother. It's new and will take some getting used to for her. She often fears I'll think she's overstepping her bounds. I constantly remind her we are a parenting team, and she's the only mother Tyler has.

I follow her without a word as she exits the pool, wrapping up in a towel. We do our best to dry quickly. I carry Tyler, and she carries his cup and our used towels. I help a very sleepy boy use the bathroom and step into his pajamas before tucking him in.

I find Schuyler, rubbing lotion on her face, already in her tank top and sleep shorts. As I change into dry shorts, I realize Dani's text killed our playful mood. *It ruined a perfect evening with my family.*

As I crawl under the covers beside Sky, I find tears threatening to spill over her lower lashes.

"Babe, what's wrong?" I pull her onto my lap as I lean against the headboard.

She sniffles. "What if she wants him back?" Her voice quivers.

"It will not happen," I promise. "She may ask to see him or meet him, but I had my lawyer make sure it was iron-clad that I got full custody." I brush a lock of hair off her wet cheek.

"What if…"

"Honey, worrying will not help. Until we meet her to find out what's up, there's no need to stress ourselves out with all the 'what ifs.'"

Both of us toss and turn all night. Ready for work, I find Sky awake when I emerge from the bathroom.

"Hi," she waves, void of her usual peppiness.

I lean down to kiss her goodbye. "There's nothing to worry about. So, don't waste your energy on it this morning. Find me, and we'll walk to lunch together."

She nods. *I hate Dani hurt her. Sky endures so much, and she just began accepting her role as Tyler's mother. Dani's text leads her to believe she'll lose him. That would devastate her.*

I won't allow that to happen.

It seems like I just arrived at work when Sky walks into the restaurant. My wrist confirms she's right on time. I let the guys know I'm headed to lunch. As I approach, I notice Sky spent extra time on her makeup and hair today. I prefer her natural beauty over this look, but I know better than to tell her that. She always looks good and rarely curls her hair or wears eye shadow and lipstick. She's nervous and trying to impress Dani.

In front of the restaurant, I stop, place my hand on the back of her neck, and pull her in for a kiss. In it, I try to convey my love for her and my faith that we have nothing to worry about. I push my forehead to hers while we steady our breathing.

"I love you so much," I murmur.

"I love you, too."

We walk, hand in hand, around the block.

35

THREE POSSIBLE MEN

Schuyler

Calvin nods toward Dani when we enter the restaurant. With his hand on the small of my back, he guides me through the crowded seating area. The warmth of his hand helps to calm me a bit. *I'm his; we're a team.*

Dani doesn't stand to greet us or smile as we join her at the table. Calvin pulls my chair out before sitting beside me.

"Hello," I greet Dani.

"Schuyler, it's nice to meet you," she replies.

How?

How does she know my name?

She knows Calvin lives in Des Moines, and she knows my name; this is weirding me out.

A server asks for our drink order as she places a steaming cup and a tea bag in front of Dani. Calvin orders two waters for us. While she steeps her tea, I take in the woman that abandoned her Tyler.

In this lighting, I can't decide if her hair is red with brown tones or brown with red highlights. Dani secures it loosely into a messy ponytail. Her eyes bright green are stunning, and her fair skin looks delicate with faint freckles smattered on her nose and cheekbones. I can't make out her body type while she's seated, not to mention she's wearing a large cream poncho.

"I've already ordered a salad," Dani informs Calvin, sliding the menu in our direction.

"I'd rather talk." Calvin's baritone voice commands her compliance.

"I see," Dani sips her tea.

"Let's start with an explanation of how you know where I live and Schuyler's name." Calvin squirms a bit in his seat. Dani clearly makes him uncomfortable.

"I decided to reach out to you a couple of months ago, so I hired a private investigator to gather information before I set a meeting with you."

She doesn't even look embarrassed or sorry for the intrusion into our daily world. *This woman is a piece of work.*

"What were you hoping to find?" Calvin asks, attempting to rein in his growing anger.

"I needed to make sure you were taking care of Tyler and creating a positive environment at home."

"Seriously?" I spit, venom coursing through my body. "You leave your son with Calvin, then have the audacity to judge his parenting skills? You gave up your right to any input in that situation years ago."

Calvin pats my thigh under the table, urging me to calm down. A sly smile sits on Dani's face. *I want to scratch her perfect skin. I want to give her a black eye.*

"I knew what the P.I. would find; I needed to be certain," she defends before releasing a long breath. "I'm pregnant, and I'm giving you the opportunity to add Tyler's half-sibling to your family." Dani leans back in her chair, teacup and saucer in hand.

I don't know what to say or how to react. I turn to Calvin on my left, finding him staring, dumbfounded, at the woman across the table. It's my turn to touch his thigh under the table. I slide my palm up and down reassuringly.

"The father?" Calvin asks, nearly in a whisper.

"About that," Dani returns the tea cup to the table, leaning in our direction. "There are three possible men. By the time I realized I was pregnant, all three were but a pebble in my rearview mirror. We weren't in a relationship, and I'm no longer in contact with any of them."

I thought I couldn't be more shocked. She proves me wrong. *What kind of life does Dani lead?* She has one-night stands while traveling the world, and, when she finds herself pregnant, she offers to sign away parental rights and never look back.

"I can give you their names in case you ever need to find the biological father," she offers like it sweetens the deal she's presenting us with. "I'm due in the middle of July. I've found a local physician, and they scheduled my C-section at a West Des Moines hospital on the morning of July 13th."

I find Calvin still in a daze, so I address Dani. "Let me see if I have this straight. You are offering us the first rights to adopt the baby you are now carrying because it's Tyler's blood relative. Am I right?"

Dani nods, looking at Calvin. "What do you think?"

There's a beat of silence. Then, he says, "I need to go back to work. I have two inspections this afternoon." He runs a hand through his hair. Looking to me, he continues, "I should be home between five and six. We'll discuss it and get back to Dani later this week."

I nod, agreeing with his plan.

Schuyler

I climb into my stuffy car, berating myself for not cracking a window. Starting the vehicle, I crank up the air conditioner. I fan myself with an envelope from the glove box. Adrenaline courses through me from the conversation with Dani. No way I'll calm down or cool down in this hot vehicle.

I pull my phone from my bag, scrolling to my contacts.

ME
lunch over meet me my house

DALLAS
I'm already here

ME
why?

DALLAS
immediate details

ME
need 2 vent

DALLAS
figured

ME
need advice

DALLAS
got that covered

Unbreakable

> **ME**
> home in 10

It's a long drive home; I hit several red lights. I struggle to focus on driving and not on Dani's offer. Dallas waits for me on the sidewalk, clearly worried. Arm in arm, she guides me to the kitchen.

"What's this?" I ask. The table is cluttered with a tablet and a laptop, a pitcher of margaritas and two full glasses, tortilla chips with both salsa and queso, notebooks, ink pens, and a box of tissues.

"I'm ready for any scenario." She shrugs like it's no big deal. "Now, sit and spill."

I pull out a chair and plop down with a huff. I'm exhausted, and I haven't even told the story or asked for advice.

"Let me start by saying," a smile slips onto my face, "she's not trying to see or take Tyler from us."

Dallas leaps from her chair to celebrate, hugging me. *I love that she's this invested in everything that affects me and my happiness.*

As she releases me, she asks, "So, what did she need to see Calvin for?"

I take a long drink of my margarita before explaining. "It seems Dani is pregnant again and wants us to adopt the baby since it's a half-sibling to Tyler."

I watch Dallas process as several emotions show on her face. From furrowed brow to confusion to excitement, she experiences the same emotions I'm still rolling through repeatedly.

"So, what answer did you give her?" Dallas asks, eyebrows high on her forehead.

"We didn't," I state, which further confuses her. "When the shock wore off, Calvin told her we needed to discuss it tonight and would give her our answer later this week." My head spins. "I need advice and to talk it out, so I'm ready to talk to Calvin tonight." I point to my friend. "What do you think we should do?"

Dallas smirks at me. "You know I won't tell you what I think you should do. I'm willing to discuss it and help you work through your feelings, though."

She refills our glasses, sips from hers, then starts. "Have the two of you discussed adding to your family? I mean, before meeting with Dani?"

"We discussed our options to have a family, like adoption, foster care, and stuff," I answer honestly. "We never mentioned a timeline."

"Newborns are a lot of work," she states. "And why is she not leaving this child with the baby-daddy?"

I share in deeper detail all that Dani told us about the pregnancy, possible fathers, and planned C-section.

"So, which way are you leaning?" Dallas inquires.

"It's overwhelming, you know. I thought I'd never have children, and I now get to help parent Tyler. I certainly never thought I'd have a newborn to care for. Our lives are such a whirlwind right now with the move, the wedding, the opening, and school starting in the fall."

"All that is true, but you didn't answer my question," she points out, squinting her eyes.

"I think I want to say yes," I confess, voice barely above a whisper. "I just don't think it's a good time for us." I stare at my fingers, tapping them on the table. "I'm not sure how Calvin will feel about raising another man's child. He already has Tyler. He's still able to have children of his own, but this is the only way it can happen to me." I pause for a moment. "Dani's giving us a tremendous opportunity. We'd get to skip all the paperwork, background checks, home visits, and long waiting lists for a chance to adopt. It feels like a gift fell into our laps. I'm trying not to get too excited, but it's hard. I want a baby more than almost anything in the world."

Slowly, Dallas smiles, and her eyes light up. "I knew it. I know it's a busy time, but this is something we've always dreamed about. Remember playing house in my backyard? You've got to do this."

"Do you think Calvin will feel the same way?" I ask that's worried me since I got into my car to head home.

"Well, he's head-over-heels in love with you. I think he'd give you anything if he knew you wanted it."

I know that to be true.

"I don't want him to say yes to make me happy, then resent me and the baby later."

Dallas takes my hand in hers. "He didn't give you a hint about how he felt before he went back to work?"

I shake my head.

"He promised to talk to you tonight," she reminds me. "Let him share all his thoughts before you share yours. That way, you'll know his honest answer and can talk it over."

I nod, biting my lower lip. "What do you think his answer will be?"

Still holding my hands, Dallas winks at me. "I think he'll want to care for the baby like he did Tyler. If you weren't in his life, from what I've witnessed and heard about him from Garret, he'd still take the baby."

My hand slips from hers to cover my mouth. Tears pool in my eyes, and my heart skips a beat at the possibility that we will tell Dani we are interested.

I could never have dreamed that something like this would happen after my accident.

"I'm home," Tyler yells when the front door swings open.

"Hi, girls," Mom greets, dropping Tyler's backpack onto the kitchen island. "What are the two of you plotting over there?" she asks, pointing at everything cluttering the table.

Wide-eyed, I look to Dallas for a clue to what I should say. She nods, smiling.

"Take a seat," Dallas says, rising to fetch another margarita glass for my mother. "You'll need this, so take a big swig."

Mom looks from Dallas to me and back before taking a couple of swallows of her drink.

I start by reminding her of the name of Tyler's mother, then explain our lunch with Dani and the offer she presented to us. My mother's face gives nothing away.

"What do you plan to do?" she finally asks.

"Calvin and I need to talk about it tonight," I state. "What do you think we should do?"

My mom takes a deep breath. "This is a decision only the two of you can make. And it's a big one. The thought of a tiny baby going into the system while it waits to be adopted breaks my heart, but it happens all over the world every day. The two of you can care for this little baby from day number one. That's an honor. Parenting isn't easy, but the positives outweigh the negatives."

"Thank you for sharing, but you didn't tell me what you think I should do," I remind my mother.

"It's not what you should do, it's what the two of you should do. And I think I gave you an answer," Mom states, placing her almost full glass in the sink. "I'll take Tyler to my house for a sleepover, so the two of you can carry on your adult conversation without his little ears nearby."

I nod as I'm still processing her words, trying to decipher what she believes we should tell Dani.

36

BABY'S FATHER

Calvin

I make sure I leave work right at five, as I promised. In my hand, I carry a large brown sack with a meal our chef practiced preparing today. I figure we need most of the evening to discuss our luncheon. Bringing dinner home will free up more time.

During my drive, I flash back to the day I found Sky at the wreck site. She shared her deepest fears, the depth of her pain, and I promised to love her. I shared alternate ways we could grow our family. Since that day, I've tried to ease her into becoming a mom to Tyler. I watched as she quickly slipped into the role, and I reveled in the immense joy it brings her. She hoped but never dreamed that she would become a mother; she never thought she'd raise a baby.

I love every minute of fatherhood. Sure, it's scary and stressful at times, but I've never regretted my decision to raise Tyler on my own. Part of me believes I owe it to Tyler to allow his sibling to join our family. I worry if he found out as an adult that the child exists, he'd resent us for not offering to help.

I really want to leave this decision up to Schuyler, let her decide if we're up to the challenge right now. She'll be the primary caregiver in the first months of the baby's life. The grand opening will consume me. Of course, I'll try to be home as much as possible. Newborns require constant care, and I can't give as much as I would like in the next few months.

Unbreakable

Schuyler

I can't sleep. I've squirmed for two hours now. I quietly slip from the bed, leaving Calvin to sleep as I head for the kitchen.

I hate a decision hanging over my head. Calvin and I talked and talked. We even made a pros and cons list as we discussed Dani's proposition. While I prefer to decide, Calvin likes to mull it over for a couple of days. I understand and support his need to wait. I fear I won't sleep until we make our final decision, though.

I sit at the kitchen island, looking at the reflections the water in the pool creates with the moonlight while I eat an Oreo and wash it down with a cold glass of milk.

"Can I join you?" Calvin asks from the doorway. His hair is the definition of bedhead, and his droopy eyes give him a boyish appearance.

I pat the stool beside me, sliding the container of cookies between us. When he dunks his cookie into my glass of milk, I rise to pour another. He's a dunker; I am not. I can't drink white milk with black chunks in it, and he knows it.

"I had a dream about us," he informs, his mouth half full of cookie.

I don't speak as I slide back onto the stool beside him. I feel he needs a few moments to explain.

"I don't want you to give up anything for me, for Tyler, or for any future family members," he begins, pushing the Oreos and his glass to the center of the island and spinning me to face him, his hands on my knees. "I want to give you everything. You deserve happiness. I'll support you in everything you desire to do."

I lean forward to place a kiss on his lips.

"When we spoke earlier, I failed to mention our finances. I guess I haven't updated you since work began on the bar, and I want you to know exactly where we sit." His thumbs caress the back of my hands. "We are way under budget on the restaurant, and we see nothing changing that in the next month or two. My investments continue to earn interest, as I shared when we got engaged. Financially, we are able for you to stay home this fall, allowing you to care for the infant. No pressure." He holds his palms out toward me. "Just a thought, an option to consider. We are lucky to have the option."

This man... He's too perfect. The fact that I've had a hysterectomy almost tore us apart last spring. Now, he wants only to give me the family I never imagined I'd have.

My eyes search his as I speak. "I mentioned that Levi's wife is stressing about hiring a sitter and returning to work after maternity leave. My mom is not ready to retire to help her out." A wide smile forms on my face. "I guess I could offer to care for my niece or nephew if I stay home with a baby."

Calvin smirks before wrapping me in a tight embrace. Near my ear, he murmurs, "So, you've decided, we're adopting a baby." His smile lights up the kitchen. "We're having a baby!"

"In four weeks!" I cheer, tears of joy filling my eyes. "July will be a busy month for us," I state as he rubs my back. "We'll become husband and wife and new parents."

"Life with me will never be boring," Calvin declares.

"As long as we're in it together, we'll enjoy every minute," I promise.

"Should we tell the parents?" Calvin pulls his phone from his shorts pocket, ready to make the call.

"No." I place my hand over his phone screen. *I can't believe his phone is in his pajamas.* "It's three a.m. It can wait 'til morning."

"We could celebrate." Calvin waggles his eyebrows suggestively.

I dart from the kitchen and up the stairs, giggling the entire way.

Calvin

At noon the next day, Sky and I meet Dani at the same barbecue place near my work. Schuyler's a ball of energy. So much so she can't sit without wiggling her foot. We order drinks, and when the server brings them to the table, I'm ready to start this conversation.

"Do you have an answer for me?" Dani asks while preparing her tea.

"Schuyler and I would like to adopt your baby if you are still interested," I state.

A slight smile creeps upon her face, and she nods before sipping from her teacup. "What I'd like to propose is not an adoption. Well, it's only a partial adoption and much simpler."

My heart stops beating, and the bottom of my stomach drops out.

Is she changing the offer?

Are we not getting the baby?

"Let me explain," Dani states, sensing the sadness on my face. "I'd like to place Calvin on the birth certificate as the baby's father. No one ever needs to know differently. I'll sign over parental rights as I did for Tyler. Then I'll fly to Paris for my next assignment, and the two of you can decide if you want Schuyler to adopt the baby or not. As far as the world knows, both Tyler and the baby are Calvin's."

Sky's hand finds mine on my thigh under the table. She looks at me, hoping to find I still want to go through with this. I smile before I nod to Dani.

"Okay. I'll update the paperwork at the hospital to name Calvin as the baby's father, so the two of you can be in the obstetrics unit immediately. Are you familiar with the hospital in West Des Moines?" Dani is calm and collected.

It's as if she's in a business meeting.

We nod.

"Dani, can we exchange phone numbers? I'd feel better if you could contact me if you can't get a hold of Calvin," Sky explains.

Dani opens her cell phone to let Sky type her information into her contacts. Then Dani texts Sky so she can save her number, too.

"Feel free to say no," I offer before I ask my next favor. "Would it be possible for us to attend your weekly doctor appointments between now and the C-section?"

Dani's eyes bug out; it's easy to see this is not something she's comfortable with. She opens her calendar on her phone.

"I have appointments set for two p.m. the next three Thursdays," Dani states. "I guess one of you could attend an appointment with me. I don't see a need for you to be at every one."

"I'd like for Schuyler to have the opportunity to go with you," I say before Sky can respond to Dani. "She's unable to…"

Dani cuts me off. "I'm aware of her condition." She quirks the corner of her mouth and tilts her head to the side in Sky's direction. "Schuyler, can you attend this Thursday's two o'clock appointment?"

She nods, clearly stunned that I have stepped aside for her to have this experience.

"Do they plan to do an ultrasound?" Sky asks.

"I'm not sure, but if I explain you are the baby's father's fiancé, they might do one for you." Dani seems put out by the thought of Schuyler attending the appointment and disrupting her unwanted pregnancy. "I had an ultrasound during the fifth month, and they recorded the baby's sex."

"Are you having a boy or a girl?" I immediately inquire.

"I didn't ask," she explains. "They recorded it in my chart in case I changed my mind and wanted the information later. I still don't want to know, but Schuyler, I'll allow them to tell you when I leave the room."

HALEY RHOADES

My fiancé smiles, trying to pretend this isn't the most exciting news in the world. *It's clear all things concerning her pregnancy annoy Dani, despite our excitement. I can't wait for Thursday.*

37

LOVE HAS NO END

Calvin

When Tyler returns from Theo's the next morning, I fix us a snack of apples and peanut butter at the kitchen island while he takes Chinook to the backyard. When he returns, he takes the stool next to mine, sharing the games he played with Levi and Clint at Theo's house last night.

When he chomps on his apple slice, I begin. "Remember the story of how Nana and Papa adopted me?"

Tyler nods while he chews, a little apple juice dripping from the corner of his mouth. I wait patiently for him to swallow.

"You love Nana and Papa like your mom and dad, just like I love you." Tyler repeats the words I've shared with him many times.

"Right." I smile. "Sky and I have been asked to adopt a baby."

His eyes grow wide. "I get to be a big brother?" Tyler asks, excitement welling up inside him.

"Would you like that?" I ask, eager to understand his true feelings. "We'd have to share time with you and the baby."

"I'm gonna be the best big brother ever!" Tyler exclaims. "I'll be just like Dan, Levi, and Clint are big brothers to Sky."

Several moments pass as we continue eating our snack.

"Will Sky love the baby more than me?" Tyler's muffled voice asks through a mouthful of apple and peanut butter.

I quickly try to calm his worries. "No. Love has no end. We have enough love for you, Grandma, Grandpa, all of Sky's family, and for a new baby." I decide to help him understand. "You love me, right?"

Ty nods.

"And you love Nana and Papa?"

Ty nods again.

"Do you love Sky?"

"You know I do," Tyler answers, looking at Schuyler as she enters the kitchen.

"Do you think you will stop loving one of us if you love a new baby?" I ask my son to prove my point.

"No! I will always love all of you!"

Sky joins our conversation. "Our love for you won't change. We have more than enough love for both you and a baby."

I continue the explanation. "Remember the story I told you about your birth mom?"

Tyler says, "She wanted what was best for me, so she left me with you."

"Right. Your birth mom is also the baby's mommy."

Confusion clouds his face. He bites his lip, looking at Sky, then at me. "Are you the baby's daddy?"

"No, but when we adopt the baby, I'll get to be its daddy, and Sky will be its mommy." I attempt to explain.

My son mulls this over for a moment. A little smile on his face, Tyler asks, "Can Sky adopt me, so she can be my mommy, too?"

Sky's breath audibly catches, and tears quickly fill her eyes. I'm proud of my little guy for requesting this; it means a lot to Schuyler and me. I'd hoped their relationship would grow, and I'm happy it is.

"Are you sure? She can be like a mommy without adopting you," I offer, just to be sure.

"I want Sky as my mommy," Tyler states with authority. "Sky, will you adopt me?"

A crying mess, Schuyler looks at Tyler and nods repeatedly.

"Why are you sad?" Tyler worries. "Don't you want to adopt me?"

"Oh, honey, of course I want to adopt you," Sky promises through her tears. "These are happy tears. Asking me to adopt you, to be your mommy, is the best present I've ever received." Schuyler attempts to wipe away her tears. "Now, come over here! I need a hug."

"I'll call the lawyer and get the paperwork started." I pull out my phone, scrolling through my contacts.

"I'll call my parents and Dallas," Schuyler offers, leaving the room.

Just when I'm about to press the call button, Tyler asks, "Can I name the baby?"

Schuyler

I struggle to fall asleep again for the third night in a row. My excitement at attending the doctor's appointment with Dani grows as it draws near.

How did I get so lucky to be her child's mother?

How can I ever thank her?

Unable to wait until morning, I shoot her a text.

> ME
> can we meet for lunch tomorrow?
>
> DANI
> I guess where?
>
> ME
> park at 9000 Douglas Ave
>
> DANI
> 1pm
>
> ME
> thanks

Since the park is several blocks from our house, I head out early with Chinook on his leash. Tyler's been practicing with him inside the house each day this week. I've packed a few snacks to reward his good behavior and three bags in case he chooses to poo. His soft fur is now about an inch long; since he resembles a healthy puppy, we can take him out of the yard now.

I contemplated bringing Tyler along with me, then remembered Dani has no desire to see or hear about him. Levi drove over to spend some time with his new nephew. As his baby's arrival draws near, I think he wants to practice being with kids. *I never expected my muscular military brother to be such a softy.*

According to my Fitbit, I've walked 2,000 steps by the time I see Dani.

"Thanks again," I say, securing Chinook's leash to the other end of the picnic table. Tired from our walk, he lays in the shade under the wooden table. "I felt I needed to share a few things."

I fidget a bit before I have the strength to say what I came to say. Her stony silence makes me uncomfortable. "Know that I will forever be grateful for the gift of the children you bestow upon us. If you ever want to see the kids, please don't hesitate to contact us."

"Thanks, but don't hold your breath." Dani's voice is flat.

"As Tyler's birth mom, I wanted to ask your permission." I find it difficult to swallow as my throat feels tight. "When we talked to Tyler about the new baby, he asked me to adopt him and become his mommy, too."

Dani doesn't speak, so I look for clues in her reaction. I find no hint of hurt, hate, or love on her face or in her mannerisms.

"You don't need my permission. I signed away all my rights. So, if it's what you all want, go for it."

That is light years away from the reaction I expected to get from her. I didn't expect her to cry and refuse, but I thought I'd see a hint of a maternal instinct in her words or actions.

"Isn't it ironic that you want kids, would be a good mom, and can't have your own?" Dani chuckles dryly. "I don't want children. I'd be a terrible mother, and I've been pregnant twice." She huffs, looking at her baby belly. "I'm getting a tubal ligation. This will be the last time *this* ever happens to me."

I can't believe my mother forgot she asked to meet me at the mall for lunch today. I mean, it's the week before my wedding, there's so much to do, and I wasted two hours by the time I drove through Chick-fil-A on my way back home. I mentally run through the items left on my list for today as I close the garage door and enter the kitchen.

"Surprise!"

I scream bloody murder. My heart jackhammers against my ribcage. As my brain processes that I'm not in danger, my face flushes with embarrassment.

"What's this?"

"It's your surprise wedding and baby shower," Dallas proclaims proudly at my side. "C'mon! I have a special seat for the bride and mother-to-be."

"When you say it like that, it sounds bad," I state, following her into the living room. "It's like I'm a knocked-up bride with a shotgun wedding."

"You are!" Calvin's mom cheers. "Only you don't have to worry about the stretch marks and labor pains."

I know she means well, but I would love to develop stretch marks while carrying Calvin's child. And labor, I'd endure any pain to have a child of my own. Dallas pats my back, knowing how my future mother-in-law's comment hurt me. I know she didn't mean it.

In the whirlwind that is Dallas, I'm seated, given a drink, and passed a questionnaire to fill out for a game we will play. A half hour later, I'm handed gift after gift while Dallas records the gift-giver on the card. I open it, and my mom passes it around for all to see.

I'm so caught up in the excitement and trying to hurry through the mound of gifts that I barely recall what I opened, let alone who gave it to me. When the crowd thins, Dallas and my mother tidy up while I go through the opened gifts one by one.

Mom brought me the family's antique baby bassinet. She explains it's held every newborn for two generations and is ready to start on the third. Calvin's mom brought the baby bed Calvin and Tyler slept in. *I can't wait for our little one to do the same.*

I find that my mom, Calvin's mom, and Dallas created a wedding and baby gift registry for us. Our family and friends, using the list, went overboard buying everything we need to complete the nursery and welcome our little girl home.

Little girl. I can't believe it. I nearly screamed with joy when the doctor revealed to me that Dani carries a baby girl. Our little family will be complete with one son and one daughter.

I received several baking dishes, recipe books, a cooking class for couples, and even a few items for the house that have a mysterious use. I'll have to read the manuals and look them up online. Mom and Dallas outdid themselves with this party. They stay until all is tidy.

When Calvin arrives home early with Garret by his side, it's clear he knew about the surprise shower as he immediately asks to see the gifts I opened. As he pilfers through the loot, he holds up the lace socks, tutu, and hair bows with one raised brow.

"We are having a girl," I remind him.

"Will she ever dress this girly?" He asks, his mouth posed in distaste.

I don't reward him with an answer.

"I know we'll need these," he states, pointing at box after box of disposable diapers. "They are expensive, too."

I'm glad he's happy with some gifts we received.

Dallas moves closer to my side while scanning the room to see if others are paying attention to us. "When I'm pregnant," she speaks low for only me to hear. "We'll share every part. I'll let you experience morning sickness and food cravings with me. You'll endure my gassy phase, listen to me complain about heartburn, come with me to appointments, listen to the baby's heartbeat, and see the sonogram, all while holding my hand. We'll have fun talking to my baby bump and feeling its little kicks." My best friend leans her head on my shoulder. "I'll practically live with you for the nine months."

"Not if I have a say in it," Garret chimes in over Dallas's shoulder.

"I love you, Dallas, but with two kids and a dog, our adult time is pretty limited," Calvin states from behind me. "I'm not sure you living here would be good for our marriage." Now in front of us, he waggles his dark eyebrows suggestively.

"I know what she means, and it won't interfere with your alone time with me," I inform my husband. Turning to Dallas, I continue, "I'd be honored to share milestones in your pregnancy with you. I'm not too thrilled about the gassy phase but will take it in stride."

"Is Dallas pregnant?" my mom's high voice nearly shrieks.

Calvin and I break into laughter while Garret and Dallas deny it emphatically. It feels good to laugh, and I have Calvin to thank for it. He's helped me into the light; he's turned my life around.

I press myself to his front, look up through my lashes at him, and lick my lips suggestively.

At his growl, I scamper to our bedroom with him hot on my tail.

38

WATER BROKE

Schuyler

I pop out of bed, excited the day is finally here. I barely slept four hours last night, yet I rise like the morning person I'm not. I've fully embraced the life I once mourned I'd never have. *My Prince Charming rode to Mexico on his white horse and turned my world upside down.*

Calvin slept at Garret's last night while Dallas stayed here with Tyler and me. I didn't want a bachelorette party, so instead, once Tyler went to sleep, the two of us drank a bottle of wine and goofed around at my house. Now, the sun is up, and it's my wedding day.

I hurry downstairs to make myself a cappuccino and Dallas a black coffee. Chinook rings the sleigh bells hanging on the sliding door, so I let him out back to do his doggy business. I marvel at his transformation from a nearly bald, shaved dog into a gorgeous golden retriever, his hair growing longer each day. It's hard to remember why I cursed at my oldest brother, Levi, for springing an ugly mutt on us when I see this beautiful one now.

Tyler pads groggily to the breakfast table, sitting in his chair.

"Good morning," I sing as I pull his favorite bowl, cereal, spoon, and milk out for him.

"Humph," he grunts in reply.

I want to curse Calvin for teaching him his manly ways, but it's our wedding day. *I can forgive it for now.*

"Are you excited about the wedding and party today?" I ask as I fill Dallas's cup with coffee.

"Can Chinook walk down the aisle with me?" Tyler whines between bites.

"Honey, dogs don't attend weddings. He'll be here when we get home." I try to appease him.

"I won't go if Chinook can't go," he bolsters, slapping his palm on the table.

"Your daddy and Nana will be disappointed when you don't show up at the wedding," I remind him.

"Chinook goes, or I don't," he repeats.

"What will Uncle Levi, Uncle Dan, and Uncle Clint do if you aren't there to stand with them?" I try to bribe him.

"They want Chinook there," he counters.

"Are you lying to me?" I tilt my head. "Maybe I should call and see if they want the dog there."

"Humph," he pouts and begins crying.

What's this?

He never acts like this.

He's been so excited about the wedding that I didn't see this coming. He never acts out.

Is this because I'm marrying his dad?

I believed him when he asked me to adopt him and become his mommy.

Was that all an act?

I decide to text Calvin, then talk myself out of it. I need to learn to parent Tyler, and hands-on is the best way to learn.

Our Fourth of July wedding goes off without a hitch, and we move on to photos and the reception. Tyler continues to act sleepy and whiney as he has since breakfast.

"Hey buddy," I murmur, approaching him. "Do you feel okay?"

"My tummy hurts," he groans, rubbing it.

"Let's find you something to nibble on. Maybe food and drink will make it feel better," I offer.

He only nods, holding his tummy as I guide him to the food table.

Mom approaches me. "What are you doing?"

Before speaking, I look around to make sure no one is in earshot. "Tyler has a tummy ache. I'm gonna let him nibble to see if it helps."

Unbreakable

This triggers Mom into action. She asks him where it hurts and feels his forehead. "I think he's warm. You feel him."

I place my palm on his forehead like I've watched Mom do a thousand times. *Sure enough, he's hot.* I nod in her direction.

"Why don't I take him back to the house? I'll get him into pajamas, give him some children's acetaminophen, and lay him down to rest," she offers, lifting her new grandson.

"Okay, but call me if anything changes," I demand.

"I will. You enjoy your reception. We'll be just fine until you come home." Mom kisses Tyler's warm forehead, smiles at me, and exits, trying not to be noticed.

I find my new husband, pull him to the dance floor, and quietly tell him about Tyler. He worries, but I assure him Mom raised four kids. She can handle this.

"How much longer do we need to stay at this party?" he murmurs.

"Hmm..." I look at the sky as if I'm thinking. "We need to dance some more, cut the cake, smile during the toasts, and toss the bouquet and garter. Then we can make our exit."

"Maybe we should slip away to start the honeymoon now since we have a sick boy at home." Calvin waggles his eyebrows, shooting me his sexy grin.

"Behave," I order and swat his chest.

Calvin drifts off moments after we pull ourselves off each other. I play with his soft, curly chest hair, reliving our wedding day. In the back of my mind, however, I'm worried about our little boy. I slip from bed, tiptoeing down the hallway. It's been an hour since we last checked on Tyler. *I won't be able to sleep, worrying about him.* Calvin told me he runs a fever when cutting teeth, and this could be new molars coming in. *He has much more experience than I do; this is all so new, and I'm a worry wart by nature.*

When I check on Tyler at three a.m., his fever's risen to 103 degrees, and he still complains about his belly. I run back into our room, waking Calvin while I select Mom in my contacts.

"Mom," I start as soon as she answers, "Tyler's fever is 103 degrees, and his belly still hurts."

I hear rustling as I'm sure she's putting on her glasses to read her clock. "I think it's time to take him to the emergency room."

I promise to update her, disconnect the call, and slip on sweats. Calvin sits on the edge of the bed, still not fully awake.

"Calvin," I raise my voice, "get dressed. We're taking Tyler to the E.R."

This springs him to life.

I sit in the back seat, holding our little guy while Calvin drives as fast as he can, breaking no laws. Although the E.R. waiting room is full, when the admission person sees we can't wake Tyler, she rushes us into the back.

An hour later, the doctor and nurses inform us he has appendicitis, and they need to operate before it bursts. I cry at the thought of such a little boy heading to surgery. Calvin signs all the paperwork. Then, the staff whisks Tyler away, leaving us to wait.

I call my mother while Calvin calls his. We hold hands while we share what we know and promise to update them again soon. A nurse ushers us to the surgical waiting room, promising the surgeon will look for us here after the surgery. Calvin wraps his arms around me, promising everything will be alright. I lay my head on his shoulder, exhausted but unable to sleep.

A commotion at the door causes me to lift my head, looking in that direction. It's my family, all of them. Mom hugs Calvin, promising him everything will be okay and that kids bounce back quickly. Levi's long strides bring him to me. I lay my head on his chest, allowing my big brother to hold me. Like he's always done, he soothes me.

"What do you need?" he asks, leaning back to look in my eyes. "Coffee, food, magazines? Just name it."

I shake my head before sitting back in the hard chair with the wooden-slat arms.

"Clint," Levi calls my youngest brother over. He passes him cash then orders, "Get drinks, snacks… a variety."

Clint nods his head, turns on his heel, and heads down the hallway. Mom takes the seat beside me, placing her arm around my shoulders and pulling me to her just as my phone vibrates.

DANI

my water broke headed to hospital

I extend my screen for Mom to read.

"What hospital?" she asks.

"She has a C-section scheduled here in a week," I pant, suddenly unable to take a deep breath.

"Text her back that you'll meet her in the E.R.," Mom suggests. "We'll update you about Tyler as soon as he's out of surgery. She'll need you with her."

"Are you sure? I want to be here when Tyler wakes up."

"Honey, as excited as he is to be a big brother, he won't mind you being with the baby." She points around the room. "There are more than enough of us to entertain him until you can make it down to see him."

I lean in to inform Calvin about Dani. He agrees I should go meet her before kissing me. "It's baby time," he smiles before swatting my butt to send me on my way.

Baby time. It's baby time. At two weeks early, I hope nothing's wrong with Dani or the baby.

At the E.R., I inform the attendant a pregnant mother is on her way in, and her water already broke. She quickly pages an OB to the E.R., and we wait for Dani's arrival. The longer we wait, the more worried I become.

Is the baby okay?

Dani's water broke a week early. *Is that dangerous?*

Will her little lungs be ready?

Are Calvin and I ready to be parents?

39

OUR DAUGHTER

Schuyler

"Finally," Dani spits as another doctor enters her labor room. "Will you tell these Neanderthals I'm not having natural childbirth and to take me to surgery?"

She words it as a question, but it's definitely not a question. It seems Dani treats everyone the way she treats Calvin, and it looks like she always gets her way.

The doctor nods to the nursing staff, and they immediately prep Dani. One nurse whisks me away to change into scrubs. I text as I follow the nurse behind the nurses' station.

> ME
> we're headed to C-section

"Um," the nurse points to my hands, "you need to leave your phone here."

"My little guy is in surgery for an emergency appendectomy right now. I'm waiting for an update," I explain, hoping to keep my cell phone.

"You can lay it down here on the counter. We'll monitor it and find you immediately, if needed." She pats my forearm. "It's a simple procedure; I'm sure he'll be fine."

I nod, write my code on a notepad, and lay my phone beside it.

Unbreakable

In the cold, sterile operating room, I'm instructed to take a seat at the head of the table while they shift Dani from the gurney onto the operating table. The anesthesiologist seated near me immediately informs Dani what about the spinal she'll receive.

I marvel at the surgical team's execution of the pre-op procedures with minimal communication. With military precision, they ready Dani for the C-section.

"You may feel a little pressure," the anesthesiologist informs Dani. He lowers one corner of the cloth, allowing me to observe as the surgeon makes the incision.

"Oh my, Dani," I whisper.

"No," she bites. "I don't want to see or hear. Not a word."

I squeeze her left hand. I realize she can't feel it, but I hope she sees my gesture out of the corner of her eye. I continue to hold her hand through the entire operation.

When the surgeon lifts the baby from Dani's womb, covered in yellow gunk, tears well in my eyes, and a gasp escapes. I feel Dani's eyes on me as my gaze follows the wailing baby across the room where nurses clean her before swaddling her in a baby blanket.

"Apgar score of seven," a nurse announces to the doctor.

I release a breath I didn't know I was holding; a seven is good, especially for a C-section. In the weeks since my first meeting with Dani, I read many parenting and pregnancy books; I did some research. I planned to spend the nine days between our wedding and the scheduled C-section asking both our parents for all the tips on parenting an infant I could squeeze in. Now, I suppose, I will have to learn as I go.

The nurse carries the baby towards Dani's head. "Um, she doesn't want to see her," I inform, looking at Dani to make sure she hasn't changed her mind. She mouths the words "Thank you."

Once again, I glue my eyes on the baby in the clear bassinet across the operating room. One nurse smiles and winks at me.

"Excuse me." A disembodied female voice fills the room via the intercom. "I have a message for Schuyler. Your son is in recovery; there were no complications."

I lift my eyes to heaven, thanking God for his protection over Tyler. When I look at Dani, her eyes meet mine for a moment.

"I figured you wouldn't want to know," I state, shrugging.

"I don't," she bites back.

I don't let her disdain for motherhood dampen my excitement for our new baby girl or for good news about Tyler. I will forever be thankful for her two gifts, but I will never understand her hate for any information about her children.

Dani orders me to leave her in recovery to be with my daughter. I hesitate for a moment, feeling pulled in three directions at once. She assures me she's fine and claims the baby needs me more than she does.

Schuyler

Upon entering the ward, a nurse quickly secures a bracelet around my right wrist to mark me as the baby's mother. The weight of this simple task hits me.

I'm a mother; this baby girl is looking to me for everything.

The nurse asks if I got the message about my son's surgery, and I thank her for letting me know as soon as possible. She passes my phone to me and gestures toward the nursery.

I look through the nursery window as two nurses measure and record the length and weight of our little girl. With an ink pad, they place her little footprints on a card, then scrub her little feet clean as she attempts to kick them about. Once a nurse swaddles our tiny girl, she carries her near the window for my inspection. With my hand to the glass, I take in the beauty that is our newborn.

I snap a quick photo with my cell phone and text it to Calvin and Dallas. As much as I wish my best friend could join me on this exciting day, I understand why she isn't here. Her fear of hospitals prevents her from visiting. To support her, Garret plans to wait to visit the baby, too. I know they will be the first to visit us when we arrive home.

"We've set you up in room four," an approaching nurse states from behind me.

I turn and follow her.

"Use the bed and chairs to hold your baby. We have television in here, but most new parents have no time for TV when the baby's in the room." She picks up a device wired to the bed. "Press this button if you need anything or when you're ready for us to return the baby to the nursery." As she walks to the open door, she says, "I'll go wheel your daughter in to you."

I can feel my heartbeat in my ears. *They are going to wheel the baby to me.*

I expected Calvin would be with me the first time I held our baby. I quickly send texts to Mom.

> **ME**
> she's perfect!
> in ob#4
> they're wheeling her in
> please send Calvin up ASAP
> & give Tyler kisses for me

I'm as excited as I am scared to meet our baby girl. Suddenly, all my years in the nursery at church and babysitting for neighbors doesn't seem enough to prepare me for this moment.

She will be littler than any of the children I've cared for, and she will rely on me to make decisions for her.

"Here we are. Mommy's here," the nurse sweetly coos to the baby. "Mommy, are you ready to hold your baby girl?" She lifts the little bundle into her arms and walks to me.

I hurry to the sink to wash my hands. I've heard cell phones are germ factories, and I don't want to pass those on to her. Hands dry, I take a seat in the recliner and hold my arms near my chest.

The nurse carefully passes the baby to me. "Don't be nervous," she instructs. "It's natural. New moms find they're much better at this than they think they'll be."

I look down at the perfect, dark eyelashes on her tiny, closed lids and her heart-shaped mouth. I don't think I'll ever be able to take my eyes off her.

"My husband..." I pause, as it hasn't even been 24 hours since we exchanged vows, and this is the first time I've referred to Calvin as my husband. "He'll be coming up since our son is out of surgery."

"His name and information are on the paperwork Dani gave us. I'll get him a bracelet and show him where to find the two of you."

"Thank you," I state, eyes glued on the baby.

Alone in the room, I sneak one of her little arms from underneath the pink and blue striped blanket. Her tiny little fingers wrap around my finger, and I feel my heart swell within my chest.

I'm dying to show the baby to Calvin, Tyler, and my family. I take my cell phone in my free hand, no longer caring about germs, and carefully snap a picture of our daughter's precious face. Then, I send it to my mom. I find I missed a text.

. . .

> **CALVIN**
> on way up

"Your daddy's coming to see you," I babble, letting her grasp my finger again. "Yes, he is. He'll be here any minute. You're going to love him. He's such a wonderful daddy."

I bend and place a gentle kiss on her tiny forehead.

"Your big brother Tyler won't be able to see you until tomorrow. He's so excited to meet you, too."

Calvin lightly knocks twice on the slightly ajar door before entering.

"Daddy's here," I whisper to our tiny bundle. "It's time to meet your daddy."

Calvin sits on the edge of the hospital bed near our chair. "How do I do this?" he asks in his softest voice.

40

DAWN

Schuyler

Calvin's fear shocks me.

"You've done this before; I haven't," I remind him. "Wash your hands."

When he sits again, I lean forward in the chair, passing the baby to him; she looks tiny in his powerful arms. Instantly, he softens, cooing to her.

I point to the card taped to her clear bassinet. I realize Calvin hasn't looked in the direction I'm pointing, so I read, "Baby Girl Calhoun weighs eight pounds, six ounces, and is 22 inches long."

"She's perfect," he whispers. He's gazing at her tiny face like he's seen nothing more adorable in his life.

"Yep! Ten fingers, ten toes, and healthy," I concur. "She's perfect. Can you believe she's ours?"

Calvin smiles at me. "Congratulations, Mommy."

"I'll never tire of hearing that," I confess, moving to sit beside him on the bed. I slide her little pink cap off, running my fingertips over her dark, peach-fuzz hair. "I can't keep my hands off of her."

"There's nothing wrong with that," my mom's voice softly states as she enters the room with Dad behind her.

"Who's with Tyler?" I stand, prepared to go sit with him.

"Sit," Mom orders. "Your brothers are with him. They plan to play a board game until his lunch arrives. I've instructed them to let him nap after he eats."

"I'm surprised they came," I admit.

"They talk about Tyler all the time now," Dad informs me. "They are competing for the title of the best uncle."

"Oh, that can't be good," I chuckle.

"It will be good for Tyler," Mom says, drying her hands. "He won't mind the attention and gifts."

She sits on the other side of Calvin. When she runs her knuckles along our daughter's chubby little cheek, the baby turns towards her fingers, her mouth seeking a nipple.

"Do you think she's hungry?" I ask my parents.

When she nods, I walk into the hall to find a nurse. On my way, I spot Dani in the next room, laying in her hospital bed.

Standing in her doorway, I ask, "How are you?"

She waves her hand as if shooing me away; I ignore the gesture. As I approach the side of her bed, she stops tapping on her cell phone to look my way. She doesn't look thrilled to see me. "Don't you have a baby to tend to? And a boy just out of surgery? I'm fine. Get out of here," she orders.

"You shouldn't be alone," I state, preparing to sit in the chair beside her.

"My assistant is on his way," she states, pointing to her phone. "We'll be working all afternoon."

"You need your rest," I remind her.

"I've done this before," she bites out, so I leave.

I feel sorry for Dani. She's in a hospital, alone, and pretends she doesn't want company. *I bet she's just being tough and doesn't want to admit she needs anyone.*

I catch a passing nurse, informing her I think our baby is ready to eat. She smiles and says they'll be right in. When I enter the room, I demand to hold the baby again.

"I'm having withdrawals," I proclaim.

Sitting in the chair with her, I hum a quiet tune.

"Look at the two of you," Calvin says, snapping a picture with his phone. He shoots a quick text to his mother and my brothers before placing it on the bed.

"I forgot how tiny they are," Calvin confesses.

"Oh, look! She's opening her eyes," I point out excitedly. "Hey, sleepy girl. Are you getting hungry?"

Calvin leans in close. "Hi sweetheart." His voice quivers. "I'm your daddy. Yes, I am," he coos. "Your little brother is downstairs. He can't come up here right now. You'll have to wait a day or two to meet him. He's very excited to see you, though. We all are."

Reality settles in. *I never knew my heart could feel so warm and so full.*

Calvin's phone vibrates. "It's a text from my parents." His fingers fly over the phone screen. "They at the hospital, so I sent them Tyler's room. I figure they will visit him first to relieve the Dawes boys, so your brothers can come up here."

"Now, who are you texting?" I ask.

"I'm sending your brothers our room number," he answers.

While I feed our daughter her first bottle, I relive the entire C-section experience. "It's a miracle, and I was right there. Ten fingers, ten toes, and a cute little button nose. Her hair is the color of Tyler's. Isn't she absolutely perfect in every way?"

"Speaking of perfection, Uncle Clint is here," my youngest brother announces and receives a swat on his back from Levi.

"I think I should slip down to see Tyler before he naps," I tell Calvin as I stand, passing the baby to Clint. "Send me the picture you took of me holding the baby so I can show him. And you guys try not to hurt our little girl with your beefy hands," I warn, pointing at my three brothers.

Schuyler

This next morning, I enter the hospital with a special treat for Dani. I approach her room after peeking into the nursery to spy on my sleeping girl.

"She's not in there," a nurse calls from farther down the hall. "They moved her out onto the medical floor. You'll have to ask for her room number at the nurses' station."

"Thank you. I'll be back in a bit."

"Oh, and we placed another mother and baby in your room," she adds before disappearing around the corner.

I text our entire family that the other half of our room is now occupied, hoping they will knock and enter quietly today.

In Dani's new hospital room, I find her working with her assistant. Well, I think they are working; she seems to bark orders at him with a fury. I rap my knuckles on her open door.

"I brought real food," I state, holding up the fast food paper bag. "How do you feel?" I ask as I place it on the table above her lap.

Dani nods but continues talking with her assistant, so I excuse myself. I feel a hint of irritation at being shrugged off, but I try to ignore it.

Today is a happy day.

As I walk back to the maternity ward, my phone vibrates.

> CALVIN
> Tyler discharged after morning rounds
> Levi & Dan, here I'm coming up

At the nursery window, I motion to the nurses to bring the baby to our room. Calvin joins me on the walk to our room. Since the door's wide open, so we go on in.

"Levi plans to take Chinook on a long walk this afternoon," Calvin states. "He may even take him to his place tonight."

While he talks, I note a purse and jacket lie on the hospital bed just inside the door. The bed is still made.

I thought the nurse said a new mom and baby would share our room.

I lay my cell phone on our bed, and Calvin does the same before he sits on its edge. We both turn our heads at the sound of the toilet flushing in the attached bathroom. The door opens, and an older woman emerges.

"Dawn, is that you?" I can't believe my eyes.

Did Mom's longtime friend come to see our new little girl?

"Schuyler Dawes?" Dawn's as dumbfounded as I am.

"It's Schuyler Calhoun now," Calvin corrects gently.

"Oh, that's right. You had a Fourth of July wedding. You're newlyweds. Congratulations!" Dawn smiles wide and claps for us. "Your mother spoke all the time about your moving back and winning a wedding contest."

A nurse pushes in two baby girls. "Special delivery," she sing-songs.

I look at Dawn, and she looks at me. At that moment, I remember Mom sending me a prayer request for Dawn a couple of months ago, because her sister was in a terrible car wreck. That doesn't explain why she's here with a baby girl, though.

41

LYNDON

Schuyler

Calvin lifts our baby from her bassinet and walks over to Dawn as she looks down at the other sleeping baby. "I'm Calvin, Schuyler's husband, and this is our new baby girl."

"Oh my gosh." My hand flies to my mouth. "How rude of me! I should have introduced the two of you."

Dawn extends her hand to Calvin. "I'm Dawn, Theo's friend and golf partner for many years." She turns to peer once more at the infant. "And this is my niece." Her voice shakes as she speaks.

My mind quickly puts it all together. *If this is her niece, then the baby must be her sister's daughter. Something must have happened to her sister in the horrible accident.* My heart breaks for her. I wrap my arm around Dawn's back as she continues to gaze at the baby. I don't speak as I'm not sure what to say; I'm not caught up on her entire situation.

Pulling away, I snap a picture of Calvin holding our baby and quickly text it to Dallas. She's already texted me twice to remind me to send photos.

"Have you shared a photo of your niece with Mom yet?" I whisper.

She turns from the infant. "Not yet. I received the call that they delivered the baby early this morning. I wanted to wait until a decent time to reach out to her."

"She plans to be here any minute." My arm back around her, I squeeze the older woman tightly. "She'll be so happy to see you."

Dawn's sad eyes latch onto mine. She attempts to smile as she nods. It's not even one-fourth of her usual smile. Dawn is an angel here on earth. Bubbly is the word that comes to mind when describing her. She's always upbeat and positive. Dawn's a ray of sunshine whom we always want around. Today, her light is dimmer than usual, and my heart breaks for her.

"Do you want to hold your niece?" I ask.

In Dawn's eyes, I see fear and pain. I recognize it instantly as I saw it in my reflection for over a year.

"I'm sure the baby's eager to meet you," I offer encouragement. When she nods and takes a seat in her recliner, I lift the baby girl and place her in Dawn's trembling hands.

"It's been over 20 years since I've held a baby," she says, smiling down at her little bundle. She caresses the little baby's cheek with her fingertips before she begins baby-talking to her niece.

"How old are your sons now?" I ask, hoping to distract her from her sadness for a bit.

"My oldest is 26, and my youngest is 21," she shares with a proud smile.

"Any daughters-in-law yet?"

"Oh, heavens no!" she giggles, her entire body bouncing. "They enjoy their freedom and expensive toys. I may never get a daughter or grandchildren. I bet your momma's over the moon to have her first two grandchildren and another on the way."

"You know it." I pat her shoulder as I move closer to Calvin.

A nurse enters with a bottle in both hands. "One for you," she says, handing one to Dawn. Looking in our direction, she informs us, "The doctor said you'll probably take the baby home tomorrow morning after rounds." Then she hands Calvin a bottle and exits.

Calvin feeds our daughter, then passes her to me to burp. His cell phone vibrates on the bed. "Mom says they're ready to discharge Tyler," he reads.

"Will you bring him up here before he goes home to rest? I'd go down, but I'm not a legal guardian." I try to smile, even though it hurts that I'm not his mom yet. I forget my sadness as I laugh at the unladylike belch that expels from our tiny girl. "I think Clint taught her to do that."

Dawn agrees with me, laughing so loudly she startles the little one in her arms. With a soft voice, she soothes the baby's attention back to her bottle.

Calvin laughs, kisses our daughter and me, and promises to return with Tyler. He's only gone a minute before the four grandparents swoop in. Immediately, the room fills with baby talk, coos, and lots of oohs and aahs.

I can't wait to see Tyler's reaction to his little sister.

"There she is," Mom greets her friend. "And look at your little cutie." She stands over Dawn, admiring the baby she feeds.

"Your granddaughter's a cutie, too."

Dawn's eyes are alight, and her smile is huge. It seems Mom is just the person she needed to cheer her up. I understand she's hurting, and her feelings are warranted. I've just never seen her without her megawatt smile and exuberant personality.

Soon, Calvin wheels Tyler into the room in a wheelchair. I'm sure it's a precaution, but I don't enjoy seeing him in the thing. He's a little boy; he should run around.

"Are you ready to hold your baby sister?" I ask, then place a kiss at his temple and mess up his hair.

"I was ready yesterday," he declares.

I show him how to hold his arms in front of his chest before Calvin passes him the baby. Tyler's hazel eyes are enormous, and his open-mouth smile takes encompasses his entire face. He speaks not a word as he stares in awe of the baby in his arms.

After a few minutes, he looks up at Calvin and me. When we nod, he whispers, "Want to know her name?"

Of course, no one hears him over their conversations.

I clear my throat. "Tyler has an announcement."

All eyes swing in his direction.

"My baby sister's name is..." Tyler looks around the room, keeping everyone in suspense for a few moments. "Her name is Lyndon." He nods his head once, smiling proudly.

Schuyler

Calvin's parents volunteer to take Tyler home, allowing us to remain with Lyndon. The tight space feels a little less crowded once they leave. I sit cross-legged on the bed with Calvin beside me. My father sits nearby in the recliner, holding Lyndon, and Mom sits on the other bed near Dawn.

"So, they delivered the baby early this morning," Mom says to Dawn. "How's your sister since the delivery?"

Dawn caresses her niece's nose and cheeks. "Her condition is unchanged." She kisses the baby's forehead. "They told me they'd bring me forms this afternoon to sign so they can carry out the wishes from her living will."

My chest tightens, and a pit sinks low in my stomach. *Living will? Her sister's on life support.*

"It's been several long months on the ventilator," Mom states. "I'm sure her body is ready to rest; her suffering will finally end."

"It took me the first month to see the reality of the situation and understand the reason for her DNR," Dawn admits. "As each month passed, while we waited for the safe delivery of the baby, I watched her dwindle away, even with the machines breathing life into her. It's time for her to join her husband in heaven."

Mom nods in agreement, and Dawn looks back to the baby in her arms. "Then the two of us will start our adventure. Won't we? Yes, we will."

"I hope you know I'm here for anything either of you might need," Mom says, her hand upon Dawn's shoulder. "Our entire prayer group is available to babysit, so you can shop, get your hair done, or just take a nap. We all remember how chaotic the first year is."

"Thank you. Would you like to hold her?" Dawn asks, and, of course, Mom says yes.

With her arms free, Dawn walks about the room, stretching. Continuing their conversation, she states, "I'm cutting my hours back to part time at work. That way, I can spend more time at home with the new baby."

"Have you found childcare for the hours you are at work?" I ask.

"Not yet. Most want a 40-hour-a-week slot filled and don't discount for a 20-hour work week. I planned to contact the private, in-home providers next week, but my niece was in a hurry to enter the world."

When I move my eyes in Calvin's direction, he nods.

"Dawn, I'll be staying home with Lyndon. If you'd like, I could care for your niece while you work," I offer. "I've promised to care for Levi's baby when his wife goes back to work. That won't be until January, though. These two will be five months old then. I think I'm up for that challenge."

Dawn stands in front of me, her hands on her hips, hope beaming from her face. "Do you think you could handle two newborns? I've taken three weeks of vacation. That would allow you to develop your own routine before you add another baby to the mix."

"I'd be happy to watch her. Have you named her yet?" I ask.

"I plan to use her mother's name, Riley." Dawn sits by my mom and smiles at her niece.

"That's a cute name and a beautiful gesture to honor her mother," I state softly.

"Let's take a photo of Mom and Dawn holding Lyndon and Riley," I suggest, knowing they'll frame them for their houses and desks at work.

Calvin takes several photos and shows them to the women for their approval.

"I bet Lyndon and Riley will be best friends, just like their grandmas," I declare.

"Heaven help us!" Dad finally speaks up after sitting quietly for hours. He points to Dawn and Mom. "I hope they don't get into as much trouble as these two do."

42

WELCOME TO THE FAMILY

Schuyler

Calvin drops me off at the door so I can run by Dani's room, then meet him in the maternity ward. I enter the hospital with a bit more pep in my step this morning. Tyler's no longer a patient; he's doing great. And we get to bring Lyndon home today.

I freeze at the door to Dani's hospital room; she's not here. When I inquire at the nurses' station, I'm told she checked out against medical advice last night.

She left without a word, no goodbye.
How could she do that to Calvin, Tyler and Lyndon?
Is it possible for her to not feel anything for her own flesh and blood?
She has no idea how lucky she is.
Shit! She left before signing over all parental rights for Lyndon.
My stomach convulses, and my head pounds.
Maybe Calvin will know what to do.

Over in our room, Tyler proudly carries the baby carrier, placing it on the bed. Calvin cracks his knuckles as if preparing for a battle.

"Let's do this," he says.

My boys seem nothing but excited while I'm scared to death.

"Dani signed out AMA last night," I tell Calvin quietly. "She didn't sign the papers, did she?"

Calvin's excitement fades. Without a word, he grabs his phone and dials someone as he leaves the room. When he returns, he's no longer worried.

"Our lawyer has the signed papers. Dani called him yesterday. He plans to drop them by."

Dawn arrives shortly after we do. Today, when she enters the room, joy written all over her face. *This is the Dawn I know and love.*

"We need to exchange contact information," I suggest, waking up my phone.

Dawn agrees. She rattles off her number for me to text her my information. As we have the same phone, I forward my contact to her, so she only needs to hit save. She stares at her phone for a minute, and I sense she has something she wants to say.

"Has your mother mentioned we only live six blocks from each other?" she asks, laying down her phone.

"No. Do you live on our street?" I ask, disbelieving.

"I live one block down and five blocks over. You drive right by my house on the way to yours," she giggles.

Calvin and I share a look. Others might write dawn's placement in our room off as coincidence. *It's another sign.* Dawn's been there for my mother and me many times over the years. *Now, it's my turn to help her out.* I love the thought of her positivity being a regular part of our lives.

A nurse brings in our discharge paperwork, which Calvin quickly signs. Again, I'm not on the birth certificate, so I'm not a legal guardian. Too many things might happen, and that worries me.

We need to move forward with the adoptions of both kids as soon as possible.

We say goodbye to Dawn. As I hug her, I ask her to call me in a couple of days. I'd like to get together and share what's working and what we need help with as new moms.

Calvin carries Lyndon in her seat as a nurse follows us to ensure we buckle her safely into the vehicle. We wave goodbye, and we are on our way home. Tyler is a ball of excitement in his booster seat next to Lyndon.

"I can't wait to get home!" he says. "You'll be so surprised."

I look questioningly at Calvin; he shrugs, unsure of what Tyler means. Rounding the corner, we quickly understand. Someone tied p ink balloons to our mailbox near the end of the driveway, and they draped a large "Welcome Baby Girl Lyndon" banner between the columns of the porch.

"Surprise!" Tyler shouts, startling Lyndon, and she wails. "I'm sorry... I didn't mean to..."

"It's okay, buddy," Calvin tells him. "She's scared, that's all."

Before we can unhook both children from the back seat, my three brothers are walking towards us.

"Welcome home," Levi greets, walking past us to place Tyler on his buxom shoulders.

"What's this?" I ask, diaper bag in hand.

"A welcome to the family barbecue," Clint proudly informs us.

"By the way, I get to hold her first," Dan states. "We arm wrestled for it, and I won."

I shake my head at my muscle-bound brothers.

"He cheated. He waited until we had several beers in us last night before he suggested we wrestle for the honor," Clint tattles.

"I can't believe the baby of the family was the first to have a baby," Levi teases.

"You're not far behind," I remind him, pointing to his pregnant wife.

My brother nods, walking past me into the backyard. As soon as he notices Dan is following him, he walks faster, eventually breaking into a jog.

"Easy," I warn Levi as he runs about the yard, Tyler still on his shoulders.

"He just had surgery," Calvin reminds him.

I shake my head at Levi's flippant nod, certain he'll keep his nephew's safety in mind, as I head into the house. "You shouldn't have made a fuss," I tell Mom, entering the foyer.

"Oh, I didn't," Mom swears. "It was your brothers' idea, and they did all the planning. They wanted a party to celebrate both Tyler and Lyndon joining the family."

"They want Tyler to know they're his uncles, and he's their nephew. We couldn't leave him out," Dad says.

"The guys planned a barbecue at our house?" I repeat for clarification. "Now, I'm scared," I laugh.

Moments later, through the sliding door, I note Clint mans the grill under a patio umbrella to avoid the July sun as it rises higher in the sky. Levi stands beside him with Tyler still on his shoulders. It looks like they're teaching him how to grill.

In the front room, Dan sits under a banner that says, "Welcome to the family, Tyler and Lyndon." He's smiling broadly as Calvin extricates Lyndon from the baby carrier and hands her over. Never in a million years would I have thought my brothers would be so ga-ga over a baby girl.

"Hey," I mention to Levi's wife, as she heads to the bathroom, "I want to talk to you about something."

"It'll have to wait; this pregnant woman has got to pee." She quickly waddles away.

I snap photos of Dan holding Lyndon. A shiver runs down my spine. *I'm a real mom taking photos of her children; I'm doing mom things.*

Unbreakable

"Did you think to invite Dallas and Garret?" I ask Dan since I haven't spotted them here yet.

"They'll be over later this afternoon. They had to work a half day," he replies.

"You okay if I go say hello to everyone?" I ask.

"Go on. Uncle Dan's got this," he professes proudly.

I greet all four parents on my way to open the patio door. "Tyler, it's time for you to come inside where it's cooler," I order.

"We've got him," Clint says. "Food will be done in 10 minutes. We'll bring him in then."

My two brothers smile hoping to keep Tyler outside. "Save your dimples. They have no power over me." I inform them.

"I'm keeping Chinook at my place until tomorrow afternoon. I think it's best if you settle in before she meets the baby." Levi glances at me, and I nod before he returns his attention to the grill.

"Hey Tyler, I'd like to get some pictures of you with Lyndon before she needs to eat again." I try to appeal to my little boy's sense of pride at being a big brother this time.

Like magic, Tyler abandons his new uncles and darts to his sister's side. I realize that his excitement will wane with each passing day, and I want to record it all.

"Sky," Tyler calls from the front room, "Dan won't give me Lyndon."

Mom leans in to place her arm around my shoulders. "Isn't he a sweet big brother?"

"I don't know who is more in love with Lyndon, Tyler or her uncles."

We both chuckle. Entering the living room, I direct Tyler to lean in to Uncle Dan for a few shots before I ask my brother to help Tyler hold the baby.

Dan stands beside me as I take photo after photo of the two kids.

"Let me take a picture of you with the two of them," Dan offers.

"C'mon, Sky," Tyler invites.

After a few shots, Calvin's mom ushers him in to join in a family photo. Then, both sets of grandparents pose with our family of four at Dan's prompting.

"Food is done," Clint announces from the kitchen. "And it is my turn to hold Lyndon while you eat." He extends his arms for the baby bundle.

"Poor little girl may never learn to crawl or walk if her uncles have anything to do with it," Calvin's mom teases.

I take in our large family, eating and talking as they help us celebrate this special day. I wonder if my brothers will be as protective of Lyndon as they are with me.

43

BRINK

Schuyler

After the meal, Levi declares, "It's time for the presents!"

"Is it customary to give gifts at a welcome home party?" I inquire.

"It's also a welcome to the family party," Clint reminds me. "We have to have presents for our little guy, Tyler."

Tyler claps, a giant smile on his face.

"This is from Uncle Levi," Calvin reads before handing the box to his son.

Tyler digs in, rapidly removing the blue wrapping paper with large, yellow bulldozers on it. "It's a football!"

Instinctively, I look toward Lyndon, worried the noise might startle her. She's too busy drinking from the bottle Uncle Clint holds for her to notice any of the ruckus.

"Your uncles love to play catch and flag football," Mom brags.

"This way, we don't have to bring one. You'll always have one here for us to play with you," Levi says.

"I love it. Thank you, Uncle Levi," Tyler says before hugging him around the neck.

He returns to his spot on the floor; Calvin hands him a gift from Uncle Dan.

"I've always wanted one of these!" Tyler informs the crowd, holding a large Nerf gun.

Dan points to a large, open box by the door. "We have four others, so we can all play."

"Can we have a Nerf gun fight right now?" Tyler asks Calvin, hopping to his feet.

"First, we have to talk about the rules and open your last gift," Dan states, capturing Tyler's full attention. "We must keep the guns and darts away from your baby sister. They are for big boys only."

Tyler hangs on Dan's every word, nodding.

"This gift is from Uncle Clint, Grandma Theo and Grandpa Richard," Calvin states, sliding a heavy gift to Tyler.

I shake my head at the video game system while my family shrugs sheepishly.

"This gift has rules, too," Dan instructs. "You need permission for screen time to play video games. If your chores are done, you take care of Chinook, your room is clean, and you have your homework done, then you can play."

"We bought you a few of our favorite games," Clint brags, causing my eyebrows to rise.

To my surprise, they aren't the violent shooting games I've watched my brothers play for years. *That's very mature of the three of them.*

"Before you play with your presents," my oldest brother, Levi, begins, "Tyler, we want you to know we are happy to have you in our family. All of us." He points to his two brothers and his parents.

"We're here for you anytime, day or night. If you need anything or get mad at your parents, we've got your back. Understand?" He extends his palm in the air.

Tyler promptly delivers a high-five.

"Okay! Let's take your new stuff to the basement. It's guy time!" Dan proclaims.

Clint passes Lyndon to Mom, stating she's ready to burp, before he joins the other guys in the basement.

Today, Calvin's walking me through the restaurant and bar. He's kept many aspects secret from the public, and there is much speculation about the business taking over the abandoned warehouse.

In a recent article in *dsm magazine*, the public learned that two high school friends plan to open a restaurant and bar in the abandoned brick building at SW Ninth & Cherry near downtown Des Moines. The article mentioned "The secretive owners remain locked up tight about the menu and theme of the venue. I quoted them saying, 'The theme fills a niche for people ages 21 to 75 who are looking for a relaxing, elegant bar in which to meet friends and celebrate life.' The owners encourage readers to follow them on social media and to be on the lookout for a grand opening at the end of August, complete with an app for the restaurant and bar which contains more details." Rumors since the article released keep a steady buzz. Calvin and Garret take advantage of the rumor mill to conduct their pre-opening advertising on all platforms.

When Calvin shared his financial status with me after our engagement, I learned that Garret and he invested 75 percent of the needed pre-opening funds, with one silent investor for the remaining 25 percent. Since we moved to Des Moines, Calvin discusses the financial side of the business with me each evening as we go to bed. To date, they are under budget on the building lease and advertising. Moving the location from the expensive Kansas City area to Des Moines continues to prove helpful.

As I stand on the sidewalk in front of the restaurant, I find all the windows covered in brown paper. It looks like an abandoned storefront instead of a restaurant or bar.

"We plan to remove the window coverings," Garret states, approaching the building.

"Hi!" I greet my friend with a hug.

"Let's go in; I'll help you find Calvin." Garret opens the heavy wooden door for me.

Once inside the door, I marvel at the restaurant space. Heavy wooden blinds cover the large front windows, and thick red velvet drapes gather at each side. The ceiling looks like molded tin from the end of the Nineteenth Century, painted red to match the drapes. The aged-brick walls and the polished concrete floor set the scene. Dark booths line the two side walls while little, round tables dot the center floor. The black tabletops hold only a miniature lamp with a velvet lampshade, complete with fringe.

I turn toward my husband's voice. He smiles at me and turns off the overhead lighting, bathing the place in muted, red light. The industrial-style, exposed bulbs providing minimal lighting down the two walkways, and a few more fixtures hang over the hostess station at the front of the restaurant and the countertop at the back.

"What do you think?" Calvin asks, pulling me into his arms and burying his face in my neck.

Goosebumps rise on my exposed skin, and my cheeks heat as I blush. I close my eyes, lost in the blissful sensation of his hot breath and firm lips on me. The sound of Garret clearing his throat jolts me back to the present.

"Calvin," I murmur as I push him to arm's length, giggling.

He swings his arms wide, proud of his space. "Well?"

"It's amazing," I announce. "It's warm, quaint, inviting..."

Calvin's mouth crashes into mine. I melt into his embrace. I miss this hot, can't-keep-our-hands-to-ourselves attraction. He's so busy setting up the business, and I'm swamped setting up the house with the kids. I find our romantic interactions banished to the bedroom late at night. I'm happy to find we're still lust-filled.

When Garret clears his throat for a second time, Calvin escorts me to the back counter. "This is the staging area where the staff will gather the food and drinks on trays to deliver to the tables."

"Oh, I thought it was a bar," I state.

Calvin shakes his head. "Drinks for the restaurant will be filled in the bar and delivered through a connecting door in the back of the kitchen." He opens the swinging doors to point in that direction.

Then, he shows me a sample of the type of menus they've ordered. The leather exterior will display the name Brink on the front and information about Fringe, the club, on the back. The interior allows for the rotating menu to be slipped in easily each weekend.

"Let's continue your tour." Calvin takes my hand and leads me toward the large, velvet curtain hanging on the brick wall.

Even knowing they created a hidden speakeasy like in the times of the Prohibition, I'm surprised when he lifts the curtain, and we step through. Two red lights allow us to find the large, black, cast-iron door knocker in the center of the wooden wall. Calvin motions for me to knock. I lift the heavy metal loop, banging it twice against its metal plate. The door slowly opens, and Garret stands, blocking our entrance.

"Password," he grunts.

I try not to laugh as Calvin says, "Tour."

44

CHRISTEN THE CLUB

Schuyler

Garret moves, allowing us to walk past him into a long, dark hallway, illuminated only by rope lighting at the bottom of each wall. Midway, a spotlight brightens the black wall with the word "Fringe" in deep red paint. Calvin points to the opposite wall where a plaque declares this the selfie station. It invites patrons to take selfies for social media and use the tags #Fringe, #FringeDesMoines, and #FringeSpeakeasy. In large, bold, red font, the plaque instructs guests to shut off their cell phones as Fringe is a phone free club. It further explains that any patrons caught using a phone may not return or use the Fringe app for 12 months.

"The guests will receive the new password by noon each day to use that night. As our popularity grows, we'll only send the password out to 250 people per day to ensure we don't exceed our 300 person capacity," Calvin explains as we make our way to the end of the hall. "The bouncers at each door will keep track of the number of people entering and exiting the club." He stops in front of the next wooden, black door. He bangs the knocker two times, and the door swings open, our path blocked by a tall, thin man. "Tour," Calvin says, and we may enter the large bar space.

The ground level of the bar extends the rest of the space. A long, dark bar lines the far end of the building, and booths line both sides. In each of the four corners, stairs lead to the upper level. Near the bar spiral staircases guide guests upstairs. The upper level of the bar is one wide expanse, interrupted only by the large, square hole cut out in the center. A railing designed for customers to lean against it surrounds the hole, giving them a prime view of anything happening at the tables below. To my right is the stage, recently built for the performers Calvin's talent scout finds for them. The square hole separates the stage from the dance floor at the front of the building.

Unlike the space below, the second level holds no seating. Several black, high-top cocktail tables scatter throughout the space. The walls are dark, aged brick just like the lower level, with heavy velvet curtains and wall lights like those in the restaurant.

I peer below, imagining a jazz band and singer entertaining the crowd. The aesthetically pleasing heavy fabrics help prevent echoes within the club. Altogether, the muted lighting gives an intimate feel. The circular booths on the lower level, with their small opening and muted lighting, will allow for private conversations while still enjoying the surrounding club.

Calvin points out the painted tin ceilings that mirror those in the restaurant before escorting me down to the bar along the back wall. Slate boards with handwritten prohibition drink names like Sidecar, Mint Julep, Tom Collins, Gin Rickey, Bees Knees, Whiskey Sour, and Champagne hang on the back wall, surrounded by exposed light bulbs and spirit bottles.

"Garret liked your idea of staff members posing as cops and raiding the bar," Calvin admits. "When we activate the raid alarm," he points to a button behind the bar, "the bartenders will close these rolling barn doors and pull the velvet curtains closed in front of them. This will completely hide the 'illegal alcohol.'" He makes air quotes.

"Oh, what fun!" I coo, clapping. "I can't wait for this place to open. This is so cool. It's more than I imagined."

"We have jazz acts, comics, tasteful burlesque, and cabaret performers scheduled for the first three months already," he boasts. "Thanks to Levi and Dan, we have several retired and off-duty officers to work security for us. Instead of a metal detector, we hired a retired K-9 to sniff out drugs or weapons at the opening to the hallway. It should be a safe, fun space."

"You should invite foodies, bloggers, and local TV personalities to the soft opening to help get the word out," I suggest. "Since Garret and you are new to Iowa, you may not realize this yet, but sports heroes and college coaches draw sizeable crowds around here. If you could get them to come in, be photographed, or post to social media, word would spread like wildfire."

Calvin presses his body to mine. "I love you," he growls, his lips grazing mine.

He playfully sucks my lower lip into his mouth, eliciting a moan to rise from my belly. Heat floods my core. "Let me show you the exit," he murmurs near my ear.

I pout, not wanting to leave. I want to finish what he started. *If we go home, we won't be alone.*

Calvin pulls the velvet drape aside for us to slip behind into the tiny hall leading to the two exits. There's very little light here. The only source is the lit, red "Exit" signs on each end.

I gasp when Calvin slams me against the brick wall, his body pressing tight to mine. In one fluid motion, he lifts my sundress over my head, tossing it to the floor, and lowers my panties to my ankles. I stand naked in my platform sandals, panting.

"Let's christen the club," he growls.

Calvin

The heat of August falls upon central Iowa with little relief, and Des Moines springs to life as the Iowa State Fair opens. Although Dallas and Schuyler revel in the fair and insist we must go, our rapidly approaching grand opening consumes Garret and my time.

Unable to sleep the night before our soft launch, I decide to swim laps, hoping to tire myself out. With the water temperature at 75 degrees, it's not much cooler than the 80-degree nighttime air. I slide off my gym shorts before I dive into the deep end. With water enveloping me, my body relaxes, and the world outside the pool no longer exists. I don't count as I swim lap after lap. Instead, I plan to swim until my body can barely move.

Halfway through my next lap, I find two shapely legs dangling in front of the underwater light. As I continue my swim, my eyes glide up her legs, over her knees, up her thighs, and discover no suit covers her mound. My eyes lock on their target, and I slip deeper into the water, only rising to the top as my hands caress her skin from shins to shoulders.

"Can't sleep?" she asks in a husky, lust-filled voice. "There's nothing left to prepare. We've checked and double-checked everything."

I nod, then graze my nose behind her ear and down the length of her neck. "What brought you out here?" I murmur, nipping and licking her collarbone.

"My bed felt empty," she whispers between moans. "I lost my other half."

My hands easily glide over her wet skin, down her shoulders, over her ribs, and cup her magnificent breasts. I plaster my mouth into hers as I massage and knead them. Her mouth opens to me on a gasp, and my tongue plunders hers. When I pluck and pull on her hard nipples, she moans loudly, and her head falls back on the edge of the pool.

My mouth is now free. I lift her by her hips as I simultaneously lower myself to latch onto her stiff peak. My rock-hard cock and tight balls ache when she pleads.

"Calvin, please," her weak voice begs. "Calvin… I need you."

I slide one hand between her thighs, caressing the delicate skin at a snail's pace. Unable to endure my torturous foreplay, Schuyler wraps one leg around my waist, her heel digging into my ass and pulling me toward her core. Her eyes are on mine in the muted lights of the pool, she smirks devilishly as she takes me in her hand.

Her palm easily glides over my shaft. Up and down. Up and down. My heavy-lidded eyes are open but a slit. I growl when her tongue peeks out on her lower lip. I suck her tongue into my mouth. She counters by tightening her fist around my shaft while her thumb slowly circles my tip.

"You win," I growl into her mouth as I lift her hips, and she guides me to her entrance.

Her eyes search mine as she impales herself upon me. With only one hand on the ledge of the pool, the water assists us in our intimate connection and our feral rise of pleasure toward release.

With a hand between us, my thumb presses her button, rewarding her with an orgasm almost instantly. I don't halt my driving and grinding, enjoying the way her tight walls clench my cock with each wave of her pleasure. I grit my teeth and hold my breath. Fire climbs my spine, and my balls release their load. I shudder as I piston once, then twice more. White-hot sparks decorate the inside of my closed eyelids. I can hear nothing over my ragged breathing and my pulse pounding in my ears.

45

YOUR BEST FRIEND AND MY BEST FRIEND

Calvin

Minutes later, back in our bed, Schuyler reminds me, "Mom will be here at eight in the morning, Clint plans to stop by to help her when football practice is over at ten, and Dawn may drop in, so the kids are taken care of." She rummages through the top drawer of her bedside table. "I'll be able to help you get everything ready until three or so. Then, I'll come home to change and get the kids ready to watch their daddy impress guests with his new venture." She places her hair in a high messy bun, turns off her lamp, then rolls to me. "Now, you will sleep," she commands. "We have a big day tomorrow."

I'm surprised; I sleep until my alarm rings at 6:30 the next morning. Sky's joining me in the pool last night did the trick. She wore me out and distracted me enough that I slept soundly. I place my feet on the wooden floor. When Schuyler's hand presses to my back, looking over my shoulder, I'm greeted by her beautiful, light-brown eyes and sweet smile.

"Good morning," she murmurs. "Are you nervous or excited?"

That's a good question; I'm not sure how I feel. Nervous excitement sounds about right. Tonight is a test run to find places to improve, and I'm eager to discover what works and what doesn't.

"Ask me after lunch," I reply as I head toward the shower.

The day flies by. With Sky's help, Garret and I walk through the entire place to make sure everything is ready. We go over our many lists to ensure we've thought of everything. Schuyler and I drive home at three, clean ourselves up, and bring the children back with us.

"Let's take some pictures," Dallas suggests.

I cringe. *Photos are not my thing, but I go along with the idea.* First, she snaps shots of Sky and me on the sidewalk in front of the door. Then, she takes photos of Garret and me in the same poses. Inside, she takes family photos of the four of us in a booth and standing by the secret door to the bar. We pose for several more photos at the selfie station as we head to the back. The last photo she suggests is of Garret and I behind the bar.

"These are perfect," she claims, her fingers flying over her phone screen. "I'm uploading some to the website and a few to social media."

Taking Dallas up on her offer of free public relations help for our place may have been the best decision we've made. She's created a buzz for more information about our opening. Several media outlets in Central Iowa have contacted us for interviews to promote our place for free. *Nothing beats free advertisement.*

The hostess announces over the intercom, drawing our attention to the long line formed in front of the restaurant. Dallas and Garret dart out the back exit to document the moment we open the front door while I guide my family to the front. I kiss each of them and thank them for supporting me this summer.

"What are you waiting for?" Sky taunts. "Open the door and let's get started." She swats my ass, and I do just that.

I'm happy to report that our vigilance in the preparations led to a successful soft opening. According to the post-event survey, the guests, which consisted mostly of family, neighbors, and food bloggers, enjoyed the atmosphere and dining at Brink. They praised us for the secretiveness as they transferred to the speakeasy. Some believe our no cell phone policy will not fly with the public while others commented it will perpetuate the mysterious allure of Fringe. With the scoring system Dallas set up for the surveys, we earn a ninety-eight percent satisfactory rating. Garret and I are ecstatic. We realize the public won't be as generous as our close family and friends and hope we don't disappoint too many of our guests in the next two weeks.

Schuyler

How is this my life? Last summer, I could not have imagined the happiness that surrounds me. With Calvin's help, I've slayed my green-eyed monster and love every minute. My transition into motherhood proves a challenge, and I enjoy every moment.

Tyler now calls me "Mom," and we enjoy mother-son adventures when we can. Healthy and happy, Lyndon grows at lightning speed. Tyler keeps his word; he's the best big brother in the world.

My three brothers often spoil their niece and nephew, much to Calvin's and my dismay. Levi continues to assist Tyler in training Chinook, and they enjoy many long walks on the nearby walking trails. My parents give us our space and enjoy living nearby, allowing frequent visits, and babysitting opportunities with their grandchildren.

Dawn and I grow close as we share our adventures in motherhood. She constantly informs me there's a reason to have children in your 20s and 30s; when you're older, you no longer have the strength. I've adopted Riley and Dawn into our family.

Dallas officially lives with Garret now. She's killing it in her public relations job and loves cultivating interest in Brink and Fringe. She's Tyler and Lyndon's favorite aunt, because she drops in at least once a week for playtime, often with food or gifts to bribe them.

Calvin's parents love their condo at Echo Valley. When they aren't soaking up time with their grandchildren, they hit the links with my parents or their new friends. Calvin believes it won't be long before his father opens a Des Moines branch of his business, and they make a move permanently from Kansas City.

I love my role as a stay-at-home mom. It allows me to witness every milestone in Lyndon's development and grow closer to Tyler. I enjoy the challenge of caring for two little girls on the days Dawn works, and I look forward to their playtimes as they learn to crawl and walk. My family and friends ensure that I still enjoy moments away while they offer to babysit or plan a sleepover.

Tonight's one of those moments. My parents host a sleepover for Tyler and Lyndon so I can enjoy Calvin's grand opening. I take one last look at myself, twisting this way and that to inspect my finger wave updo, complete with a black feather, in the mirror. The doorbell rings, signaling Dallas's arrival.

She snaps some selfies of the two of us in our matching dresses. She looks lovely with her blonde hair in long, soft waves that flow over the shoulders of her silver, fringed dress. Together, we embrace the flapper look of the 20s from head to toe. We bound, hand in hand, to our waiting Uber.

Dallas texts Garret as we pull up to the club, so he can meet us to open the back door.

"Wow," he greets. "You ladies look awesome."

Dallas pecks him on the cheek.

While the club remains empty, we find the restaurant packed and full of excited conversations. We alert the hostesses that we are available to help anywhere they need, then walk together, table to table, welcoming our guests. Several patrons ask to pose with us for photos. Dallas encourages everyone to post their pictures with hashtags on all social media sites, so we may add them to our platforms.

As the first group of guests make their way to the secret entrance to Fringe, Dallas and I make our way into the club. When not needed elsewhere, we plan to pump up the party in the bar. We help promote activities on the dance floor and introduce the guest performers.

A half hour passes, and the club hops. While we mingle, Dallas and I point out cards on nearby tables with a schedule of entertainers for the next month and dance lessons offered on Monday, Tuesday, and Wednesday evenings, as well as Saturday mornings. We mention a few of the dances available to learn like the Shimmy, Charleston, and Lindy Hop, and we encourage those who show interest to take a business card from the table.

As we pass the bar, Dallas announces we will dance upstairs until the show starts at eight p.m. With water in hand, we climb the spiral staircase, choose our playlist, and connect to the club's speaker system. Then, we dance. Uninhibited in our role as flappers, we demonstrate the dance styles from the prohibition era and invite others to join us. A few brave souls attempt the moves while others enjoy watching.

Just before eight, we take our place on the entertainment platform downstairs where Dallas introduces the band and singer for the evening. The almost full club claps and cheers loudly, but the band doesn't play. I turn to see what the delay is. I find Calvin and Garret standing at the microphone, waiting for the applause to quiet down. I encourage Dallas to turn and watch.

"We didn't rehearse this," she murmurs near my ear.

"Good evening, ladies and gentlemen. My name is Calvin Calhoun, and this is Garret Hendricks. What do you think of our new place?"

The crowd erupts with cheers and clapping.

"We're sorry to interrupt; I assure you the entertainment will begin in a moment. First, Garret would like to say a few words." Calvin passes the microphone to his friend.

Dallas looks to me, and I shrug; neither of us know what he plans to do.

"Let's invite our beautiful girls to join us." His voice is deep and soft as he speaks.

At his suggestion, Dallas and I walk to them. Standing behind me, Garret continues, "This lovely lady is Schuyler. She's Calvin's wife."

The crowd cheers. Garret moves over to stand behind his girlfriend.

"And this lovely lady is Dallas. Tonight, I plan to ask her to be my wife." While the crowd gasps and cheers, Garret swiftly drops to one knee in front of Dallas, an open ring box in hand.

"Yes!" Dallas squeals, hopping up and down excitedly. "Yes, I'll marry you!" She doesn't even allow him to properly ask her, causing me to laugh as tears of joy fill my eyes.

I turn my head toward Calvin and murmur, "My best friend is marrying your best friend. My world is complete."

UNRAVELED

GLUTTONY

PROLOGUE

I hate Las Vegas; I hate girls' trips. *How stupid must I be?*

"Let's fly to Vegas for two days. It'll be fun, just us girls shopping, eating, gambling, and dancing." I spoke those words. How innocent I thought their meaning to be.

Our other girls' trips were fun. We let loose, we partied, and we returned to Iowa prepared to resume our daily lives.

Not this time; not this trip. There's no returning to our normal, daily lives after last night. My life is forever changed.

A chance meeting led to two nights of dinners and clubs with a famous rock band. Most would say we were very lucky to spend our time with them. I can say I enjoyed every minute until the sun rose this morning.

Married. I had to ruin it by drinking too much, marrying a member of the band, spending the night with him in my bed, and not remembering a moment after the six of us enjoyed dinner.

It takes two to tango; I know. He claims he doesn't recall our trip to the wedding chapel or the night we shared, and I want to believe him. From the two days we've spent together, I feel I can trust him.

Married. Together for two days, and we wake on the third naked and married.

1

MONTANA

Three days earlier

"Thank you for forcing me to take a girls' trip," I murmur under my breath as we walk from the lobby through the casino of the New York, New York hotel.

"Just doing my best friend duties," she states, nudging my shoulder, as we stand at the bank of elevators. "My job is to force you to spread your wings and step out of your comfort zone, and you do your best to reign me in and keep me out of jail," she states as we ride the elevator to our floor.

"That's true." I allow her to step from the elevator with her two large, pink, rolling suitcases, before I exit with my one carry-on bag.

I seem to keep several things on my plate at all times, often forgetting to set them all aside and enjoy the day. I love that Peyton sees my weaknesses and helps me take a breath, take a chance, and enjoy life.

As she fumbles with her luggage and oversized purse, I quickly pull my room card from my pocket, swipe it, then throw the door open wide for her to enter. My breath catches as I take in our hotel room. I expected it would be like the tiny rooms on the cruise ships we've shared during trips with our families. I mean, you don't come to Vegas to spend most of your time in the hotel room. Ours, however, is larger than a typical hotel room; it's not quite a suite, but two full-sized beds are separated from a common area with a sofa and chairs. It looks like Peyton went all out in planning this girls' trip.

"I'm setting my timer for 45 minutes," I inform her as I place my makeup bag on the bathroom vanity. "Just a little time to relax and freshen up. We've got a lot of ground to cover on the strip and only three days here."

"Relax," she admonishes, scrolling through social media. "We're not on a schedule. We'll go with the flow and see what we see along the way. If we miss anything, we'll just have to come back at the end of summer."

I fear if she had her way, Peyton and I would travel every weekend. I pull a bottle of water from the mini fridge; the cold beverage washes away the heat of Las Vegas in May.

"Montana!" Peyton's high-pitched voice startles me from across the room. "Do you know how much they charge for water in the minibar?"

I turn, rolling my eyes. She knows that a six-dollar bottle of water is well within my means. I mean, I don't spend money frivolously; when I need something, I can afford it. I pull a second water bottle from the small refrigerator, tossing it onto the bed near my friend.

"What are you doing?" Peyton asks, eyes glued to her phone.

"I'm changing out of my comfy travel clothes into my knock-'em-dead-in-Las-Vegas clothes," I tease.

It's not really a knock-'em-dead outfit, more like a makes-me-feel-cute-and-sexy outfit. I'm pairing a silky, black with white polka dots tank top that hugs tight to my breasts and abdomen with a black miniskirt that ends mid-thigh and high-heeled, black sandals. The heels with the skirt place my long, toned legs in the spotlight. Peyton says my legs are my best asset. To finish the look, I secure my hair in a loose ponytail, with tendrils framing my face.

"How do I look?" I pretend to stroll down a catwalk, posing at the sofa where she sits, phone in hand.

"Holy hotness. You're pulling that out on our first night in town?" Her smile tells me she likes the look.

"I have other head-turning outfits for the next two nights," I inform her.

"How you fit everything into one small suitcase I'll never understand. And no, I don't want you to teach me," she states. "I think I'm wearing peach tonight."

"I love your peach sundress," I remind her. "Time's a-wastin'," I prod, taking away her phone.

She complains but hustles to change. I'm sure, in her mind, the sooner she changes, the sooner she'll have her cell phone back.

Unraveled

The sounds of video-slot machines fill the air as I follow Peyton onto the casino floor, and bright lights flicker as far as the eye can see. Butterflies spread their wings in my belly as my excitement increases. Although I know the general premise of slot machines, I'm not sure on the logistics, and I'm eager to learn.

"Walk slower," I beg Peyton, so I may observe people playing the games. Every few steps, I pause and watch as a person approaches a chair, places cash into a machine, then plays. *I guess it's that simple.*

"Ready to play?" Peyton plops into a high-back, black, leather seat, patting the machine next to her.

I take my seat, pull a twenty-dollar bill from my clutch, then slide it into the slot. The machine registers my money and bright lights flicker into action. I feel giddy; all the stories of people winning on such machines flash through my mind. It's the potential to win that creates the buzz in my veins. I'm a realist, though; I'm aware of the probability of me winning.

"If we win $500, I'll purchase tickets to the Thunder Down Under for us," Peyton giggles as the wheels on her machine spin and lights flash.

Instantly, I know full well if we do to attend, Peyton will make every attempt to become a prop in their performance. While she'd thoroughly enjoy it, I'd be mortified. I take a deep breath, realizing odds are we will not win at slots.

We move from machine to machine, inserting a twenty and cashing out with less than a dollar. When the allure of the bright lights and loud machines eventually wears off, we sidle up to the casino bar for a drink then make our way outside.

"Excuse me." Peyton approaches an older couple on the walkway between our hotel and the MGM. "Would you mind taking some photos of us?"

The wife smiles, nodding. Peyton and I hug tight and smile proudly with the New York, New York hotel skyline behind us. Next, we turn to pose with the Las Vegas Strip lights behind us. We thank the couple, offering to take a photo of them, then continue on.

At street level, near Caesars Palace, Peyton places her hands on both of my shoulders. Facing me, she states, "We're gonna play the fifty states game while we're here."

I lift an eyebrow, having not heard of this game without riding in a car, and looking at license plates.

"Our goal is to take a picture with a person from each of the fifty states." She pulls her phone from her pocket.

This seems like a complicated task, requiring initiated conversations with too many strangers.

"This is our list of the states in alphabetical order," she explains, holding her cell phone for me to see. "When we pose for the picture, we'll signal the number on the list with our hands. Number fifteen is Iowa, so one person will hold up one finger and the other will hold up five. Then, we'll know the photo was number 15 which means Iowa." She smiles proudly. "Then, later, I'll post them on Instagram, so everyone knows how we are progressing in our game."

Will anyone care? I think to myself. Peyton's obsession with social media consumes most of her day. She easily posts ten times more than I do daily.

"It's practice for my career in marketing," she claims.

I've learned over the years that it's easier to give in when she's wanting to take selfies than it is to fight her. That means I have fifty selfies in my future.

"I'll show you how easy it will be to do this." Peyton smiles then scans the surrounding walkway. Her target in sight, she struts towards a group of three guys.

"Go Titans," she says, pointing to the ball cap on the guy in the middle.

The three guys cheer, proud of their team.

"Are you from Tennessee?" she asks in her flirty voice.

"Yep," a dark-haired guy responds.

"My friend and I," she motions for me to join her, "we're playing a game in which we need to take a picture with someone from every state. Can we take a photo with you?"

They comply. Peyton directs me to take the photo, looking at her phone she announces Tennessee is number 42 on our list. She asks the guy on her right to hold up four fingers while she holds up two. I count to three out loud and snap several photos with my phone. Peyton thanks the men, making an excuse for us to move on rather than hang with the three of them for the night.

"One state down forty-nine to go," she smiles, wrapping her arm around mine as we step up onto the escalator that will take us down to the strip below. "Go ask that older couple where they are from," she orders.

I want to protest, but it's futile. Unlike the group she approached, this couple is not wearing anything to clue me in on where they might be from.

"Hi," I greet. "My friend and I are trying to take a picture with someone from all fifty states. Where are you from?"

"We live in Nebraska," the woman announces proudly.

"We're from Iowa," Peyton informs them. "Can we take a quick photo with you?"

The couple agrees, so Peyton poses between them as they hold up fingers for twenty-seven. We chat with them for a bit before continuing our walk.

Peyton's photos impede our progress down the strip. I take a photo now and then of the buildings while she takes photos of desirable men. I take a picture of the two of us in front of the Eiffel Tower at the Paris Hotel. Peyton takes selfies with an Elvis impersonator along with a hot security guard outside of Planet Hollywood.

"Peyton, I'm tired," I complain hours later.

"Just wait," she begs. "I want a selfie of the two of us in front of the fountains, then we'll head back."

"I'll agree to the selfie, but we are taking a cab back to our hotel. It's almost midnight, and that feels like two a.m. to our bodies with the time change."

"We can't take our fifty states photos in a taxi," she whines.

"We took twenty pics; that's enough for our first night," I state, hands on my hips.

She mumbles her complaint then agrees to the cab ride.

2

MONTANA

The next morning

I find myself in a dressing room at a shop near Planet Hollywood as Peyton tosses dress after dress over the door to me. She's on a mission to find me the perfect little black dress. She claims I need a new LBD for clubs tonight. I assure her I packed appropriate attire, but she won't have it.

"I refuse to try this one on," I inform her through the door, tossing the dress back at her. "You know I won't wear a strapless dress." Peyton is aware women constantly tugging up a strapless dress ranks high on my list of pet peeves.

I tilt my head in the full-length mirror, turning this way and that, admiring a simple black halter dress with a flowing skirt that ends mid-thigh.

"I kind of like this halter one," I tell her as I slip it over my head then pull on my own clothes. "I refuse to try on another dress," I state, emerging from the fitting room to find Peyton browsing a nearby rack.

"Where's the dress?"

"What dress?" I ask, walking to her.

"You said you like the halter dress," Peyton reminds me, pointing toward the dressing room. "Go get it. You need to wear it tonight."

"I told you I don't need a new dress; I packed one." I make my way toward the register, hoping she'll follow me to pay for her armful of clothes.

"It never hurts to have a new LBD," she informs me, plopping her shopping spree finds on the counter. "Go grab it, and I'll pay for it."

Unraveled

I love my friend, but sometimes, she's too bossy. "Let me think about it," I defer. "I may find a dress I fall in love with at the next store."

Peyton's distracted by the cash register. The sound of the clerk scanning the tags on her dress, shoes, and handbag is music to her ears; she loves shopping sprees.

After lunch, Peyton stops to play at a roulette table, so I sit at an empty slot machine nearby. The lady at the machine next to mine wishes me good luck as I feed it my money.

"Have you won yet today?" The older, blonde woman asks, pressing the spin button in front of her.

"This is my first gamble of the day," I explain. "My best friend and I spent the morning shopping along the Strip."

"Well, the last two people who sat at your machine lost over $200." Her hand pats my forearm. "It should be ready to hit for you." She crosses her fingers and waves them between us to bring me good luck.

Her smile is infectious. I watch during her next spin as her wide, blue eyes shimmer with the flashing lights in front of her. She rapidly claps her hands and bounces in her seat. She's a ball of energy. The first two rows of her game line up, matching perfectly. Her hands fly to her mouth in anticipation of the third wheel. I can't believe my eyes. She matches all three columns and rows.

"You won!" I cheer from her side.

"I won," she parrots, clapping. "I never win."

Together, we watch as gold coins fall from a pot at the top down to the bottom of the video screen, while simultaneously the amount of money she's won continues to climb in the center. It hits 100 dollars, spins past 200 dollars, and doesn't seem to want to stop.

I notice in small type at the bottom right corner of her machine it says, "Win $4,350." I can't speak, so I point at my discovery.

The woman leaps from her chair, preceding to hop up and down, clapping, eyes glued to her machine until she tugs me from my seat to hop with her. Adrenaline flows through my veins as if I was the winner. It's amazing to witness such a win. She seems like the perfect person to deserve such luck. A casino employee in black pants, a white, long-sleeved shirt, and black vest approaches and congratulates her.

"I must gather some information from you," the employee states, with pen and pad in hand. "Please fill out your name, address, and phone number. I also must see your state issued ID."

The woman takes the pen and notepad then looks to me, bewildered.

"Take a few deep breaths," I suggest, placing my arm around her shoulders.

She nods, breathes, then fills out the information with a trembling hand. A small crowd gathers behind us to witness the magic that is Las Vegas. It's one of the few places you can turn twenty dollars into over four thousand.

The employee informs her she must finish playing the eight dollars she has in the machine and heads to get a check from the cashier, promising to return soon.

We sit quietly, staring at our machines, wide smiles upon our faces.

"My name is Dawn," she informs me between her spins.

"I'm Montana. I can't believe you just won $4300," I giggle.

"I know, right?" She laughs. "My best friend forced me to take a weekend trip. She all but threw me out of my house, promising she'd take care of the kids for me."

"Sounds like your friend knew you needed it. I'm glad you won." I bet another dollar and fifty cents in my machine. "How old are your kids?"

"Oh, I have two adult sons. One is 26, the other 21," Dawn states, turning in her seat to face me and my machine. "I'm also guardian to my sister's six-month-old daughter."

"Sounds like you have your hands full. Your friend must be caring for the baby back home, then? It's nice you have help."

"Iowa's known for being kind and helpful," Dawn informs me.

"I'm from Des Moines, Iowa," I inform her, unable to believe the coincidence.

"No way!" Her voice raises an octave. "I live in Des Moines, too. You wouldn't happen to be single, would you?"

Her eyes widen, and her megawatt smile is hopeful. I wonder if her sons inherited her bubbly personality.

"Well?" she questions when I don't answer.

"Um…" I'm saved from answering when the casino employee returns.

She hands Dawn the check and a copy of the information slip she filled out. I busy myself playing on my slot machine while she instructs Dawn on the taxes for her winnings.

I'm down to three dollars, allowing me two more spins until I need to insert more money or move on to another spot. I press the repeat bet button and watch

Unraveled

my machine spin to life. It emits unfamiliar sounds and purple flashing lights strobe along the sides of the video screen.

"Jackpot!" Dawn squeals near my ear. "You've won a jackpot!"

I look from her back to the video screen. A matching game appears. It instructs me to choose coins until I match three of the same color, then I win the jackpot of that color.

Dawn points to the four jackpot options on the very top of the screen. "The least you will win is $149.22," she points out.

My first choice reveals a green coin; looking up, I see the green jackpot is over 900 dollars. I'd love that. Next, I uncover a red coin with a matching jackpot of $252.98. I'd be ahead if I won that pot. After that, I reveal a blue coin then a green one.

"Choose a green one," Dawn orders as if I control what color I will pick next.

I hover my hand over one coin near the center then move to hover over another coin in the corner.

"Follow your first instinct," Dawn encourages.

I press my finger on the center coin. It's green. *It's green! I just won $915.72!*

Dawn leaps from her seat, wrapping her arms around my neck as I remain seated. "You did it!"

"I can't believe it," I whisper, my breath escaping me.

"I told you this machine was ready to hit," she reminds as she releases me.

We stare in amazement as the video machine continues to announce my win with loud noises and flashing lights. Eventually, it displays my grand total of the jackpot and deposits that amount with my remaining dollar-fifty in the machine.

"It's under $1200, so you can just cash out and redeem a ticket," Dawn informs me.

High on adrenaline, we walk together towards the redemption machine to cash my white slip of paper in for actual money.

"We should get a drink to celebrate," she suggests as I pocket my wad of cash in the front pocket of my shorts.

"Okay," I answer, causing her smile to grow wider.

With drinks in front of us, Dawn turns on her barstool to face me. "You never answered me. Are you single?"

I nod my head. "I don't seem to be as lucky in the dating world as I am at slot machines."

"We should exchange numbers, so we can get together when we're both back in Des Moines," she states.

I know that she really wants my number to set me up with one of her sons. As much as I love this exuberant new friend I've made at the slots, I don't think it would be wise to allow her to set me up on a blind date with her son.

"Let's take a selfie to post our winnings on social media," I suggest. "Crud." I freeze with my hand in my back pocket. "I left my phone in the room."

"Here; use mine," she offers with a smirk before she leans in for the photo.

"I'm posting on Facebook," she shares. "I'm typing 'winner, winner chicken dinner' with it. What's your Facebook name so I can tag you in it?"

This woman never stops. I'm sure she drives her grown sons crazy with her aggressive attempts to set them up. We exchange names, and she tags me on her photos on Facebook and Instagram.

"While your phone's out," I begin, "would you mind taking another picture together? My friend and I are attempting to take a photo with someone from all 50 states. We'd planned to use a selfie of us, but that would be cheating." She nods, and I continue. "If you'll hold up one finger, I'll hold up five since Iowa is number 15 on our list. And, I'll take the selfie." I strain to extend her phone one handed and press to take the photo. I pull my arm back, and we inspect the photo. It looks good with our bright smiles from our big wins.

"While you have my cell, text the photo to yourself." Dawn grins.

I see what she's really up to; she'll have my cell number to use to set me up. As I want a copy of the photo, I text it to my number.

"I should go find Peyton and share my news. What will you do next?"

"I'm heading to Chippendale's tonight," Dawn whispers, blushing. "I have front row tickets."

I shouldn't be surprised, but I am. For a moment, I try to imagine my mom attending such a show with front row seats. I want to bottle up some of Dawn's aura to carry with me.

"Catch ya later," Dawn says as she heads in the opposite direction through the casino from where I need to go.

I can't stop smiling; I'm not sure if it's Dawn or my winnings that cause it, and I don't care. I should ask Peyton to return to the store and buy the halter dress with a portion of today's lucky win; that way, I'll make Peyton happy, too.

My right hand reaches for my cell phone to text her, only to find it's not in my back pocket. Then, I remember; I left it on my bed in the room. I make my way to the elevator bank.

3

MONTANA

Excitement from my win still pulsing in my veins, I press the elevator button, noting the numbers above each door are increasing instead of going down. Normally, I'd pull out my phone to check for emails and look at social media while I wait; I'm surprised I didn't notice it missing earlier.

Eventually, a ping signals the arrival of an elevator car. I enter, pressing floor 12, hoping the doors close before others join me. I hope to avoid the awkwardness that occurs when trapped with someone else; I almost always feel like I should strike up conversation to end the silence. I breathe a sigh of relief when the doors close, and I'm alone.

I round the corner from the elevators, heading down my hallway, hearing loud chatter in an open office. One woman sits behind a large, metal desk as staff in housekeeping uniforms chatter with timecards in their hands. I smile and wave as I continue walking by.

At our room, I scan my keycard, turn the handle, and push the door. KLUNK! It only moves an inch.

Who is in our room? There's not a cleaning cart in the hallway. How did someone get into our hotel room?

Through the crack of the slightly opened door, I speak into the room. "Hello?" With no reply, I try again. "Anyone inside?" Nothing. No noise. "Um, hello? This is my room. Please come unlock the deadbolt." I wait a bit; still, I hear nothing, and no one comes to the door.

I walk back to the open door with staff inside.

"Um, excuse me. The deadbolt has locked me out of my room," I explain.

"That happens sometimes when leaving the room," a manager-type lady states, lifting a walkie talkie to her face. "Give me your room number, and I'll send maintenance to help you."

Great. I wish I had my phone to entertain myself while I wait.

Carson

As I step from the elevator car, I adjust the bill of my ball cap atop my head. I keep the bill low while on the casino floor so others might not recognize me. Now, on my floor, I adjust it.

I'm walking to my room, because I need a break from the guys. I love them, would do anything for them, but all of us together, letting loose... They get to be too much for me.

I can't wait to crash in my hotel room, throw back a few beers, and try to write some lyrics. It's time I remedy the emptiness of my notebook, for far too long now the blank pages haunt me. I hope a few hours of alone time will spark some creativity.

We record our next album in seven days, and I have yet to write a single lyric. My writer's block has resisted for over a year now. I should lock myself in my room, order room service, and write non-stop for the next forty-eight hours. If only it were that easy, but I can't force the creativity.

Thoughts on my empty notebook, I cut the corner, walking close to the wall. *Crap!* I stumble to the left.

"Oh, I'm sorry." I continue down the hallway, my mind racing. *Why is she sitting on the hall floor?* I slow my strides. *Is she hurt? Locked out?* I turn and hesitantly approach the woman sitting against the wall across from a closed hotel door.

"Um... Are you locked out of your room?" I ask.

"Yes..." her small voice answers.

"I'll walk with you to the front desk to get a new keycard," I offer.

"Thanks," she smiles sweetly.

Holy cow, the girl has dimples.

"That won't help; it's the deadbolt. It locked when housekeeping left our room.

They called maintenance for me, so I'm just waiting." She quirks her mouth at one corner.

"Would you like company?" When she shrugs, I slide my back down the wall to sit near her. "How long have you been waiting?"

"Not long, maybe ten minutes," she shares. "I left my phone in the room, so..." She stares at her empty hands and wrists in front of her. "They have weird deadbolts here. I've never seen a metal bar stick out with a metal flap as a deadbolt before. I guess that metal plate can move without really being touched.

"I wondered what that protrusion was. I've nearly hit my head on it twice already," I chuckle. "I think I'm gonna get a beer from my room; can I bring one for you?"

There's her smile again, and I can't pull my eyes from the dimple on her cheek. *What is it about dimples?*

"Sure," she agrees. "I can walk with you."

"You'd better stay here," I offer, rising to my feet. "I'd hate for you to miss the maintenance person."

I mentally urge myself to saunter toward my room, sure her eyes are on me; I can't let her see I want to hurry back to my spot on the floor beside her. In my hotel room, I snag the six-pack and bottle opener from my mini fridge. Then, I try to keep my cool as I walk towards her.

"Just how long do you think we must wait out here?" she laughs at the six-pack in my hand.

"I'm always prepared," I reply, with as much charm as I can. "When did you get to Vegas?"

"Yesterday," she answers. "And you?"

"I've been here a few days now," I answer, suddenly realizing I haven't asked for her name. "I'm Carson," I say as I extend an open beer bottle.

"Oh, I'm... um..." she stammers a bit. "I'm Montana."

"Nice to meet you." I clink the neck of my bottle with hers. Suddenly, I can't think of anything to talk about. "I know what we can do."

"What?"

"Let's play the name game," I suggest nervously. "What you do is name a celebrity with my name, and I'll do the same with yours. First one that can't think of a name loses. I'll go first. Hannah Montana," I begin.

"Ah, I see; you have a secret Miley Cyrus crush?" she teases me.

"No, I don't. It's your turn," I urge.

"Carson Daly," she rattles off, pride upon her face.

"Joe Montana," I counter.

Next, she answers, "Johnny Carson."

Think. Think. C'mon, you can do this. Montana. Montana...

"Ready to accept defeat?" she jeers.

I notice we've both sped through our first drink, so I open a second beer, stalling for time. "You win." I pass her the open bottle and grab another for myself.

We continue to chat as minutes pass, and I lose all track of time.

"Are you here on business or pleasure?" she inquires.

"I'm here with a group of guys," I hedge, not knowing how much I should divulge. "We're blowing off some steam before we get back to work. How about you?"

4

MONTANA

"I'm here with my best friend, celebrating the end of our sophomore year of college," I share.

As we chat, I attempt to check him out without letting him know I'm doing so. *Why would such a cute guy sit on the hallway floor with me, considering all that Las Vegas offers?*

His deep, dark blue jeans are worn white and thin at the middle of his muscular thighs and each knee. My eyes want to stare at his biceps, tight beneath his black t-shirt, when they flex as he constantly adjusts his ball cap. There's something about him... Maybe it's his deep-set, brown eyes or dark scruff on his jaw. *Why does he look so familiar?*

"What type of work do you do?" I ask, attempting to keep our conversation flowing.

A crooked grin slides upon his mouth. "I'm a musician."

I tap my index finger on my lower lip. It's on the tip of my tongue. I feel it coming any second, and I'll remember. "No way!" Heat crawls up my neck and cheeks. "You're..." I fan my overheated face. "You're..." I attempt to quell the clog in my throat. "You're Carson Cavanaugh."

I turn to face him, my legs folded yoga-style between us, my beer bottles on the floor beside me.

He peers down both sides of the hall before his brown eyes crinkle at the side, and his tongue darts out to swipe his plump, lower lip. The motion temporarily stuns me.

"I knew you looked familiar! A musician... Phish! Yeah, you are a musician, a freaking talented and well-known musician," I babble.

Of all the hotels in Las Vegas, of all the floors in this hotel, Carson Cavanaugh's room is just down the hall from ours.

"Shouldn't you have a suite high in a tower somewhere?"

"Nah." He's suddenly enthralled with watching his fingers tear the label from his brown beer bottle. "We've been on a tour bus, crammed in like sardines; I need my space. The guys have their suite, but I like to get my own room to get away." His eyes peer up to me through his long, dark lashes. "Eighteen months on tour is plenty of time together."

"I bet. Even my best friend Peyton and I would not last on a bus for a year and a half," I agree.

"Well, we're here for five days before we head into the studio to record our next album," he shares.

"I bet it's hard to be incognito here."

"Cat's out of the bag now." He removes his ball cap and combs his fingers through his dark brown hair that falls to his jawline. "When the four of us are together, it's hard. On my own, I can usually make it through most of the day with no one recognizing me."

I try to suppress my growing excitement. "I'm sitting in a hotel hallway with one of the greatest lead guitarists on the planet." I shake my head at my lame attempt to play it cool.

"Nah," he argues.

"You know darn well *Communicable* is one of the hottest rock bands, and you know your fingers work those strings as many only wish they could."

"So, I take it you're a fan?" He smiles, stunning me for a moment.

"Maybe just a bit," I tease.

"Just a bit?" he counters. "Tell me, who's your favorite band, then."

I smile as I try to come up with a list to impress *the* Carson Cavanaugh. "As I'm an Iowa girl, I'm partial to ZipTie."

"Of course," he parrots.

"Then, Seether, Five Finger Death Punch, Nirvana, and Communicable."

His smirk tells me he's impressed by my rock knowledge. I'm sure, because he's famous, women pretend to be fans when they aren't. *Wow. I still can't believe I am sitting here drinking Carson Cavanaugh's beer.*

Carson

She's too good to be true. Her sexy dimples lure me closer; her conversation keeps me entertained, and her genuine love of music seals the deal. I definitely need to spend time with this goddess.

Words flow. Word after word flows through my mind.

> *ball of yarn, unbinds me, laughter crumbles my walls,*
> *come undone, unravel me, you're the only one*

Lyrics are back; she's cured my writer's block.

She nudges my shoulder, drawing me from the song forming in my head. A man in a work shirt and dark pants pushes his cart towards us. The front right wheel squeaks and shakes erratically.

"Thanks for coming," Montana greets politely. "I'm not sure how this happened."

"It happens from time to time," the man's gravelly voice responds. "We've even created this handy-dandy metal tool to unlock it with."

We stand, watching as he feeds a two-foot long strip of metal through the barely opened hotel door. He grumbles as he inserts it over and over toward the top of the door and attempts to slide it down to catch the metal flap. We hear a pop then the sound of a piece of metal hitting the tile floor below followed by his murmured curses.

The maintenance man rummages through each shelf of his cart. "I thought I had a spare here somewhere." He unclips the radio from his hip pocket and calls to a man on the other end for help. "He'll be here soon." And with that, he leaves us to wait in the hallway again.

"Take a seat," I encourage, as my back slides down the wall.

"Do you think it'll be another half-hour?" she asks, resigning herself to sit on the floor again.

"Tired of my company?" I tease.

"More like I'm tired of my bottom falling asleep." She wiggles and shifts into a comfortable position.

Much to my dismay, a maintenance person quickly approaches. He slips a metal piece through the door crack, pulls it back fast, and poof! The door swings open.

Montana

Still unbelieving, I search around our room, ensuring nothing is missing. I slide my cell phone into my back pocket, grab my debit card from my purse, and tuck it into my front pocket. I glance at the metal plate of the lock as I exit the room. Surely, it won't happen a second time.

"Oh, um…" I sputter, startled by the man standing in the hallway near my door. It's Carson. "What are you doing out here?" I look down the hall in both directions.

"I thought I should wait for you, so you wouldn't be walking alone." His mouth quirks up at one side.

His smile warms my belly. He's too damn sexy.

"I'm a big girl," I state as we move toward the elevators.

"I know," he responds. "I wouldn't want my sister walking alone through this large hotel or the casino, though."

"You shouldn't have," I argue.

"I wanted to," he informs, peering into my eyes while we wait on an elevator.

I search first his eyes then his face in its entirety. It seems he's not bluffing. *I can't believe Carson Cavanaugh of Communicable wants to spend time with me.*

While the elevator lowers floor by floor, I attempt to be discrete as I make sure I'm ready for a night in Las Vegas. My black, scoop-neck t-shirt remains wrinkle-free. With my left hand, I tuck it in on the side, allowing the rest to remain untucked and casual. I'm wearing my favorite white shorts with black platform sandals.

Peyton often rants at how muscular and long my legs look in these shoes. I glanced at my hair while in my room, unaware Carson waited for me mere feet away. I'm sure I pale in comparison to the Barbie-like beauties that congregate around him. *Oh well. No one knows me here, and I'll never see him again. I should make the best of it.*

5

MONTANA

Stepping from the elevator, Carson motions for me to walk toward the casino floor. His palm rests upon my lower back, just above my bottom; his heat nearly brands me.

"I should find Peyton near the tables," I explain.

"What?" He inquires, turning to face me.

The loud bells, whistles, and conversations of the casino surround us. In my heels, I don't have to stretch to speak near his ear.

"I need to find Peyton at the table games," I repeat, louder this time.

He nods, offering me his hand. Hand in his, he leads me through the slot machines. I'm awarded the opportunity to admire his tastefully snug jeans. *Oh, what an ass this man has.* His biker boots pound heavy on the floor while we cut our way through the busy casino as it comes to life for the evening.

When I bumped into him in the hallway as I left my room, I noticed he'd changed into a heather-gray, V-neck t-shirt with a navy and gray-plaid, button-down shirt over it. The buttons remain undone, and his sleeves are rolled up, allowing a hint of his forearms. They are tanned with a faint smattering of brown hair. He pauses abruptly, allowing me to admire the day's scruff highlighting his powerful jaw. The thought of the stubble scraping my most intimate parts creates the need to rub my thighs together.

"I'm texting the guys to meet us at the craps table," he informs before turning his eyes down to his phone screen. "Now, let's go find your friend."

Following behind him once more, I wonder if I am ready for him to meet

Peyton, or better yet, for us to meet his band. I quicken my pace at Carson's side as we approach Peyton and her table. I wiggle my fingers a little, trying not to mess with any luck she might have. She waves me over then freezes, a wide smile upon her face at the sight of the Adonis walking beside me. She promptly cashes out her money.

"Who do we have here?" Peyton's wide eyes match her wide smile.

"Um..." I falter, not knowing if he wants me to introduce him or let him remain anonymous.

He extends his right arm. "I'm Carson." He pours on the charm, complete with his sexy smile. "You must be Peyton."

My wide-eyed friend looks to me, waggling her eyebrows; as he's standing beside me, he sees it all.

"So," she moves her index finger between Carson and me, "the two of you know each other how?"

We look at each other. "It's kind of a funny story," I begin. "I left my phone in our room, so I went up to grab it. Our deadbolt locked itself, and I waited in the hallway for someone to come unlock it."

"I nearly stepped on her. She was sitting on the floor near the wall, and I wasn't watching where I was going." He shrugs as if this thing happens all the time.

"So, you bumped into each other?" she inquires, not impressed with our chance meeting.

I smile, knowing my friend is about to owe me favors for the rest of her life; she'll flip when she learns who Carson is and that his band is joining us. Although she's not the metal head I am, she doesn't complain when I play their songs or attend concerts. Hanging around famous rockers tonight will cause her to lose her mind.

"Well, well, well, what do we have here?" A lanky guy in kelly green skinny jeans and a white Magnum P.I. shirt approaches Carson. "Where did you find two such lovely ladies?" he sing-songs.

"Eli, this is Montana and her best friend, Peyton." Carson pats his band mate on the back. "Ladies, this is Eli Patrick."

Eli looks like Shaggy from *Scooby Doo* with Paul Walker's blue eyes. His arms sport chorded muscles from years of banging his drum kit. Long, curly, light brown hair framing his face and deep dimples in his cheeks when he smiles in my direction only up his adorable factor.

I wave. Noticing the rest of the band a few feet behind him, I raise my chin, signaling for Carson to turn around.

"The party can officially start now," the lead singer announces, throwing an arm over Eli and Carson's shoulders.

I pay no attention to Carson as he makes introductions. I know each member from TV award shows and entertainment sites.

Warner Bradshaw, the bad-boy lead singer, wears black from head to toe. His skin-tight jeans, boots, and V-neck t-shirt are his trademark attire. A thick, gold chain around his neck draws my eyes toward the dark chest hair peeking out. I've often thought of him as a Jason Momoa look-alike. Although he's not as bulky in stature, his long, highlighted hair and large forehead resemble the star. His look is never complete without his tousled brown waves touching his shoulders, the mirrored shades, whether inside or out, and a sucker in his mouth. Gossip sites claim the sucker is always red and cherry flavored, as it has something to do with his childhood. It's not something I gave much thought to until now. *I mean, what grown man enjoys suckers in public?*

Flanking him is the quietest member of the band with the infamous, smoldering stare. Jake Johnson, the bass player, gives off powerful don't-engage-with-me vibes. I'm surprised as his looks are even more potent in person. His bright blue eyes are like Eli's. It states in his bio that his eyes are blue; I know that for sure. They've never looked this blue through a camera; maybe he wears contacts to cause a more dramatic contrast. His dark complexion and sandy, blonde hair might make you think of a surfer if he wasn't so stoic. He's not overweight but not as skinny as Warner and Eli. He is a big guy that works out, as if he needed to look even more intimidating.

"You did good," Peyton murmurs near my ear, drawing me back to the group conversation. "I call dibs on the guy in black."

I open my mouth to inform her there are two men dressed in black, but her knowing smirk and wink tell me she's claiming both of them. This should be an entertaining night.

6

CARSON

After introductions, Warner demands we hang at the MGM Grand before we do anything else. He's the stereotypical diva that goes with being a lead singer; he must always get his way. He promised some drunk millionaire last night that he'd return to play poker tonight, so we head across the street.

Montana and I hang to the back of the group while her friend seems at home, entertaining the rest of the guys.

"We'll give him an hour or two tops," I promise. "And, we don't have to stay with him at the poker table. There's plenty to do and see in the MGM."

She nods. "Would you mind taking a photo with me with the Las Vegas strip behind us?"

"Jake," I holler to the rest of the group, walking across the pedestrian bridge, "the girls need a pic."

Peyton bounces to Montana's side. They murmur for a moment before Peyton backs up, camera ready to take a photo. I wrap my arm around Montana's shoulders, pulling her tight to me as Vegas sprawls out behind us. Eli stands behind Peyton, teasing us, trying to crack us up as Peyton attempts to take the typical Vegas picture. She snaps several, and when she lowers her phone, Eli orders all of us to pose with the girls.

"Excuse me." Eli approaches a young couple. "Would you mind taking a couple of photos of us?"

I fear this couple may figure out who we are and post to social media, then, crowds of fans and paparazzi will swarm us all night. The female instructs us to squeeze together before she snaps photos with Eli's phone. When thanked, they continue on their way without incident.

"I'll wait until later tonight to post it," Eli tells me as we resume our walk toward MGM.

Our band manager ordered us to post on all of our social media platforms each day during our stay. Everything we do advertises our band; she's spreading the news about our new album every chance she gets. Fans know we are in Vegas; several seem to find us each night, but for the most part, they leave us alone.

As we enter the hotel, I lean toward Montana. "Why'd you hold up five fingers in our photo?"

She proceeds to tell me about their 50 states challenge, and the five represents California as the fifth state on her list. Interesting. It sounds like a fun game to play in one of the busiest cities in the world. Since she didn't ask, I assume, as a true fan of Communicable, she knows from my bio that I live in California.

At the edge of the casino, we split into two groups. Warner and Jake head for the high-limit poker tables while the rest of us venture further into the casino.

"What shall we play first?" Eli asks the girls.

"Crap!" Montana blurts, turning to face Peyton. "I forgot I was coming to tell you something when I realized I left my phone in the room." She scans the casino, pointing to a bar near one edge. "Let's go in there; we'll order a drink, and I'll tell you."

I'm anxious to hear what she has to say. I wonder if it's something she told me in the hotel hallway. I doubt that it is; nothing stands out as something she'd need to tell Peyton.

The ladies climb to sit at a high-top table with Eli's assistance while I place a drink order at the bar. As soon as my ass hits the chair, she begins.

"I won $950 at slots today," she cheers, clapping her hands in front of her chest.

"Uh-huh," Peyton responds, her eyebrows raised and mouth open.

"I did. Here, I'll prove it."

Our drinks arrive, but we do not drink. We all watch as Montana opens her phone and searches for a photo. She scrolls through Instagram and pauses on a post of her holding her voucher of over $900. She reads the comments and hashtags a woman named Dawn posted.

"I didn't have my phone, so the lady next to me took the photo and tagged me. She won more than I did. Oh, and she's from Des Moines. Can you believe that?" With a few more swipes, she displays a photo in her text messages, marking Iowa off of their state game.

We pass her phone around, witnessing the amount on the machine and the celebration photo afterwards. Sure enough, she won nearly a thousand dollars.

"I can't believe you." Peyton pushes Montana's shoulder. "You always win. She's the luckiest person in the world." With her drink near her lips, she adds, "I mean she met you in a hotel hallway; she has to be lucky."

I smile at Montana, her eyes move to mine across the small, square table. She doesn't deny her friend's statement. She simply shrugs.

"The lady's name is Dawn; she's so sweet and perky. She's..." Montana searches for words. "She's sunshine, and she's contagious. She even tricked me into giving her my phone number to set me up with one of her single sons."

"Did you give it to her?" The words leave my mouth before I can stop them. *Way to play it cool, dummy.*

"She texted me our Iowa photo, so yes, she has my number. I'll just evade her attempts at setting me up on a blind date like I do my mom's."

Her eyes remain on me as she answers. *Play it cool. Play it cool. Don't let her know jealousy filled you at just the thought of her dating another guy.*

"Drinks are on you tonight," Peyton informs her friend.

"No," Eli and I state in unison, causing the girls to laugh.

"Chivalry is not dead," Peyton says. "Hey, give me your phone; I want to see that post again."

Peyton looks at Montana's winning photo, taps her finger once then scrolls several times. I can't help but wonder what she's up to. Suddenly, she stops scrolling, her eyes widen, and her jaw drops. She slides the cell phone across the table to Montana.

"I think you should reconsider letting her set you up with her sons. They. Are. Hot." Peyton points at the screen in Montana's hand. "It doesn't matter which one she sets you up with; they're all mega hot. Tell her you want to make it a double date. I want one of them." Peyton waggles her eyebrows, and Montana swats at her.

An anvil sits in the bottom of my stomach; I force myself to inhale a long, slow breath. *Why am I so bothered by a woman I just met being set up with another guy?* It's irrational, but I can't control the jealousy I feel.

7

CARSON

A commotion in the far corner of the bar draws my attention. A DJ sets up his gear, preparing to entertain the growing crowd. The overhead music pauses for a moment, then the DJ starts his first song. It's no surprise it's country; the decor of the entire place screams wood, cowboy, and country. Patrons around the bar begin moving to the music and singing along.

"The two of you should feel right at home," Eli states, pointing towards the DJ booth.

"Not everyone in Iowa farms and loves country music," Peyton snaps, clearly offended by his assumption.

"What's the line in The Beach Boys' Song?" Eli presses his luck. "Midwest farmers'..."

"Finish that statement and I'll demonstrate a city girl, kicking your ass." Peyton raises one perfectly shaped eyebrow in challenge.

Montana bites her lips, trying not to laugh.

"I'm sorry," Eli lies. "I didn't mean to tease you."

Eli loves to tease everyone. The more you demonstrate it bothers you, the more he teases.

"We do go to Beer Can Alley sometimes with friends, but country is not our jam," Peyton informs us.

"What is your jam?" Eli smirks at me before returning his gaze to Peyton.

"Pink, Avril Levine, and Maroon 5," Peyton answers proudly.

Eli raises an eyebrow at me. I gesture in Montana's direction, urging him to ask her.

She holds her palm in front of his face. "I've already been interrogated and passed with flying colors." She lowers her hand, smiling at me.

Eli's brow furrows as he tries to understand what she means.

Peyton rescues him. "She's a metal head. She loves alt rock, metal, grunge, and vintage. She drags me to concerts with her. After the last ZipTie concert, it took three days before my ears stopped ringing."

"I approve," Eli says to Montana then looks at me.

"I love this song," Peyton states, and Montana nods. "They play it on pop stations, too."

"So, you do listen to country," Eli states, smirking.

"You can't totally escape the genre when you live in Iowa," Montana explains. "We know the most popular country songs. Heck, we've even performed dance routines to them."

Dance routines? There's a new tidbit of knowledge.

"Tell me more," Eli prompts, leaning his chin on his hands, elbows on the table.

"We won the talent show at the Iowa State Fair when we were 17," Peyton brags while Montana gives her a death stare. "It's a huge accomplishment. The Iowa State Fair is a big deal; it's considered one of the best in the United States."

"So, the two of you," Eli seeks clarification, pointing between them, "did a dance routine on stage at the state fair?"

"I'll tell you everything, but you have to pinky-promise you won't tease us about it." Montana looks from me to Eli and back.

"Pinky-promise?" Eli furrows his brow.

Montana extends her pinky across the table to me as Peyton does the same toward Eli.

"Wrap your pinky with mine," Peyton instructs. "Now, promise you won't tease us."

Eli and I promise, trying to refrain from laughter. It's my first pinky-promise, and I want to keep it for Montana.

"We took lessons at the same dance studio for years. We entered the talent show twice in the under 18 category." Montana's eyes remain on her hands on the table in front of her as she continues. "When we were 17, our routine was a clogging dance to the Charlie Daniels Band hit *The Devil Went Down to Georgia*."

She takes a sip of her beer. "During rehearsals, those in charge decided our act would be more appropriate in the adult category. At the time, we didn't think that was fair, but we went ahead with it." She lifts her eyes to mine. "We were so good, we won."

"She's down playing it," Peyton states. "We were on fire, and the crowd absolutely loved us."

I squint my eyes, searching Montana's face for clues. She doesn't seem overly proud of it like Peyton. Maybe she's embarrassed; I can't quite read her.

"What were your costumes?" Eli seeks more details.

"We wore cut-off jean shorts, cowboy boots, a red and white checked shirt that tied at our waist, and cowboy hats." Peyton raises one eyebrow at Eli, daring him to comment.

"They weren't Daisy Dukes. My mom made sure the shorts weren't too short and that our bellies were covered," Montana clarifies.

"In my mind, they will be Daisy Dukes and a midriff top," Eli informs the ladies.

"You pinky-promised not to tease," Montana reminds him.

Eli mimics zipping his lips and throwing a key over his shoulder.

"So, the two of you must be excellent dancers," I mention. "What forms of dance can you do?"

"We took tap, jazz, and hip-hop classes," Peyton answers. "We also know how to two-step and line dance."

I nod. I'm such a moron; all I can do is nod. Words escape me. My mind's too busy imagining Montana dancing with me.

"Show us," Eli orders, pointing to the dance floor where a few couples are.

"Um," Montana hedges, "it's hard to dance to country in high-heeled sandals." She shrugs apologetically.

Eli purses his lips.

"We can show you a video of our performance." When Peyton suggests this, Montana freezes.

Eli and I lean our heads together to watch a short clip of their state fair performance. They weren't just good; they were awesome. They worked the crowd while moving in perfect unison. I pass the phone back to Peyton.

"I need to tinkle," Peyton blurts, climbing down from her stool.

Montana joins her without a word. *Why do girls do this? What's so special about joining each other in the restroom?* My parents have told me a million times not to try to understand the mysteries of women. Just accept it and go with it.

With the women out of ear shot, Eli leans closer to me. "I gotta see them dance."

I agree whole-heartedly. Everything about Montana intrigues me. I want to see it all and learn everything about her.

"I'll be back in a minute," Eli says, leaving me alone at the table.

I signal the waitress for another round of drinks then stare off into the distance, my thoughts on Montana.

Eli returns with shopping bags before the girls get back from the bathroom.

"What's in the bags?" I ask, then think better of it. Knowing Eli, I may not want to know.

"I told you I've got to see them dance," Eli reminds me. "Since sandals won't work…" His hand emerges from a shopping bag with new cowboy boots, or more correctly, cowgirl boots. "Now, they'll have no excuse. We'll request the Charlie Daniels Band then sit back and enjoy."

Eli's face shows he's proud of himself. I hope the ladies don't beat him to death with the boots. Speaking of the girls, they emerge from the restroom, crossing the bar towards us.

Carson

Sliding back onto her barstool, Montana thanks us for ordering another round, noting glasses of water are now on our table.

"What's in the bags?" Peyton asks, eyes glued to the large bags at Eli's feet.

He dips his hands into one oversized sack, handing red cowboy boots to Peyton. From the other bag, he passes brown boots with jade embellishments to Montana.

"Did I guess the right size?" he inquires.

Montana nods, and Peyton speaks, "How'd you know our shoe sizes?" Her nose crinkles and brow furrows.

"I'm not a stalker and don't have a foot fetish," he vows. "I've got small feet for a guy, so I often compare mine to women's. I figured Montana's feet were my size, and Peyton, yours look a little smaller. It's one of my many gifts," he brags.

"So, why did you buy us boots?" Montana inquires, her head tilted to one side, eyes like lasers on Eli.

"I dare you to perform your state fair winning routine," he smirks back at her. "You mentioned you can't dance in the sandals, so I found you boots."

Montana shakes her head. "You didn't just find us boots; you bought us boots. And, I can tell these are expensive, too."

"Don't mind her," Peyton urges, patting Eli's arm. "I absolutely love them."

"So, you'll dance?" He asks, face lighting up with the possibility.

"Um…" Montana hops back into the conversation. "New boots give blisters, especially without socks,"

Clearly, she has no intention of dancing for Eli.

"Ah…" he quickly responds, pulling another item from the bag. "I have socks." He waggles his eyebrows at each of them. "I dare you to dance. Do you accept my challenge?"

Peyton immediately nods her head. She folds her hands together and flutters her blonde eyelashes at Montana with pouty, pink-painted lips.

Arms crossed over her chest, she slowly shakes her head, a wide, closed-mouth smile growing on her face. I stare as her dimples slowly form in her cheeks.

"I'll need two shots." She holds her two fingers towards Eli's face. "And, time to get ready," she concedes.

Eli and Peyton practically float to the ceiling in their excitement. I smile, anxious to watch Montana move.

Eli is quick to fetch two rounds of shots. After the four of us take the first tequila shot, chasing it with lime, Eli disappears. Through the dark bar, I see his silhouette at the DJ stand. He's a man on a mission.

Peyton and Montana exit their barstools, Peyton snags one of the bags, and they return to the ladies' room with boots in their arms.

I'm alone for only a moment before Warner and Jake show up.

"Drinking heavy tonight?" Warner teases, slapping me on the back, harder than necessary.

"You can thank me now," Eli gloats in a raised voice, returning to the table. "Montana and Peyton are performing a dance for us in a couple of minutes."

Warner thanks him, wrapping his arm around his shoulders. Jake's blue eyes squint in my direction. I've often thought of him as an empath. As if his thoughts aren't enough to brood over, he takes on all of ours, too. I try to let him know I'm okay with Eli's plan.

Eli catches the others up on what we've learned about the girls, that they won the adult dance competition at the Iowa State Fair. He brags that we saw a short clip, and it was hot.

"Eli," I interrupt, "you did hear them say they were seventeen in the video, right? That's jailbait."

"Please tell me they're eighteen now," Warner groans.

"They just finished their sophomore year of college," I inform the group.

Based on Warner's relief at my answer, I assume he has plans for Peyton.

Montana

"I'm gonna kill you for this," I hiss toward Peyton.

Her reflection smiles back at me apologetically. I turn around, lean on the bathroom sink, and remove my sandals. I must admit my feet will be relieved to be out of my heels. I pull on one long black sock, then the gorgeous jade embellished boot. Eli certainly spared no expense and has fabulous taste. The chocolate ostrich contrasts beautifully with the jade tones. I tuck the sock a bit lower on my calf, so it's not visible before repeating the process on my right foot.

"It's like Eli knows me. I mean *really* knows me," Peyton declares. "These red booties are perfect. They're soft, maybe calfskin. I mean I'd buy something like them. Wouldn't I?"

I nod even though I know her boots are way over her price range. I can't believe Eli bought two pairs of expensive boots on a whim. I hope he gets his money's worth watching us. I shudder; I hope he doesn't get his rocks off on this. That would be too creepy.

"Ready?" Peyton asks me.

"No," I state honestly.

"C'mon," she tugs on my arm. "Can you believe we're hanging out with a famous rock band?"

We giggle. She's right; we're here to have fun, and so far, tonight has been more than fun.

Reentering the bar, I halt, and Peyton does, too. Warner and Jake are at our table. I don't want to go over there with the entire band present. Leaning towards her ear, I tell Peyton to go borrow a hat. I stride toward the bar.

"What can I get you?" the bartender greets while drying a glass.

"I realize this goes against cowboy code, but could I borrow your Stetson for a bit?"

Clearly, it's the last thing he expected to come from my mouth. His dark eyes assess me for a moment.

"I'll be the only one to wear it. And trust me, you'll be glad you loaned it to me."

With that encouragement, he places his hand on the top and transfers his black cowboy hat onto my head.

I turn on my boot heel, throw a little wave toward the band's table, and make my way to the DJ booth.

"You must be the dancer," he yells over the music. I assume Eli's already talked to him. "I'll put your song on after this one." I nod then search the suddenly crowded bar for Peyton.

When she seems to apparate by my side, I jump. She tips the bill of her hat to the guys occupying our table; Peyton's always performing, flirting, and working the room. I only turn my performance on for one song then flip back to the real me. The current song fades, and I pull Peyton with me to the center of the dance floor.

"Hey, ya'll," the DJ draws out in a fake country twang. "We are in for a unique surprise tonight. A dude approached me moments ago, telling me about a dare he issued to the two pretty ladies currently standing in the center of the dance floor."

A small spotlight focuses on the two of us while a few other dancers quickly exit the dance floor.

"These are Iowa girls, and they won the Iowa State Fair talent show. They will be sharing that performance with us tonight."

The patrons clap and cheer loudly; the air crackles with their excitement. I nod to the DJ, and we assume our first pose to catcalls and whistles.

8

CARSON

I grind my teeth, watching Montana lean towards the male bartender to chat. When he places his hat on her head, I feel my hackles rise. *I only met her hours ago. How can I feel this strongly for her? What is it about this woman that calls to every part of me?* I feel protective of her; I feel close to her. I feel like we're a couple—she's mine.

Taking a pull of my beer, I return to the present. The two girls stand in the center of the otherwise empty dance floor. The DJ stops talking as the song begins. As a guitarist, I can admit Daniels is a genius with the fiddle in his hands.

Montana smiles non-stop, her hands on her hips, her thighs and calves flexing with her movements. The sound of their boots on the wooden floor adds to the percussion. They're not really clogging or tap dancing as I expected. It's a routine to a country song with an occasional boot stomp.

They dance in unison until the lyrics reach the part that the bet is made. Now, Montana performs steps, challenging Peyton to keep up. They feed off of each other and the crowd's enthusiasm. While their steps grow faster and more complicated, their smiles never waiver. They command the stage, drawing every eye to them.

They end, bottoms leaning into each other, backs arched provocatively, with heads against each other and cowboy hats spinning on their index fingers.

The ladies bow as the gathered crowd awards them vocally and applauds. Peyton raises her palm, and Montana gives her a high five; then, the girls leave the dance floor. My eyes follow Montana as she heads for the bar. She leans over the bar top. The male bartender is more than eager to lean towards her. She removes the borrowed hat, placing it on top of his head. Before she pulls away, he places a kiss on her cheek.

I growl. It's a real, feral growl, and I'm grateful country music blares through the space to cover my reaction.

Montana

I can't wash the huge smile from my face, and there's an extra swing in my hips as I walk towards the band's table. Peyton's already there. Everyone's attention is glued on her, except Carson's. His eyes scan me head-to-toe multiple times as I approach.

He extends a fresh beer to me. When I grasp it, he pulls me tight to his side before I can take a sip.

"I owe Eli huge for talking the two of you into dancing," he murmurs huskily near my ear. There's a sexy smirk upon his face; when his tongue darts out to wet his lower lip, heat floods my belly. "I should have recorded it to watch over and over again."

I playfully tap his forehead. "Guess you'll have to rely on your spank-bank material up here." I look up at him through my lashes. His whiskey-brown eyes turn liquid.

The rest of the band turns their attention on us. Eli wraps his arm around my shoulders. "You didn't disappoint."

"Oh, we never disappoint in anything we do," Peyton claims, her eyes moving to Warner.

She's definitely pulling out all of the stops to make Warner aware she's up for anything. She seems to flirt with Jake almost as much as she does Warner. I pray she doesn't start a fight.

Carson

After hearing my bandmates mention hunger a couple of times, I text our band manager, Meredith, to see what she has set up for dinner.

Immediately, she responds, saying reservations are set for eight p.m. at Nobu in Caesars, and the limo is currently waiting outside the casino.

As the ladies climb in the black, stretch Hummer, the guys comment as they always do to the women they meet.

"Enough," I admonish them. "Remember your manners; Montana and Peyton are not groupies."

Testosterone rises within me, and I'm a little scared. *Why me? How can I have such strong feelings in so little time?*

Sensing my affections towards Montana, my band mates start to tease me.

Peyton sits between Jake and Warner toward the front. Montana sits between Jake and Eli. When I motion for Eli to move, he refuses. Just like in the cartoons, steam fills my head. I decide to sit on Eli's lap, knowing soon enough he will move over. My bottom only on his thighs, I don't lean back, and can't get comfortable. I look beside me to find Montana biting her lips at our antics.

"I think something's popping up," Eli declares.

I hop from his lap, banging my head on the ceiling. "Move," I demand. I'm not sure if it's my tone or my face that causes him to move. But when he does, I take a seat next to Montana.

Montana

"Stay here I'll be right back," Carson directs before walking to the hostess stand.

I note Carson stands close and addresses a woman holding an open iPad in front of her. In her navy pencil skirt, white silk blouse, and stiletto heels, she puts off an "I'm important" vibe to those around her. Her dark bra shows through her thin blouse with its top two buttons undone.

While he speaks to her, glancing at the screen, his hands remain in his front jeans pockets. Carson remains at the hostess station as the woman approaches our group. I look to the rest of the band, trying to judge their reaction to her.

"They've made the private room available," she speaks to the remaining three band members without acknowledging Peyton or me. "Join Carson, and they will take you to your table."

I waste no time grasping Peyton's hand and walking toward Carson. Behind me, I can faintly hear the conversation continue.

"Carson's in charge tonight. I have a meeting I can't miss." Her female voice is stern. "Let's not have a repeat of last night."

"Our table's ready," Carson announces upon my arrival at his side. "Guys, c'mon." He signals, swinging his arm.

We follow a gentleman in his mid-thirties toward the rear of the restaurant. I struggle to follow Carson through the dimly lit environment, so I grab the hem of his shirt with one hand. We're led to a private room through ornate sliding doors. In the center of the floor is a large table sitting two feet off the floor, surrounded by pillows. The thought of the band sitting on these pillows causes me to smile. This might be fun.

"May I take your drink orders while you look at the menu?" the host asks.

Warner wastes no time. "Two bottles of top-shelf vodka, a bottle of your best red wine, and a bottle of Jack Daniels."

Mentally, I attempt to figure if we really need that much alcohol. I'll only have a glass or two of wine; I don't want to forget a moment of my time with Carson and the band.

When the waitstaff delivers our drinks, Warner orders, "Oysters with Nobu Sauce, New Style Sashimi, oyster shooters, Rock Shrimp Tempura, Squid Pasta, spicy crab, Shrimp and Lobster with Spicy Lemon Sauce, brick oven-roasted lobster, scallops with jalapeno salsa, Hamachi Kama, crispy Shishito peppers, Kushi Yaki, chicken and shrimp, Nobu caviar tacos, and tuna tacos."

"Sir, if I might suggest," a waiter interrupts, "perhaps you'd like to order the tasting menu?" He points to the bottom of the menu. "For the entire table."

Warner nods to the man.

My eyes fly to the bottom of the menu in front of me. I nearly choke, finding it reads $200 per person. *It's $200 per person. That's $1200 for the food and doesn't include the drinks.* I take in a long, deep breath, then let it go slowly as I pass my menu along with the others to Carson on my right.

His eyes squint, and he mouths, "Are you okay?"

I nod and paste a smile on my face. I'm not sure how I feel about him paying over $200 for my meal. Make that over $400, as Peyton is here because of me. When we get a quiet moment, I'll need to offer to pay for my part.

I sit in awe at the amount of food and drink brought to our table. I scan the many serving dishes covering the entire top; there's no way we could possibly eat it all. Peyton and I, eyes wide, witness the guys fill their plates, not afraid to reach over everyone to get what they desire.

"Don't be shy," Carson murmurs into my ear, leaning into me.

I meekly spoon spicy crab and brick oven roasted lobster onto the empty square plate in front of me. Carson refills my wine then passes the bottle to Peyton.

"Ladies," Warner calls for our attention, "you'll want to try these oyster shooters and the oysters with Nobu sauce." His wicked smirk dares me to blush.

Always up for anything, Peyton tries each while Warner's eyes are glued to her lips the entire time.

Eli's eyes dart from Warner's to Jake's then mine.

I simply shake my head at their antics; I'm sure an aphrodisiac is the last thing these men need.

When my second glass of wine fades, Carson urges me to drink from my water glass. It's now I realize he isn't drinking alcohol with the rest of us. *Interesting.* The table holds two empty vodka bottles, a wine bottle, and an empty bottle of Jack. Some platters are bare. I easily assess we have more leftovers than what we actually consumed.

The guys are talking more than eating, and with empty beverages, I assume we will leave before reordering. It's a shame so much food will go to waste. What's worse is the price of the uneaten food. I feel guilty. There are many in need, and we squander our meal.

"Have a seat," Warner encourages our waitress as she attempts to exit our private room. His hands pat both his black, jean-clad thighs.

Surprisingly, she sits precariously on one of his knees. He whispers to her softly; as she giggles, her body visibly relaxes.

"Wanna lick?" He pulls his red sucker from his mouth with a pop and taps her bottom lip with it.

She refuses to open or stick out her tongue which causes Warner to laugh deviously.

"Playing hard to get, I see." His hands on either side of her, he lifts her to stand. "Off you go, then." He swats her on the butt.

She emits a squeal as she scurries away.

He turns to Peyton, "You'll have a suck, won't you?" He extends his sucker, and she opens wide for him, her tongue extended. When she closes her mouth, his eyelids grow heavy, and his tongue glides across his lower lip.

"Luke," she says with her mouth full of sucker. "Wanna lick?"

Luke's bright blue eyes react to her flirtation.

My eyes fly to Warner to see his reaction to her sharing his candy. Where I expect to see disgust or betrayal, I find approval. He likes her game. The three definitely imagine something other than a sucker in their mouths and show no shame for speaking loud enough for all of us to hear their foreplay.

9

MONTANA

I marvel at Carson's patience in corralling his band mates from Nobu into the limo. The three are easily distracted by other patrons, hot women, and their cell phones as we exit the restaurant.

Warner informs the group he wants to head to a poker table instead of the night club.

Carson reminds the group, "Meredith scheduled an appearance for us tonight. We can't back out."

"Two hours," Jake pats Warner on the back. "After two hours, we'll head to the casino."

They don't look to Carson for approval.

While the others climb into the limo, Carson turns to me. "Meredith is supposed to be with us for all public appearances. I'm gonna let her have it about ducking out tonight." He shakes his head in frustration then motions for me to climb inside.

Upon exiting the Hummer, a hotel staff member immediately greets us and instructs us to follow her. She leads us through a maze of hallways, out of sight of the other guests. We exit through employee doors and are asked to wait here for a moment. Standing between two large, marble pillars, we're somewhat hidden from others standing in line, surrounded by velvet ropes leading to the doors of the club.

Our guide speaks into her headset, and immediately, a bouncer at the club door looks our way then nods. He speaks to the two security guards commanding the waiting guests.

If Peyton and I were coming to the club, we would be waiting in that extremely long line. As we're hanging with the band tonight, we're escorted past the long line, straight into the club. The club manager and two waitresses greet us and explain where the VIP area is. We follow the scantily clad women.

It amazes me, the speed at which cell phones appear and the number of camera flashes attempting to capture the band walking through the main level of the club. A shiver climbs my spine at the thought that I'll be in the photos, too. I don't know these people; I don't want them to have photos of me.

Carson and the guys smile, wave, and occasionally pose for the crowd as they pass. This is normal for them. I can't imagine living life constantly in the public eye, always available, not able to relax.

Peyton and I attempt to fade into the background, but Carson takes our hands and leads us with the group. Finally, at the stairs to the VIP area, we are no longer visible to the crowd.

We're escorted to a large, oval, high-backed booth facing the floor-to-ceiling glass wall with a view of the club below. Carson motions for Peyton, then Eli, to take a seat. Next, he urges me to slide in before him. Warner, then Jake, scoot in near Peyton.

"Ketel One, Grey Goose, Johnny Black, and …" Warner looks to Peyton for her order.

"Two Stella Artois, please," I order. Turning to the guys, I state, "We're lightweights." I shrug, apologetically.

For once, Peyton doesn't argue with me.

"And, six small bottles of water," Carson adds to the order.

The bottle girl looks back to Warner, bats her fake eyelashes, then wiggles away. I can't help but roll my eyes at the desperation that drips off of her.

"Relax," Carson whispers into my ear.

Goosebumps grow on my skin at this nearness. "So, what exactly happens in the VIP section?" I ask.

"Anything and everything," Warner smirks, eyebrows wagging suggestively.

I quickly move my attention to the dancing crowd below. Like all clubs and bars I've been to, the women outnumber the men, clad in a variety of skimpy dresses, tight pants, and killer heels.

"We can go dance," Carson murmurs.

My head spins to him. *He's kidding, right?* My brow furrows, imagining the chaos of fans, mostly women throwing themselves at him; not to mention the photos.

"Not down there." He motions with his chin to the lower level. "There's a dance floor over there." He points to the right of our booth. Through the glass, I see an open area with VIPs leaning on a railing, looking below.

Before I can tell him I don't want to dance, our waitress returns with our drinks. Carefully, she places the large bottles in the center of the small, round, knee-high table with glasses and tiny water bottles around the edge.

Warner motions for her to come closer by patting his knee. The young woman sits without hesitation. *Is this required in her job description, or does she hope, one day, to be swept away by one of the rich bar patrons?*

"See the girl in the red, sequin dress and her friend?" He points to the dance floor below.

The bottle girl's eyes follow his extended arm and finger before she nods.

"Please invite them to join us." He flashes a devilish grin to the group.

With a nod and an attempt to hide her disappointment, she rises to leave.

Eli stands, stumbling over first mine then Carson's feet in his attempt to catch the waitress. With an arm thrown over her shoulders, he escorts her right up to the glass wall. I can no longer hear the conversation, but as he points below, I assume he's picking out a girl for him, too. As they walk back to our booth, Eli orders six apple martinis and another bottle of vodka.

Sadness washes over me; these men don't lead a normal life. Dating must be difficult, maybe even out of the question. Their version of Tinder is merely pointing and crooking a finger.

Soon, the waitress returns with a tray of drinks and six--yes, six--smiling women following her. Eli welcomes them to join our group as the waitress brings over chairs. I'm not sure how he did it, but Warner has one girl on either side of him in mere seconds. His fingers twist in the curls of one woman as he whispers flirtatiously in the other's ear.

I jump when Carson's heated breath skims my skin.

"Remember when I told you I need my own space to get away?" His lips nearly graze my cheek. My breath catches, and my body heats at his proximity. "It's rarely just the four of us, and I can only endure so much of this." He lifts his chin toward the group.

Before I can reply, a sharply dressed man with what looks like a bouncer, wearing a black t-shirt and black suit approach. He introduces himself as the club owner and thanks the band for coming. A woman approaches, large camera in tow, and directs the men to pose with the owner for some promo photos.

Staring longingly at Warner, one of the new female guests asks the other, "Do you think he wants us both?"

"Does it matter? He's worth millions," the other replies. "Wait until my followers see this on my Insta."

Wow. Just wow. I mean, Peyton likes to get wild and have a good time, but I've never known anyone like these women. A one-night stand, a three-some... They don't care as long as he's rich and famous. I'm sure they don't even know his last name is Bradshaw and chances are, they don't even listen to his music.

The band returns, sliding back into the booth. As Carson and Jake resume their spots by Peyton and me, Warner and Eli each take a girl onto their lap.

I try not to stare, but it's hard. The women all up their game. Their hands often touch or rub legs, chests, and play in hair. After only minutes, Eli stands up with the girl from his lap and leads her, hand in hand, from the room.

Part of me longs to go with him. I'm not sure how much more of the fake giggling I can endure. Warner's friend on his lap rubs against him like a cow at a scratching post.

"Are there clubs like this in Iowa?" Carson asks, turning his back to the three girls Eli abandoned before they can focus their attention on him.

"Um," I grin, "nightlife in Des Moines doesn't even come close. I doubt they even have a VIP section."

Peyton interjects, "They do have a VIP bottle service, but you sit amongst the commoners."

"Do the two of you go to clubs often?" He continues on the topic.

Peyton handles this question. "We go out, just not always to clubs. We call them bars in Iowa, by the way. We enjoy sports bars more than anything."

Warner ignores the squirming play toy on his thighs. "You enjoy sports bras?" he asks Peyton.

She blushes and slowly enunciates, "Sports bars."

"Whew!" Warner rubs fake sweat from his brow. "Sports bras create a mono-boob. Trust me, there's nothing sexy about a mono-boob."

Peyton sips from her water bottle, looking through her eyelashes toward Warner, a smile forming upon her red face.

"And, breasts as glorious as yours must never be a mono-boob." He seems to enjoy the blushing at his topic.

Peyton spews her mouthful of water across the cluttered drink table. "I'm... so...sorry," she sputters.

Warner and Jake delight in her embarrassment. Much to her dismay, Warner dismisses the woman from his lap, positioning himself facing Peyton. Jake's arm slides behind her on the back of the booth. From here, it becomes a game.

Our waitress returns to clear our little table and then a second waitress leaves fresh drinks.

"No more water for you," Warner informs Peyton, licking his lips. He slides a glass of Vodka toward her.

"Find me a bag of Peanut M&Ms," Jake orders the waitress, throwing a one-hundred-dollar bill on the tray she balances in her hand.

With a nod, the bottle girl excuses herself to fill our drink orders and fetch his candy. I find it odd she didn't hesitate or ask any questions at Jake's order. Peanut M&Ms are not a common nightclub snack. Mentally, I map the strip; CVS and Walgreens aren't nearby either.

Carson's hand brushes mine on my lap beside him. "Overwhelming, right?" His lips form a small smile. "I like to believe I'm still normal, but I'm in the band; all of this comes with it."

"I'm sorry if I'm wide-eyed," I tell him honestly, keeping my voice low. "It's a lot to take in. There are so many fans everywhere, eyes are constantly on you, and phone cameras follow you." I shake my head. "Then, there's the women willing to do anything. There's nothing normal about any of it."

"I feel like I don't fit in at these types of events," he confesses.

"I'm not buying that," I challenge. "You definitely belong with a guitar in hand and a mic nearby."

He chuckles, and his smile grows wider. "I feel at home playing music. Performing is in my blood. I'd do it naked without a thought. I lose myself in my guitar and lyrics."

Naked. Did he just say naked? Oh, holy hell. Now, all I can do is see him naked. I imagine corded muscles, taut skin, and ripples down his abdomen. *Hair? Hmm, I wonder if he waxes, shaves, or has chest hair. Or, better yet, a happy trail from his navel leading to his...*

"It's the meet and greets, the appearances like tonight, and the parties that I feel like a fish out of water at. I long to only write and perform." He runs a hand through his soft waves of brown. "It's not possible, so I grin and bear it."

"I mean," he stumbles. "Usually I detest these nights. Tonight, I'm enjoying my time with you and trying to ignore everything else."

As if on cue, Eli saunters back to our group. Warner asks if he lost something. Eli leans towards the guys on the other side of our booth. I can't hear his explanation for returning without the girl, but I can imagine what he says since Warner and Jake reward him with high fives.

10

CARSON

I refuse to high-five Eli's antics. I worry they will cause Montana to believe all of us act like him.

When he plops in the booth next to me, he adjusts himself. "It was an eight on the BJ scale," he loudly announces.

Peyton giggles beneath her hand, her eyes on Montana. Mine are, too, as I attempt to read her reaction. Her lips curl in over her teeth, and her eyes stare at the beer in front of her.

It's hopeless. No amount of apologizing for the band's actions will erase their crazy behavior. I'm living in La La Land if I think she won't be bothered by them and want to spend more time with me.

"I have to admit that's one of the best bathrooms I've ever fooled around in."

I shake my head at Eli's proclamation.

"So," Montana bumps her shoulder against mine. "Have you enjoyed many BJs in public restrooms?"

Jake spits bourbon over his lap and onto the table. Peyton, now sitting on Warner's lap, leans so far back that Jake has to support her head in front of him. "Don't waste alcohol. It's a party foul." She slurs her words a bit. Warner and Eli look to Montana.

"Carson's a party pooper," Eli reports. "He'd rather write or read than get a blow job. You're the first girl he hasn't treated like she has cooties."

"We even started a pool," Warner adds. "We bet on when he'll come out as a gay man."

"He's not gay," Jake's deep voice corrects before he places Peyton back in her upright position.

She spins on Warner's lap, placing her legs over Jake's lap.

"Ignore them," I plead.

"He says that all the time," Warner says. "He acts like it's a sin for us to let loose, have fun, and get our rocks off."

"It's not a sin; it's against the law in public, and it's just not for me," I remind the band while explaining to Montana.

"Hold on, darlin'," Warner tells Peyton as he digs in his front pocket. "Something's popping up."

At his words and devilish smirk, Peyton blushes deep red. This causes Warner's eyes to light up as his smile grows wide.

"Wanna suck?" Warner offers his red sucker. With no answer, he slides the candy along Peyton's lower lip.

I bump my shoulder to Montana's. "Looks like he's set his sights on your friend."

"Should I be worried?" she asks with concern upon her face.

"Peyton seems to give as good as she gets," I quip.

"I'm worried she may have met her match with Warner. She's usually the one in control and making the moves," Montana explains.

"We'll monitor both of them," I promise.

Montana

Though Carson's handsome face and tantalizing conversations entertain me, from time to time, I glance at Peyton. I've noticed she's moved from beer to vodka. Good thing I'm only sipping my beer. One of us needs to make sure we both make it home safely.

She also focuses her attention on both Luke and Warner. I recognize her signature flirty moves. She sets her sights on playing with both men at the same time. I do not understand how she does it.

I watch as a new waitress clears away our empties. Warner murmurs something to her that I don't hear. She leans close and slips a cocktail napkin into his front right jeans pocket, near Peyton's bottom. When she pats the outside of the pocket twice before removing her hand, it's clear she doesn't even try to hide her actions.

Warner smiles at her then leans in to whisper in Peyton's ear. Peyton slaps her palm over her mouth and giggles as she watches the waitress slink away. One hand in Luke's hair, she moves the hand from her mouth and pokes Warner's chest. "You're a bad boy."

Warner grabs her index finger, removes his sucker, and sucks on it.

"Come with me," Carson encourages, taking my hand in his.

I rise, following him from the booth. I nearly walk into the back of him as he suddenly stops at the edge of the booth. When I move my head, peeking around him, I witness a different waitress rub her breasts against Carson's upper arm as she places a white slip of paper in his hand. I'm invisible to her or inconsequential. She giggles, places her hand upon his chest, then pulls away like it's the hardest thing in the world for her to do.

Carson looks to me. "It's best if we just ignore her," he snickers.

I cock my head as my brow furrows.

"I've found if I act like it never happened, they won't approach me again," he explains, embarrassed.

"Luckily for me," Eli murmurs near my ear, standing behind me, his hands on my upper shoulders, "he hands me the info."

I turn my head, looking over my shoulder, my jaw agape as Carson passes the paper to an excited Eli. *Does he have no shame? How many women does Eli need in one night?*

Carson

I release Montana's hand, pulling my cell phone from my pocket. I scroll to Meredith and text her it's time to pick us up. I've had enough for tonight.

Although I've enjoyed my conversations with Montana, the antics of my band not only annoy but embarrass me. I'm still unsure if Montana has enjoyed the evening or not.

As much as I want to spend more time with her, I need to write. So many lyrics and chords are swarming my brain. It'll take hours to put them all on paper. Perhaps if she had fun, she'll be up to spending time with me tomorrow.

"I've texted Meredith," I announce to the guys.

"But, Dad, I'm not ready to go home," Eli playfully whines.

"That's between you and Meredith," I retort. "I'm outta here."

I signal a nearby waitress; we are ready for the check.

"I don't think Peyton's ready to return to the hotel, but I am," Montana states beside me.

I attempt to judge her honesty; I catch her in the middle of a yawn, back of her hand over her mouth.

"Not used to the rock star life?" I tease.

"I've been up since eight; can you say the same?" she defends.

"Well..." I hedge, then decide to be honest. "Not exactly. I was up most of the night trying to write, only staring at an empty notebook."

She places her palms upon my chest, looking up at me through her lashes. "Your lyrics speak to the masses. I have faith in you; the words will come."

Her smile, those dimples, her thick lashes—I'd kiss her if I didn't think she'd slap me for being too forward. Dazzled by her looks, I can only nod in reply.

When she pulls her hand from mine, my skin burns. It aches for her return. *How can she affect me so in less than 12 hours?* I join her at the enormous glass wall, the crowd below us moving to the beat, bodies swaying, enjoying each other and the night.

I imagine our bodies close, moving with the beat, hands roaming, in a world where I'm a normal guy, a world where fame isn't an ominous, stone wall between us.

"Yo, Carson," Warner calls over the loud music pumping into the room via the speakers.

Over my shoulder, I spot the club manager and Meredith at the booth. My stomach plummets. My night with Montana is ending. The pull to be near her is as strong as the call to write.

I escort Montana toward the group. Eli rises to stand beside us while Warner, Luke, and Peyton remain seated.

"I'm headed to the poker tables," Warner states firmly, his face close to Meredith's when he stands, wobbles, then rights himself.

"First stop is the hotel," I inform the guys. "The rest is between you and her." I point to Meredith.

I'm ready for them to be her responsibility. I've kept them from scandals and jail so far tonight. It's time for my babysitting shift to end.

Montana

As our entourage reaches the base of the stairs, the crowd turns, phones pop out, and the show begins again. The crowd calls out individual names, hoping a band member will look their way for a photo or autograph.

Hands extend, trying to touch, grab, and stop a celebrity. The guys wave and smile to their fans. Meredith, the club owner, and three beefy bouncers force our group to keep moving toward the door.

I grasp the hem of Carson's shirt with both my hands. It seems the closer we get to the door, the closer the crowd squeezes in. I keep my head down and eyes pinned to his back. I'm aware I'll be in photographs; however, it will only be in profile. The last thing I want is to be in a gossip mag or on social media.

Carson's hand reaches around his back to pull my hand from his shirt and tugs me to his side.

"Just a little further," his low voice promises, tucking me tight to his side.

I guess I wasn't hiding my growing anxiety. I melt into his warmth; he forms a protective cocoon around me.

At the open door, we find sizable crowds on two sides of the red velvet ropes, creating a pathway for us to walk between on our way to safety in the hidden hallways. While the band stops, smiles, and waves, Peyton and I slip safely out of sight.

"Wow," she laughs. "Can you believe we're with the band?"

Enamored by the crowds and the attention they give, she's star struck. I thought fans were always like those at the concerts I've attended; this is different. They seem to disregard all rules and personal space. Tonight, I've witnessed several women making it clear they will do anything with these four famous strangers. The air is heavy with female desperation; I try to shake the fear it brings.

"Carson seems into you," Peyton declares by my side. "He seems like a nice guy, too. Warner and Jake are naughty."

Her smile conveys she likes their kind of naughty. I smile, shaking my head at my best friend. I've never understood how we can be so different yet get along as we do.

Finally, the employee door opens, and loud crowd noises filter in with the guys.

"Is it always this crazy?" I murmur, leaning into Carson as we make our way back through the maze of hallways to the limo.

He shakes his head. "Meredith had an arrangement with the club owner," he explains. "She posted our location on social media. Most of the time, we wait until we've left to post that detail."

"I knew I wasn't the only fan of Communicable. I just never dreamt fans could be this crazy." I fight another yawn.

"Most of that crowd isn't fans of our music." Carson mimics my yawn. "They're attracted to the fame."

I contemplate his words as we slide into the black stretch Hummer outside the hotel. *Would I ever track down someone famous when I read on Instagram that they were nearby? Nope.* I'm a big fan of the band but wouldn't stalk them if I had the chance. Peyton, yes. She'd even drag me along. But I'd hide in the back, at a safe distance. It's what I did when she tried to get us backstage at a concert. I'm good at fading into the background.

Carson taps his index finger between my eyebrows. "What has you concentrating so hard?"

I realize my head is tipped to the side, and my brow is furrowed. "I was just contemplating if I would have hunted the band down when I saw the posts," I confess honestly.

"No," Peyton's voice is much too loud for our enclosed space. "No way. You'd spend the night talking non-stop about Communicable and their music, but you'd stay away."

Everyone's eyes fall on me in the dimly lit interior. I nod then shrug, agreeing with my friend's assessment.

Carson leans closer into me. "Lucky for me you were locked out of your room, then."

All my anxieties from the crowd and cameras fade as I look into his deep, brown eyes and sexy smile. *I'm in so much trouble.*

11

MONTANA

When the limo stops at our hotel, I breathe a sigh of relief; crowds are not waiting for us. One by one, we climb from the back. Eli and Warner require help, having had much more alcohol than the rest of us.

"The poker tables will have to wait until tomorrow." Meredith informs Warner; surprisingly he puts up no fight.

"Party in the penthouse," Eli cheers.

"Count me out," Carson replies. "I will walk Montana and Peyton to their room then write lyrics in my room the rest of the night."

"Actually, if it's alright with you," Peyton places her hands on my shoulders, "I'd like to join them in the penthouse for a while."

Her green eyes search mine while pleading for me to agree. When I nod, she kisses me on the cheek.

"You're the best." Then, she turns to Carson. "You'll see she's safe in the room?"

"Of course," he promises, his hand taking mine.

"Don't do anything I wouldn't do," I warn Peyton.

"Yeah, right," she scoffs.

Carson escorts me through the lobby and casino, towards the bank of elevators.

"She'll be okay?" I ask, concerned for my friend.

"Judging from the attention she received from Jake and Warner, I suspect she'll be just fine. Eli will keep everything under control."

"But he's drunk," I protest.

"He's surprisingly alert, even when his body sways."
I guess I'll trust Carson on this one.

Carson

My mind is a jumble of words that I need to get on paper. It's killed me all night to not even be able to jot them down on a napkin or paper coaster while we were out. I'm headed to my room to write the rest of the night.

"Thank you for an entertaining evening," Montana murmurs as the elevator passes floor after floor. "We got to experience a side of Las Vegas we never thought we would; you guys sure know how to party."

"Correct me if I'm wrong…" I look into her light brown eyes. "Peyton seems to know how to party on her own."

Montana snorts in laughter, covering her face with her hands. Her cheeks pinken with embarrassment.

"We all have our talents," she says. "Yours is writing music and playing guitar; hers is having a good time."

The elevator doors open onto our floor, I motion for her to exit before I follow. I'm torn. In a few, short steps, I'll say good night and head to the solitude of my hotel room. I need to write; I want to write. A large part of me longs to stay with Montana, however; time flies when I'm with her. I'm afraid to say good night as I may never see her again.

"Thanks for everything." Montana's teeth tug at her lower lip. "I had…" she stammers.

"I enjoyed having someone with me," I admit. "It's difficult being the only sober one, trying to control those three when they drink." I lean my shoulder against the door frame. "What are your plans for tomorrow night?" I hope I'm not being too forward. I don't want to let her disappear; I need to see her again.

"Um…" She shifts her weight from one foot to the other as her right hand plays nervously in her hair. "I must ask Peyton, but I don't think we have any concrete plans."

"Cool," I respond like a goober. "If you give me your number, I can text you in the afternoon to meet for the evening. The guys enjoyed having the two of you with us."

She nods. "Hand me your phone; I'll type it in."

I place my cell in her outstretched hand. She taps a few numbers then passes it back to me. "If you hit send, I'll have you in my contacts, too."

Glancing at my phone, I see she typed her number in the text app. I hit send. Electricity hums in my veins at the knowledge she now has my phone number, too.

"Well," Montana interrupts my thoughts, "I should get inside, so you can…" She motions down the hallway.

"Goodnight." I lean forward, placing a gentle kiss on her cheek. When I pull away, she's stunned. Her eyes scan my face while her index finger connects with her cheek where my lips touched.

I nod towards her hotel door. While she scans her card to enter, I pull away from the door frame where I leaned. "Be sure to use the deadbolt," I remind her. "I'll wait until I hear it."

She flashes me her dimples before slowly closing her door, and I lose sight of her. She turns a lock and slides the deadbolt into place, and I slip down the hall toward my room.

I drop my ink pen, massaging the palm of my right hand with my left. I make a tight fist then release my fingers a few times in an attempt to work out the cramps. I glance at my phone, seeing it shows four a.m. I've been writing for three hours straight. I flip through the pages of my notebook, admiring the full pages of lyrics.

Montana is my cure. Bumping into her in the hallway opened me up. The dam crumbled, allowing my creativity to flow. Page after page, song after song, she's opened my thoughts and feelings up, so I may lay them all out on a page.

Montana

In the room, I sprawl out on my bed. I open my phone, bypass social media, and search for Carson Cavanaugh and Communicable on the internet. I comb through post after post, looking for a reliable source.

In a magazine article, I read that Carson formed his first band in Middle school; Eli, the drummer, was an original member. In high school, they added Jake, the bass player, to the band, and after graduation, Warner, the lead singer, joined them.

He grew up in San Diego where, after high school, Carson stepped from front man to back up vocals and lead guitar. The original band name in middle school was Virus, and it changed in high school to Communicable. The reporter states that Carson writes most of the lyrics for the band; I knew that fact. Following their current world tour, the band plans to head back into the studio to record their third album.

Carson's bandmates refer to him as the father of the group as he tries to keep the guys out of jail, away from bad press, the ER, and even rehab. Carson is quoted as saying, "I like to have fun; I just rarely let go because someone has to monitor the guys."

After the article, I scroll through pictures of the band. Photos of Warner with different women clinging to him fill the screen. It's easy to see that photographers enjoy capturing the lead singer more than the rest of the band.

I'm relieved that I don't gaze at photo after photo of Carson with scantily clad women; I fear I might be jealous. I have no right to feel possessive. We've not even known each other for twenty-four hours, yet I feel so comfortable, like we've been together for a year.

In all my years watching TV and concerts, I never fully understood the lack of anonymity celebs have. Tonight, I witnessed first-hand the constant cell phone cameras pointed at them. There's no privacy. They're constantly asked to give autographs and photos, fans not caring if they interrupt meals or conversations. In public, they're like animals at the zoo.

The women throwing themselves at the guys tonight weren't groupies, more like attention whores. They would do *anything* to hang with someone famous. I scrunch my nose at the next thought to enter my head. *How many STDs and unplanned pregnancies have these four had?*

My finger slides over the mouse pad as I visit fan pages, rock news sites, and the gossip rags. The four appear at openings, release parties, award shows, and clubs together; often, females pose with them. The only constant in all the photos is Carson. With his blank expression, he appears withdrawn. When a woman is beside him, his hand isn't on her; in fact, they don't even touch. The other guys allow the women to drape themselves over them.

I type "Carson Cavanaugh+girlfriend" into my search engine. No results fit my criteria. Surely, he's had a girlfriend. I wonder how difficult it is for the two of them to keep their relationship out of the public eye.

He's much too gorgeous and kind not to have women interested in dating him. I shake away such thoughts. Carson is a rock star, and I'm a twenty-one-year-old trying to decide if I'm going back to college in the fall or finding a job. There's no way that we'll be together in a year. He has his life in Los Angeles after touring with the band while my world is in the center of Iowa.

I clean my face, slip into my pajamas, and rest my head on a pillow. I resign myself to the fact the only place the two of us can be together is in my dreams and happily fall to sleep.

12

CARSON

The Next Morning

I'm on the sofa, watching Eli and Jake argue over the ingredients in an Old Fashioned at the bar in their large suite. We're waiting on Warner to emerge from his room for the day. He kicked two women out an hour ago, so at least we know he's awake.

"You must open that notebook and pick up the pen in order to write lyrics," Eli spouts sarcastically, pointing at the green notebook sitting on the cushion next to me.

I flash him my shit-eating grin then open it, flipping through five pages of new lyrics written last night.

"No way!" Eli sputters. "Atta boy!"

"How?" Jake asks, astonishment upon his face. "What's changed? I mean, don't get me wrong, I'm glad your writer's block lifted."

Eli smirks at me. "She really has an effect on you, doesn't she?"

Jake looks from me to Eli questioningly.

"After meeting her yesterday afternoon, he said lyrics flooded his head," Eli explains.

"Montana?" Jake seeks further clarification.

Eli nods; all eyes focus on me.

"Within 10 minutes of talking to her in the hallway, words came to me for the first time in months." I shrug unable to explain it further.

"Months, you mean years," Eli jeers.

"It's her lips," Warner suggests, dragging into the room. "Her oral skills cured our Carson-boy, didn't they?" He pauses to look at me for a reaction. "I knew she had talents. It's always the sweet, innocent ones that turn into wildcats in the bedroom." Warner laughs with the guys.

"Hey," I bite out. "Be nice. I won't allow you..."

"Easy tiger," Warner raises both palms towards me.

"What's the saying about protesting too much?" Eli teases.

"What are the lyrics to that Beach Boys song? Something about midwest farmers' daughters..." Warner prods further.

"I think he's had enough," Jake tells the group.

"Are we going to sit around here all day? Or do we have plans for tonight?" I ask, ready for a different topic.

"Meredith plans to meet us here at eight," Eli states, sitting beside me and flipping through my notebook.

"Dinner then a club," Warner adds. "We must make an appearance at ten, then we're free the rest of the night."

I don't like those plans, and I can't wait until eight to see Montana. "I think I'll head down to the casino. You can find me at eight." I snag my notebook from Eli and rise from the sofa.

"Will Montana be gambling with you?" Jake asks, surprising me.

He's our introvert, happy to lurk in the quiet room until he's forced to see the public.

"I hope so," I answer honestly. "I'm supposed to text her when we know our plans so Peyton and she can join us."

Eli and Jake announce they'll join me in the casino, causing Warner to huff.

"You can't expect me to stay in the suite alone after you kicked out my playthings," he whines. "I guess I can hang with Peyton while you entertain yourselves with Montana."

I watch as Jake's jaw muscle tightens, and his eyes squint at Warner. It seems he likes Peyton; good for him.

"Let's get ready; we'll meet at the casino bar in an hour," I suggest. Not waiting for a response, I exit the suite.

As I walk down the hall, I text Montana our plans for the evening and tell her I'll knock on her door in an hour. She quickly responds with a thumbs up emoji.

I'm five minutes early when I rap on her door. I'm anxious to see if she's ready. I imagine we'll have to wait on Peyton.

"Come in," Peyton invites, holding a tissue in my face. "You'll need this."

I take the proffered tissue, and confused by her words, I raise my eyebrow.

"It's for the drool. Trust me," she promises.

Montana emerges from the restroom, causing my eyes to bulge and jaw to drop.

"I told you." Peyton nudges my shoulder. "She looks hot as hell."

I try to collect myself. I know Montana affects me. Yesterday, in the hallway, she quickly worked me up. I found her adorable and cute; it was her personality that pulled me to her. I shouldn't be surprised that when she dresses up to go out on the town, she's a knockout.

My eyes take her in from top to toe. Her hair is up with curls in the back and two tendrils down to frame her face. Her eyes pop with smoky colors on her lids and black eye liner edging them. Her pink-gloss lips from yesterday are now red with lipstick, luring me to lick and suck upon them.

Her long, bare neck begs to be nipped. Her black halter dress exposes her bare shoulders that invite me to touch and hints to cleavage that I long to lick. *Heaven help me. How will I keep my hands to myself all night?* I'm being tested, and I fear I'm failing miserably.

"Well?" Peyton nudges me again.

I shake away my inappropriate thoughts, scrambling to collect my wits.

"Um," I struggle to find words to express how she looks.

"I told you." Peyton hugs Montana. "He's speechless."

"Ladies," my voice shakes, so I clear my throat. "You look amazing. I'm going to spend the entire night keeping the guys away from you."

"No need." Peyton swats at me. "I can handle myself." She smiles proudly.

I take Montana's hand in mine, pulling her towards me. When she's mere inches from me, I murmur, "You look amazing."

Her brown eyes look up through her velvety-black lashes. Her eyes sparkle, and her skin glows. I want to push Peyton out the door, lock the weird-looking deadbolt, and ravish Montana all night long.

"This will be a very long night," I groan near her ear. I catch a whiff of her light, vanilla perfume. As if she needed help being edible.

Montana

I stifle my giggle at Carson's reaction, while inside, I love that I affect him so. Peyton and I decided to dress up this evening as it's our last in Vegas. We wear our little black dresses and new shoes we purchased in the hotel shops. Although I protested, Peyton styled my hair and applied my makeup; she's much better at it than I am.

I stare up at Carson nervously, and his warm breath caresses my cheeks with his every exhale. In a moment of strength, I place my palms flat upon his chest, rise on my tiptoes, and whisper into his ear, "Should I go change?"

I pat his shoulder as I pass by him to the bedside table to fetch my clutch. Aware that his eyes follow me, I put a little more sway in my hips. I peek inside my bag to ensure I have cash, my debit card, and my ID. When I glance in his direction, he's staring at me.

13

MONTANA

Peyton enters the elevator first, presses the button for the casino, then leans against the rail on the left side of the car. Carson's hand never moves from the exposed skin at the small of my back where the warmth from his hand heats my entire body.

Man buns were never my thing. However, Carson sports one today, and I'm loving it. *Holy hotness. Who knew he could look even better than yesterday?*

His dark dress pants cling tight to his thighs and glutes. His button-down, royal-blue dress shirt accentuates his athletic build. His biceps bulge against the silky fabric. My breath catches at the thought of the silky fabric brushing against my bare skin.

"Everything okay?" Carson asks.

As we plummet, I cover my mouth to hide my giggle. In the metal reflection on the opposite wall, I see Carson raise an eyebrow and erupt with giggles.

"She's always uncomfortable in quiet elevators," Peyton tells him. "Something about needing to break the silence, even with strangers."

Carson's hand slips from my back to my hip, spinning me to face him. "What shall we talk about?"

I stand, frozen in his gaze. I focus on his hair, his man-bun. His wavy, brown hair with perfectly placed highlights calls for my fingers to tangle in it. The scruff dusting his jawline draws my eyes to his mouth and plump lower lip. Oh, those lips; I long to suck his lower one into my mouth and nip it playfully. I startle as the doors open, and the loud casino noise surrounds us.

Unraveled

"Nice chat," Carson teases, motioning us from the car.

Carson

I let the ladies exit before me as I stay near Montana. My hand returns to her back; this dress pushes all of my buttons. With so much bare skin on display, I long to strip it off of her and reveal the rest of her.

"Where are we meeting?" Peyton inquires over her shoulder.

"The casino bar in the center," I share. "What can I get you to drink?"

Peyton orders an apple-tini, and Montana requests a Captain Morgan and diet cola. I flash a glare at a guy I catch staring at Montana from across the bar.

"Fuck," Warner greets. "Those dresses are the shit." His eyes scan Peyton from head to toe and back up.

Eli appears at Montana's side, turning to face her he states, "Carson's gonna have his hands full, keeping guys off of you tonight."

Montana

"Stop," I beg. "It's just a dress."

"Uh-huh," he laughs. "And, the Great Wall of China is just a fence."

I swat him playfully. I love him, because he's different, bright, nerdy, and so much fun to be around. How he comes up with all of his sayings baffles me. "The Great Wall of China a fence!" I love it.

"I'm headed to poker," Warner announces.

Jake nods, and Peyton follows them toward the high stakes area.

"What should we do?" Eli asks.

"I like video slots," I remind them.

"Let's make a lap until a machine calls to us," Eli suggests.

"I like the James Bond, Britney Spears, and Monopoly games," I inform him as we walk. "Oh, and I won on the Buffalo game yesterday."

"Then, let's go find them," Carson agrees.

"Hold on," I order, pulling my cell from my clutch. I open my Casino app, select NYNY, type in James Bond, and the map shows me where to find the game. "It's this way."

"How'd you do that?" Carson asks.

"It's an app. You can find a map of each hotel and casino floor, your favorite games in each, and it even helps you locate your friends."

He hands me his cell. "Download it for me, please."

I take his cell to download the app as I move us toward the machine I want to play. I pass the phone back as we approach and find the 007 game empty, so I quickly take a seat.

"Ah, ah, ah..." I place my hand over the slot when Carson attempts to slide his one-hundred-dollar bill inside for me. "If it's not my money then it's not my luck."

Without argument, he allows me to remove money from my clutch and insert it into the machine. I choose max bet, the machine springs to life. The bonus game hits, I spend the next few minutes choosing cards, matching Bond characters, and piling up more winnings. Over and over, I pick and match cards. My heartbeat races faster as the money grows. $100, $200, $300 and still rising. I match a few more cards and characters. $400, $500, $600... That's when the coin bonus spins begin. When all the games and free spins end, my first spin on this machine rewards me with $1,592 and some odd change. Eli and Carson cheer loudly behind me while I sit, stunned.

Eli orders drinks from a passing waitress while we wait for the casino personnel to fill out the paperwork, gather my information, then fetch me my check and tax form.

"Here I thought you were the lucky one." Eli swings an arm over Carson's shoulders. "Your writer's block lifted when you met her, but she's the lucky one. Two big wins in two days—girl, you are the shit."

"I am lucky," Carson states. "Luckily, I went to my room at the right time to bump into Montana." His eyes bore into mine. "The luckiest man alive."

Carson

We sit at the casino bar after Eli and I lose a couple hundred each on machines. Montana carries all the luck in our trio.

She slowly sips her Captain and diet while Eli and I enjoy beers. When she finishes her third drink, she states she'll have no more until she eats.

"Where are we eating?" I ask, turning to Eli.

He beams. "It's my night to choose, so it'll be Twin Peaks."

I can't even act surprised; it's so totally Eli. Burgers, fries, beers, and boobs in a super casual setting. I can't help the enormous smile upon my face. Meredith joins us tonight, and watching her endure Twin Peaks will provide hours of entertainment for the four of us. Tonight's looking better than last night already.

"I'm sending a group text to meet in the lobby in fifteen minutes," I tell them as my fingers work on my phone screen.

When I look up, I spy two guys across the bar, staring at Montana. I fight a growl as I slip from my stool. "Let's make our way to the lobby," I suggest, not letting on that I'm attempting to sneak her away from all lecherous eyes. As hot as I find her bare skin in the dress, I'll have to fight off men all night.

Montana

"Where are we eating?" Peyton asks, louder than she should.

"Well," Eli moves closer, "I'm glad you asked. Tonight, we'll dine on the best American cuisine accompanied by the coldest beer served in frosty mugs."

Peyton raises an eyebrow.

"Twin Peaks," Jake informs, his eyes searching my face for a reaction.

"I love that place!" Peyton cheers. "We have one in Des Moines. They have great appetizers."

I find Carson's eyes still on me. I smile, letting him know I'm not offended by the busty theme of the restaurant.

Meredith doesn't join us at the table, although there's an empty chair. Instead, she stands at the bar, her attention on her cell phone.

Warner instructs the server to bring a round of tequila shots for the group. She turns on her fuzzy-lined hiking boots, shaking her ass on her way to the bar.

"Which app is your favorite?" Jake asks Peyton.

She shrugs, glancing at the menu Warner holds out on her other side. "I like them all."

"Then, it's settled," Warner smiles, wrapping his arm behind her on the chair. He signals the server over again. "We'll take one of each appetizer."

Too much food, especially French fries, and three giant, frosty mugs of beer later, I excuse myself to the ladies' room, and Peyton joins me. I pause at the entrance, staring at the signs on the two doors.

"Which one is the women's?" Peyton asks, confused like me.

I attempt to focus my beer-logged brain. Both wooden signs have a stick figure followed by a "2" and a "P". I point as I speak, "2P means 'to pee'. That one 'stand to pee', this one 'sit to pee'."

"Holy crap." Peyton pushes the 'sit to pee,' door open. "They should warn you about these signs before they serve you three beers."

"Right?" I agree, giggling and following her inside.

The rest of the night passes too fast. With Meredith accompanying us, Carson and I take part in several rounds of shots. The band is recognized the moment we enter the club. Everywhere we look, we're captured on cell phones. I've now learned the VIP area is safer as the cameras can't record everything we do. We're on the second floor; guests downstairs only see us when we lean on the railing, open to the dance floor below. A new, up-and-coming alt-rock band sits near our table. They don't approach but nod, smiling to greet the guys.

Like last night, bottles and drinks rarely remain empty for a minute before the servers swoop in with fresh ones. Life seems easy in VIP-land.

14

MONTANA

The Next Morning

"Make it stop," I groan, placing a pillow over my face to block out the much-too-bright sun as the incessant pounding continues. "Uh," I whimper, clutching the pillow tight at my ears. I've never had a hangover that caused such a loud pounding in my head.

"Montana," a woman yells. "Open your door." Immediately, the annoying pounding resumes.

I throw the pillow from my face, moaning as I roll to place my feet on the floor of the spinning room.

"Hey, why'd you do that?" Carson grumbles from the other side of my bed. I freeze, staring dumbfounded.

Well, I guess that happened. I search my foggy brain; I can't recall the two of us returning to my room.

"Montana," the woman's voice calls again from the other side of the door.

I grab a t-shirt from the floor, pulling it over my head while approaching the door. I quickly check to ensure it's long enough to cover my naked parts. When I turn the handle, the door flies open.

"He's over there," I mumble. Carson's band manager barges past me into my room as I walk into the bathroom and close the door behind me.

I scoop cold water from the faucet to my mouth, hoping to remove the dry, cotton sensation. The cold water brings the urge to potty. I pee and pee and pee. I turn on the water and quickly wash my hands, wanting to return to Carson to seek information about last night.

"Ouch!" I look from the mirror to see what scraped the palm on my right hand. It's a large ring. Not just *any* ring. A giant diamond on my ring finger. I squint at it, the water still flowing from the faucet; I stare as if the diamond will tell me all that I can't remember.

Carson

The faint sound of a phone ringing slices into my sleep. *Is it the room phone?* While my groggy brain dashes between sleep and waking up, the sound of the ringing phone ceases. Replacing it is the sound of heavy pounding on the door.

"Carson, I know you're in there! Open the goddamn door!" Meredith, our band manager yells in her annoying, nasally voice. "Montana," she yells. "Open your door." Immediately, the annoying pounding resumes.

Suddenly, a pillow lands upon my face.

"Hey, why'd you do that?" I grumble from my side of the bed.

I toss the pillow back to Montana's side. While I attempt to keep my eyes open, I adjust myself under the sheet, and I wonder which one of the guys stirred up trouble, causing Meredith's tirade so early in the morning. I also wonder how she knew to look for me in Montana's hotel room.

Propping myself up on another pillow, I squint, unable to focus on Meredith storming into the room, coming to stop at the foot of the bed.

How is it this woman looks perfectly put together in her black pencil skirt, blue silk blouse, and matching high heels? It's much too early. Her hands planted on her hips and her blue, open-toed shoe tapping, she glares at me as though it's my turn to talk.

"Where is your cell phone?" she huffs.

I couldn't begin to guess where, in this room of empty bottles and clothes strewn on the floor, to find my phone.

"Clearly you haven't been on social media today?" When I don't respond, Meredith continues, "You two have created a cluster fuck. What were you thinking?"

"What's up?" I ask my manager.

"What's up?" she spits back, her voice raised. "What's up? I'll tell you what's up… "

"We've got a problem," Montana blurts, returning from the bathroom, her hands tangled in her messy hair.

"I'm glad to see one of you is thinking clearly this morning," Meredith spouts.

I look from her back to Montana whose long, shapely legs disappear under a large black t-shirt announcing, "I'm the Groom." I'd chuckle at it if my head didn't hurt. With effort, I lift my eyes toward her face. The fingers of her left hand wave in the air. It's there that I see she's wearing a ring. *Fuck! Did I sleep with a married woman?*

"Yes, you idiot," Meredith hisses. "She's your wife."

Wife? Did she say my wife? Fuck! I pull my left hand off my morning wood to find a gold band wrapped around the base of my ring finger.

"How'd you let this happen?" I ask my manager.

"Me? I didn't let this happen. Your group snuck off while I was loading Warner's drunk ass in the limo," she defends. "I can't be in charge of the four of you all the time. Of all the band, you're the last one I'd worry about fucking up this majorly."

"The internet is crawling with photos and videos of the two of you last night," she adds. "Seems you didn't rush back to the room to start the honeymoon." She sighs heavily. "That would have been *too* easy."

Montana and I scramble to find our phones. She finds a video first. "My family's gonna kill me," she whispers. When she turns the volume on, I hear, "Meet my husband, Mr. Cavanaugh," in Montana's voice. "Meet my wife, Mrs. Cavanaugh," in my voice. Then, "Can we take a selfie with the happy couple?" in an unknown, male voice.

"Meredith," I raise my voice to get her attention, "Montana and I need some time. Can I text you later?"

Hands on her hips, Meredith states, "Flight is at two, so don't take too long." She gives Montana a disapproving snarl before leaving the room.

At the sound of the door latching, I ask, "Can we talk?"

"My parents are gonna kill me," Montana murmurs, barely above a whisper.

"Please shut your phone off, so we can avoid social media. The vultures are swarming, and they show no mercy. They're mean, evil really, with their comments. They're out to entertain their followers and viewers, not caring if it's truthful or who it hurts. Trust me, I've been through it many times with the guys in the band. However, this is the first time I'm the subject," I ramble. "Where is it? I'll turn it off for you."

"I should at least text my parents to let them know I'm okay," Montana protests.

"Let me open the phone, type the text, and send it for you. That way I can protect you from missed calls, texts, and social media alerts a bit longer," I offer.

After I send the text for her, Montana rests her forehead to the wall of windows, eyes staring down the Strip.

"I need to look up a few things; it will just take a minute," I tell her back. "Then, we'll work this all out."

Palms pressed to the cold tile, I allow the hot water from the shower head to soak my hair and pelt my body.

Where did I go wrong? When did I cross the line? I drank way too much. Oh, what she must think of me... I never let my guard down like last night. It's like I did everything I harp on the guys not to do. Three condoms. There are three used condoms in the trash by the bed. Why can't I remember the sex? Three condoms mean it should be memorable.

We are good together. Two days felt like years, so natural. Then, I self-sabotaged by marrying her. The paparazzi will love a chance to spoil my clean, rocker boy image. I'm far from perfect, definitely no choir boy. They'll have a field day with this.

No way she'll want to keep in touch after the annulment. It will end our good thing. Is there any way possible, even drunk, she meant her vows at the ceremony?

I've gotta find a way not to lose her; it's clear I need her in my life. Within an hour of meeting her and chatting, lyrics swam in my head as never before. She's more than a muse; sitting by her, my soul found its match, and I felt complete for the first time. Without touching or kissing, I knew we'd make a great pair. It just felt right, similar to my moving to lead guitar and bringing Warner in on lead vocals. It's meant to be. But there's no way Meredith will let me keep her.

I like her; I like her a lot. I've never felt this way, this close with another woman, even after several dates. She's one of a kind; she's my kind. I need her on a visceral level. She breathes life into my creativity while she ignites a yearning within me.

Unraveled

Even now, lyrics come to me. *I need to write; I must record them.* She gifts me word after word, verse after verse.

I emerge from the hot shower, soaking wet with a towel around my waist, leaving a water trail from shower to sink. I frantically search the restroom, looking for my notebook. Not seeing it, I scramble for any paper and pen or other writing utensil.

Not finding anything better, I use a black eyeliner pencil on the enormous mirror over the vanity.

I must ask Montana if she has any paper I may use to copy these lyrics onto.

With a towel around my waist, I rub a hand towel through my wet hair, stepping from the bathroom.

Montana stands at the large windows, her forehead pressed to the glass and the desert sun's rays enveloping her. She's still wearing the "I'm the Groom" shirt, her legs, golden tan, spilling from its back hem mid-thigh. I need my cell phone; I want a photo to remind me of this moment forever. Unaware I'm watching her across the room, she presses her arms to the window over her head. I stifle the moan in my chest as the hem rises several inches, revealing a peek of the lower portion of her bare ass. As if her tone legs didn't do it for me, her exquisite backside assures me every inch of her is magnificent.

I don't recall last night, and my hands itch to explore her as if for the first time, my mouth to taste her, and my body to please her. She's definitely a temptation I can't let escape. I dress quickly in my jeans from last night, skipping my day-old boxers. Then, I purposely bump the bathroom door, the noise a signal I'm behind her.

She turns from her contemplation above the Strip and curls a knee beside her on the bed. *This woman is killing me with her no underwear poses. I must think of something else, anything else.*

"Do you have any paper I could use?" I ask, slicing into the much too quiet room.

She pulls a journal from her luggage. She opens to the first clear page and passes it to me, eyes questioning.

"Some lyrics came to me in the shower; I wrote them on the mirror and need to copy them, so I don't lose them."

"May I see?" She whispers.

I'm sure she's worried I won't share my work until it's perfect. That's not me. I crave input and reaction. I want to see how my words affect her and ask what she thinks of them.

When I nod, she follows me. "I need to buy you a new eyeliner pencil," I mention as she enters the bathroom.

I watch her almond-shaped, brown eyes grow wide, her head tilt to the side, and her lips part. I swear I hear her whisper, "Oh."

I follow her eyes as they read down the mirror, then start over at the top. This time she speaks the words, barely a whisper. When she's done, she looks to me, and I find tears in her eyes; she's trying hard to keep them from falling. My chest swells and warmth fills my body that my words move her so.

Montana

I lean my forehead against the cool window glass. Though my eyes peer toward the Vegas Strip, I see nothing. The cool air-conditioner feels good upon my face. *I'm married. I got drunk and married to a guy I met only two days ago. I married a freaking rock star.*

My parents will be ashamed; they raised me better than this. They instilled in me that marriage isn't a frivolous endeavor and should be a lifelong promise.

My older brother will kill me. I fear his impending lecture more than my father's. An annulment is a quick fix for a fuckup. Carson's too good to be a fuckup. He's so sweet.

When he sat by me in the hallway, a cozy, warm feeling enveloped me. Not a liquid sensation, a full, complete feeling. I'm me with him. I'm not fake. Carson is a gentleman. I haven't had a first date since high school that the guy didn't try for more at least once. Two days together, dates of sorts, and he only kissed me once. Well, once that I remember, then we got married.

Talking to him is as easy as talking to Peyton. It's as if he's familiar, not a total stranger. Carson loves his friends despite their flaws and helps look out for them. He's hot as hell—that shouldn't matter—it's a nice perk.

A pit grows in my stomach at the thought of getting an annulment and never seeing him again. I feel that if we get an annulment, it will be my biggest mistake in the eyes of my parents with the wedding a close second.

Could it work?
Could we try?
Should we try?
Do I want to try?
Would he?

"Okay," Carson clears his throat, pulling me from my thoughts; I turn from the windows to face him. He pats the bed beside him in invitation.

I comply, leaning against the headboard with a pillow hugged tight to my chest.

Beside him on the bed, I can feel his heat, even with our bodies not touching. Neither of us speak, lost in our own thoughts.

"This may sound crazy, but hear me out," he begins, voice tight. "What if we stay married?"

Stay married. Did he just suggest we stay married? I expected he'd lobby for a quickie annulment and hop on his jet, never to see me again.

"You see," he stumbles a bit as his voice falters, "I like you. A lot. I mean…" He runs both hands through his damp hair. "What I'm proposing is not to get the annulment, then go our separate ways. Instead, we continue to learn more about each other. Kind of like we're dating. There's no rush, because we can get a divorce anytime. But…"

I toss the pillow aside, turn to face him, eager to hear more.

"It feels real to me. There's something about you. I feel… Every part of me… I think I'd never forgive myself if I didn't give this a try. I mean…" he turns his body to face me. "I mean everything up to the drunken wedding was pretty amazing."

Carson

"Right," she nods. "I know an annulment will upset my family even more than learning we married."

"Mine will see it as an escape clause," I admit.

"Ya, a quick fix to easily erase it." Her eyes seem to search me. "Do you think we…" she motions between us with her index finger. "Could we make us work?"

"I think so." *Oh, how I hope so. I believe she's what's been missing in my life.*

"Me, too," she agrees.

"An annulment now or a divorce three months from now… Either way, my parents will be just as disappointed." I share.

"Maybe if they see us try to take the marriage seriously, they'll back off a little," she offers, a smile slipping onto her lips. A little light sparkles in her eyes. "I didn't want to do the annulment and never see you again."

"Me either; that was all I could mull over in the shower. Two nights isn't enough. You leave me wanting more, so much more." I confess. "You're easy."

She raises a single eyebrow.

Montana

"I didn't word that right." He immediately raises his hands, crossing them as they wave between us.

"And you call yourself a songwriter, a master of words, if you will," I tease.

"Well, until we met in the hall, words evaded me for over a year," He states, baring his truth to me.

"Wait." I quickly stand. "You mentioned that last night. I remember we were in a taxi; the four of us snuck out when Meredith loaded the guys into the limo."

I anxiously wait to hear if he remembers more.

"Remember? We were going shopping," I nod, attempting to coax his memory.

He shakes his head. Maybe memories will come back later today. "Are we really gonna do this?" He seeks assurance.

"I want to," I say. "But what happens next? We're scheduled to fly in opposite directions this afternoon."

His eyes plead with mine. His eyebrows are high, eager for my answer.

I open my mouth, but no words escape. I raise my hand to my lips as I search for the strength to tell him how I feel; I nod.

Carson

I'd give anything to see her smiling dimples rather than the sadness and pain she expresses now. "My parents won't like my disregard for the sanctity of marriage," I share, matching her thoughts with total honesty.

"My parents constantly lecture my brother and me that marriage is forever, requires work, and requires patience to be successful," she states, eyes downward. Looking up through her long lashes, she quirks her mouth to one side and shrugs.

"Exactly," I agree. "I even promised my family I'd never treat relationships like rock stars usually do," I sigh. "And, look what I did; we're all over the internet." I stand, walking to the foot of the bed to grab my phone. "I've worked hard to portray a clean rocker image, and a drunken Las Vegas wedding followed by a quick annulment will tarnish that image. The paparazzi have tried for years to catch me in a situation every other rocker appears in regularly."

"I get it," she states. "I've strived to uphold the values my family holds dear. Our marriage will not please them, and I don't want to disappoint them."

"So, you'd be willing to stay married?" I ask.

She nods slowly.

"I have an idea about how we can move forward." I return to sit beside her, back against the headboard. "We're scheduled to record our next album in L.A. next week. We stay in a house together and use its studio. The label arranges it all." I shake my head slightly, running my hands over my stubbled jaw. "We've done this for past albums, and because it's L.A., Warner will sneak out to party, only to show up hungover in the studio the next day. Eli will parade girls through every night then be too exhausted to contribute during our studio session. Jake... Well, Jake is a mystery; I have no idea where he traipses off to." I take her hand in mine. "We're supposed to work morning, noon, and night. The goal is to release our best work in the least amount of time."

My thumb rubs absent-mindedly on the back of her hand.

Montana

I do my best to concentrate on his words as he shares his idea with me, but I fail. My body's reaction to his gentle touch grows exponentially. My mind drifts to him caressing other parts of my body, causing me to miss his entire plan.

"So," Carson drawls out, "what do you think?" His eyes ping pong back and forth, searching mine.

I blow out a long breath as I search my brain for any clues to the plan he shared; I've got nothing. "Sounds good to me," I lie. *Well, is it a lie if I don't know what I'm agreeing to?*

"Awesome!" Carson taps on his phone several times, then his thumbs type. "I'm scheduling a band meeting in my room in 15 minutes. I need to apologize to the band for the negative publicity. We'll share the plan with them and see if they'll agree."

Carson

Of course, Meredith shows up early for the meeting. I don't want to deal with her crap, but I know it's best to get it over with sooner rather than later.

When I open the door, Meredith plows inside. "I want to handle this before the label calls me in hopes of appeasing them. And, they could call any minute. I've got the paperwork for the two of you to read, and I have a lawyer on standby. When I text, he'll come witness the signatures and file your annulment paperwork."

"Hold your horses," I tell her. "Montana and I talked. We're married; it's a done deal, so move on."

Meredith looks at the two of us, "But..."

"No!" I raise my voice. "There's nothing to say, nothing to argue about. We're adults, and we've come to an agreement to make the marriage work."

Her mouth opens and closes like a fish out of water. She fans herself with an envelope in her hand while she paces from the windows to the door and back. It dawns on her what she's waving.

"Here," she passes the large brown envelope to me. "If you plan to remain married, you need to see this."

"What is it?" I ask, not opening the clasp to peer inside.

"I had a technician run a background check on her for you," Meredith confesses proudly.

"And, what did you find?" Montana coaxes.

Meredith's eyes look from me to her. "I haven't had time to look through the information; I only just received it."

"Let me save you the time." Montana takes the envelope from me and tosses it toward Meredith's chest. "I was born and live in Des Moines, Iowa. My father owns a large farm north of the city, and my mother runs her family's real estate business. They own several properties throughout the metro. I graduated from Lincoln High School and just graduated from Des Moines Area Community College, both with a 4.0 average."

Montana looks to me, her back toward Meredith. "I have no college debt, no credit card debt, and I own my vehicle. I'm not behind on any bills, I live at home, and I've never looked into my credit rating as my parents still pay for everything. But I imagine, should one care to look into it, my credit rating is impressive."

I smile, shaking my head at her. She's sharing information to help us as a newly married couple, but she's also putting Meredith in her place. She licks her lips, smirks, then winks at me before turning to face Meredith, nearly toe to toe.

"Did I forget to share anything?" Montana taunts. "Ask me."

Meredith leans around Montana to look in my direction. "You'll have your hands full with this one."

I'm not sure how to take that from her. For one, Meredith is a type A personality, works twenty-four seven, and wins most of her pissing matches. *Does she mean it as a compliment that she sees Montana as an equal? Or, does she mean Montana's behavior is out of line, and she will cause trouble for me and my band?*

I take the envelope from Meredith, tear it into four pieces, then toss it into the trash can by the desk. I breathe a sigh as there's a knock at my door.

Montana

A knock at the door startles me; one arm remains wrapped across my stomach as my other hand flies to my mouth. Carson smiles sweetly in my direction as he prepares to open his hotel room door.

"Atta boy," Eli greets, pulling Carson in for a one-armed man hug with heavy pats to his back. "I can tell by the looks of the two of you that your wedding night rocked."

Peyton pushes her way past the guys, making a beeline for me. "Oh. My. God. Why didn't you text me back this morning?" She wraps me tight in her embrace, rocking us back and forth.

"Carson shut my phone off until the dust settles." My small voice keeps my words between the two of us.

"Well, your mom lit my phone up, because you wouldn't answer."

Peyton's hands upon my shoulders keep me in front of her; I can't hide my reactions from her eagle-eye gaze.

"I'm still in shock," I confess. "Waking up married... I mean... How do I deal with that?"

She cocks her head to the side, pursing her lips, and blinking several times.

"Hey Meredith," Warner's loud voice draws our attention. "Choir boy's impromptu wedding tops anything I've ever done, right?"

Meredith shakes her head.

"Take a seat," Carson orders, organizing the entire group.

"Dude, we should move up to the penthouse, so there's room to sit," Eli grumbles.

"Sit," Carson demands, pointing to the king-sized bed.

Taking Carson's hand, I'm pulled to his side.

"Ah... They're still wearing the shirts we bought them," Eli points out, looking to Peyton.

So caught up in our situation, I need to look to see what shirts we're wearing. Carson has on the "I'm the groom" t-shirt I threw on when Meredith woke us up. I have on a matching "I'm the bride" t-shirt.

"You bought these?" I look at my best friend.

"Duh," Peyton replies, squinting her eyes.

"So," Carson interrupts, pulling attention back to him, "by now, you know Montana and I were drunk and apparently got married last night."

"Hold on," Eli butts in. "You're playing this off as a drunken mistake?"

Peyton scoffs, walking toward me. "Don't do this," she pleads. "Don't blame it on too much alcohol. It was a great night."

"Was it?" I ask, needing details.

Her eyes squint, assessing.

"Imagine Meredith banging on my door, waking us up, and finding ourselves married."

Eli stands now. "You don't remember?" he asks me, concern painted on his pinched brows.

I shake my head.

"Peyton and I would not have allowed the two of you to go through with it if we thought you were that drunk."

Peyton chimes in, "You seemed very aware of the whole thing. I mean, you came up with your own vows and everything."

I look to Carson to see if he remembers our vows; he's as lost as I am.

Carson speaks to Peyton and Eli. "Please take a seat, so we can continue with the meeting."

Carson

I scan my band members. "First, I want to apologize for the publicity storm you woke to this morning. I'm sorry my actions last night might have placed you in a negative light because of your association with me."

Lying starfish-style on my bed, Eli raises his head. "Negative, dude. Your marrying Montana did not put a blemish on Communicable." He scoffs. "There's a bit of speculation, but your 'Prince of Rock' image remains untarnished. Fans want to know all about the girl that stole your heart."

"Well, trust me when I say, my actions last night were careless on my part. I would have liked to drink less and remember every second of it."

Laughter fills the room.

"You don't..." Jake laughs.

"Neither of us remembers much from the time we left the club," Montana confesses.

"Seriously?" Peyton asks, voice rising as she moves to stand beside her friend. "You didn't seem wasted. Did she?" She looks to Eli for confirmation. Turning back to Montana, she states, "You have to know I'd never let you do such a thing if I thought you were drunk."

Montana takes Peyton's hand, nodding.

"Before we get into the details of last night, I'd like to share an idea with the band and put it to a vote," I interrupt the murmurs throughout the room.

With no objections, I continue. "Montana and I decided to give this marriage thing a go. We're going to spend some time together and see if it's possible for us to remain husband and wife. We've opted not to get the annulment Meredith arranged." I look from Eli to Jake to Warner.

"To allow us more time together, I reached out to Corey. He graciously offered for us to record in his lake home near Des Moines this summer. Montana and I will head to L.A. I'll pack, then we will fly to Des Moines to arrange everything at the house before you arrive. Corey assures me everything we need is in the studio, and he has a local guy that will assist us with recording any time we'd like."

I scan the room again to find no argument and no questions from the band.

"Carson, no!" Meredith interjects, authoritatively.

Montana

"Meredith, this is not up for debate. Montana and I plan to take some time, learn more about each other, and not get an annulment. We've enjoyed the past two days and don't want to throw that away." He squeezes my hand as his eyes meet mine for a moment.

Meredith points her glare in my direction. Her tight lips and squinted eyes attempt to intimidate me.

"An annulment is the best way to put an end to this social media nightmare," she hisses. "We'll play it off as publicity for the new album. I'll release a statement that it was research for lyrics you're working on."

Hands on hips, left foot pointed outwards, she stands firm in front of Carson and me.

"Hear me. Listen to me this time," Carson snarls. "There will be no annulment. No. Annulment."

He leans closer to her, still holding my hand. "You work for us, not the other way around. If you have a problem with the band's plans, you're welcome to request the label reassign you. Now, step back so I can talk to the band."

Meredith steps back, her icy glare stopping on me as she walks by.

Carson draws in an audible, calming breath, squeezing my hand then relaxing his grip. He licks his lips, nods, then returns to the previous conversation.

"Here's where I'd like to propose something, and then, we'll vote on it." He waits for each of the guys to nod before continuing. "I've contacted Corey to take him up on his offer to record in his studio. ZipTie's in the middle of their world tour, so he said we can use his lake house and studio for the summer."

The guys shuffle a bit in their positions. I can tell they are hesitant about this change in plans. I listen intently as I didn't hear him when he shared the plan with me earlier.

"We can't change plans one week before recording," Meredith states.

Carson holds his palm out in her direction. "I've already contacted the label, and since Corey's not charging us, they'll save money."

Meredith scoffs. "There's no way Corey's footing the bill all summer. And, we still need to discuss the annulment."

"We won't pay for the house or the studio time," he shoots a glare at Meredith. "The label will cover food, utilities, and staff during our stay. As the label comes out ahead, they are on board with the change of location."

Meredith, shocked at his thoroughness, is silent.

"By leaving L.A., we'll focus on the album more and will finish it faster. Of course, Montana's from Des Moines, so by recording at Corey's, we'll be able to see each other and give this relationship a try."

"I'm in," Eli blurts. "I've never been to Iowa."

Unraveled

Jake grunts, "I'll go if everyone wants to."

All eyes swivel to Warner who rolls his eyes. "You seriously expect us to give up L.A., fly to Iowa, and rough it for the summer?"

I'm astonished the guys don't correct his statement; instead, they remain quiet.

"I will not leave the ladies behind in L.A. to hook up with the cows in Iowa," Warner whines.

It takes all of my willpower not to bite back at his dis of my home state. He essentially called Peyton and I cows, inferior to the women in L.A. I admit I'm not a fake blonde with fake hair extensions and fake body parts; I may not look as hot as the ladies he sleeps with then tosses to the side, but I'm far from a cow.

I turn my attention to Peyton to find her shooting daggers at Warner. My friend rarely holds her tongue. It seems we both choose to fight internally with his comment and disrespect for the Midwest.

Tired of the silence and lack of engagement by the guys, Warner speaks. "But if all of you want to go, I won't stand in your way."

"So, it's settled then," Carson concludes, smiling widely. "Meredith, I'll text you Corey's house manager's number, so you can arrange everything. We'll fly to L.A. today then to Iowa next week. Time to pack," he urges.

"You make a cute couple," Jake murmurs in passing, briefly touching my shoulder.

"If I'm sequestered in Iowa for months, I'm staying in Las Vegas for the week," Warner informs Meredith. "Make the arrangements; I'll be upstairs."

"I'm staying, too," Jake's gravelly voice adds as he walks out the door.

Meredith scowls. I'm not sure if it's the added task of extending their stay or the fear of the trouble they might cause with more time in Sin City. I hope she has to stay and babysit the two of them. As it's clear the woman isn't a fan of mine, I sort of hope the guys cause trouble and make her deal with it.

15

MONTANA

"With that settled," Peyton starts, "look at these photos I took last night."

Her fingers scroll through photo after photo. Unimpressed, Meredith leaves the room. Eli pauses beside Carson.

"Here." He places his palm flat upon Carson's chest. "It'll work. The two of you, I mean. Watch this, and you'll believe like we do." His index finger moves between Peyton and him.

When he pulls his palm from Carson's chest, I see he's given him a flash drive.

"What's this…?" Carson asks.

"It's a video of last night." Eli grins.

A video of our wedding. I'll need to thank him for recording it. As we can't remember, it's our only window into the ceremony, our vows, and our drunken behaviors last night.

"Can you send me the photos?" Carson asks Peyton. "Montana has my number."

It seems he's as eager as I am to relive last night.

"Watch the video. I'll head to our room and send the pics to Montana." Peyton hugs me before leaving. "Grab tissues; you'll need them, both of you." With that, she leaves the room.

"Where's your laptop?" I ask before the door latches behind Peyton.

He pulls his computer from a duffle near the head of the bed. Opening the lid, the machine sparks to life, and with a few keystrokes, he unlocks it. He inserts the flash drive into the port and opens it with a touch on his screen. He fiddles with the settings for sound and wide-screen before looking to me to find out if I'm ready to watch our actions from last night.

Carson

"I'm ready." her voice cracks a little.

I take her right hand in mine, using my left to start the video.

Eli's videography skills are shaky, but I'll never mention it to him. I'll be forever grateful he thought to catch the moment on video.

He poses for a selfie with Peyton, the two laughing and talking animatedly about not believing what's about to happen. Next, he swings the camera to me standing near a small, raised altar I assume the man that waits with me is the officiant.

I'm standing tall, excited, and not swaying as I expected to be since I can't recall any of this.

"These are your last moments as a single man," Eli reminds me. "Any final thoughts?"

"What's taking her so long?" I mumble.

"Easy tiger," Eli attempts to settle my nerves. "She's wanting to make a grand entrance on this very important occasion. You can't fault her for that."

"I'll be fine when I see here," I growl. "I don't like her out of my sight."

Eli pats my shoulder, before taking his spot beside me and pointing the camera down the small aisle lined with a few white folding chairs.

The bridal march begins, the French doors open, and my heart stops.

Montana

I stare at Eli's video, Carson close at my side, still holding my hand in his. I watch myself walk down the aisle in a gorgeous, Marilyn Monroe style, white halter dress, the hem falling high on my thigh; my feet are adorned with delicate sandals and satin ribbons criss cross up my calves. The look is complete with the biggest smile I've ever worn.

My eyes lock upon Carson's while I make my way to his side. Eli turns the camera toward the men, then back to me as I assume my position beside Peyton who's still wearing her LBD.

Eli moves behind the officiant, framing the two of us in his lens. Occasionally, he zooms out to include Peyton in the video.

"You may exchange your own vows," the officiant states.

I look quickly to Carson, confused. *If we drank enough and we don't remember any of this, how were we able to say our own vows?* I prepare myself for drunken babble and slurring.

"Carson," I listen as I begin my vows, "I'll be the Oreos to your milk, holding you in my arms on a bad day. I promise to wear silk and to always come watch you play. I'll be beside you, no matter what life brings. I'll tickle your tattoos and always listen when you sing. I'll be your biggest fan, following wherever you lead. I'll do everything I can to be everything you need."

Wow. Where did I come up with those rhyming words? Did I spend an hour writing them? They're unique and express perfectly my new feelings for Carson.

He pauses the video. "How did you come up with your vows on the spot like that?" he asks me.

I raise his hand in mine and place it over my heart. He nods, gulping; I watch his Adam's apple move. He pushes play.

"I guess it's my turn," he says, looking to the official for confirmation. "My first, my last, my always. You're Leia to my Han Solo, Adrian to my Rocky, and my partner in crime. I promise to put the seat down, hold your hair back while you puke, and do my best to keep you safe. I'll strive to make you happy—I love your laugh. And, I'll make sure you never get locked out again."

I'm choked up, both on the video and now sitting beside him. His words, his beautiful and perfect words, fill my heart with joy.

Like me, he didn't seem drunk; he didn't even slur a single word. *So, why the hell can neither of us remember this special moment?*

We are pronounced husband and wife. Without prompting, I launch myself into Carson's arms; chest to chest, I wrap my arms around his neck and legs around his waist. His mouth crashes to mine; our lips battle, our bodies longing to show the vows we just shared.

It's not the wedding Peyton and I've planned a million times since our childhood; it's better. It's not traditional, and it's not scripted., It's spur of the moment with heartfelt honesty, just like our conversation on the floor of the hotel hallway the day before.

"Can we watch it again?" I ask.

He purses his lips, shaking his head. "We need to pack for the airport," Carson states. "We'll watch it again on the plane. Besides, Peyton is probably dying to have you to herself. I'll walk you to your room."

"It's about time," Peyton greets when I enter our room. "Did you watch the wedding video?"

"I can't believe how perfect it was," I explain. "Impromptu, honest, and perfect."

"I know, right?" she agrees. "Now, tell me. Do you really plan to stay married? I mean, last night I felt both of you knew exactly what you were doing, and it was meant to be. Now that I know neither of you remember it, and I assume that means you were drunk, I question your reasons to stay married."

"We're going to make it work," I reiterate. "We feel the same way we did last night, exchanging our vows. I can't explain it. It happened in an instant. There was no fighting love at first sight."

"Well, I guess I'll be flying back to Des Moines by myself." Peyton extends her lower lip out in a pout. "Some of us have a job to start in two days."

"Boo hoo," I mock. "At least you have a direction you are working towards. You know what you want. I'm still confused, even more so now. Speaking of confused, which guy did you end up choosing?" I wiggle my eyebrows at her.

"Guy?" she asks. "It's guys." She giggles.

My eyes grow to the size of saucers. *She can't mean... No, she wouldn't. Would she?*

"There's no need to choose. Men do it all the time. I chose both of them." She shows no remorse for her decision.

"And, they went for it?" I shouldn't ask; I don't want details, but I need to know where her mind is.

"It took some coaxing on my part," she blushes.

"I don't want details. I just need to know you are happy and safe."

"Happy is not the word for it. I'm sated for the moment. I had the best night of my life and hope to repeat it many times to come. Thanks to you, they'll be in Des Moines all summer."

"Peyton," fear laces my voice, "I'm afraid they'll hurt you. They're used to women throwing themselves at their feet every day. What will you do when they move on?"

"I'm not that vested in the relationship yet, so stop worrying. For now, I'm a single woman, having fun. It may be for a night or a few nights. I'm a big girl; I can take care of myself."

"So, while I got married in Vegas, you joined a thruple," I can't believe how our lives changed during our three days in Nevada.

"A thruple?" Peyton's brow furrows.

"Yes, a thruple. It's a threesome and a couple called a thruple. Or, do you prefer to use triad to describe it?"

"How do you know about this?" she asks, hands on her hips.

"I read romance novels, and I know things," I proudly state.

"Maybe you should start sharing your books with me," she teases. "I can't have you know more about my sexual conquests than I do."

"Crap! Look at the time," I screech. "We need to pack and be downstairs in an hour, and I still need to shower."

"Go shower; I'll pack for the both of us," she offers. "Just don't be surprised when some of your new clothes fly home with me today."

16

CARSON

In Los Angeles

"Montana, we're here," I murmur near her head which is resting on my shoulder. "It's time to wake up." I can't believe she didn't wake when we stopped at the security gate at the entrance to the neighborhood.

It warms my heart that she feels comfortable enough with me to sleep on my shoulder. We shared a long night of sex last night that neither of us remembers, and except holding hands while watching the wedding video, this is the first contact we've had since. My body craves her touch and loves having her near.

Her groggy eyes take a moment to focus on me before turning to my house.

"It's not the over-the-top mansion I thought it would be," she states, taking in my simple three-story beachfront house in Huntington Beach, CA.

"I'm not a mansion type of guy," I tell her. "Oh, fuck."

"Are those your...?"

"Yep. Those are my parents," I groan under my breath. "They're supposed to be in San Diego." I turn to her. "I'm sorry; this is not what I planned."

I slide from the back seat, extending my arm for her to join me. I'm sure Mom heard about the wedding and nagged Dad until he drove her here to shut her up. This will be interesting; meet the parents, firing squad style.

We round the front of the black escalade before I see my new dog standing at Dad's side; I forgot he arrived this week. I stride toward my parents, more excited to meet my Malamute.

My mom, ever the sharp dresser, stands in her designer Velour tracksuit, complete with rhinestones and a word across her butt, in full makeup and high-heeled tennis shoes. My father's in his signature golf shirt and shorts with designer logos, brown leather loafers, and dark tan skin.

"Hello dear," Mom greets me, kissing each cheek European style.

"Mom," I hug her. "And, you come over here and meet your new daddy," I say to the furry beast near her feet.

"Who's this?" Montana bends to pet the friendly fur ball.

Untrained, the large puppy places his two enormous paws on her shoulders to lick her face, causing her to fall backward into the grass. Giggling, Montana shifts her face from side to side in an attempt to avoid licks, all the while rubbing the puppy's tummy above her.

I guess she's a dog lover. That's good since I forgot to discuss this with her before our arrival. So caught up in her, I completely forgot he'd arrive this week, and I would come home to my new companion instead of my lonely house.

"Okay, that's enough," I state. Pulling the mammoth fur ball from Montana's chest, I hand the red leash back to my dad.

Montana stands, brushing grass off of herself nervously, taking her place by my side.

"To what do I owe the honor?" I ask my mom.

"Well, dear," Mom answers, "we had a few free days and while reading the morning headlines, we were excited for you and wanted to speak with you before the band starts recording."

Crap! I neglected to introduce Montana right away. I pray she doesn't read into it. My parents caught me off guard, and I didn't mean to forget the introduction.

"Mom, Dad, this is my wife Montana." I smile proudly.

Montana smiles back at me; we both realize it's the first time I've called her my wife.

"Montana, this is my dad and mom, Kurt and Aaron."

I watch nervously as Mom's eyes assess her. She has her feelers out; she wants to start the interrogation and be nosey, but she waits. This may be the longest evening ever.

Montana

In a whirlwind, I meet Carson's new puppy and his parents. I know Carson didn't plan for company when we arrived in L.A. I roll with it because, as a newly married couple, we are bound to be ambushed by our parents, siblings, and friends.

When we entered the house, Carson wanted to take me on a tour, but Aaron announced they had supper ready and sent Carson's housekeeper home early, promising to care for the puppy until we arrived. This doesn't please my new husband.

"Carson, help your father fetch the meat off the grill," his mom orders. "Montana, you can help me place these on the patio table." She motions to salad and dishes on the kitchen counter, and I comply.

"What is it you do?" Aaron asks, as soon the men are out of earshot.

"I recently graduated from a community college with my Associate's Degree," I explain. "I'm deciding this summer if I'll head back to school or find a job."

"So, you're taking a gap year? That's convenient." His mother raises her eyebrows.

Is she insinuating I did not meet Carson by chance?

"What do your parents do for a living?" she continues as she hands me two bowls and signals for me to follow her out another set of doors to a patio table.

"My father owns a large farm north of Des Moines, and my mother runs the family's real estate business. They also own several properties."

After we place the dishes in the center of the table, I follow her back indoors.

"Any desire to go into the family business?" she queries.

I shake my head. Although I'm not sure what career I'd like, I do know it's not farming or real estate. I've helped both of my parents off and on throughout the years. I respect what they do; it's just not for me.

Aaron stands with her hands on her hips. "He's seldom home. What do you plan to do while he's away?"

"I guess that's what I'll be deciding this summer," I reply. "I could work toward my bachelor's degree or work full time by fall. I just don't know yet."

"How'd you pay for the Las Vegas trip with no job?" she pries.

Carson

Dad and I enter the kitchen in time to hear Montana defending herself.

"Not that I owe you an explanation," she remains calm. "When I was 18, my brother and I created an app. We sold it a year later to a tech company for close to six million dollars. I also have a small trust fund when I turn 25, and I own 10 percent of my family's real estate business. Trust me; your son's money is safe."

"Mom, that's enough," I demand, raising my voice. "I won't have you attack her when I turn my back."

"Uh, what?" Mom feigns innocence.

"You need to trust that I know what I'm doing and accept Montana as my wife and your daughter-in-law. Or, we won't welcome you in our house."

Montana places her hand upon my shoulder. "It's fine, Carson. I'm sure my parents would worry about the same things if our roles were reversed."

I kiss her temple, placing my arm around her shoulders, escorting her with me to the patio.

During dinner, it's as if nothing happened; we eat steaks, salad, and asparagus with wine and water. Montana's stories and our questions about the city of Des Moines, her family, and her brother's African adventures keep us entertained.

"Finish your wine," I urge Montana and Dad. "I'll help Mom with the dishes."

We load our arms with the empty dishes and make our way inside. While I load the dishwasher, Mom moves leftovers into containers and places them into the refrigerator.

"Tell me how you met," Mom instructs.

"It's like the opposite of the Big Bang theory," I explain. "With us, instead of the collision of the two objects exploding outwards, the explosion happened inside. When we met, it's like we collided, and a fire lit within me. Our meeting, our collision, sparked a reaction here." I point to my chest. "The more we talked, the more we were together, the fire grew and flowed through my veins. Call it love at first sight, fate, destiny, or blind luck, but it happened within two days. I'm all in; I'm a goner. Cupid's arrow permanently pierces my heart. I am in love."

Mom chuckles. "Your descriptions are verbose and vivid. You could have said 'I knew it the moment I saw her.'"

I could have, but that isn't adequate for the physical and chemical reaction between us. We aren't the typical "boy meets girl, boy dates girl, boy marries girl" story. We are much more than that.

17

MONTANA

With our empty wine glasses in hand, Kurt and I join the others in the kitchen, Denali, the Malamute, trotting behind us.

"Let me give Montana a tour, then we can meet on the rooftop," Carson suggests to his parents.

"So, this is the kitchen." He swings his arms wide.

I'm already very familiar with this open space, with the large island with seating for five, and the bar area to the side, near the floor-to-ceiling glass doors, leading to the outdoor grill.

A few steps away, also on the first floor, we walk through a giant living room, complete with a wall of glass, two French doors to the patio where we ate, a small powder room, and a mudroom with a shower off to the patio side.

Near the table where we ate, the stone patio holds a wicker sectional with large, cushioned chairs, a glass railing all around, and a glass gate that opens to a wooden ramp which leads down to the private beach he promises to show me tomorrow.

Next, he ushers me upstairs to find an open seating area, three bedrooms and three baths with French doors onto a balcony off of the seating area.

On the third floor, he shows me a library at the top of stairs, French doors to yet another large balcony, and more stairs that continue to the roof. Before we climb, he opens two heavy wooden doors, unveiling his master bedroom and bath, the largest walk-in closet I've ever stood in, and his personal library space. He tugs me from the room much too soon.

We continue up the stairs to find patio chairs and tables, string lights, large planters with tropical plants, a putting green, and a fabulous view of the sandy beach and ocean below. His parents sip from wine glasses, sitting around a stone table with a fire burning in its center.

"We brought up the wine and the puppy," Carson's father boasts.

We enjoy our drinks on the rooftop patio, sitting in chaise loungers with throw blankets to ward off the cool ocean breeze. His parents decide to shop and eat at a quaint beachfront dive bar they frequent when in town. They invite the two of us to join them tomorrow. An hour passes before his parents excuse themselves for bed.

Carson

"Where would you like to sleep?" I ask, nervous of her answer.

She shrugs beneath her blanket, a small smile gracing her lips.

I continue. "How about we take Denali out for a potty break then chat in my room until you're ready to sleep?"

She nods, a smile growing larger. Standing, she folds her blanket before placing it on the seat.

"We should grab a snack, too," she hints. "Can Denali sleep in your room tonight with us?"

I shake my head, smiling. This woman can have anything she asks for. I'm putty in her hand.

After eating a snack of cheese and crackers, Montana takes Denali out front to potty while I move the dog paraphernalia to my room. I had no idea puppies needed this much stuff.

Montana

I struggle to find a patch of grass or dirt out front for Carson's puppy to do its business. I never knew grass to be a luxury; I take it for granted in Iowa. Lucky for the both of us, Denali is a male. He lifts his leg and waters a lamppost near the end of the driveway. Thank heavens he didn't need to go number two. *I wonder if Denali will fly with us or remain in L.A.*

Later, in bed chatting, I keep looking at the puppy in the kennel on the floor in the corner of Carson's room. It seems cruel to place him in a cage while we are here. I realize he might chew on things, but with us near, he can't do any damage.

"If this were my house," I blurt, "Denali would sleep with me."

He hops from his side of the bed, frees Denali from the cage, and helps him up onto the bed. The large fur ball licks my cheek then lumbers to Carson's side and lays lengthways beside him. While I rub his belly and pet his head, he licks my arm and cheek before yawning.

"It's your house too," Carson informs me. "In California, what's mine is yours in our marriage."

With that, our conversation turns to our arrangement and the important items we should know about each other. We talk financials; I share in further detail the app I created and sold. He's surprised when I tell him it's the casino map and friend tracking app I downloaded to his phone. I share that we split the earnings 70 percent mine as it was my idea and I did most of the research, 15 percent my brother's, and 15 percent to the coder we hired.

I wake the next morning alone in Carson's bed. We talked until the wee hours of the morning last night. In fact, I'm not sure if I fell asleep first or if he did. I learned about his parent's house, his father's marketing firm, and his brother and sister. Looking around the room, I notice Denali is missing as well.

In his bathroom, I run my fingers through my hair and wash my face. My reflection tells me I'm presentable, so I head downstairs for breakfast. From the bottom step, I see breakfast is spread out on the island, buffet-style.

I smile, waving at Carson's house manager. He told me all about her last night. She's a single mom named Sonny with a four-year-old son, Matt. I find he sits, coloring, while nibbling on his breakfast.

Sonny stands behind the island, wearing a warm smile, dressed casually.

"Good morning," I greet, taking a plate. I butter toast then spread peanut butter on top. I place fresh fruit and yogurt on my plate then sit by the little boy.

"I like your picture. Can you tell me about it?" I encourage.

Matt points to parts of the drawing and tells me about it. Soon, Carson's parents join us to eat.

"Is Carson still asleep?" his mother asks, taking the barstool beside me.

Sonny answers before I can admit I have no clue where he is.

"Carson took Denali on a walk at the beach." She looks at her watch. "He left 20 minutes ago and should be back soon."

My plate empty, I place it in the dishwasher, much to Sonny's protest.

"I think I'll venture to the beach," I state, walking to the patio door.

I find the pair right away. Carson's private beach is a quarter of a mile long. Carson greets me with a kiss on my cheek. Denali greets me with large, wet paws to my thighs. My husband informs me they've walked back and forth several times.

"He needs obedience school," Carson mutters. "He shouldn't jump up like that."

"How old is he? Six weeks?" I defend. "He needs stability. You'll just have to train him and reward him with little treats."

"We," Carson interjects. "*We* will train him; *we* will give him stability."

I nod. It's hard to remember we are a couple; what's his is mine and mine is his. Having only had two serious relationships lasting two months, I'm not practiced in referring to myself as part of a pair.

We walk the dog three more laps on the beach.

"Your housekeeper seems nice, and her son is too adorable. How long has she worked for you? And how does she make it by only working part time?"

Carson informs me, "She's my house manager, not housekeeper. She lives in the mother-in-law suite above the garage. I didn't show that to you as I didn't want to disturb her last night. She works for me all year, and I provide benefits. I even pay for Matt's preschool nearby."

We turn around and head back in the direction we just came from.

He continues, "She once mentioned to me that I should open the house to be an Airbnb while I'm touring. I gave her permission to do that and allow her to keep those profits. I can't lose her, so I try to spoil her like she spoils me."

We return to the house, towel drying Denali's paws before we enter.

"Oh my, look at the time," I urge. "We're supposed to head out with your parents in an hour. I'll take Denali to his kennel, and you get in the shower."

Carson pulls me against his chest. I feel him vibrate as his husky voice invites, "If we shower together, we can save time."

I raise an eyebrow, unsure if I'm ready for showering together.

He smiles his sexy smirk.

Unraveled

The next morning, while eating breakfast, my phone vibrates, signaling a FaceTime call. "Excuse me; I need to take this." I scoot my chair from the breakfast table and Carson's parents.

"It's my brother," I whisper to Carson as I pass.

"Hello," I greet nervously, aware of the lecture coming my way.

"I didn't wake you, did I?" Joe asks.

"We're eating breakfast. It's eight here," I answer. "What time is it in Africa?"

"About five. We're getting ready for dinner," he explains.

In the background, I see bare dirt and huts in the distance.

"I miss you," I whisper, fighting back my tears.

"I'm sure you do, but we've got other stuff to cover." My brother's voice takes on an authoritative tone. "What were you thinking?"

"Joe…" Tears fall, and my throat swells shut.

"Let's put aside the fact that you were blitzed in an unfamiliar city with strangers that are rock stars. Mom says you're not getting the annulment. Montana, you can't stay married to a complete stranger. Who does that?" He pauses for a moment. "Insane people, that's who."

"Joe, he's not a stranger." I clear my throat in the hopes my voice sounds serious. "I know we rushed the wedding, but we're slowing things down now."

"That's the craziest thing I've ever heard. He could be a serial killer, a rapist, a deadbeat loser, an abusive S.O.B.--"

"I know you're upset with me," I interrupt his list. "But it upsets me that you think so little of me."

"Montana, that's not what I meant," he quickly clarifies. "You've always been level-headed. I never thought in a million years you'd elope in Vegas. Peyton, yes—you, never."

"Did Mom tell you we spent two days together? And that there were instantly signs this wasn't only attraction?" I swallow, then quickly continue. "If it were someone I met hours before marrying, I would have annulled. Carson's different. We spent a lot of time together, and I couldn't bear the thought of leaving Las Vegas and never seeing him again. We're just going to spend some time together. If it doesn't work out, then we'll get a divorce. We both felt it's worth trying to stay together."

"You expect me to believe in two days you knew enough to marry this guy?" Joe asks.

"Joe, we both agree Carson and I rushed into marriage. Two days is *not* enough time to make the commitment," I explain. "We are interested enough that we didn't want to go our separate ways without trying, though. I believe in love at first sight. When he sat beside me in the hotel hallway and we made small talk, there was an instant connection. I felt complete for the first time. We spent that evening together with Peyton and his band. He never once tried to hold my hand or kiss me. We talked and talked and talked. He's different from any guy I've ever crushed on or dated. You'll see."

I position myself on the patio chair. "I wish you were in the States. Then, you'd see he's all I say he is and more. We're headed to Iowa tomorrow. I can't wait for Mom and Dad to meet him."

A little boy packing a heavy pail walks close behind Joe. He's adorable, all dusty in a much-to-big t-shirt and bare feet. I'd hoped to visit my brother in Africa this summer. His village in the background of our calls entices me. My trip to Africa will need to wait. I married Carson and need to invest my time in our relationship.

"You know they'll rake him over the coals," Joe warns.

"I'm very aware of that."

"If I were in Iowa, this never would have happened. What kind of brother lets his little sister elope with a rock star?" He shakes his head, his scraggly brown hair flying everywhere in the breeze.

"The only way you'd have prevented it was not allowing me to go to Las Vegas with Peyton. And, we both know you wouldn't have been able to stop Peyton's girls' trip."

"Get an annulment; then, you can date him if you want him in your life. You can't stay married to him," my big brother orders. "An annulment or a divorce. Take your pick."

"Joe, I need you to hear me," I bite. "I love him. We're staying married, so deal with it."

I've never spoken to my brother like this. In fact, I've never been this mad or disappointed in him. I understand he's trying to protect me, but this is my decision; I'm a grown woman. If he can't accept my decision, then it's a good thing he's halfway around the world in Africa.

"Are those waves I'm hearing?" Joe's smile signals he's done with his big-brother lecture.

I turn the camera, sharing the beach view.

"Damn! Mom didn't tell me his house is on the beach," Joe chuckles.

"Yeah, well, Mom doesn't know much... yet." I chuckle. "Other than being on the beach, his house is pretty normal."

I rise from my patio chair, giving him a 360-degree view.

"That's way too much glass to be a *normal* house. Nice try," he teases.

"I meant on the inside," I explain. "It's casual, not flashy or formal. His parents are here, or I'd take you on a tour."

Joe turns his stance, and more of the village comes into view. Now, I see a group of school-age children sitting around a woman with a guitar on the steps to the medical tent. The children clap and wiggle with her music.

"Who's that?" I ask, not recognizing her from the staff I've met in his previous video calls.

"She's the musician I've mentioned before. When she's free, she visits with her music. She encourages them to trust the doctors." Something's different in his voice, but I don't press the subject. I'm proud of the work he does for Doctors Without Borders. Selling my app allowed him to volunteer. Instead of working exhausting hours at a hospital to pay off his student loans, he graduated debt free with money left over to volunteer in under-privileged regions.

"They look so happy." My eyes stay on the children. "Are they still teaching you to play soccer?"

"Yes, and I'm still pretending to suck at it," he laughs. "They enjoy teaching me and laugh at my mess-ups."

The woman, finished with her song, stands, waves to the children, then walks towards my brother. He quickly places the camera back on his face.

"She's gorgeous." I tell him something he already knows.

"Shh. She's coming this way." I can barely hear his low voice. "I'll let you go."

I'm surprised by his sudden desire to disconnect.

"I love you, and I miss you," I state before saying goodbye.

"Montana, be careful. I'd hate to fly home and kick his butt if he hurts you. I might wind up in jail." He winks and smirks at me.

I hold my phone tight to my chest. With his closing words, Joe's letting me live my life and offering his support. I'm confident that when my family meets Carson, they'll understand.

18

CARSON

At Des Moines International Airport

Montana directs our driver to take us to the end of the terminal for the rental car counters. Since Peyton picked up her vehicle last week when she flew home while we went to L.A., I'm renting a vehicle today for me and the guys to use for the summer. I select a sweet, red, Jeep Wrangler Rubicon Recon 4x4. I can't wait to take the doors and top off.

"Should we stop and grab a few things on our way to Corey's house?" she asks as we pull from the airport.

"No, we'll get back out later if we need to," I promise, ready to get to the house and relax.

Montana helps me navigate through the city; then, we let our GPS guide us to the house. She also texts her mother and Peyton that we are safe in Des Moines and makes plans to talk tomorrow.

At the security gate I buzz, give my name, and we drive up the long, winding lane. Standing outside the front door are two women to greet us.

"You didn't tell me Miss Kelly would be here," Montana's voice is high-pitched, excited, and she hops from the jeep before I can get out myself. "Miss Kelly!" she calls, arms wide, walking to her.

"Oh my Lord, Montana, what are you doing here?" the woman who I assume is Miss Kelly asks, walking to hug Montana.

"Carson Cavanaugh, ma'am," I greet, extending my hand.

"Phish!" Kelly waves off my greeting. "It's Kelly, not ma'am."

"So, how do the two of you know each other?" I query.

"I've known Montana since she was knee high to a grasshopper," Kelly answers.

"My mom serves on several charity boards with Miss Kelly," Montana explains.

"Let me make proper introductions," Kelly states. "I'm Corey's mother, Kelly, and this is Corey's house manager, Fran. She'll see to anything and everything you might need while you are here."

Montana

Corey's house is not the mansion I assumed it to be. It's a large house for the Des Moines area but looks similar to many other houses in design. As we follow Miss Kelly and Fran into the home, we find the decor is comfy and relaxed with lots of photos of his family, friends, and other entertainers. Adding to this inviting interior are large pillows, overstuffed cushions, and hardwood floors, not the cold tile many prestigious mansions would boast. The space looks lived in rather than uninviting.

19

MONTANA

The Next Morning

Carson and I sleep in until Denali signals he needs to potty by licking my face to wake me up. We hook him to the leash and head out on a long walk near the lake. Since we won't be leaving Corey's property, I keep on the t-shirt and boxers I wore to bed last night.

We laugh at Denali's attempt to lift his back leg to wet on everything over six inches tall.

"No way he has more urine left to mark with," I giggle.

"Don't make fun of him!" Carson acts offended. "He's a growing boy, trying to make his mark on the world."

"What is it with males of every species needing to pee as many places as possible? My brother used to pee on Mom's plants in the backyard and everywhere on Dad's farm," I share.

"Not all of us pee everywhere," Carson defends.

"Ever peed in the snow?" I raise my eyebrow in his direction. At his nod, I continue, "Go on a tree?"

"Okay; some of us go outside once or twice in our lifetime," he admits.

"Only twice? I call bullshit."

We've reached the lake, so I lead Denali to the water's edge. He stops with his front two paws in the water; his head low, he laps up as much water as he can.

"Poor thing dehydrated himself walking down here," Carson deadpans.

I laugh loudly at Carson's words and the loud lapping of water by Denali.

"Let's sit on the dock," Carson suggests, and I follow, tugging the leash behind me.

At first, Denali's scared to walk on the wooden dock as it moves with the gentle waves. I kneel beside him. "It's okay," I coo, patting for him to step towards me. "C'mon, that's it."

Within arm's length, I praise him with belly rubs and strokes under his chin. "You're a brave boy. Yes, you are."

Carson chuckles behind me. I look over my shoulder at him, blocking the bright sun with my free hand. Carson smashes his teeth between his lips, moving his fingers as if zipping his mouth shut before tossing the imaginary key over his shoulder. He can make fun of my baby-talking to Denali all he likes. Soon, he'll do it, too.

I rise, pulling the fluffy puppy with me to the end of the dock. I slip off my shoes, dipping my foot in the water below. I pat the board beside me, inviting Carson to join me.

As the two of us sit, gently kicking our bare feet in the cool lake water, Denali, who's seated beside me, whimpers. His front paws are inches from the edge. He leans his nose towards the water then whines again.

"It's okay," I promise, placing my hand in the water in front of him.

He steps up, closer to the edge. When he lowers his head, I swirl my hand in the water in front of him. He watches my movements closely. With no warning, he jumps into the lake, splashing the two of us.

Carson laughs while I freak out. *What if he can't swim?* It's his first time in a lake. Tears well in my eyes as my fear grows.

"Atta boy," Carson cheers, turning to watch Denali paddle to shore.

I attempt to wipe my tears, hiding them from him. My breathing calms while I watch Denali shake himself dry on shore. I take in a deep breath now that he's safely on land.

"What's wrong?" Carson asks, pulling me into his embrace.

I sniffle, shaking my head, not looking up to meet his eyes. He lifts my chin, forcing me to let him see my tears.

"Were you scared?"

I nod. "What if he couldn't swim?" I whimper, my voice unsteady.

"Honey, he can swim," he chuckles. "He did the doggie paddle."

I giggle at him. I turn quickly in his arms at the loud splash as Denali jumps in from the deck again.

"He's okay. No need to worry. He's okay." Carson's calm voice soothes me. "I'm not sure how we'll get him out of the water to go eat breakfast, though,"

Carson chuckles. "You're protective of him; I like that." His lips hover near mine. "I love you."

My breath catches, and my fingers clutch tight to his t-shirt. Those three words catch me off guard. Three little words, eight letters; they are powerful. They're heady. We're married; we should love each other. "I love you," he said with me in his arms, sharing a simple, private moment. He beat me to it; he said it first. He loves me.

Back at the house, I dart into the shower before I eat breakfast. When I descend the stairs and enter the kitchen, Miss Kelly points to the security screen. My mom waits at the gate. Miss Kelly enters the code and urges her to drive on up to the house.

"I need to pop into the restroom; I'll be right back," I tell her.

When I return, I hear Mom and Miss Kelly chatting excitedly as they enter the house. While they catch up on the many charity boards and activities they are involved in, I sneak out back with Denali for a minute.

I walk closer to the studio door while Denali looks for the best place to lift his leg. Although the urge to open the door and peek inside is strong, I fight it. Carson needs to work, and I have plans with Mom. Denali finishes, and we walk back inside.

"I thought you were going to text me when you were at the gate," I remind Mom. "Miss Kelly, you want to join us for lunch?"

"No, thank you," she answers. "I'm running errands; I just popped by to make sure you had everything you need. I have too much to do today while the dogs are at the groomers."

"Let's eat," Mom suggests, placing her arm around my shoulders and waving to her friend.

"Want to meet Carson before we go?" I ask, hopeful and wanting a reason to be near him.

"No, let's wait until after we eat," Mom suggests. "We have a ton to talk about."

"A ton." That's an understatement. I'm not sure exactly what my mom's reaction is and am sure she has much to lecture me about.

Mom is unusually quiet as we drive down the long lane from Corey's house. I find the silence unbearable.

"In the mood for Gilroy's?" I ask nervously.

"Ooh, I love that place," Mom states. "Is that on 8th Street?"

"Yes; we can sit on the patio and drink Moscow mules with lunch," I add. "Mom, let's start our conversation now, so we can enjoy lunch."

"We'll enjoy lunch, no matter what," Mom declares. "This lunch isn't to punish you, Montana. We have a lot of questions and answers to cover."

"So, shall I tell you about him?" The urge to start our talk grows with every silent, passing moment.

"First, I have something to tell you," Mom opens.

I swallow hard. Here we go. Here's the disappointment statement. Here's the guilt trip.

"When you won at your slot machine..." Mom begins. "The woman, Dawn, in the photograph you posted on social media..."

This is nowhere near what I expected her to say. I thought she'd lecture me on responsibility and the sanctity of marriage.

"Dawn and I serve on the JDRF and Variety Club boards together." Mom smiles at me before returning her eyes to the road. "It's a small world, isn't it?"

"Yes," I agree. "She told me she was from Des Moines. In fact, she asked if she could text me a photo of us to sneakily get my cell number. Then, she mentioned I'd be perfect for one of her single sons."

"She's out of luck on that matter, now, isn't she?" Mom laughs. "Married women can't go on blind dates."

"Hmm, I hadn't thought of that," I lie. "Guess that means you can't keep setting me up then, too."

As we laugh together, my mood lightens, and my worries fade. The dread I had for this lunch disappears.

After we order our drinks, Mom adjusts the umbrella to better block the sun from our faces then starts her list of questions. "So, how did you meet?"

I share the story of being locked out of the room, waiting on the hall floor for the maintenance staff, and how Carson nearly stepped on me.

"You'll be happy to know he's polite, not only to me but to everyone around him," I promise.

"He's handsome," Mom giggles.

"Duh! Of course, he's handsome." *Did she expect me to settle down with an ogre? I mean, I'm not superficial or vain, but I do have 20/20 vision.*

"He's a regular guy. Good values and family are important to him," I share. "Sparks flew the instant we met, and although we were impulsive on our second night out, it's both our family values that has us staying together instead of signing for a quick annulment."

While we nibble on our shared appetizer then our meal, I continue telling Mom about the band, Carson's writer's block, the lyrics he's started writing, and how he changed their plan to record in Des Moines instead of L.A. to be near me. "Here." I hand her my cell phone, open to photos I took of his house.

"I can't wait for you to see his beach house in person. The photos don't do it justice. Keep scrolling," I prompt.

"That's his house manager, Sonny, and her son, Matt," I state. "She lives on the premises, and he keeps her on full-time, all year-round. She had the idea to rent his home out as an Airbnb while he's on tour. Because it was her idea, he lets her keep all the money she earns from that."

"Wow," Mom reacts with a mouth full of food.

"He treats her like family. It's sweet," I confirm.

"You look radiant," Mom blurts. "He's good for you."

"Mom…"

"What are we waiting for? Let's go so I can meet my new son-in-law," Mom says, waving for our bill.

"Lunch is on me," I state. When Mom argues, I inform her, "I won even more money on my second day in Las Vegas."

Smiling, she shakes her head.

On the ride back to Saylorville Lake, I decide to ask my mom for advice. "What was it like being married to Dad in the beginning?"

Mom shares about nerves, getting to know everything about each other, about marriage, and trust. She tells me she protects Dad as much as he protects her. She hurts when he does, celebrates when he does. Marriage is a work in progress, and so is love. It's not all desire, and it's based on loyalty.

"I feel like a middle school girl with a crush," I share. "I want to be near him twenty-four-seven, and I can't stop thinking about him; I'm like a bee, constantly buzzing around him. My heart constantly pounds my ribcage."

"That's the early stages of love," Mom assures me. "The honeymoon phase isn't just a weekend or week. It's a year or two. It's hard, but you need to find your own identity, even as his wife. You can't lose yourself in him, or you'll never last."

I nod.

"I know you planned to decide this summer whether to continue with college or find a job of interest to you," Mom says. "Is that still your plan?"

I nod again. "I'm leaning more towards entrepreneurship. But I'm not 100 percent sure yet."

"Well, you've proven yourself in that arena already with your app," Mom agrees. "I think you could make a go of it."

"I have a product I've been working with Peyton on," I share. "Maybe I'll use the summer to give it legs and see if I'm happy while doing it."

"Sounds like a brilliant plan," Mom states, pressing the call button at the gate.

Carson

As Fran opens the gate, my nerves skyrocket. Montana promised me her mother will come around quicker than my mom did. She describes her as positive and always smiling. But she's never eloped with a rock star before. She has no way of knowing how her parents will react to our marriage. My hands shake as I reach to open the front door.

"Carson," Montana calls as she jogs towards me. "This is my mom, Tony. Mom, this is Carson Cavanaugh, my husband."

I smile at Montana and her words before I turn to greet her mother.

"Mrs. Randall, it's a pleasure. Come, let's sit." I motion to the interior of the house.

"We'll have none of that," Mrs. Randall orders.

Crap! She's not happy with me or the marriage. Bloody hell, this will be a long afternoon.

"You'll call me Tony," she states. "Mrs. Randall was my mother-in-law." She laughs at what I'm sure is the scared look upon my face.

"Okay," I agree. "Tony, please join us inside."

Montana's mother walks ahead of us. I look to Montana with raised brows. She shakes her head, an enormous smile upon her face. She mouths, "Everything is good." Her words do little to settle my nerves.

"Mom, would you like a drink?" Montana asks before we take a seat.

"Yes, tea or water please," Tony replies.

"Would you like to sit here in the living room, out on the pool deck, or in the kitchen?" I ask.

"We ate on the patio, and it's heating up," Tony informs me. "Let's find a spot in the kitchen."

I motion for her to follow the steps her daughter took only moments before, and I follow. We sit at the kitchen island, and Montana places ice-cold drinks in front of each of us.

"Carson," Tony begins, "Montana has told me so much about you today. It's nice to meet you."

"Thanks," I respond. "I hope most of it was good."

"Phish." Tony waves her hand. "Seems you're much more than a rock star."

20

MONTANA

Late that Night

Nestled in the warmth of our king-sized bed, Carson cuddles my back against his front for several long moments as we talk.

Tonight, I pull away, lying on my side to face him. The pale moonlight allows me to see his face. Too many thoughts clog my mind.

What if we have no sexual chemistry in the bedroom, if we're not compatible sexually? Will our marriage and friendship end? What if he has terrible habits that I can't bear? What will happen if I want to go back to college or start my career in Des Moines? What if his writer's block returns? What if I snore?

"What's going on in there?" Carson taps my forehead before tucking hair behind my ear.

"There's still so much we don't know about each other," I admit. It's not a lie; I'm summing up all of my concerns.

He nods. "Let's remedy that now."

I scrunch my face, unsure what he means. *How can we remedy it now?*

"Do you have any allergies," Carson inquires.

"Chocolate makes me itch with hives. You?"

"I'm allergic to bees," he shares. "I carry an EpiPen everywhere I go." His hand brushes lightly over my cheek then falls between us. "How old were you when you first tried alcohol? And, what was it?" He smiles.

I guess we're playing twenty questions to learn more about each other.

"I was 16 at a party at Peyton's house while her parents were out of town," I answer. "I'm not sure what it was. I suspect it was a punch of sorts. Red liquid in red cups. There were so many bottles around the concoction, it could have been any or all of them." I raise my eyebrows. "You?"

"I was 16--"

"Uh-huh," I interrupt. "You can't use my answer. Tell the truth."

"I'm trying to," he defends. "I was 16; I snuck a bottle of vodka from my parents' liquor cabinet. Eli and I drank the entire bottle during our band practice. This was before Jake and Warner joined us."

"How'd you get that scar?" I point to his left jaw.

His fingers trace the jagged scar as if he'd forgotten he had it. "A broken beer bottle, pulling Jake and Warner from a bar fight when we were 19."

I'm not surprised he protected his bandmates then, just like he does today. It's one of the endearing qualities that drew me to him.

"What were you like in middle school and high school?" he queries.

"I was a nerd of sorts," I begin. *Why is describing myself so difficult?*

"I read a lot, took advanced-placement courses, took part in clubs and sports. But my genuine passion was to hole up in my room, reading, writing in my journal, or researching online." I shrug. "I was boring, really."

"What did you read?"

"In middle school, mostly John Greene and Stephen King…"

"That rhymes," he chortles.

"In high school," I continue, rubbing my tired eyes, "I discovered true crime and romance novels." I blush, hoping the faint moonlight hides my pink cheeks. "Online, I binged TED Talks, documentaries, conspiracy theories, and STEM related articles."

"Diverse. I like it." Carson repositions himself on his two fluffy pillows, body still turned to face me.

"Let me guess." I bite my lips as I contemplate a younger version of Carson. "You were a jock, captain of sports teams, before you gave it all up to start a band with Eli. It became your addiction, and you became successful."

He smirks, "I played sports all the way through high school, even when we started the band. I was the typical SoCal teen, hanging at the beach, surfing, and skateboarding, anything to be outside. It wasn't until Jake joined the band that I gave everything up for my music. Hmm…" he pauses to think. "What's your favorite food?"

I don't even have to think about it. "Peanut butter," I share. "All things peanut related are my favorite."

"I'm a potato junkie," Carson tells me. "All shapes and forms of potatoes. What's your favorite color?"

This really is twenty questions. It's working; we are learning about each other.

"That's a tough one," I confess. "I'm partial to blues, everything from Carolina blue to royal blue. But I also like to wear a lot of black." I struggle to get the last part of my answer out through my yawn.

"That's enough for tonight. We're tired," Carson states.

"Just one more," I plead before another yawn. "Who's your hero? Or someone you look up to?"

The corners of his eyes crinkle with his gigantic smile. "It's corny, and you'll judge me."

I cross my finger over my heart. "I promise no judgement if you'll tell me why that person is your hero."

"President Bill Clinton," he blurts then waits for my reaction.

I do my best to keep my eyes from widening and my jaw from falling open.

Carson explains, "He's the first President I was old enough to remember. We learned about him in grade school, and my parents did a magnificent job of keeping me from hearing about the Monica Lewinsky scandal. For much of my life, he was a great President. I love the tone of his voice. It draws others to listen; it's melodic."

"No judgement," I whisper, fighting sleep no more.

Carson

After that, we lie in bed each night, talking about anything and everything. We talk until we can no longer keep our eyes open, then wake the next morning, cuddling each other. We bare our souls, sharing every part of us. It's intimate. For now, it's the only intimacy we share.

We share about our siblings and what it was like growing up. I grind my teeth when she tells me about dating in high school, attending dances, and losing her virginity.

We share our most embarrassing moments, worst and best dates, and even our first broken heart.

I tell her about the vacations I shared with my family, and she tells me about those with her parents and Peyton. We were both in scouts, and neither of us has a tattoo. We even share the same fear that we do not understand how to be a husband and a wife. With all that we've shared at night, we've so much more to learn about each other.

As much as I love writing lyrics and playing music, I look forward to our nightly talks and waking in each other's arms. It's simple; it's sweet. But it's causing me to need the rest of her. I long for her to give herself over to me completely, the way we did on our wedding night, although we don't remember it.

21

CARSON

Days Later

"Are you ready for this?" I ask Montana. "These are the last few minutes of having the house all to ourselves. Our peace will be no more."

"The house is enormous—plenty of room to spread out," Montana reminds me.

Moments later, we're snacking in the kitchen when the gate buzzes, signaling the band's arrival.

Montana asks, "Fran, are you ready for this?"

She nods. "Corey's family and ZipTie have prepared me for everything."

When we open the front door to greet the guys, the first person I see is a label representative, giving orders into his Bluetooth earpiece and barking orders to the younger male hovering nearby.

Eli, our drummer, is the first through the door, two duffels in his hands, Jake the bass player, strolls in sans luggage. They take in the foyer and stairs. Eli smirks at Montana. "How's the married life, child bride?" Turning to me, he chuckles. "She looks happy; atta boy."

"She's not a child," I defend.

"Where's Warner?" she asks.

"Said he'd rather play in L.A. and not fuck cows in Iowa," Eli shares.

"Warner will arrive in two more days," the label rep informs as he lays down his next set of bags.

"Pompous ass," Jake mutters on his way back out to the SUV. He returns with a small travel kennel in his hand and a diaper bag in his other. "Eli, this isn't a 5-star hotel. Unload your own crap."

Eli jogs over. "Snoopy, are you ready to escape that nasty cage? I bet you are ready to pee on everything sticking up in the backyard, aren't ya?"

I'm thankful we thought to put Denali in his kennel in our bedroom. Eli didn't tell us he planned to bring Snoopy, his Jack Russell Terrier. It shouldn't be an issue. The house is plenty big enough for all of us, and it will give Denali someone to play with while we work.

"That's everything from the Escalade," the rep tells us. "You've got our numbers if you've forgotten anything, need anything, or… well… you know." He shuts the door behind him, evidently eager to head back to the small Des Moines airport and the west coast.

"Since it's not the Ritz, can you help us carry our bags to our rooms?" Eli asks, walking up the stairs with Snoopy and his paraphernalia.

Jake has his over-sized duffle on his back and picks up Eli's two bags, muttering on his way. "Which room?"

"The first on the left is ours, and the door is closed," I tell both of them. "The other four bedroom doors are open; pick your own."

"There's one more master suite at the end of the hall," Montana informs. "Since Warner's not here, one of you should take it. That'll teach him to dis on Iowa." She giggles at her own orneriness.

"Meet in the kitchen in five minutes," I call to the guys. "Bring Snoopy; I'll go over some house rules."

"Fran," Montana calls out as she enters the kitchen area. She disappears in the large walk-in pantry. "I'm gonna set out a few beers for the guys and some chips."

"I can do it." Fran quickly attempts to get between Montana and her task.

"No, I've got it. You'll keep busy come mealtimes," Montana reminds her. "Besides, I need something to keep me busy."

"I can't believe Warner's not here," Montana tells me when she re-enters the kitchen. "Our nightlife doesn't compare to Las Vegas or Los Angeles, but we still have fun. Peyton and I will show the four of you fun in Iowa. What are we going to do about the dogs?" she asks.

"Dogs?" Eli asks, entering the room, snagging a beer, and taking a long drink. "Snoopy's only one dog."

"Remember, I bought an Alaskan Malamute at the end of the tour," I remind him. "Denali is in his kennel in our room."

"Snoopy loves other dogs." Eli tells me something I already know.

"Denali's a spirited puppy and a large breed; you sure Snoopy's up for that?" I ask, petting Snoopy in his arms. "The dog run is to the right of the pool. Once he does his business, he's welcome in the pool area."

"I'll take him out," Montana volunteers, arms already extended.

Eli's more than happy to hand over his pet to stay in the air conditioning with his ice-cold beer. Montana places a kiss on my cheek as she passes by.

"C'mon Snoopy," she babbles. "Wait until you see your potty spot. It's huge, and then, you can swim or sniff around all you want. Later, I'll introduce you to a new friend. His name is Denali. He's gonna be so happy to have a friend to run with him every day."

Eli's talking, but I don't hear a word. I tune my ears to Montana's baby-talking with Snoopy. *Could she be any sweeter?*

22

MONTANA

The Next Day

Peyton takes the afternoon off early to come join me at the pool. I introduce her to both dogs, and they entertain with much too much energy, sprinting around, hopping in the pool, and chasing each other.

The guys are in the studio, and I can't keep from glancing at its door behind our lounge chairs from time to time. Carson's showing the guys more lyrics he's written. He promised it wouldn't be long.

"So, how's married life?" Peyton says, noting my attention on the door behind us.

I smile at my best friend. She gave me the days I asked in L.A. to be with Carson without needing to call and report everything to her. I told her I needed alone time with Carson. Little did I know his parents would drop in and ruin that plan. I vowed to share everything with her upon our arrival in Des Moines, so the time has arrived.

"It's hard to put into words," I admit.

"Uh-huh," she shakes her head. "I'm not letting you off that easy. I want details." She sits upright and turns her body toward my chair.

"I promised I'd share," I remind her. "Just know my descriptions won't do it justice." I mock her position, turning to face her, my hands folded over my knees.

"So, we didn't get the alone time we'd hoped for," I begin my explanation.

"When we pulled into his driveway, his parents were at his front door to greet us." I pause for her reaction.

"His mom gave the house manager the day off, they cared for the new puppy, and waited on Carson to get home. They claim they needed to chat with him before he went into seclusion for recording the new album, but they were there to meet me."

"And?" Peyton prompts. "Are they nice, or is his mother a raging witch?"

"She was nice enough. She interrogated me, but I held my own," I smile proudly. "After I answered her questions and assured her I wasn't in need of her son's millions, we had a nice 48 hours together."

"So, now tell me about you and Carson…"

"We've talked a lot. I told him about my parents, my brother, our lives in Iowa, and my indecision on my future." I take a sip of my iced tea and wipe the beads of sweat from my brow. "I love him. It's crazy; it's too soon, but I love him."

"Uh, duh," Peyton mocks. "I knew that on the night they married the two of you. Both of you are head over heels in love. That's the only reason I allowed you to elope."

Too bad she didn't make sure I wasn't blotto so I could remember it. I enjoy having the video, but actual memories of that ceremony would be better. I guess she had no actual way of knowing, though.

"We stay up late talking until we can't keep our eyes open any longer."

"Now, we're getting to the good stuff," Peyton cheers.

"Stop," I admonish. "We are taking it slow; we're dating. We've held hands, cuddled in a lounge chair on his rooftop patio while watching the waves at night, and kissed. Nothing more."

"Wait. What?" Peyton sputters. "You're married and newlyweds! You should be screwing like wild animals."

"Peyton, we consummated the marriage in Vegas, and neither of us remember it. We're trying to get to know each other. We didn't date, so we do that now," I explain. "And, you know me; I don't give it up right away."

"But you already gave it up right away," she reminds me.

"Be nice," I scold. "He's an excellent kisser."

"Good. Then, he'll be good in bed, too."

I swat at her. "That's my husband you're talking about. I don't want you thinking of him during sexy time."

"Oh. My. God. Please never refer to sex as sexy time," Peyton begs. "I think my ears are bleeding."

"Cannon ball!" Eli screams, running to jump into the pool.

How did I not hear the studio door open? I spin to find Jake and Carson approaching our lounge chairs. I rise to greet him with a kiss I've been attempting to stifle for over an hour.

"Get a room!" Eli hollers from the far end of the swimming pool.

"We have a room up there," I inform him.

"Well, use it. We don't need any of your marriage germs rubbing off on any of us," he declares, climbing from the pool, his red skinny jeans, t-shirt, and converse sopping wet.

"It's not contagious," I remind him.

"I'm going to put my suit on," he informs the group.

"Freeze," Carson yells, and Eli strikes a statue pose. "I'll bring your suit. You're dripping wet and shouldn't walk through the house like that."

"I'll come with you," Jake states.

I raise an eyebrow at Peyton. *Is Jake going to swim?* No way.

I assist Peyton in applying sunscreen to the backs of the three men. I start with Carson, and she starts with Jake. Eli comments that he's okay with sloppy seconds to which we shake our heads. As Peyton is taking her sweet time, ensuring Jake's safety from UV rays, I apply a thick coat of sunscreen to Eli's very pale back.

"Dude, you're gonna fry," Carson informs him.

"Sun screen will protect me. I'll just need to reapply it every hour." He looks over his shoulder at me. "Will you set an alarm and make sure I do?"

I nod, hoping the others will assist me. It feels strange to be running my fingers over Eli's back.

"Spin," I instruct.

"No, I can get my chest." He snags the bottle of sunscreen from my right hand and heads to the patio table under the umbrella.

I turn my attention to Peyton; she's finally done fondling Jake in front of us. Now, the two are sitting at the edge of the pool, talking low enough we can't hear them.

We spend the afternoon floating on rafts, lazing at the pool's edge, and playing fetch with the two dogs in and out of the water.

"I'm headed to the cooler," Eli announces, using his arms to pull himself from the deep end, his back to us. "Who wants another?"

Jake, Peyton, and Carson all order another beer. When Eli turns, walking toward our end of the pool and the cooler, I gasp.

"Eli," I call to him. "Did you reapply sunscreen to your chest when I reapplied to your back?"

"Why?" he asks, looking down.

The guys laugh loudly at their band mate. Peyton laughs so hard she snorts.

I try not to giggle when I inform him, "You have two large, white handprints on your chest, and the rest of you is bright red. Let's go inside," I suggest. "The sooner we get aloe vera on you, the better you'll be."

Not helping, Jake and Carson cheer, "Atta boy," as he walks by. Eli awards them double middle fingers, grabs a towel, and follows me into the house.

23

MONTANA

In our bathroom, I pose Eli in front of the vanity mirror while I grab the aloe vera from my makeup bag. Thank goodness I took it to Las Vegas in case we spent a day at the pool.

"This will be cold," I warn.

"Then, rub your hands together," he urges.

I shake my head. "You want this to be cool to sooth your burned skin," I inform him. "We must reapply this often, like I did for you at the pool, not like you did." I can't help the giggle that escapes as I place my coated palms on his pectorals and spread the aloe all over his chest. When he squeals like a girl, I lose myself to laughter. "Atta boy!" I throw his favorite saying back at him.

Once I've slathered a thick layer over all of his screaming, red skin, I wash my hands then turn to face him.

"Can you do me a favor and record something for me?" he asks, opening his phone and extending it to me after I dry my hands.

He looks around the oversized bathroom and positions himself in front of the glass shower stall. "Start recording with only my face. Then, pan to include my chest when I mention it," he directs. When I nod, he begins, "Hello, all my Communicable Diseases. I'm posting today to share an interesting lesson I've learned. I've lived my entire life in California and traveled all over the world with the band. But after less than 24 hours in the Midwest, I've experienced my first sunburn."

He pauses, smiling as I zoom out to share his painful burn with the fans of the band. He places his palms on the white skin where he placed his sunscreen covered hands then removes them. "Evidently, sunscreen doesn't run or spread through osmosis. Lesson learned, my friends, and now, I'm paying the price." Looking up to the sky, he shouts, "Damn you Midwest sun!" Then, he signals for me to end the video.

"How'd it look?" he asks, snagging his phone from me to check it out.

"Love it," I tell him. "But I've never been fond of the band's followers being labeled the Communicable Diseases."

"Warner and marketing came up with that for our fan club," he informs me, something I already knew. "Aren't you a member of our fan club?" His expression of worry that I'm not as loyal to the band as he thought nearly rips my heart in half.

"I've been a proud fan club member since the club's inaugural year," I state.

"Um," he smirks, "so, you've been a Communicable Disease for many years now. Get used to it."

I shake my head. He's right, but it doesn't mean I have to like the title.

"What's the plan for the rest of the afternoon, like dinner?" he asks while carefully pulling a t-shirt over his head then chest.

"I need to run to my parents' house to grab more clothes, shoes, and stuff. I've been living out of the bag I packed for Las Vegas for over a week now."

"I'll ride with you," he excitedly offers. "I can't wait to see more of Iowa. Lord knows I don't need to spend more time at the pool."

"Okay," I respond. "Peyton will go with us. It shouldn't take but an hour, and we will be back in time for dinner with the guys."

Stepping back on the pool deck, Eli and I find Peyton's face tucked into Jake's neck and his hand on her ass as she sits on his lap. He's carrying on a conversation with Carson, distracted by her lips to his neck and ear.

"Peyton," I call, and she pulls her face from him to look in my direction. "I'm running to Mom's to grab stuff."

"I'm going with her," Eli informs the guys from the shade of the patio umbrella.

"Good," Peyton cheers. "Then, I'll stay here and soak up some more sun."

"The only thing in the sun is your feet," Eli informs her.

She sticks her tongue out at him.

I look to Carson to see if he has any interest in going to my parents' house and meeting Dad.

"I've got some fine tuning I need to work on." He rises, striding toward me. "I should be done in an hour; will you be back by dinner?"

His hands slide into my hair at my jawline, making it difficult to nod.

"Good, I'll get my stuff done and have the rest of the evening to spend with you," he murmurs less than an inch from my lips.

My eyes move from his eyes to his mouth, willing it to press to mine. He doesn't disappoint. A gentle kiss slowly simmers between us.

"Uh-hum," Eli interrupts sassily. "As I'm the only single male here, I'd like to mention that you both suck, and your public displays of affection are disgusting."

"Dude," Jake replies, "I'm still single."

Eli throws him a look. "I guess that's a tumor on your lap, rubbing your crotch and licking your neck, then."

"Easy," I sooth, pulling Eli from the shade into the house. "Carson and I will try to be more discrete."

As we walk through the house and hop into my white Jeep Cherokee, he explains, "No, you and Carson are newlyweds. You're supposed to be all over each other all the time. You need to be. I'm just having a weak moment. Maybe it's the pain of the sunburn making me bitchy."

I want to tease him about his low pain tolerance or offer to set him up but think better of it. He's flown from L.A. to Des Moines, he drank several beers, and he's now sunburned; I need not add to his long day.

When we enter my parents' home, Mom and Dad are both in the kitchen. She's pulling meat from the refrigerator for the grill, and Dad is fixing mixed drinks for the two of them.

"Well, hello," Mom greets. "To what do we owe this surprise visit?"

Before I can respond, Dad extends his hand to Eli. "Welcome. I'm Don," Dad greets. "It's nice to finally meet you."

"Um, Dad," I interrupt. "This is Eli Patrick, not Carson."

Embarrassed, Dad tries to cover. "The drummer, right?"

I glance to Mom then back to my dad; someone's been doing his homework. I make a mental note to ask Mom if she printed out information for Dad or if they researched online together.

"Yep, that's me," Eli smiles. "Carson's working in the studio, so I offered to ride with Montana. I'm eager to see more of Iowa."

"Welcome to our home," Dad extends a low-ball glass. "Would you like an Amaretto Sour?"

"Sure! I haven't had one of those in ages," Eli answers, taking the proffered glass.

"None for me; I'm driving," I remind Dad.

My statement causes him to smile. My parents like that I am careful with alcohol and motor vehicles. We've had more than one family friend in DUI accidents and have discussed it many times.

"Eli, wanna come see the rest of the house and help me in my room?" I ask.

He tells my parents, deadpan, before following my lead, "She just brought me for my muscles."

After a quick tour of the house, backyard, pool, and pool house, I pause before opening my bedroom door. "Now, what you are about to see is not, and I repeat, is *not* to get back to Carson."

Packing items to take with me is only half my mission. The other task is to remove all the band posters, record covers, trophies, and ribbons from my room before I bring my husband over to meet my dad.

"What have we here?" he teases, eyes wide, taking in my room.

"I've shared that I am a rock and metal fan," I defend. "I just haven't told Carson about the posters on my walls."

"Posters of sweaty, hot lead singers, bassists, guitarists, and drummers. All of which are not your husband, Carson." Eli sarcastically points out the obvious.

I swing my closet doors open, my hands and arms outstretched like a model, pointing out the Communicable poster.

"Poor Carson's heart will shatter if he finds out you hid him inside your closet, and it's a poster of the entire band, not just him. The other posters only have one guy in them and are on display 24/7."

I want to slap Eli. This is why I asked him not to tell Carson what he was about to see. I flop onto my bed with a deep sigh. Eli flops down at my side.

"Your secret is safe with me 'child bride,'" he vows.

"We need to come up with a new nickname for me," I remind him. I'm worried that the next one might be worse than the current one.

"Nickname can wait," Eli states, taking my hand in his as we lie on my bed. "You pack the stuff you need, and I'll handle the posters."

I turn my head to him, his already facing me. He nods his chin, pulls me with him from the bed, and pushes me towards the closet.

24

MONTANA

That night, after dinner, the guys invite Peyton and me to join them in the studio. Carson plans to unveil some lyrics, and they plan to create the music to accompany it.

I'm excited. I've seen bands on stage but haven't witnessed the creative process behind the songs. Well, other than watching *Songland* on TV. The way the three producers and the artists collaborate with the new songwriters mesmerizes me. I can't wait to witness it in person.

Peyton and I take seats on an over-sized chair in the studio while the guys each take control of their instruments. Carson and Jake sit with their guitar and bass in their laps. Carson moves a stool to him and spreads notebook paper full of lyrics in front of him while Eli takes the throne behind his drum kit.

They don't discuss a plan of action, and Carson doesn't read the lyrics to them first; he strums his guitar and reads from his pages. Jake plays a few chords now and then, and Eli watches.

I close my eyes, lost in the lyrics Carson sings. I don't catch every word, but what I hear touches me deeply.

"First to fall... doubt... not a guy believes in love at first sight... slap in the face, heart began to race... make me a believer..."

It's the lyrics he wrote after we bumped into each other in the hallway and went out as a group that first night. He's writing about his reaction to me. My heart swells as tears well in my eyes.

"Wow," Peyton whispers, turning to face me. "You may have a hard time telling me how you feel about him, but he definitely has no trouble describing it."

I nod, smile, and wipe the tears from my eyes before they can fall to my cheeks.

"I can't believe my best friend has a rock song written about her," Peyton giggles.

I'm silent; I can't speak. The love and emotions swirling inside of me are too much. Carson plans to share these lyrics with the world. The world will know exactly how he feels about me. It's heady, it's sweet, and it's so much more than I can ever give to him.

I'm lost in my own thoughts for so long that when I become alert in the studio again, the guys are experimenting with lyrics to another song.

"*Risk... must..., gifted... not a tryst... dust... Play my part... trust... hair mussed... heart... lust... I was lost... box... come undone, unravel me.*"

The words "unravel me" repeat many times in the chorus; that should be the title of this song. *Unravel Me. Carson unraveled me; according to these lyrics, I've done the same to him.*

"*Face front... don't look back... celebrate the end of loneliness... the end of bachelorhood... no longer solo or a lone wolf.*"

I'm hot from head to toe, my skin prickles, and my heart thumps in my ears. I stare at Carson—my man, my husband. Every part of me longs to jump on his lap, wrap my arms and legs around him, and rub against every part of him. I need him; I want him. Every part of him, inside and out, calls to every part of me.

Peyton rises from our chair, stretching her arms above her head and yawning for all to see. Taking his cue, Jake returns his bass to its stand before following her to the door.

I look to my phone; it's past nine. Peyton is not ready to head home. Instead, she's going to Jake's room. My desire for Carson grows stronger each day. I find the need to make love to him consuming more and more of my thoughts and time. Remembering my conversation with Eli earlier about making out in public, although I want to take Carson up to our room for the rest of the night, I won't.

Late the next afternoon, I'm sitting at the edge of the pool, fighting tears, and watching the dogs in the backyard.

Eli emerges from the house, sneaking up behind me in his stealthy way. "How's Snoopy? Is he behaving?"

I startle, nearly falling forward into the pool. I quickly attempt to settle myself.

I nod while wiping my cheeks discreetly. "You know that Snoopy was a beagle, and not a Jack Russell, right?"

"Thanks; the band let me know that right away," Eli shares, taking a seat beside me. "He looks more like Snoopy with his coloring than most beagles with their brown and black patches."

"Why are you out here, not in the studio with the guys?" I ask, not liking silence with him so near.

"I need fresh air to clear my mind; it helps with creativity," he states.

I nod.

"What's with the tears?" he asks, bumping his shoulder into mine.

"It's nothing," I lie.

"Nothing doesn't cause tears; it's something."

I shake my head.

"C'mon! I'm a superb listener," Eli urges.

"It's…" I let out a huff of air. "I need to get my act together." I pause, lifting my long hair off the nape of my neck in one hand, resembling a ponytail. "This house is full of people working, working toward something, and I seem to tread water."

"I get that," he states. "But you have a job, and you are working. You're a newlywed, and you're working on your marriage. That's a job, especially with a rock band in tow."

I shrug, "Not an actual job. There's so much we don't know about each other. It's like we are dating now since we didn't before."

"I see the way the two of you look at each other. You're crazy in love. You're good for him. He's been lost for too long," Eli shares.

"It's crazy; it doesn't seem real," I admit.

"If you don't need to work, enjoy some time to relax." He taps my temple. "Your next decision between college or job will come to you when you're ready," Eli promises.

"I don't feel like a grownup. I'm supposed to be wise and responsible."

"If you mention that to your parents, I bet they tell you adulthood is a lot of faking it," he says, kicking his bare feet in the water. "Heck, when I'm not behind a drum kit, I do not understand what I'm doing. I don't date, I can't make friends—the band is my family. Sometimes, I think I'm fine right where I am, but all too often, I daydream about more."

"You deserve more," I state, hoping he realizes it.

"That's easier said than done. We can't all bump into the love of our life in a hotel hallway." He bumps against my shoulder again.

"Well, the first step is being open to the possibility. Now, tell me what type of woman we are looking for," I pry.

"We?" he counters.

I nod.

"Not high maintenance, easygoing, fun, and hot. She has to be hot. Do you have a sister or cousin like you?" he asks, only half teasing.

"Ah, that's sweet. I think it'll take someone more interesting to keep your attention." I bump his shoulder back.

"Drop it," Eli instructs. "I need to focus on the album."

That night, Peyton and I find a moment alone in the kitchen, fetching snacks. "What's it like being married to the famous Carson Cavanaugh?" Peyton asks. "It's hard to believe you're a wife now."

"I'm bored all the time. Denali, Snoopy, and I spend too much time together," I groan.

"So, do what you planned to do this summer, before you went and got married. You had summer plans," she reminds me.

"Well, I planned to hang out with you," I smile sweetly at her.

"Duh," she teases.

"And, to do some career and school research," I remind her. We spoke about it before our trip to Las Vegas.

"So, do that," she states as if it is just that simple.

"I guess I could work a bit at Mom's office, too. I've tried to stay at the house, because I'm worried about the paparazzi swarming me like they did in Las Vegas and L. A.," I confess.

"It's Iowa—you're safe," Peyton argues.

"I think I'll wait until Warner arrives before I plan days out and about."

"Okay," she draws out.

"You'll still come visit me all the time, right?" I ask.

"Or at least until Carson tells me I can't be here. I mean, you have a pool. You must force me to stay away," she chuckles.

"Maybe the reason I'm so wishy-washy on my next step is because God planned for me to meet him," I suggest.

"So, you've met him," she counters. "Now, it's time to do your research, find what makes you happy, and spend some time on your future, too."

"Maybe I'll work with our Bra-Claw idea for a while until I'm ready to do something else," I state.

"That's a fabulous idea," Peyton agrees. "You loved working on your app, then marketing, and finally selling it. I know I came up with the Bra-Claw idea, but you brought it to fruition. I'll help when I can."

"Then, it's settled. For now, I'll be an entrepreneur," I smile at my best friend. "Let's take the dogs for a walk before they're put in kennels for the night," I suggest, seeking more time with her.

"How do I seduce my husband?" I ask when we're safely outside the house.

Peyton guffaws and stops abruptly which jerks Snoopy to a halt.

I continue walking. "I mean, should I just tell him? Or is it better if I hint at it?" I query further, looking directly at my friend, desperately seeking her advice.

"You're serious?" Peyton asks. "Okay, well, what have you done in the past with guys to give them the green light?"

My jaw drops in disbelief. She knows I'm inexperienced with men. I'm not the leader in my relationships. *How did I think I could do this?*

"Hey." She waves her hands in front of my face to get my attention. "So, you've shared that you cuddle at night while talking. That's a perfect time to drop your hints. Every touch can be a signal. Brush against him; place your hand on his arm, his chest, and his jaw."

She leans closer to me. "Dress provocatively, forget a towel when you shower and holler for him to bring you one, or walk naked in front of him as much as possible."

"I don't know," I hedge. "What if he ignores me?"

"You make it impossible for him to ignore you. He's a guy; he won't need over one or two hints," she explains, taking my hand in hers. "I think he's struggling with the whole 'taking it slow' plan. He's a good guy, so he's giving you the time he thinks you want." She squeezes my hand, smiling. "Trust me, he's ready."

I swallow hard and nod. Maybe she's right. Heaven knows she's way more experienced than I am. I'm not keen on flaunting my naked body, but I could hint a little as we chat in bed. I nod. *I can do this; I'm ready.*

Carson

. . .

While the girls walk the dogs, I waste no time squirting a dab of shower gel in my hand. I lather up my hand as I allow the spray to cover my chest and flow southward. I've used up all of my restraint for the day; I'm desperate.

I glide one fist down my shaft followed by the other. The slick soap allows my motions to glide smoothly up then down. I place my left palm on the tile wall, under the showerhead. With thoughts of Montana's tight body on my mind, I imagine what she might look like naked, showering with me. I tighten my grip and quicken my strokes.

Although I'm sure it will pale compared to the real thing, I fantasize my fist is her hot, wet heat, clenching around my shaft. On its own, my pelvis thrusts into my palm, once, twice. Fire shoots from my center as I spew my seed onto the tile near the shower floor. My body shutters, and a low groan echoes in the shower enclosure.

The warm water pelts my back. I close my eyes tight, and I lean my forehead on the cool blue tiles. I can't believe I'm resigned to my second shower of the day. I need to find another way to channel my desire for Montana. I can only take so many showers in a day before my housemates figure out what I'm really doing in here.

We met days ago, yet it feels like we've been together much longer. After eloping, I thought it best if we took a few weeks to get to know each other better before I initiated sex. I spend my day sporting a boner at the sight of her, at the thought of her. It's barely been a week, and the blue balls are nearly killing me.

Perhaps I should slowly start laying the groundwork. I can kiss her more, hold her more, and cuddle with her in bed at night. It will be torture as my body will only desire her that much more, but I don't want to rush her. I rushed her into marriage; I can't rush her into sex. I need her to trust me and come to me when she's ready. I just pray it's sooner rather than later.

25

CARSON

I'm in the kitchen when Warner's driver buzzes in at the front gate. I shoot a text to Eli and Jake, alerting them of his arrival.

"Did you see where Montana went?" I ask.

Fran nods, pointing to the front room. When I walk through the doorway, I find Eli, Peyton, and Montana in a tight huddle. They are planning something. Jake descends the stairs, a giant smile upon his face. Jake rarely smiles and never this wide. The hair on the back of my neck stands on end; something is up, and I don't like it.

Eli pulls the two wooden doors open, and we step onto the front porch to greet Warner. Off to the left, I notice a large truck and matching trailer with "Randall Farm" printed on the side, sitting at the edge of the driveway with a large black and white cow tied to the back of it. Now, I know what the gang was whispering and giggling about.

We move back inside and out of the way for Warner and his entourage. Three young men assist a label rep in caring several crates of liquor and boxes of food into the foyer. Warner doesn't grab his bags; instead, he waltzes in with a blonde woman under each arm and a sleazy smirk upon his face.

"Atta boy," Eli champions Warner's choice in travel companions, slapping him on the back.

Warner's heavy footfalls echo in the large foyer as he escorts his women to the living room sofa. The girls giggle at his sides. I roll my eyes, and Montana elbows me in the ribs.

Unraveled

Warner goes to check out his bedroom, not taking bags with him. "What the fuck!" he yells before a door slams, and we hear his boots clomping toward the top of the stairs.

"Real fucking funny," he announces, leaning his arms on the railing. He looks down to the group. "Ha, ha, ha, you got me," he deadpans. "Thanks for the cow in my room. I'd blame it on Eli, but the truck out front has Montana's name all over it." He turns to look at her from his perch. "You're officially part of the family now, and it's open game on pranks."

Montana nods, smiling. "I know you are concerned about leaving L.A. women for the cows in Iowa, so I arranged a welcome party for you. Call it Midwest hospitality."

"Thanks for putting me in my place; now, escort the cow out of my room then sanitize everything before you carry my bags up."

Montana scoffs loudly. "Um," she climbs the stairs, "I'll lead the calf from your room, but the room's already clean. Your bags are your own problem."

I love that she's comfortable enough with the band that she gives as good as she gets. Leading the calf slowly down one stair at a time, she speaks to it. "You're much too good for the likes of Warner. I should have brought a mule for him. That's the closest thing we have to an ass. And, don't let anything he said bother you; he's used to blonde, twiggy bimbos climbing all over him. My grandma would call them hussies. You're much too good for him; never forget that."

Montana pulls the calf through the front door. At the sight of its mother, it bawls.

"Dude," Eli looks to Warner. "I think it's a male."

The group laughs.

"Perfect," Warner whines. "Now, she thinks I'm..."

"No, I don't," Montana interrupts, returning. "And, it wasn't a male. I know the difference."

"Carson," Warner says, "you've got a real winner here. If we're ever stranded, she'll know how to help us survive."

Montana

. . .

After listening to Warner grumble for hours about missing his life in L.A., I pull Peyton aside. The two of us plan to show the guys fun in Des Moines tonight.

Warner and Jake motion for Peyton to join them on the sofa. I quirk an eyebrow in Carson's direction. He smirks back at me. *What is going on?* He waggles his eyebrows at me. Maybe it's best I don't know what he knows.

"What's up?" Eli asks.

"We're taking you out tonight," Peyton answers. "We're gonna show you fun-- Iowa style."

"No thanks," Warner says. "I'd rather stay in and wash my hair."

"Too bad," Peyton retorts directly to his face. "I wanna go out, so we're going out. And you, mister, will have fun."

Warner rolls his eyes in our direction.

"How long until dinner is done?" Peyton asks.

"An hour," I answer.

"Okay, upstairs, all of you," she orders. "We need to help you fit in. We don't want the entire city to recognize you on your first night in town."

"What's wrong with the way we're dressed?" Warner asks.

"Just trust us," Peyton pleads.

"So, this is the Brickhouse," I inform the group as we walk the three blocks to the little corner bar. "Tonight's open mic night. There will be a couple of bands performing in thirty-minute sets. Then, a local band will perform sets the rest of the night. Sometimes, they do covers, sometimes only their songs."

"Great," Warner drawls out. "High schooler-wanna-be-rockers are my fav."

Peyton swats his arm. "You promised."

"And, so did you," he reminds her, referring to an agreement the two made in private.

I reach for the door handle, but Carson quickly pulls it open for me. He's such a gentleman. I pause inside until all of our group enters. I point to two open bar stools at the corner of the bar. Peyton and I hop onto the stools while the four men surround us. A band scurries around the small stage, preparing for their session.

Carson

A tequila shot down and beers in our hands, we visit in the tiny, yet noisy, bar. A high-pitched sound of feedback proceeds the announcement, "And now, Blue Biscuit."

The crowd applauds, and the band starts right in with a cover of Buckcherry's *Crazy Bitch*. The band is good instrumentally, but their voices aren't great. At the end of the song, the guitarist apologizes, claiming their lead singer couldn't make it tonight.

"Put us out of our misery, Carson," Warner shouts over the noise. "Go be their lead singer."

I shake my head. "Let them work it out."

"Our next band's running late, so order drinks. Our headliner, DnD, will take the stage at 10," the manager announces to the crowd while Blue Biscuit tears down their equipment.

"Have we heard DnD?" Peyton asks.

Montana smiles wide, nodding. "They're the Dungeons and Dragons band."

"I want to leave by 10 then," Peyton tells the guys.

"Should we?" Eli asks, lifting his chin towards the stage.

"You think the kids would loan us their gear?" Jake asks, his face excited.

I approach the manager, now back behind the bar. "Hey, mind if we fill in for the absent band?"

His brow furrows, and he states, "I knew you guys looked familiar. Have you played here before?"

I shake my head, fighting my smile. He motions for me to take the stage, so I approach the bassist at his case.

"Dude, would it be possible for us to borrow your instruments for a bit?" I ask. "We'll buy your drinks while we perform."

The kid rises, quickly tilting and turning his head to toss his long bangs from his eyes.

"Fuck!" he shouts. "You're..."

"Yes, can we use your instruments?"

"Yeah, man. Of course." He rambles, waving his bandmates over. They put their heads together, and I can't make out what he tells them. When they part, all four are star struck and speechless. I wave for my bandmates to join me then slip a fifty-dollar bill from my wallet.

"For drinks," I state loudly near his ear.

I approach the mic stand. "Hey, if you don't mind, my friends and I wanna play for you. Let's give a big round of applause to the Blue Biscuits for loaning us their stuff."

A few members of the crowd clap while others look on judgingly.

"Who the hell are you?" a man near the back yells, and several audience members nod, also wanting to know.

"Let's just say you'll recognize us in a moment. We are bored and hopped over to Des Moines for a while."

The crowd cheers approving of us in their city, even if they don't recognize us.

Each of us play a few notes, getting the feel for the strange instruments. The crowd boos, thinking we don't know how to play. Pissed at the crowd's response, Eli bangs out a four count, leading us into our first number one hit. Just like that, the crowd figures out our identity and goes wild.

For the next 30 minutes, we play through our catalog in chronological order. The crowd grows larger by the minute. By the time we're done, police are at the door, and the fire marshal's pushing customers out the door. I'm sure someone posted on social media, causing word to spread like wildfire.

We didn't keep the fact that we're recording our album in Iowa a secret. We don't plan to hide, but we might consider security on our next outing.

Blue Biscuit greets us as we exit the tiny stage, handing each instrument back to its owner. Always ready, Eli produces a black permanent marker for us to autograph the instruments.

We slowly push our way through the crowd, back to our girls. It's clear we can't stay here. I call the manager over and ask for his help with the police to slip us out a backdoor. I have to give it to the Iowa fans. They are not as intrusive as they are in other cities. They don't follow us to the back or swarm our car as we drive away. It's a pleasant change of pace.

26

MONTANA

The Next Morning

I take my laptop down with me to breakfast. The guys are still sleeping as they worked past three last night. They'll rise about noon, eat lunch, then return to the studio; it's their new daily schedule. Peyton and Mom both work every weekday, so I plan to chat with Fran for a while before I take Denali and Snoopy to the dog park or walk on a trail.

I nibble on my breakfast as I bring my laptop to life. "What's on your to do list today?" I ask between bites.

"I'm making a grocery trip about ten-thirty, I'm fixing burgers and fries for lunch, then there's laundry and cleaning to be done upstairs in the afternoon," Fran shares. "What are your plans?"

I shrug. "None really. Walk the dogs or go to the dog park. Maybe swim in the backyard or read while I get some sun." I'm embarrassed I have nothing important to do. I don't want people to think I'm freeloading off of the band. "I've already started laundry for the guys."

"Montana," Fran chides, "it's my job, not yours."

"I know, but I have too much free time." I tell her something she already knows. "I don't mind. It's only two loads twice a week. Anyway, I'm used to doing my laundry, washing dishes, cooking, and cleaning. It's hard to let someone else do it for me." Fran gives me a stern look with hands on her hips, but I see her smile break through.

"I want to make a treat for the guys; could I add a few items to your grocery list?" I feel bad for asking; I have more than enough time to run to the grocery store myself.

"What are you making?"

"Scotcharoos," I explain. "They take five ingredients and are easy to make. I'll make two batches. Trust me, they are so good; two batches will not be enough."

"I've never had them," Fran confesses.

"If you have 10 minutes this afternoon, I'll show you how to make them." I try not to sound too eager. I know Fran has work to do. I probably bother her too much. I really need to find something to busy myself.

I busy myself caring for the dogs and visiting Fran while she works. At PetSmart, I introduce Denali to the clerks and sign us up for a training class. I purchase too many toys and chews. It's easy to get carried away; there are so many fun things to play with.

After lunch, I hold both leashes as we walk toward the lake. Denali and Snoopy love the water; so, I throw a tennis ball from the dock, and they dive in to fetch it over and over. When my arm grows tired, we return to the house.

Tomorrow, Denali, Snoopy, and I plan to join Mom for lunch then play at the dog park on her side of town. She loves dogs, and it gets the three of us out of the house for a bit. I feel I spend more time with them than I do Carson. I don't see Carson except for his 30-minute lunch breaks or on the nights they emerge from the studio before midnight.

Eager to see my man, I interrupt the studio session by taking them my Scotcharoos. I realize their work is important, but I can't help myself. I'm in desperate need of human attention.

I quietly make my way down the hall, slowly opening and closing the door to the booth where everyone watches through the glass while Warner sings.

Eli hops from his chair, sniffing the treats I hold. "Break time," he yells, forcing Warner to stop his vocals abruptly.

"What do we have here?" Carson asks, then places a kiss at my temple.

"I made Scotcharoos," I tell them. "Trust me, they are to die for."

As if on cue, Eli elicits a moan of pleasure while he chews.

"That good, huh?" Carson asks.

I bite my lips and nod.

Warner relieves me of the tray. "You bake, child bride?"

"I can bake," I answer, not bragging that I am a superb cook. It's a detail I need to share with my husband before the entire band.

"Holy shit," Jake mumbles with his mouth full.

Carson nods in agreement as he chews.

I lean near his ear. "I made another batch just for the two of us. I'll hide them in our room."

I love the twinkle in his eyes. I guess it's true what they say. The way to a man's heart is through his stomach.

I catch myself ogling him every chance I get. *How weird is that?* We're married, and I feel guilty for lusting after him. It's only been two weeks; essentially, we've only dated two weeks, and I'm revved up like a brazen hussy.

My mind drifts to fun fantasies and sinful scenarios. My hands itch to grip his ass and pull him towards me. I crave his hard body pressed tight to mine. Even my dreams involve sex with Carson. The more we're together, the more I get to know him, the more I long to connect with him in every way. *I wonder if he feels the same...*

27

MONTANA

Two Weeks Later

Peyton and I spend the afternoon poolside with margaritas, currently we are on our second pitcher, delivered by Fran. After floating in the pool on mats, now we lounge under the patio umbrella as we dry off and plan to shower then change before dinner.

The guys emerge from the studio.

"Explain to me why we spend hours in the studio when we could be out here, enjoying the gorgeous view?" Eli asks the guys.

"While I agree the view is gorgeous, I'd advise you to keep your eyes on Peyton and off my wife," Carson warns.

Eli throws his hands up, stepping towards Peyton's lounger. An indescribable noise rumbles from Jake, causing Eli to excuse himself and head into the house.

"Don't move," Warner orders in our direction. "We'll grab our suits and meet you back out here."

I pretend I don't see his eyes waggle suggestively to Peyton as I try not to giggle.

Seems the lead singer is smitten with my bff. The bad boy of rock-n-roll seems to have lost his desire for a wide variety of ladies. Though he won't admit it, he's lost his desire to go out and plunder in Des Moines. He's happy to hang at the house with Peyton.

Unraveled

Minutes after Carson, Jake, and Warner head into change, Eli emerges from the house, his arms carrying a cooler with beer which is busting out of the top.

"Thirsty?" I tease.

"We're celebrating," he informs.

"Celebrating what?" Peyton sits up, moving her sunglasses atop her head.

"We officially have two songs done for the album," Eli boasts, popping the top off his bottle of beer.

"Cool." Peyton grabs a beer from the cooler while I still sip my last margarita.

Carson

"Last beer," Jake states, opening his bottle.

"I guess we must move the party inside," Peyton offers, always up for keeping the fun flowing.

"Can I hear the songs you finished?" Montana attempts to whisper, slurring her words.

I chuckle, rise, and offer my hand to my wife. She sways a bit on her feet, so I pull her tight to my side.

Warner chuckles, "She's a lightweight." He points at Montana.

"No, she's not," Peyton swats his chest from her perch upon his lap. "The two of us polished off two--, count them-- two pitchers of margaritas before we switched to beer with you. And, Fran has a heavy pour."

Montana then comes to her own defense. "We started drinking at noon today." She stares at her phone then asks me, "How many hours ago was that?"

Of course, everyone hears her.

"C'mon. Let's go listen to the tracks," I urge.

The others follow our lead.

I love watching her reactions. Although she's read my lyrics, now with the music and all of the band's voices, my words come to life.

Montana

. . .

"I'm bored," Eli whines. "Let's play a game."

A game? Did famous drummer Eli Patrick just suggest we play a game?

He opens the fridge, passing beverages to everyone.

"We're playing two truths and a lie," Eli states. "Montana, you go first."

I nod. *I can do this.* Two truths and a lie. "I'm a certified skydiver. I'm allergic to chocolate. I've sold an app I created for millions of dollars."

"Carson and I have to sit this one out as we know the answer," Peyton offers.

"Well, now, this is interesting," Warner croons. "If I had to guess immediately, I'd say allergic to chocolate is the most boring of the three. It has to be true."

Wow. This guy doesn't have a filter.

"She's smart," Jake states his opinion. "I could see her creating and selling an app."

"With Peyton as her best friend, I wouldn't put skydiving past her," Eli adds. "Hmm, I say the lie is she's allergic to chocolate. I didn't see her eat a Scotcharoo, but I doubt she'd make them if she's allergic to them."

"I'm not a certified sky-diver," I share. "I am allergic to chocolate. It's not deadly. I break out in hives for 24 hours."

"Eli and Warner, drink up," Peyton taunts, and they quickly down their entire drink and grab another.

"Let's make this more interesting," Warner urges. "Let's play truth or dare instead."

Four sets of eyes look to Peyton and me to see if we will play.

"I'll go first," Eli announces. "I dare Peyton to kiss Montana."

"Really?" Peyton asks. "You go straight to that one with no warm-ups?"

"If you don't feel comfortable, you can always choose truth," Carson offers.

"We don't mind," Peyton informs. "It's not like it's the first time."

The guys look on with wide eyes and open mouths. We share a kiss halfway between sisterly and porn stars, and they don't hide how much they enjoy watching.

Peyton asks Eli, "Truth or dare?" She makes a point to show that he did it wrong last time.

Eli chooses truth, and Peyton asks if he's ever taken part in a three-way.

"Nope," he answers. "I've never been lucky enough to get an invitation."

He turns his attention back to me. "Montana, truth or dare?"

As much as I want to take the easy way out by choosing truth, I need to choose dare and impress the guys. "Dare."

"Give Carson a lap dance right here." He points to the chair Carson currently occupies.

"I'll need music," I inform the group.

Walking toward my husband, *Closer* by Nine Inch Nails fills the room, and I begin.

I've never given a lap dance before or witnessed one at a strip club. I have watched several shows containing them, so I harness my inner goddess and begin. I sway my hips slowly from side to side then forward and back, side to side and forward and back again. I bend at the waist, keeping my legs straight, and slap the floor between my feet. I look to Carson between my legs. Slowly, I slide my hands up my legs as I return to a standing position.

I spin around in time with the music, placing first my right knee in the chair beside his thigh, then my left. My hands on the back of the chair at either side of his head. I grind my happy place against the fly of his jeans. A small breath of air escapes my lips at the sensation of his rock-hard cock where I desire it most.

Instantly, the rest of the room fades away; he's the only one here with me. I repeat the movement of my hips over and over, the song setting my pace. Carson's hand settles on my hips; his fingertips dig deliciously into my flesh. My breathing picks up, and Carson's nostrils flare.

"Uh, hello? The song's over," Peyton's voice breaks our spell.

My eyes widen with the realization that I just gave the band fodder for future spank-bank material. I feel my cheeks heat as I crawl from Carson's lap.

His hand flies out, grasping my wrist, pulling me to his lap.

"Don't wiggle," he growls into my ear, his hot breath prickling the skin of my neck.

The group sits silent for a moment before Eli reminds me it's my turn to choose someone.

"Carson, truth or dare?" I toss over my shoulder.

"Truth."

"Rate that lap dance on a scale of one to ten compared to the others you've had," I order.

Without a thought, he answers, "Ten. The best I've ever had." He kisses my shoulder.

I want to ask how many lap dances he's had in his lifetime, but I'll save it for our private pillow talks.

Carson chooses Warner who picks truth, much to my surprise. When asked if he's in a monogamous relationship, Warner answers no but that he wouldn't be opposed to it.

Hmm. That's interesting. Seems my husband's as curious about the three of them as I am.

"I choose Eli," Warner announces proudly. "And, you can't choose truth."

"Dare," Eli says.

"I dare you to show Montana *all* of your piercings." Warner's proud of himself.

My eyes dart to Carson, unsure what's about to occur. From what I know of Warner, I can only assume one of Eli's piercings is below the waist.

Eli approaches where I sit on Carson's lap. "You can't punch me for this," he tells Carson while unbuckling his belt. He lowers his pants to reveal his erect and pierced cock.

I don't dare count how many piercings he's adorned his genitalia with. It's not polite to stare, but how can I not? He's a mere five feet away from me, exposed and proud.

"If you get your cock pierced, there will be *no* blowjobs," I inform my husband, my index finger pointed in Carson's direction.

"D-A-M-N!" Warner draws out.

Suddenly, I realize Carson might already be pierced, and I don't remember from our drunken wedding night.

Carson spins me on his lap, crushing his strong lips to mine. His kiss is a powerful and demanding one. I follow his lead, open my mouth, and express my desire for him as he doesn't hide his need for me.

We're all lips, tongues, and hands exploring. Moments pass before I come up for air to find the studio is empty. We are alone. The others slipped out without us noticing. I don't give them more than a second's thought and return 100 percent of my attention to my man.

While my lips rejoin his, my hands unfasten his belt and unbutton his jeans. I slip my right hand down, palm to his abdomen, until my fingers reach the target. A hiss escapes him when I grasp his heavy, rock-hard cock fully in my hand. I'm startled when his hand grabs my wrist, pausing my movements.

"Are you sure you are ready?" he asks, his voice gravely. "I mean, we've been drinking…"

"I've been ready for a while," I interrupt him. "I'm very aware of exactly what I'm doing. Now, hush, and let me get to know my husband intimately."

He releases my wrist, and I resume my exploration, stroking him. My left hand unzips his jeans, and taking my cue, he shimmies his jeans and boxer briefs low on his hips, offering me unfettered access to him.

Part of me wants to back up and take him in; a bigger part of me seeks an intimate connection, so I continue my strokes, adding a second hand. Carson's head relaxes on the back of the chair, heavy-lidded eyes peering at me.

I wiggle myself from his lap, still caressing his heavy weight in my hands. My knees on the carpet, my eyes on his, I part my lips, daring my tongue out to touch the tip of him. Wanting more, I slide my tongue in a circle around his tip. Still wanting more, I lower my mouth, taking him in inch by inch.

Eyes still on his through my lashes, I slowly slide farther and farther down his shaft. When his tip taps the back of my throat, I swallow, allowing my throat muscles to tighten around him.

Carson snarls, pulls me from my knees, crushing his mouth to mine. On their own, my hands remove his shirt as he tears off mine. Breathing heavily, we stare at each other for a moment before removing our remaining clothes ourselves.

Naked, we stand a foot apart, chests heaving. I extend one hand, placing it over his heart; its rhythm is as fast as mine. When I lick my lower lip, it stirs Carson back to action. He pulls me tight against his hard chest. His hands grasp my backside, lifting me. I wrap my legs tight around his waist. My breasts smash against his strong pectorals, and one of his fingers traces my hot, wet folds.

"Yes," he growls, positioning his tip at my opening. Then, eyes on mine, he thrusts into me.

Carson

Nestled within her, my heart swells, and my world's complete. I'm hers, and she's mine; we're finally together in every way.

Montana's so tight, wet, and warm; I need to calm myself. I've waited for this; I've fantasized of this. I don't want to lose control too soon. I need to make her feel good first.

Impatient, Montana wiggles her hips. I remove my mouth from hers and smile. She knows what she wants, what she needs, and I'm the luckiest man alive because I'm the one that will deliver.

I back up one step then another. My heel meets the bottom of the chair. I release her ass with my right hand, place it on the arm of the chair, then lower us to sit. When I scoot back in the seat, Montana positions her knees at either side of my hips. I grasp her hips, pulling them forward.

"Oh... god... yes!" she moans, sliding her hips forward and back while grinding herself on the forward strokes.

With her hands over my shoulders, her fingertips bite into my skin. I slide one hand between us, seeking the button to catapult her, to rocket her over the edge. My fingers part her swollen lips, and I place the pad of my thumb on her swollen bud, making tiny circular movements.

"Yes! Yes! Don't stop!" she screams at my contact. "Please! Please..." A feminine growl escapes her throat as I keep the pace. "Y-e-s!"

She grinds herself tightly to my pelvis; her nails pierce my shoulders, and her inner walls, with vice-like strength, grip my shaft. Wave after wave her muscles contract, milking everything from me.

Her forehead falls upon my shoulder while we come back to earth and attempt to slow our racing hearts and rapid breaths.

"I'm glad," I gulp in a breath, "that this studio is soundproof," I tease.

"What?" She lifts her head. "Were we loud?"

"Well, one of us was," I state.

I'm not sure if she's blushing or her cheeks are pink from our physical activity. Her eyes are bright, and her lips are swollen. Sex looks good on her.

"We should dress," Montana offers, slipping her arms into her bra and refastening it. I remain seated as she shimmies her lace panties then her shorts up her long legs and over her hips. I continue taking in her body until she slides her shirt back over her abdomen. "Everyone will know what we've been up to."

"They left knowing," I explain.

She tilts her head and bites her lower lip as she watches me redress.

"Like what you see, Mrs. Cavanaugh?" I tease.

"Umm," her eyes find mine. "I guess it'll do."

Giggling, she runs from the studio. I grab my shoes then dart after her. She's already out the exterior studio door and across the patio, entering the house.

"You better run," I holler after her. "Just wait until I get my hands on you."

I can hear her laughter when I enter the house. I nearly catch her on the stairs.

"What's all the racket?" Eli asks, peeking his head into the hallway from his bedroom.

At his words, Montana pauses at our bedroom door. I don't acknowledge him. Instead, I throw her over my shoulder like a fireman.

"Carson!" she squeals, out of breath and laughing.

I step into our bedroom, nudging the door shut with my foot. In three long strides, we're next to the bed, and I throw her. The wrought iron headboard bangs loudly against the wall, and the bed frame squeaks.

She props herself up on an elbow to watch me slowly and stealthily lock the door. When I slide my t-shirt up then over my head, she licks her lips, her eyes locked on my abs.

Stuck in a trance, she lifts her fingers to caress my stomach muscles as I near. Her touch feels like feathers; her fingertips swipe over each bump and hard plane. I suck in a ragged breath as she lightly scrapes her fingernails on the same path.

My eyes lock on her liquid brown ones as she continues to bite her lower lip.

She dips her index finger in the waistband of my jeans, her pouty lips forming an "O" when she contacts my still-hard cock.

Montana

His nostrils flare as I run my finger along his shaft; then, he pounces. He drags me up to the head of the bed, his mouth entertaining mine while his hands divest me of my halter top and shorts.

My flesh prickles against the cold air. The sensation energizes my desire. Cason pulls his lips from mine to gaze down my body. I squirm under his view. He licks his lips, eyes on my mouth as he sits up, knees planted on either side of my hips. I glide my hands up his sides and over his ribs in an attempt to grasp his neck and lower his mouth back to mine. My arms aren't long enough, and Carson smirks, realizing what I want and withholding it from me.

"Please," I whimper, breathy.

His tongue emerges from his parted lips to lazily swipe his lower lip, the lower lip I want to nip and suck. My body is afire with fevered need. Every part of me needs to feel every inch of him, skin to skin, mouth to mouth, and limbs wrapped tight.

Aching to hold him, I wrap my twitching fingers around the metal bars of the headboard. The cold, smooth metal grounds me for the moment. Carson stares at my hands, gripping the headboard. He falls to his elbows, inches above me.

"Don't move," he growls. His right hand covers both of mine, gripping tightly. "If you let go, I'll stop."

I search his face; he's not kidding. My man likes the thought of my hands handcuffed or tied above my head. I can appease him; it'll be fun. The rough pads of his fingertips skim down my arm and over my shoulder. I fight a shiver while biting my lower lip. I'm pinned beneath him, at his mercy and hot with all the possibilities. I've never trusted a partner as I do him. I've never given over all of my power and allowed a guy to pleasure me. Somehow, I've trusted him from the moment we met in Las Vegas.

28

CARSON

We're making great progress in the studio today. So far, Eli and Warner aren't bumping heads, and we're recording great tracks. Warner's singing the last verse of what may just be our first single on this new album. Jake and I man the sound board while Eli shares directions with all of us. He's proving to be a talented producer.

"Shit!" Warner blurts.

Well, we were making significant progress.

Eli flips the mic switch, "What's up?"

"My cell phone won't stop buzzing." Warner pulls it from his back pocket. "It's Meredith; let's take a 10 minute break."

Jake and I groan in frustration as we hoped to lay this entire track down today. I look to the clock. It's nearly six p.m.

"Might as well make it a supper break," I inform the group, rising from my chair. Before leaving, I look back to Warner, still in the studio. His back turns towards me, and his hand rubs the back of his neck.

I pull my cell from my pocket, turning it back on. Some of us actually follow the rules and turn our phones off to limit distractions while we work. Moments pass before three missed texts from Meredith ping. I read them in order.

> MEREDITH
>
> call me NOW!

Unraveled

> urgent issue CALL ME!
>
> NEED 2 SPEAK 2 U & WARNER!!!!

I delete them as Warner's on the phone with her now. Eli and Jake have left; I hang around to hear what Warner has to say. It turns out to be several minutes before he ends his call.

"Fuck!" Warner screams, throws his phone against the padded studio wall, and kicks over two music stands.

I exhale before opening the door. "That bad?" I query.

"She's pregnant," he states, facing me, his hands in his hair.

Gone is the always confident trouble-maker. Before me stands a broken man. I might even say a scared man.

"Sit," I instruct, motioning to the large chair behind him. "Give me the details."

He falls into the leather chair, letting out a long, loud breath.

"Remember last fall? Our four concerts on the east coast?" Warner doesn't look to me or wait for me to answer. "There was a woman at all four venues. Security let her through backstage and to the tour bus. I messed around with her once, but I wore a condom. My own condom. There's no way the baby's mine."

"The timeline fits for her to be eight months by now." I tell him what he doesn't want to hear.

"I wasn't the only guy she fucked. I fucked her once; God only knows who she fucked at the other three concerts where she earned her way backstage," he spits. "She claims it's mine; she's looking for the biggest fish to get her payday."

While I don't like his slut-shaming the woman, groupies allow many types of men to enjoy certain favors to gain the access they seek. I've heard security and roadies brag about blowjobs and sex from women desperate to get to the band.

"We need to talk to the guys and then to the crew to see if they remember her at the venues. If their stories match yours, you may be able to keep her from going to the press." My friend doesn't seem eased by my words. "What will you do if the baby *is* yours?"

"It's. Not. My. Fucking. Kid," he bites. "She'll get nothing from me."

Warner storms from the studio, slamming the outside door. I tap my phone to call Meredith. I need all the details to handle this for our band. I text the guys, too.

> **ME**
> band mtg 30 min

Warner remains in his room during our meeting. It's better this way; his inability to fathom that it might be his child doesn't help us get ahead of the media.

"Shouldn't Montana be here?" Eli asks when I try to start our meeting.

"Yes; she's part of us now," Jake agrees.

"Montana," Eli yells from the kitchen.

Soon, she peeks her head in.

"Have a seat," I urge, eager to get this over with. "Meredith has been contacted by a lawyer representing a woman claiming to be eight months pregnant with Warner's baby." I pause, giving this heavy news a chance to settle.

"Dude, how many times has this happened already?" Eli says. "Eventually, the women admit they aren't pregnant or refuse to take part in a paternity test."

"This woman is eight months pregnant, the baby bump is real, and she's requesting Warner submit his DNA for the paternity test." I repeat what I learned from Meredith.

"Damn..." Jake's shaking his head in disbelief. "So, who is she?"

"Meredith didn't give me her name, only that she attended our four east coast concerts last fall, was given backstage and bus access at each one, and states she had sex with Warner," I share, watching Montana to gauge her reaction.

"I remember her," Eli announces too loud. "Not her name, but I remember I couldn't believe she was a regular person, not a celeb, and made her way back at all four venues. That never happens."

I look to Eli as he speaks, corroborating part of her claims.

"I saw her and Warner leave the green room together," Eli continues.

Jake enters the discussion. "Warner always wears a condom, and it's not one someone gives him. He carries his own at *all* times."

I'm surprised when Montana jumps in on the conversation.

"Condoms are only 98 percent effective at preventing a pregnancy," she informs. "That's when they're used perfectly every time. New studies show the average man applies his condom correctly only 85 percent of the time." She looks to me and shrugs.

"Fuck," Eli reacts, throwing his hands in the air. "How come they don't tell us guys that? I mean, a guy should know there's up to a 15 percent chance the condom will fail. I deserve to know that." He doesn't hide his frustration.

"The condom box warns that they are 98 percent effective when used properly," Montana states. "The other information is in several magazines and available online."

"Who reads the back of a condom box?" Eli scoffs. "Do you?" He points to me. "Have you?" He points to Jake. We both shake our heads.

"It's his baby, isn't it?" Eli surmises, plopping back into his seat, defeated.

"Not necessarily," Jake states. "If she hooked up with someone at all four concerts, there may be other men on the hook for this one." He faces Eli. "You saw her all four times? Where was she? Was she with any guys?"

"Not that I remember," Eli confesses.

"Try to remember," Jake orders, desperate to prove Warner innocent.

"So far, she's agreed not to go to the press," I explain. "Meredith's arranging a meeting near us for Warner to meet with the woman and her attorney. Unless his DNA isn't a match, I'm afraid Warner will need to step up and take responsibility."

"This sucks!" Jake says what we are all thinking.

"Warner's refusing to do the paternity test, claiming there's no way he's the father," I share. "The easiest remedy is for him to agree to the DNA swab."

"I'll talk to him," Jake promises.

Montana

I feel like I'm right in the middle of an entertainment show publicity scandal. Like Jake said, "This sucks!" I understand the woman's need to seek the father of her unborn baby. On the other hand, though, I can't imagine Warner's fear that he might be the father. I suspect he fears the DNA result, and that's the reason he's protesting it so.

I try, but my mind can't help but wonder how many women Carson slept with while on tour. Having witnessed the women throw themselves at the guys while in Las Vegas, I'm not sure Carson could have refused many of them.

I refuse to sit here and wonder about this all night. I snag a bottle of vodka from the bar and head toward Warner's room. I knock lightly three times.

"Leave me alone," Warner snarls.

I ignore his demand, turn the knob, and find it's unlocked. I slip inside, shutting it behind me.

"I come bearing a gift," I state, extending the vodka bottle for him.

"Thanks," he bites, his chin motioning for me to head back through the door and leave him alone.

I join him, sitting on the floor, leaning against the foot of the bed.

"I don't want to talk about it," he states before chugging from the vodka bottle.

"Okay," I agree.

We sit quietly for several long minutes. I take a long pull from the bottle when Warner offers it to me.

"Carson didn't mess around," he declares, nudging my shoulder with his. "Not with groupies or a girlfriend."

I let his words sit for a minute.

"We teased him about it," he chuckles. "I do not understand how he does it. He can go forever without sex. It's unhealthy how long he deprives himself."

I like Warner's words. I hope he's being honest with me. I mull it over for a while.

"Are you, Peyton, and Jake in a thruple?" I blurt the question which has been bothering me for weeks now.

"Thruple?" he parrots in question.

"You know, a threesome?" I reword my question.

Warner laughs at me, a deep belly laugh. "A thruple?" he slurs his words a bit.

"It's a real word. I've read about them," I defend. "It's a combination of threesome and couple."

"You've read about them?" he inquires.

"Yes; I read all the time," I explain. "Occasionally, I enjoy a steamy romance, and that's where I've learned all about them." I change directions. "I see the way you react to Peyton."

"I…"

I'm not sure if he's stuttering or slurring.

"Don't deny it," I argue. "I know she excites you. And, my best friend seems to reciprocate those feelings." I glance sideways at this face in the pale light from a YouTube video paused on his iPad on the floor beside him.

"She's important to me, and I don't want to see her hurt," I continue. "So, are you in a relationship or not?"

He takes a long pull from the bottle before stating, "We're adults. If she wants you to know, she'll tell you. Otherwise, keep your nose out of it."

It becomes harder to understand the more he slurs.

"If you hurt her…"

"What?" he taunts. "You'll what? Cut off my balls? Tarnish my image in the press? Tell Carson to punch me?" He chuckles, shaking his head.

I try a different approach. "Have you ever been in love?"

To my shock, he answers, "Yes," his voice low.

"What happened?" I continue, hoping to learn more.

"She was the sister of my roommate and bandmate." He plays with the now empty vodka bottle in his hands. "She's the reason I looked for a new band all those years ago."

I remain silent, although I want to pry. I feel lucky he's opened up to share so much already.

"I messed around with another girl outside a bar during intermission. I was drunk, but that's not an excuse."

Again, we are quiet for several long moments.

"Do you think I deserve this?" he asks into the darkness.

I shake my head. "No one deserves this. But you need to find out one way or the other."

"I can't be a father," he states, defeated.

"I don't agree," I admit. "You have options, you know. You could offer money if you are the father. You could be involved in the child's life. The days of forcing a man to marry the pregnant woman are far gone. Before you decide how involved you want to be, you need to find out if the baby's yours."

Warner remains quiet beside me.

"I believe you'd make a great father. I've seen glimpses into your paternal side with the guys and with fans," I share. "A baby would be lucky to have you as its father and in its life."

"Were you a virgin when you married Carson?" he slurs. "You seemed so sweet and innocent…" His head bobbles on his shoulders.

"Let's get you into bed," I suggest, tugging his arm.

"Carson won't like you in bed with me," he smirks.

Perhaps drunk Warner will open up.

"Do you like Peyton?" When he nods, I continue. "Are you in a monogamous relationship with her?"

"Nope," he answers, popping his 'p' and upsetting me. "I share… trup… thrup…"

"Are you in a thruple?"

He nods.

"Are you sleeping with other women?" I dig deeper, needing to know.

"Only Peyton…" he mumbles.

There; I have what I wanted. Warner cares for her.

Warner continues slurring words I can barely make out. Worried he took pills, I scan the room. I'm relieved to spot an empty liquor bottle rolled under the foot of the bed. He's drunk and out like a light. He's too heavy for me to lift into his bed. Instead, I place a pillow under his head and toss a blanket over him.

29

MONTANA

A Week Later

I pat the pillow next to mine before I open my eyes. Carson's already up, and we left the curtains open. It's much too bright in here. I raise my hand to shield some of the late-June sunlight. Hearing the shower, I look towards the bedroom door. Denali isn't there; I guess he already took our boy out this morning.

I stretch my arms over my head, breathing deep. *How is it I just woke from a full night's sleep and I'm still exhausted?* My muscles feel heavy. Perhaps breakfast will give me energy to wake up.

I snag a hair tie from my bedside table, securing a high ponytail as I descend the stairs. A big yawn hits me at the bottom step, and I place my hand over my mouth as I cross the front room. I'm wiping the corners of my watering eyes when I enter the kitchen.

Carson

. . .

Fresh from my shower, I towel dry my hair then secure the towel around my waist. I smile at my reflection; I can't wait to wake Montana and reveal my plans for us today.

A female scream tears through the house. I lean into our bedroom; she's gone. *It's Montana!* I sprint from our room and down the stairs, hopping from the third step to the tile floor below.

I narrowly miss falling from water dripping off of me on the marble of the front room. I use a Scooby-Doo-like maneuver until I gain traction and run into the kitchen.

I'm unable to speak or catch my breath when I stand in the doorway, finding Montana wrapped in another man's arms as Fran and another woman watch.

She pulls away, wiping tears from her eyes. "What are you doing here? And, why didn't you call me? I could've picked you up at the airport." Before the man can respond, she asks, "How did you get here?"

"Mom brought me over," he admits.

As if on cue, Montana's mom appears beside me.

"Carson, aren't you a little under-dressed for breakfast?" Tony teases, pointing to my towel.

"Carson," Montana acknowledges my presence, "why aren't you dressed?"

I run my hand over my stubbled jaw. "I didn't have time when I heard your blood-curdling scream."

"Oops," she giggles, covering her mouth. "It surprised me to see my brother, that's all."

"Your brother," I repeat. "Nice to meet you. I'm Carson."

"Oops," Montana giggles again. "Joe, this is Carson. Carson, this is my big brother, Joe."

"So," Joe lifts his chin towards me, "he's not the usual rock star, huh?"

He's pointing out my nudity. Montana swats his shoulder.

"Be nice," Tony Randall orders her son, complete with a mom stare.

"Oh my gosh," Montana gasps, drawing my attention back to her. "You must think I'm incredibly rude. In my excitement, I didn't notice you," she explains to the familiar woman sitting at the breakfast bar. "Wow, even that sounds rude. You're much too pretty not to be noticed. I'm so sorry," she rambles and extends her hand. "I'm his sister, Montana. I saw you playing guitar during our last FaceTime call."

"I'm Starr."

That's why she looks familiar.

"And this is my husband, Carson," Montana introduces. "But I'm sure you've heard Joe rant all about him."

Starr smiles her mega-watt smile. "I might recall him mentioning something about a wedding," she teases. "And, Carson and I've already met."

I find the confused look on Montana's face adorable. I should let her gnaw on Starr's statement for a bit as payback for taking years off my life when she screamed. But I won't.

"Starr and I met at the MTV Video Music Awards a couple of years ago," I inform the group. "Now, if you'll excuse me, I should get dressed."

Montana

I'm so excited to see my brother that I barely entertain the idea of following my man upstairs and ripping the towel from his waist.

"Why didn't you tell me Joe was coming back for a visit?" I ask Mom.

She doesn't answer, simply points to my brother. I turn to face him, waiting for an answer.

"I wanted to surprise you for your birthday, silly," Joe confesses, playfully punching my forearm.

"This is the best birthday gift *ever*!" I announce, hugging him again.

"Did someone say 'birthday'?" Carson asks, back in the doorway, still wearing only a towel.

"Didn't she tell you?" Joe smirks. "Tomorrow's her birthday."

Carson

I want to wipe the smirk from his face. He's purposefully making everyone aware I don't know my wife's birthday. But I won't hit him. He's her big brother, and he's concerned for her; I'm glad he is. Also, if I punch him, my towel would probably fall, and that's not what I want to share with my new family.

I smile at my wife, and she smiles back. I nod my head, while inside, I'm frantically searching for an idea for her gift.

Montana

Carson excuses himself for the second time, and I aim my attention back to my brother. His hair is much longer and messier than he usually styles it. I like it. He looks softer, more relaxed. He's always been too serious and very focused on his career. Before me stands a new version of Joe.

"I'm afraid to ask…" I cringe at my shaky voice. "How long can you stay?" I scrunch my nose, bracing for his response. I can't wait for it. "Please, please, please stay in the U.S. I mean, Iowa. Please stay in Iowa. I need you here, near me," I plead. "A girl needs her big brother. Don't go back to Africa."

Joe pulls me to his chest, wrapping me in a tight hug. He kisses the top of my head before responding, "I might be able to arrange it."

My breath catches while I replay his words to ensure I didn't misunderstand.

"You'll probably be bored of me in a week," Joe teases.

I don't find it funny. "You'll really consider staying?" I ask hopefully.

Starr slaps him on the back. "Stop teasing her and tell her already."

I blink my eyes several times as if that will help me understand.

"I'm home to stay," he states slowly.

"Now, *that's* the best birthday gift ever!" I announce, and the kitchen fills with laughter.

"You mind keeping it down in here? You've got the dogs all riled up," Eli says as he opens the patio door.

Denali and Snoopy rush past him, straight to me. We've spent so much time together, they're anxious to see that I'm alright. I'm sure my scream earlier worried them. I bend down to pet them. Denali's heavy paws at my shoulders push me flat on the floor. I laugh as the two dogs nuzzle and lick my cheeks, chin, and neck. You gotta love the way dogs share their love.

30

MONTANA

"You know, many couples get a dog to prepare themselves to become parents," Carson's mother tells my mom.

I'm lounging in the sun in the chair next to theirs. My eyes are closed, and they believe I'm asleep. Wanting to hear what they say next, I keep pretending.

"A grand baby may be in our future." My mom claps excitedly.

"They rushed into marriage," Carson's mom reminds mine. "It would be okay if they took their time in starting a family."

"Do you have any grandchildren?" Mom inquires.

"No; do you?"

"No. I can't wait. I do look forward to it," Mom states. "I assumed my son would give me my first grandchild, but he doesn't stay in the U.S. long enough to meet a girl. Although, I don't know what to make of Starr traveling from Africa with him."

"She knew the band; maybe she tagged along to see them," Carson's mom offers. "I've got another son and a daughter, both married, but they plan to wait until in their 30s to start a family. They have too many things they want to accomplish first."

"Did you plan all of your children?" Mom asks.

"No. Did you?"

"Heck no," Mom answers. "Maybe God will gift us grandkids sooner rather than later." Both giggle; then, I hear them tap their glasses together.

My queasy stomach beckons for a snack. I find Starr placing snacks on her paper plate, too.

"I'm still on Africa's time," she explains. "Usually takes a good four days for me to settle when I return."

My plate full of snacks, I pause to talk. "Do you fly from Africa to the States often?"

She nods, chewing her last bit of food. "I try to visit Africa once or twice each year. It's hard to squeeze it into my busy tour and recording schedule."

"I apologize." I place my finger over my lips as I swallow a bite of cracker. "I'm not familiar with your work." I meant to search for her online last night, but Carson had other plans for my hands. I smile at the delicious memory.

"No worries. I'm not exactly mainstream," Starr explains, swirling the ice cubes in her drink. "I'm known in Jazz and Folk circles."

I nod. I'll need to research her and listen. I enjoyed the music in mine and Peyton's Jazz dance classes. I'm sure I'll enjoy hers.

"I collaborate in other genres; that's how I know the guys," she chuckles. "I can't believe they have a connection to Joe. Yesterday was a surprise for me as well."

"I enjoyed watching you play your guitar with the children in the village," I say then take another small bite of cracker.

"The children are my favorite part of my visits," she states, fiddling with her phone. "I also enjoy the photos I take." She extends her phone to me. "Scroll," she directs.

Her phone in hand, I marvel at the photos of the African scenery, the people, and even Joe, who she's caught providing medical attention to the communities. I swipe slowly, enjoying each photo of a land I hope someday to visit.

The next photo includes Starr and Joe. They stand side-by-side, their joined hands between them. There's an elderly man with his hands up in front of them as the community surrounds them. It looks like a ceremony of some sort. I search the photo for more clues.

"What's this?" I question, tilting the phone for Starr to see which photo I'm on.

Her eyebrows rise high on her forehead, and her lips from an "O." Instantly, I know she didn't mean to share this photo.

"Um…" She takes back her phone, scanning the pool area for my brother. "I guess…" She returns her gaze to me. "It's supposed to be our little secret," she states. "Follow me."

I grab two more crackers before following her into my parents' house. She doesn't stop in the kitchen as I expect; instead, she leads me out into the garage, shutting the door behind us.

"Okay," she starts. "Joe hasn't told your parents yet, so you have to keep it a secret." I nod, and she continues, "The tribal chief performed a marriage ceremony for us on our last night in the village."

My head tilts to the side, and a smile slowly spreads upon my face. That little devil. He lectured me about my eloping in Las Vegas, yet he does the same thing in Africa. Wait until I get him alone, I'll--

"We plan to tell your parents." Starr interrupts my thoughts. "Joe's waiting for the right time."

"Trust me, there is no *right* time," I chuckle. "So, the two of you are married?"

Starr nods, a gorgeous smile on her face and twinkles in her eyes. "I spent a month in the region last year, and we grew close. This year, I've visited twice and..."

I wave my hand in the air. "No judgement here," I promise. "I'm so happy for you and thankful you brought him back to the U.S. I've really missed him."

She can't stop smiling; she's positively beaming. "Our marriage isn't legal in the States; eventually, we'll need to make it legal."

I nod, unable to speak. I'm ecstatic. Already, I see that she softens him, getting him to relax and enjoy life. The fact that he's not headed back to Africa in a few days is even sweeter. It seems everything in my life is falling into place.

31

MONTANA

When we return to the backyard, I pull on my swimsuit coverup. I find that Carson and Eli man the grill full of burgers and chicken breasts.

I join my brother near the kitchen door, placing all the fixings on the long table. Working as a team, we position the buns, condiments, onions, tomatoes, lettuce, chips, and dips. Mom and Dad set up a cooler of water, beer, and pop.

Taking turns, we fix our plates soon after then scatter around the patio and poolside, gathering around tables and chairs. Sporadic conversations continue while we enjoy dinner. Dad commends Carson on the burgers and asks which seasoning he used. The two discuss the best flavors of seasonings and barbecue sauces. Luckily for me, the band is on their best behavior, and we enjoy hours with my family.

"Time for gifts," Mom announces.

Carson takes my hand and leads me to the round table by my parents. He pulls out a chair for me, kissing my exposed neck before sitting himself. A pile of perfectly wrapped boxes appears in front of me. Peyton unloads two paper bags. Apparently, they plotted to hide the gifts so I wouldn't protest.

I scan the group of family and friends gathered to celebrate my twenty-first birthday while my father lights the candles on my birthday cake. This is my new family; it's grown this year, and I'm blessed that it did.

"Hold up," Eli orders before the crowd sings the birthday song. "It says 21. You're already 21."

"Um..." Peyton smirks at me by my side.

"Nope; she turns 21 today," Mom answers.

"But you..." Eli continues his attempt to understand.

"Did you tell them you were 21?" Dad asks.

I shake my head. "It never came up," I explain. It's the truth. "I never got carded in Las Vegas."

Mom bites her lip, shaking her head at my actions. It's no surprise to my parents. They know Peyton and I drink. They've lectured us on safe drinking and not driving.

"So, you really are a child bride," Eli states, proud of the nickname he labeled me with.

"Can she blow out her candles now so she can open my present?" Peyton pleads.

I'm curious to find out what she bought for me. "I'll blow out the candles, but you're not singing to me," I announce.

They argue with me a bit, but I get my way. Of course, Peyton ensures her gift's on top of the pile on the table in front of me. I take my time, ripping the beer-can decorated paper, and I pull a frame from the box. It's two five-by-seven, golden-brown frames connected with hinges. I pull them open to find my wedding vows on the left and Carson's vows on the right. This simple gift of our typed vows inside a frame means the world to me. She approves of the words, our marriage, and wants me to see our vows every day.

Tears well in my eyes, and I fan my heated face.

"What is it?" Mom asks.

I pass the frames to her then turn to face Carson. He wipes my tears with his thumbs and kisses my cheek.

"I love you," he murmurs.

"I love you, too," I return.

"I didn't mean to make you cry," Peyton promises.

"I know." I've almost recovered from my tearful moment.

"These are the vows you recited at your wedding?" Mom queries, her brow pinched.

I nod, realizing she's not seen my wedding video that Eli recorded. I find the words we shared in our inebriated state perfect. It's clear she only reads the ramblings of drunks.

"I've got the video," Eli offers. "I can share it with you."

He's only trying to help, but I fear my parents won't find us responsible, level-headed adults, pledging our lives to each other. I want their approval, but I've grown to love our Las Vegas Wedding Chapel nuptials.

"Next gift," Joe prompts, trying to help me move on from the awkward situation.

I select the smallest box on the table, carefully pulling the ribbon and wrapping from it. Suddenly, I realize there is no card, and there's no "to" or "from" on it. I pause, the lid in my hand, almost revealing the gift inside. "Who's this from?" I ask my family.

"It's mine," Carson confesses beside me. "I suck at gifts. Guess I forgot to get a card." He shrugs, smiling his sexy, quirky grin.

Excitement bubbles within me at the possibility of the small, three-by-three-inch box. I bite my lower lip as I slowly slip the lid from its base to reveal a shiny, silver key on red, crimped papers. I take the key into my hand then toss it from one hand to the other.

"The key to your heart?" I look at my husband for confirmation.

He shakes his head. "The key to our house," he corrects. "It's much more than that, really. It's the key to all of me, to everything I have. You have all of me."

"Shew-wee!" Mom fans her face with both of her hands, tears in her eyes.

I smile, and my belly warms at my mom's reaction to Carson's gifts and words.

"He's a songwriter, that's for sure," Joe states, complimenting Carson on his choice of words.

I continue opening more gifts. The final one is from my parents. It's an eight-by-eleven-inch box, decorated in royal blue wrap with a Carolina blue ribbon, my favorite colors. Under the lid, I find a deed. I pick it up, scanning the details amongst the legal jargon. Mom shakes the bottom of the box, drawing my attention to a key. I pick it up, holding it on top of the deed. I see an address. Needing more details, I look to my parents.

"We purchased a small building for yours and Peyton's business." Mom smiles proudly.

Peyton joins me, reading over my shoulder.

"There's an office, a storefront of sorts, and a nice-sized warehouse behind it," Dad shares. "As you've created your second business venture, we thought it was time for you to set up shop for all of your enterprises."

"Thanks," Peyton says before I get my chance.

"Thank you," I respond, rising to hug each of them. "You shouldn't have. I have more than enough…"

"We know," Mom stops me. "We want to help you girls get started. It's an investment in the two of you and in real estate, so it's a win-win."

Part of me worries it's a way to keep me in Iowa and not in L.A. with my husband. I chide myself for such a thought. I'll save it for later; for now, I plan to celebrate.

"Seems keys were a theme," Eli teases, hugging me. "Wish I'd known. I would have bought you a car."

"Stop it." I swat at him. "I like the vintage tee more than I would a new vehicle."

"Even a vintage Mustang?" he teases.

"Well…" I tease back.

32

MONTANA

Later that week

We're sipping iced tea by the pool, my foot in the water, and Peyton is tanning, topless, on a nearby lounge chair.

"So, last night..." I begin the conversation I've longed to with my best friend.

"Finally!" She sits upright, not covering her bare chest. "Tell me everything. Leave nothing out."

"Cover yourself first," I prompt.

Peyton joins me at the pool's edge.

"Peyton, are you happy?" I ask.

Peyton crinkles her brow. "I thought you were going to tell me all about you and Carson. You want to know if I'm happy?"

"I mean with the... uh... guys." I worry my bottom lip.

Peyton smiles wickedly. "I thought you didn't want details."

"I don't," I quickly state. "I worry about you being happy and safe. I mean, you've never spent two weeks with the same guy before."

"I'm not with one guy; I'm with two," she corrects.

"Have you discussed what you want from your... uh... relationship?" I pry.

"Yes, Mom," she teases. "We've agreed it's just the three of us until one of us informs the others they want out. So, don't worry; we're monogamous."

"And, they take good care of you?" I continue. "Do they treat you with respect?"

Peyton smiles lovingly. "They take *excellent care* of me." She waggles her eyebrows.

"That's all I need to know." I quickly end that topic of conversation.

"Now, let's talk about you and Carson," she prompts.

It's Wednesday of the next week, and I've a billion things to do. Carson's already in the studio when I wake. I forego a shower, grab a quick bite, then lock myself in the office. I reached out to Carson's father last night, hoping to get some ideas on marketing our product. We're set to meet in a videoconference on Monday.

I swallow my last bite of cherry toaster pastry as I enter the office. What a mess. I take in the piles of papers I've spread out on the floor. Today, I need to focus on a presentation for Carson's father, explaining our product so he can best help me with a marketing strategy. The piles on the floor will need to wait.

I settle myself in the large, leather office chair behind the desk. I move a stack of papers, freeing up room to open my laptop. While I wait for my presentation software to open, I check my cell phone calendar for today through Monday.

Crap! I have a doctor's appointment this afternoon. Although it will be a quick visit, I call the office to cancel, promising to call in later this week to reschedule. I just can't deal with that today.

I settle in, creating a presentation complete with videos, online and in-person sales figures, and demographics. I'm nearly finished with the rough draft when there's a rap at the office door.

"Yes?" I call.

Fran appears in the doorway. "When you didn't break for lunch, I thought I'd better interrupt."

She places a tray on the two large stacks occupying the corner of the desk. In its center, there's a paper plate with a sandwich and chips. Next to the plate is a glass of ice, a bottle of diet cola, and two bottles of water. Everything practically fills the tray.

"Thank you, Fran." I didn't realize I'd worked five hours since breakfast.

She quietly exits, closing the door behind her.

I continue working while I eat; I need to finish the first draft of the presentation today and gather items to print for my meeting with Kurt.

Mom wants to meet Peyton and me at our new location in the morning. I'd reschedule, but I've already done that once. Hopefully, it will only take an hour, so I can get back here to work.

I've got a conference call with a potential manufacturer in the afternoon and another with the company supplying our packaging the next morning. I need to gather our current fees and information along with sales projections to complete those conference calls.

It's a good thing the band works all day until late at night. I need the hours to get organized and prepare myself for meetings.

33

MONTANA

Monday

I greet Kurt and Aaron at the door with uncomfortable hugs. They are still new to me, more like strangers rather than my new in-laws. Fran notified me mere minutes ago that they were at the gate. We'd planned a video call for today; I had no idea they'd fly to Des Moines. The guys are recording in the studio, so I won't let Carson know they're here until after our marketing discussion.

Fran and I offer our new guests a snack and drink before I invite both into the office. Aaron settles in the large, leather armchair by the library wall. I encourage her to share her opinions on the product, marketing, etc. as she'll be one of our key demographics. I begin by showing the product, our current packaging, and the examples on the dress forms with and without the product. I explain our attempts at naming and slogans: "Bra Claw," "a-BRA-cada-BRA," and "Now you see it; now you don't."

When I finish my presentation, I'm met with silence. It's silent for too long. I grow hot; I'm nervous they don't find our product worthy of his marketing. Aaron smiles, but like her husband, also remains silent. I begin to freak out. Silence can't be good. *Crap! This is bad. My in-laws don't like our product! This will throw a wrench in our newborn relationship.*

"Wow," Kurt finally gives feedback. "You have a solid platform for us to add to." He smiles wide.

I think he's proud of me. Perhaps I'm proving to Carson's parents I'm not seeking his money and fame.

"My turn," Kurt states, and he hands me a manilla folder.

I slowly open the cover, finding an outline with three major categories.

"I suggest we focus on these three avenues of marketing," he informs, pointing at the outline. "My team threw together this plan of attack, and we're ready to assist with each."

I'm stunned. He didn't just come here to hear my ideas and lend me a hand; he planned ahead and even brought his team in to assist us. My eyes blink rapidly, hoping to fend off my tears.

"As you see here, we plan to create banners and pictures for you to use on all social media platforms. We've contacted our two hottest influencers with ties to the Midwest. Both are on board, eager to receive the product and start promoting."

While he continues to explain, I hear not another word. One of the influencers is Peyton and my idol. She's the Olympic Gold Medal Gymnast that trained at our gym when we were in our first years of gymnastics. *Peyton's gonna lose her shit! Forget Peyton—I'm losing mine.* She's agreed to promote our product. We'll be working together. I need to sit down before my legs buckle. Both Peyton and I follow her on social media, we often discuss the products she promotes, and now, she'll be promoting for us. *No. Freaking. Way.*

"So," Kurt's voice calls me from my errant thoughts, "what do you think?"

I can't admit I didn't pay attention, so I smile and nod. I'm sure my eyes gleam. There's no way I'm concealing my excitement.

"I love it," I manage to reply. "I can't believe you put all of this together so quickly. I figured I'd pick your brain during our call."

I close the folder, clutching it tightly to my chest. "How much do I owe you?"

Kurt looks to his wife before he looks to me, smiling. "Pro Bono for family."

I shake my head. "I have the funds--"

He interrupts. "Consider it our wedding gift for our new daughter-in-law."

Tears fill my eyes; I press my lips together and nod. As much as I want to argue, I can't. I asked for his help, he's already done the legwork, and he can't undo it. Besides, I really, really want to work with the two influencers he has access to.

"Thank you," my weak voice trembles. "I can't tell you how much this means to me, to us. Peyton and I never expected this much help. We'll be forever grateful." I pat the manilla folder I hug tightly.

"We're happy to help," Aaron states, rising from her chair. "Based on the research we've conducted, I think your product will be a hit. I, for one, can't wait to try it." She stands before me with hands on my shoulders. "Now, let's go interrupt the boys and surprise my son." She slides her elbow around mine and walks me from the office.

When his parents come into view through the large, glass window, separating the production area from the recording studio, shock and worry flood Carson's face.

"What's wrong?" he asks through the studio mic, filling the booth.

I open the door to the studio. "Nothing's wrong. I asked your dad to help me with some marketing—I didn't plan to mess with your recording schedule. I'm sorry."

He shakes his head, smiling. "It's okay. A break will be good for the four of us. We've spent too many hours in this little space without windows to the outside world."

I wrap my arms around his neck, looking up at him through my lashes. "I love you," I whisper.

"I know," he teases, guiding me into the booth. "Let's break for the day."

"I'll be at the pool," Eli announces.

"Remember sunscreen," I tease him. "Set an alarm on your phone."

"Yes, child bride," he sing-songs.

I hear Jake murmur to Warner, "I'm texting her now."

I still worry about Peyton getting hurt in their little threesome arrangement, but she swears she's got it all under control. There's no way it's as casual as she claims. I hope, when the album's done, the three can still get along for Carson's and my sake. They really seem into my friend.

34

MONTANA

Weeks Later

After Carson's parents' visit, Eli announces he's been working on a special project that he is ready to share with us. I'm seated on Carson's lap as he sits on the sofa with Jake and Warner. Eli flips a few buttons on the soundboard then plays his work.

Music fills the small room from speakers in the ceiling and walls. The band loves his production, asking to hear it again. I can't put my finger on it, but there's something different about this piece; it strays from their usual recordings. I listen closer the second time he plays the track.

"Hold up," Warner directs. "Increase the volume on the second moan."

Eli fiddles with the soundboard and replays the section twice until they agree it's better.

All blood drains from my face, and my jaw drops. I point at Eli as I rise from Carson's lap. "You and I need to talk. Now." I push Eli's shoulders toward the music studio.

Carson follows us.

"In private," I inform, shutting the door before he enters the room.

"Ooo..." The other band members sing and laugh.

I motion for them to head back to the house. When it seems they've all left, I round to face Eli again. "How could you?" I spit.

Eli fanes confusion.

"You plan to exploit a private moment," I bite, spittle flying from my mouth with my words. "I thought we were friends." I wrap my hands around the back of my neck. "Were you spying? Did you watch us? Is that your thing?" I'm appalled.

Palms out toward me, Eli explains, "I only flipped a switch to start the recording; then, I left."

"Why me? Why us?"

"No one will ever know," he promises, tracing a finger in a cross pattern near his heart.

"But I know," I state. "You can't expect me to let you use it for the entire world to hear."

Behind me, the door opens. Carson joins us. "What's going on?"

"Your buddy, Eli," I share, "he... Those breathy sounds, those moans... That's me. That's us having sex. Eli recorded us." There, I said it. Now, Carson will handle the rest.

My husband's face isn't as angry as I expected. Instead, he smirks proudly.

"Seriously? You're okay with every man in the world hearing me, even jacking off to my sounds?"

He doesn't respond. We stare at each other, the rage inside me dying to explode, to escape, while he smiles back at me. I lick my lip before biting on it. Carson's nostrils flare, and his eyes lock upon my mouth. I stare at him for several long moments; the anger inside me wanes with each passing second.

Carson's gorgeous looks, sexy smirk, and memories of his actions that elicited those sounds from me wash away my desire to kill Eli for doing this to me, to us.

"You're really okay with this?" I ask my husband. He takes my hands, pulling me flush against him.

My head pressed to his chest, he whispers. "I didn't know it was you. And, if I didn't recognize it, no one else will."

I look up through my lashes. His warm brown eyes comfort me. I nod, letting out a long breath. My mouth quirks to the side.

"Okay." I turn to face Eli on the other side of the room. He's lying sideways in the oversized chair without a care in the world. "I'm sorry if I over-reacted. I've been so tired lately." I try to excuse my tirade. "I'm not happy you recorded me without my permission and planned to use the tape. In fact," I look to Carson for his support, "now that you've dubbed the sounds you want, you'll give us the recording. I'm not okay with you having it around." A chill shivers through me. "And no one, and I mean no one, better ever find out that's me you used for the song. You're lucky I'm so vested in those lyrics, or I'd tear your arms off for exploiting my first time with my husband. Without arms, I wouldn't have to worry you were jacking off to the recording."

"Um... second time," Eli corrects.

"What?" I'm lost.

"It's actually the second time you've been with Carson." He smiles sheepishly, still lying in the chair.

I make a move to attack, but Carson wraps both arms around my waist, pulling me back into him.

"I can't believe you want to argue with me when I apologize and give you permission..." I struggle against Carson's hold, attempting to attack his friend.

"Go," Carson orders, and Eli quickly complies. "And, don't record us again," he yells after his friend.

35

MONTANA

The Next Morning

I wake deliciously exhausted from our session in the studio followed by hours of lovemaking here in our bed. I take my time stretching my arms over my head then pointing and flexing my toes. Beside me, Denali groans as he stretches, too. He takes up more of the bed with each passing week; he's going to be huge.

My phone informs me it's nearly 10 o'clock. Carson's already in the studio. I'm surprised Denali let me sleep so late; I guess we kept him up late last night, too.

"Let me go potty, then I'll take you outside," I tell him as he nuzzles my neck and I scratch his belly. Never far from my side, he follows me into the bathroom, whining as I wash my hands. It's hours past his usual potty break, so I don't delay him any longer.

Every muscle aches as I descend the stairs, and my head hurts. Once outside, I take a seat on a patio chair as Denali does his business then runs to greet his friend, Snoopy, now on my lap.

Lately, I've busied myself in the office, spending less time with my canine friends.

"If you let me work, then I'll take you to the dog park later today." Both look to me while I speak, tilting their heads as if they understand my words.

I relax a few more minutes, watching the dogs explore the pool area and the grass beyond.

Fran knocks on the open office door, stating I should come eat some lunch. Glancing at the clock, I find it's two p.m. My body still aches as I pad my way to the kitchen. I spot both dogs lounging near the pool, so I eat my sandwich poolside today.

"Montana," Fran's voice calls to me.

My eyes blink, fighting off the bright sunlight.

"You fell asleep," Fran explains. "I don't want you to get a sunburn."

"What time is it?" I groan.

"It's after three," she states.

"Crap!" I sit up too fast, causing my head to spin. "I have work to do."

I bury my head in my work; time in the office flies. After a late dinner with the dogs, I take them for a long walk on the grounds and near the lake. It feels good to be outside. I love time with Denali and Snoopy. I really need to schedule breaks into my work days.

Carson

I call it quits at midnight. We've hit a wall and need the break. As I enter the house and make my way to our room, I hope Montana's still awake.

We've been working too many hours on the last two songs for the album. So much so that I can't remember if I saw her, outside of sleeping, yesterday or the day before. It's sad, really. We're newlyweds; we should spend more time together in and out of our bedroom. Unfortunately, for the past week, we've only been together while one of us sleeps. I keep saying, "One more day; one more long day." Then, we'll wrap up the album, and I'll devote entire days to her.

She left the nightlight on in the bathroom for me. I close the bedroom door as quietly as possible then tiptoe into the bath. Of course, Denali hears me. Tucked into Montana's back, his head follows me, but he remains quiet. I brush my teeth, strip out of my clothes, then slide into bed. I find myself jealous of the dog cuddled between us.

The next night, I'm sneaking into our bedroom long after midnight. Closing the bedroom door, I notice Denali is not in our bed; neither is Montana. Excitement grows as I walk toward the bathroom to find my wife.

"Montana," I murmur to her shadow lying on the bathroom floor, Denali's head on her back.

Denali whimpers.

"It's okay," I promise him as I squat down.

"Montana?" I shake her, but she doesn't respond. I roll her over, pulling her into my lap. She's pale as a ghost. She doesn't wake when I call her name a bit louder. Then, my body and brain snap into action. I pick her up and walk to the bedroom door.

"Help!" I scream into the hallway. "I need help!"

I snag a blanket off our bed, placing it over her in my arms.

The guys appear in my doorway.

"She won't wake up!" I speak quickly, unsure what to do. "Get Fran!"

Eli sprints toward the stairs.

"Did she take something?" Warner asks while Jake reaches out, his hand on her forehead.

"She feels normal, no fever," Jake states.

"I found her passed out near the toilet; there's vomit in her hair." As I speak, my eyes lock on Fran as she's entering the room.

She passes her phone to Eli." I've given the address; you answer their questions."

Fran looks to me then lays the back of her hands on each of Montana's cheeks. "She's had a flu bug for two days. No fever, but she barely eats or drinks. I put her to bed at nine tonight when I found her asleep in her office chair."

A flu bug. I didn't know. She's been sick for a few days, and I didn't know. Fran's words do calm me a bit. At least now I know it's the flu and not an overdose. *Thank you, Warner, for putting that thought in my head.*

After what seems like an hour, the EMTs arrive. While they take Montana's vitals, Fran shares her symptoms from the week.

"Is she on any medications?" the female EMT asks.

Fran looks at me, but I don't know. "I haven't seen her take any meds," I share.

When the next questions deal more with her family history, I decide I'd better call her mom. "Tony?"

"Carson, what's wrong?" Her frantic voice makes the weight in my stomach heavier.

"Montana's had the flu for two days," I explain, following the stretcher and three EMTs from our room. "I found her passed out by the toilet, and the EMTs need some information, okay?" It kills me every time the fact that I barely know my wife is pointed out. "I'll hand my phone to the EMT for you to answer their questions."

I descend the stairs, hearing the EMT speak to Montana's mom but not listening to a word of it. The sight of her loaded in the ambulance feels like a kick in the gut. My hands cover my abdomen. Fran pushes my back, urging me to ride in the ambulance with Montana.

When Tony joins us in the emergency department, Montana's still unconscious. I share the information Fran told me. In her motherly tone, she tries to calm my nerves.

I watch as the nurse replaces the empty IV bag with another. She promises Montana's improving with the fluids in her system.

Later, rustling near my head wakes me. I lift it from the bed, finding Montana looking down at me.

"Kiss… Beth…"

I barely make out her raspy whispers.

"What?" I ask.

Tony appears on the opposite bedside.

"Kiss…" Montana's eyes flutter closed. "B-e-t-h…"

And, she's out again. Neither Tony nor I understand what the two words mean. We attempt to work through it out loud, but we're too tired. The wall clock reads six a.m. We need Montana to wake; then, we need to go home and sleep.

Hours later, the nurse returns, taking Montana's vitals. At her movement and touch, Montana wakes again.

"There she is," the nurse says, greeting her sleeping patient. "How do you feel?"

"I... I'm okay," she croaks.

The nurse passes her some ice chips, instructing her to chew them slowly. After documenting on the chart, the nurse states a doctor will be in soon then leaves.

Tony swoops to her daughter's side, and I continue holding Montana's hand.

"What happened?" Montana asks.

"I found you passed out in the bathroom," I answer. "Fran says you've had the flu."

She nods, her hands quickly flying to the back of her head.

"You're dehydrated," Tony explains. "You'll have a headache until you rehydrate." She passes the cup of ice chips back to Montana. "You were mumbling about kissing Beth in your sleep."

"Hmm...?" Montana slowly tilts her head, her brow furrowed. "Oh. Not kissing Beth." She grins. "The song *Beth* by Kiss."

And? Was she dreaming about a Kiss concert?

She pats my forearm. "I now understand the lyrics," she states, her voice husky.

Damn. Just like that, she breaks my heart. Like the lyrics in the song, I've been working too much, making and breaking promises.

Tony interrupts my thoughts. "Well, now that you're awake, I need coffee," she states, approaching the door. "Carson, I'll bring you some, too."

A minute after Tony leaves, the doctor enters. "Hello, Mrs. Cavanaugh. I'm glad to see you alert," he says while reading her chart. "Gave us a bit of a scare, but both mom and baby are fine."

Wait. What?

"Nausea and vomiting are common in the first trimester," he continues. "I'll recommend some ways to prevent future bouts of dehydration. There are many reputable books on pregnancy with many helpful tips. Everything looks good here. I'll let the nurses know we're ready to discharge you." He looks from her to me. "Any questions?"

A million, I say to myself. He mentioned pregnancy more than once, so I didn't imagine it. *Did she even have the flu? Or was she just pregnant? Did she know? Did she know she was pregnant and just told Fran it was the flu? Why didn't she tell me? Surely, if she knew she was pregnant, she would tell me. Unless she's afraid to tell me. Is she afraid of how I might react?* I lean forward, elbows on my knees to start a dialogue, when Tony returns.

"Thanks," I mumble when she hands me a coffee.

Tony informs her daughter, "I met the nurse in the hallway. They're working on the paperwork to send you home."

While Montana looks shocked like me, her mother seems the same as she was an hour ago, tired and ready to leave. I look to my wife for guidance. She shakes her head once, eyes locked on mine. I assume we aren't sharing the news with Tony today.

"Will you be able to take us home?" I ask.

"Of course," Tony assures. "I wouldn't make either of you take a cab after the night we've had."

I would've called the band, not taken a taxi. *Shit! My phone's been turned off since I rode in the ambulance. The guys must be freaked out. I need to send them an update.* I ignore the text alerts; I know what they are asking. I tap on Eli's name.

ME

sorry

phone off

all better be home soon

36

CARSON

The Next Night

"About ready?" I murmur near Montana's ear, looking at our reflection in the mirror.

"Just a sec," she promises. "Are your parents here yet?"

I nod. "Fran said they arrived while we were napping."

Montana sighs audibly as her shoulders fall.

"You look perfect," I vow, kissing her cheek before turning her to face me.

"So far from perfect," she counters.

"You're perfect for me." When she scoffs, I relent. "Okay, in all honesty, you look like you've had the flu." I tell her what she already knows. "Most of them know you were sick. They'll be happy to see you awake and eating."

"Let's get this over with," she says before placing her lips to mine.

We hear loud conversations from the crowded front room as we make our way down the stairs, hand in hand. Noticing our arrival, the conversations dwindle.

"Let's eat," Montana suggests, swinging her arms toward the dining room.

Tony leans in close. "You look like you feel better," she says then continues with the crowd toward the table.

My father takes a seat at one end of the table while Montana's takes the other end. The rest of us line ourselves down each side. Peyton sits between Warner and

Jake. Joe and Starr sit opposite them. Montana and I sit by them with Eli across from us. Tony says grace, and we fill our plates, passing food around family style.

Montana places a roll, some mashed potatoes, and a bit of chicken on her plate. It's not much, but it's more than she's been eating this week. I notice her mom keeps a close eye on her plate, too.

Montana and I make eye contact several times as we eat. Well, as I eat and she nibbles while around us, our family and friends converse on a variety of things, everything except last night's ER visit and the flu.

Montana leans into me. "Will you go ask Fran to join us?"

I do as I'm told, asking Fran to join us for a few minutes in the dining room. She argues until I tell her Montana wants to tell her something.

"Thank you for giving up your Friday night plans to join us tonight," I begin. "We have many things to celebrate tonight."

Montana takes my hand under the table. I nod my chin toward Warner.

"We officially finished our album last night." At Warner's announcement, everyone claps and cheers.

Montana nods to her brother, but he doesn't take the hint.

I rise. "Mom, Dad, we're glad you dropped everything to fly here today. We didn't want to worry you. The rest of us already know that Montana was in the ER last night. Well, early this morning, really." I look at my friends and family around the table. "I found her passed out on the bathroom floor from what we thought was the flu." I kiss Montana's hand in mine. "No need to worry about catching the flu bug tonight."

"Just don't drink the water," Montana giggles.

The guys look to each other in confusion. Peyton spews a mouthful of water across the table at us. Starr claps, and Tony tears up, a hand on her lips. After a few moments, I announce, "We're having a baby!"

Now, the table erupts with cheers and clapping. Pats on the back and words of congratulations surround us.

When we all calm down, Tony takes a turn. "Well, then it's settled. Kurt and Aaron, if you'll extend your stay, I'd like to throw a renewal of vows for Carson and Montana at our house. This way, the family may celebrate the marriage."

My parents agree to stay, and my mother offers to assist Tony with the preparations. I look to Montana to see if she's okay with the plans. When she smiles, I assume I need not shut down our mothers' plotting.

"And, I have one more announcement." Montana surprises me by standing. Again, she looks at Joe, and he's clueless. "As you're planning for Carson and I to renew our vows, I think you should know that another couple at this table should share their vows."

Understanding dawns on Joe's face, but Montana and I are the only ones to see it. Everyone else's eyes look to Peyton and the men beside her.

"Oh, hell no!" Peyton argues. "Stop looking at me; I didn't elope."

I have to laugh at her denial. Someday, she'll change her tune.

"Who?" Tony asks her daughter.

It's clear Tony's the only one who hasn't figured out her son and Starr are the ones.

"For Pete's sake, Mom." Montana points. "Joe and Starr were married in the African village before they flew home. Jeez." She sits down, frustrated.

I slide her water glass towards her hand, gently reminding her to sip often to avoid another ER visit.

Montana

Snuggled close, my head on Carson's chest, my mind rewinds the past 24 hours. What a day it turned out to be.

"Are you ready to talk about our news?" Carson asks, tucking hair behind my ear to reveal my eyes.

"What will I do while you go on tour?" I ask. "Stay in Des Moines or L.A.?"

"What do you want to do?" he asks.

"I don't know," I confess.

"Well, I'd prefer if you were with me in L.A. while we prep for the tour. Then, I'd love to have you on tour with me," he confesses.

"How would that work? Would I drive my own R.V. and follow your tour busses or be on the bus with you and all the guys?" I inquire.

Carson shrugs. "The guys have had women ride the bus with us from time to time. Most of theirs were one-night stands. But I'm sure we could lobby to sleep in the actual bed at the rear of the bus. The guys love you, and as long as you could tolerate all the smells that come with four guys crammed on a bus, it could work."

"I don't want to come between you and the band. I won't force myself where I'm not welcome," I state, tracing lazy circles on his abdomen.

"Do you feel welcome here in the house?" he asks.

"Yes," I answer honestly.

"See, the guys love you. It helps that you tease them back. It'll be hard for Warner to top the calf in his bedroom, but he will try," he chuckles, his hand rubbing my back. "We don't have to solve it all this week. I mean, we haven't even known you were pregnant for 24 hours yet. I have plenty of room in my house for us to start a family. Um, I'm getting ahead of myself. Do you like my beach house? We could sell it and buy another. Or, do you want us to live in Des Moines near your family?"

"You'd consider that?" I lift my head, resting my chin on my arm on his shoulder.

"Of course! I told you I'd really give us a chance. I don't care where I live."

I love this man.

37

CARSON

Sunday Evening

I hate seeing Montana like this. I understand her morning sickness messes with her all day long. On top of that, she's anxious about today's double wedding.

"Please relax and take two deep breaths," I urge as I pull into her parents' circle drive. "Remember, the doctor wants you to relax, because it's better for the baby. Besides, we've already had our real wedding; this one is pretend. You have nothing to be nervous about."

"It's not nerves," Montana states, tears welling in her eyes. "It's that my mother didn't approve our vows and the Las Vegas wedding."

"Please don't cry, honey." I rub my thumbs under each eye. "No one can take away our wedding. It was real, it was a spur of the moment, and it's ours."

Montana nods her head in agreement. I pull two pieces of paper from my shirt pocket. I open the first and pass it to her.

"Let's recite our own vows. These are the vows from our Vegas wedding."

"I can't believe you brought these," she chuckles. "I love you so much."

"So, we'll play along with your mom's wedding but recite our original vows." I open my door, hurrying over to help my wife and baby from the Jeep.

Montana

I lead Carson through the house into the backyard where I'm stunned silent. I blink my eyes several times to make sure I'm not imagining it. Sure enough, I'm standing on the patio in my mother's backyard, and it's not decorated with all things white and wedding. Instead, it's set up like it was for my birthday barbecue. The only difference is one white backdrop set up amid the greenery of her garden.

Mom *always* goes big. Her parties require hours of planning with decorations that match down to the napkins. Since Mom announced our vows for this weekend, I've dreaded her decorations and plans. I expected her to plan her vision of the perfect daughter's wedding. Even though she promised to keep it simple, I prepared for an over-the-top big ceremony.

"Everything okay?" Carson whispers, concerned as I stand here like a statue.

"She kept it simple," I whisper back.

Carson nods, lifting my hand to kiss it. I lean into him, thankful for his strength. He takes the paper gift bag from my hand, placing it on a nearby table, then guides me to a chair.

Our family walks over to greet us, commenting on my sundress and asking how the morning sickness is today. We visit for 15 minutes until Mom announces the minister arrives.

Carson helps me stand; I giggle. If he's this protective at four weeks, I can't imagine how he'll be when I'm the size of a bus with cankles and stretch marks and can't put on my own shoes.

Mom introduces Starr then Carson to the minister. She explains how we'll stand by the backdrop and states she'd like to take photos during the ceremony. All on the same page, we take our positions. Then, our family and friends gather around us.

As the minister speaks, a loud humming begins. I do my best to ignore it, but it buzzes overhead. Looking up, I spot a drone hovering above us. Annoyed, I return my attention to the minister. The persistent drone hovers lower, circling around Carson and me then the minister.

"Excuse me," I interrupt the minister. I can't take the incessant buzzing interrupting the ceremony. "Can we do something?"

"It's got to be the paparazzi," Eli states. "News of the ceremony must have leaked."

Suddenly, a loud thud sounds above us, and the drone splashes into the swim pool. We stand dumbfounded, watching the drone float.

"You're welcome," Peyton brags, hands on her hips. "Oh, Tony, I invited your neighbor over to join us as thanks for shooting down the drone for us."

I turn toward our neighbor's house, finding the boy proudly holding his tennis ball-shooting dog toy. He shot it at Peyton and me last summer as we lounged by the pool. I wave him over, thankful he took out the annoying drone.

"Carson," Peyton calls with her hand extended, "I need $100 to pay the neighbor kid."

Laughter fills the air.

EPILOGUE

Montana

With the album complete, the guys hang at the pool with Peyton and me during the day, and we entertain them in Des Moines at night.

Carson takes frequent calls from Meredith and the label regarding publicity for the album release and the upcoming tour. He calls a band meeting almost daily.

Using the tips found in the many pregnancy books Carson bought for me, I'm feeling better, and the morning sickness doesn't ruin my every waking hour.

News leaked to the press about his purchases; now, the paparazzi swarm and speculate that he knocked me up before the shotgun Las Vegas wedding. Peyton allows me to vent and helps me remember to ignore the headlines; she helps me focus on my life and not the rumors.

At the many band meetings, we've arranged for the Unraveled Tour to contain shows for two months, then take a month break, then repeat. With our baby due in mid-April, the tour takes a four-month break from April to August, allowing the guys to be home. They brought me to tears when Eli suggested it, and Jake demanded the label give in to their planned breaks for the tour. These guys look out for me in every way.

We're in L.A. now. I work with Sonny and Matt to prepare the house for the baby while Carson and the guys practice on the stage for the tour. He's home each night for dinner, usually with at least one guy joining us.

Unraveled

Peyton and I video chat daily. She's running the Des Moines headquarters, complete with a full-time office manager and five warehouse employees. The influencers made our product a must have all across the U.S. Online sales skyrocketed, and retailers sought us out for the product. Carson's arranged for Peyton and me to meet our gymnast idol at the upcoming concert in Tennessee. I plan to fangirl hard; it will be embarrassing.

I have three new ideas for our next entrepreneurial venture, but they will need to wait until after the baby arrives. That gives me lots of time to brainstorm. I'm blessed to work with my best friend. Peyton refers to me as the talent of our operation.

Tomorrow, we will see the customized tour bus Carson and I will live on during the tour. The rest of the band will share another bus. Carson thought I deserved more privacy and a space of my own during our pregnancy. I think he wanted our own bedroom without three sets of ears listening nearby. Our own bus brings many advantages.

Each night, Carson sings songs from the new album to the baby. The sound of his voice often lulls me to sleep while causing the baby to kick. I don't have a favorite song; they're all about me. Carson poured his feelings into each one, further explaining the uniqueness of our chance meeting.

The first single released, *Unraveled*, currently boasts four weeks in the number one slot. *Undone*, *Before You*, and *Everything* slowly climb the charts, threatening to knock it off the top of the charts.

My summer began with a heavy decision on my shoulders—find a job or continue with college. Little did I know the whirlwind my life would become. Everything seems to fall into place, much to my surprise. I don't know what the future will bring, so I'm enjoying every minute with my family and the band.

When it comes to love, I'm lucky. Love at first sight really does exist.

UNLEASHED

GREED

PROLOGUE

Sylvie

I shoot a quick text to Lidia; she's probably asleep as she has early morning classes tomorrow.

> ME
> you will not believe what just happened to me

Immediately, my cell phone rings.
"I thought you'd be asleep," I greet.
"Still studying for a test tomorrow," she explains. "What happened?"
"Well," I begin, "I started painting this afternoon. I got lost in my canvas. The next thing I know, two police officers were knocking at my door."
"What did they want?" she quickly asks.
"Well, you know the new speakers I had installed today?"
"Yeah..."
"I was listening to my playlist while painting," I share. "I didn't pay attention,

and I had the speakers on out by the pool. Anyway, you know how loud I listen to my music. One of my new neighbors called in a noise complaint to the police."

"No way!" Lidia gasps.

"Of course, it just happened to be the time I'm working on an angry portrait, listening to my metal playlist. Let's just say the lyrics were not radio edits." I take a quick breath. "I've made a great first impression on my new neighbors."

"Were the cops nice about it?" Lidia inquires.

"Oh, you should have been here," I giggle. "They sent two very *attractive* cops to my door. One of them was a silver fox and the other a young hottie."

"What?" she sputters. "Seriously, Mom?"

"Yes. The older of the two was tall with silver in his dark hair and his goatee. The younger one was stacked with muscles on top of muscles, dark hair, and dark eyes. I was awestruck as I opened the door. I'm sure I stood there frozen, looking like an idiot in my painting clothes with paint in my hair." Adrenaline still pulsing through me, I try to steady my breath.

"Wow! You're a lucky lady," Lidia chuckles.

"I should have gotten the young hottie's name," I state. "You'd definitely be interested in a date with him."

"Mom, for the last time, stop," she whines. "I don't need you to set me up."

"You say that, but on a scale of one to ten, he was definitely a ten," I share. "The silver fox was a ten, too."

"Mom!" she squeals.

"Okay. Okay," I give in. "Trust me, you would have thought they were hot with a capital H-O-T."

"So, did you get a ticket?" she asks, changing the topic of conversation.

"They let me off with a warning," I share. "I promised I'd be more careful with my outdoor speakers in the future. Get this, though. The young hottie winked and smirked at me when I promised it wouldn't happen again. What does that mean?" I ask. "How should I interpret that?"

"No way," Lidia scoffs. "A cop wouldn't do that. You must have imagined it."

I don't argue with my daughter, but I'm 100 percent sure I didn't imagine it.

1

SYLVIE

Two Months Earlier

I play with the fresh green leaves of the peony bush sprouting from the ground. "Omar, I can't believe it's been a year already," I begin, sitting myself down at his headstone. "There were times, countless days when I wasn't sure I could take another hour without you. I cursed the mornings I woke up and the nights without you by my side." I pause, calling up all my strength to do this. Like the leaves on this bush, although I am the same person, I change daily.

"I've mourned your absence *every* single day." I fight back the tears stinging my sinuses, threatening to escape the cages of my lids. "With the help of Lidia and my therapist, Edith, somehow, I made it through." I look up to the bright blue sky. The clouds float effortlessly across like all is well in the world.

"I need to apologize to you." I trace the engraved letters of his name as I speak. "I got lost in our lives. I changed everything about myself and no longer resembled the girl you fell in love with. For that, I am sorry." I sigh deeply. "I got caught up in what the wife and life of a law firm partner should be and lost sight of who I was. How you stayed with me all those years without mentioning it... I'll never know." I release a hollow chuckle. "Don't get me wrong; we had a great life. You worked hard to provide every opportunity for our daughter, and you bought me a beautiful home."

"I hope you know how much Lidia and I love you and miss you. Even if it looks as if we're moving on, we struggle with your absence." I sigh, gathering my emotions and finding the words I need to share.

"I have a meeting at the firm tomorrow; they claim to have settled the estate. It will be my first time there since you passed. My therapist claims it's another bit of closure that I need." I shake my head. "I don't think I can go back there. The memories of you in every inch of that office make it hard. Walking through the parking lot where I last saw you will be… difficult."

The image of Omar lying on the cold concrete, a white sheet covering him as the police and EMTs hovered nearby, burns in my memory. I bounce back and forth on whether I wish I had not been the one to find him that night or not. Most often, I'm glad I found him rather than having officers delivering the news on my doorstep. However, the last image of him that comes to mind isn't at his funeral, serene in his casket. I see him lying on the ground alone in the darkness.

I'm startle when my cell phone pings.

"That's my cue," I state, returning my eyes to his name. "It's time to meet Lidia for dinner." I stand, dusting off the grass and dirt from my pants. "We're okay, more so day after day. I love you." I kiss my fingers and press them over the letters engraved on the stone, the same ones forever written on my heart.

2

SYLVIE

Late in the week, I patiently wait on the sofa as Edith places her glasses over her nose and opens her tablet to take notes.

"So, how are you today, Sylvie?"

Her question has many answers, answers that she will pry, dig, and pillage for until I open up and let her in. I've decided not to mention the estate meeting at Omar's firm early next week. I can't discuss my feelings on returning to the office. They're too raw, and I don't think I could endure an hour on the topic.

"I'm pretty good," I state honestly.

"In our last session, we discussed the approaching anniversary of Omar's passing." She spins her stylus in her left hand as she speaks to me. "Tell me about that."

"Well, I went to visit his grave," I share. "I bet I spent an hour there, talking to him. I did that early in the morning then spent the rest of the day in Iowa City with Lidia."

"What did you talk to Omar about?"

There's the digging she's so good at. "Well, I told him how much I miss him—*we* miss him," I correct. "And I told him it's hard, but Lidia and I are doing okay."

"How did you feel then you left the cemetery?"

There she goes again with the questioning. "It felt good," I confess. "Like a heavy load lifted. I know that's not polite to say…"

"Isn't it?" Edith cuts me off. "Isn't being honest, taking ownership of your mourning, and saying the words out loud, okay?"

She's like a spider on a web; she maneuvers our conversations from one strand to another then explains how they all intersect.

"I might not admit it to everyone, but yes. The work we've done really helps," I state.

"It's the work you've done," she corrects. "I've only guided you on the path; the work has been all yours. Will you continue to visit his grave monthly?" she inquires, typing on her tablet.

"I'm not sure. I think I will visit when I want to but not write it on a calendar as a weekly commitment." I shrug, looking down at my hands folded in my lap. "I've felt I owed it to him and Lidia to visit this past year, but I don't feel that way anymore. I'm ready to focus more on myself."

She nods, adding additional text to her notes. "So, the goal was socializing this week. How did that go?" Edith asks from her overstuffed plaid chair, facing me.

I reposition myself on the small sofa with a pillow tight to my chest. I keep my eyes on the table between us. "I stayed after church for a cup of coffee and cookies." I uncross my legs, letting them remain apart. "I spoke to a few families."

"Good." Edith is always positive. "How did you feel?"

I shrug.

"Any upcoming church events to attend? Any potential friends?" she prompts.

I shake my head. "And I didn't look into any book clubs or card clubs."

"Why?" she asks, always trying to uncover true reasons for my actions—or lack thereof. "Why are you hesitating to socialize?"

Again, I shrug. "I feel like the new girl in a large school. No one approaches me, and I'm hesitant to engage."

Edith taps her stylus on the tablet in her lap. "Would you like to set this as a goal again?"

When I nod, she continues, "Let's look at the local library and bookstore for book clubs." Edith suggests this as if she'll go with me. "Facebook groups and community calendars might be a good place to look, too."

I nod. I understand that I need to find hobbies and make friends. I've avoided these in the past, devoting all of my time and talents to Lidia and our family.

Once again, Edith looks at her notes from our previous session. "Did you bring your notebook with your lists?" she inquires.

I pull the spiral notebook from my purse, turning several pages to the lists we made in sessions this year.

"As you read through the lists, how do you feel?" she asks.

My mind rewinds to the past session in which we started a running list of items that I wished to revisit on the anniversary of Omar's death. As I mourned during our appointments, I also took a long hard look at myself. We discussed the woman I am compared to the woman I want to be. When I met and dated Omar, I envisioned becoming a woman and having a life very different from the one I became and lived.

"I think I'm both excited and scared," I admit.

"What excites you?" She prompts more discussion.

"Each item," I answer. "I can't wait to start."

"What scares you?" She digs deeper.

"I worry about what Lidia might think of my new tasks and hobbies." I shrug, lifting my eyes from the lists to my therapist.

"Why would Lidia's reactions bother you?"

"Her father's death was hard on her. She seems fine on campus as her life there remains the same as it was over a year ago." I move the pillow from my lap back to the corner of the sofa, placing my open notebook on the cushion beside me. "When she returns to Des Moines, though, the fact that Omar isn't here becomes a reality. I think moving to a new house will help her as all of his memories are in the home the three of us shared."

I take a sip of water to quench my dry mouth, then continue, "I worry that my new tasks and hobbies will be yet another change that upsets her."

"What have we discussed about how others feel about your life?"

Yeah, yeah. I know. "I need to live the life I want, doing the things of interest to me, and I shouldn't let others prevent me from my happiness. I need to put myself first." I repeat the answer we've covered in every session of the past year.

"That is one of the items on your 'reminder list,'" she tells me.

I turn to another page. On it, in large handwriting, are the words, "Live the life I want. Don't let others prevent me."

"I'd like for you to share your lists with Lidia as well as all the feelings we've discussed," Edith encourages, not for the first time. "She might enjoy helping you place check marks by items on your list."

She's right; I know Lidia supports me and wants me to be happy. It came up when she admitted she knew of my painting hobby. I thought I'd kept hidden for years.

"Which one do you hope to try first?" Edith continues, directing the session.

"I'd like to learn to use more technology and start practicing the guitar," I share. "I plan to schedule an appointment at the Apple store. I hear they are the best at teaching you how to use devices and fix them if there is an issue." I look at her. "And I'm playing around with the idea of applying to be a part-time piano teacher at the music store. That's where I will take my guitar lessons, too."

Edith alternates between taking notes and looking at me as I speak.

"I've tried to research using the internet on my phone, but it's so old that it takes forever and is too small to read on. So, I think the Apple store will be my first task."

"Sounds good," Edith praises. "Before our next session, you will plan to look into groups at church or book clubs at the bookstore and visit the Apple store."

"Yep," I agree, closing my notebook.

Excitement defeats the fear within me. My blood hums through my body. *I'm ready.* Today, I'm ready to start on my lists.

3
SYLVIE

I hate Mondays. My stomach roils as I enter the law firm—Omar's practice. I haven't been here in the year since Omar passed. I tried to prepare myself, knowing everything would remind me of him, but obviously, I failed. The air feels heavy and hot. It hurts my chest to breathe. I keep my eyes focused on the carpet before me and the artwork on the wall opposite me for fear I might lose what little hold I have on my emotions.

The receptionist cuts my misery short, taking me to the conference room. Sitting at the long table, I feel like I took a punch in the gut. Just like his office at home, this was Omar's world. I can't help but remember him in this setting.

I take the long breaths Edith taught me. Then, rather than panic, I name objects across from me. *Leather chair, painting, intercom...* I say to myself.

"Sylvie, so nice to see you again." The partners take turns greeting me then take seats opposite me. The three men open binders in front of them on the table. I realize all three attend this meeting out of respect for their former partner and to comfort me, but I'd rather speak to one lawyer and hurry through this. I want this finished once and for all.

"Will Lidia be joining us today?" One partner politely asks.

I shake my head.

"Right, so as we've previously mentioned, Omar wisely invested his money over the years..."

I do my best to listen to their words, but my mind flashes between them and memories of Omar.

"Life insurance... Trust fund... Stocks and bonds... House... Van... Car..."

I hear words, but I'm not listening. They place a large binder in front of me. I stare at page after page of its figures and words; it's all too much. I'll need to read it at home when I can focus.

The hour-long meeting passes in a blur. I shake all of their hands and promise to seek their assistance if Lidia or I ever need anything. Still in a trance, somehow, I drive myself safely to the house. I place the binder on the counter and pour a large glass of red wine.

I open the financial binder, passing the title page and firm's contact information quickly. In front of me, I see figures, figures that blow my mind.

During our marriage, Omar allowed me $3,000 monthly in my account for household expenses, Lidia's needs, and incidentals. I paid utilities, groceries, and gas from that allowance.

I pinched pennies for years, making do with what he allowed. I clipped coupons, shopped deals, and did without many things I longed to do or own. From my measly monthly allowance, I saved $7,500 over the years. It pales in comparison to Omar's savings.

I knew my name was on the house and minivan. I had no clue there were these other assets. Listed as his sole beneficiary, I now possess much more than my meager savings account.

A trust fund of over $450,000 is in Lidia's name and available upon settling his estate. I'm not surprised that Omar took care of us in case of his passing. It's the amount of money that shocks me to my core. I'm not sure how Lidia will react when I share this news with her.

The house, minivan, and his car are all paid for. The firm secured copies of Omar's death certificate and updated titles for each with my name on them. We bought our house over 20 years ago for $275,000. An enclosed appraisal shows its value is now over $400,000.

Omar's other accounts and investments total over $3.6 million, and this does not include his million-dollar life insurance policy.

I take deep breaths and name things I see around the room as I hope to prevent a panic attack. *Light bulb, house plant, chair, centerpiece...*

I scrimped to save and worried about money every day of our marriage. I did my best to make do with my allowance while he provided a comfortable life for us. Omar knew of these assets and never shared that information with me. *How naïve I have been, how stupid.*

I should have been more involved with taxes and finances; I should have asked questions. Instead, I allowed Omar to take care of me and our daughter; I should have taken an active role in our savings.

Nauseous, I pull crackers from the pantry to calm my stomach as my head pounds. Figures swarm in my mind; it's too much money. I'm not sure what to do. The partners referred me to a financial management firm to assist me. My head swims.

I sip the last drops from my wine glass and pour myself another. A deep breath —in and out, in and out—calms me.

In therapy, I discussed selling the house, downsizing, and using some proceeds for items on my list. This is to be my year to "find me," and I thought a little money would help me do that. With this much money, I can do anything I choose. The enormity of the events and hobbies on my list pales compared to the lists of investments Omar compiled during our time together.

Why did I hide my head in the sand for so many years?

4

SYLVIE

After such a long day, I should be asleep, but I can't lie another minute in this bed. I slip out from under the covers. My slightly ajar closet door catches my eye. I grab both knobs in my hands, flinging the doors wide open.

I cringe at the plethora of pantsuits in muted colors before me. I've always craved vibrant, trendier styles but sacrificed my desires for the "proper attire" a wife of a lawyer would wear. I wrap my fingers around the hanger of a beige jacket and matching pants. I lift it from the closet and place it over the end of the bed to donate. *I'm definitely donating these.* Pantsuits in pale blue, navy, cream, and black, one after another, I purge from my closet. I snag a couple of hangers at a time and move them to the growing pile on the end of my bed.

Staring at the pile, I recall overhearing a conversation at a Bible study that one charity in town collects attire for women to wear for job interviews. They collect donations and help the women practice for the interviews, setting them up for success by giving them a hand up, not a handout. *Teaching women in need the art of successful interviews is a charity I can get behind.*

Back at the closet, I squeeze five hangers between my hands then toss the pantsuits into the donation pile. Armful after armful of pantsuits vacate my closet, creating a giant pile at the end of the bed. Amidst the pant suits are silk blouses, sweaters, and silk scarves.

Free. I finally feel free of these shackles. They were costumes I endured to play my role of doting wife. My love for Omar prevented me from straying from the neutral colors and styles. Now, I can dress as I please. There's nothing holding me back.

The rod empty, except for two button down blouses and a pair of black slacks, I turn my attention to the shoe boxes on the shelf above. I pull them down two at a time and pile them next to my other donations. I need not read the labels. Inside are granny shoes in muted tones. Sensible, one-inch, square-heeled shoes to match each of my pantsuits.

I refuse to wear them again. I'm ready to own blue jeans, t-shirts, and other items in vibrant hues. I plan to purchase clothes that reflect my personality.

There's an empty closet before me. Excitement grows for me meeting with a personal shopper. I'm done with the boxy, old lady clothes and eager to start on my new wardrobe to express the true me.

5

SYLVIE

"Mom!" Lidia calls from the kitchen.

I love the weekends she comes home from college. This house is too big and quiet for one person.

"Hmm?" I mumble, while watering my snake plant in the front room.

"It's still not up here," my daughter states in a maternal tone, hands propped on her hips.

"You're gonna make me regret telling you about my therapy sessions and assignments," I inform her as I make my way to the kitchen. I stand opposite her at the island, my forearms leaning on the granite countertop.

"The reason you started sharing in the first place was to hold yourself accountable." Lidia poses, hands remaining on her hips and a scowl upon her face.

"Fine," I huff in defeat. I point to the drawer by the refrigerator. "It's in there."

She doesn't ask for permission. Instead, she opens the drawer and places my list on the center of the fridge door, securing it with two magnets. She takes one step back then another, tilting her head to the side as she reads.

Mentally, I go over the handwritten list on notebook paper as she does.

The list:
Learn to use technology
Paint more
Share my art

Learn to play guitar
Explore restaurants
Discover me, inside and out
Participate in the world outside of my house
Make friends and find a best friend
Ride a motorcycle
Get a dog
Attend concerts
Take a road trip
Sky dive, bungee jump, hot-air balloon ride
Travel to: New Orleans, Nashville, Washington D.C., Tampa, Denver, Dallas
Get a passport
Travel to: Mexico, Aruba, the Caribbean, Greece, Egypt

My heart rate quickens as she reads it; I've only shared it with Edith. In the past year, I've come to realize there is a lot about me my daughter doesn't know as I've kept it hidden. I plan to ease her into it one at a time, but my list might cause her to have many questions.

Lidia turns to face me, a giant grin upon her face. It's his grin and his eyes; Lidia looks so much like her father. My heart melts.

"Let me hear it," I challenge, eager to move past this awkward conversation.

She shakes her head, smile growing larger. "I like it."

She likes it? What on Earth does that mean? She likes it? Does she think it's a farce? The mother she knows doesn't do the items on that list.

Lidia chews on her lower lip for a moment. "I've long known you've hidden your talents. I found the key to your craft room when I was 12." She pauses for my reaction.

I nod. I knew she'd known about the painting for a while.

"Grandma and Dad shared stories of how the two of you met and what you were like." Lidia pulls a water bottle from the fridge. "Dad's face lit up when he spoke of meeting you and the dates he took you on."

I never knew. She loved her daddy-daughter time; I had no idea they spoke of such things. *When he shared with her, did he miss that part of me? Did he long for the woman he fell in love with, and if so, why didn't he tell me?*

"I can't wait to see you take time for these things that interest you. I'm here if you need me for anything: for a ride, a pep talk, advice, or to practice on. I know you need to do it on your own, but I'm ready to help when needed." She laughs. "And I'm willing to be your plus one as you travel."

Her wide smile touches her twinkling eyes. I marvel at her excitement as I approach and pull her into a tight hug.

Holding my shoulders with both hands, arms extended, she states, "Some of these are pretty dangerous feats and lofty goals."

6

SYLVIE

As each week passes, I grow stronger and stronger. It's time, time for me to pack everything up to keep, donate, or sell. I've encouraged Lidia to box up the items important to her over her last three visits. With those items out of the house, it's time to thin out, move out, and put the house up for sale.

Following the suggestions of the staging company, I take all family photos down, clear off all surfaces, and plan to clear as much furniture from the house as possible before they stage it to sell.

The clothes I plan to donate to charity. I spoke to my minister and his wife; as I sell everything, I plan to donate all proceeds to the ministries of the church if they assist me. We've decided to hold an indoor rummage sale of sorts at my open house to announce the house is for sale and hopefully get rid of the furniture the same day. Most of the furniture is over 10 years old, but it's still in excellent condition. We're hoping the sale saves us from moving the furniture multiple times; and after it's gone, the staging company can get the house ready for showings.

I recall during Lidia's first year of college telling Omar this house was too big. It feels even more so in the year since his death. It's time for a simpler home with new furniture. Although I love this house, I need a new one, one where memories of my old life won't haunt the new me rising to the surface.

Ready to address Omar's memory haunting me, I sit ready to reply to an uncomfortable email I received yesterday. My fingers flex while I search for a plan. I stare at the email. Clicking reply, I fidget in my seat. Honest. I'll just be honest.

I don't want to see it; I don't want to know what might have taken place in his work apartment. It was Omar's secret, and I don't want to know. I'd rather live with my memories of his occasional sleeping at the office during big trials. In my memory he worked until the wee hours of the morning, cleaning himself up in the bathroom before he returned to court.

"Please donate all items from the apartment, including the funds from the sale of the property. Use the funds to do pro bono work at the firm. Sincerely, Sylvie Rice"

I click send, breathing a sigh of relief that Omar's law partners will take care of the matter. It's no longer my problem.

7

SYLVIE

Boxing again today, I'm in the kitchen, I snag another box. *Three! It's crazy; who needs three boxes of cookbooks?* In my constant search for recipes to impress Omar, I gathered an entire library of cookbooks.

The irony, more often than not, is that my culinary endeavors lay on chilled plates in the refrigerator until Omar called it quits at the office. Although he called to alert me, he would work late. The call came as dinner was already baking. With his limited time at home, I found food was a way to receive praise from him and impress colleagues when hosting a dinner party.

I won't need these cookbooks. Cooking for one isn't easy, but very few recipes serve only one; I don't need leftovers.

After dinner, I'm not making much progress on packing up the photo albums. In my nostalgia, I take my time, flipping through each one. In years past, with free time on my hands, I took my time in creating each album page.

Pregnant with Lidia, I look so young. I smile, realizing I was younger than Lidia is now. In the photos of Omar holding Lidia, it's easy to see his love for our daughter. With each photo, a moment of time replays in my head. Here she toddled in her playroom; here she attempted to climb the stairs for the first time.

In the next album are Lidia's birthdays, two pages for each year. In the early years, Omar's parents and my mom were the only guests. When she started school, classmates began attending the parties.

Another album holds photos of Lidia at the piano, practicing and at recitals. These photos are bittersweet now that I have learned how much she hated playing. It wasn't until the past year that she confessed her distaste.

The only constant in the scrapbooks, with all of their photos, is my hair. I don't know when I decided to keep the style, requiring little maintenance and no coloring, for decades.

It's time I choose a new hairstyle.

Later, with all my linens in boxes, I notice two smaller boxes on the highest shelf of the closet. Not remembering the contents, I pull both down to the floor before peeking inside. *Whoa.* These are boxes holding my journals; these notebooks contain my thoughts and desires from age 18 until Lidia's sophomore year of high school.

I flip through a notebook, marveling at the handwriting filling each page and often the margins. I pause, reading the entries. One topic I ranted about was a concert nearby, one that I longed to attend, and how inappropriate it was for Omar's wife. Another topic included locations I hoped someday to visit. Sadly, I didn't attend the concert or travel to any of the places I wrote about.

In another notebook, I find a bucket list I created at age 18. Little did I know then the complete 180-degree turn my life would take in the next three years.

I look at my accomplishments over the past 21 years. I nurtured and taught Lidia to become a woman confident in her strengths, owning the fortitude to survive in the modern times. I guess, learning from my mistakes, I raised her not to give up on her dreams; I taught her that she can have it all—a family and a career.

While I raised our daughter, I helped Omar earn a partnership by mingling at dinner parties and social functions, all the while keeping his confidence high, even during the tough cases.

Omar and Lidia's accomplishments might be seen as mine; I don't see it that way. I'm a wonderful mother and was a great wife; those are my two accomplishments. Somehow, they don't seem enough in my own eyes.

I long to find this younger version of me, the woman full of confidence and hope, the woman that does what she wants instead of worrying how it might look to others. This is the woman I've discussed with Edith and plan to find again.

8

SYLVIE

The next day, I'm giddy; in this store with all of its possibilities, I feel like a kid in the candy shop. I've wiggled every mouse then touched every iPad and iPhone on display. My breath catches when a woman greets, "Welcome to the Apple Store. What can I help you with today?"

"I'm moving into the new century as my daughter says," I state. "I'm interested in an iPhone." I show her my now antiquated cell phone. "And perhaps an iPad, Apple TV, and laptop."

"Okay. Let's start with your phone..." Her face lights up with the dollars I plan to spend today.

Over two hours later, I'm driving home with all four items, accessories, and future appointments to attend classes in the store to learn how to use each of my products. I've so much to learn about using these technologies. Lidia gave me a sneak peek; now, I'm curious to learn it all.

The next day, with three pictures of me, ages 18 to 20, I walk into the department store, excited. In the past, I've dreaded shopping. Now, I know that was because I wasn't purchasing the items I craved. *Why did I give up on my taste in fashion so easily?*

I approach the customer service area, our agreed upon meeting place, and am immediately approached by the personal shopper. When she asks what I'm looking for, I give her more than she expects. I hand her the photos, claiming I want to return to the styles I wore all those years ago.

When Lidia asked why I wanted a personal shopper, I shared that while I know what I like, I don't know where to look and how to accessorize according to current trends. The shopper could help me spot items.

When discussing it at my last session with Edith, I explained I wanted to "find me."

To which she asked, "Have you been lost?"

We discussed how I was not lost, just playing a role for years. I still admired styles and trends I like from a distance as they didn't fit the professional agenda. In my journals, my true thoughts and desires for clothes were expressed. They were just hidden away; it's time they surface.

I share with the personal shopper that I don't have formal functions or work to dress up for. I'm interested in casual styles that are expressions of me and would like to start with a few outfits today. Together, we choose jeans, many brightly colored shirts, retro tees, and comfy sweats. Although she works for the department store, she mentions I might find concert shirts and other t-shirts I desire at thrift stores or consignment shops. I make a note to check them out in the weeks to come.

As I drive from the mall to my house, I glance at the multitude of shopping bags in the back seat. I didn't just buy a couple of outfits. My new wardrobe is well on its way. I have two pairs of Converse shoes, two pairs of boots, and a sassy pair of sandals. I also have not one but four pairs of jeans along with some shorts for summer. A couple of swimsuits and a denim jacket complete my purchases.

Next to the white bags from the department store, the pink bags from Victoria's Secret pop brightly. I return my eyes to the highway before me, proud I splurged on the pretty bra and panties sets.

Once home, I spend the rest of the afternoon shopping online. I order handbags, belts, a designer blazer, and two sundresses.

With the help of the shopper, I now know what I want and clammer to buy them. I spend over an hour on Amazon after I've visited several major clothing stores' websites.

Edith's words play in my mind. "Remember baby steps; it's a process. You *will* make mistakes. Think of them as learning opportunities."

I didn't take baby steps today. I plunged into shopping for my wardrobe headfirst.

Unleashed

Continuing my transformation, today I'm addressing my outdated hairstyle. I've been excited to find something new that expresses the woman I'm trying to find. In bed, I meticulously browse celebrity sites and Pinterest, critiquing hairstyles and colors. Excited about the short, sassy style I like, I need to find a salon; I no longer want to pop into the no-appointment-needed shop in the strip mall.

During the next week, with the assistance of my new devices, I visit Yelp and Facebook to read reviews on nearby salons. Finding the one for me, I call an Aveda salon with all natural products nearby.

9

SYLVIE

Today is the day; today, I morph my hairstyle to match my personality. I approach the salon chair, excited to embrace this change.

"What are we doing today?" my new stylist asks while draping a black cape around me, securing it with Velcro behind my neck.

I pull my arm with my cell phone in hand from beneath the cape and pull up the screenshots I saved. "I like this style," I state. "Will it work with my face shape?"

The stylist takes my phone, swipes through the photos, then looks closely at my face in the mirror. She pulls my hair away from my face and off my neck in the back, still scrutinizing my reflection.

"Yes, if you are ready to make the drastic change, it will work well with your cheekbones."

I breathe a tiny sigh of relief. I had my heart set on this style; I'm not sure what I'd choose if she hadn't agreed.

"The style is versatile," she shares. "You can curl it, scrunch it, or simply blow it dry. You mentioned color when you scheduled your appointment. What were you thinking?"

I shrug. "This is where I'd like your input. I've never colored my hair. I'm ready to; I'm just not sure what I need."

She runs her fingers through sections of my hair along my part and near my face.

"I don't see many grays, so we can do one color all over or add highlights."

She still plays with small sections of my hair. "All over color requires you to come in regularly as the roots will show when they grow out. Highlights and lowlights are more natural and blend better as they grow out. Should you decide to keep the new, shorter style, you'll be in often for a trim, and we can touch up both as needed."

I nod in the mirror. "Let's add natural highlights for the summer," I decide, and she smiles her approval.

Moments later, she chops inches off the side of my hair. "So, are you new to town?"

That night, while I wait in the tiny room for my guitar teacher to start my second lesson, I practice my fingering over the frets.

"What new song did you learn this week?" my teacher asks, entering the room.

I shrug, too embarrassed to share.

"C'mon," he encourages. "You told me you pretty much watch a video and then play the song. So, let me have it. What song?"

"*Hotel California*," I answer. "And *American Pie*."

He smiles, slowly shaking his head. "Only two?" he teases.

"And part of *Redemption Song*," I confess.

"Let me hear," he prompts.

As I play the two songs I've practiced every day this week, my heart warms; music seems to soothe my soul.

"I'm wasting your time with lessons," he states. "You are a talented woman. Your ear for music is far superior to any I've ever encountered." He passes me his business card. "I've written my cell number on the back. If there ever comes a time that you have a question on a technique or song, feel free to call me."

Carrying my guitar case, I wave goodbye to the staff as I make my way to the car. I enjoy playing guitar and challenging myself to conquer a new song. I'll let the internet be my teacher from now on.

During my drive, I contemplate songs I might like to play. Although I love the simplistic sounds of the acoustic guitar, many songs of interest to me include electric guitars.

Hmm. I might need to buy one.

Early Monday, I'm reading the local news on my iPad, enjoying a cup of coffee, when my cell phone signals a text.

> **LIDIA**
> are you free today?

> **ME**
> yes

> **LIDIA**
> I'm driving to Des Moines after class
> spend afternoon together & dinner

> **ME**
> yay!

> **LIDIA**
> I'll text when on my way

I'd planned to paint all day; Lidia's visit is a better plan.

10

SYLVIE

"Did you buy out the Apple Store?" Lidia teases, marveling at my new devices on the kitchen island when she arrives. "I'm jealous."

"Please," I scoff. "You've had a smartphone and a laptop all of your life."

"Do you know how to use them?" she asks, pulling water from the fridge.

"I've attended three classes at the Apple Store," I remind her. "I know the basics and plan to take more classes as I grow more familiar with each."

"Grab your phone," she directs, pulling hers from her back pocket. "Let's download Snapchat and sign you up."

She walks me step by step through downloading the app then creating an account. My head spins a bit as she shows me all the filters, stickers, and camera angles to use within the app.

"I use Snapchat more than texts," she states. "Let's send your first Snap. What would you like to take a pic of?"

I point to my guitar on the sofa in the front room. With her help, I take a picture, type a short label, add a sticker, then send it to her. She shows me the Snap on her phone.

"Snapchat is easier than sending a photo via text. Here. Let me move the app to the front screen of your phone."

I watch her fingers fly on the screen in hopes that I may be able to repeat the task in the future.

"There. All set." She smiles proudly. Pointing to the sofa, she asks, "How are your guitar lessons going?"

"It's only been a month," I remind her. "I've stopped taking private lessons and use YouTube now."

Lidia shakes her head. "I'm jealous. I wish I could watch a video or hear a song and mimic it. Unlike you, it takes me months to learn a piece of music."

"Not this again," I sigh. "I thought you enjoyed the piano lessons. If you'd told me how you felt, I'd have ended them before you turned 13."

"I'm over it now," she vows. "If I had your ear and talent, I'd probably still be playing. Who knows? I might have even joined a band."

We chuckle together. Like her father, Lidia is driven by numbers. When she left for college, I worried she chose her major to impress him. However, as she talks about her classes, her excitement is evident. Along with her looks, it's another way she reminds me of Omar.

"Play me something," she challenges.

Other than my former teacher, she's my first audience. As I position the acoustic guitar in my lap, I take a few deep breaths and flex my fingers.

I let my hands caress the strings as I play The Black Crowes' song *She Talks to Angels*. I focus on my fingers and the notes then lose myself in the song.

When it ends, I slowly raise my eyes to Lidia who still stands in the center of the room. Her mouth forms a small "O" and tears fill her eyes. She fans her face, unable to speak.

Knowing she needs a moment, I play *Patience* by Guns N' Roses. It's a long song, so when she sits beside me, I end in the middle of it.

"So jealous," Lidia laughs. "Is there anything you can't play?"

"I'm learning a couple of new songs each week," I share. "The songs I'm working on now are not acoustic."

"So…" Lidia draws. "You need to buy an electric guitar."

"Um…" I purse my lips to the side. "I've already bought one. It's in the corner." I point across the room.

She hops from the sofa. "Oh my, Mom! This is not just an electric guitar." She looks back to me as she points to it. "I follow enough music and pop culture to know a Les Paul is a big deal. How much did this cost you?"

I shake my head, not willing to share the price. *I enjoy playing the guitar and never plan to stop; I splurged on myself, and it feels good.*

11

SYLVIE

After driving through the dealership lots for the twentieth time over the weekend, today, I'm ready to purchase a new vehicle. I park my minivan near the building then make my way to the red Honda Pilot parked in the front row of the vehicle lot. I cup my hands at the sides of my face and put them against the glass to peer inside. I move from window to window, repeating the process.

I don't need my minivan as I won't be transporting Lidia and her friends every day. I want versatility to carry my new canvases but still hold four people comfortably if needed. It's another change for my new life.

Next, I look at the Pilots on either side of the red one. These both have cloth seats, and I prefer the leather. As I walk from vehicle to vehicle, I catch a salesman watching me from the corner of my eye. I'm sure he's hovering, waiting to jump in for the sale. I walk back to the red vehicle.

"How are you this morning?" a male voice calls to me.

I turn to find the salesman in a grey, pin-striped suit approaching. He's balding on top, and he attempts to hide it by spiking his longer hair on each side upward.

"Nice choice. Very safe," he states, mere feet from me. "What exactly are you looking for?"

I point toward the building where I parked. "I'm ready to trade in my minivan, and I think this is what I want. May I take a test drive?"

"Will your husband be joining us?" he inquires, his eyes searching the lot.

"No," I state, trying to hold back my anger. His question insinuates I need a man to make such a purchase.

"Yep. Let me go grab the keys." He smiles, shakes his head, then turns and walks away. "Oh…" He stops, glancing over his shoulder at me. "Um, would it be possible for me to get your keys to have the guys look over the minivan, assess its trade-in value?"

I squint at him as I try to work through it in my mind. *Is this something they always do? I thought that Kelley Blue Book thing was how they determined my van's value.* I've looked it up online and know exactly how much I will want for the trade-in.

"Okay," I answer, searching my purse for the keys.

I park the Pilot where I found it. Now, I'm certain this is my new vehicle. I'm in love, but I try to hide that fact from the salesman so he doesn't think he has the upper hand.

"When could your husband come by for a test drive?" he asks as we exit the vehicle.

"He doesn't need to know," I reply.

The salesman's face scrunches, not happy with my answer; he thinks he's lost the sale.

"We can discuss the trade-in value of your minivan," he suggests, motioning to the showroom. "Then, you can take the information home to discuss." He remains tight at my side as we walk. It's almost like he's glued himself to me so I can't escape.

"Have a seat," he directs in his cubicle. He begins looking through the envelope from my glove box that someone used my keys to get for him.

"I'm ready to sign paperwork right now," I blurt, catching him off guard.

"Well, we can't do paperwork until your spouse comes in. Since he is on the title to the minivan, he will have to be present to sign the paperwork."

Is he's man-splaining this to me?

I pull Omar's death certificate and the replacement title from my purse and slide it across the wooden desktop. "I'm a widow." I try to hide my contempt for his assumptions.

"Oh… Sorry…" he sputters while I'm sure his mind is working on a new game plan to close the sale.

I use his guilt to knock $5,000 off the price of the Pilot and get every dollar Kelley Blue Book stated my minivan is worth. Driving home, I giggle at his expression when I paid cash. I'm used to assumptions that I need a man to care for me; I love that I am now able to prove them wrong.

12

SYLVIE

The silence in the house makes it hard for me to fall asleep. Only on the second story, it feels as if I'm high in a skyscraper. Every noise I make echoes louder as I box up room by room.

I turn on the lamp, prop my back against the headboard, and bring my iPad to life. I need to find a new place; I'm ready to leave this much-too-large, two-story home and the memories it constantly replays. Lots of happy times in Lidia's childhood cause me to smile while Omar's empty office and side of the bed haunt me. I long for a place to make new memories.

With the assistance of the search engine, I enter my desired filters, and a large list of properties fills the screen. Though Lidia claims I don't need to have a room for her, I still plan for her bedroom and a guest room. The homes span all the cities that make up greater Des Moines. Moving from Norwalk into the city will cut my drive times by several minutes as I make new friends and engage in new hobbies.

When I created my list of pros and cons of moving with all the features I desire, I needed a studio with plenty of light to paint in, a room for Lidia, and one for guests. Of the four-bedroom homes, I rule out the brick ones. I like stonework but not the red brick exterior.

I'm partial to open floor plans and ranch homes. I prefer the laundry to be on the same level as the kitchen and master bedroom, because although they aren't a problem now, in the future, as I age, stairs may be an issue for me.

As I scroll through the list, clicking on picture after picture, I also consider the location. I want easy access to the major roads in the city. If my goal, as discussed with Edith, is to socialize, I'll drive around more.

I hover my index finger over a blonde-stone covered ranch near the Easter Lake portion of south Des Moines with a large, paved surface attached to the three-car garage and a tiny, well-manicured front lawn. It's less for me to mow, so I tap on it and swipe through the pics. It has only three bedrooms.

Oh, what's this? A beautiful four-season room. That would make a great studio and an in-ground swimming pool. Hmm...

Excitement pulses through me as I send the property to my real estate agent and then to Lidia.

Seconds later, I jump at my vibrating cell phone.

> LIDIA
> why aren't you asleep?

> ME
> why aren't you?

> LIDIA
> flipping through pics now

> ME
> it has everything I want & then some

> LIDIA
> (heart emoji)
> pool
> I call the 2nd master when not at school

> ME
> (heart emoji)
> that's what I wanted to hear

> LIDIA
> need to go study
> keep me posted

> ME
> study hard, I (heart emoji) you

. . .

Our conversation over, I scan through the texts one more time. I'm proud I used the emojis like she showed me a couple of days ago. I chuckle, remembering her overly dramatic proclamation about her ushering me into the new century.

13

SYLVIE

Three weeks later, with piles of paperwork complete, I grab a quick lunch then hurry to my new house. I've scheduled electricians today and find they're waiting in front of the house when I pull in.

"I'm sorry," I greet as they exit their van.

"No worries," the driver says. "We're running ahead of schedule."

The team of two men and one woman follows me into the house. I show them around, and we discuss the location of the speakers throughout the house: upstairs and down and on the patio around the pool. They promise to install some disguised as landscaping rocks on the patio near the pool. I motion to the walls I want the flat screens mounted on in the living room, family room, master bedrooms, and guest bedroom.

The female instructs the two men which tasks to start on. I guess she's in charge. *Right on-girl power.*

Three hours to install and a 15-minute tour, then I receive instructions on the command center in the kitchen. They leave a thick booklet on the counter by the console; it's a bit daunting with all the buttons and knobs. Before they leave, they assist me with starting my playlist, then my music blasts throughout the house.

I slowly spin, taking in the open floor plan of the ground floor. Once the furniture arrives, it will feel like home; it's my new home in which to create fresh memories and start my new life, the new life 19-year-old me imagined all those years ago: artful, bright, expressive, and riddled with adventures.

After inflating the air mattress in the living room, it takes three trips to carry my easel and paint supplies in from the garage. The mattress and easel are the only furniture in the large, empty space that comprises my living room, kitchen, dining room, and attached sunroom.

I quickly send a picture of the new space to Lidia on Snapchat, highlighting the air mattress and the fact that tonight is my first night in the new house.

I still have possession of the old house, but I'm excited to start this new part of my life. I figure I'm not going to sleep tonight in either location; standing in the large empty space, I'm glad I brought my paint supplies to keep me busy.

I set up the easel in the sunroom—my new studio—spread out my paints, drop a canvas tarp on the floor, and fan out my brushes. As Seether plays through the speakers, I open my duffle on the floor to pull out my overalls and head into the bathroom to change. My skin prickles as the excitement of an empty canvas upon my easel and millions of colors at my disposal to bend to my will fills me.

I mix colors on the palette in my left hand before I brush dark strokes, shadows, and a rough outline of a woman as darkness envelopes her, bringing her down.

14

SYLVIE

Hours pass unnoticed as I lose myself in my art while music surrounds me. Slipknot, Five Finger Death Punch, and others set the mood while I paint.

The faint sound of a doorbell under the loud music catches my attention. I lay my brush and palette down before answering the front door. Two uniformed policemen stand before me. My skin chills, and the hairs on the back of my neck stand up. Bile climbs my throat as the memory of the night Omar died flashes to mind.

"Ma'am..." the older, slim, salt-and-pepper-haired officer greets.

"Come in," I rasp, trying to collect myself.

Lidia? When did I last hear from Lidia? What were her plans for tonight?

"I need to turn off the music." I excuse myself, scurrying back to my art room, silencing the playlist on my cell phone. Deafening silence fills the large, empty space. I look to the officers as they take in the empty interior. "Now, how can I help you?" my voice cracks.

The younger officer smirks. "We received a noise complaint from your neighbor."

It's not Lidia. She's fine.

Shock floods me then morphs to embarrassment, horror, and mortification.

"We could hear your music in the driveway," the young, hot cop with a badge reading "Kirshner" informs me.

"Crud!" I move to the new wall console control for the speakers. "I didn't know the pool speakers were on. I'm so sorry." My fingers point to each button on the system as I frantically search for the outdoor speakers. "The system was installed today, and it's my first time using it." I turn to face the men. "I promise it won't happen again."

Realizing Five Finger Death Punch's *Burn MF* played moments ago, my hand covers my mouth, and my eyes grow wide. The sound and lyrics are very inappropriate for non-metal fans to hear.

What will my new neighbors think of me?

"Ma'am are you the homeowner?" the older officer with a badge reading "Calderon" inquires.

"Yes. I have paperwork over here on the countertop." Sensing the empty home sends up red flags, I retrieve the documents as I continue, "My new furniture arrives in the morning."

The men look at one another then back to me. "Keep it down," Officer Calderon instructs.

"And apologize to your new neighbors," Officer Kirshner adds, with a wink and a sexy smirk.

I walk behind them to the door and let them out. I watch as they pull from the curb at the end of my driveway, giving them a wave before I shut and lock the door.

Way to go, Sylvie. Get it together. First day of your new life and you've already been approached by law enforcement.

15

STEPHEN

I recognize *Closer* by Nine Inch Nails playing loudly in the backyard as we approach the large ranch in an upper-middle class neighborhood.

We ring the bell twice and pound a fist upon the heavy wooden door. I'm sure we can't be heard over the music.

Eventually, the door swings open, and a stunning woman in denim overalls splattered with paint in every color of the rainbow stands before us, a gun-metal gray paint smudge upon her face where a finger must have touched her cheek. Scanning quickly, I notice paint on the bandana in her hair and speckles of paint splattered on her right shoulder. She strikes quite an image with her shiny, golden-sun-kissed skin, baggy overalls, and a tight white tank top beneath.

I thought I'd seen it all in my time on the force. She's a disheveled mess. A sexy, metal-loving, disheveled mess.

"Ma'am..." Fredrik greets.

"Come in," she rasps.

I scan the large open floorplan, finding her alone in an oddly empty space.

"I need to turn off the music," she excuses herself, scurrying back to the art easel, silencing the playlist on her cell phone. Silence fills the empty space. "Now, how can I help you?" her voice cracks.

I smirk. "We received a noise complaint from your neighbor."

Embarrassment evident on her face, her hand covers her mouth, and her eyes grow wide.

"We could hear your music in the driveway," I inform her.

"Crud!" She moves to the wall control for the speakers. "I didn't know the pool speakers were on. I'm so sorry." Her fingers point to each button on the system as she frantically searches for the outdoor speakers. "The system was installed today, and it's my first time using it." She turns to face us. "I promise it won't happen again."

"Ma'am are you the homeowner?" Fredrik inquires.

"Yes. I have paperwork over here on the countertop." She retrieves the documents. "My new furniture arrives in the morning."

I look at Fredrik then back to her. "Keep it down," I instruct. "And apologize to your new neighbors," I add with a wink.

She walks behind us to the door and lets us out. She watches as we pull from the curb at the end of the driveway, giving us a wave before she shuts the door.

Later

"Fredrik, go home to your wife and kids," I call to my partner across our joined desks. "I'll write the report. Besides, it's the end of our shift. You should be there when your kids wake up." I'm already pulling up the driver's license of our last call, the noise complaint. He doesn't argue, quickly leaving before another call comes in.

While filling out the report, I see her birthday. Quickly, I do the math. *Wow. I would never have guessed it. Wait until I tell Fredrik. I would have put her at 35, not a day over 38. She looks fantastic for 42. Hmm. Intriguing. Good for her; she seems to enjoy life. This is why I should never judge a book by its cover.*

She's a little minx.

16

SYLVIE

The next morning, I happen to spot a cute little popcorn shop as I walk toward my car. *I love popcorn.* I step inside and buy a couple of bags of assorted flavors. I can't help myself; I purchase a large tin with three sections of different flavors. I smile, and my insides warm at my plans to drop it by the police station. *Come to think of it, I'd better get two tins, one for the day shift and one for the night shift.* I also grab a medium bag of the cheese and caramel mixture for the dispatchers. *Hopefully, in doing so, there will be some left for Officer Kirshner and Officer Calderon's shift.* It's a small I'm-sorry-for-being-a-nuisance and thank-you-for-keeping-our-community-safe token of my appreciation.

My stomach turns as I park my car. Suddenly, I feel like I might be sick. *Why am I acting this way? I'm simply treating the local station to popcorn, nothing more. No one needs to know that young hottie and the silver fox have been on my mind constantly since they left my place last night.*

I quell my nerves before I load the popcorn in both of my arms. I didn't think this through; it's too much to carry in one trip. Before I can return one of the large canisters to my trunk, a male voice offers to help me. I accept his assistance, explain why I'm here, and he escorts me into the station.

"Hi. I'm a local resident," I tell the women at the front desk. "I've brought popcorn for everyone."

At the mention of food, two nearby officers move closer. I fight the urge to chuckle and continue my explanation.

"I have a tub for the day shift and another for the night shift." I set the two canisters on the counter. "I even have two bags for the dispatchers."

"Oh, wow," the desk clerk smiles. "I'd better label these. In fact, I may need to hide the one for the night shift, or there will be nothing left for them."

I want to explain it's important that the night shift get popcorn since they are the reason, I wanted to get the gift in the first place.

"Who should I say these are from?" she asks, pen in hand.

"Sylvie Rice," I answer before I can think better of it. "Wait. No. Just say a local community member brought them in. They won't need to know my name."

"Gotcha," she winks. "Thanks for this."

17

SYLVIE

Today, I plan to add another toy to my garage. Excitement pumps through my veins as I pull into the dealership on Merle Hay Road. Unlike the two other times, today, I visit during business hours.

I slide my fingers along the trunk, the driver's door, and the hood. I pause in front to admire the sleek, little red sports car convertible.

"She's a beauty," a male voice calls, "isn't she?"

"Nope. *He's* an 18-year-old boy dressed in a tux on prom night. He's desperate to look the regal part but itching to go have some fun and take off his tux jacket and bowtie."

The salesman smirks, believing he's got me on the hook for an easy sale. "It's ready to drive home today."

"No, but it will be," I counter.

He tilts his head, amused a woman believes she knows more about cars then men, and places his hand on my back. "Honey, I promise it's ready. I'll even throw in two years of oil changes and tire rotations."

Honey? Honey! Did this man just call me honey?

I stride towards the showroom, my thoughts stormy as I rage over his demeaning words and his hand upon my back like he knows me. It's one thing to insinuate I need a spouse for such a big purchase; it's another to use that language with me.

At the reception area, I ask, "May I speak to a manager?" When I'm directed to the salesman approaching the door that I already spoke to, I shake my head. "I need his supervisor."

Judging by the receptionist's reaction, she knows what I'm upset about. "Follow me."

"How may I help you?" the supervisor greets, extending his hand across the desk.

"I'm here to buy a car," I begin, causing his smile to widen. "And a salesman of yours called me 'honey.' He doesn't know me, and I'm offended he spoke to me in that manner and placed his hands on me."

"I'm sorry that happened…"

I interrupt. "Sorry doesn't work for me. I'm here to purchase a car with cash today, and your skeevy employee gives me the creeps."

"This is not his first complaint, but it will be the last. You have my word on that," he states, his phone in his hand to text.

I furrow my brow as I assess his sincerity. My gut tells me he'll be true to his word. I nod my head, ready to move on.

"I'm interested in the little red Miata on the lot," I inform him. "One tire doesn't match. If you throw in four new tires, I will pay full asking price in cash today."

I leave the lot; my new toy being delivered to my home later today with a full tank of gas and four new tires. I'm giddy with pride. I'm proving to be the strong, assertive woman that I once was and am striving, again, to be.

18

SYLVIE

"How much has your new guitar hobby cost?" Lidia asks on her next weekend visit home.

It's really none of her business. It's something I enjoy, and I have the money to buy myself nice things. There is a difference in instruments, and I didn't buy from the cheaper end of the spectrum.

"I know it's not my business," Lidia states. "I see you now have a Fender next to the Les Paul."

"I'll just say there are many more expensive guitars than my Fender Telecaster," I share. "I can always sell it for good money if I ever stop playing."

"I don't want you to stop playing," she quickly shares. "It only made me think of your future new hobbies and how much they might cost; you may not stick with them."

"Honey, I told you. Your father had both of us taken care of," I remind her. "Come with me."

"Where are we going?" she asks before she stands to follow me.

"I want to show you the financials…"

"Nope." She quickly and boldly says, "I don't want to know."

"Yet you are worried about me spending $1,500 on a new guitar." I raise an eyebrow at her.

"I know you said it's more than I have in my trust fund. I just can't help but worry. You've purchased new cars, a new house, new furniture, and all the decorations," she explains.

"If I told you it's more than four times your trust fund, would you stop worrying?" I offer.

Lidia coughs caught off guard. I've tried to share the financials with her many times; she is adamant she doesn't want to know. A part of her is worried, and I need to calm those nerves once and for all.

She clears her throat. "That much?"

I nod.

"Wow!" She stands, taking my hand in hers. "I guess I shouldn't worry about you spending $2,000 on your new hobby then."

We chuckle.

"I don't plan on spending it all," I promise.

"It's your money to spend any way you want. I just wanted to make sure there was enough as I plan on you living for many decades." She tilts her head to the side.

"I'm living off of the interest," I share. "You'll inherit…"

"No… Nope…" she shouts, her hands flying to cover her ears. "Do. Not. Finish. That. Statement."

I nod. She's right. It's only been a year since she lost her father. She shouldn't think about losing me, too.

19

STEPHEN

"Oh my!" A loud female voice catches my attention to my left. "You're certainly proud of your member, aren't you?" Her laughter tickles the air.

I blink, not believing my eyes. The woman we made a noise complaint on last week, emerges from the big cat building. Her cheeks are bright pink, and she covers her mouth as she laughs. She pauses mere feet away, quickly typing on her cell phone before tucking it into her denim cutoffs. When she looks up, she immediately notices us.

She lifts her chin in our direction. "Officers."

"Hello, ma'am," Fredrik greets.

"I have to know. What was the conversation you were having?" I motion to the big cat paddock she just exited.

She rubs her forehead, wiping sweat from her brow on this warm June night.

"I tried to get a photo of me with the lion," she confesses. "He was only interested in cleaning his privates right by the glass." She chuckles. "Well, I guess I'm assuming he was cleaning and not..." She clears her throat. "Certainly not a PG-13 exhibit at the moment," she laughs.

"What a hoot," Fredrik chuckles when she walks away. "And don't think I haven't seen you light up at the sight of her twice now."

"Fuck." I know I'll be the butt of his jokes now. He won't move on; he'll pester me about her every chance he gets.

Sylvie

What have I done?

I stand in the kitchen of my new house, observing two dogs scurrying about, sniffing every corner as they explore their new home.

My plan for the day was to pick up my new Basset Hound puppy from the breeder. Bocephus, Bo for short, is 8 pounds of the most adorable puppy I've ever seen. His large paws pad along as his long, droopy ears drag to the floor.

On my way home, with Bo in his carrier, I felt guilty for purchasing a puppy when so many dogs wait in pounds for new homes. With each passing mile, my guilt grew.

Hagrid, the name given to him by his former family, is a mixed breed. The employees at the Animal Rescue League guessed he's part Rottweiler. He's 5 years old, and his family moved into a new rental with a strict "no pets" policy.

As Hagrid sniffs high and low, Bo trots behind him, sniffing the floor. When Hagrid laps water from the small dish I purchased for my new puppy, I realize I need to make another trip to the pet store. The tiny food and water dishes will not work for both dogs. Hagrid will need his own set, bigger kennel, and larger, soft bed.

I only have one leash, so I can't take both with me to shop at PetSmart. There's no way I can leave a new puppy alone in my absence. I'll need Bo in his kennel then have to trust that Hagrid is house trained. Clearly, I didn't think all of this through.

Deciding to postpone my trip to the pet store for an hour or two, I pull out my phone and send a Snap of my new fur babies to Lidia. She often asked for a dog growing up, but Omar strongly opposed it.

Immediately, I laugh as I answer her incoming video call.

20

SYLVIE

Slowly, I'm decorating my new home, making it my own. All my new furniture graces the place. Now, I'm purchasing decorative pillows and items for the shelves and walls.

I've purchased many things in the past two weeks from Amazon and other online retailers. I know the UPS guy by name. It's not uncommon for me to receive at least three deliveries in a week. He teases me about having a shopping addiction and promises to report me before I'm too far gone.

I move my box cutter along the seam of the third box to arrive today. With each box, I feel the excitement of Christmas morning in my youth. Although I purchase the items online, by the time they arrive, I forget what should be inside. This box contains a chenille blanket for the back of my sofa. I imagine I'll use it when winter arrives.

My stomach growls, reminding me it's lunch time. I groan; meals for one are a challenge. When I cook, I have leftovers for another meal or two, and most of the leftovers lose their taste the next day.

Recently, I decided to try new restaurants for lunch. It reminds me of the mother-daughter lunches Lidia and I had one Saturday a month before she entered high school and got too busy. Now in college, we enjoy meals out when I visit her in Iowa City.

Eating alone bothered me the first time, but now, I figure I'm rewarding myself with takeout or delivery. I've become a foodie of sorts, trying new places and new menu items. I share each of my lunch endeavors via Snapchat with Lidia.

It's a perfect day. The sun is out, and it's not too windy for a top-down ride in my Miata to pick up take-out. I plan to dine on a park bench since I can't fit a lawn chair into the tiny trunk of this car.

I choose a tiny tenderloin restaurant on the south side. It's been featured as a stop of Presidential candidates before the caucuses, so I'm excited to check it out.

I let the sounds and smells of the restaurant stimulate visions in my mind to later paint on my canvas. If that doesn't inspire me, eating at the park allows nature to spark my creative juices.

I lean on the edge of my car, watching runners, walkers, and bikers on the trail around Grey's Lake as I slowly enjoy my meal. With each bite, I grow more anxious to return home to my studio and record the senses of today's culinary adventure.

The greasy smell of the restaurant evokes the image of sharp points, maybe geometric shapes on my canvas. The sandwich reminds me of a small farm town. It's simple; a pork tenderloin and bun, yet it doesn't lack taste or charm. I think I'll paint a rural community this afternoon.

At home, I quickly grab a water before I address my blank canvas with my paintbrush in hand. As is always the case, butterflies flutter in my belly before I make the first brushstroke. I take a deep breath and begin.

When I yawn for the second time, I take a step back to admire my progress then glance at my phone screen. *It's 10.* I've painted for nine hours. At this knowledge, my stomach growls, and my bladder signals it's well past a bathroom break.

As I clean my brushes, I decide I need to set another alarm on my phone like I do for lunch. It will signal, "Time for a dinner break!" each day. I often lose all track of time in my studio; I'm blessed that way.

21

SYLVIE

My air-conditioned house or even the swimming pool would feel good about now. It's 86 degrees, and I'm walking on hot pavement in downtown Des Moines. I offered to meet Lidia and a couple of her friends to browse the art at this year's Art Festival. I must admit, I had no idea how hot it would be at this time of the evening; I might not have agreed to go if I did.

At our meeting spot, I wipe my brow as I scan the crowd for any sign of my daughter. There's a huge gathering. This annual event makes the news every year; it wasn't until Lidia suggested it that I chose to come down and check it out for myself. Maybe I'll find some things for the new house.

Lidia and her friend's approach with wide smiles, giggling and whispering. Though I strain, I cannot hear what they are going on about. I do hear all of them *shhh* each other as they wave in my direction.

"Mrs. Rice, you look amazing!" Lidia's best friend announces.

"I'm so glad you joined us," one of her friends greets.

"I don't want to ruin your time together," I state.

"Nonsense! We'll look around, try some food, and have a great time," another friend assures me.

We make our way down one side of the street, moving from vendor to vendor. I find so many interesting pieces and mediums.

"Mom, you should set up a space here next year," Lidia encourages, nudging me with her elbow.

"I bet the booth space is expensive, and the event is popular enough they're sure to have a wait list." I fiddle with copper bracelets on display.

"I'm sure it's cheaper than the new Fender guitar you bought last month," Lidia chides. "Anyway, your art is worth as much as your new hobby, isn't it?"

"We'll see," I placate her, walking to the next booth, wanting the topic to change.

"Hey!" one of the girls whisper-yells at the group. "There he is again."

I attempt to follow her pointing, but I can't see through the crowd from where I stand.

"Stop!" Lidia reprimands.

"He can see you pointing," another hisses.

I crane my neck, but the crowd is too large for me to know which guy they are infatuated with. I love it. They're young, dynamic, single ladies. Surely any guy attending the art festival would be worthy of them.

"Duck!" Lidia yells.

The four girls bend their knees to fade into the crowd.

"Who are we hiding from?" I ask, standing above them once again, craning my neck for a better view.

"Shh!" the girls demand in unison.

"The cop," one whispers, causing me to believe he's close by.

I shake my head, not seeing any police officers. I wonder... No, it couldn't be the cop that called on my house. I smile at my silly thought.

"What?" Lidia asks, slowly standing up beside me.

"I find it funny that you're acting this way about a policeman after I told you about my interaction with hot cops at my house," I murmur, not wanting all the girls to hear me.

"What did your hot cops look like?" one of my daughter's friends asks.

I bite my lip to hide my grin.

"What were their names? You saw their badges, right?" Lidia asks, drawing all the girls' attention.

"Officer Kirshner was the young hottie," I share. "And Officer Calderon was the silver fox."

"OMG! Mrs. Rice..." one of the girls giggles.

Lidia's fingers fly on her phone screen. "Is this him?" She shoves her phone much too close to my face.

I place my hand on hers, lowering her phone to the proper viewing distance, then freeze. With wide eyes, I nod.

"That's young hottie," I state.

"That's the cop. He's right over there," Lidia points.

Unleashed

I look but can't find any cops in that direction. I continue to look to the left and right, finding nothing.

"I'd say he's a silver fox," Lidia chuckles.

I turn to find the gang admiring Officer Calderon's photo on a Des Moines Police Department press release.

"They both were at your house?" Lidia asks, disbelieving.

I nod. "I told you, I should have gotten his number for you," I remind her. "Capital H-O-T, right?"

All the girls nod.

"And I bumped into the two of them at Zoo Brew, too." I smirk as the girls stare at me in awe.

While I continue to look at art, it's clear the girls make finding the cop priority number one with art now second place.

22

SYLVIE

I love my life, I feel guilty for saying it with the loss of Omar, but I really love my life. I'm still adjusting to my time alone each night, slowly I'm getting the hang of it. I make the most of it by playing my guitars or painting.

I remind myself with Lidia at college and Omar working late, I spent most evenings alone. Of course, my mind wanders during these times to Omar during trials "sleeping at the office". It's in the silence and darkness at night that my former life and relationship with Omar haunt me. I was so naïve and blind. Perhaps I longed for ignorance. I didn't look, I didn't ask, and I didn't care.

Wait. What? I cared. I fucking cared. Didn't I? I mean, I loved Omar, I kept the house for him, and I raised our daughter. Maybe I didn't ask some questions I should have. Maybe I looked the other way. Maybe I allowed our marriage to become friendship. A don't ask, don't tell, sexless friendship. Man, I was such an idiot.

Not again. Never again. I plan to live, to engage, to experience everything for the rest of my life.

Sitting on the floor, I prop myself against the sofa, my iPad in hand. I open the browser to begin my search. One dog on the sofa and the other beside me, I type "current trends in dating." It's been decades since I dated; I'm not ready yet, but I need to brush up. What seems like millions of sites appear before me. I scroll past the top five which are ads and click on "dating apps."

The first one is Bumble. *It sounds like a bee.* Next. Faith-based. Next. Tinder. *Hmm, don't you start a fire with that?* Next. Silver— *Uh-huh, I'm not that old. Do people really use these apps to date? This is not for me.*

Next, I type in "modern dating terms." Hook up. *Do I want to hookup?* Jekylling, Elsa'd, Rossing, Keanu-ing, whelming, dog fishing, dial toning, flat lining, and stashing. *I will need a handheld dictionary with me on dates. When did dating become so difficult? When I'm ready, I just want to meet, talk, and if we like each other, to go on a date.*

Continuing my research, I read extensively about waxing and manscaping. Next, I learn about piercings. When the first sketch pops up, I decide I'm not ready to learn about dating. I shut the browser and turn off my tablet. Now, I'm scared to death at the thought of dating. Perhaps I'll wait a couple months before I research more.

23

SYLVIE

The next weekend, sitting across from Lidia at a favorite restaurant, the waiter delivers our fried pickle spears appetizer and offers to bring us two more drinks. We've covered the usual: her classes, my art, her activities, the weather, and plans for the rest of the week.

Now's my chance to ask for advice. "I've been researching dating," I blurt.

"Why?" she asks between bites.

"Don't you think it's time I consider it?" I defend.

"No. I'm not asking why you're dating," Lidia explains. "Why are you researching?"

"A lot has changed in the over 20 years since I last dated." While waiting for her comments, I enjoy another bite of fried pickle.

"Yes, it has, but the internet's not where you should research. Did porn pop up?" Her smile is wide as if she knows all about my little research fiasco.

"Yes. It was just a sketch, but I immediately knew I was in over my head." *I scheduled this luncheon in order to ask for dating advice, so here it goes.* "Have you ever seen a pierced penis?"

Lidia coughs, having swallowed wrong.

I push her tea glass towards her. "Well, have you?"

"No," she scoffs. "Have you?"

I shake my head. "I glanced at the sketch before I freaked and closed the browser."

Lidia fans her red face, eyes wide, worried about this topic, apparently.

"What do you know about manscaping?" I blurt.

"Mom!" Lidia scans nearby tables to see if anyone overheard me. "Stop doing research."

"If I date, it's important I know what I'm in for," I tell her.

"You won't encounter a pierced cock or manscaping on your first date," she whispers.

I raise an eyebrow at her.

"I mean," she clarifies, "that I hope you won't on your first date. Or fifth date for that matter." She scans the restaurant again. "What brought this on?"

"I've read about them in romance books," I confess. "I looked them up, so I'd understand what I was reading."

Lidia shakes her head at me.

After chewing another bite, I move on to my next question. "Where do you propose I meet potential dates?"

"Church, the grocery store, the YMCA before or after your yoga class, or while walking in your neighborhood," Lidia suggests. "It's a long process, and you don't want to use dating apps." She sips from her iced tea glass before continuing. "Have I used one? Yes, but most of the time, I don't. I meet guys at parties or at bars."

"I met your father at a college homecoming bonfire."

She nods. "I know. You've both told me the story. My advice? Go to events in the community."

"Just so you know, I'm not in any hurry," I clarify.

"Okay, but you deserve to meet others and create new relationships," she states. "Put yourself out there. Go to events, meet people, and have fun. That's when potential dates will pop up."

I smile, proud of my daughter. Her advice is solid. I purse my lips, realizing both Edith and Lidia believe I should to prioritize my need to meet more people by attending events.

24

STEPHEN

It's times like this that make me wonder if the overtime is worth it. Fredrik really needs the extra money, so I do it to keep him company. The heat from the pavement penetrates the soles of my black work boots. We need to find a piece of cardboard to stand on like we do in the winter.

It's six, and the sun is slowly sliding from the sky. A high of 100 degrees today means we're still in the upper 90s this late in the afternoon. For the hundredth time, I wipe the sweat from my brow, my nose, and cheeks. I berate myself for not drinking more water today.

It feels like the Kevlar is fusing with my chest; no amount of shade helps tonight without a breeze. I return my thoughts to my task for the evening. I scan the mall parking lot, making sure this bike night runs smoothly.

The lot is finally full; the crowd doubled in the last hour. I remind myself I'm here to watch the people, not admire the bikes. My scan of the event stops on a cluster gathered around bikes near the stage, where a local cover band sets up.

My eyes look for any sign of conflict. I crane my neck, looking to the center of the group.

"I'm gonna check this out," I tell my partner, my chin motioning towards the growing crowd.

I make my way toward the stage and walk up from the opposite side of the group. It seems they're admiring a bike. A tall, slender woman stands at the handlebars, her back toward me. She wears skin-tight jeans and a tight, black tank top. I don't approach. Keeping my distance, I monitor the situation.

"You're staring at the bike, right?" Fredrik teases beside me. I didn't even hear him approach.

It's at that moment that the crowd steps back, and the woman turns.

What the fuck? It's her. I don't believe it.

"Now I know why you're staring," Fredrik teases. "Damn man…"

"Right?" I groan.

It's Sylvie Rice. Again. I'd never seen the woman before her noise complaint. Now, she's popping up everywhere. The orange Harley Davidson logo on her tank top draws my eye to her breasts. The tight jeans and black biker boots only add to her allure.

"You're drooling." Fredrik nudges my shoulder with his.

"I'm looking at the bike," I lie then move my eyes in its direction.

She stands beside a charcoal bike with the metal logo on the tank. Below it, a moth or butterfly spreads its wings while sitting on a cocoon. I find myself wondering if she painted it herself as I know she's an artist.

A guy points to the art then the area above his old lady's heart. They must be contemplating a tattoo. Ms. Rice nods and pulls out her phone, and they exchange information. The local cover band now plays 70s and 80s rock on the nearby stage.

Amidst the public here that doesn't ride, the weekend riders, and the hardcore bikers, she seems to fit right in. That night at her new house, I thought she was a sexy loon. While typing the report, I decided she was the typical housewife. Now, I'm not sure how to label her. *She's an enigma.*

"Yeah," Fredrik agrees.

Did I say that out loud?

"Come on, lover boy." Again, he nudges my shoulder; this time, I follow him.

Back at our central location, I try my best to spread my attention over the entire crowd. *She rides a bike.* I shake away the thought. *Work. I need to work.* I scan the crowd, not allowing myself to look in her direction. It's difficult, there's something about her that calls to me.

I slowly, intentionally, slide my eyes from one bike to the next, counting to three in my head before moving on. With every breath, I will myself not to look back in her direction. I move my eyes like a typewriter from right to left, only halfway, then left to right.

25

SYLVIE

Damn, it's hot. I should have worn shorts, but I wanted to fit in at my first bike event. I worried I wouldn't be taken seriously in my denim shorts and biker boots.

My research on bike events online did not prepare me for the crowd that flocks to my bike before I get my helmet off. I fight the urge to tell them to keep their hands off my bike. I answer many questions about my ride, where I found it, and where I live. It seems for every person that walks away, two more approach. Eventually, I excuse myself to walk around, leaving the group with my bike.

Holy hotness! My eyes land on two officers leaning on a barricade. To my surprise, it's the silver fox and the young hottie.

Officer Kirshner strikes a commanding presence, his skin glistening in the heat. His bulky muscles spill out of his uniform shirt, his hands grasping his bulletproof vest at his collarbone. It's easy to see his upper arms and thighs match his visible muscles.

He's like a red popsicle. I long to lick, suck, and bite into him. *Stop that! Get a hold of yourself, woman.* He's much too young. His partner is my age, and the silver fox is *fine*. He could pass for that actor Harrington on the TV show S.W.A.T. As handsome as he is, my eyes keep migrating back to Officer Kirshner.

I hide my smile when, at my approach, Officer Calderon nudges Officer Kirshner, motioning toward me.

"Are you two stalking me?" I ask, hands on my hips. "First, you take the disturbance call to my house. Then, it was maybe a coincidence to see you at Zoo Brew. But here, tonight? This crosses the line."

"We're just doing our job," the silver fox states.

"Uh-huh." I shake my head.

"Thanks for the popcorn," the young hottie smirks. "Some might think you coming to our place of work was stalking." His smile widens as he taunts.

"Just a citizen thanking her local law enforcement. I bought enough for everyone. And they weren't supposed to put my name as the donor." I move my fists from my hips, crossing my arms across my chest.

I notice Officer Kirshner's eyes hone in on my chest with my movements. My skin prickles under his gaze.

"No. Really," Officer Kirshner adds. "Thank you for the popcorn. It's rare that we get a treat like that."

"You are welcome." I smile. "I best get back to my bike." I glance over my shoulder at the crowd behind me. "This is probably not the place to let them think I'm friendly with the po-po."

As I walk back to view other bikes, I chide myself. *Way to play it cool, dummy. Do they still refer to police as po-po?* I never thought in a million years that I'd run into those two again.

As I try to play it cool, viewing other motorcycles, I send a Snapchat to Lidia with the words, "Guess who I bumped into at bike night."

Walking from bike to bike, I occasionally glance in the direction of the officers. I find Officer Kirshner's often looking at me. I'm not sure what I should make of his attention. It's foreign, and I like it.

26

SYLVIE

While a late-July thunderstorm brews outside in the night, I sit in front of my laptop, hands in my hair. I opened YouTube on the browser minutes ago. I want to follow through on the challenge Edith put out for me this month. I want to share my music but am afraid of live audiences. By posting a video of my music online, I can share while avoiding the crowd for now.

Slowly, I will my fingers to create an account. It's not the YouTube channel that I'm anxious about; it's putting myself out there for comments. I'm not delusional. I know there will be both good and bad comments, and I'm not sure I want to hear the public's feedback. I enjoy playing; it's something I do for myself. By uploading a video, I'll open myself to others, and that's scary and exciting at the same time.

I strum my fingers on the table as I wait for my video to upload and process. *I'm really doing this.*

I begin to contemplate the number of views I might get. Lidia will watch it, perhaps even a few of her friends. *Ten. I bet I get a total of 10 views.* I remind myself that I'm not doing this for the views, likes, or shares. *I'm challenging myself to try something new; and that is reward enough.*

After the video processes, I watch it from start to finish two times. One of the many things I learned at my Apple Store class was to send and receive texts on all three of my devices. I copy the direct link and text it to Lidia. Not bad for my first video upload. I'll need to position my camera a little tighter on my upper body and guitar next time.

Next time. I giggle, proud I'm considering there will be a next time.

Unleashed

I'm in the backyard playing fetch with the dogs the next morning when Lidia calls.

"Mom!" she squeals and continues to speak unintelligibly.

"Calm down," I instruct. "What's wrong?"

Still squealing, she repeats, "Look at your video views!"

"Why?" I stupidly ask, moving inside towards my laptop.

I hear her talking to people on her end of the phone call. Before she answers, my browser refreshes, and I have 5.7 thousand views and over 200 subscribers.

"That's way more than 10," I murmur.

"What?" Lidia asks.

I forgot she was on the phone. "Wow! Lidia, I expected like 10 views. I mean 10 total views." I place my free hand on my chest. "What happened?"

"You're a hit! That's what happened," she congratulates. "I viewed it, showed it to my roommate, and shared it with the girls. From there, it snowballed. I told you how good you are. Now the world can see it, too."

"I don't know about the world…"

"Mom, you're talented. I bet you have twice as many views by tomorrow." She pauses to speak to someone in the background. "I mean, it hasn't even been 24 hours yet."

Her excitement, even over the phone, is contagious. Others like my guitar playing. My heart races as I plot to record my next song to post.

27

SYLVIE

Days later, I pick up my ringing cell phone with "unknown caller" across the screen. "Hello?" I greet.

"Hi. Is this Sylvia Rice?" the female voice asks.

"Sylvie," I correct. "Yes."

"My name is Dawn," she starts. "I fell in love with one of your paintings while visiting a church member in the nursing home today." She pauses for a moment as I wonder where this is going. "I asked the staff, and they gave me your name."

"Okay…" I draw out.

"Well, I'd love to schedule a meeting, maybe for lunch or drinks."

"Okay…" I repeat.

"Are you available tomorrow?" she excitedly asks.

"I guess," I hedge.

"Let's say 11 at the Hy-Vee grocery store on Fleur," she suggests. "They have a full-service restaurant and bar inside.

"Okay," I mutter.

"Good. Then, I will see you tomorrow at 11," Dawn states then ends the call.

I stand, phone in hand, disbelieving. I can't wrap my mind around it; I replay the conversation in my mind. I guess I'm meeting a woman named Dawn at 11 tomorrow at the grocery store to discuss the paintings I purged and donated to a nearby nursing home.

"Do you belong to any clubs or charities?" Dawn, sitting across from me, begins, excitement bubbling in her every word.

"No," I confess.

"I'm on the Juvenile Diabetes Research Foundation board and am involved with the Variety Club," she shares, eyes bright, smiling wide. "I wondered if you might donate a painting for the upcoming JDRF and Variety Club auctions?"

Her smile... This woman's smile should be bottled up and sold. It, matched with her personality, draws me to the vivacious lady.

"Of course, if you think someone would bid on it. I doubt it would bring much money," I admit.

"We set the minimum bid, and the community often pays two to three times what the item's worth," Dawn boasts. Her contagious, megawatt excitement begins to light a flame within me.

"Would you like to join me for the next planning meeting? We can use all the help we can get," she asks hopefully.

Edith and Lidia's constant prompting to make friends and get involved in the community comes to mind. "I'll give it a try." I nod, a wide smile on my face. "Honestly, the works I donated to the senior center are not..." I search for the words, attempting not to belittle my donation. "My better works, I kept."

"Might I see them?" my new acquaintance, Dawn, asks eagerly.

Who could refuse her? "My studio is in my home," I explain.

"Could I follow you home and take a peek?" Her eyes brighten at the thought of seeing more.

28

SYLVIE

I'm not sure why I didn't object. I stand in my driveway as Dawn pulls into my neighbor's driveway to park. *Why is she parking there? My neighbor will not like it if my guests park there.* I open my mouth to protest.

"Hello, neighbor," she beams, both arms waving at me.

My brow crinkles. *Is she crazy? I must be crazy, allowing this loon to follow me home.*

"That's my house." She points to the house next to mine.

I look from her to the house and back.

"It's kismet," she cheers, clapping, smiling widely.

"You live in that house?" I seek to understand.

"Yes," she reiterates, her head bobbing. "We're neighbors."

As we step into my house, she confesses, "I'm the one that called the police about the noise."

She doesn't apologize to me as I stand dumbfounded in my kitchen. I don't blame her. I was playing my music too loud that night.

"Sylvie?" Dawn prompts, pulling me from my stupor.

"My studio is in here." I swing my arm to the four-season room.

"I knew it!" Dawn claps her hands in front of her face. "I had a feeling it'd be this good." She stands, head tilted in front of my easel.

"That's not finished," I inform as I pull a cloth sheet off my paintings leaning in the corner.

"Oh, my," she gasps.

"These are my most recent," I boast.

"And you'd donate two of these?" She asks again the question she brought up over lunch.

I nod. "Any of these," I vow. I don't share that my most prized paintings are down on shelves in the storage room. "Do you think they'd help you raise money?"

"Of course, they'll be great silent auction items," Dawn promises. "I can't believe you aren't attending art fairs or selling them in area stores."

I'm not used to sharing my artwork with anyone. In fact, it's only recently that I've begun to share it with Lidia. I'm as excited as I am scared. I'm not sure I'm ready for public input—good or bad.

"Which two are you willing to donate?" she asks.

"You'll know what your guests might be interested in," I state, wanting her to make the decision.

Dawn's excitement bounces like a red rubber ball off of the walls as she inspects each canvas before leaning it against an open space along the wall.

"I think this one for the JDRF auction and this one for the Variety Club."

I nod.

"Our guests will love these," Dawn promises. "You should approach stores at Valley Junction about carrying your art."

I'm silent; I'm not sure what to say. I'm scared. Sharing music is one thing. Sharing my painting is another. I'm not used to sharing my art; as of today, it's public.

"I can't wait for my friend, Theo, to see these," Dawn continues. "We are on both boards together. She'll love these. Thank you."

29

SYLVIE

I'm five minutes early as I exit my Miata at the meeting location in the Valley West Mall parking lot. I investigated the Miata club online, and now that I am here, I'm rethinking this event. I hoped I'd meet some new friends; I had no idea exactly how big this club was.

I walk past several cars toward the large group gathered nearby.

"Welcome," a female voice greets. "You must be Sylvie."

I nod, shaking her hand. I'm introduced to several couples, waving at many more, then it's time to hit the road. I climb back into the driver's seat, falling in line behind a black convertible.

I notice, of the cars in front of me and behind, that I'm the only single driver. I guess I'll meet twice as many people when we reach our destination.

I give myself permission to sing along with the radio as the warm summer air whips by.

Arriving in Clear Lake, we visit a tiny ice cream shop before parking in another area and walking several blocks to the lake's edge. In the July heat, the ice cream quickly melts. I use my napkins to wipe my brow several times and do my best to remain in the shade of nearby houses and trees.

I stand with a group of three couples, listening in on their conversation for a bit before they state it's time to return to our cars and hit the road.

"So, we just drive for two hours, visit, then drive two hours again?" I ask the couple I recently met.

"Sometimes, we stay overnight and have more time to visit," the woman states.

These are NOT my people, and this is not my scene. What a waste of a Saturday. I tried it but won't be returning. Instead of following in the long line of convertibles, I opt to take a different route through town. I'm on the interstate before the club arrives, and that allows me to drive the faster speeds I enjoy on my way home.

30

SYLVIE

The next day, while I'm shopping at Scheel's, making my way around another circular clothing rack, I nearly bump into a young girl holding two t-shirts in front of her. I watch for a moment as she appraises both.

"Having trouble deciding?" I offer, and she turns to face me.

"Dad says," she begins, "that I can buy Mom one Chiefs shirt for her birthday."

"I see. I had trouble deciding, too." I motion to my armload of Chiefs attire. I place them on the shelf in the center of the rack. My cell phone buzzes with an incoming Snap from Lidia.

"Do you know how to use Snapchat?" I ask the little girl.

She smiles wide while nodding her head, her dark curls bouncing, so I extend my cell phone to her.

"My daughter downloaded the app and showed me how to use it," I explain. "But I don't remember how to change the camera for a selfie."

"It's the rectangle here, with the arrows," she says as she taps it.

"Well, that was easy." I smile, taking my phone in hand. "Would you mind posing in a selfie to send to my daughter to prove I went shopping today?"

"Okay," she quickly agrees.

I snap our selfie and type a quick note on it. "Made a friend while shopping today."

"You should add some stickers," she suggests, so I squat beside her.

She deftly swipes through, finding a filter that adds "West Des Moines" and the date.

"Cool! Thank you."

She immediately returns to her impending decision.

"Here." I extend my hand with a 20-dollar bill I pulled from my purse.

"What's this?" she asks, staring at my extended hand.

"You helped me with Snapchat, and computer techs make good money. Now, you can buy your mom both of the Chiefs shirts." I wave the money in my hand towards her.

"Thanks." She grins, snags the bill, then proceeds to run to join her father who is standing nearby.

This. Can. Not. Be. Happening. I'm dumbfounded.

Leaning against a railing at the edge of the center aisle stands the two police officers. They're in street clothes, but I can easily tell it's them. *Is this more than a coincidence?*

As I load my selections back across my left arm, I frequently glance in their direction. The young girl hands her money to the silver fox then holds up both shirts for his approval. Both men then stare at me. While I can't read the silver fox's expression, the young hottie tries to hide his smile while shaking his head. When the silver fox beckons me with the raise of his chin, I slowly approach.

"You really didn't need to..." her father starts.

"She helped me with my phone," I explain. "IT people make good money." I smile, hoping I didn't overstep my bounds.

"I see," he mumbles.

"I'll pay for one shirt," the little girl pleads with her father. "And you'll pay for one shirt." Smiling, she anxiously awaits her father's approval.

"Let's put the $20 in your savings account, and I'll buy both shirts for your mom."

At his words, his daughter hops up and down, clapping before the two approach the cash registers nearby.

"Are you stalking me?" the young hottie teases.

"As you can see," I extend my armful, "I've been shopping longer than you've been here. Thus, you must be stalking me."

We stand quietly for a moment.

"So, the two of you are together even on your days off?" I inquire.

"No, we're not always together," he explains with a chuckle. "About once a month, I offer to watch his kids so he and his wife can spend some adult time together." His inquisitive eyes pierce mine.

No way. Not only is the young hottie keeping the city safe, but he's also a caring family man. He's too perfect; he's too good to be true.

He clears his throat, drawing my attention back. I find myself staring at his extended hand with a white business card in it.

"What's this?" I ask.

"Well, if you take it," he pushes his hand and card closer to me, "it's my cell number. I thought maybe it'd be fun to get lunch or a coffee together."

"I see." I take the proffered card.

Sitting in the mall parking lot, I don't start my car. Instead, I text my daughter.

> ME
> need to meet ASAP
> need advice

At home, putting away my new clothes, she replies that she'll be here for dinner.

31

SYLVIE

"What's with all the Amazon boxes?" Lidia asks, scanning the brown stacks along the wall by the front door.

I flip my wrist, signaling it's nothing. "I found a few items for the kitchen and some picture frames."

"Well, there are three new ones out on the front porch," Lidia informs, peering through the front window. Turning to me, she raises an eyebrow. "Is all this stuff making you happy? Or are you bored?" she asks, concern upon her face.

"I'm updating," I defend. "See for yourself; open them for me." I pass her the box cutter. "I'll fix iced tea."

Lidia opens each box, placing the items on the dining table. I return, handing her a tea glass garnished with a slice of lemon.

"I love these frames," Lidia says, running her fingers over the deep design in the wood. "And these new serving bowls will look great with your new dishes."

"I sent several photos to be printed," I inform. "I plan to display them throughout the house."

"These aren't for the house," Lidia teases, lifting one red Converse shoe from its package.

"It's part of my new wardrobe," I defend.

"Since we wear the same size, I might need to borrow these sometime." She smiles hopefully.

"A year ago, you wouldn't even consider borrowing from me," I remind her.

"So, that's a yes, I can borrow them?" she asks.

I nod, loving that my daughter approves of my new style.

"It's really starting to come together," Lidia agrees, looking around the space.

I need to start my planned conversation, but I chicken out. *Later. I will do it later.*

"Let's head out by the pool," I suggest. "Choose one of your playlists. I've turned on the outdoor speakers."

Bocephus floats on a foam mat as I sit near the edge of the pool, my feet beside him.

"Will Hagrid get in?" Lidia inquires.

"Sometimes he does. He usually gets wet then lays in the shade," I explain, my feet slowly moving the mat in the water. When I guide the mat close to us, she rubs his forehead between his long ears.

"You are the cutest, most spoiled puppy I've ever seen."

Here's the moment. I can do this.

"So, you know how I shared that I've run into that cop a few times?" I pause, still not sure how to broach the subject of age.

"Yeah. Did you bump into him again?" she asks.

I can't fight the silly smile of a teenage girl that slips upon my face.

"Details," she orders.

I excuse myself to grab his business card.

32

SYLVIE

"Hmm..." Lidia twists her lips, staring at the business card Stephen handed me.

"Well?" I prompt.

"Well, I like it." She smiles, crossing her arms over her chest.

"Huh?"

"I'm just going by all you've told me. I've never met him, but he's smooth. He's put the ball in your court," she explains.

"What do you mean?"

"He's allowing you to contact him. He doesn't have your number. So, you have all the power." Lidia takes my hand in hers. "Do you like him?"

I shrug. She releases my hand, grabbing her cell phone.

"What are you doing? Don't text him!" I panic.

"Easy," she chides. "I wouldn't text him from my phone. I'm looking him up; I need to see a picture of your young hottie again."

I lean into her side, looking over her shoulder.

"He's not on Facebook or Instagram," she tells me, her fingers flying over her screen. "We'll have to look to the internet."

"Holy shit!" She turns to look at me over her shoulder. "Yep, young hottie is *hot*!" Her free hand fans her face.

I swat at her shoulder.

"Well..." She draws out while fiddling with the photo on her phone. "Officer Kirchner's definitely on the hot scale. You definitely need to call him."

"I can't."

"Why?" She sets her phone down, placing all of her attention on me.

"He's way too young for me." I state the obvious.

"How old is he?" she asks.

"I don't know," I admit.

"Then, how do you know you're too old?" she counters, placing air quotes around "too old."

"Hello! You've seen him. He's your age." Internally, I cringe at the thought of Stephen being Lidia's age.

"Age doesn't matter," she states. "Besides, it's fashionable to be a cougar."

"Thanks," I deadpan.

"The only thing that matters is how you feel," she offers. "Clearly, he's into you; he gave you his number. Go out to lunch or get a coffee with him. It might be fun."

A small smile slips upon my face at the thought, while fear laced with excitement pulses through my veins.

"So, you'll call him?" she encourages, full of hope.

I bite my lip.

"He's off today," she reminds me. "Text him. Chat with him for a bit. You can get to know him better, then go to lunch another day."

I squint, processing her words. He *is* off today. If I wait, I may text him while he's on the job. I don't want to distract him; his job is too important.

"I may text him later tonight," I hedge. "What do you want for dinner?"

"Actually," she draws out, picking up her cell phone, "a couple of us are grabbing dinner and hanging out. I hate to back out on our dinner, but…"

"Go out; have fun," I encourage. "You aren't in Des Moines often enough to see all of your friends."

She rises from the pool's edge, sliding my cell phone toward me. "Text him. You can spend the evening chatting back and forth. Text him once, and I will drop it."

I draw in a deep breath, open my cell phone, and text.

> ME
> can you chat?
> this is Sylvie

Giggling at my nervousness, Lidia teases, "Congrats, Mom. Now, you are in a text-lationship."

33

SYLVIE

I drop my cell on the concrete when a FaceTime call rings.

"Answer it!" Lidia squeals.

"Hello," I greet, cringing at my own face in the corner of the screen.

"Hey," Stephen greets, smirking. "I'm free to chat."

"I meant on text," I explain, smoothing my t-shirt, making sure the white fabric isn't wet from the pool. "I could have been in my pajamas with a facial mask on. You shouldn't just FaceTime a woman."

"And if you were, I would have loved seeing and learning that about you," he responds. "What are you doing right now?"

I shake my head at him. "I'm getting ready to eat dinner with my daughter."

I rise from the pool, heading for the house.

"No, she's not," Lidia hollers from behind me. Quickly, she comes to my side. "I'm backing out on her dinner to see friends. So, she's free."

My wide eyes cause Stephen to laugh. It's a deep, masculine laugh, causing my belly to flip-flop and butterflies to flutter their wings inside it.

"Let's get dinner," he suggests as if it's just that easy. "Super casual. We could get takeout and take it to the park."

It's my turn to speak. I know it is. I have no idea what to say. *Could I do "super casual" takeout at the park? When he handed me his card, he suggested a drink or coffee, not dinner of any kind.*

"She'll do it," Lidia answers for me.

"Uh..." I'm speechless.

"I'm in your area," he admits. "I can pick you up."

I prepare to argue, but Lidia, peeking through the blinds at the front window, catches my attention. She mouths, "He's here," while her finger points to my driveway.

Holy crap! I wanted to suggest I'd meet him, so I'd have my own vehicle when I wanted to leave.

"Are you in the area or sitting outside my house? This seems very stalker-ish to me, Officer," I tease.

I shouldn't tease. I should worry a bit that he remembers where I live and drove over here. *If I didn't text, would he have stopped?*

"You caught me," he confesses. "I just left Fredrik's—I mean Officer Calderon's house—and since I was in this part of town, I thought I'd drive by your house." His face now serious, he continues, "I just couldn't help myself." He shrugs. "The fact that you texted made me pull over. It's not safe to text and drive, you know."

"Well, come inside," I prompt. "I don't want my neighborhood watch to call the police on your dark truck lurking on our street."

Lidia opens the front door, waving him in. I disconnect the call as I make my way to the front room. Mentally, I run through my clothes, hair, and makeup, although it's too late to change it.

He opts not to enter the house, remaining on the front step. "It's a beautiful evening. Let's grab a bite and find a park bench."

Wide, nervous smile upon my face, I nod. He gifts me with a smile so wide it reaches his dark eyes, framed with long curling lashes. The warmth in my belly soothes my nerves a bit. He's much too sexy.

"I'll follow you in my car," I declare. "Give me a second." I wave to him before walking to the kitchen to grab my purse.

I can't make out the words Lidia shares with Stephen before she closes and locks the front door. She hugs me, excitement exuding from every pore.

"Since he's a cop," she shares, "I won't worry that he's taking you to a secluded part of the park to kill you." She laughs. She actually laughs while a small part of me worries that I'm too trusting. "Stop," she orders. "He's a good guy. You'll be in public, never alone."

"Then, why did you put that thought into my head?" I swat at her.

"This is so exciting." She claps in front of her chest, giggling. "You have to text or call me afterwards. I want to hear all about it. My mom's going on her first date!" She continues to clap while I shake my head at her.

34

STEPHEN

I back my truck from her driveway, pulling along the side of the street to wait for her. *I hope she won't change her mind.* It seems like forever before her garage door lifts. *I breat*he a sigh of relief as her SUV pulls from the driveway. I wave to her in my rear-view mirror, then realize we haven't decided on a restaurant. I leave my truck; I hop out running to approach her door.

"We didn't decide what to eat," I tell her.

"You decide. I'll just follow you," she states.

Really? She'd really let me, almost a total stranger, choose her meal?

"Are you in the mood for Mexican, burgers, chicken, or Chinese?" I ask for a hint.

"Mexican sounds good," she answers.

"Tasty Tacos is close," I offer, running through all the options between here and the park in my head.

"Perfect. I've never tried it," Sylvie admits. "Lead the way," she prompts.

"How have you lived in the Des Moines area for all of your life and avoided Tasty Tacos?" I ask, bending my legs under the picnic table.

"I just never wanted to," she explains. "I think it's the name; it's kitschy."

"Well, you've missed out," I state. "They're not your average tacos. They fry the flour tortilla for the shell. I bought you two; don't worry if you can't eat both of them."

She peeks into her white sack before she pulls the tray with the wrapped tacos out. I take my first bite, watching her eyes assess the food in front of her. She worries her lower lip as she positions the paper, revealing half her taco, then takes a bite.

My eyes scurry between her mouth as she chews and her eyes for her reaction. She nods her head, still chewing her first bite.

"Good," she mumbles, hand over her mouth.

Unlike her, I swallow my food before I speak. "Never judge a book by its cover," I tease.

"Tacos are my weakness," she confesses. "This could be very bad for me."

"How can tacos be bad?" I ask.

"It's close to my house and tastes so good," she explains before taking another bite. "Mmm..." she moans, mouth full.

I shake my head. *I love it. I love that she's being herself, eating carbs in front of me, and holding nothing back with her reactions. She's real unlike so many women I meet. She's comfortable in her own skin; not trying to impress me by being fake.*

35

SYLVIE

Pulling into my garage, I'm suddenly aware I don't recall the drive home; our conversations replayed in my head during the drive. My nerves were not as I expected. I marvel that I am already so comfortable with him. I answered his questions, and I didn't hold back like I often do in my sessions with Edith.

I open the door to the house and am greeted by the excited sounds of Bocephus and Hagrid in the laundry room. I place my purse on the counter then free them from their kennels.

"Let's go potty," I urge. "C'mon. Let's go outside."

I open the sliding door, and they sprint to the edge of the grass to quickly relieve themselves. I plop down on the step and watch.

Stephen is right, it's a beautiful evening. Hagrid takes a seat beside me to watch the puppy trot around and sniff everything. Try as he might, Hagrid just can't keep up with Bo's puppy energy.

I guess I should text Lidia.

ME
I'm home & safe

LIDIA
details

Unleashed

ME
we ate, we walked, we talked

LIDIA
uh-huh

not getting off that easy

ME
ate Tasty Tacos

(smiling emoji)

LIDIA
and...

ME
found a picnic table at Ewing Park

LIDIA
and...

ME
I had fun, we talked, evening passed quick

LIDIA
plan date #2?

ME
we left it open

LIDIA
do you want date #2?

ME
I think so

LIDIA
(clapping emoji)

(winking emoji)

ME
you having fun?

LIDIA
yep

got to go!

. . .

I shake my head. She was adamant I text her as soon as I got home, but she's too busy to really chat.

"Oh, well." I cuddle Hagrid to my side. "You guys will keep me company, won't you?" I rub his belly.

Of course, Bo sees me rubbing his friend and wobbles over for his turn. I pick him up, and we head inside. I plop on the sofa, Bo on my lap and Hagrid at my side. I use one hand on each of them, scratching their bellies and heads.

Buzz. My cell phone vibrates on the cushion beside us.

> STEPHEN
> I had fun tonight

Ahhh. He texted instead of waiting a day or two to call or ghost me.

> STEPHEN
> what are you doing?

> ME
> rubbing bellies

> STEPHEN
> sounds kinky

> Me
> Hagrid & Bocephus don't think so

> STEPHEN
> 2 men
> you're talented

> ME
> 2 men, 8 legs, 2 tails

> STEPHEN
> ah

>   your dogs

> ME
> yes, what else?

>   STEPHEN
>   plead the 5th

> ME
> what are you doing?

>   STEPHEN
>   watching Die Hard for the millionth time

> ME
> I love that Christmas movie

>   STEPHEN
>   excuse me?
>   I think I misread that

> ME
> it's a Christmas movie

I stare at my phone for several long moments. *Did I offend him, or did something come up?* I was only teasing. Well, sort of teasing.

"Hello," I greet, a wide smile upon my face, when a FaceTime call comes in.

"What part of *Die Hard* is a Christmas movie?" His head tilts to the side, and his brow furrows.

"The office Christmas party is the main scene." I remind him of something he knows if he's seen the movie more than once. "The entire movie takes place on Christmas Eve."

"*Die Hard* is *not* a Christmas movie," he argues.

36

SYLVIE

Days later, I glance over my shoulder. Riley sits in her highchair, playing with a little police car. She loves pushing the button and listening to the siren. I turn back to my griddle, flipping the grilled cheese. It needs a few more minutes to toast.

Ding dong. The doorbell rings. I quickly pull the skillet off the hot burner before heading for the door.

"Who could that be?" I ask Riley. She smiles at my words.

Through the peephole, I find Stephen on my front step. I open the door, signaling for him to come on in. He's in uniform, on duty today. We've chatted three times since our park dinner. I should find it odd that he randomly shows at my house, but I don't.

"Well, this is a surprise," I state, tending to the grilled cheese again. "Is this an official visit?"

"Fredrik had an appointment, so he dropped me off for lunch. Mind keeping me company for 30 minutes?" Stephen asks. "Who's this?" He notices my little guest in her chair.

"This is Riley," I answer, keeping my attention on my work. "My neighbor, Dawn, had a committee meeting, so I offered to keep Riley for her."

"I like your car," he says to her.

She launches it onto the kitchen floor, claps, and giggles. She points at it saying, "Po."

"That's how she says, 'Police.'" I point to Stephen and say, "Police."

Riley points at Stephen. "Po."

I laugh as I turn my attention back to the grilled cheese. I place one on a saucer, then I make two more sandwiches, placing them in the skillet. I cut the cooling sandwich into tiny pieces and sit it on the tray for Riley.

"I love grilled cheese," Stephen claims.

"Good because that's on the menu today," I tease.

Riley holds a bite out for him. When Stephen chews it, he makes a huge production of loving it. She claps happily. Then, he feeds her a bite. I plate our grilled cheese, add a pickle, and grab a bag of chips before placing them on the island.

37

STEPHEN

The long afternoon and my shift finally end; I hurry through my shower and quickly dress. I don't want to waste any more time before I call Sylvie. Sitting in my recliner, I select her name then press call.

"Hey," Sylvie's disembodied voice greets.

"Am I looking at the ceiling or carpet?" I ask, turning my head in an effort to make out the video screen.

"It's a towel," she chuckles. "Give me a minute."

That sparks my attention; there are many possible scenarios involving a towel. Perhaps she's stepping out of the pool or, better yet, the shower. Thoughts of water droplets on her naked skin stir my cock to life. It's a good thing she'll only see from the chest up as we chat tonight. In my fantasy, I clutch the towel in both hands, caressing her everywhere with the pretense of drying her off.

"Earth to Stephen," Sylvie calls.

"Sorry." I scramble to focus on our call, leaving the fantasies for later.

I watch as she carries her phone from her kitchen onto the patio.

"Did I call at a bad time?" I ask.

"Nope," she states. "I finished my painting, so I'm done for the night. I was washing my hands when you called."

Thus, the towel. I prefer the thought of her in the shower. I clear my throat and attempt to clear my mind as well.

"Will I get to see the painting?" I love the sparkle my question sparks in her hazel eyes.

She purses her lips to the side. "Sharing ..." She stammers. "I'm not accustomed to sharing my pieces."

"C'mon," I nudge. "I'm no expert, just very interested in your work."

"We'll see," she answers. Her hand cups the back of her long, slender neck. "What's for dinner?"

"Honestly, I haven't thought of it," I confess, my mind solely focused on talking to her. "I'm not an expert at grilled cheese like you are."

A wide smile slides upon her lips. "You surprised me."

Squinting my eyes, I attempt to decipher her expression. It seems she liked my impromptu visit.

"I probably should have called, but I didn't want to give you the chance to make up an excuse," I explain.

"I..." she stutters. "I..."

"I took a chance, hoping you wouldn't make me sit on your porch until my partner returned," I tease.

"I thought about it," she deadpans. "But what kind of citizen would I be if I didn't provide lunch for a boy in blue?"

I chuckle.

"Next time, give me a heads up, and I'll prepare something more enticing than a grilled cheese sandwich," she states.

So, she wants there to be a next time. She's inviting me to stop by on future lunch breaks. Nice.

"You're good with kids," Sylvie states.

Fuck! Here it comes. Discussing this could end the good thing we have before it even starts. *Why'd she have to choose this topic?*

"I have six nieces and nephews," I inform her.

"You look intimidating in your uniform, but you melted to putty in Riley's hands when she smiled," Sylvie teases, her fingers pinching her lip at the corner of her mouth.

"I have a way with the ladies." I wink, attempting to make light of this topic.

Sylvie rises from her seat on the patio, calling for Bo and Hagrid to follow her into the house. I'm silent as the background shows her walk through the kitchen to sit on her sofa. She lays the phone down, and in the distance, I hear her talking to the dogs.

"You're quite a catch. Why haven't you settled down and started a family?" she asks.

There it is. The big question. "I love kids. Maybe it's because I'm a big kid myself."

"You'll make a great dad someday." Her statement hangs heavily in the night air.

"I guess I would…" I mumble, my mind scrambling for a way to change the subject or take the focus off of me. "Why didn't you have another?" I ask her.

After a long pause, Sylvie shares, "I wasn't ready for Lidia. I had a long list of things I planned to do." Her eyes shift to the side as she bites her lips uncomfortably. "Don't get me wrong. I planned to have children, but not until my early 30s. When I took the pregnancy test, I cried for hours."

She looks to me for my reaction. "I mourned the life I hoped for. Morning sickness haunted me all day, and for the first three months, I rarely left the house. That's when my life changed." She shakes her head. "I focused all of my energy on Omar, Lidia, and our home. There wasn't time for anything else. I gave up all hope of following my dreams."

She sighs before continuing. "I knew there was no way I could handle a second child. I may have been greedy for thinking it, but I drew my line in the sand."

"How were you greedy?" I interrupt. "You gave them 100 percent; you gave them everything. That's not greedy—it's selfless." I then take in a deep breath.

"I'm the greedy one. I like my life. I have expensive toys and a job I love. I enjoy every minute I spend with my nieces and nephews. It's just… I can't… I couldn't…" Now, it's my turn to be uncertain of her reaction to my confession.

"I couldn't continue in law enforcement with a family. I couldn't bear the thought of my children worrying that I might not come home from work."

Sylvie jumps in. "There is a risk every day for everyone. Any profession has a risk for a car wreck, natural disaster, random gunman, or infectious diseases; the list is long."

"Yeah, but it's less random for officers. We put ourselves at risk every traffic stop and domestic disturbance call. Don't get me wrong; I love what I do. And to continue loving it, I can't have children," My eyes lock on hers. "So…" I draw out, "I got a vasectomy. I may be greedy, but I won't let my love of career cause stress or pain to a child."

Sylvie nods. It's not the response I expected from her.

"You seem to know exactly what you want. If that means you want to remain single, that's your prerogative," she states, a small smile upon her lips.

Hmm. She champions my thoughts.

"Childless, yes," I agree. "Single? I'm just keeping things simple for now."

She squints her eyes at me, worrying her lower lip. My eyes lock on it, glistening in the light. I long to run my thumb over it before sucking on it.

Focus, idiot. What were we talking about? Oh, yeah. Kids.

"Kids can't fully understand the dangers and reasons I chose this job. A woman, the right woman..." I secretly hope she's the right woman. I have a feeling—intuition, maybe. There's something about her that causes me to hope for the first time that Sylvie is the right woman for me. "The right woman can weigh the pros and cons and choose whether or not I'm worth it."

"You're definitely worth it," she immediately responds. "The pros far outweigh the cons."

I tip my head to the side. She didn't hesitate; she didn't... She barely knows me, yet she believes the pros outweigh the cons. She likes me. I should ask her out on a real date. *Hmm... I can't rush her, and I need to plan.*

"I've never shared all this with anyone; not even my family knows," I admit in a whisper.

"I'm honored you shared with me, and I'll keep your secret," she promises.

"I did the same thing," she states. "I had a tubal ligation after Lidia was born. I wanted to ensure I wouldn't have more children." She chuckles hollowly, "I guess we were both greedy in that way."

38

SYLVIE

Snacks and beverages border the patio, while pool toys and towels line the pool's edge. Mother Nature blessed us with a beautiful early-August Saturday. Umbrellas at the patio tables will provide shade from the bright sun. I select a local radio station and set a volume we can easily carry-on conversations over.

"Yoo-hoo..." Dawn calls beyond my privacy fence.

I unlock the gate, prop it open, and motion for my neighbor and new friend to come on in.

"You're the first to arrive," I greet.

"What can I do to help you set up?" she asks, following me through the patio door and into the house.

"I think it's all set up," I state, glancing around the kitchen.

"Perfect. Then, let's fix a drink and relax until other neighbors arrive," she suggests. "What shall we have?"

"Water, lemonade, beer, wine, or margaritas," I list.

"Margaritas it is!" Dawn cheers.

Again, I marvel at her vim and vigor. If I could bottle it up, I'd be a millionaire many times over. *Wait. I am a millionaire.* I don't feel like one. I'm not sure the reality will ever set in. I shake away those thoughts.

Dawn selects two glasses from the counter and wets then dips them in salt while I mix ingredients in the blender.

"We make a great team," Dawn smiles, holding her full glass toward mine.

We clink our rims and take a long sip.

"Mmm," Dawn moans. "You have no idea how much I needed this today."

"Where's Riley?" I ask, just now realizing she's not in her arms or stroller nearby.

"A playdate with my best friend's granddaughter," she states between sips.

"You're lucky to have a friend with a child the same age."

"You're telling me," she agrees. "When my sons watch Riley, I worry the entire time I'm away. When she's on a playdate, I can relax."

The doorbell rings.

"Crud. I forgot to hang my sign." I return my glass to the counter then grab the tape and sign from the kitchen island. "It instructs guests to use the side gate to enter the pool area," I inform her as I walk to the door.

Dawn follows me to the front door. She introduces me to the couple that live down the street before she urges them to follow her around the side of the house. I hang my sign then scurry through the house to meet my guests poolside.

The party's perfect. While some neighbors visit under the shade of the umbrellas, others dangle their feet in the water or swim with the children. This was a great way for me to break the ice and meet my neighbors.

My brow furrows as loud voices draw our attention to the open gate. It's Lidia. She said she couldn't make it, yet she stands in front of us now.

"The party can start now. I'm here!" she shouts, her arms above her head.

"I thought you couldn't come," I greet as I approach her.

"We moved study group to tomorrow evening," she informs, lowering her large bag to the stone patio.

"Let me introduce you to everyone." I motion for her to walk with me toward the crowd. "If I can have your attention," I call to my guests. "This is my daughter, Lidia. She attends college in Iowa City."

The crowd smiles, waves, and cheers, "Go Hawkeyes!"

Lidia's classmate slips through the gate to join us, and my nerves spike. When Lidia told me she couldn't come, I invited Stephen to bring a couple of friends.

Lidia will spend time with Stephen. Although she's been here during a phone call, I'm nervous about them spending time together.

"Psst," Dawn seeks my attention. "What's wrong?"

I shake my head.

"Let's go make another pitcher of margaritas," she prompts, locking her elbow with mine and pulling me inside. "Spill it."

"It's nothing really," I state.

"Nope. Not buying it," she orders.

"Lidia wasn't coming. She said she had a study group," I inform my friend. "She caught me off guard," I lie.

Dawn's furrowed brow and squinting eyes inform me she knows there's more to it. Thankfully, she lets it go for now.

39

SYLVIE

Later, my phone in my back pocket signals I have a text.

> STEPHEN
> we're here

My heart pounds hard against my ribcage as butterflies flutter in my stomach. Looking up from my phone, my eyes meet Lidia's.

"What's up?" she inquires.

"Um," I stammer. "So, I neglected to tell you... I invited Stephen to bring a couple of friends to the party."

"Cool," she grins.

"He's here." I extend my cell phone, showing her the text. "Um, can we not make a big deal about it in front of everyone?"

"Phish." Lidia swats my shoulder. "No one will even notice."

I follow my daughter into the house, through the kitchen, and toward the front door.

Lidia answers the door when they approach. "Hi. C'mon in." She swings the door wide, leaning on it.

"Hi, guys," I greet. "Head straight on back to the pool."

Lidia raises an eyebrow at me after all three men pass. "His photo didn't do him justice. He is so..." she draws out the word, "good looking."

"Shh," I admonish as they are only a few feet ahead of us.

She mouths, "Wow," before we step onto the patio.

Stephen turns to face us. "Guys, this is Sylvie and Lidia."

The guys smile and wave.

"Make yourselves at home," I urge nervously, pointing out areas of the backyard. "The coolers are full, the bathroom is in the pool shed, and snacks are already on the table. If you need anything else, don't hesitate to ask."

Stephen's friends move towards the snack table to drop off their towels and shoes, giving us a moment of privacy while surrounded by many of my neighbors.

"I know you've briefly talked on the phone," my voice breaks, exposing my nerves, "but Stephen, this is my daughter, Lidia."

He extends his arm to shake her hand, stating, "This isn't awkward at all, right?"

The two laugh as I nervously scan the crowd.

"I hope you're ready," Lidia says with hands on her hips. "Now that I know you are seeing my mom, I've got you under my microscope." She attempts to remain serious but cracks up and laughter escapes.

Stephen blows out the breath he was holding in relief. Lidia encourages her friend to join Stephen's friends near the snacks to make introductions.

As the sun sets, the neighbors say their goodbyes. One by one, they leave; my backyard grows quiet. Dawn helps me wash the wine and margarita glasses before she excuses herself to pick up Riley.

Alone in the house, I duck into the powder room and splash cold water on my neck. With hands on the counter, I stare at my reflection. The pink upon my nose hints at hours in the afternoon sun. I didn't reapply sunscreen.

"Mom?" Lidia's voice calls from the kitchen. "Need any help?"

I scurry from the restroom, smiling at my daughter who is dripping wet just outside the patio door. Shaking my head, I emerge from the house to face Stephen and his friends.

"Wait a minute," one of Stephen's buddies demands. "How young were you when you had Lidia?"

The other friend and Stephen swat him in the back of the head.

"First, you never—and I mean never—ask a woman her age," Stephen lectures.

"And dude, it's none of your business," Lidia adds. "Just know she was in her 20s and leave it at that."

"I didn't mean it in a bad way," Stephen's friend defends. "She looks more like Lidia's sister than her mother. I meant it as a compliment."

I pull Stephen closer to where I sit on the edge of the pool. "This is the whole reason I invited you to the barbecue," I remind him. "We want everyone to meet and get our age difference out in the open." When I smile in Stephen's direction, his eyes glue on my mouth. "His comments don't bother me," I promise.

40

SYLVIE

"Lidia have a new boyfriend?" Dawn asks as she walks to her mailbox the next day.

My garden-gloved hands pause. I sit back on my calves and look her way, raising one hand to block the bright sun. "What?" I ask, not understanding her question.

With mail in hand, she walks towards me at the front flower bed.

"I've seen a young man in a dark pickup visiting your house, and he was at the pool party," Dawn explains. "I figured he was Lidia's new fella. I guess I missed the chance to set her up with one of my sons."

"Lidia prohibits me setting her up," I inform her.

"From what I've seen, she's hooked herself a handsome young man," Dawn continues.

I rise, pulling off my dirty gloves. "He's not Lidia's boyfriend." I answer her initial question.

"Oh, I saw them chatting at your pool party." Dawn purses her lips to one side. "Is he doing work on the house?"

"Um..." I hedge, not knowing what to say. The truth is all I can think of. "He's here to spend time with me."

There. It's out. Public. Now, for her reaction.

"I see," Dawn says, her face morphing into a wide smile. "I've chilled a bottle of wine. Why don't you lose those gloves and come enjoy it with me?"

Unleashed

She'll probably follow me inside if I attempt to evade her. I toss my garden gloves to the sidewalk and follow her into her house. *This won't be bad. She's not my mother. She's my age. I hope she won't judge me.*

"Where's Riley?" I ask, taking a stool at the kitchen counter.

"She's on a play date," Dawn states.

"Two days in a row. Aren't you lucky?" My nerves can be heard in my voice.

Filling my wine glass to the brim, she prompts, "Drink up."

"In a hurry or trying to get me drunk?" I ask.

"Both," she replies. "I want to know everything. How you met, all of his details, and…" She wiggles her eyebrows at me. "I mean *all* of the details."

I sip my wine, aware of her eyes glued to me. "Well, you're the reason we met," I confess.

"I am?" she questions.

"His name is Stephen Kirshner, and he's a police officer."

"Seriously?" she squeals, her brows high and mouth open wide.

I nod, sipping more wine.

"When you called in the noise complaint, two very handsome officers rang my doorbell," I share.

"Two?" she queries.

"Yes. The older one was a silver fox," I share. "That's how I described him to Lidia."

"And the young one?" Dawn presses, on the edge of her seat.

"He's a young hottie," I blush.

"I'd say he is," Dawn laughs. "I've only caught a few glimpses. He looks fine," she draws out.

We drink wine for a few quiet moments.

"So, he's a cop." Dawn urges me to continue.

"Yeah. I met him and his partner the night you turned me in. A few weeks later, I bumped into the two of them working at Zoo Brew," I divulge. "Then, get this: the two were working at a bike night I attended. I accused them of stalking me."

"Three times," she counts. "Three times you saw the two of them in uniform? You're so lucky." She fans her face.

She must have an active imagination.

"I love a man in uniform," she sighs. "So, did he hit on you while he was working?"

"No, not in uniform," I answer. "I bumped into the two of them shopping at Scheel's. Stephen was helping his partner's daughter shop."

Her lips pursed; Dawn's eyes implore me to continue.

"There's nothing to tell, really. He gave me his cell phone number." I shrug.

"He gave you his number and...?" she urges, hands prompting me to continue.

"Flustered, I called Lidia for advice," I share. "She explained that since he gave me his number, he let me have control. He had no way to contact me."

"So, when did you call him?"

I sigh heavily. "Lidia urged me to reach out to him that day as I knew he was off work. Not wanting to distract him while he's on patrol, I texted him." I smile, remembering. "Instead of replying to my text, he video called me."

"Whoa..." Dawn's eyes are wide as is her smile.

"With Lidia's help, he coaxed me to follow him to Tasty Tacos then to a park to eat and chat." I shrug, lifting my wine glass to my lips.

Unable to wait for me to continue, Dawn speaks. "I'm not really a super nosey neighbor," she promises, index finger crossing her heart. "I happened to be out watering my plants when he pulled up once."

I wrinkle my nose at her.

"He's appeared in a few of my security camera videos," she further confesses, attempting to make light of this fact.

I tilt my head to the side, furrowing my brow. "Do your cameras point to my front yard?"

She pulls her lips into her mouth sheepishly. "In order to capture my side yard and the end of my driveway, I also see most of the street and yard in front of your house."

I'm not sure if I should feel safer knowing her cameras allow her to police part of my yard or be offended that she keeps track of my guests coming and going.

"I'm not a voyeur," she states. "My boys installed the cameras, worried for my safety." She shrugs, making light of it. "I get an alert on my phone when there is movement in the area."

"So, you know when I pull from my driveway and prune the plants in my front flower beds?"

"Yes, but I delete those as soon as I recognize Lidia and you," she vows. "I can't promise I won't happen to be out every time he triggers the cameras on his visits," Dawn giggles, waggling her eyebrows at me.

"You're horrible," I chuckle. My wine finished, I place the glass on the counter. "I'm not sure there should be a next time."

"Phish," she swats the air. "Have fun. At our age, we deserve it."

"That's just it," I inform her. "He's too young for me."

"Nonsense," she argues. "In junior high, a year's difference is normal. In high school, a year or two difference is acceptable." She pours more wine as she continues. "In college, up to five years difference seems appropriate. After age 25, anything goes."

I wonder if these rules are written somewhere. She recites them as if she's visited this topic often. I cringe. Perhaps she tells her sons this.

"So, by your rules," I tease, "I'm too old for your sons."

She swats at the air between us. "How old is Stephen?" she asks.

"Twenty-eight," I answer.

"My sons are only 21 and 24," Dawn states. "I don't believe you're too..."

"Stop!" I shout. "You would not want me dating your boys."

"Stephen's nearly 30," she reminds me. "I doubt he acts like a young, 20-something, going out partying."

"But we don't know," I state the obvious. "He could still like to party and play with his expensive toys." I sip my wine, playing with the stem of my glass as I continue.

"Excuse me?" Dawn raises her voice. "You've only eaten fast food, walked in the park with him, and allowed him to swim in your pool."

Why does the last point sound seedy?

"That's too soon to make assumptions. You only have the facts to judge by." She leans forward in her seat towards me. "He's a cop. He probably likes to follow rules and laws since he's a cop. He showed he's okay with allowing you to lead when he gave you his number instead of asking for yours. And you mentioned he babysits for his partner's kids. All in all, he seems like an adult instead of a man-child. He's worth a date; you need to keep an open mind."

"It's a 14-year difference. Fourteen years is a *big* difference," I hedge, my voice rising in pitch.

"You certainly don't act your age," Dawn explains. "Thus, the 14 years shrinks. If he's a bit more mature for his age, it shrinks even further."

Her rationale seems strong. I find myself wanting to cling to it.

"Ahh..." She smiles, pointing to my forehead. "You're considering it," she cheers.

"I'll keep an open mind," I promise.

Dawn claps, bouncing in her seat like a child.

"I need to find you a man," I tell her.

"Uh-uh," she argues. "I have no time for a man. Riley is more than I can handle most of the time. There's a reason we have children when we're young and have energy." She shakes her head. "When she naps, I'm so tired I need to nap but also need to do the long list of things I can't do while she's awake. It's a constant battle.

Do I rest then complete the tasks when she goes to bed at night or complete my tasks and be exhausted the remainder of the day?"

"I hope you know, I'm available to help with Riley. I can give you a couple of hours to catch up when you need to." I offer.

"Then, we will both be tired," Dawn quips, and we laugh.

41

STEPHEN

"So, tell me more about your family," Sylvie prompts.

I watch her play with the long ears of her Basset hound on my phone screen. I'm jealous; I long for her slender fingers to fondle me with her affection.

"I'm the youngest at 28. My parents are in their 70s. I have an older brother that's 48 and an older sister that's 42. I was a mistake." I smile, attempting to make light of the obvious age difference with my siblings.

Sylvie raises her eyebrows, urging me to continue.

"I have a nephew that's 23 years old; I'm not much older than him." I purse my lips to the side, shrugging.

"My mom claims I have an old soul. I tend to gravitate towards people older than me. Heck, Fredrik is my best friend, and the guys I hang with are all older than me."

My eyes move to her lips for a moment before I continue. "So, when I told my mother I met a woman, the first thing she asked me was, 'Is she older than you?'" I chuckle. "Now, I didn't share any more details about your age. I only told her how we kept bumping into each other and asked for her advice in planning our first date."

I sigh, a slight smile upon my face. "Of course, she shared all the details with my siblings, and they hound me incessantly for details about you. I'm still avoiding those questions."

"You could talk to them," Sylvie states. "Stop avoiding them; it's torture."

"If I do, all the bribes will end," I share. "They've bought me lunch a couple of times, my sister cleaned my apartment for me, and they even bring me casseroles and stuff."

"You're bad," she laughs.

"So, I'm supposed to invite you to a family barbecue two weeks from Thursday." My eyes peer deep into hers, awaiting her reaction. "Are you ready to meet my family? Or is it too soon? Remember, I'm new to relationships. If it's too soon, just tell me. It's no big deal, really," I blabber.

"It's not too soon. It's…" She struggles to express the reason for her hesitation. "I think we need to discuss what we are before we…"

"Okay," I drawl out. "You are my girlfriend."

Sylvie beams, causing my body to grow hot.

"I am?" she teases. "And what does being your girlfriend mean to you?"

"Exclusive, becoming best friends, and …" I waggle my eyebrows suggestively.

She laughs at my insinuation.

"What do *you* think we are?" I toss her question back at her.

"Honestly, even with all of my research, I'm still not sure how the dating scene works now. I have tons of fun chatting with you. I'm exclusively yours." She pauses, her eyes scanning my face through the phone screen. "I wasn't sure if you were on the same page."

I long to pull her tightly against me, peppering kisses on every inch of her. As much as I look forward to our video calls, I'd rather be with her.

"Will you be my girlfriend?"

"What's in it for me?" She giggles, her cheeks pinking.

Sylvie

"He told me I'm officially his girlfriend," I state.

Lidia coughs. "What was your answer?"

I smile like a middle school girl, maybe even blush a bit. "I'm his girlfriend."

"That's so cool," she cheers, hopping up and down, clapping.

"What is?" I ask.

"My mom has a boyfriend that makes her smile non-stop." Lidia pauses to inhale. "I've worried about you alone in Des Moines. Now, when we talk, you have stories to tell me about during your phone calls. I can hear happiness in your voice over the phone. He's good for you. And he makes me feel less guilty for being in Iowa City," Lidia confesses.

"I'm not alone; you have no need to worry," I promise. "I do spend time with Dawn and Riley, and I have a few committee meetings coming up in the next couple of weeks. So, I'm not alone."

42

SYLVIE

The next evening, my cell rings. I quickly wipe my hands on my apron before answering.

"Hello," I greet.

"Sylvie, this is Nelson, Dawn's son. I'm watching Riley, and I need your help."

"What's up?" I ask, noting Riley whaling in the background.

"I'm babysitting while Mom's at the JDRF Gala tonight." I hear worry in his masculine voice. "She's teething, running a fever, and I can't find any children's medicine. I've tried everything."

"I'm on my way," I state, slipping on shoes.

I quickly walk to my neighbor's door while removing my apron from around my waist. I find the door open with Nelson holding a fussy Riley in his arms.

"Can you hold her for a while?" Nelson pleads. "I need a bathroom break."

He passes Riley to me then darts down the hallway. I hug little Riley, placing a kiss on her forehead.

"It's okay," I coo. "I know it hurts, but we'll fix that. I promise."

I continue baby talking as I rummage through the kitchen drawers and cabinets. Next, I dig through Riley's diaper bag on the dining room table. I find a bottle of children's Tylenol; to my dismay, it's empty. I lay it on the tabletop and continue digging through the bag. Next, I search the nursery with no luck.

Nelson returns with out-stretched arms, and I pass Riley back to him.

"I've looked everywhere," I state. "All I found was this empty bottle."

"Would you mind driving to the store to get some?" he asks.

"Sure," I respond. "Anything else you need?"

"Nope," he answers, handing me a set of keys. "Take my truck."

"No, I'll take mine," I reply.

"I insist," Nelson argues, forcing his keys into my palm.

I take the proffered keys and head for the door. I don't like to drive strange vehicles. I know from my talks with Dawn that his truck is new, and he's very careful with it. Although I have the strong urge to take my SUV when I get my purse from my house, I abide by his wish and take his truck.

I must hop and pull myself inside the big truck with the handle mounted inside the door. I place his key fob in the exterior pocket of my purse, start the mammoth beast, and nervously pull from the driveway.

I feel I'm a long way above the road. Other cars cower in comparison when I pass. At the closest grocery store, I park at the far end of a row of parked cars as I remember Dawn telling me he usually takes up two parking spots to prevent door dings. My conscience won't let me take up two parking spots, so I park farther down in hopes of no one parking beside me.

I dart inside, pick up some Orajel and children's Tylenol, pay the cashier, and dart toward the end of the lot. I toss the sack into the truck before I climb up into the driver's seat.

When I pull from the parking lot, I notice the check engine light is on. *Crap! Nelson's going to kill me if I broke his new truck.* I quickly look for other warning lights on the dash. It doesn't appear to be overheating, so I carefully watch the dummy lights as I drive back.

Walking to Dawn's door, I realize I left the grocery bag in the truck, and I jog back to fetch it. My nerves increase as I'll have to tell Nelson about the truck.

Back inside the house, I rub Orajel on Riley's upper and lower gums. Nelson holds her tight in his arms as I use the dropper with the children's Tylenol. The two actions upset her further.

"Let me hold her for a while," I offer, my arms outstretched. "She loves my dogs. Want to come over to my house until she calms?"

Nelson nods, and I open the front door. The sight of his truck reminds me to tell him about the warning light.

"On my way home," I begin, hesitant, "your check engine light came on."

"Huh?" he asks, brow furrowed.

"Just the one light," I promise.

He joins me on the front step.

"Sylvie, that's not my truck," Nelson states calmly. "Tonight's not the night to be pulling tricks on me."

"It's no trick," I state. "And the check engine light stayed on the entire ride home."

Nelson opens the driver's door then looks back to me, his worried face lit by the interior light of the truck.

"What do you mean it's not your truck?" I'm confused.

He reaches in then dangles another set of keys in front of me. Even in the little light from the truck, I know they are not the set he handed me earlier. I quickly approach the truck.

"This is not my truck," Nelson slowly says. "You have to take it back before someone reports it stolen."

Stolen. I stole a truck. Fuck! Bile climbs my throat. I have to get back to the store before the police are involved.

"Take Riley to my house," I instruct. "Play with the dogs until she calms down. After that, she'll probably fall asleep."

I lift myself into the stranger's truck. "I'll call you to let you know what happens at the store."

43

SYLVIE

As I pull into the grocery parking lot, I see a police car in the area I previously parked Nelson's truck. They stand at the back of his truck with an older couple. I pull in next to them.

As I hop out, I quickly explain with my hands held up, "It was an accident. See? I have the keys. I just took the wrong truck."

When I join the group behind Nelson's truck, everyone looks at me.

"You see?" I explain further. "It's my friend's new truck. I didn't want to drive it, but he insisted. I parked it way out here because he's paranoid about door dings. I ran inside to get supplies for a teething baby. When I came out, I climbed in the truck where I parked. I didn't see there were two trucks parked here." I pause for a quick breath.

"I assumed the key fob in my purse unlocked the door and allowed me to start the truck. When I told my friend his check engine light was on, he went to check and told me it wasn't his truck. I didn't mean to steal it." My eyes beg them to believe my story.

I hear a familiar, deep laugh behind me. I don't turn around. *This is just my luck.* Officer Kirchner and Officer Calderon join the group. Part of me is glad he is here; he'll believe I didn't mean to steal a truck. Another part of me knows he will tease me about this.

"I'm not pressing charges," the man standing by the other officers states. "We left our keys inside, and this wouldn't have happened if we'd locked it."

I smile at the man and his wife. "I'm so sorry. I should have paid closer attention."

"No worries, dear," the woman promises, patting my forearm.

"I'm not filing paperwork on this one," one officer states.

"I wouldn't even know how to start paperwork on this one," another officer teases.

When the two officers retreat to their patrol car, I'm left standing with Officer Calderon and Officer Kirchner. Both smirk at me.

"This can't be the first time this has happened," I offer in my defense.

"I've never seen it," Officer Calderon states, fighting a grin.

"You really didn't know it was a different truck?" Stephen queries.

"I was in a hurry to get Riley's medicine. She's very fussy," I share. "I knew it was a dark truck with dark interior."

"You really need to pay closer attention to details and your surroundings," Stephen offers, shaking his head, arms crossed over his broad chest.

"It's over now. Everyone has the right truck, and no one was hurt," I defend.

"It's not going to be over for a long, long time," Stephen's partner laughs.

"How long will the teasing on this one last?" I ask, hands on my hips.

Stephen laughs, "There will be no expiration date on this one."

44

SYLVIE

"I got your text," Dawn explains when I open my front door.

"Nelson needed a break," I share. "I hope you don't mind that I kept her over here for a couple hours."

"Of course not," Dawn smiles. "I'm upset with myself. I had the teething meds in the backseat of my car. I meant to leave them with Nelson."

"She's fine now; no worries," I promise.

"I'll have one of those," Dawn says, motioning to my wine glass. "While we drink, you can tell me what happened tonight," she states. "Nelson said you were hilarious."

"Odd." I pull out a wine glass. "He didn't find it funny at the moment."

"So…?" she prompts.

We settle into comfortable spots on my sectional sofa with wine glasses in hand and dogs curled up near us on the floor.

"Well, you know I went to the store to get teething supplies," I start. "Nelson insisted that I drive his truck. I tried to argue, but he wouldn't have it." I shrug. "So, I drove his truck and parked at the far end of the parking lot. I remembered what you said about his paranoia of door dings." I smile at Dawn. "I shopped then hurried back home," I continue.

"What's the funny part?" Dawn prompts.

"I suggested that we bring Riley to my house. I planned to let her play with the dogs while the medicine kicked in for her to sleep," I share.

"On my way home from the store, the check engine light came on in the truck.

I remembered to tell Nelson as we headed for my house. Of course, when I told him, he immediately went to check on his truck." I take a sip of wine before this next part.

"When he got closer, he told me it wasn't his truck. He opened the driver's door and stated again that it was not his truck," I explain.

"But it was his truck, right?" Dawn asks.

I shake my head. "It was *not* his truck."

"How?" she asks, confused.

"He took Riley to my place, and I went back to the store," I explain. "The police were called and standing with a couple by Nelson's truck when I pulled back into the parking lot."

She's not laughing. Maybe she won't see this as funny.

"I explained that I was in a hurry and that I had driven my neighbor's truck. I assumed the key fob in my purse unlocked it and allowed me to drive it. The other couple left theirs unlocked with the keys in it. I didn't pay attention that there were two dark trucks parked there, and…"

"Oh. My. Gosh. You stole a truck!" Dawn blurts.

We both look to Riley who is sleeping on the floor. She doesn't even flinch at Dawn's loud voice.

"I didn't steal it. I mistakenly borrowed it," I argue. "And I returned it immediately."

"I wish I could have seen Nelson's face when he found out it wasn't his truck," she laughs.

"It was too dark to really see, but in the dome light of the truck I could see he was mad," I share.

Dawn's still laughing. I love her laugh; it's contagious. I join her in laughter. We laugh so hard, we have to place our wine glasses on the table.

"My side hurts," I say through my laughter, holding my side.

Dawn snorts. This causes both of us to laugh harder.

"I haven't…. have more…" I can't continue to talk through my laughter. I attempt to breathe in long breaths as I wipe the tears from my eyes.

Dawn joins me in taking deep breaths but loses her battle and continues to laugh.

"Stephen was on the scene," I sputter.

Leaning forward in laughter, Dawn tumbles to the floor. She rolls into a ball on her side, laughing. She knows he teases me; this will give him new fodder.

I move onto the floor beside my friend. Still laughing, I smile back at her. Slowly, her laughter turns to giggles. I'm not sure how long we lay on my floor, but I enjoy every minute of it.

45

SYLVIE

Dawn and I stand in the water up to our waist, trying to remain cool on a hot, sunny Friday afternoon. Riley laughs, slapping the water around her pool float. Occasionally, we push her back and forth between us.

"I have a personal problem," I blurt, unsure how to bring up this topic.

"Do tell," Dawn encourages.

"I shaved my bikini area," I begin. "Now, it's growing back in, and it itches something fierce."

Dawn's deep belly laugh elicits a snort. She slaps her hand over her mouth, and I join her giggles.

"I shouldn't be laughing," I tell her. "It *really* itches."

I turn all of my attention toward Riley while Dawn collects herself.

"Why would you shave?" she asks.

"I read on the internet that it's popular now," I inform my new friend. "They make it sound like guys expect it from the women they date."

"You should stick to older men," Dawn states. "Guys our age aren't picky."

I stare wide-eyed at her. She's my friend; I expected this from a stranger, but she seemed supportive.

She raises her arms, palms toward me. "I'm kidding." One of her hands begins rubbing my upper arm. "I'm sorry. I was trying to be funny. I think it's awesome." She pulls Riley along beside her as she wades towards the steps. "You should wax. That way, you don't have razor burn and itching."

"I read about that, too," I explain. "It's got to hurt something fierce; don't you think?"

"It's ten minutes of pain for four to six weeks without shaving daily. If you can survive childbirth, you can handle waxing in that area." Dawn tilts her head, waiting for my response. "My salon offers waxing services."

"I need to think about it," I admit, wading toward the stairs. "You can text me your salon's information."

I'm unsure if grooming my bikini area is part of my new life, but I might give it a try.

46

SYLVIE

So, here I am, nervously playing with a cocktail napkin at the corner of the bar with a perfect line of sight to the little stage.

I saw a flyer at the music store, back when taking my guitar lessons, and after my YouTube channel blew up, Edith encouraged me to challenge myself with a live performance.

Bongo, the bartender, returns with my first beer.

"You're new," he states. "I'd remember if I had seen you in here before."

I claim to have just moved into town. It's true; I moved from Norwalk to Des Moines. He doesn't need to know I moved less than 10 miles. He slides my Bud Light draught on the napkin closer to me then returns to the other patrons.

The night quickly passes; I'm on my second beer at the end of the first band's performance. I watch as the next group of gangly, high school boys nervously tune instruments, arms barely strong enough to hold their guitars and basses. I can't stifle my giggle.

"What's so funny?" Bongo asks.

I share, and he chuckles.

"I promise the two after this one are great bands that perform here often." He smiles before taking more orders.

While watching this band, a large, bulky guy squeezes between my barstool and the next. I keep my focus on the stage. In my periphery, I see him hold on up two fingers while ordering and taps the bar near my empty mug.

"Another?" his deep voice growls near my ear.

I nod as my skin prickles.

"You've got to be kidding me," he says when I turn to face him. "Now, I wonder if you are stalking me." He looks offended.

"I was here first," I defend before calling out, "Bongo, who got here first? Him or me?" I point my thumb at each of us.

Pleading the fifth, the bartender raises his palms up and retreats.

"If I recall, this was the type of music playing through my speakers when you banged on my door," I state.

Smirking, he gives in. "I haven't noticed you here before."

"Seriously? You keep track?" I scoff. "You're the second person to comment that it's my first time here."

"We pay attention when hot women are involved," he states.

Hot women? He thinks I'm hot? Easy. Play it cool. Pull it together, woman.

"So, how often are you here?" I ask.

"I come every now and then when I'm working day shift. Much less often when I'm on nights," he admits.

"Oh." I chug from my ice-cold mug.

He watches, brow furrowed.

Not wanting to alarm Officer Kirshner, I explain, "I'm using Uber tonight. I'm ready for a night out, and none of my friends enjoy my taste in music." *Especially not my daughter.* I keep that thought to myself. "I'll be using Uber as my designated driver."

"Last call. Last call for alcohol," Bongo yells, after ringing the loud metal bell mounted behind the bar.

Stephen orders a drink for each of us.

"I'm using Uber, too," he declares, clanking his bottle to my mug before we each take a drink. "I think we should go out next Thursday night," he announces, catching me by surprise.

"You do? That's interesting." I smirk in his direction. "I happen to have plans for Thursday."

"So, cancel them." He graces me with his sexy, crooked grin.

"I don't want to," I coyly reply. "Maybe…"

"Yeah?" he eagerly prompts, a glimmer of home in his brown eyes.

"Maybe you could go with me," I state, eyes scanning his entire face.

"Go where?"

"I have two tickets to the Communicable concert Thursday night at the State Fair," I boast.

He spews the drink he just took, causing me to snort.

"That's hilarious," he says.

Confused, I tilt my head with a furrowed brow. "I don't think it's hilarious."

"Well, that's because you don't know the punch line," he states.

I raise an eyebrow, urging him to explain.

"I hoped to take you to the State Fair on Thursday," he confesses.

Now, I chuckle. "Let me see if I have this straight. You'll get me into the fair, and I'll get you into the concert."

"It's a date," he states.

"I haven't said yes yet," I tease.

"But you will." He leans closer, our noses now an inch apart. "Won't you?"

I nod.

He sighs. "Finish your beer, and we'll share an Uber," he insists.

Bossy much?

At my house, I pause nervously before opening the car door. "I'd offer to let you come in, but all the beer makes me very, very sleepy," I admit.

"If you offered, I'd have declined gently," he promises, smiling.

Ahh... He is so sweet and definitely too good to be true.

47

SYLVIE

The next week, I'm crossed-legged on Edith's couch, fiddling with the tip of my shoelaces.

"I've been asked out on a date," I blurt.

"How did you feel when he asked you?" Edith counters. "And did you accept?"

How did I feel? Hmm...

Sensing my hesitation, Edith tries a different route. "How'd the two of you meet?"

"Oddly enough, we've bumped into each other several times." I answer honestly. "Do you believe in signs?"

Edith quirks her head to one side. "Explain what you mean by signs."

"He asked me to go to the State Fair with him on Thursday for a date, and I just so happen to have two concert tickets and VIP passes for that night at the fair."

"Quite a coincidence," Edith smiles.

"That's only one of the times we bumped into each other," I sigh, preparing to spill my guts. "He was one of the cops that came to my new home for the noise complaint. Then, I saw him at a Zoo Brew event *and* the Southside Bike Night."

"As if those weren't enough signs," I continue, "We were both shopping at the mall. That's when he slipped me his cell phone number."

"So, you called him?" Edith seeks more details.

"I texted him," I state. "He immediately video-phoned me."

"Did you answer?" she asks, no longer taking notes on her tablet.

I nod. "He was driving through my neighborhood and pulled over in front of my house to make the call." I shrug. "He doesn't text and drive," I explain.

Edith's face no longer looks amused; she's concerned.

"He's not a stalker," I quickly state. "Well, it's kind of a running joke between us. With each chance meeting, we accuse the other of being our stalker. He's a cop," I remind her. Again, I shrug. "When he bumped into me at the Brickhouse, he asked me on a second date."

Edith squints with her head tipped to the right.

"Second date? So, you went on a first date before the Brickhouse?" Her hands play with the stylus in her lap.

"No," I answer. "Yes." I bite my lip. "He claims we went on a first date; I don't agree."

Edith's head tilts to the left, eyes still assessing.

"So," I draw out as I attempt to explain, "when he video-called me, I gave in. I followed him to pick up fast food. Then, we went to a park to eat. Since we drove separately, I don't classify it as a date."

"How long were you at the park?" she pries.

"After we ate, we walked and talked," I share. "It was like an hour or two."

She smirks. Edith actually smirks at me. *Is that even professional?*

"You think it counts as a first date, don't you?" I query.

"It's not my place to tell you what to believe. I'm simply here to guide you," Edith states. "When he asked you on the second or first date, did you say yes?"

I nod, smiling.

"How do you feel?"

Here we go again. Time to uncover deeper feelings and put my fears into words.

"I'm too old to date, and he's much younger than me." I pause. When she doesn't jump in, I continue. "I gave in, though; I figure I shouldn't ignore all of the signs."

"What concerns do you have?" Edith continues her prying while jotting notes. "Do you foresee any issues arising during the date?"

"I'm worried how Lidia feels about me dating. I don't want her to think I've forgotten her father. And then, there's the whole age difference. It will be painfully obvious I'm a cougar."

"If the age difference concerns you, perhaps you should talk to him about it," she offers. "Does it matter what others think more than what the two of you think?"

I shake my head. Every visit, we discuss that my feelings matter more than what others think of me.

"I think it's a very public venue; that might make it an easier first date." I make eye contact for a moment before looking down at my hands in my lap. "But that also means more people will see the age difference…"

"Will you know all of them?" Edith butts in. "Will you ever see them again?"

I shake my head.

"Do their thoughts affect your happiness?" She continues to drive her point home.

When I shake my head again, she continues, "All that matters is the thoughts and feelings the 2 of you have. And your thoughts and feelings are the *most* important. You've worked hard to bring your feelings to the front instead of always putting others first and suppressing your own."

Nodding, I look up. "I chose the concert and splurged on the VIP access. In the past, I've heard about concerts of interest to me and did nothing more. I've missed many things of interest to me. By attending this concert, I'm embracing life—enjoying it. Thus, I'm putting my wants first."

48

SYLVIE

I have one more errand before I head home. I did my research online and followed the information before my first appointment; here, now, climbing the steps, I'm having second thoughts.

Get it together, Sylvie. You've read all about waxing and even looked at photos online. Get your butt up these stairs; you're a grown-ass woman.

My legs are weak on the final set of stairs, and my hand trembles when I reach toward the door handle. I pause before grabbing as I read the sign hanging from the knob that says, "Please take a seat. I'll be with you shortly."

Sitting in the little waiting area in one of the two chairs, my nerves skyrocket, while my knee bounces. The door opens and I'm summoned to enter, remove everything from my waist down, sit on the end of the table, place the towel across my lap, and wait. She'll be back shortly, she tells me.

"You're a new client. Have you waxed before?" the spa woman asks when she comes back.

"No."

"Do you know what style you want?" she asks next.

I flash back to the research I conducted on the web and the options. "I'd like to leave a landing strip," I nervously answer.

"Okay. I'll warn you: the wax is hot but safe. Remember to breathe; holding your breath won't help." Her back turns to me as she rolls a cart toward the table I lay on. "Ready?"

I nod, and she begins. I anticipated it would hurt more than it does, and I breathe a sigh of relief. We carry on a polite conversation as she applies the hot wax, smooths a strip upon it, and rips it off over and over again.

"Alright. Now, I need you to bend your knees, wrap your arms under them, then roll back on the table."

This I wasn't prepared for; everything is exposed. Every little bit of me is on display, and she wastes no time waxing every inch.

Will I do this again? I'm conflicted. It's weird, baring myself in this way to the esthetician. It's kind of like a pelvic exam without the cold, clinical feel. I'm really not sure how I feel about it. Walking back to my car, I look at my phone screen.

No way! The appointment lasted only 10 minutes. *That was easy.*

Early the next morning, Dawn and I sip our coffee poolside.

"Get this," I begin. "Last night, I was sitting at the bar of the Brickhouse, listening to live music, when *he* happened to sit on the stool beside me. We were both surprised that we share a love of the same music. We talked a lot, and that's when he asked me out on a date." With wide eyes, I look to Dawn, anxious to hear her thoughts.

She leans closer to me, her eyes twinkling. "Where'd he want to take you?"

I chuckle. "It's funny really. He asked to take me to the State Fair on Thursday."

"And you think *that* is funny?" Dawn quirks a perfectly-maintained eyebrow at me.

"Well, I actually have two VIP passes and tickets to the Communicable concert that same night at the fair."

"No way!" She stands upright, mouth agape.

"I planned to bribe Lidia to attend with me," I share. "It's not her type of music, but I didn't want to go alone."

"So, he's taking you to the State Fair, and you're taking him to the concert," Dawn summarizes, and I nod. "Wow. I can't wait to hear all of the hot details of the date?"

49

STEPHEN

"Hi, young hottie!" Dawn yells toward me as she scurries from her front porch toward Sylvie's driveway. I'm sure I turn three shades of red.

It's Thursday afternoon, and I suppose she's been glued to her front window and security camera app most of the afternoon. Sylvie warned me about Dawn's voyeuristic capabilities.

While I love that her cameras help keep Sylvie safe, I fear her keeping tabs on us might get annoying. I chat on the lawn with Dawn for a couple of minutes before Sylvie emerges from the front door, rescuing me.

Damn! Sylvie's a sexy little minx.

"You look..." I chuckle, not sure how to convey she's hot without sounding like a teenager.

With soft spikes on the crown of her head and wispy, short curls on the sides and back, this is my favorite way she styles her hair. While she's a natural beauty, I enjoy the allure of her smokey eyes and pale pink cheeks that match her lip gloss.

My eyes catch on her sun-kissed shoulders, bared by her black halter top. The silver, metal grommets lining the neck bring back memories of her and the motorcycle. Her denim, cutoff shorts perfectly hug her hips and ass, while the hemline is at a respectable length. In my mind, I imagine they're an inch or two shorter, allowing some of her cheeks to peek out. I brush away that thought. I wouldn't want her on display like that in public; that's for my eyes only.

Is it too early in the relationship to claim her as mine?

The heels of her lace-up sandals cause her tan calves to pop deliciously. I long to feel her long legs wrapped around my waist.

This may be a long night.

"Ready?" Sylvie asks, patting my shoulder, drawing my attention back to the present.

"You two kids have fun," Dawn calls, walking back toward her yard.

I place my hand in the small of Sylvie's back, ushering her to the passenger door of my truck. Pulling the door open, I lean my mouth to her ear.

"You look amazing," I murmur, fighting the urge to put my hands on her hips to lift her up into the cab.

"Thanks." She smiles, looking at me over her shoulder. Then, with her hand on the "oh, shit" handle, she pulls herself into the truck.

On the road, I blabber to avoid awkward silences. "I've arranged to park in an officer's yard that lives a block from the fairgrounds," I share. "It's a prime location, and they make a lot of money renting out parking spots during the state fair."

"Parking is crazy; I hope your buddy still has one available," Sylvie states.

"I called mid-week, and he agreed to save us one for tonight," I explain.

"Lucky us," Sylvie smiles.

I love the way her eyes light up when she smiles. Like. Like. I like the way they light up.

50

SYLVIE

"So, be honest," I begin while he drives. "Are you a fan of Communicable?"

"Honestly," he says, glancing in my direction then back to the road before him, "I could only name three of their songs. When I downloaded their album to prepare for tonight, I realized I know several more than I thought."

I'm lucky he likes metal and rock. Lidia would have been bored tonight.

"I still can't believe you purchased two VIP packages to see Communicable," he says, eyes remaining on the road.

I'm grateful he doesn't ask or want to know how much I paid. I wanted to make up for all of the concerts I've missed in my past, so I paid $1,700 per person, so $3,400 plus the processing fees.

I'm worth it.

I remind him, "I planned to invite Lidia to attend with me, but it's not her type of music."

My excitement grows with every step we take on our way into the fair and the outdoor grandstand. Our paper tickets are exchanged for lanyards. Placing it around my neck sends my adrenaline into overdrive. As a free drink bracelet wraps around my wrist, I take a peek at my hand. Sure enough, it trembles.

With his band secured, Stephen places his hand in mine, and murmurs, "I feel like I can't breathe."

My eyes meet his. His excitement helps to calm my nerves a bit. I don't want to embarrass myself by turning into a fangirl.

We're led with one other couple to meet the band in a green room of sorts. Each of us takes a turn posing for a photo, standing between lead singer, Warner Bradshaw, and lead guitarist, Carson Cavanaugh. When they find out we're a couple, Carson pulls us together for a photo with both of us in it, then—even though it's only two hours before the show—the drinks flow.

Scanning the room, I note every member of the band is here. Two women stand near the door, attention glued to their tablets with an occasional hand to the headset over their ear. *They must be with the band.* Four young men lean on the bar, talking animatedly. I recognize two as the drummer, Eli, and the bassist, Jake. Three other men in suits mill about, sticking out like sore thumbs. *No way they're with the band dressed like that.*

"Enjoy yourself," Stephens murmurs near my ear, pointing toward the bar. "I'll have a couple then stop before the concert so I can drive home."

I love that he's conscious of that and wants us to have a good time.

I text Lidia, begging her to take a screenshot of any Snaps I send her, so I'll get a copy to keep. Then, I Snapchat a few photos: sitting on the sofa beside Warner Bradshaw, chatting with Jake Johnson, and taking a shot with Carson Cavanaugh and his wife, Montana.

When the band claims this is their first time performing in Iowa, I correct them. "Not true. You performed at the Brickhouse while recording two summers ago."

"Burn" one of the other fans taunts.

"Montana claims this is the best state fair in the country," Eli mentions, motioning to Carson's wife.

"The fair has a huge following," Stephen answers. "Morning shows from New York travel here to air from the fair for a week. Heck, the entire state practically shuts down during the fair. You should find time to check it out before you move on."

"Not to pressure you into it," I taunt. "Stephen Tyler walked the midway and rode a couple rides after he performed here a couple of years ago." I bite my lower lip. I can't believe I am in a private room with the members of Communicable and am taunting them as if we're longtime friends.

"Let's do it," Eli and Jake encourage in unison.

I shrug, smiling while inside, I have butterflies at the thought of witnessing the band at the fair like Iowa residents.

"Best date ever," Stephen whispers, leaning into my neck.

51

SYLVIE

My skin prickles, and my body hums with his nearness. It's familiar and feels like we've been together forever. Turning in his direction, I smile. His eyes drop to my mouth then back to my eyes. In them, I see his want. A minuscule movement is all the confirmation he needs.

The moment his lips crush to mine, a jolt of lightning zings through me. He keeps it short and leaves me wanting more. I'm still floating in the clouds when it's announced we need to make our way to our seats. I follow Stephen's lead as I try to gather my wits.

He grabs each of us a beer, and we find our seats. There are only four of us in the entire grandstand; it's both eerie and exciting. Our tickets are in the third row, where we find our free tour t-shirts waiting for us.

Iowa's oppressive August heat remains heavy in the air this evening. Stephen looks miserably sexy. His face glistens with sweat, which he constantly swipes away. It's not easy for all guys to dress appropriately for this weather. I can't imagine him in shorts or sandals. A white, short-sleeved tee stretches across his broad shoulders, his arm muscles threatening to burst out of the straining sleeves. His fitted jeans add to his discomfort in this heat, while the fabric hugs his ass and thighs.

I laughed so hard I snorted when I read his T-shirt in my driveway. "I'm with the band." Stephen is not only gorgeous with a capital 'G'; he's funny, protective, and astute.

Yummy. I'm one lucky woman—at least for tonight.

As the crowd fills the grandstand, I notice fans in the rows around us are all younger than me.

"Let's send a pic to Lidia," I say, offering my phone to him.

Thank goodness he's a pro. He knows to move the phone so that the stage shows behind us. With his long arms, he easily takes the selfie.

A woman in the row behind ours offers to take a photo of the two of us. I gladly pass her my phone.

52

STEPHEN

In this photo, I place my arm around Sylvie's waist and pull her tight to my side. The smell of her vanilla-scented skin mixed with the musk of her sweat tickles my nostrils. Her long, lean body molds to mine like two pieces of a puzzle.

I've only posed for photos with my sister and my nieces. With Sylvie, I don't mind. In fact, I want everyone to know she's with me. *She's mine.*

Whoa! Where did that come from? I don't date. I choose one-night stands. I don't pose for photos that might send the wrong message to the woman. Sylvie's different; I gravitate towards her.

How is it possible that she instantly changed everything? She makes me want to try. Try to date. Try to have a relationship. Try to be a couple in public. She's magnetic; she's my kryptonite.

I release her, and we turn to face the stage. Roadies scurry here and there, then disappear. Sylvie bounces on her tiptoes, her hands clasped in front of her chin, and her eyes wide. She holds nothing back; she's a breath of fresh air.

Song after song, Communicable delivers. The electric crowd, paired with Sylvie's belting out every lyric, plants a permanent smile upon my face.

As the opening notes of a ballad fill the air, I shift my body behind hers. I place my hands on her hips as she sways gently to the music. She allows her head to lay upon my chest, and her body presses back into mine while we continue to move as one.

That's it. The end. I'm a goner. The sensation of her body pressed back into mine from shoulder to thigh spirals my desire. I no longer hear the band. I no longer hear the crowd. It's only Sylvie and me, swaying in unison.

"Should we stroll the midway before we go?" I offer, my lips grazing her ear as we shuffle slowly with the crowd toward the exit.

Sylvie tips her head back, allowing me to gaze into her hazel-colored eyes. For once, my number one concern is not assessing the crowd for danger. I focus my attention on her—on touching her, on holding her, and on everything I long to do with her.

"Let's ride the Ferris wheel," she urges.

I find it hard to deny her anything.

As our car slowly rises above the hordes of people below us, I wonder how many times she's ridden this ride and if she's ever been kissed high above the fairgrounds below.

"Did 17-year-old Sylvie ride the Ferris wheel every year, enjoying kisses in the night?" It's out there before I can think better of it.

She scoots her body closer in suggestion. "No, but I'm up to share my first Ferris wheel kiss with you."

53

SYLVIE

Too soon, the warm sunlight bathes my face upon my pillow. I mew, stretching my deliciously sore body, the sheet falling to my side. I freeze, memories of last night scrolling through my mind. My eyes fly open to find a condom box upon my nightstand.

No!

"Good morning," Stephen's gravelly voice greets.

"Umm," I turn my head then clutch the sheet over my chest as my body turns to face him.

He lifts his hand, his fingers brushing a stray hair strand from my forehead.

"I, uh..." I struggle to put together a coherent thought. His bare chest and scruffy jawline obliterate all thought.

Several moments pass until I find my words. "So, that happened," I blurt.

He bites his lips together, his eyes dancing.

"This isn't me," I state. "I haven't dated in over 25 years, and a lot has changed. You may be used to this type of dating, but I'm not. I wasn't, and I'm still not a sleep-with-a-guy-on-the-first-date, one-night stand type of woman."

"I don't consider this our first date," he smirks, his soft, sleepy eyes on mine.

Seriously? He wants to argue?

"The Brickhouse was more like a first date, and you already know I kind of feel Zoo Brew and bike night were mini-dates." His dark brown eyes lock on mine. "I learned more about you at each event," he adds as explanation.

"Ha," I choke. "I already knew you were a cop, so I didn't learn anything new from you at Zoo Brew and bike night," I counter.

"I feel..." He rolls his entire body to face me. "It feels as if I've known you for months or even years. I can't explain it. There's so much I don't know about you, yet you seem familiar."

I know what he means. I feel the same, as if he's my...*soulmate*. I attempt to swallow the lump in my throat. *Too soon. It's too soon for all of this.*

He rests his palm upon my cheek. "I don't plan to fight this, whatever is between us. Something started the night I delivered the noise complaint to you, and try as I might, it didn't fade; you've kept popping up in my life."

"I..." I sputter. "I've never..."

He releases my cheek, shaking his head. "This is new for me, too." He raises up on an elbow. "I don't fall asleep or spend the night." He looks towards the ceiling then back. "I'm drawn to you in a way I can't bring myself to leave." He shrugs. "I like to keep things casual—I have to with my job. I haven't let myself be in a relationship; my work is too dangerous."

I place my palm on his chest near his heart. "Officers deserve families; you deserve it all. Your career path doesn't change that. It's not fair—"

He cuts me off. "I live day to day because I can't promise to come home at the end of each shift. I can't control criminals and can't ask anyone—"

I interrupt, "Then, don't ask. Allow." My eyes implore him to really hear me. "Allow others to choose to be in your life. Other officers have families."

"Many Iowans have a false sense of security," he explains, his hand resting over mine. "Crime exists here just like everywhere else in this country. People are unpredictable, and with the rising incidents in the mental health crisis, it's even more unstable. I do my best to keep safe—the thought of asking a woman, let alone children, to live with that uncertainty... I won't let myself be that selfish."

I squint at him in front of me. "You're hiding behind that excuse." I state. "You're trying to protect yourself—not others."

He shakes his head. "I should leave. Hell, I should have left hours ago." He chuckles. "I couldn't bring myself to let go of you. This..." he moves his index finger back and forth between us. "This is different; it's new to me."

"Then, *let* it be different. Don't push me away. Don't try to protect me from your job."

What the hell am I saying? Am I ready? Do I want to be in a relationship? It's not like me to jump in the deep end.

"Just let it be," he smiles. "It's that easy, huh?"

"Yep. I'll make a deal with you," I smile back. "I won't fight it if you won't."

I watch his Adam's apple move as he swallows hard. He nods, pulls me close, and his mouth collides with mine.

Stephen

"Look away, please," Sylvie murmurs.

"Uh-huh," I argue.

"C'mon," she pleads.

"Don't be shy," I prompt.

She shakes her head, and her eyes turn downward. I place my forefinger under her chin, lifting her eyes back to mine. Her tongue darts out to wet her lower lip, before her teeth tug on it. It's easy to guess she doesn't want me to see her naked, now that it's day. The confident woman, holding nothing back while seeking her orgasm of last night is no more. Next to me she now clutches the sheet tightly to her chest.

"Syl..."

"I'm...I..." she stammers. "I'm not in my 20s and my body..."

"Hey," I murmur, reaching for her. "I like *every* part of you." I tilt her face up to mine. "No one's perfect. I'm not perfect. You're beautiful inside and out. I want to learn every curve, every scar."

She shakes her head.

"I'll close my eyes," I offer, placing my hand over my eyes.

When she giggles, I peek between my fingers. She's darting into the attached bathroom, but I catch a glace of her long lean body and round ass. Perfect. She's perfect. She has nothing to hide, but I won't push her.

54

SYLVIE

Breakfast dishes barely in the dishwasher, Stephen orders, "Give me a tour of your studio." Then, he pulls me with him.

"There's really not much to see," I state, passing him to take the lead.

I pull the French doors open. I'm suddenly nervous about sharing my happy place with him. I fear it might seem silly to a non-painter.

"Pardon the mess," I murmur. "It's organized and makes sense to me."

"Show me," he says, lifting his chin toward the white canvas on the easel. "I want to see you paint."

I take a palette in hand, squeeze a dab of royal blue and black onto it, and grab a nearby brush. I move in front of the blank canvas. Stephen moves behind me; I feel his warm breath upon my neck.

I mix some blue with a tiny bit of black paint, and I add a bit more blue with my brush. I place my brush on the canvas and look over my shoulder at Stephen. Uncomfortable with his smoldering dark eyes, I must force myself to look away. I slowly begin with a wide stroke and gently taper it as it curves. Stephen's right hand covers mine. Together, we continue pressing the dark blue upon the canvas. His warm lips press to the nape of my neck. His tongue darts out to wet my skin then he blows, prickling my skin.

"That's not how to paint," my husky voice informs him.

He takes my brush and palette. I turn to find a sexy smirk upon his face as he places the brush upon the tip of my nose.

"Hey," I admonish.

Unleashed

He proceeds to dab paint on each of my cheeks.

"This means war," I declare.

"Wait," he begs, backing away. "Let me remove my white shirt and shoes. And you should remove your jeans."

Both stripped to our underwear, I grab paint and a brush to defend myself.

55

STEPHEN

I'm frozen in place, paintbrush in my hand. Sylvie stands in a dainty pastel pink bra and panty set with blue paint on the tip of her nose and each cheek. The image of her like this will be burned in my memory forever.

I could get used to this, spending our evenings out on the town, falling into bed in each other's arms, eating breakfast together, and playing for the rest of the day. I could, but I won't. I'll dabble a little, dip my toe in the proverbial pool, but I won't go all in. I won't allow myself to hurt her.

"1…2…" she taunts.

"3!" I lunge forward, paintbrush extended, and miss.

Sylvie ducks, slathering my thighs with quick, sideways strokes.

"Gotcha!" she announces, standing behind me.

"Damn, you're fast." I laugh, turning.

She expertly paints my back, my neck, and my ribs. Clearly, I'm out of my league here. I'm distracted. *That's what it is.* I'm allowing my body's reaction to her to slow me down.

"Come here," I order, wrapping my hand around the wrist of the hand holding her brush.

Flush against me, she attempts to wiggle free. She struggles for only a moment, freezing when my fingers unclasp her bra. Her mouth opens, and a gasp escapes. My eyes move from her perfect pale pink lips to her hazel eyes.

Now, I have the upper hand. With one arm holding her tight to my chest, the other guides the paint brush slowly up her spine.

Unleashed

"Mmm..." she moans, her body relaxing into mine.

I push the straps of her bra off her shoulders. She arches her back, allowing her heavy breasts to free from their silky cups. Stealing her brush, I hold two paintbrushes a hairsbreadth from her nipples. The pale pink nubs harden, straining to reach the bristles with her heaving breaths. Simultaneously, I paint each tip, swirl over the areola, then pinch each nipple between my thumb and brush handle. I marvel at her complete trust and unabashed desire.

"Mmm..." she moans again, eyes closed, basking in the sensations.

I paint a trail under each breast, down her ribs, and to her navel, causing her heavy-lidded eyes to open. I tickle her lower abdomen, stroking side to side. Goosebumps rise, and her breath hitches.

The two brushes fall to the floor, allowing my fingertips to dive beneath the waistband of her panties. Eyes locked on hers, I ease closer and closer to the apex of her thighs.

She holds her breath in anticipation. I search her eyes for permission, then slip my index finger between her hot, wet folds. Slowly, her eyes close, and her tongue peeks out to swipe her lower lip. Gently I slide my finger down her seam, my thumb rubbing her clit. On contact with her bundle of nerves, her knees bend. Out of fear of her falling, I place my free hand on the small of her back.

Moments pass before Sylvie, while still enjoying my ministrations, moves her hands from my shoulders down my chest to pause on my abdomen. Ready to explode, I change our position. On my knees, I slide her panties down her thighs and calves before she steps free of them. I tug on her forearms, encouraging her to join me on the canvas covering her floor.

She tugs my boxer briefs down my legs before climbing over me. Her knees planted on either side of me, one hand on my chest, she slowly lowers herself upon my rock-hard cock. She pauses with an inch to go, allowing her body time to acclimate to my girth.

"Wait. Condom," I warn, my hands pressed to her thighs.

Sylvie shakes her head. "I can't get pregnant, remember?"

My over-stimulated brain scurries to recall such a conversation. *Only one child, didn't want more, got a tubal...* I nod, my body on high alert. I've never not worn a condom. No condom means no barrier, and no barrier means more pleasure.

"It's deeper," she groans, sliding further until I'm fully implanted within her hot center.

As my hands at her hips encourage her to move, I drum up all of my willpower to keep from losing my control too soon. Knowing I won't last long, I place the pad of my thumb on her swollen clit, swirling it in unison with her movements.

"Yes!" she moans loudly, grinding harder against me.

"Oh, my...Yes!" She yells through her groan. Her head is thrown back, her back arched.

Wave after wave, her orgasm constricts my shaft. Hands still upon her hips, I drive into her, once, twice, then a third time. I shudder, a full body tremor as I lose every last drop into her.

Forcing my hands to relax their grip on her hips, I will my eyes to open. I find Sylvie looking down on me, a soft smile on her face as she bites her lower lip. Her hands fall off my chest, her elbows bend, and her torso meets mine.

"Best. First. Date. Ever," I state, my mouth near her ear.

Her body bounces with her laughter.

Moments after Stephen leaves, I stand staring at the paint smears upon the drop cloth on my studio floor. Two fingers press against my lips, my belly warms, and my cheeks head as I replay the scene of our bodies, our pleasure, creating this masterpiece. I need to keep it; I long to save this memory.

I could make a blanket or pillow covers; the tan cloth with its blue and black patterns is large. Or I could stretch the cloth over a large canvas to display on the bare wall above my bed.

I bite my lap, a smile growing. I like the idea of it as the last thing I see at night and it greeting me every morning. Its story will be my little secret.

56

SYLVIE

I'm thankful to be assisting Stephen with his partner's kids in my pool this afternoon. If alone I fear I might have spent the entire day convincing myself that I shouldn't be dating anyone, let alone someone 14 years younger than me.

When he informed me he offered to watch Fredrick's three kids today, I insisted he bring them over to enjoy my pool. So, here we are, Stephen and the three kids in my pool as I sit in the sun, attempting to dry off a bit before I let the dogs out of their kennels to join us in the backyard.

While six-year-old Winston and eight-year-old Michelle scamper about, the youngest boy, Daniel remains within arm's reach of Stephen at all times. He has pool floaties on each of his arms, but Stephen assures me he knows how to swim without them.

Before he left to pick up the kids today, he shared that at age 5, Daniel is nonverbal and struggles to socialize with strangers. This is one of the reasons Stephen volunteers to watch the kids, as finding a sitter is hard for them.

While I hoped having his siblings and Stephen here might make him more comfortable, Daniel still hasn't looked my way or interacted with me.

When I slip into the house, I allow my two dogs to follow me to the grass on one side of the backyard. "Go potty," I order, attempting to keep my body between Bo and the kids swimming in the pool, distracting him.

"Bo, go potty," I direct over and over until he complies.

"Good boy," I cheer, then slip both dogs a small treat.

We walk back toward the patio around the pool. Bo immediately whines at the pool's edge, standing near the children playing in the water.

"Let them in; it's no problem," Stephen says.

Daniel perks up, eyes glued on my puppy.

I lift Bo onto a mat to float, pushing him gently away from the edge.

Daniel ventures farther away from Stephen, eyes glued on Bo. Hovering nearby, he smiles, giving all of his attention to the puppy on the floating mat.

Not wanting to interrupt the fun, I wait as long as possible before I suggest everyone dry off so we can apply fresh sunscreen. Michelle and Winston take one more time off the diving board then swim to the ladder at the side of the pool.

Stephen guides Bo towards the pool steps and Daniel follows. Wrapping him in a towel, he prompts Daniel into a chair and places Bo beside him.

I apply lotion to the two older children then set a timer on my phone for when they may enter the water. Daniel refuses to drop his towel. Both Stephen and I try, but we aren't successful in applying more sunscreen. Even when Stephen enters the water, lifting Daniel's siblings over his head and tossing them into the deep end, Daniel remains wrapped tight in his towel in the shade of the patio umbrella.

Every part of me longs to talk to him, sit nearby, and entertain Daniel. But I don't. Instead, I give my attention to Hagrid and Bo.

57

STEPHEN

"Sit," Sylvie directs. Hagrid sits, and she rewards him with a tiny training treat.

Daniel moves to the end of his lounge chair to better see Sylvie and the dogs.

Next, Sylvie looks to Bo. "Sit," she commands firmly. When Bo doesn't obey, she repeats, "Sit." She places her hand on his bottom, pushes it to the patio, then gives Bo a treat.

My breath catches when Daniel approaches them.

"You want to give him one?" Sylvie extends the small treat toward him. Daniel remains close but doesn't react. She gently opens his tiny hand, slips him a treat, then assists his fingers in closing.

My cell phone alarm signals it's time to go. Not wanting to interrupt Daniel's interaction with Sylvie and the dogs, I quickly silence my phone alarm and instruct Michelle and Winston to dry off.

"High five," Sylvie instructs Hagrid. He obeys and gets a treat.

"Bo," Sylvie directs her attention to the little hound, "high five." She helps the puppy give her a high five with one of his front paws then offers him a treat.

Next, she looks at her older dog. "Hagrid, sit." He obeys and receives a treat as reward.

"Bo, sit," Sylvie directs. With no reaction, she repeats, "Bo, sit."

"Bo! Sit!" Daniel orders.

In shock, Sylvie watches her puppy sit and receive a treat from the little boy. She turns to me, her mouth agape. A large lump in my throat and tears welling in my eyes, I stare back, awestruck. Michelle stands beside me, hand to her mouth and eyes wide.

I'm not sure how to react and decide to follow Sylvie and Michelle's lead. We stand, marveling at Bo and his miraculous effect on little Daniel. I snag my phone to record.

"Hagrid," Sylvie continues. "Lay down." Again, she rewards him for his compliance then passes the small treat bag to Daniel.

"Bo," Daniel orders, "way down." Daniel's little boy voice is firm.

The puppy tilts his little head, large ears flopping heavily.

"Bo, way down." Daniel points to the concrete.

Still nothing.

"Bo, sit." When the puppy sits, Daniel passes him a treat.

I sneak a peak in Winston's direction. He stands, wide-eyed, tucked under his big sister's arm.

Fighting tears, Sylvie smiles proudly in my direction.

Out of treats, Sylvie plops down on the patio, rubbing Hagrid's belly. Nearby, Daniel mimics her actions. Bo crawls up on the little boy's lap, happy to accept his loves.

A wide smile upon my face, I mouth, "Oh. My. God."

Sylvie's smile assures me she understands the weight of this moment. This is a big deal.

58

SYLVIE

My vibrating cell phone draws my attention from my painting.

STEPHEN
thought I'd pick up dinner & head your way

ME
what if I've already eaten?

STEPHEN
I'll bring dessert

ME
bring dinner + dessert = it's a deal

STEPHEN
see ya soon

Smiling widely, I put away my paint brush. I pause, admiring the bright sunshine and field of flowers I created while Stephen drove the children home. Daniel's words and interactions with Bo prompted my sunny, upbeat painting. I cover my canvas, preparing for his return.

Moments later, I'm exiting the bathroom when my doorbell rings.

"Wow. That was quick," I greet, opening the front door.

It's not Stephen. Crap! "I'm sorry. I thought you were someone else," I explain.

"Expecting Stephen?" the stranger asks, tucking her curly hair behind her ear.

I'm statue-still, holding the door open.

"I'm Elizabeth, Officer Calderon's wife," she explains. "My children enjoyed swimming with Stephen and you today."

"Where are my manners? C'mon in." I wave my free arm toward the living room.

"I don't want to intrude," she states, standing near the sofa. "I'll only need a minute."

"No problem," I reply, taking a seat in a nearby chair. "The kids had so much fun. I told Stephen we should invite your whole family over to grill and swim."

She nods. "I want to thank you. Stephen sent me the video..." Her voice cracks as her eyes fill with tears. "We'd hoped and prayed his silence was temporary. As year after year passed, the odds were not in our favor."

I nod, smiling, unable to speak due to the heavy lump in my throat.

"You're magic," Elizabeth claims, "an angel sent to us."

"He did all the work," I argue. "I was blessed to witness Daniel in action." I shake my head. "He decided when to use his words."

Her tears flow freely down her cheeks. "I believe in a higher power that guides our lives. I think your neighbor calling the police station was a catalyst to introduce Stephen to you and bring Daniel to your home."

A higher power? Hmm... I've always believed in fate and our destined paths. Whether it's a higher power, fate, or destiny, I'm honored Daniel entered my life on the day he spoke his first words.

"I wish you were here in my place," I confess, unsure what else to say.

"I've always told Stephen there was a perfect woman out there for him," she informs. "You're the perfect woman that Daniel felt safe enough with to open up and speak."

"Whoa..." I raise my hands, palms toward her. "I'm far from perfect, and we've only been on one date..."

Elizabeth quirks her head. "You chatted at the bar, you went to the concert, you babysat together, and he spent the night." She waggles her eyebrows suggestively. "He never, and I mean never, spends the night. And you are the first woman that he's talked about non-stop."

He talks about me non-stop? Apparently, he's told Fredrik and her everything.

"I probably should not have spilled the beans about that to you," she hedges.

I bite my lips and nearly hit the roof when my doorbell rings.

"That will be Stephen," she states, standing.

Stephen lets himself in. I don't have time to process that because I'm wrapped in a tight bear-hug. Wide-eyed, I look to Stephen.

"You'll never know how happy it makes me that you've entered our lives." She rocks me side to side, still clutching tightly. "Thank you for today."

I pull in a deep breath, free from her embrace. "I meant it when I said we should grill and chat while the kids swim. All of you are welcome any time."

Hagrid and Bo scratch at the patio door, curious about the two doorbell chimes, so I let them in.

"This must be Bo," Elizabeth states, lowering herself to the floor. "You are adorable. You're even cuter in person."

Bo climbs into her lap, enjoying her rubs. "He's so cute and those ears."

"He'll never grow into them," Stephen states. "Or his paws."

"Stop that," I admonish. "Basset hounds have long ears and big feet."

"Alright," Elizabeth stands. "As much as I want to stay and love this little cutie," she passes Bo to me, "I should get back home. You two have fun." She winks at me and pats Stephen's shoulder.

"Don't let the door hit you on the way out," Stephen says.

59

SYLVIE

"Be nice," I chide, waving to Elizabeth as she slips through the door. "She came over to introduce herself and thank me. I told her it wasn't anything I did. Daniel did it himself."

In two long strides, Stephen wraps his arms around me, pulling me flush against his chest. "Don't argue with me; just listen." His voice drops low. "You have this way of making everyone around you feel comfortable. I feel it, the kids feel it..." He places a kiss on the top of my head. "Daniel relaxed today. That's not usually the case for him. He refuses to engage in new situations and people."

"But you were here," I argue.

"Ah, ah, ah," he teases. "It's listening time for you. Usually, he glues himself to his parents, his sister, or me. He didn't do that. He moved around the pool on his own, swimming closer and closer to the dogs. You have this calm—I don't know, maybe it's a calm aura—around you. Instead of shutting you out, he watched you. He chose to approach you and the dogs. He mimicked your behaviors. He doesn't do that with someone he just met. He doesn't approach animals, either. So, whether you choose to believe it or not, you were partially responsible for him speaking."

He squeezes me tighter, and I tighten my hold on him. Several quiet moments pass.

"She thinks I've found my perfect match," he whispers. "Now that she's met you, I'll never hear the end of it. She already warns me not to do anything to screw this up."

I lift my head from his shoulder, looking up to him through my lashes. "After one date?" I shake my head slightly. "Is she this way with all of your dates?"

He smiles a sexy little grin. "I told you, I don't date. I definitely don't share details of my hookups either." His eyes ping-pong from mine to my mouth and back. "She claims I had 'a glow' about me this morning." He makes air quotes. "She knew I had a date last night and recognized I wore the same clothes from the pics we sent her husband with the band. She's very perceptive."

I bite my lips.

"She went on and on about all the ways I'm different when I talk about you…"

I interrupt, "You didn't tell her about last night, did you?"

"No," he states, leaving no doubt. "She put two and two together. I did share details about our time swimming with the kids."

"She argued with me when I stated we'd only been on one date," I share.

"How many times must I tell you? We've had other dates!"

I pull away from him, shaking my head once again.

"What's for dinner?" I ask, changing the subject.

Stephen's smirk assures me he knows what I'm doing. "I made an executive decision. We're skipping dinner and going straight to dessert."

60

STEPHEN

"I enjoyed today," I inform Sylvie as we eat our second bowl of ice cream.

"The kids are so adorable," she mumbles, ice cream still in her mouth.

"I bet they'll hound Fredrik and Elizabeth nonstop to come swim again," I chuckle.

Mouth empty, Sylvie swallows a sip of water. "What a rush. I mean... It was my first time with Daniel, but knowing he spoke for the first time... What a rush."

I nod; there are no words to describe the monumental moment we witnessed.

"You're so good with the kids," she continues. "And it's clear they absolutely love spending time with you." She smiles fondly.

I fear I know where she's headed with this line of conversation. "Like I've shared before, I like being around other people's children. I love what I do. And to continue loving it, I can't have children." My eyes lock on hers.

"But..."

"So..." I interrupt her, drawing it out. "that's the reason for my vasectomy. I may be greedy, but I won't let my love of career cause stress or pain to children."

"You told me I wasn't greedy in making my decision. Thus, you aren't greedy for making the same decision." Sylvie smirks, tossing my words back at me. "I was just making an observation, not trying to force the issue. Besides..." She bites her lips, her eyes purposefully looking away from mine. "If you wanted children of your own, we'd be through."

Snagging her wrist, I pull her onto my lap. "I'm enjoying this relationship thing. I'm in no hurry to move on."

Clearly, my words didn't convey the meaning I'd hoped. I cup her chin, turning her to face me. "I need you to understand what I'm trying to tell you." I wet my lips, loving her eyes focused on my mouth. "I'm having fun."

Crap! That sounds bad.

"Urgh…" I growl. "I'm into you. I want to spend as much time as I can with you. I'm here until you tire of me."

My eyes beg her to understand I'm on the verge of sharing three little words out loud. I've never spoken them to anyone aside from my family, and I worry if I say them, I'll scare her away. I'm not sure if there are unspoken rules or a timeline for relationships. *Man, relationships are much harder than I ever dreamed.*

"I…" I sputter nervously. "I… I like you." My heart rate skyrockets. "I probably like you more than I should for the amount of time we've spent together."

Her eyes glisten as a wide smile graces her face. Her reaction, while unexpected, is very welcome. I urge her to stand with me, place my hands on each of her cheeks, and gaze into her eyes.

"It's not too soon," she whispers, eyes locked on mine. "I'm fighting it, too."

We don't speak the three words we're dancing around.

On their own, my lips find hers. My mouth consumes her; my tongue tastes all she has to give. My lungs protest eventually, and I'm forced to end our kiss. Forehead to forehead, we struggle to pull in air.

"I'm falling in love with you," I admit in a whisper. "I'm done trying to deny it, and I pray I didn't just scare you away."

Sylvie leans her body tighter to mine. She places a kiss on my chin, my jaw, then the corner of my mouth. She lifts a leg, her thigh grazing deliciously against my swelling cock. She doesn't parrot my sentiment, choosing to show me instead.

61

SYLVIE

I stand before my vanity, taking in my reflection. I marvel at the woman I've become. I love sex. I think about sex with Stephen twenty-four-seven. It's not the fact it's been missing from my life since my early twenties, it's Stephen. I can't get enough of him. I fantasize about his lips tasting every inch of my skin, the rough pads of his fingers grazing over my sensitive parts, and his cock. What a cock! I should be alarmed at how much time I spend thinking of his cock and the magical things it does to me.

Crap! I'm doing it again. I roll my eyes at my hard nipples poking into my vintage Nirvana tee. I rub my thighs together, attempting to quell the damp heat of my core. Vibrator. This calls for my vibrator. I step from the bathroom toward my bed. I pause, my hand on the knob to my nightstand.

Harness it. Harness these feelings and place them on a canvas. Paint. I must paint.

My vibrating phone jolts me from my painting. I hurry to my table, placing my paint brush on a nearby paper plate. My body hums with excitement to read what Stephen texts.

Unleashed

LIDIA
got an A

I sigh disappointed it's not from Stephen. It's stupid; his shift doesn't end for two more hours. She's my daughter for Pete's sake. Her texts should be the most important. *What kind of mother gets disappointed by a text from her only child?* Shaking my head, I process the text I received.

ME
awesome job!

1 more to go

LIDIA
easy 1 left

ME
1 more A?

LIDIA
that's the goal

ME
good luck & keep me posted

LIDIA
will do

I should try to remain distant, instead of fall head over heels so fast. I shake my head, knowing I can't change my feelings. There's something about Stephen that draws me to him. It's useless to fight it, and I don't want to fight it. I like how he makes me feel and I like how I am in his presence.

62

SYLVIE

I glance at my cell phone clock; it's almost eleven. My insides cheer as I prepare for his text. My thumbs hover over my screen. I'll shoot him a text. He tends to text me as soon as his shift ends, then again when he arrives home. I'll text him first tonight.

> ME
> any noise complaints today?
> (laughing emoji)

I return my phone on the table, grasp my paint brush, and stand at my easel. I purse my lips. The creative juices fled; I no longer feel the urge to paint. After cleaning my brushes and palette, I stand in the living room, staring at my phone. It's eleven-fifteen and no text from him yet. I'm rethinking my silly texts. Perhaps I messed up. I should've let him text me first. It's his thing and I...

My cell phone vibrates in my hand, causing my heartbeat to speed and my body to hum.

Unleashed

> **STEPHEN**
> I wish
> worked out well for me last time

> **ME**
> looking to replace me already?

> **STEPHEN**
> never be a call like the 1 that brought me to u!

I can't think of a witty reply.

> **STEPHEN**
> (kissing emoji)
> headed your way

Wait. What? I quickly scan myself head to toe. I'm a disheveled, paint-covered mess. I turn towards the hallway then back to the front door. My feet are cemented to the spot. I need a shower but there's not time. He'll be here…

Crap! I hear the thunk of his truck door closing in my driveway. Stunned I walk to my door. I unlock and open it as Stephen prepares to knock.

"I thought you didn't text while driving," I greet.

He laughs. He actually laughs at me.

"I used the hands-free talk to text today," he explains. "Did I catch you in the middle of something?" He points to my face and paint covered shirt.

"No, but you didn't give me time to clean up," I inform. "I'm a mess."

"Nope," he argues. "You're cute." His thumb wipes a paint smudge on my cheek.

Cute? Do I want to be cute?

Forefinger to my crinkled brow, Stephen asks, "What's going on up here?"

I attempt to shake off the topic, but he insists I share. "I'm not sure I want to be 'cute'." I make air quotes as I speak.

He chuckles. "Bull Durham, right?"

Tilting my head to the side, my eyes squint as I search for his meaning.

"You know the quote from Bull Durham," he prompts.

"Never watched it," I confess with a shrug.

"No way!" He stands mouth agape and his eyes wide.

I shrug again.

"Well, I'll make it my mission to remedy that as soon as possible," he states, pulling me into a hug. "Let's snack and then we will watch it."

I arch my back, smiling up at him.

"You didn't have any other plans, did you?" He grins down at me.

Text or videocall with him, I think to myself. I love that he wants to share a favorite movie with me. Secretly, I hope he will share all of his favorites with me, as well as take me to his favorite spots and restaurants. I long to experience everything with him.

63

STEPHEN

It's Thursday, I'm off, and today, I'm walking the zoo with Sylvie. I've been intrigued by her comments from the evening she bumped into us working Zoo Brew. I'm dying to experience the entire zoo with her.

Walking side by side, hand in hand, we turn left from the entrance.

"Maybe we'll catch a glimpse of some Animal Planet action." She giggles excitedly as we pass the first exhibit of flamingos.

I shake my head and can't help the big grin upon my face. Try as I might, I can't ever predict what she'll say or do next.

"What's your favorite animal?" I ask while we admire the river otters' agile swimming maneuvers.

"At this zoo or world-wide?" she inquires.

"World-wide," I answer, kissing the back of her hand in mine.

"I love hippos. They're awkward-looking but deadly beasts in water," she answers without taking time to ponder. "Big cats fascinate me. I don't consider myself a cat person, but I love big cats. They are beautiful, graceful, powerful killing machines."

We walk away from the otters up a slight incline and stop at the bald eagle enclosure.

"Oh, and I'm intrigued by the new rhinos here." Sylvie squints as she takes in the enormous bird perched mere feet from us. "Talk about awkward. They're just weird to look at." She turns to face me, my forearms leaning on the metal bar around the eagle's cage, fencing her in. "Did you know they can't see? I mean, they aren't blind, but everything is very blurry for them."

I refrain from shaking my head at her. Instead, I place a kiss in the middle of her forehead. She wraps her arms around my waist. Her bright hazel eyes gaze at me through her lashes. Her teeth bite the corner of her lower lip. I try to refrain from laughing and fail miserably. She wants to tell me another fact; I can see her biting her lip to stop herself.

"I'm a nerd," she murmurs.

I nod. "I wouldn't have it any other way," I admit. "And I did know about the rhinos. I've brought my nieces and nephews here several times."

She turns back toward the majestic bird, leaning her head on my shoulder.

"The first time I saw this guy," she lifts her chin towards the bald eagle, "I was surprised by how large he was. I've seen them flying in our area during winter and perching in trees. They didn't look this big." I feel her shrug against my side. "I guess I thought I was closer to them than I really was. It's an optical illusion."

Hands on her hips, I spin her to face me. With a sudden awareness of several children around us, I refrain from melding my mouth with hers. Her eyes on my mouth, her tongue sweeps over her lower lip. My insides warm, knowing she desires me as I do her.

64

STEPHEN

"Daniel's gonna love her," Sylvie states in between little puppy licks and her giggles.

I struggle to keep my attention on the road. It's a constant struggle to focus on anything when I'm in her presence. She's all-consuming.

"Should we name her?' Sylvie holds the puppy at arms-length near the dash.

I smile in her direction, then quickly return my eyes to the street before us.

"I know, I know," she continues. "Daniel's been talking more each day. She's just too cute. Yes, you are." She coos at the female Basset hound in her arms. "I'm glad Fredrik and Elizabeth chose to get him a puppy."

"I still can't believe you found them a free dog." I reply. "Runt or not, she's purebred and worth something."

"When I explained about Daniel's first words with Bocephus, she offered this little cutie to encourage Daniel to interact and speak more. She was excited to donate her as a therapy dog."

"You had a lot to do with it," I state, enamored by the affect she has on people. I put my truck in park. "Let's go surprise Daniel."

"What should we name her?" Daniel's sister Michelle asks him.

"Ten-a-the," He immediately answers.

All eyes turn to him, several brows raise, and confusion consumes all.

"What, honey?" Elizabeth asks.

"Ten-a-the," he states, pointing to the top of the refrigerator.

Beside me, Stephen bounces with quiet laughter. I elbow him in the ribs.

"What's funny?" I whisper.

Unable to speak, Stephen shakes his head.

Elizabeth walks toward the fridge, looking for the object Daniel points at. "Show me," she prompts.

"Daddy jui-th," Daniel points above the freezer.

"Fredrik!" she calls, stern voice raised.

Stephen's laughter continues, so I elbow him harder this time.

I watch Elizabeth chew Fredrik out, hands moving wildly between them.

"What's going on?" I whisper.

"They learned this week that Daniel can read. Like, really read. Fredrik and I sipped from his bottle of Jack Daniels night before last. Seems Daniel saw the bottle and now wants to name his puppy Tennessee," he chuckles. "We were supposed to be watching the kids not drinking."

I can't help but giggle. I love this family and Stephen's involvement with them. He's more than a friend, he's family.

65

STEPHEN

It's late Friday morning, and we've left the comfort of Sylvie's bed in search of sustenance. Sylvie hops up to sit on the counter between the stove and the refrigerator. I let the dogs in through the patio door then lean my hips against the kitchen island, facing her.

"Now what?" she asks, head cocked to one side, fingers strumming the granite countertop beside her exposed thighs peeking out from under my t-shirt.

I smirk. She's the cutest thing I've ever seen.

"My breakfast is typically a protein bar," she states. "I have a couple of eggs; we could whip up an omelet, or…"

I take this opportunity to demonstrate exactly what I prefer for breakfast. I close the distance between us, sliding my hands up her bare thighs. Her eyes question me as her lips form a perfect little 'O'. Hooking my thumbs into the waistband, I quickly slide her panties toward her knees, my eyes locked on hers. While hers ping-pong between mine, I remain focused. My eyes implore hers to see my need, my want, my absolute addiction to her. My palms slowly urge her knees to part. Her hazel eyes search mine for… for I don't know what. In answer, I fall to my knees, my face eye-level between her open thighs, in awe of the gift before me.

"Steph…"

My mouth connects with the apex of her thighs, the center of her pleasure. When my tongue laps once, twice upon her sensitive bud, her head falls back, thumping against the cabinet door. At war, my mind wants me to comfort the bump while my libido urges me to continue my ministrations until she screams my name. I focus on my task, the pleasure I desire to give to her, and the end game.

"Mmm," she moans, fingers splayed wide upon her thighs.

I alternate licking, sucking, and strumming, fueled by her whimpers, moans, and hitching breath. Her fingers find their way into my hair and at the back of my head, urging me not to stop. Instead of patting myself on the back, I double my efforts to deliver her ecstasy.

"Mm-hmm," she murmurs. "Right there. Oh. God. Yes."

My index finger caresses her inner walls as my thumb presses repetitive circles upon her clit.

"Fuck...Fuck...F-U-C-K!!!!" Sylvie pants loudly.

I press my mouth to her, my lips sucking her nub, elongating her orgasm. My free hand fumbles with my boxers as her inner walls contract over and over, grasping my fingers tight.

I rapidly withdraw my fingers and mouth, thank God I no longer need a condom, and slide inside, impaling myself deep within her heat.

Still contracting... the pressure... the heat... I let go. Her hands grab my ass, her fingernails biting my flesh as she milks every ounce of me, taking everything I have to give. My nerve endings from my ass cheeks send the alert of pain to my brain. My eyes closed, I draw in a long breath, registering the slight bite of pain her fingernails cut into my skin. Sensual. Delicious. Hot. I shudder, my legs shake, and my hands fall to the counter to prevent my fall. I press my forehead to hers, forcing my heavy eyelids to open.

I find her sated eyes peering back at me. The release is not enough; she leaves me wanting more. I heft her over my right shoulder. Her legs kicking in protest in front of me, I stride to her bedroom.

66

SYLVIE

"Stephen! Put. Me. Down!" I yell, my body hefted over his shoulder.

"You want down?" he rebuts. "Now you are down," he states as my body bounces on my bed.

I blink, and he's over me, pressed to me, his heat and weight upon me. He nips, he sucks, he kisses, and he bites.

I close my eyes but a minute, and he's in me and over me; he's everything to me. With every breath I pull in, I feel him. With every cell in my body, I feel him. He's everywhere, and I'm bathed in him.

My back arches, and my heartbeat quickens. I need this; I need him.

"Syl..." his husky voice whispers. "I'm... cum with me."

He only needs to ask; I obey. One... Two... Three... I'm over the peak. I'm there. I'm at the pinnacle of ecstasy; I'm in heaven.

A guttural groan escapes his chest. He's feral, shuttering.

It's heady, this ability, this knowledge that I affect him so. It's as if I'm his kryptonite. I fly high outside myself with this feeling of power.

His mouth covers mine, consumes mine, consumes me. His tongue invades, and he owns me. My hands rove his back, his ribs, and find purchase upon his buttocks. I hold him to me as I seek to ground myself by anchoring to him.

Many moments pass as we fall back from the edge of heaven. Our labored breathing finds a slower pace, and our racing hearts their healthy rhythm.

"I need a shower and food," I state, smiling.

"If we share a shower," Stephen smirks, his thumb caressing my cheek, "we'll eat sooner."

Doubting his logic, I slip from my side of the bed, padding into the bathroom and feeling the heat of his gaze on my naked backside.

The warm water and soapy bubbles ignite rather than calm my sensitive skin and desire. I bite my lower lip when a sensual idea enters my mind. I steal the soapy loofa from his hand, replacing it on the hook. Both under the spray, I lazily slide my fingertips over his shoulders, his chest, then his ribs. I drop one hand behind me as the other entwines with his. Backing up, my free hand guiding me, I take a seat on the tiled corner bench, pulling him with me.

Through my wet lashes, I look up for his approval. I sweep my index finger from his navel, following the thin smattering of hair down his happy trail. His eyes turn liquid, and that's my cue.

I take his cock in my left hand, enjoying the heavy weight of him in my palm. My tongue darts over my lower lip, barely swiping his sensitive tip. I giggle when it twitches, his rock-hard cock reaching for me. I should prolong his torture, but I'm too turned on myself.

67

STEPHEN

Every muscle in my body flexes as Sylvie's hazel eyes, through her dark, wet lashes, seek mine. Her hot tongue slowly licks only the tip of me. It takes all of my strength to refrain from sinking myself into her mouth over and over again.

Sensing my need, she doesn't toy with me; her right hand grasps my hard shaft tightly, and her lips slide over me an inch at a time. I want to keep my eyes on her; I want to watch her mouth take me and her cheeks hollow out, but my eyes close as her warm, slick tongue and powerful lips work me. My left hand caresses the side of her head while my right palm on the tile wall holds me in place.

She sets an aggressive pace, sucking me in and out, her fist pumping in time. Though I've had her twice this morning, it's clear I won't last long under her ministrations. Her free hand clutches my ass, pulling me towards her on her downward strokes. It's my undoing.

"Syl," I moan, my voice husky. "Syl, I'm going to..."

In the blink of an eye, both her hands dig into my ass, holding me to her as she takes me deeper. So deep, I can feel the back of her throat. Lightning shoots down my spine, my thighs tense, and my orgasm explodes. Not wanting to hurt her, I attempt to pull out, but she refuses to release her tight grip on my backside.

Slowly my heavy eyes open to find hers staring up at me, a proud smile on her face. I slide the pad of my thumb over her swollen lower lip, and she rises to stand in front of me under the spray. I pull her to me, her head to my chest. I feel my hands tremble as they press into her back. Every part of me buzzes. She affects me in a way no woman has before.

Syl slips from the shower, allowing me to clean myself up. I turn the knob, silencing the spray, wrap a towel around my waist, and step from the shower to find Sylvie in my t-shirt, sitting on the vanity.

She doesn't hide her head-to-toe inspection of me. She bites her lip, liking what she sees.

"I think every day should be 'towel day'," I state, enjoying her ogling me.

"'Towel day' will need to wait until after you feed me," she counters, her head tilting to the side.

I grab my phone from the vanity, tap a few buttons, then replace it. "Done," I inform her, tilting my head as she did.

"What's done?" she queries.

"I ordered pizza," I state. "It will be here in 45 minutes."

She nods approvingly.

"Now back to 'towel day'," I growl, leaning into her. I press a kiss upon her lips before quickly throwing her over my shoulder and packing her back into the bedroom.

"Stephen!" she laughs, her legs flailing.

"Shush, woman," I tease.

She swats my backside, causing my towel to fall to the floor. When she gasps, I pause.

"Did I..." she whispers.

I bend, standing her on the floor at the end of the bed, my eyes questioning.

"I'm sorry. I didn't mean to hurt you," she murmurs.

It takes a moment, but I figure out she's talking about the red marks her nails caused on my ass.

I gently pinch her chin between my thumb and forefinger, holding her eyes to mine. "They don't hurt, and at the time, the sensation..." I struggle to explain. "It was hot."

She shakes her head, unbelieving.

"You didn't break skin." I tell her what she knows. "They'll disappear in a couple of hours," I promise.

I urge her eyes back to mine.

"It will be even hotter when I give you so much pleasure that you leave scratches up and down my back." I smile. "It'll be like the Buckcherry song you like and hot as hell."

"I can't believe you want me to hurt you," she murmurs, shaking her head.

"It's not painful during sex. It actually heightens the pleasure," I inform.

I slide my hand up under the tee, softly caressing her breast. I slip my other hand under as well, raising the shirt up, allowing my mouth to find her nipple. I gently suck before pulling away.

"It's like this," I state, my mouth returning to her breast. This time, my teeth gently tug at her nipple. When I pull away, my thumb continues to circle the puckered nub.

I look into her eyes, hoping she now understands that her fingernails don't hurt me; they're part of the entire sensual experience.

"I see," she whispers.

68

STEPHEN

"Yo, you're doing it again," Fredrik chuckles from the driver's seat as we sit outside the funeral home.

Of course, I'm doing it. Sylvie's not someone you can forget.

"Like your mind is on the job right now," I motion towards the hearse parked beside us. "I'm sure you're thinking of Elizabeth and the kids. I mean, they're the reason we're working overtime today."

I don't mean this in a bad way. We're working funeral duty on our day off; it's not as if we're in any danger. I'll focus when I stand in the middle of the intersection to stop traffic for the funeral procession. Until then I prefer thinking of Sylvie to thoughts of death.

"You going over there after this?" he asks.

"Didn't make any plans yet," I mumble.

"Text her," Fredrik encourages.

"Huh?" I turn to face him.

"It's clear you can't keep her off your mind," he states the obvious. "Text her, make plans," he chuckles. "Elizabeth's worried you'll screw this up. I wouldn't be surprised if she doesn't talk to you daily to keep you from letting Sylvie slip away."

I shake my head. Elizabeth's already spoken to me about how much she likes Sylvie and that she's available for any advice I might need.

Unleashed

STEPHEN
I'm fixing you dinner tonight

ME
Ok

STEPHEN
be there @7

ME
Ok

My insides flutter with excitement. I wonder what he'll prepare. I try not to get my hopes up; he could simply mean he's getting takeout. I hope he actually cooks. A vision of Stephen standing at my stove, causes me to smile. Seven hours--this will be a long afternoon.

"Pour yourself a glass of wine," Stephen instructs. "Then come to the patio and keep me company."

I quickly grab a beer for each of us, following him out back.

"One for you and one for me," I say, placing his beer on the patio table with his ingredients. "What are you fixin'?"

While lighting the grill he shares, "New York strips, cream cheese stuffed Anaheim peppers wrapped in bacon and baked potatoes."

He smiles over his shoulder at me. "I hope you're hungry."

"Starving," I reply. "I forgot to eat lunch today."

"I thought you set an alarm to remind you to take a break. He turns to face me, tongs in his hand.

"I did. I took the dogs out, then started painting again without eating." I shrug. "I get enthralled in my work."

"How do you like your steak?" he asks, as he turns the foil-wrapped peppers and potatoes over.

"Well-done," I answer.

"Well, you'll try it medium tonight. Trust me, you'll love it." He clicks the tongs open and closed in my direction. I open my mouth to argue, but he continues, "No blood, I promise?"

I enjoy my beer as he grills, seasons, and turns the food. All the while, my stomach growls for the food he prepares, and my body yearns to gobble him up. I laugh at my thoughts; the new Sylvie always wants more.

"What's so funny?" he asks, beer near his lips.

I shake my head. "I'm drooling." *For him more than the steak*, I admit to myself, while biting my lip.

Stephen's thumb tugs my lip, startling me. *How'd I not hear him approach?* All thoughts cease as his warm mouth molds to feast on mine. Too soon, he pulls away.

"Steaks are done," he states and smirks.

My brow furrows and eyes squint as my foggy mind processes his words.

69

SYLVIE

Just off the phone with Lidia, I text Stephen before he starts his night shift on duty.

> **ME**
> cancelling my oral surgery tomorrow
>
> Lidia's ill & can't drive myself

When a few moments pass, I figure I've missed him before he entered the station.

> **STEPHEN**
> don't cancel
>
> I can drive you

> **ME**
> you'll be tired from work

> **STEPHEN**
> I rarely head straight to bed
>
> let me drive you

> I can nap while I stay with you
> until the anesthesia wears off

ME
> I couldn't ask

STEPHEN
> you didn't, I offered
> let me do this for you

ME
> appt. @ 9 takes 45 min

STEPHEN
> I'll come straight from work
> about 8

ME
> thank you
> (heart emoji)

STEPHEN
> good night
> (kissing face emoji)

Stephen

After receiving a printout of Sylvie's post-operative instructions, the nurse helps her into the passenger seat of my truck. With her door shut and seat belt on, we head to her house.

"How are you feeling?" I ask, eyes on her while idling at a red light.

"Good," she says. "I should send a picture to Lidia."

She pulls out her phone, leans towards me, holds the camera to the side, and smiles for a selfie with me.

"Lidia's gonna love this one," she states as she types and sends the photo of the two of us.

"So, no pain?" I ask. I was told she'd be groggy and in pain.

"Nope," she replies, popping her 'P'. "What should we have for lunch?"

"Well, lunch is hours away. We're stopping for your prescriptions, then I'm taking you home to tuck you into bed." When I glance in her direction, she seems herself with no sign of grogginess.

I pull in the drive-up pharmacy lane and request her scripts. I'm told they will be ready in ten minutes, so I park us in the grocery parking lot to wait.

"I'm gonna run in to grab some pudding and soft food for me," she suggests. "It'll just take a minute, and I'll grab my scripts on the way out."

Odd. I squint my eyes, assessing her. She's not having trouble talking and she's able to send Snapchats, so she should be able to shop. I nod.

She climbs from the cab of my truck, purse in hand, without any trouble.

I people-watch while I wait for her to emerge from the store. Several long minutes pass, then she steps through the automatic doors, carrying several grocery bags.

I pull the truck up beside her, and she places all of the bags on the floorboard with her purse before climbing into the seat, a large smile on her face.

"I thought you were getting pudding and something soft. It looks like you bought way more than that," I tease. "Did you remember your prescriptions?"

She proudly lifts the paper pharmacy bag from the plastic ones on the floor.

I assist Sylvie from the truck and carry her shopping bags into the kitchen for her.

"Go change into comfy clothes, and I'll get the sofa ready for you to lay down," I order.

"For *us* to lay down," she corrects.

I pull a bag of white chocolate Reese's from one shopping bag then another. With all bags empty, I stare at the food covering her countertop. There are several bags of white and milk chocolate Reese's candy bars, a roll of chocolate chip cookie dough, two types of pudding cups, varieties of Chex cereal, and a large can of mixed nuts.

"Just leave them on the counter," she instructs. "That way, it will be easy for me to grab some," she says as she grabs a water and plops on the sofa.

I read through the post-op instructions again, marveling that she's not showing the symptoms I read about. I search her kitchen cabinets until I find some pain reliever. I pour two into my palm, then walk toward my patient.

"Thank you," she says, quickly downing the pills.

"I'm going to take the dogs out back for a bit," I inform as she positions herself on the pillow with a throw blanket.

I'm only outside 10 to15 minutes, but when I return, she's asleep. I position myself on the other end of the sectional sofa, encouraging the two dogs to lay with me and leave Sylvie alone. Unable to find something interesting on TV, I tilt my head back and close my eyes.

70

SYLVIE

I open one eye then the other. My mouth hurts; I need some pain relievers. I slowly raise to a sitting position, freezing at the sight of Stephen asleep nearby with my puppy on his chest and Hagrid near his feet.

I snag my cell phone from the table in front of me and take two pictures; I have to record this moment. Of course, at my movement, the two dogs move, waking him up.

"Hey," he greets with sleepy eyes and a gruff voice. "How do you feel?"

"I hurt." I stand, and when he moves to join me, I order him, "Stay. I'm getting pain meds and laying back down."

He props his head on the back of the sofa, watching me move about the kitchen. I swallow two pills then take in all of the snacks on my kitchen island.

"What are these?" I ask, pointing to the counter.

"You went in the store for pudding and your prescriptions," he states. "Those are all the items you came out with."

I return to my end of the sectional. "I don't remember shopping," I admit, brow furrowed. Glancing down at my pajama shorts, I add, "I don't remember changing my clothes either."

Instantly, Stephen is alert. "You don't remember telling me you would go into the grocery store to get pudding and your meds?"

I slowly shake my head.

"You were talking and acting fine," he swears. "I wouldn't have let you go in by yourself if I'd thought you were out of it. You talked fine and took selfies on our way to the store."

I cringe. *Selfies? What did I take, and who did I send it to?* I open my phone, searching for photos. Then, I go to Snapchat. I see that I sent photos to Lidia, but I can't see what I sent.

"I don't remember leaving the oral surgeon," I grumble.

"Well, you are home and safe," he offers. "I should have known better than to let you shop."

I shrug, lay back down, and quickly fall back to sleep.

Stephen sleeps on my sofa. I feel bad that he worked all night then had to care for me this morning. I do my best to eat my pudding and take the dogs outside without disturbing him. I move a lounge chair under the patio umbrella and relax outside with the dogs.

Why did I buy all of those candies while I went in for pudding? They aren't even treats I normally eat. I hope that all of the items were between the door and the dairy where I found pudding. I cringe at the thought of me seeming drunk, traipsing around the grocery store.

I'm outside an hour when Stephen joins me. "How do you feel?"

"I'm okay; pain relievers work if I take them without letting them wear all of the way off."

His hair is messed from sleep, and I smile.

"What's the cookie dough for?" I ask. "I found it when I grabbed a pudding cup."

He shakes his head, chuckling. "You bought it. When I tried to ask you why you bought all of those chocolates and cereals, you pointed your finger at me and said, 'Don't be judgy. I need soft, melt-in-my-mouth foods for a couple of days, so you can't be judgy.'" He bites his lips, attempting not to smile.

I shake my head, remembering none of it. "I'm afraid to ask," I chuckle. "I planned to make Chex Mix?"

He shrugs, a wide smile upon his exhausted face. "I guess I suck at taking care of patients."

We laugh.

"Wait!" I shout. "Did I pay for the groceries and prescriptions?"

"Everything was in a bag when you exited," he informs. "So, I assume you did."

"I better check," I state as I open my banking app on my phone. I breathe a huge sigh of relief when my account shows debits for today's purchases.

"Shouldn't you go back to sleep?" I ask.

"I'm off the next three days," he explains. "If I sleep now, I won't sleep tonight."

"Wow. That has to be a hard transition," I state.

"I'm used to it." He makes light of it.

71

STEPHEN

> SYLVIE
> still mtg @ Brickhouse?

> ME
> 6 sharp

I've worked double shifts. It seems like weeks since I've seen her instead of three days. We may meet at the bar, but I have other plans for the two of us tonight, I think to myself. It's my nieces' birthday, and I plan to introduce Sylvie to the family. She seemed okay with meeting them at the Sunday barbecue that Mom cancelled when Dad had to go to urgent care for stitches a week ago.

My stomach flip-flops at the thought. I've never taken a woman to meet my family. I try to calm my nerves. We'll hang at the bar an hour or so. Then, we'll need to leave.

When I enter the smoky bar, it's a couple of minutes before six. Scanning the crowd, I can't see Sylvie anywhere. I slide onto a stool and order a beer at the bar.

Unleashed

At the sound of a crackling mic, I turn towards the little stage. I freeze, beer in my hand, halfway to my open mouth.

"Hey. My name is Sylvie, and my therapist challenged me to take the stage. So, if I suck, it's all her fault." She shrugs. "But I'll have something to talk about in my next therapy session."

The crowd's laughter and applause fill the tiny bar. She strums her electric guitar once, and the crowd goes silent. A nervous smile upon her face, she nods to the audience in front of her, letting them know that she's ready. During this short silence, my heart beats loudly in my chest, and my throat grows dry.

She masterfully manipulates the six strings of her Fender guitar to play the National Anthem, reminiscent of a performance by Jimi Hendrix.

Taking a pull from my beer to wet my dry throat, I stare at her fingers prying each note out with their expert movements. Our previous conversation about her first time at the Brickhouse and checking out open mic night replays in my mind. At the time, I assumed she was pulling my leg. This little minx is full of surprises.

The bar is dark save for the stage lights focused on Sylvie's solo. She seems at ease, feet spread in a wide stance to allow her arms to move her fingertips over her instrument. Thoughts of my mother's CD collection spark to mind. Sylvie's short, blonde hair reminds me of Blondie from the 80's. Both are kick-ass rockers.

It's hard for me to imagine the version of Sylvie that raised Lidia and married Omar. The Sylvie I know could never be muted; she's a force. I love this woman. I love her with every part of me. I love her to the point that I can no longer live without her.

The applause with whooping and hollering pulls me from my thoughts. Sylvie's cheeks turn red as the patrons refuse to end their celebration of her performance. Several sharp whistles join the voices and clapping.

She bows, her hands pressed together in front of her, then exits the stage. The lights over the bar brighten, allowing me to watch her place her guitar into its case.

Unable to remain seated, I stride in her direction. I forcefully push my way through the crowd that flows toward her. I fight down the growl rising in my chest, my need to assert my claim publicly bubbling up.

Sylvie leans her guitar case against the wall, turning toward the crowd.

My hands plant on her hips, I pull her tight to my chest, and my mouth takes hers. I ravage her for several long minutes, breaking our connection in need of oxygen. My forehead presses to hers, our mouths an inch apart, my eyes boring into her soul.

"Stephen," she whispers breathily. "People are staring."

"Let them stare," I growl.
Her hands slide to my chest, clutching the fabric of my shirt.
"Wanna get out of here?" she murmurs, a goofy smile upon her face.

72

SYLVIE

"Come inside. I'll only be a minute," I offer. "I just need to change from these smoky, bar clothes."

I enter the code, and the garage door rises. I hurry inside, not looking to see if Stephen follows. In my room, I step out of my jeans, leaving them on the floor. I wiggle my t-shirt over my head, stepping into my closet. My fingers glide from hanger to hanger, unsure what to wear to meet Stephen's family.

I should have planned my attire earlier today.

I slip into a pair of white shorts, a red halter top, and a pair of red flip-flops. Turning this way and that in front of the full-length mirror, I'm looking good and ready to go. Catching Stephen standing nearby, my skin sizzles under his approving gaze. I spin slowly to give him the full view.

"Okay to meet the family in this?" I inquire, placing my hands on his hips.

Stephen clears his throat. "It's perfect. And they are gonna love you. Don't worry."

"Ugh," I groan. "My hair smells like the bar; even I can smell it."

"We'll be outside. No one will notice," he promises. "Anyway, they all knew we were meeting for drinks tonight."

I tilt my head, smiling. "You told them?"

He nods.

"Let me see the picture of your nieces again," I beg, palm out between us.

Stephen quickly scrolls through his cell phone pictures then passes me his phone. I stare at the identical twins standing at his sides, the picture from earlier this summer.

"We can't show up without a gift," I state, heading for the stairs.

"I dropped the gift off earlier this week, so that's covered." He repeats what I already know.

"It's not in me to show up with no gift." As I descend the stairs, a plan forms in my mind. "I will only be a minute,"

Stephen follows me downstairs. He hasn't seen this part of my house before. In the storage area, I move a drop cloth and thumb through canvases standing long ways on a shelf. I pull out first one then a second painting. I slowly turn to show him.

I hold two canvases, each with a little blonde girl in a white sundress with yellow sunflowers, barefoot, on their knees in lush, green grass near a flowerbed. One painting has a butterfly in the little girl's palm. The other has an earthworm, and dark dirt speckles her hand.

73

STEPHEN

"Syl..." I shift my weight from one foot to the other, holding a painting in each hand. "Wow. That... Those are amazing and look exactly like the girls."

Sylvie turns them to face her, tilting her head to the side, scrutinizing her work. "May I see the picture of them again?"

Once more, I extend my phone.

"Hmm... I need to make one small addition. I'll be quick."

She darts up the stairs, both canvases in hand, and I do my best to follow. In her sunroom studio, she doesn't wear an apron but quickly and artfully adds brown undertones to the blonde hair in each painting.

"Now, it looks like the girls." She steps back proudly. While she blows a nearby hair dryer on each area for a couple of minutes, I have to admit that, with a few perfectly placed brush strokes, the paintings now look just like my nieces. I shake my head. She certainly has a finely tuned artist's eye.

I hold the paintings while she pulls two large brown paper bags and colored ribbons from the entry closet. She wraps white tissue paper around each canvas before sliding it into the large gift bag. Then, she creatively ties a large pink ribbon to one and a purple ribbon to the other. She writes 'Happy birthday!' on blank cards, slides each into a white envelope, then writes each name on one before securing it to the ribbons on each bag.

"I'm ready to go," she declares.

74

SYLVIE

Pulling up to his parents' house, I see several cars and trucks in the long driveway and parked on the street. Stephen carries the two bags in one hand, and his other splays across the exposed skin at the small of my back, guiding me around the side of the house to the backyard where I spot piles of gifts and helium balloons decorating a long table.

Patio chairs surround tables filled with adults as teens and younger children play tag amongst the manicured landscaping and trees.

"They're here! They're here!" Two little girls, in matching green sundresses, sprint toward Stephen and me, yelling and flailing their arms. They freeze in front of us. "Mom said we could open gifts when you got here."

"Are those for us?" One niece points to the large bags in Stephen's hand.

He nods. "Sylvie, this is Hanna and Madeleine," he introduces, pointing to each twin. "Carry these to the gift table, please."

They instantly do what their uncle asks, looking at the names on the cards, exchanging bags, then hurrying to the table.

"Momma?" they call while making their way to the table. "We can open now; Uncle Stephen is here."

"Only one before we eat." Stephen's older sister, Hillary, waves excitedly in our direction.

"I wanna open this one," they state in unison, and I freeze.

"You'll get used to it," Stephens whispers near my ear.

I turn, unsure what he means.

Unleashed

"They talk together and have their own twin language," he smiles. "You'll learn to ignore it."

"Let Uncle Stephen and Sylvie find a seat before you open that," she yells to her daughters.

"Hurry, Uncle Stephen," one girl urges.

"Yes, hurry and sit down," the other girl orders.

He pulls out an empty patio chair for me, then plants himself in one beside me.

"Okay. One… Two… Three…" Stephen yells, and the girls untie the bow and reach for the large gift inside.

"Freeze!" their mom orders, and they obey. "Who's it from?"

"It's from them." They point at us.

"Nope," his sister states.

The girls shrug at each other and reach for the card.

"Read it out loud," their mom orders.

"It's from her." Both girls stare wide-eyed at me.

"Happy birthday," I cheer, wishing the attention back on the girls and off of me. Soon, they tear into the tissue paper.

"Oh…" they gasp.

"I love it. I love it. I love it!" Hanna spins in a circle, admiring the art, her arms fully extended. "I love butterflies," she states, stopping in front of me. "Uncle Stephen, did you tell her I love butterflies?"

He shakes his head.

"Then, how did you know?" Madeleine asks.

I simply shrug, no idea how I luckily labeled the gifts for the twins.

"Thank you," the other twin says on her way to the man standing by her mom.

Stephen's sister's voice raises an octave. "Sylvie, you painted these?" It's both a question and a statement.

I smile back at her.

"I showed her the girls' photo on my phone," Stephen explains. "Next thing I know, she pulls out two paintings." He catches his breath. "I thought they looked just like the girls, but she said she needed to fix something. She made a few colored strokes through their hair, and here they are. Perfect."

His sister scrutinizes his boasting and admiration before smiling in my direction. Apparently, she enjoys seeing Stephen like this.

"Sylvie are you a painter?" one twin asks.

"She's an artist," the other twin corrects.

I nod.

"Can you teach me how to paint?"

"Me, too? Me, too?"

Stephen answers for me. "On my next weekend off, we'll all go to Sylvie's house to paint."

His nieces cheer.

"Time to eat," an older gentleman calls.

"That's my dad, Gordon," Stephen states, pointing toward the grill where his dad waves. "Mom is at the food table." Again, he points. "Mom, turn around and say hi to Sylvie."

I wave to his mother then the rest of the family as he introduces me to them.

"Stephen, why don't you go help Dad set out the food?" his sister directs. "I'll keep Sylvie company."

I smile to let him know I'll be okay.

She wastes no time, getting right to the point. "I like seeing Stephen so happy. You're good for him."

"I don't know about that. We have a lot of fun together," I respond.

"Like I said, you make him happy." She squeezes me with one arm around my shoulders, then guides me through the patio doors to the large family inside.

EPILOGUE

Stephen

We found each other. In this crazy world somehow, we bumped into each other. Over and over, we bumped into each other. Fate, destiny, a higher power, or even blind luck, whatever it was that brought us together, I will be forever grateful.

We're not a traditional couple; that doesn't matter to us. We work. We fit. Others won't understand, for them our fourteen-year age difference is a non-starter. I have an old soul; she has a young heart. We work. They'll label her a cougar or Mrs. Robinson. Let them. We work. She's not a cougar she's my little minx.

It takes a strong woman to commit to a first responder. Not everyone can deal with the constant unknown, the danger, and the fear.

Sylvie is a pillar of strength. She assures me she can handle all that comes with my being an officer, and I'm starting to believe her. I feel myself letting her in, getting closer with each passing week. She's melding with my partner and my family. Our lives interlace; she's mine, and I'm hers. I was smart for keeping everything casual for years; it allowed me to be free when Sylvie slid into view. Little did I know, a noise complaint call on a warm, late-June night would forever change my life for the better.

UNCAGED

SLOTH

TRIGGER WARNINGS

Trigger warnings for my books are available on my website www.HaleyRhoades.com.

For more information on topics in Uncaged:

Post-Traumatic Stress Disorder: https://www.ptsd.va.gov/public/where-to-get-help.asp

Sexual Assault Hotline: https://www.rainn.org/about-national-sexual-assault-telephone-hotline

PART I

KRISTEN

1
KRISTEN

"So, Kristen, I saw Senator McGuire and his son Zane on the news today, leading a fundraiser for The Des Moines Police Department," Kendall's mother, Anne, informs, passing the green bean casserole to her husband on her right. "I'm surprised you didn't attend with him."

"Mom," Kendall draws out. "Don't pry."

"It's okay," I tell my best friend. "We're not seeing each other anymore," I tell Anne.

"They only went on two dates," Kendall tells her parents.

"He sent up red flags," I explain. "The alarm bells were so loud, I had to end it."

"See ya," Kendall says.

"Wouldn't want to be ya," we say in unison.

As we giggle, she extends her fist to bump mine.

"Well then, you two single girls enjoy the party tonight," her father, James, urges.

"Make good choices," Anne says, pointing her fork at each of us.

"Yes, ma'am," we respond in unison, giggling.

James and Anne are nearly perfect parents. They allow Kendall and me to come and go as if we live on campus, rarely asking questions, or prying into our lives. They've been open and honest in raising their only child, and continued with me, when I needed a place to stay to finish high school. They care deeply, trusting we will ask for guidance when we need it.

"How are classes going?" James attempts to change the subject.

Kendall answers, "Boring. What else would it be?" She rolls her eyes.

"And your math grade?" Anne teases, arching an eyebrow. "We can't have you retaking it next semester like I did my freshman year."

Kendall shakes her head, while the three of us chuckle at the long-time running joke. Kendall takes after her mother in the math department. Instead of answering, she shoves a large bite of steak into her mouth in hopes of ending the conversation.

"Kristen, I hope you're helping her with math assignments." Anne points her fork at her daughter. "You have to pass math to graduate, so let her tutor you."

"It's calculus, not math," Kendall spits, a hint of venom lacing her words.

James' eyes meet mine in silent question of the reason his daughter isn't laughing with us. I shrug apologetically.

"We're on top of it," I assure Anne, hoping to put an end to the topic once and for all.

Tension floats from the dining room, as we consume our meal, family-style as we do most nights in the Ward house.

"So, where is this party tonight?" I ask.

"About that…" Kendall starts, putting the car in park.

Oh, no! It's not good when she's this secretive. When will I learn not to follow her blindly into messes?

"We're here," she states.

I exit the car, noting the street signs signal we are near the Drake University Campus.

"Details, please," I order, hands on my hips.

"It's a Tau Kappa Epsilon fundraiser for the Des Moines Police Department's Shop with a Cop," Kendall informs.

Where have I heard those words lately? Tau Kappa Epsilon. Tau Kappa Epsilon. FUCK!

"Nope." I shake my head sternly. "No way." I glare at her. "He's in town today, and the local branch of his frat is also hosting a law enforcement fundraiser. That means he will be here." I'm still shaking my head, arms crossed over my chest, feet planted firmly on the sidewalk.

Uncaged

"We don't know that," Kendall argues. "Frats don't send a notice to the other chapters every time they plan a party. Anyway, the Drake chapter is probably below him." Her hands on her hips, lips pursed, she's trying her best to convince me.

She places her hands together in front of her chest, begging, "Plleeaasse. Pretty, pretty please."

I roll my eyes. "Fine, but you owe me big for this one."

She hops up and down, clapping, a large grin on her face. She tucks her arm in mine, a spring in her step as we head down the block.

I hear the music as we round the corner. Two doors down, I spot a short line already formed. *I guess it's not a small fundraiser, then. Great.* Mentally, I prepare myself for the crowd and the chance I might bump into Zane again tonight.

Beside me, Kendall fluffs her hair and straightens her tank top when we take our place at the end of the line. I crane my head to the left toward the front of the line, finding we are third in line from the pay station. Sitting at the table, collecting money and marking hands, is the hot guy Kendall's been cyber stalking all week. I shake my head. I guess now I know why we are here.

As we step forward, I nervously straighten the straps of *my* halter top. Well, it's not my halter top; Kendall insisted I wear it tonight. I don't prefer revealing clothes like this. I detest the birthmark below my right shoulder blade and strive to cover it at all times.

It could be worse; it could be a large black mole with dark hairs. Instead, it's a faint red, L-shaped mark on my otherwise perfectly smooth, olive skin. My mother bragged that we had identical marks that proved how alike we were. Along with her brown eyes and brunette hair, these were the only similarities between us. I've taken great strides to make sure I'm nothing like her.

Focusing my mind on the present, beside me, Kendall smooths bright red gloss upon her lips then urges me to "apply my sparkle."

I try not to sparkle. Standing out is not my goal. I pull my lip gloss from my pocket, applying it as prompted. "I shine; you sparkle," I remind her, causing Kendall to giggle.

The line moves once again, and Kendall eagerly faces the table.

"Hi," she greets, a sweet smile upon her face, fluttering her eyes at Stephen.

"Hey," he returns, his outstretched hand freezing mid-air. "Uh... I didn't know you were a twin." A wide smirk grows upon his lips.

"We're not," I correct.

"We get confused for sisters all the time," Kendall giggles, twirling a stray hair between two fingers. "This is my best friend Kristen, I told you about."

He nods, taking our cash. "I'm glad you made it." Now, he stamps a blue heart on the back of our hands.

"Wwweeelll," Kendall draws out flirtatiously, "you made it sound like the place to be, so we couldn't resist."

She tosses her long, soft, brunette waves over her shoulder. I may be wrong, but it looks like Stephen is smitten with her. *Cool.*

"You ladies have fun," he says, motioning us to the entrance. "But not too much fun before I join you." He says the last part under his breath.

And there it is, confirmation he's into my friend.

Kendall links her arm through mine, and we climb the four wide steps onto the porch. She glances over her shoulder, giving a flirty wave as we step through the door. While she drags me to the beverage table, I scan the room and sigh an easy breath, not seeing Zane McGuire.

2

KRISTEN

Two beers in, Kendall and I occupy the center of the makeshift dance floor. Even with the windows and front door open, the large room is much too warm, and our dance moves further heat our bodies.

"I need a drink," I inform her, my mouth near her ear, voice raised.

"Wait until this song ends," she pleads.

Of course, I wait. I don't want to walk through the large crowd alone. We operate as each other's wing-women and vowed long ago never to leave one another alone in these settings; girls can't be too careful. Minutes pass, and the song ends.

"Drink time," She sing-songs. Turning, Kendall runs right into Stephen's chest with an "Umph."

"Are you alright?" he asks, embarrassed his approach lacked finesse.

She nods, mesmerized by his concerned gaze. "We're…uh…" She stammers.

Coming to her rescue, I loudly state, "We're getting drinks."

He nods then leads the way, parting the crowd for us.

Kendall looks at me, mouthing, "Oh, my god!"

I roll my eyes.

Stephen steps aside, signaling with his arm for us to approach the table.

"So chivalrous," Kendall flirts, placing her palm on his chest.

"What will it be?" the frat guy behind the bar asks.

"Two Bud Lights," I reply.

"Make it three," Stephen states loudly. "Looks like you're having fun." He juts his chin toward the dance floor.

"We were, but it's too hot to dance now," she says while she stands on her toes, her lips near his ear as both her hands press on his pectorals.

She's pouring it on so thick that there's no way he's missing her signals; she knows what she wants.

I avert my eyes from the two of them. Leaning my hip against the table, once again, I scan our surroundings. This party is nearly standing room only. Kudos to the frat for a successful fundraiser. Glancing to my right, I freeze when my eyes meet Zane's. A heavy lump clogs my throat. Before I look away, he lifts his chin, smiling, making sure I know he sees us.

I place my hand on Kendall's shoulder. "Bathroom. Now." My tone leaves no room for argument.

Her eyes widen at my glare. My pale face, large eyes, and tight mouth put her on high alert. My body chooses flight, not fight; I leave immediately. Stephen must understand my reaction; he again parts the crowd, easing our escape to the bathroom.

"I'll stand watch," he promises, leaning on the doorframe.

That gives me some comfort. At least Zane can't follow us in here.

"He's here," I whisper to her from the sink. I cup cold water in my hands then slurp it in an effort to remedy my dry throat.

"So what?" Kendall attempts to brush off my anxiety. "It's a crowded party. We'll just stay on opposite sides of the room."

"You really think it's that easy?" I scoff. "I can't explain it because I can't put a finger on it. There's something wrong with him—something…scary. Although he hasn't shown me a reason, my instincts tell me it's there." I'm interrupted by raised male voices outside the bathroom door.

Kendall runs over to ensure the door is locked.

"Is she in there?" Zane's familiar voice can be heard through the door.

"The ladies are in the bathroom," Stephen states.

"Move," Zane orders.

"Dude, it's a women's restroom at the moment."

"I'm not repeating myself," Zane bites.

"Then you'll have to go through me," Stephen challenges.

"And us." Male voices I don't recognize join in.

I plaster my back to the door, place my hand upon my chest, and attempt to slow my rapid breathing. Fear fires from every cell while my rapid heartbeat threatens to break my ribs.

"I'm overreacting; I've only been on two dates with Zane. Based only on a feeling, my reactions are irrational, right?" I whisper, my eyes wide, nodding my head in hopes Kendall agrees with me.

"Hey," Kendall's low voice calls to me.

My rapid, shallow breaths and fearful face cause her protective instincts to kick in. She wets a nearby paper towel then presses it upon my brow, cheeks, and the back of my neck.

"Hold this," she murmurs as loud male conversation continues outside the door. She raises my right hand, urging me to hold the cold compress to my neck.

"Did he..." Her words choke her, and horror envelops her entire body.

I tilt my head to the side. "Did he? Did he what?"

"Did he hurt you." she murmurs. It's a statement, not a question.

I vehemently shake my head. "No." My raspy voice cracks. "He just gave me a bad feeling." I quirk my mouth, raising my brow. "My skin prickles at just the mention of his name." I shake my head, peeling myself from the door. "I must be out of my mind."

Kendall wraps her arm around my shoulders. "You have good instincts. If he gives you a bad feeling, you need to heed the warning signs," she agrees. "Why don't I pop my head out to see if the guys can escort him away, then we will leave? I'll have someone walk us all the way to the car."

"I can't see him," my shaky voice squeaks.

I move, and she nods before clasping the door handle. Kendall knocks, states she's coming out, then attempts to squeeze through the barely opened crack.

Moments later, Kendall peeks her head back into the bathroom. "All clear," she promises. "Stephen escorted him personally to his car. He's no longer here, and thanks to several of Stephen's frat brothers, I don't think he will bother you again."

She smiles proudly, taking my hand and pulling me into the crowded hallway.

I whisper, "I'm so embarrassed to see a line of women while I selfishly hid in the bathroom." I mouth, "I'm sorry," as Kendall continues pulling me toward the front room.

3

KRISTEN

I plant my feet firmly, signaling for Kendall's attention. The crowd grew while we secluded ourselves, and the volume rose, too.

"With the threat of Zane gone, I owe you more time with Stephen. After all, it's the reason you chose to attend tonight." I attempt to make light of the situation.

I tilt my head toward the beverage station. Her pinched face gives me the giggles. Mere inches from her, I raise my voice, "Let's get a drink and stay a bit longer."

"Yeah?" Concern covers her brow and thins her lips.

"Yeah. He's gone. No need for us to leave," I suggest. "I can stay a bit longer."

Her wide smile ensures I've made her a very happy girl.

"Besides, I owe Stephen for standing guard for me," I offer.

"For both of us," Kendall grins. "Where is my knight in shining armor?" She cranes her neck, leaning forward and back in an attempt to find him.

"Who are you looking for?" he asks, startling Kendall from behind.

Giggles erupt from me again, and I place my hand over my mouth. She glares in my direction, ensuring my giggles continue.

"Need an escort to your car?" he offers, still concerned for me.

"Actually, I'd like to buy you a drink for protecting the two of us," Kendall states.

"Ah, that's sweet." He smiles at us. "But my drinks are free." He shrugs his shoulders sheepishly. "Let me fetch you drinks," he offers. "What will it be?"

"I can't allow you to get our drinks. We owe you," I remind him.

"I'll take a dance as repayment." He smirks first at me then hopefully towards Kendall.

"I'd love to dance," she quickly responds.

When they look my way, I raise my palms in front of me. "I'm fine. I can get my own drink. Go have fun." I point in the direction of the crowded bodies moving to the music.

They continue gracing me with their concern.

"Go, I said!" My raised voice sparks them into motion.

Her hand in his, they quickly disappear among the crowd. I watch from a distance, finding Kendall craning her neck in my direction as I order a drink. Then I find myself an open section of the wall near a corner to lean.

Several songs later, I join Stephen and Kendall on the dance floor for one song. I feel like a third wheel when I join them; they're clearly moving past the friendship stage. Uncomfortable, I excuse myself to get a drink before returning to my role as voyeur of the festivities.

Drink in hand, I slowly scan the room. Several soap operas play out before me. Girls argue and compete for attention from the same guys, men attempt feats of strength and stupidity with alcohol as their copilot, and couples make out—even if just for the night.

The stale air and excess bodies heat the entire first floor. I decide to step onto the back porch for some fresh air. What little beer was left in my cup falls to the floor when bodies collide with mine as I attempt to maneuver my way outside. There are too many people here. *They've definitely not abided by the fire marshal's warning for capacity.*

I breathe deeply, drawing in my first breath of the cool evening air. Although a small crowd lingers on the porch, with the fresh air and open sky, I feel free. I seat myself on the railing, opposite the gathered crowd, then flip my legs over, spinning around, my back facing the house.

Before me, kegs surrounded by a melting ice bath sit in kiddy pools and trash barrels. Red and blue plastic cups overflow two large trash barrels and litter the lawn. I choose to keep my eyes skyward. A few bright stars shine in the dark sky despite the bright lights of the city.

I'm not sure how long I lose myself in the night sky. Looking over my shoulder, I realize everyone went back into the party. Spotting a cigar still burning in the ashtray on the rail, I swing my legs over the railing, stomping over to extinguish it before the entire frat house burns down. *Seriously, some people are so rude.*

Deciding it's time I rejoin Kendall and the party, I turn toward the back door.

Thump.

Mentally off kilter from running right into a guy and needing to apologize, slowly, I lift my eyes from my hands flat on his chest to meet familiar eyes.

Ice freezes in my veins as burning fire climbs my throat. My mouth opens, but I can't call for help; I can't breathe.

"Careful," his deep baritone voice warns. "You look unsteady. Let me help you."

I shake my head as his arm behind my shoulders forces me forward with him —at his command. A cough escapes before I draw in much-needed air. My lungs burn as I attempt to pull in ragged breaths.

"There's a bench over here," he informs and strongly ushers me in that direction.

Every part of me fights him until, with a cloth to my mouth and nose, my brain grows foggy before my world turns black.

My throat and mouth sting while a heavy hammer pounds in my head. I faintly remember a sweet smell...

Zane! Zane was there! Zane put something over my mouth. I bolt upright; my head protests the movement. I wobble a bit, my eyelids blinking rapidly due to the fluorescent lights above me. I shield my eyes with my right hand and slowly look around the room.

Where am I?

I'm sitting on a bed, positioned against a wooden plank wall. My eyes follow the lines in the wood around the small rectangular room. In the corner hangs a camera, and next to the bed sits a small desk and chair. Two small shelves of books

Uncaged

hang on the wall above it. The opposite end of the room sports a weight set, stationary bike, and what looks to be a tanning bed. As I stand, I find my bare feet on an area rug, while the rest of the room is hardwood floors.

I've never been here and haven't seen this room in photos. All the wood gives it a cabin feel, minus the windows.

Crap! There are no windows.

I scan the room again to find no computer, no TV, and just one door. Slowly, I step towards it, knowing it will be locked. Each baby step brings me closer and closer to the reality I already know deep in my bones.

I take in a deep breath and release it while counting to ten. Inch by inch, I extend my right hand, closer and closer to the silver handle. Turning the knob, tears fill my eyes and dread weighs me down. My hand connects with the cold metal. Tears fill my eyes, as the horror sets in.

I'm his prisoner. I'm his hostage in this little room. There must be a way out. I'll bide my time.

I will find a way to escape.

4

KRISTEN

I run.

I run despite the pain of my bare feet on the rocks of the road below.

I run despite the fact I don't know where I am or where I'm heading.

I run to escape him.

I run toward safety.

I run in hopes that my nightmare is over.

There are no street lights, no signs, no houses. It's a cloudy night, so the moonlight and stars can't guide me.

I run because my life depends upon it.

My lungs burn, and I struggle to breathe; but I don't stop. *I can't stop*. I'd rather die out here than return to Zane's psycho Stepford-wife playroom.

Ahead, I see a light. It's a distant light. I'm not sure if it's reality or if my eyes are playing tricks on me. A glimmer of hope sparks within me; I continue through the pain.

I look over my shoulder. Not finding I'm being followed, the glimmer becomes a flame. *I can do this*. I run, and I run. The light becomes street lights that lead me to a tiny town and a gas station at its edge.

Please be open. Please be open, I chant as I race toward the door. It doesn't budge. Peering through my hands pressed to the glass, I find no one inside. I move from window to window in hopes of finding someone or a way inside. Back at the front entrance, succumbing to exhaustion, I slump, my hands on my knees as my lungs demand more oxygen and my side aches for rest.

Uncaged

I lift my head at the sound of a vehicle approaching. *It's him! He's found me!* I turn to hide then realize the noise is coming from the opposite way I ran from. It's coming from the town.

I will my bleeding feet to move me toward the road and thus the noise. *I need help. I need them to stop.* Standing in the middle of the road, waving my arms frantically, I will them to stop.

"What the heck?" An old man sticks his head through the driver's window of an old blue pickup truck. "You're gonna get yourself killed. Get out of the road."

Slowly, I approach, my mind scrambling for words to explain my situation.

"Do you..." My voice cracks. It sounds so small. "Do you have a phone I can borrow?"

I wait as his eyes take me in from head to toe. I'm sure I look like a runaway, a drug addict, or maybe something worse.

He turns on his hazard lights, mumbling. His door creaks, groaning in protest as he forces it open. He flips his cell phone open then extends it to me.

"Thank you," I respond. "Where are we?" I swivel my head, taking in our surroundings.

"This is Harford," he answers, brows furrowing even more.

"Hop in. I'll give you a ride," he urges. "You don't live around here, do you?"

I shake my head no—no to the ride *and* no to living nearby. My shaking fingers struggle to press the tiny numbers.

"Please answer. Please answer," I chant out loud.

"Hello?" Her sweet voice is my savior.

I hurry to speak, unsure how much time I have before Zane finds me. "Kendall, it's me. I need a ride."

"Kristen? Is it really you?" Her voice breaks. "What the hell? Where've you been?" Though she's shouting, I hear the tears and fear in her voice. My friend starts a tirade about my not checking in and expresses worry over my disappearance for weeks.

"Shut up!" my scream interrupts her blubbering.

My best friend grows silent.

"I'm at a gas station at the edge of Hartford on Highway 5. I need you to come pick me up. I'm in danger. I'll hide until you pull up. If the coast is clear, honk three times."

I realize my plan sounds crazy. The man standing in front of me and my friend on the phone have no idea how crazy my life has been these past weeks.

"I can wait with you," the older man offers.

"Someone's after me," I explain while shaking my head, his phone still at my ear. "If he comes this way, he will find me. I need to be alone, and I need to hide." I return my attention to the call. "Kendall, just hurry and get here. Remember to honk…"

She interrupts. "Three times. I've got it. I'm already pulling away from my driveway. GPS says I'll be there in 20 minutes."

"Okay. I'm giving this guy back his phone. You won't be able to talk to me until you arrive," I remind her.

I close the phone, extending it to the kind man.

"I don't feel right leaving you here." He looks down the road in both directions. "What kind of trouble are you in?"

"I'm sorry. I can't explain." I raise my eyes to meet his. "Trust me; he's powerful, and you won't be safe if he finds me with you. Please go. My friend will be here soon. I'll be okay." I wrap my bare arms over my abdomen, willing my words to be true.

"Hop in the truck. I'll take you to my place. You'll be safe there until your friend and the sheriff arrive."

"I can't," I explain, head shaking adamantly.

I can't put him in danger. I can't because I can't trust him. I won't trust him. His rusty truck from the 70s and aged flip phone lead me to believe he's a gentle old grandpa, but I can't let my guard down.

Reluctantly, he returns to the driver's seat. "My house is two blocks ahead then turn right, first house on the left. The key is under the mat. I hope you'll go there and be safe. Use my landline to call the sheriff. You're not safe out here."

I force a small smile. "Thank you for your help. I'll be okay."

I hope I'll be okay.

I don't hang around to watch him leave. I scurry around the side of the building, and when I hear his truck drive away, I duck inside a stack of three old tires. My ears on hyper-alert, I wait for Kendall to rescue me; she's the only one that can.

Minutes pass slowly. I listen as another vehicle drives by. I can't make out the direction, but it definitely doesn't stop. I jump and a small gasp escapes when a dog begins barking nearby. *What's he barking at? Is Zane nearby, looking for me?*

I beg my racing heart to be still. I need to listen. I must hear everything in case I need to flee.

A twig breaks immediately to my right. My hand covers my mouth to ensure I remain quiet. Someone or something is close. The sound of the gravel crushing under a step draws near. I suddenly realize climbing out of the center of the tires will impede my getaway. *I didn't think this through.*

"Kristen?" A whisper calls my name. "Kristen, I'm here."

It's Kendall. Although it sounds like her, after weeks, part of me worries my brain might be deceiving me.

"Ffuucckk… I was supposed to honk," she berates herself quietly.

"Kendall?" I murmur. "Is it really you?"

My best friend, my rescuer, peers down at me. I want to cheer, throw myself into her arms and celebrate. I can't; I'm still in danger. I won't be safe until I'm with her parents.

"Shh," I order as I climb from the tires. It's not an easy task. My legs and feet feel numb from crouching so long. "Follow me and stay quiet," I instruct, taking her hand.

I walk us slowly around the building. I freeze, peeking around the corner, looking for Zane in every shadow. I tell myself I must take a chance and run to the SUV ten feet from us. I look back to my friend.

"When I take off, run fast, get in the car, and lock the doors," I order before I sprint to the passenger side of her vehicle.

While running, Kendall presses the button. I hear the *beep-beep*, unlocking the vehicle. I close my door seconds before she closes hers and flicks the lock. I want to breathe a sigh of relief, but there's no time.

"Get me out of here!" I don't mean to yell; it's my adrenaline. "Go! Go! Go!"

5

KRISTEN

Kendall doesn't look my way. She doesn't chastise me for yelling. Instead, she immediately pulls onto the street, driving me from Hartford, away from the hell Zane put me through. Minutes pass before either of us speak.

"I'm so glad you are okay," Kendall informs me, her right hand taking mine.

"Thank you for rescuing me," I counter.

"Where are we going?" she asks, her eyes never leaving the highway.

"Take me to your parents," I urge. "They'll know what I should do."

Kendall peels her eyes from the road to look at me for a moment. She squeezes my hand in hers. "What happened?" I hear her attempt to swallow the lump in her throat.

"I'll share everything," I promise. "Just get me to your parents."

I lean my head against the passenger window, closing my eyes, safety finally wrapping tightly around me.

"Umm…" Kendall lets go of my hand, needing both of hers on the steering wheel. "Could someone be following us?"

I turn my head to look out the back window.

"I'm going 70, and those headlights are approaching fast." She states the obvious.

"It's Zane! Don't let him catch us," I order.

I'm thrown back in my bucket seat when Kendall pushes the gas pedal to the floor.

"Hang on!" she yells seconds before the vehicle makes contact with the back of our SUV.

It happens so fast. Kendall screams; we swerve into the oncoming lane and off the side of the road. She tries her best to steer the vehicle as it bounces on the uneven hillside. She swerves to miss a tree on the left then the right. My stomach turns as we are airborne.

My head hurts. I've felt this before. I groan through the pain as I raise my hand to my forehead. It's wet. My fingertips slip over my wet brow, and I struggle to open my heavy eyes.

It's dark save for the headlights in the tall weeds at the front of us. *Car. I'm still in the SUV.* I turn my head despite the pain. The vacant seat beside me sparks my mind to life. I take in all of my surroundings, looking for my friend and to find a way to get to her.

The vehicle lays on its side, the windows shattered and airbags deployed. I open my mouth to call for my friend.

Excruciating pain throbs on the side of my face. All I can manage is a gurgle; I clear my throat to try again.

"K…" I attempt to call. On a scale of ten, my jaw pain is a ten. "K…!" I force out, enduring the pain to save my friend.

My shaking hands fumble with the release button on the seatbelt. I press and press but nothing happens. Finally, I look down, focus my attention, then unfasten my seatbelt.

I glance to the empty seat beside me. The belt isn't secured; the buckle is intact. I wonder if she forgot to buckle hers. There's no time to sit and think; I must find her.

I maneuver my legs onto the door, then using the dash and seat, I stand up to grab the opposite door at the top. I slowly climb out, crunching glass with every move. I sit atop the wreck, craning my neck, trying to locate her. It's dark, even in front of the car. The weeds and trees block the headlights from shedding any light.

I look up the hillside for Zane. Afraid he might hear me, I decide not to make more noise. If he doesn't see or hear us, maybe he'll leave. I know without a doubt Zane caused our wreck; he ran us off the road.

I hop down from the wreck, pain shooting from my feet, my ankles, and my hips; the pain is everywhere. *I must keep moving.* My feet tangle, and I fall. Unable to see, I allow my hands to unravel the purse strap from my ankle, then slip it over my head on one shoulder. With great pain, I stand again, sliding my feet through the ground cover in search of my friend.

My pounding head fogs as I force my body to keep moving. I can't find her; I need help. *Cell phone.* I shoot a quick prayer to heaven before I dip my right hand into the purse. When I find a smooth rectangle, I breathe a sigh of relief. I fumble a bit but manage to punch the numbers 9-1-1.

I'm trying to curb the pain when the dispatcher answers. Through gritted teeth, I share, "I've been in a wreck."

"Where?" he asks.

"I don't know," I sob, barely able to move my jaw and not scream due to pain. I continue to garble, "We left Hartford, headed to Des Moines on Highway 5. We drove for a few minutes. I don't know where I am."

"Can you describe what you see?" he prompts.

"I can't find my friend," I cry. "She's not in the car, and I can't see her."

"What's your name?" he asks.

"I need to find her!" I wail through severe pain.

"Okay. An ambulance and officers are on their way to you," he states calmly. "Look around. What do you see?"

"Hill," I answer through gritted teeth. "Off the road, down…"

"Can you see the road above?"

"No… Her… Anything…" I grit out.

"Listen for a moment," he instructs. "What can you hear?"

"Popping," I mumble. *Why does my jaw hurt so much?*

"Are there any flames?" he quickly asks.

"No." I turn my head in the opposite direction of the car. "Sirens!" I scream through my pain.

"Good. I'll let them know they are getting close to you," he states.

"Where is she?" I cry as my world grows dark and my eyes close.

PART II

KENDALL

6

KRISTEN

Bright lights. Too bright.

No. No. Zane found me.

"No!" I attempt to shout, but my mouth won't open.

Despite my fear, I open my eyes. The lights are too bright. I try to cover my eyes, but my heavy arms won't budge.

Where am I? Why can't I move? My eyes struggle to remain open long enough for me to assess my surroundings.

"Easy." A female voice calms me.

I turn my head slowly toward her voice, blinking. She stands in royal blue scrubs, a stethoscope around her neck.

"Hosp…" My jaws refuse to move; the pain is too much. I try to bring my hand to my throat, but again, it won't raise.

"Yes, honey, you are in the hospital," she soothes, patting my left forearm. "We had to wire your jaw shut."

I close my eyes tightly to avoid the pity I spy in her eyes.

"My arms?" I hum more than say.

"Your right arm is in a cast," she informs while looking at the monitor beeping near me. "Your left shoulder was dislocated, and that arm has your IV in it."

She turns her gaze to me, smiling. "Can you tell me your name?"

"My friend?" I groan, ignoring her question.

The door to my hospital room bursts open.

"Ah. Your parents are here," the nurse informs.

I begin to argue, but my head pounds, my body aches, and tears burn my sinuses as they charge to my side.

"I'm so sorry…" I attempt through a sob.

"Shh," the nurse soothes.

I feel arms on mine, large warm hands rubbing, and the darkness pulls me under.

"Her vitals are improving, her MRI shows no brain swelling, and we've lowered her pain medications," a deep male voice states. "I've instructed the nurses to administer pain medicine when she requests it. She will be in and out of sleep as her body attempts to recover from the trauma."

"She's sleeping so much," a familiar motherly voice states.

I want to get her attention; I need them to look at me, but my throat is so dry it hurts. I squeeze my eyes shut tightly and grunt. Opening them again, four pairs of eyes fly toward me. They scurry to the sides of my hospital bed.

"Good. You're awake," the older doctor greets. "I've updated your parents. I'll have the nurse take your vitals, and I'll visit you next during my evening rounds." With that statement, he exits through the open door.

"Find her?" I grunt. At their confused expressions, I repeat myself, painfully annunciating each word through my clenched teeth. "Find her?"

Ever the mother, Anne's teary eyes seek her husband's assistance.

He shakes his head. "She didn't make it," he murmurs, wrapping my left hand in his.

"Find her?" I grunt as I cry.

"Yes. They found her," he shares. "She was thrown from the vehicle as it rolled down the hill."

I look from him to her; I can't believe they don't blame me for killing her. They seem to be handling Kendall's death relatively well.

My stomach plummets, my head clouds, and I fight to open my eyes after each blink.

"Sweetheart," she coos beside me with tear-filled eyes.

James wraps an arm around his wife's shoulders, places a peck upon her temple, and smiles in my directions. His eyes are bloodshot and his jaws unshaven. They both look weary.

Try as I might, I can't stay awake.

Uncaged

I force my eyes to open against the pain and oppressive overhead lights.

"Hey there," a smiling woman greets. "My name is Kiera; I'll be your nurse," the beautiful blonde woman, now in Kelly green scrubs, informs me. "On a scale of one to ten, how would you rate your pain?" She smiles down at me from the right side of my hospital bed.

Again, I try to move my mouth to speak, but it won't budge; I swallow a large gulp.

"Here." Nurse Kiera holds a large plastic mug with the hospital logo and a flexible straw near my lips. "Take one small sip," she instructs.

I nod and comply. The cool water feels divine. I quell my urge to guzzle and stop after one sip, following her instructions.

I hold up seven fingers as I grunt, "Seven."

"Okay. Now, one more small sip." She offers the straw once again.

I take a longer pull of water this time.

"Easy. We don't want your stomach to revolt. You have a lot of pain medications in your system. We will slowly increase your water and then introduce food." Kiera taps the screen on a nearby tablet, entering my information.

"Is pain at a seven tolerable? Or would you like more medication?" she asks, eyes back on me.

How do I answer when my mouth won't move? Looking down at my hand, I form an okay sign with my fingers, displaying them to her on top of my covers.

"If that changes or your pain worsens, ask your parents to page the nurses' station." Kiera nods at me then shifts her eyes. "Anne and James, be sure to page me if she doesn't."

When they nod, the nurse continues. "She needs to sip slowly for the next 15 minutes," she orders. "I'll pop back by in a half hour unless you need me sooner." Kiera exits the room, following the path of the doctor before her.

I want details; I need answers. I'm so tired. I try to keep my heavy lids open but fail in my attempts. Warm darkness envelopes me.

"Your mom's fit to be tied, worrying about brain swelling and other horrible injuries." I look from James to Anne and back, confused. "So glad you're awake." He grins.

"Stop that," Anne chastises him. "The doctor just reported your MRI results show no swelling." Her hand covers her mouth when a hiccupping sob escapes.

I attempt to lift my heavy head to assess my injuries without any luck.

"Just a minute," he prompts. "They said we could raise your head up a bit. Just let…me…remember how they did it."

"Here. Let me," Anne states.

"I've got it." James swats her hand away from the large bed remote in his hand. "See…"

The motor grinds lowly as the top portion of my hospital bed rises. With every inch, the movement sends pain from my limbs and abdomen. At my wince, he removes his finger from the up button.

"Oh, dear," Anne cries. "You need more pain medicine. I knew you were trying to be brave."

He interrupts her. "Want me to lower it back down?"

I shake my head, immediately regretting it. The room spins as the pounding inside increases and my stomach roils. I squint my eyes and will my inner turmoil to settle.

"I'm paging the nurse," she states.

I grunt loudly, barely shaking my head.

Four eyes attempt to assess my sincerity or bravery.

Anne returns to her chair on my left, while James stands beside her.

"Your left shoulder was dislocated; the doctor already reset it." He lifts his chin toward my side. "You'll be in a sling for a while."

I want to nod but think better of it. Instead, I attempt a smile.

"Your right wrist was broken. They reset it in surgery, and you have a cast." He looks in its direction. "You'll let your old dad be the first to place graffiti on it, won't you?"

"Not…" I moan through clenched teeth. "Kiss-then," I mumble, frustrated I can't communicate. I need to tell them, I'm not Kendall.

I attempt to speak again through pain and clenched teeth. Instead I plummet into darkness.

7

KRISTEN

I nod my chin toward the water glass; my throat feels more normal with every sip.

Anne rushes to my right side and the water mug on the table. My eyes widen at her urgency, and James chuckles.

"It's been killing her not to tend to you," he shares through a smile. "The nurses had to get the doctor to make your mom sit still and let them work."

I shift my gaze to her as she stands on my right now. I grace her with what I hope is a small grin.

"Your spleen ruptured, so they rushed you straight to surgery," her tearful voice informs. "You broke your jaw; they have wired it shut."

"Other than that," he continues as she attempts to quell her sobs, "you have a couple of cracked ribs and a sprained ankle."

"And stitches," she adds between her sobs.

"Right," he remembers. "You had several cuts on the soles of your feet. One of them was so long, they had to put in four stitches to close it."

My lips in a pucker, I open and close them to signal her as she still holds the cup in her hand.

"But the nurse…" she argues.

"Anne, give the girl her water," James urges. "If she feels queasy, she'll stop drinking."

She shoots a death-stare at her husband.

I scrunch my brows, begging please, and she complies. She forces a small smile as I swallow the cool sip. *How can I be this tired?* I'm only sipping water, and I already feel the need to rest.

My body doesn't hurt as much this time when I open my eyes.

"Water," I groan, looking towards the cup. I hope they understand me.

James rises from his chair, lifting the water to my lips.

"Do you need more pain meds?" he asks, placing my mug of water back on the side table.

I shake my head; it doesn't pound. As for my other injuries, I feel all of them. Tears fill my eyes.

"I'll call the nurse," he offers.

"No," I attempt to argue, shaking my head.

He nods. I watch his Adam's apple bob as he swallows hard.

"I'm not…" I moan, frustrated I can't open my mouth.

"Kendall," his stern voice interrupts. "I want to talk to you before your mom comes back. We don't need the details. Right now all we need is for you to rest and heal. You're safe; that's all that matters. I think your mom will need a couple of days before she can bare to hear everything. Your mom's been through enough with the wreck. I don't think she could cope with anymore. Understand?"

I tilt my head, my eyes assessing his.

"She's struggling to mourn the loss of Kristen. I had to push her out the door to visit the chapel and fetch more coffee." He draws in a long breath. "I think it's best if we do what we can and not make it worse," he states matter-of-factly. "Should I page the nurse? She wanted to talk to you about drinking your food since your jaw is wired shut."

I shake my head, still trying to process his words. *Safe.* His words hang heavy in the sterile air. *I'm safe.* They think I'm Kendall. *I'm safe.* He knows Anne better than me. He knows what's best for her. *If Zane thinks I'm dead, I'll be safe.* My mind reels.

"You've not eaten in three days," he informs.

Three days. I've been in the hospital for three days. Zane? Bile crawls up my throat, my stomach hard as a rock. I feel tears threaten to fall.

Recognizing the fear on my face, he shares, "I assume Kristen's Zane was involved."

He knows.

I nod.

"He hasn't been here, and we've not heard anything," he promises. "I won't let him near you." He gently rubs my forearm. "You are safe." His hand squeezes as his eyes implore me to believe him—to trust him.

I nod unable to speak.

"When you are ready, you can tell me all about it," he states. "I'll do everything in my power to keep you safe. It's a *dad's* job, after all." He winks at me.

"She's dead!" I attempt to scream, jarring awake but it is muffled. I'm sure they can't understand. "She's dead, and I'm to blame!"

I'm propped up on too many pillows in my hospital bed, my jaw wired shut, the pain excruciating. My eyes beg the two of them to forgive me. I can't lose them; I've just lost my best friend—my sister. I need to move my jaw; I need to make them hear me.

"Shhh," Anne soothes from my bedside.

Her bloodshot eyes shed tears. They are the tears of helplessness as I'm in pain. My eyes implore her to see.

"Kristen!" my restrained voice garbles. "Kristen!"

She nods, but she doesn't understand. She can't understand. I move my focus toward the defeated man at the door. His exhausted eyes, bloodshot, barely look at mine before falling toward the floor. *Why won't he lock eyes with me? Is it because he can't or won't? Does he blame me?*

The most painful tears I've ever experienced fill my eyes. My nose, cheeks, and jaws throb as warm tears stream over them. I attempt to refrain from blinking, losing the battle. The water blurs my vision, and instinctually, my lids move, emitting even more pain. I glance down at the IV in the back of my hand. Surely pain meds flow through the clear tubes. *More. I need more; this pain is too much.*

"Hurt," I attempt to convey.

Even I can't understand my word. I need to write it. I raise my right arm only an inch, signaling the motion of writing with my fingers. The heavy cast does nothing to prevent the pain of my movement. I release an exasperated growl.

He looks at me, nods, then moves to a nearby closet. Swinging my eyes toward

Anne, who is still seated, I find she's lost her ability to hold back her sobs. *Perhaps it's just now hitting her.* I close my eyes, praying he comforts her.

The sounds of medical machines assure me they monitor my vitals for several long moments as the sound of muffled sobs tear at my heart.

James returns to my side, iPad in hand. He quirks his mouth to one side. It's not a smile but a sign he hopes he's helping. I'm sure helplessness overwhelms him.

"You're awake," a nurse greets, peppy smile upon her face, scurrying into my room to my bedside. "How's your pain?"

"Humph." I attempt to convey it is excruciating.

"Let's type on the iPad," she suggests, and I nod. "On a scale of one to ten, is it above a five?"

I nod, even though it feels like my brain ricochets off my skull with the movement.

"Type instead of nodding," she reminds me before continuing her inquisition. "On a scale of one to ten, ten being highest, what's the pain?"

I type the number nine.

Her eyes remain glued to my face, assessing my honesty.

She steps closer to my IV stand, pressing buttons with her thumb. "This will help, and you should feel it within a minute or two."

Her free hand reaches out to soothe me, pausing inches above my forearm so as not to cause more pain. She makes her way to the computer terminal mounted on the wall near the sink. She scans her card then enters my vitals from the plethora of machines surrounding the head of my bed.

"How's the pain now?" Anne asks from her seat at my side.

I will my sluggish brain to process her words, blinking my eyes. Darkness envelops me; the pain meds pull me under.

8

KRISTEN

"Run!" I will my trembling legs to carry me far away from this hell hole.

"Run!" I scream, begging my bleeding feet to find purchase on the gravel beneath them.

I can't fall. I won't be like the girls in every thriller that stumble, allowing the murderer to catch them. I won't let him find me; I won't let him take me back.

Lacking a moon, the pitch-black sky prevents me from seeing anything more than a few feet in front of me. The rough rock beneath my soles assures me I'm on a rural road. The road must lead somewhere. Each painful step leads me farther away from Zane and his cage.

The warm night air does little to quell my burning lungs. My entire body screams for rest, but I can't. I won't. I must find help; I need to escape.

I shriek at Zane's form, standing in front of me. "No! No! No!"

My entire body flinches; my eyes fly open. The oppressive fluorescent ceiling lights cause my eyes to water along with the sharp pain in my head, my arm, and my jaw. My eyes dart around the room. I'm in my hospital room, not with Zane. I'm safe.

Ever the mother, Anne hovers above me. "Let me call the nurse," her frantic voice offers while she presses the call button on the rail of my bed.

"Nightmare?" James's fatherly, baritone voice draws my eyes across the room.

I've never seen him like this. His normally commanding posture slouches, his usually warm and caring face mourns, and this strong man stands defeated before me. And it's all my fault.

A nurse enters my hospital room. Without a word, she presses buttons on my IV. A sluggish warmth flows up my arm, wraps around me, and carries me away.

Time passes while I'm unconscious. An authoritative female voice breaks into my dream. "We'll need to talk to her as soon as she wakes up. As the lone survivor, she holds the details to fill in the gaps in our investigation."

"Her jaw is wired shut. Communication will be difficult," a male voice informs. "Even typing will prove painful."

"As soon as she wakes," the now fuzzy female voice orders. "We'll be in the hallway."

I will my eyelids to open, lose the battle, and slip away.

When I wake again, I'm determined to explain everything.

I chicken-peck the word "not" on the iPad, which is resting on the bed below my casted right wrist. The three letters of this little word require too much work.

James's heavy hand rests upon mine. His brown eyes stare into mine. Without speaking a word, he shakes his head, steals the tablet, and slides it from my reach.

Hmm... My groggy, medicated brain tries to process his actions. *No? No what? Avoid pain; don't type? Not right now? Or no? Could he... Does he know I'm not Kendall?* A bit of hope flickers in my eyes.

"Leave it." His raspy voice is barely above a whisper.

My eyes scan his face.

A heavy weight presses into my chest, burning tears fill my eyes, and my pain returns. Glancing at my other hand, I twitch my thumb on my new patient-controlled analgesia pump, releasing another dose of medication to flow through the IV tube and wash everything away.

Later, a knock alerts us of someone at my hospital door. The doctor left moments ago. Surely, he wouldn't be back so soon.

"Mr. and Mrs. Ward," a police officer greets, stepping into the room and securing the door behind him. "I'm Officer Sterling. I need to ask your daughter questions about her accident." He looks at me. "The doctor assures me you're stable and alert enough."

I nod, unsure how I will handle this. I should tell them I'm Kristen; I should let Anne and James know their daughter is dead. In doing so, Zane will learn I'm alive. *He'll come for me... if I allow them to believe I am their daughter, if I pretend to be Kendall, I'll be safe.* Zane wanted Kristen not Kendall.

I focus once again on the officers in my hospital room. They will be asking me questions, and my jaw is wired shut. I look at James, at *Dad*, for guidance.

"Officer." *Dad* rises to shake his hand. "Our daughter hasn't shared the details with either of us. We didn't want to push for details until she was ready to share. After all, she's hurt, and her best friend died in the wreck." Then, he looks at me with a thin smile and a nod, sliding an iPad under my right hand.

"Let's begin with why you were on Highway 5 at that time of night," the officer prompts.

I nod, my hand—index finger extended—positioned above the iPad on my bed. Even this little gesture is painful. I take several steadying breaths. *I can do this. Go slow. Answer their questions. I need to be smart about this. Think before I type every answer.*

I type with my index finger, one letter at a time. "Call from unknown number."

Anne, I mean, Mom lifts my water mug close to me, and I take a sip.

"It was her," I type.

"Her?" Officer Sterling interrupts, wanting more detail.

"It was..." I hesitate, glancing up at *them*. I take a deep, steadying breath. "Kristen."

Without interruption, the officer questions, and I peck out my answers.

9

KENDALL (FORMERLY KNOWN AS KRISTEN)

"She'd been gone..." I type.

"Her best friend, Kristen, disappeared for ten days," *Dad* interjects. "We were all very worried and searching everywhere for her. It was unlike her to not contact Kendall several times every day."

With his support, I power ahead.

"Kristen was frantic," I continue, my index finger tapping the tablet screen as fast as I could through my tears and the pain. "She needed me to pick her up at a gas station in Hartford. I drove to pick her up."

The officer stops taking notes in his little notebook.

"Did she tell you why she needed a ride? Or why she disappeared?" Officer Sterling inquires.

Glancing to *Dad*, with his nod, I continue.

"She disappeared from the frat party we attended." I take a deep breath, cursing the pain while deciding whether I should name Zane. *If I do, will he come after me? This is so much harder than it should be. My brain hurts; I'm thinking too hard.*

"Kristen had broken up with a guy earlier that week after only going on two dates with him." I try to keep my answers short. "She stated Zane put something over her mouth, and the next thing she knew, she woke up in a strange wooden room."

"This Zane..." the officer prompts.

Fuck! I wasn't going to mention him. I'll never be safe now.

"Zane McGuire," *Dad* states. "Senator McGuire's son. We filed a missing person's report immediately. We named him as the possible abductor."

"Thank you, but I need to hear from Ms. Ward herself," Officer Sterling reprimands then looks at me again.

Ms. Ward. It takes me a second to realize he's referring to me.

"Kristen told me and my parents that Zane McGuire set off warning bells," I type, my hand trembling. "She claimed she couldn't put a finger on it, but she had a bad feeling. So, she ended it. She didn't want to go to the frat party for fear he might be there."

"You can't blame yourself," *Mom* soothes, standing at the head of my bed, reading every word I type. "None of us could have known that, while he was in town, he'd attend that party. Even she didn't know he was capable of this."

The officer clears his throat.

"She needs a break," Anne...no, *Mom* warns the officer, defending her butting in to help me answer. "She's due for pain meds, but she needs to be alert for this interview. So, forgive us if we attempt to fill in the story." Always hovering, she presses the straw to my lips again.

"She didn't know where this room was. It had no TV or computer," I continue, tapping. "She said Zane delivered food and water to her once per day..."

From a detached point of view, I do my best to share the painful story of driving away in the car at high speeds down Highway 5.

Officer Sterling asks, "Where was this cabin?"

I stifle the groan rising from my chest. Clearly, he doesn't understand the pain it took to tell him everything the first time. Now, he wants me to retype it.

I write, "I don't know. I picked her up at the gas station in Hartford."

"And this vehicle you state sped up and hit you from behind... Did you see the driver?" he asks.

I shake my head then write, "Too dark. Night."

"But Kristen told you she was running from..."

I growl through my wired teeth, writing, "Zane!" I long to underline it three times, angrily.

The officer closes his notepad and tucks the pen into his chest pocket. All the while, his eyes assess me.

"Follow me outside," he tells *the parents* as he walks from my room, closing the door behind them.

I waste no time pressing the button of my PCA pump to seek relief. I'm long overdue for pain medications. Writing with the police officer for over an hour took its toll on me.

After the three days of lying unconscious and the four long days of vitals, liquid hospital food, mourning the life I'll no longer be able to lead, and contemplating the life ahead of me, the doctor announces I will be discharged this morning. Kiera, my nurse, vows to make quick work of the paperwork so I might be on my way. I hope I hide my fear at returning to the world outside.

Since Officer Sterling left two days ago, we've anxiously looked for news of Senator McGuire's golden boy's arrest. As of yet, we've heard not a word, which leads me to believe Zane remains free and knows of my claims against him. I fear he's waiting for me to emerge from my hospital bed to gain his vengeance.

"Everything's ready at home," *Anne* promises.

She's mom. Anne is Mom; I need to get myself together. *Why can't I remember this? And what could she mean? Does she think I'm sleeping in the bedroom the two of us used to share? Did they remove the second bed?*

Will I return to the bedroom I spent most of my time in with her? *The bedroom. The room we laughed, played, and even cried in. Every memory of her still lives in the room; there's no way I can sleep there. At the moment, I can't fathom entering the house without her, let alone sleeping in the bedroom.*

"Anne, I thought we agreed not to rush her," *Dad* reminds his wife.

"What did I say?" She looks to me for an explanation of her misstep.

"I'm ready to escape the hospital," I type. "I'm just tired, thinking about walking & the car ride," I lie.

"They will escort you to the car in a wheelchair," *Mom* explains, believing my worry to be walking.

"Honey," *Dad* jumps into my rescue. "Perhaps we wait and see how Kendall feels before we push her to return to normal."

Normal. Nothing will ever be normal again. A world without her, a world where I must pretend, a world with the evil Zane McGuire can never be normal.

10

KENDALL

"Home sweet home," *Mom* cheers, opening her car door.

I stifle my groan.

"Anne, fetch the door; I'll help Kendall," *Dad* suggests.

"I'm not sure I can do this," I type on my iPhone before extending it for him to see.

"You have to act excited to be home, for her sake," he whispers.

Excited? Excited... I may never feel excitement again. She was my best friend, and she's dead. She's gone forever.

"Here we are," *Mom* comforts, arranging sofa pillows around me and my cast. "Here's the TV remote. I'll be right back with a drink and then blend you a snack."

I roll my eyes as she walks away.

"I saw that," *Dad* teases. "Let her hover for a day or two. Then I'll tell her to lay off."

I nod as I flick on the TV, not caring what channel it's on, and toss the remote on the coffee table with a hard thump.

"Our first story tonight involves an investigation into allegations made toward Senator McGuire's son," the newscaster announces. "The investigation into accusations against Zane McGuire, the son of United States Senator McGuire, for kidnapping and wrongful death have been dropped. Local authorities claim that, due to insufficient evidence of his involvement, no charges will be filed."

The stale air burns my lungs, and the tears in my eyes feel like fire. *This is not justice*. The powerful and rich control everything without repercussions. This is Senator McGuire and his cronies paying to cover up Zane's wrongdoings.

Dry heaves overtake me. With my cast and broken ribs, I'm unable to scramble to the bathroom. Fortunately, *Dad* places a large bowl in my hand as I bend. My stomach roils, spasms, and desperately attempts to purge itself, but thankfully, it's empty. I'm not sure how it would work with my jaws wired shut.

Slowly, my stomach calms, while my mind reels with the news that Zane will not be charged. He'll be upset we called the police; he'll retaliate. My blood boils as goosebumps form on my chilled skin. Frozen with fear, I realize I'll never be safe; he'll come for me.

Dad's voice breaks through my freakout. "Kendall," he calls, voice full of concern. "Kendall, you're safe. He wanted Kristen, not you. You. Are. Safe. We'll keep you safe."

"Who are you calling?" he asks *Mom*, who stands across the room with a phone in hand.

"Did you see the news?" she spits towards *Dad*, anger in every syllable, then returns to her phone call. "Tomorrow. Here. Top of the line. Money is no issue."

The world around me shrinks into a tunnel.

"Security system. Good idea," *Dad* states.

The tunnel grows smaller and smaller until I fade into the black abyss.

11

KENDALL

It's one year, five months, and fourteen days since the accident; every day is much the same as the day before in my life. Time passes and yet is stagnant. I'm one yet, I've become no one; I cease to exist to all but my parents and neighbors. Outside these walls, the world continues to flourish without me.

I peel myself from under my quilt, placing one of my fuzzy-socked feet on the hardwood floor in hopes to stop the ceiling from spinning. Every night, I enjoy my drink, and every morning, I vow I've consumed my last bottle of rum. Yet I repeat the vicious cycle day in and day out.

A master of the morning after, I close one eye, and my world stops spinning. I slip my other foot to the floor and slowly rise, seeking the restroom and my toothbrush.

Upon returning to the living room, I note a period piece playing on the television. My head crooks to one side, and an eyebrow rises. I don't recall selecting this series on Netflix. Pressing pause, I find it's *Bridgerton*. I hit the bottle much too hard if I chose a historical romance to entertain me. Romance is a farce; opposites don't attract, and life has no happily ever after. It's trying, it's lonely, and it's difficult. I turn the TV off, preferring silence to the fairy tale.

I argue with myself, trying to decide if today is Saturday or Sunday. Mom dropped by two days ago on Saturday. That makes this Monday. *Crap!* That means I must tolerate Ashley's fluttering about the apartment for two hours. I refuse to waste my time cleaning, so she's a necessary evil. I long ago gave up feeling guilty that my parents pay her to clean for me weekly. I'll endure her time here, as I do every week with my noise-canceling headphones and a video game. Monday also means my parents will be here for dinner tonight. They, however, don't allow me to ignore them by playing video games during their visit.

Time flies in front of my screen. When I pull myself from level 14, I find Ashley already came and went, the apartment is pristine, and I am alone as always. I remind myself how messy my life was beyond my apartment door, how friendship and fun turned into a nightmare. I'm better off in my safe place—my apartment.

With a box of Honey Nut Cheerios in hand and a water bottle, I resume my occupation in the gaming chair with my headset and my game. Today's goal? To conquer levels 14 through 20.

I bolt upright in my bed, sheet twisted tightly around my legs from my tumultuous slumber. I'm covered in sweat from head to toe. I pull away strands of hair stuck on my cheek while I struggle to pull in breaths as I scan my dark, empty bedroom.

I don't leave my bed, my body still spun tight, on alert, and in shock. My nightmares feel real, even after a year. I attempt to regulate my breathing and calm my racing heart with the exercises my therapist suggests.

With each long breath in and out, I battle to ignore the images of a cabin and Zane flashing in my mind. I shake off a chill at the thought of him.

My phone display informs me it's four. As I won't fall back to sleep, I slip from my bed, deciding to play my game.

Uncaged

I find my monotonous life exhausting; each 24-hour period resembles the one before. I go to bed in the wee hours of the morning, not to rise until noon most days. I binge-watch shows, sometimes while playing video games, other times staring unseeing at the TV. Each day, I wear black leggings with a black or gray sweatshirt; each night, I wear the same items to bed. My goal each day and night is only to avoid my nightmares.

In the cell that is my apartment, I'm able to avoid people and the news broadcasts. I've surrounded myself with all that I need. My three monitors and gaming PC entertain me for days in the worlds the coders create. When I need a break, they stream shows to fill the silence. I have a sofa, gaming chair, dining table, and four chairs. I have a bed and a closet to throw my clothes in. I need nothing more.

Online shopping delivers groceries, clothes, and anything I might need to my door. Apart from Monday dinners, I live on two things, cereal and rum. I mix the rum with cola, juice, or drink straight from the bottle. It helps to numb my thoughts, my guilt, and my pain, if only for a while.

I hang nothing on the walls, own no knick-knacks. I have no mirrors as I must protect myself from my reflections. The blinds and drapes keep out the sunlight as well as glimpses into the world outside my apartment. Four locks, the video doorbell, and an alarm system protect me from the evil lurking just outside my door.

In here, I'm in control of all but my nightmares.

I don't clean, I rarely eat, and I constantly drink; it's a vicious circle. Each 24 hours mimics the one before.

What shall it be tonight? I open my food delivery app, scrolling through the nearby choices. As I ran out of milk this morning and dry cereal at lunch, it's takeout or starve. I'll order food then place my online grocery order for delivery tomorrow.

Tacos? No. Chinese? No. Italian? Not tonight. Pizza? Maybe… I'm in the mood for French fries. Good, soft, large French fries. *Hmm.* I scroll to my go-to local burger joint that hand-cuts their fries; I love them. My fingers tap quickly to choose my sandwich and fries. *What the hell?* I add a piece of cheesecake on for dessert. The app informs me my dinner will arrive in 40-55 minutes.

I toss my cell on the table and return to my video game. Thinking ahead, I decide to remove my noise-canceling headphones from one ear so I might hear the delivery person when they arrive.

Crap! I pause my game once again. I open the app for the nearby grocery store. I detest ordering groceries. It's easy, really. I order the same things every week. I think it's the fact that there are thousands of choices, and I simply choose my milk, two boxes of cereal, a bag of chips, and my caffeinated beverages. I'm sure by now, I'm predictable to the online shoppers. They probably make fun of me as they work. Maybe even play rock-paper-scissors to see who gets my easy order. I remind myself I don't know them, finalize my order, and return to my game.

12

KENDALL

Another week passes. It's Monday, which means Ashley will clean this afternoon. Then Mom and Dad bring dinner over after work tonight. Mondays exhaust me.

Stepping from the shower, of course, there's no towel on the rack. I pick up a nearby navy towel, bringing it to my nose. *Ugh. No. Uh-huh.* That's way past its expiration date; I drop the musty cloth to the floor. I toss a few hoodies and socks aside; on the bottom of the pile, I snag a white towel. Sniffing, I'm pleased to find it's not foul, so it will do.

While I dry my hair then my body, the sheet falls off the mirror over the vanity. The reflection causes me to pause. It's me; the new me—a shell of the women I used to be. I lost the real me the night of the frat party. Over the past year, less and less of the old me surfaced while more and more of a new depressing one developed.

In my reflection, I stare at a woman with incredibly long brunette hair, a hint of a scar at the scalp above her right eye, pale skin, and pained brown eyes with matching dark circles beneath. I step to the right in order to avoid the mirror, finish drying off, and head into my bedroom.

What prompted me to glance in the mirror? I didn't need affirmation of what I suspected. I'm barely human these days.

At my open closet door, I look at the piles of clothes I'll pull my dark hoodie and leggings from. The good thing about only wearing one style of clothes? It really doesn't matter what I choose; it's all the same. The only trick is to find the cleanest ones when I'm amongst company.

I know I should allow Ashley to wash everything when she cleans, but I want her gone, not hanging around for load after load of laundry to finish. On rare occasions, in moments of weakness, I load the washer, and sometimes, I even manage to switch them to the dryer. It's not that I can't; it's that I have no desire or strength to mess with it most days.

Kendall

"Just leave it," I yell, frustrated, from my gaming chair.
"Ma'am, I can't. We made a mistake, and I'm here to fix it," a male voice hollers back.
"So, leave it. Error fixed," I holler back at the idiotic delivery guy.
"I need to make sure it's right," he shouts.
Oh. My. God. Seriously? He won't just leave my item; I have to open my door to receive it?
I toss my controller to the rug and stomp childishly to the door. It takes me a minute to unlock the chain, deadbolt, then the two door locks.
"I'm sorry we neglected..." The guy starts then pauses.
Dude, you interrupted my game. Speak.
"Um," he stammers, smiling apologetically. "I've thrown in a $10 gift card to apologize for our mistake."
He really is gorgeous with his dark blonde hair, brown eyes, and scruffy jaw. His smile warms something within me, perhaps my heart.
Stop! Stop! Stop! Gorgeous guys are nothing but trouble. Good looking guys are too good to be true. I won't fall for a guy with a sexy smile; I'll never fall for that again. Smile all you want. Your $10 gift card doesn't make this worth pausing my game.
"Okay," I mumble, not sure the appropriate reply.
"I placed my business card in the bag. Please call if you have any issues or if, heaven forbid, we make another mistake." He shifts his weight nervously as he runs his hand through his blonde locks.
"Hey, is that *Defiance Academy*?" he asks, craning his neck to see around me.
I bristle. *Intrude much?*
Just his eyes peering inside my apartment feels like an intrusion to me. I don't

like him peeking into my personal space. I want to hide behind my locked door. My skin grows hot, and fire pumps in my veins. It's how I feel when anyone stands at my door or enters my apartment, even my parents.

He's very different from Zane, so why does he trigger fear in me?

He's nothing like Zane. In fact, he's the opposite of Zane. There's no product in his hair, his white dress shirt has a few wrinkles, and his sensible work shoes would never come near Zane's feet. *Snap out of it.*

"Yeah. You know it?" I hesitantly reply, ready for this interaction to be over.

Pull it together; he's still in the hall.

"I'm on level seven," he brags. "You?"

"Umm," I hedge, gulping.

"What's your gamertag?" he asks.

I won't share my handle; there's no way I'll tell him.

At my hesitation, he offers, "My gamertag is Die4U." He holds up four fingers. "Look me up sometime."

I nod, not verbally agreeing to do so. He gives me an awkward wave with his hand near his hip.

I quickly shut the door and lock all the locks.

John Hoover

I stand staring at her closed door. One, two, three locks click along with the sound of a chain sliding into place. She's a single woman living alone, but four locks seem extreme. At the beeping of her security system activating, I turn on my heel, heading for the exit.

My cousin pops to mind as I walk. She's still in high school but anal about the locks on all her doors. My blood heats to boiling at the memory and thought of what might have happened if I hadn't found her in time that night. I shudder.

I wonder if this customer experienced something like my cousin.

She couldn't stop hugging herself. She seemed guarded, cool, but interesting. She wouldn't give me her gamertag, but maybe she will look for me in the game.

Although I know her name and where she lives, it's unprofessional to use knowledge I gained through work to contact her. So, the ball is in her court. Let's see if she nibbles.

I sure hope she nibbles.

13

KENDALL

A week later, as with every Monday, it's barely 5:00, and I'm exhausted. I sit on the sofa, showered and dressed in clean clothes, preparing myself for the weekly meal and conversation with the parents. Every creaky board and faint footstep outside my door levels up my nerves. Although it's much the same each week, the interactions still upset me.

I walk to the door at the sound of two sets of footsteps growing closer. Intaking a deep breath, I open the door before they knock.

"Hello," Dad greets, carrying a baking dish wrapped in aluminum foil to the counter.

"You look nice," Mom states.

She doesn't mean it in a bad way; I know she hopes her praise will spark me to put forth effort every day. She read many books and articles on anxiety, depression, and PTSD in the weeks following my hospital stay when I received my mental health diagnosis. I'm grateful she doesn't push; she supports me by letting me know she's near if I ever want to talk.

"What's for dinner?" I ask, turning the locks on my door while attempting to sound interested.

"Brisket with new potatoes and green beans," she brags fondly.

"Your favorite," Dad reminds me.

But it's not my favorite; it was *hers*.

While I love Mom's brisket, potatoes in every form are my favorite. I smile for her sake as I pull down plates, handing them to her. I remove the utensils from the drawer and place them, following her around the table.

Dad places water glasses on the table before pulling a chair out for his wife. I love that, after 25 years, they demonstrate their love for each other openly and often. At one time, I strived to find a love like theirs; now, I resign myself to a long, lonely, single life.

Finished with grace, he fills my plate then Mom's before his own. As always, too much food sits on my plate; I won't eat half of it.

"Anything new this week?" Mom begins between bites.

I nod as I chew then swallow. I search for the strength to share my new developments. I rarely contribute to the meal's conversation except to talk about a new book or video game I've found. My parents stop eating, staring at me.

"I had a visitor a week ago," I start, my voice shaking.

"Really?" Mom's face lights up. "Who was it?"

"Well, it was not so much a visitor as it was a delivery," I confess. "The grocery store made a mistake, so a manager brought the item by."

"A delivery? That's all?" Her excitement fades.

"Well..." I draw out. "He refused to leave the item in the hall, instead making me open the door."

Dad smiles while Mom's brows arch.

"He gave me a gift card for my troubles," I share. "And..." I draw out. "He saw my new video game and told me he plays it, too."

"So, you let him in, and the two of you talked for a while." Mom seeks further information.

I shake my head. "We just talked at the door." I shrug. "Oh, and he gave me his business card." I jut my chin toward the magnet holding it on the fridge.

She nearly tips her chair over as she scurries from her seat for a closer view.

"His name is John Hoover." I don't miss the inflection in her voice; she's excited at the prospect of a new friend. "So..." she prompts.

"Anne, let's not pry," Dad pleads.

"That's all," I inform them both.

"His cell number is on the card," she tells me. "You should call him."

"Anne," he chides.

"What?" she bites in his direction. "You could text him about the video game."

"Maybe," I reply, knowing full well I have no intention to do so.

I may have thought of him while playing the game and placing my grocery order, but no. I hate how much of my time over the past week thoughts of him consumed me. Try as I might, I can't erase him; he keeps popping in.

"I think it's great the two of you chatted," Dad chimes in. "And if you keep the card on your refrigerator, you can contact him in a couple of months *if* you decide to."

His warm smile comforts me. I love that he isn't pressuring me. I'm not ready; I may never be ready. I don't want to be ready. I don't want to put myself in a position where a man like Zane might hurt me again.

"Let's have a glass of wine," Mom suggests.

I know she wants to finish her statement with "to celebrate." I'll gladly drink the wine, not as a celebration but as a means to calm the anxiety within me.

She places three wine glasses on the table, and Dad fills them. We don't toast, but I can see that Mom really wants to.

Moments later, together, the three of us make quick work of clearing the table and loading the dishwasher. They don't linger after dinner, saying their goodbyes, and I secure all locks then set the alarm.

I take a shot of rum to forget the comment Mom made about taking online college classes. I take another to erase the guilt that they pay for my apartment, my utilities, and my food. I take a third shot just because. Just because Zane's out there, he's free, and I'm locked in my apartment 24/7. The fourth shot I drink to forget. I want to forget; I need to forget. I can't cope with any of this tonight.

I check for the fourth time since they left that every lock is secure on my apartment door then flop myself onto the sofa. I pick up the remote, quickly scrolling through channel after channel of reality TV, news, sporting events, and shopping networks. It's too much mindless dribble. I switch from live TV to my streaming services.

Hmm. Clueless, Forrest Gump, The Silence of the Lambs, *or* Men in Black. *Which should I choose?*

Forrest Gump *is over two hours long, so I gong it.*

Clueless… *I'm not in the mood for funny, so I gong it, too.*

I pour myself a large glass, emptying the wine bottle they left behind. I place my glass near my monitors before I hurry to my room in search of comfort. I shed my bra, pull a hoodie over my long-sleeved t-shirt, and place my long hair in a messy high ponytail.

"There. That's better," I say to myself, plopping into my padded chair for the night.

My hand shakes unsteadily when I take my wine in hand. I snag my nearby prescription bottle, quickly swallowing a Xanax and washing it down with a sip.

Controller in hand, I pick up where I left off with my game. I move from wine to rum as the night passes quickly.

I take the bottle in hand, ready to drain the last of it, but the cap is stuck.

It's her.

"Damnit!" I yell at my deceased friend. "I need one more glass."

I try to unscrew it bare-handed with a kitchen towel in hand and by tapping it gently to knock it loose. Try as I might, I can't get the lid off my bottle of rum.

"Fine!" I spit into the empty room. "Have it your way. I'm done drinking for the night!"

When will I learn I can't win an argument with her? I'm crazy to think, as my guardian angel, she'd be any less stubborn than she was here on Earth.

I sling on my headphones, planting my butt in my chair and in front of the monitors, and I return to the only world I belong in—my game.

14

KENDALL

"Get up!" she yells, her mouth near my ear. "I'm tired of this shit. Get your ass out of bed!" My best friend stands, legs wide, hands on her hips.

"Shut up," I groan, throwing a pillow over my head.

"Uh-uh," she argues. "This is an intervention. I'm pissed, and we are going to have this out right now." She crosses her arms over her chest.

"No," I spit from under the pillow.

Pulling the covers off me then tugging at the pillow, she pushes me out of bed. I fall to the hardwood floor with a thump.

"You're hiding when you should be living," she screams. "You should be living for the two of us!"

Her foot nudges at my ribs. "Get up! It's time you start living for both of us. Stop wallowing; you're letting him win by hiding in here."

I close my lips tightly, fighting to focus on my friend through the tears pooling in my eyes.

"By hiding in this apartment, it's like you are still in his clutches. You can't let Zane win," she states. "You have to leave this apartment; you have to live, to smile, and to have sex!" She laughs. "Enough sex for the both of us."

"Get off your ass and make me proud," she yells. "You wouldn't let me become a pathetic loser; you'd do everything in your power to shake me out of a funk."

I sit up, pulling my knees to my chest.

She continues, giggling, "You'd haunt my ass."

She wraps her arms around me. "Girl, you are paler than a ghost. Let's go outside." *She leans her forehead to mine.* "Let's walk in the park, go to the zoo, and visit a bar."

She pulls her head from mine, looking into my eyes. "Let's swipe right, take a chance," *she prompts.* "Lightning doesn't strike twice, so girl, you need to PPAARRTTYY!"

My friend places a peck on my temple before pulling away. "Don't make me come back to this disgusting pig-stye." *She motions her arms around my bedroom.* "Get your ass up and live a real life, for you and for me."

I sit up too fast, and my bedroom spins. *Whoa.* I place one hand on my forehead and one foot to the floor in hopes of stilling its movements. I don't glance around the room; I don't need to. I know she's not here; it was just a dream or maybe a haunting.

I've missed her every day for over a year. My hallucination brought her back to me in an intervention prompted by anxiety meds and too much alcohol—that is all. A jackhammer pummels my head while the muted light from the mini blinds pierces my eyes, and the ceiling won't stop spinning.

"Get up!" she yells at me. "Get up NOW!"

Falling to all fours on the wooden floor, I crawl to the bathroom, turn on my shower, and sit on the tile floor as warm water strikes my face then streams to the drain below me. The sound of the running water blocks out any orders from my friend. I remain fixed to the tile for several long minutes, cursing my alcohol consumption of the previous night.

After my shower, I dress quickly then sit at my computer. I've opened the curtains and blinds. Tiny dust particles float in the warm rays of the early March sun. She's right. This is a pig-stye.

"I hope you are happy. I showered and let sunshine in. As my head is in a vice, that's all I can manage today. I guess I'll need to figure out what to do tomorrow," I call to my invisible friend.

Eerily, at that exact moment, I hear a knock at my door.

"I'm headed out for a haircut. Need me to stop by the store?" I open my door, forcing a smile for my neighbor, Stephenie. The smile is foreign; a once easy daily occurrence now is forced.

"I'm good," I state, not needing her to pop by the liquor store for me. It might be a while before I drink again after last night.

Stephenie's surprised. I'm not sure if it's my passing on alcohol or my freshly showered presence and the sunlight in my apartment that shocks her.

"Okay." She waves over her shoulder as she leaves.

I know she counts on the $20 I pay her to pick up items for me; it helps her as a single mom. If I stick with my plan to consume less alcohol, I should find another way to help her earn cash.

Back at the computer, my fingers hover above the keys when it hits me. Grinning, I shake my head. That was a sign, sort of a message from my self-appointed guardian angel.

"I guess tomorrow I'll go to the salon," I say out loud. "I can't live the life you want if I scare everyone looking like I belong to a cult," I tell my friend.

I head to my bedroom in search of clothes. I lay each item on my mattress. I want to choose an outfit to wear as I rejoin the living tomorrow. I stare at the black and gray array of hoodies and leggings. *It's a disaster; I'm a disaster.* Maybe I should attempt to stop in a store to purchase some clothes, too.

Hmm. Probably not.

Baby steps for now.

15

KENDALL

My app for my video doorbell signals someone in the hallway moments before they ring my bell. I watch on my phone as the delivery person leaves my grocery bags. I wait to unlock my door until footsteps signal they've left the hallway.

I quickly pull my three grocery sacks through the doorway then secure the locks. As I place the items on the counter and into the cabinet, I notice a folded piece of paper taped to my cereal. Unfolding the note, in black permanent marker is a gamertag. *His gamertag.* This must be his way of urging me to find him in the game.

Hmmm. It's kind of sweet that he sent me a note.

I go about my afternoon, plotting out my adventure for tomorrow. Hours later, fed up with watching game shows, I settle into my gaming chair, booting up my PC, a bowl of cereal in hand. On a whim, I seek out the grocery guy's gamertag, and I'm transported backwards to level seven.

Still on level seven. Hmmm. He needs more help than I expected.

John

Uncaged

"This game sucks!" I throw my controller into my chair, stomping to the kitchen. *Stupid level. Why can't I figure out how to master it?* I've been struggling with it for over two weeks now.

I pull another beer from the fridge, pop the top, and chug. I might need to eat something as it's my third on an empty stomach. I keep thinking the beer will help me relax and finish this level, but it hasn't yet.

If only...

I'm doubly frustrated. I can't play this game without thinking about her now; it's been two weeks, and I can't get her out of my mind. I know she plays this game, and when I told her what level I was on, it was clear she was farther than me. Of course, I don't have her gamertag, so I can't reach out to her for help. Judging by her sweet gaming chair and multiple monitors set up, she's probably beaten this game along with another by now.

Argh! I should play a different game, one that doesn't remind me of her every step of the way. But I can't. I'm not a quitter; I can't let this game beat me. With a snack and drink in hand, I return to my game, determined to get through this level tonight.

An hour later, I'm no closer to passing level seven, but I persist in my attempts to clear it. Maybe I should check the internet and YouTube to get some cheats.

Bloop, bloop. My game alerts me that a new gamer has joined my level and chat.

His gamertag is "invisfraud00," and the avatar he's chosen... Wait. That's a female avatar. There's no way to know if this could be a guy or a girl. Guys sometimes choose female avatars.

Hmm. I don't recognize the gamertag, so I'll wait and see what they want.

> INVISFRAUD00
>
> Dropped in 2 leave tips
>
> Do u mind?

This never happens. Players drop in to play the game with an occasional chat, not to "give tips." My fingers twitch on my controller as I decide how to respond.

> INVISFRAUD00
>
> Delivered any Sugar Smacks lately?

Ah-ha. It's her. It's Kendall.
I quickly reply.

> **DIE4U**
> Did we forget them in your order again?

> **INVISFRAUD00**
> No. figured you'd catch on to me

> **DIE4U**
> Came down to lower levels to help poor novices?

> **INVISFRAUD00**
> I may not be much help

> **DIE4U**
> Somehow, I don't believe u

> **INVISFRAUD00**
> I have a few tips in my pocket

I move my eyes from the sidebar chat to the avatar with a buxom bust and legs that go on for miles. It's far from the ponytail, oversized hoodie, and leggings she wore when I saw her in real life. Our avatars differ greatly. Hers is tall, fit, scantily clad, and definitely a kick-ass woman. Mine sports a green mohawk, concert T-shirt, jeans with cuffs at the bottom, and sneakers. She's a physical fighter with weapons while mine uses tech and gadgets for survival.

> **DIE4U**
> Your avatar has no pockets

> **INVISFRAUD00**
> F-ing sexist game creators
> Limited options for female attire

I struggle to find words to respond to that. Female gamers are often targeted and bullied by guys. It's a hot controversy, and I want nothing to do with it. She seemed skittish at her apartment; I don't want to scare her off.

> INVISFRAUD00
>
> Ready to crush this level?

> DIE4U
>
> Hell ya!

I begin playing through the level, as I have more times than I want to admit. At the halfway mark, she prompts me to investigate the torn bumper sticker on the wrecked truck to my left. Upon my approach, a weapon and a strength box rise. I chose the strength as she prompts and continue. Time passes quickly in our game. With her help, I easily complete this level and two more.

Looking at my cell phone, it's past 1:00 a.m. *Crap!*

> DIE4U
>
> I'd better get some sleep
>
> Work @6

> INVISFRAUD00
>
> Sweet dreams

> DIE4U
>
> Thanks for help. Hope you're on here again

> INVISFRAUD00
>
> We'll see...

We'll see?
Her final words haunt me as I attempt to settle into sleep.
We'll see.
I hope to hell she does come back.

Kendall

Stop! Stop it!
I slap my cheek with my right hand.
I can't let him make me smile.
I don't need anyone.
I'm better off on my own.

I place my controller in front of my monitor, shutting it all down for the night. There's no way I'm ready to fall asleep and no way I will fall asleep if I keep playing the game. All I do is think about John Hoover, how he's doing, and when he'll play again.

I pour myself a bowl of cereal, plopping on the sofa and watching a random show on TV.

After a week containing two more gaming sessions and chatting with John, tonight, I bravely suggested that we communicate through our headsets while we play on level 15 and 16.

"How are you so good?" he inquires as his avatar hops over a boulder.

My skin prickles at the sound of his voice in my ears—in my apartment. *I hope this isn't a mistake on my part.*

"Unlike you, I don't work. I have all day and night to play," I explain.

"Well, I'm glad I'm reaping the rewards of your many hours of hard work," he teases. "It'd take me months to solve this game."

"Watch out for the log coming up," I warn. "It begins to roll as you draw near."

He deftly jumps over two rolling logs onto a floating raft.

"That's an interesting bush," I hint, and he explores it, gaining two more lives.

"Thoughts on a Higher Power?" John urges, seeking to learn more about me.

"I believe in a Higher Power," I answer. "Personally, I believe in God."

Well, I used to believe in God. Now, my faith waivers, unsure how He could allow evil men to get away with the things they do.

"Me, too," he agrees. "I don't feel there needs to be strict ceremonies or worship in one building."

"Tell me more," I urge.

"God is omnipresent. Therefore, we may praise Him anywhere at any time," he shares.

"I like that."

It doesn't escape me that we have much in common. He's intelligent and thought-provoking.

Maybe. Just maybe…

16

JOHN

In my mother's driveway, barely out of my driver's seat, I smile, shaking my head. Mom's a force—a brilliant, shiny, active force. Her security camera catches my motion, and in less than a minute, she's walking down her sidewalk to greet me.

"Well, isn't this a nice surprise?" her cheery voice greets as she opens her arms to pull me in for a hug.

I'm blessed. In the mom department, I have the best. I can't wait to share the reason for today's visit. She's going to go ballistic.

"Hey, Mom," I greet, wrapping my arms around her, too. "I thought I'd surprise you for lunch."

"What a splendid surprise. Riley's napping, so we will have to eat here," she states. "Thirty-minute break, right?"

I nod. "How is my little cousin?" I ask, walking toward the front door, my arm around Mom's shoulders.

"Still teething," she replies.

"I don't know how you do it," I share, opening the door for her. With the passing of her youngest sister, Mom chose to raise her newborn niece, Riley.

"It's good practice for my future grandchildren," she states.

I don't miss her underlying hint. She's constantly attempting to set my brother and me up with young women she meets, all in her endeavor to become a grandmother.

I follow her into the kitchen where she opens the refrigerator door.

"I have cold cuts and salad," she informs me, turning to see my reaction.

"Let's order something for delivery," I suggest, not wanting her to bother.

"Or... Let me see..." She opens one of the lower drawers. "We could have grilled cheese or hot ham and cheese..."

"Actually, that sounds good," I state. "Which do you prefer?"

"I'll make both, cut them in half, and we can share." She smiles in my direction, pleased with her offer.

I pull the griddle from under her oven, laying it across the burners while Mom places butter, cheese, ham slices, and bread on the counter between us. I turn the burners on then grab a butter knife from a nearby drawer. Together, we make quick work of our meal prep.

"So, tell me why you're really here," Mom prompts.

Nothing gets by this woman. I swallow the bite of hot ham and cheese, washing it down with a sip of water. Forearms on the table, I lean towards her.

"I think..." *Hmm... How should I word this?* "I think I've met someone." *Well, duh. I meet people every day.*

"A girl?" Her voice rises in pitch as she claps her hands. "Tell me everything."

"There's not much to tell," I confess. "I made a grocery delivery to her apartment. She seemed really cool. We play the same video game, so I gave her my gamertag. It took a while, but several times over the past week, she's contacted me through the game."

"And you feel it?" she murmurs excitedly.

I nod. "There's just something... I can't put my finger on it..."

"I told you. When you know, you know. That's how it happened with your dad and me." Her excited smile reaches the corners of her dancing eyes.

"She's skittish," I share. "So, I'm enjoying our gaming and online conversation for now."

"She'll be worth it; stay patient," Mom advises.

I smirk. I love her positivity. She hasn't met Kendall but gives me advice as if she knows her well.

Kendall

Two nights later, we are playing our game again. Really, we are chatting more than we are playing.

"*Star Wars* versus *Star Trek*?" I blurt as we duck into a cave, falling to the underground.

"Both," he answers, concentrating on his battle with a giant snake.

"I'm a huge *Star Wars* fan," I confess.

"Me, too. But there are many more versions of *Star Trek* to watch and follow," he states.

"Ah, but thanks to Disney+, we now have many more parts to the *Star Wars* saga to enjoy," I counter.

"I don't subscribe," he states.

"I do," I reply before thinking better of it.

Now I wonder if he hopes I'll invite him over to watch some with me.

"Spock or Jim?" John asks.

"Neither," I reply. "Uhura. Nichelle Nichols was a pioneer on and off the screen."

When he doesn't respond, I say, "Now you know just how nerdy I am." I chuckle.

"I wasn't thinking nerdy," he states. "Your answer revealed...your intelligence."

Hmm. I chew on my lip, contemplating my next question, worried I'm sharing too much too soon.

"Do you believe in ghosts?" I ask.

"Random," he declares.

"Not really. Answer please," I instruct.

"Yes." I imagine he smirks. "Is that the right answer?"

I nod, realizing he can't see me. "Yes."

"Why do you ask?"

I shrug, now regretting my random question.

"C'mon. You had to have a reason," he pries.

"I believe in them," I state, attempting to make light of it.

"Have you had any experiences?"

I nod nervously and send him a smiling emoji in the chat box to the right of the game.

"After my grandma passed, I swear she remained with me for over a year," he confesses. "She helped me help my mom through it. She had a tough time. My dad had left us years before, and as a teen, I didn't know how to help. Then, often as I pondered if I should do one thing or the other, I felt a gentle nudge or found a little sign would tell me which to do. Anything like that for you?"

"Yep. At least once a week," I reply.

"Really?"

I quickly respond. "My best friend passed away in an auto wreck. I'm not sure if she's a ghost or a guardian angel."

"I'm sorry for your loss," he says. "How long ago?"

"Just over a year." I shake my head. I'm done with this subject. I end our chatter. "Let's clear this level now."

I like that he doesn't judge me for sharing my supernatural experiences. The more we chat, the more I wonder if I'm ready to have a friend.

17

KENDALL

A week later, our journey ends. *Finally! Level 20 complete.* I proudly smile, having helped John advance this far. It feels good to have a friend, even if only online in a video game. Activity on the sidebar chat catches my eye.

DIE4U
I think we should go on a date.

I stare unmoving. *Oh, no. Oh, no. Oh, no. Why can't he be happy with what we already have? Why did he type instead of ask that question?*

DIE4U
Not fancy. Watch a movie @ your place?

A date? He wants to come to my house and hang out. My head on a swivel, I take in my large, empty space.

Uncaged

> **DIE4U**
> Crickets?

I could shut down my PC, claiming it froze up and I never got the message, but I'm not keen on living with another lie. The one I currently carry weighs heavier on my shoulders every day.

> **INVISFRAUD00**
> Umm...

Think! Say something!

> **INVISFRAUD00**
> I guess we could.

> **DIE4U**
> Next Saturday night? I'm off the next day so can stay up later.

Fuck! Saturday? Stay late? This is moving too fast.

> **DIE4U**
> Just a movie & snacks. I promise.

Just? Does that mean he has no interest in... Stop! Don't go there. Definitely not ready for any of this.

> **DIE4U**
> Say yes.

I jump at the sound of silverware clanking in the metal sink behind me. *It's her.* She's giving me a sign. She wants me to do this. I type rapidly before I can think better of it.

> **INVISFRAUD00**
> OK.

> **DIE4U**
> 7:30 next Saturday. Your place.

> **INVISFRAUD00**
> OK.

> **DIE4U**
> C U then.

What did I just do? Do I really have a date in my apartment Saturday night?

Again, I cringe, looking at my place. The clock on my PC shows it's near midnight. I have only eight days to get my apartment ready for company and find something to wear.

My parents might help. *Who am I kidding?* They'll fall all over themselves to help me prepare for a date.

I think I'm going to vomit.

Kendall

I'm doing it; I'm really gonna do it.

The next morning, I close my apartment door, turning the key, locking it behind me. *Step one is complete. I'm officially in the hallway.* I try to decipher if it's

Uncaged

nerves or adrenaline ramping up my heartbeat. I pull in two deep breaths, deciding I'm still in control; I can do this.

Fully outside, I've completed step two. I look up into the bright sunlight, enjoying the breeze upon my face. As I don't have an appointment, I plan to walk to the nearby salon in a strip mall. Careful to check all my surroundings, I internally count my steps as my eyes constantly sweep the area in front of me and over my shoulder.

I release a long breath when my hand grasps the door handle. I'm doing this. I'm really doing this. Stylists' eyes turn to the door when the bell above it rings. I'm greeted and instructed to take a seat on a sofa. I'm only there a minute before a stylist invites me to her chair.

"What are you thinking for today?" she asks, lifting my hair and securing the black cape around my neck.

"I'd like my hair to fall just above my shoulders," I share, my hands swinging above them. "Perhaps some long layers and no bangs."

"Very well," she agrees. "Your hair is quite long."

"Yeah. I grew it out, thinking it would be easier to put it in a ponytail."

"Long hair requires a lot of work and maintenance." She states what I've learned. "What about the color?"

"I'd like natural highlights," I share.

She lifts my hair this way and that as she asks, "All over highlights or framing your face?"

"Let's do it all over," I answer, unsure what the difference really is.

We carry on easy conversation over the next hour as she highlights, cuts, and styles my hair. As stylists go, I hit the jackpot. Sometimes, they talk to each other and not the clients in their chairs, and other times, they pry into all aspects of your life in hopes of gaining gossip to spread later. Today, she calms me with her funny stories, celebrity chit chat, and easy demeanor.

"What are your plans for the rest of the day?" she asks as I swipe my card.

"I'm not sure," I answer honestly.

While sitting in the stylist's chair, I felt confident that I could run a few more errands. Now, standing near the exit, I feel panic rising.

I planned to walk five blocks to Target to purchase new clothes to replace my leggings and sweatshirts; standing on the sidewalk again, exhaustion sets in, and I decide to skip shopping for clothes. There's one more thing I hoped to do before I give up for the day. Now, I'm wavering. *I really want to do it.*

"Excuse me, sir," I begin, fighting laughter. "Can you direct me to the Sugar Smacks?"

John turns around, hand still on the canned goods he stocks on the shelf. It's clear he's surprised it's me. A wide smile on his face, he shows me to the cereal aisle.

"I like your hair," he states, pointing to my new hairstyle.

I'm impressed he noticed. "Thank you," I blush. *What the hell am I doing? Act normal, like you've left your apartment before.*

I stand nervously by the cereal, not sure if I want to actually pick up a box and interact with a checker as I leave.

"I don't want to keep you from work," I state, unsure what to do now that I'm here. "I'll be online tonight."

His smile grows. "I'll be on after 7:00," he shares, and I nod. "I'd better get back at it," he says, pointing his thumb over his shoulder.

I wave, a genuine smile on my face and warmth in my chest.

18

KENDALL

After attempting to play three different games and stream two different shows, I resign to the fact that I need my anxiety medication. I've fought an internal battle in the hours since I returned home. I feel good about the errands I ran and even my stop at the grocery store to see John. While I looked over my shoulder often, I didn't have a panic attack, and that is a huge win for me.

My hours online with my therapist prepared me for these baby steps. While my stomach ached and I broke out in sweat, I walked several blocks without breaking out in tears. When I thought about turning around to run back home, I took a few deep breaths and thought of the skills I learned in therapy. It feels good to begin to use the tools I've collected in my toolbox throughout the year.

I make a mental note that I need to apologize for my eye rolls during our video sessions. Many times, I took notes or walked through the motions of a new technique with my therapist while mentally claiming I would never use any of it. In the end, he was right, and I must acknowledge that.

I swallow my anxiety medicine with a sip of water, knowing it will help to ease my mind and slow my racing heart. In the past, I've needed these pills after nightmares, panic attacks, and dinners with my parents. It feels good to use it now only to help calm me a bit. I conquered a huge task today, and I'm proud.

I didn't feel as if a stalker followed my every move. Although I did feel like eyes were on me, I felt they were not a threat to me. I recalled the words of my therapist during our hours upon hours together, used the techniques I learned, and I didn't allow my anxiety to deter me from my goals for the day. It may take me another week before I attempt it again, but I will plan another trip out of the apartment.

My best friend's favorite words were "fortitude" and "fierce;" today, I channeled both of them. I hope she's proud of the baby steps I took.

Suddenly, on the table behind me, a strong wind blows through the pages of my sketchpad. Except there is no wind, no breeze, and no windows open. I shake my head.

She's here, and she's proud.

Kendall

Days later, frustrated with my game, I pop over to try to find John in the new online game we've discovered. I search for a bit with no luck before tossing my controller on the table and picking up my cell phone. I use the number on his business card, which is still hanging on my fridge.

ME
Not gaming tonight?

JOHN
Softball game

Who is this?

ME
Um...

JOHN
Invisfraud00?

ME
Yes

JOHN
Thanks 4 your #

Uncaged

ME
I'll let you get back to game

JOHN
Waiting on the first game to end

ME
Slow pitch?

JOHN
Yes

Me

Position?

JOHN
Center field

ME
Nice

JOHN
Miss me?

ME
No

JOHN
Text because I wasn't gaming?

ME
Ya

JOHN
You missed me

ME
Whatever

JOHN
Thanks 4 texting

I should warm up my arm

ME
Good luck. Have fun

> **JOHN**
> Thanks. Can I text after?

> **ME**
> If you hit a homerun

> **JOHN**
> Deal

> **ME**
> (laughing emoji)

Hmm. I haven't used emojis since... I shake my head, knowing she's smiling down at me.

John

I have her number. Progress. Slow and steady progress.

"John, let's go," my teammate yells from the field.

Shit! The game's starting. I grab my glove from the bench and jog to center field. It passes quickly, thank goodness. I pull my cell phone from my bag as I make my way to my truck. My thumbs unlock and pull up Kendall's text chain.

> **ME**
> We won

In the long minutes that pass, waiting for a reply, I start my truck and drive towards home.

> **KENDALL**
> Homerun

Using my truck's handsfree capabilities I reply.

Uncaged

> **ME**
> You said I could text if I hit 1

> **KENDALL**
> No way, liar

> **ME**
> Driving now. Will text video when home

> **KENDALL**
> Don't text & drive

> **ME**
> Handsfree

> **KENDALL**
> Thata boy

That a boy? She's weird, and I love it. Exiting my truck, I type her back.

> **ME**
> Home. Video game in 30?

> **KENDALL**
> If homerun really happened

> **ME**
> Game 30 min. Homerun on its way
>
> (sends the video of homerun in 3rd inning)

The next morning, my vibrating cell wakes me.

DAWN
On pins and needles
Any update?
No pressure

ME
Right... No pressure
3 texts already this morning

DAWN
Pardon me
I have hopes & dreams

ME
I'm working on it

DAWN
I'm just checking in
Haven't seen you this week

ME
Guilt trip?

DAWN
Just stating facts

ME
I have her cell

DAWN
OMG!

ME
Right?!

DAWN
1 step closer

ME
1 monumental step closer

DAWN
Nice!

Uncaged

ME
Mom, I told you not to do this

I have to move slow with her

You need to back off!

DAWN
I can't help it

At least I don't text/call every time I want to

ME
Focus on Nelson

DAWN
Ugh! He'll never find a girl

ME
He dates

DAWN
No. He hooks up

ME
MOM!

DAWN
What? It's true

ME
You can't know those things

DAWN
Why not? I'm hip

ME
I'm sure using the word hip means you aren't

Bye

DAWN
Love ya

ME
(heart emoji)

19

KENDALL

What was I thinking? I must be crazy. Why did I agree to see him in real life?
Where did the week go? It's Saturday, and I am not ready.
I'm gonna need reinforcements.
I pick up my phone to ask for help.
Asking her for help proves I am out of my mind.

> ME
> Help. I have a date
>
> Well, maybe it's a date

> MOM
> Yay! What can I do?

> ME
> ????!!!!

> MOM
> I'll be there in 10

So out of my mind.
I guess I'd better shower before she arrives. I scurry to the bathroom, rush

through my shower, pull my hair into a ponytail, and throw on somewhat-fresh clothes just as my doorbell rings.

Glancing at my doorbell app on my phone, I see it is, indeed, my parents. I unlock one lock, then the next, then another, then the last. I take a deep breath before I swing my door open wide for them to enter. They stand awkwardly in my loft.

"Where should we begin?" I ask, clasping my hands in front of me.

"First, we'll need to know what you have planned," Mom says gingerly.

I don't blame her. My emo personality for over a year is beyond her comprehension.

"I've invited the guy I've been chatting with in my online game over for the evening," I state nervously.

"Are you fixing him a meal? Ordering out? Watching a movie?" Mom restates her previous question.

"We're just hanging out," I answer. "Gaming and maybe a movie." I shrug, unsure of anything more than that.

How in the hell did I used to ask guys out, go on dates, and all that crap?

"So, we need to make the loft, you know..." I flip my hands around the apartment space. "And have a few snacks."

I shrug, unsure. Then, Mom pushes, "And maybe a new outfit?"

I nod, not fully committing to the clothing.

Mom is in her element. "We'll shop online then send Dad to pick it all up while we keep working here." She spins slowly, her eagle eye on my space. "We'll keep it simple; I promise."

I nod, knowing full well her simple and my simple are miles apart. They aren't even on the same continent these days.

I open my laptop on my table; Mom, Dad, and I gather round.

My head spins with all we've bought today. Dad was great, driving around the city, picking up the items that Mom insisted I needed to make my loft "comfy." She opened the blinds, filling the space with light. My sofa now includes three throw pillows and two lap blankets. Fake succulents flank my TV and the kitchen sink. A live plant Mom vows I can't kill sits on a windowsill. Rugs lay on the hardwood floors scattered around the space. I now own coasters, a deck of playing cards, a Scattergories game, and a coffee table book that decorates my new table.

I never thought of my loft as cold, but Mom's little touches warm the place up. It actually feels like a home.

Dad assembles cube shelves to hold my clothes in the closet and a bookcase to hold books, comic books, and art supplies with my new tools. Yes. I now own tools. I do my best to keep a fresh beer nearby for him as he works.

"Kendall," Mom calls from the kitchen. "Let's prepare the snacks."

I thought the reason we chose snacks was to keep it easy and not require me to cook.

"Pour the tortilla chips in this bowl and seal it with the lid," Mom slides a new, large, plastic bowl with a lid towards me, and I comply.

My task is completed quickly, and I watch her pour salsa and queso into small glass bowls then cover them with lids and tuck them into the refrigerator.

When Mom slides another large bowl and lid with a bag of popcorn to me, I repeat my previous task. I stack the two bowls beside the fridge, awaiting her next instructions.

"Let's pour the M&Ms into this bowl," Mom suggests, pulling a glass dish I've never seen before from my cabinet.

"All done," Dad announces, returning from my bedroom, tools in one hand and his empty beer in the other.

"Thank you." I smile.

"We're all done in here, too," Mom smiles, placing his beer bottle in the recycle bin.

"Can we help with anything else?" he asks, scanning the space.

I shake my head. I'm not sure if I'm ready. We've prepared my space but not my mind. Mentally, I'm a freaking mess. I'm not ready for this. I don't know how to stand, where to put my hands, or what to do next. My heart races, and my hands shake at my sides.

"Should you take a...?" Mom senses my anxiety.

I shake my head. I do need a Xanax, but I don't want to be out of it this evening. I really do want to be sedated but need to be present, and I need to be sharp. Honestly, I want to shoot him a text and cancel. I could easily make up an excuse then never speak to him again.

The sound of my bathroom door closing loudly startles me. Mom lets out a little scream as her hand flies to her heart. Her wide eyes look at me while Dad goes to investigate.

It's futile. He'll find no reason for that door to shut on its own. When open, it remains open. There's no breeze in there, nothing to explain the phenomenon other than it's my ghost or guardian angel reacting to my previous thought. She doesn't want me to cancel tonight. She does this type of thing all the time.

20

JOHN

The nerves we shared upon my arrival fade while we play our online games for the first hour. Her gaming PC performs faster than my laptop, but I hold my own in our battles.

"I'll be back in a minute." Kendall excuses herself to the restroom. "Queue one of the movies if you want."

Snagging the remote to her smart TV, I log her out and then into my account, choosing to stream *Ready Player One* for us to watch. I walk into the kitchen, and I pull another beer for each of us from the fridge, grabbing a bottle of water just in case. I'm setting them on top of the coasters in front of the sofa when Kendall returns.

"Let's carry some snacks in, too," she suggests.

The coffee table barely holds the large bowls of snacks, dips, and sweets. I dip a chip into the queso, careful not to drip any on the way to my mouth.

"Should I push play?" she asks.

I nod, my mouth full, leaning back on the sofa. I can't believe I'm in her apartment. My patience paid off, and I smile to myself; she's worth the wait.

I've seen this movie many times, and it's a good thing because all I can do is think about the woman sitting a few feet away on the same sofa. The soft scent of her vanilla body wash causes my mouth to water.

I love that she didn't dress up, applying tons of makeup for this evening. She's casual with her brown hair in a loose clip, exposing her long neck. Her long-sleeved t-shirt and leggings hug her curves while screaming she's easy going. The fuzzy Harry Potter socks upon her feet cause me to smile, assuming she loves the series I've read multiple times.

I love watching her facial reactions throughout as she watches this movie for the first time. She leans against the opposite arm of the sofa, feet curled beside her, a pillow in her lap.

"I need another beer," I announce. "Can I get you a drink?"

She doesn't pull her eyes from the TV. "I'll take a beer," she states, leaning forward for a handful of popcorn, eyes glued to the movie.

We seem to have similar interests. I smile, happy she likes the movie I chose for tonight.

"So, what did you think?" I ask as the credits roll on the screen.

"I loved it." She smiles, setting the pillow aside. "I'm not usually keen on watching animated shows."

"What do you usually watch?" I ask, eager to learn everything about this woman.

She shrugs, pursing her lips in thought. "I don't watch much. Until tonight, I hadn't watched a movie in two years."

Two years? She must be exaggerating. She spends all of her time in this apartment. Surely she binges movies.

"Well," I attempt to keep the conversation flowing, "what about *The Mandalorian*?"

She lights up at my question. "I love *The Mandalorian*."

I release a breath I didn't know I held when she answers.

"What's your favorite *Star Trek* series?" I ask next, enjoying that she shares knowledge of interest to me.

"Honestly, *Star Trek: The Next Generation* is my fav with the new *Picard* series a close second," she shares. "I guess I'm a sucker for all things Jean-Luc Picard." She shrugs, thinking it silly. "How about you?"

I love that she asks. "*The Orville* is my new favorite."

She shakes her head. "I haven't heard of that one."

"Well, then you should check it out," I encourage. "If you haven't watched movies in a long time, then you've missed many of the new Marvel movies."

When she doesn't correct me, I continue. "I think we should watch all of the Marvel movies in order."

I can't believe I suggested that. It makes me sound desperate to spend more time with her—a lot more time with her.

She tilts her head to the side, brow furrowed and eyes squinting in my direction. I hold my breath, waiting for her reply.

"I've lost count. How many movies are we talking about?" She smiles.

"Twenty-six and counting," I inform her.

"You knew that off the top of your head without looking it up?" She smirks. "I'm impressed."

"Yeah. Well, to be honest, I looked at some of them to stream tonight," I confess.

"I tell you that I haven't watched a movie in about two years, so you propose we tackle all 26 Marvel movies, one at a time?"

"Not in one weekend." Unable to hold back my reaction, I laugh. "One or two at a time over several weeks or months."

"I might be up for that," she giggles, her wide eyes sparking to life. "I think we are up for the challenge."

Nodding, I smile, knowing I've secured 26 more dates with her.

21

KENDALL

I lock all four locks, press the keys to set my alarm, then slide my back slowly down the door. I sit, knees bent in front of me, a goofy smile upon my face.

I allow myself moments to revel in the good feels John left me with. I vowed never to open myself up, to never accept a date, and never let a guy give me good feelings ever again.

Okay. Time's up. I force myself off the floor, patting my cheeks to ward off the good feelings. I can't let them linger. I can't allow myself to let down my guard; nothing good will come of it.

I snag another beer from the fridge and the remaining popcorn before plopping back on my sofa, remote in hand. I search one streaming service then another until I find *The Orville*. I bite my lower lip, excitement bubbling inside as I press play on season one, episode one.

Four episodes and another beer later, I pick up my phone to text him.

> ME
> Guess what I'm watching.
> (sends pic of the TV screen with show paused)
> Thanks for the suggestion.

I place my cell phone on the coffee table in front of me, and I press play to start another episode. I'm not upset John doesn't text back; he's probably sleeping. I lay my head on two decorative pillows, cover myself with my new blanket, and lose myself in outer space.

John

Too soon, my alarm blares, waking me from an amazing dream starring Kendall. I silence it, scrolling through my morning alerts as I climb from under the covers.

No! Oh, god, no! She texted, and I didn't text her back. *Stupid "do not disturb" setting. She'll think I'm ghosting her.*

I click on her text to reply.

> ME
> I was sleeping.
> Sorry I missed your text.
> Glad you took my advice.
> It's addictive. I know.

My chest swells with pride in knowing that she took my suggestion to heart and did, in fact, like the show. Not only that but she texted me within hours of me leaving her house. I take that to mean she enjoyed hanging out with me, and it gives me hope that I might get to see her again soon.

Next, I read a text from a co-worker, asking me to cover his shift today. As he covered for me a couple of weeks ago, I really do owe him this favor. I grab my slacks and work shirt from the closet on my way to the shower.

Uncaged

Kendall

"I must say, I'm surprised you invited me to lunch," Mom professes. "I thought I'd have to wait until our Monday dinner to hear about your date."

"It wasn't a date," I remind her. "We hung out, played video games, and watched a movie."

She finishes her bite of salad and washes it down with a sip of water before she speaks. "Care to share any details?"

She knows prying will reap her no rewards. She's trying to hide her curious excitement by playing it cool.

"It was…" I search for words to describe our evening without giving her false hope. "It was okay."

"Okay is good," she states, smiling as if she knows a secret. "This salad needs more dressing." She rises from the table.

Searching the condiments in my refrigerator door, she says she believes she left salad dressing in here after dinner a few weeks ago. I wouldn't know. I only use my fridge to store milk for my cereal, beer, wine, and water.

"What's this?" Anne asks, her index finger gliding down the long list posted on the freezer door under a magnet.

Crap! I forgot I put that there. *Please don't pry. Please don't pry.* In a moment of weakness, I printed a list of the 26 Marvel movies in chronological order and tucked it under a magnet. I figured we should keep track of what we've watched. I should have put it somewhere else. *How am I going to brush this off as nothing?*

"It's a list of movies I plan to watch," I answer.

"What sparked this?" she asks, fetching the butter from inside the fridge.

"I just realized I haven't seen most of them." I attempt to make light, shrugging it off.

"You don't like movies," she reminds me. "So, what gives?"

"John mentioned wanting to watch the Marvel movies in order," I tell her. "He was just joking around, but I thought it sounded fun. So, I'm going to watch all of the movies."

I shrug, hoping to brush it off. I want her to drop it.

My cell vibrates with an incoming text.

JOHN

Sorry again about the text.

I use "do not disturb" at night.

> I realize this is the 2nd time I'm telling you today.
>
> What are you up to?
>
> Watching The Orville?

"Who's the text from?" Mom sing-songs.

I shake my head.

"I know it's him. You've got a goofy smile on your face," she informs me, unable to wipe the grin off her face.

John

My coworkers comment often about my sappy grin and good mood. For nearly eight hours, I've let them have their fun; I was counting down the minutes until I could call her after work. Timeclock punched, I open my cell phone and select her from my contacts. I tap buttons, dialing her on a video call, and I nervously wait as it rings.

"Hi," Kendall greets, her face barely on the side of the screen as she attempts to adjust her phone to better display her face.

"Hey," I greet back. "I'm getting ready to leave work. I thought I would check in to see if you needed anything. I could grab it and drop it off for you on my way home."

I mentally urge her to not read too much into my offer. I'm walking a thin line between being helpful while keeping in touch and constantly contacting her and forcing my way into her space.

"Um, let me look."

I watch as the ceiling then surroundings hint she's walking into her kitchen.

"I have plenty of cereal and milk," she talks out loud. "There's water. Um, I only have one beer." She pauses, looking at me. "If I invited someone over tonight, I'd probably need beer for him."

Love it. I. Love. It. She's chill; she's being cool about my offer and playfully inviting me over.

Uncaged

"Should someone like to come over and accept your offer to come over," I tease. "Do you need anything other than beer?"

Her smile grows. "I planned on cereal for dinner. We can order in, though, so beer is all we need."

"Gotcha," I respond. "I'll be over in 15 to 20 minutes and text when I'm close."

Maybe we'll start on our Marvel movie marathon tonight. I still can't believe I get 26 movies with her.

22

KENDALL

Before I know it, it's Monday evening. I motion for Mom to join Dad and me at the table, hoping to move this meal along. My butt in my chair, I scoot closer to the table, smiling over to Dad.

"How's John?" she pries.

"Anne," Dad's tone warns.

"What?" She brushes off his warning, continuing with her motherly duty. "New friends and watching movies again... I'm liking the new changes and trying to be supportive."

Be supportive by keeping your nose out of it, I think to myself.

"Is it the man from the grocery store?" Mom asks, her voice rising an octave in her excitement.

I try. I try very hard to keep my reaction neutral where John is concerned while making it clear I want her to stay out of my business.

"She's blushing!" Mom cheers, clapping her hands in front of her face. "James, she likes him."

Dad mouths, "I'm sorry," to me before addressing his wife. "Anne, you're doing it again," he warns, his voice warm. "Kendall will share when she's ready."

Mom pretends to zip her lips shut while her wide smile and sparkling eyes continue to advertise her excitement.

I curse myself for posting the list. It's an open invitation that Mom doesn't need. She only wants what's best for me, but I'm not a fan of her helicopter-mom tendencies.

Uncaged

The awkwardness of our weekly meal increases as Mom and Dad sneak happy glances.

John

Eight o'clock doesn't come fast enough. Kendall's eating with her parents; I have no reason to want to leave work early. She told me they would stay until at least seven.

> ME
> Heading out. Need anything?
>
> KENDALL
> Hmm...
> Something sweet
> But only if you're coming by
>
> ME
> Gotcha
> Be there in 20

Decisions. Decisions.
Sweet. Sweet.
Hmm...
Too many options.

I feel like this is a test. She's trusting me to choose for her and come visit. It took weeks to earn it; I can't mess up now. I like her. I've made progress in our relationship.

Is it a relationship? We're friends. That counts as a relationship. My goal is more than friends, but that will take time—maybe months. She's hurting, she's skittish, and she needs me not to push. It's killing me to move slow, to not push.

Patience—all in good time. She's worth it; I can do this.

My blood hums loudly as each step carries me closer to an evening with Kendall. The grocery bag of oatmeal raisin cookies in my left hand, I ring her doorbell with my right. My index finger is still hanging in the air at the sound of her four locks unlatching. I smile to myself at the knowledge she hung by the door, waiting for me.

"Dessert," I announce, extending the plastic bag.

"Thanks," she smiles. "C'mon in."

I note she doesn't peek her head out to look in the hallway. Instead, she's quick to shut and lock it tightly. She places the cookies on the counter. When she realizes what she forgot, she hurries over to set her alarm.

My hope is that, someday soon, I will earn enough trust that she shares what scares her beyond her apartment door. *Perhaps tonight will be the night.*

Kendall

It's killing me. I can't live this lie any longer. I owe it to her; I've not been the best friend she deserves. Often mistaken for sisters, although our personalities were very different, we were similar in many other ways. I love James and Anne. Always have. They've been great parents to me. With her gone, I feared I would lose them, too. With each long breath in and out, I battle to ignore the memories flashing in my mind. Images of the cabin-like bunker, of Zane ordering me to... And his daily visits. I shake off a chill at the memory of him. I've been disguising myself to hide from Zane. I can't pretend for the rest of my life.

23

KENDALL

"Hey," he calls my attention. "What's bothering you? You're distant."

Here we go.

"I'm ready to share," I begin, swallowing hard. "A stalker. That's the reason for all of this." I swing my hands, signaling my apartment.

"He's stopped, right?" he immediately asks.

"Uh...sort of." I shrug my shoulders. "He's still out there." My eyes search his face for a reaction. I have no way to know how he will react. He could decide I'm not worth his time; I may not be worth his patience anymore.

I add, "He's from a powerful family, so he barely got a slap on the wrist."

He rises, barreling around the apartment, ire apparent. I allow him his reaction. Lord knows I'm angry 24/7. My eyes follow him back and forth, back and forth. Eventually, he pauses in front of me, hands planted firmly on his hips.

"Tell me about it. Please," he prompts. "I'm going to need to stand while you talk, though."

"We went out twice before I broke it off." I raise my downcast eyes from my hands in my lap.

His eyes glued on me do little to hide his reaction.

"I couldn't explain it at the time," I shake my head. "Something about him set off alarm bells, so I ended it." I fight the chill crawling up my spine. Again, I stare at my hands in my lap, my fingers picking at my cuticles. "He didn't take me seriously about the breakup." I let out a heavy breath. "The next week, my best friend and I went to a frat party at Drake, and he was there."

This is the tough part to share. If I continue…if I share the truth, I might lose him as well as Anne and James.

"He…" I take a sip from my water bottle. I find it hard to swallow, much like dry cotton. "He…kidnapped me at the party that night, took me from the back porch."

I chance a glance up. His eyes have softened; his jaw no longer ticks. He sits beside me on the sofa, taking my hands in his. His thumb rubs soft circles on the back of each hand.

"It's okay; you're okay now," he soothes. "You don't have to tell me. I can see this is difficult for you."

I shake my head; I need him to know. "I'm ready to tell you *some* of it."

He keeps a hold of my hands, nodding for me to continue.

"I woke up in a room with no windows, no phone, no computer." I draw in a long, unsteady breath. "He kept me hostage for nine days.

He visited me once per day to drop off a meal and snacks. He wanted to break me down, but I wouldn't let him. I devised a plan and escaped when he visited. Then…"

My chest heaves, my throat is dry, and my eyes weep rivers of tears at the memories, at my confession. I've only shared these details with my psychiatrist. It took him nearly six months to pry the memories from my dead soul. I look at my fingers, wound together with his; I will my trembling hands to still.

"Take your time," he urges, looking from me to our hands between us.

"When I ran away," I gulp, "he found me, caused a car wreck, and fled the scene. My best friend died, and I was in the hospital for a long time."

"Did he come to see you…there?" He growls, losing his battle of controlling his anger.

I shake my head.

"Would I know him?"

Uh-oh! I'd better tread carefully.

"Umm…" I stammer. "He's affluent, somewhat famous, and part of a powerful Iowa family."

I can see the wheels turning in his mind; he wants to pay this guy he doesn't know—Zane—a visit. I can't let him get hurt because of me. I shake my head again.

He nods. "It can wait." He pats my hand sweetly. "I'm glad you shared, I now understand some of your…quirks." He forces a smile upon his face; I do the same.

"There's more, but…" I hedge, not sure if I should share more. "In hiding away, I've sort of been…" I clear my throat nervously, "…breaking the law."

I search his face, leery of his reaction.

"If it kept you safe, it's forgivable," he states without skipping a beat.

I want to believe him; I need to believe him. I can't keep this next part from him any longer. Constantly lying to him pains me. I hope the truth will set me free and not cause him to flee.

"I'm..." I take a steadying breath. "You see, my..."

Ugh! Spit it out already! Like pulling off a bandage. Quick.

"I'm not Kendall," I blurt.

My hand flies to my mouth. *It's out.* The lie that consumed me for over a year is out.

Head quirked to the side, he asks, "How so?"

"I woke up in the hospital, my jaw wired shut. Kendall died in the wreck," I explain rapidly, willing him to forgive me.

"So, it's a case of mistaken identity," he both states and asks.

I nod, gathering my thoughts to explain further.

"We look alike," I share. "We were always mistaken for sisters." I smile faintly at the memories. "Days passed before I emerged from the narcotic-induced haze." I shake my head. "By then, everyone thought I was Kendall."

Scanning his face, I find understanding.

"I think James knew the truth," I share. "I still think he does. We never talk about it. I got the feeling he didn't want to hurt Anne any more than he had to after the kidnapping and wreck." I shrug.

John's thumbs continue tracing small circles into the backs of my hands between us. He tugs his lower lip into his mouth before releasing it to speak. "So, if you're not Kendall, then you're..."

"Kristen," I state, closing my eyes and dropping my head toward my lap.

John's finger presses under my chin and lifts my gaze back to his. "Hi, Kristen," he smiles.

John

Kristen.

She's Kristen, not Kendall.

That's a curveball I didn't foresee. She had a stalker, her friend died in a car wreck, and she's living a lie on top of all of that out of fear of him. *Kendall is Kristen. Kristen is Kendall.* My head spins a bit.

I'm not in shock, just caught off guard. I expected her fear to be based upon a real trauma, not her living someone else's life on top of that.

"Say something," she prompts.

"I'll need something else to call you," I state. "You're not Kendall, and you're no longer Kristen. You need a…nickname." My attempt at lightening the mood falls flat. I'll revisit the name later.

"I…" I struggle for words to convey my understanding and support. "I can't imagine…" I gulp audibly, biting back the pain I feel for her and the anger I feel towards him. "You're a survivor, a strong woman of fortitude. You amaze me."

She scoffs. "I hide in my apartment. I'm not strong."

"I beg to differ. You didn't let him break you, you escaped, you started over, and I know you'll emerge from this more powerful than before."

Tears well in her eyes as she hiccups.

"Come here," I urge, tugging her tightly to my chest. "Thank you for confiding in me." I place a peck on the top of her head. "You've been through so much. I'm amazed by you."

"Amazed?" She chuckles. "I hide in my pajamas and apartment all day. The thought of walking down the hallway causes a panic attack. The fear of bumping into him cripples me."

"It amazes me that you escaped, you survived." He denies my attempt at brushing off his compliment. "You're healing. Day by day, hour by hour, you're taking steps to protect yourself."

I place a kiss upon her forehead, breathing in the scent of her. I whisper, "I think I love…"

24

KENDALL

What. The. Hell.

Seriously, what the hell? Did he really just say that? Love? Love!

He can't love me.

Never again. No one can love me. A guy's love for me stole my life. A guy's love for me locked me in my prison. Love is infatuation, and infatuation leads to pain.

How can he just say, "I think I love the name Kay for you…"?

Wait. My brain focuses on his entire statement. He didn't say "I love you." He said, "I think I love the name Kay for you."

Wow. My mind freaked out over nothing. Well, not nothing but the wrong thing.

"Hey," John's warm voice calls. "It doesn't have to be Kay; I was only trying it out."

I shake my head. "I like it," I murmur, adrenaline still coursing through my body from my freak out.

"Kay it is then," he confirms. "A 'K' stands for Kristen and for Kendall."

"I love that," I cheer, a wide, goofy smile on my face. "How'd you come up with that so fast?"

He shrugs it off as nothing.

"I love it even more now that I know the meaning behind it."

"Should we spell it K-a-y or just a letter 'K'?" he asks.

I pull my cheek from his chest, looking up to find his warm, brown eyes and a broad smile on his face. I wet my lips, his warm gaze heating me on the inside. I watch his eyes dilate while he watches my tongue slide across my lower lip. *I do that to him.* I ignite something within him with one innocent swipe of my tongue.

He sparks a flicker within me I believed would never light again. He makes me want to try, to want more, and to hope. I want to be the woman he thinks I am. He makes me better.

Hours after he leaves, I still can't erase the goofy grin from my face. He gave me a nickname; he calls me Kay. He didn't flinch when I confessed I'm pretending to be Kendall in order to hide from Zane. He accepts my "quirks," as he called them. The flicker in my belly grows into a small flame.

My TV flickers; it's Kendall. She likes my train of thought. I nod, smiling. For her, I need to try. I need to try a bit more each day until I'm living the life we both dreamed of.

"Okay," I say into my empty apartment. "I'll keep an open mind," I promise her.

Funny thing is I want to. I really want to be with John, to leave my apartment, and be normal.

I'm not worthy of John's friendship or his attention. Just over a year ago, I called Kendall to pick me up; I'm the reason she was on the road, fleeing from Zane. It's my fault she's dead. I had no way to know two dates with Zane would bring this upon us. But I did call her instead of the police. I called her instead of going with the old man, and I called her instead of Anne and James. My phone call put her in danger. My phone call killed my best friend.

Of course, my psychiatrist often reminds me I am not responsible for Zane's actions and thus not responsible for Kendall's death. I want to believe this; I want to end my pain. Baby step by baby step, I'm processing it all and attempting to open up once again. I long to feel worthy of him.

"Can I ask you a question?" John asks, days later placing our empty plates in the sink.

I hear the hesitation in his voice, and I nod.

"I hope by bringing this up, I won't upset you," he states, returning to my side, seated on the sofa. "Have you considered moving out of state? I mean, if your stalker lives in Iowa, maybe starting a new life somewhere else would be best for you."

He searches for my reaction, anxious for my response.

"His family's power doesn't end at the state line," I inform. "And I don't want to leave the country."

He nods in understanding then growls, "Grrr! I want to fix this."

"I don't need you to fix it. I need you to be patient with me," I inform him.

"It's frustrating. I mean, you know better than anyone how frustrating it is." He paces around the room. Pausing, he places his hands upon his hips. "You live it every day. This is so unfair," he barks.

"I know it's hard not to do anything," I agree. "It means a lot to me that you support me and you care. Maybe someday, I'll tell you everything."

Needing to change the subject, I lead us to the sofa.

25

JOHN

"Can I try something?" She asks, standing in front of me.

I quirk my head, brow furrowed. "Depends..." I hedge.

"Don't you trust me?" she teases nervously.

"Yes..." I draw out through a chuckle.

"I promise I won't hurt you." She attempts a sweet smile.

"I trust you," I state with a serious face.

She takes my hands in hers while moving her legs to straddle my lap. Fingers entwined, her brown eyes lock on mine.

Nervously, she smiles. Her eyes ping pong from my eyes to my mouth and back. Slowly, she leans towards me, her eyes homing in on mine. I'm transfixed as her tongue wets her lips seconds before they make contact with mine.

Her grip tightens on my hands as she softly presses her lips to mine. Sensing her hesitation, her nerves, I don't hurry the kiss. I allow her to take control. She doesn't rush, she doesn't urge my lips to part, and she doesn't release her tight grip on my hands.

Slowly, it becomes more natural. With each passing second, her entire body relaxes. She's opening up, lowering her walls, and allowing herself to feel.

She parts her lips, tongue darting out in search of mine. I read into her kiss and body language; she's pouring everything into it. She's telling me exactly how she feels about me. Withdrawing her tongue, she peppers pecks upon my mouth before leaning back. Her warm brown eyes smile at me.

Hands still entwined, I squeeze hers. "And..." I urge.

She shrugs, attempting to play it off as just okay, nothing special, but she loses her battle, bursting into giggles.

Kendall—I mean Kay—giggling is truly a beautiful sight. I squeeze her hands in mine as I lean towards her, my mouth seeking hers once more. This time, she releases my hands, raising hers to my shoulders.

I kiss her softly, understanding she needs to be in control. Her mouth on mine presses harder, her kiss more passionate.

I rest my hands on her hips, fighting the urge to help her grind her crotch against mine. Her hands slide into my hair, and her chest presses firmly to mine. We're closer than we've ever been, our bodies melding into each other. I focus on the part of her she's sharing with me, not all of the ways I want this to progress.

Her hands slide to my jaws as she ends our kiss. She smiles, biting her lower lip and nodding. I hope she's imagining lots of kissing in our future.

"Time for bed," she murmurs, and I nod.

I know she's not ready for sex, but I hope she's up for sharing her bed and cuddling. It'd be a long, sleepless night for me on her sofa.

Kay rises, tugs me up, and urges me to follow her to the bedroom. She slides under the covers without removing her clothes and socks. She folds the cover back on the open side of the bed, patting invitingly.

I remove my socks, tucking one inside the other, then drop them to the floor.

"I get cold, so I sleep in my clothes, but you don't have to," she explains.

I don't want to scare her by climbing into bed with her, only wearing my boxers. I keep on my t-shirt and remove my shorts. I slowly lay myself on the free pillow, positioning my portion of the blanket between us. This is another big step for her, so I tread lightly. When she rolls onto her side, facing me, I roll toward her.

We talk for nearly an hour, before losing ourselves to sleep. At four a.m. I wake to her cuddling into me in her sleep. Enjoying her touch, I'm unable to sleep. I savor the intimacy she shares in her subconscious and long for more of this when she's awake. Someday. She's slowly allowing herself for feel, and someday we will be together in all the ways couples demonstrate their love.

Love! Love?

I refrain from chuckling at my reactions to my thought, so I don't wake her. I am in love. *I love her.* She's not ready for me to confess it, but my body warms just knowing I'm in love with this woman.

26

KENDALL

Continuing our virtual dates together, tonight is week four of our online self-defense class. As we mimic our teacher, John and I have a ton of fun making jokes. We laugh way too much as we practice and learn. At the end of class, I'm holding my side from laughing so hard.

"I have an idea; I'll be right back," he informs me, leaving the room.

I quirk my head, wondering why he's in my bedroom. *What might he be up to?* Rather than ruin his surprise, I remain in the kitchen, grabbing a drink.

I spew a mouthful of water when John emerges from the bedroom with several pillows taped to him. The gray tape secures one pillow to his abdomen and chest and one to each arm and leg.

"What…?" I can't even find the words to finish my question.

"I thought we'd really practice your new moves," he states with a wide smile.

"You expect me to punch you?" I laugh.

"You can do everything but go for the eyes and nose," he informs me. "Come over here so I can attack you."

"Not the words a girl longs to hear," I tease.

"Less talk and more action," he taunts, causing me to raise an eyebrow. "C'mon. I'm going to approach you from behind."

"Not getting any better." I laugh as his choice of words could have a very different meaning.

He plants his pillow-covered legs apart, and with hands on his hips, his arm pillows act as muscles.

I decide to give him what he wants; it's time to stop laughing and simulate self-defense. I turn around, reminding myself I am safe and this is only a simulated attack because I need to prepare for the real thing.

When he wraps his pillowed arms around me, I stomp on his right foot, thrust my elbow backwards into his abdomen, then—taking his arm in hand—throw him to the floor, planting my right foot on top of his chest pillow.

"How did that feel?" I chuckle before noting his face is beet red and hearing his groans. "Did I hurt you?" I ask, squatting beside him, noting blood vessels straining in his neck and forehead.

"Your elbow…" he grunts. "Too low."

It's now that I notice his knees are curled to his torso. *Holy crap!* I must have elbowed his crotch. I move from fear I hurt him into full body laughter.

Stupid idiot. That will teach him to tape pillows to himself and taunt me. I laugh so hard I fall back on my butt, rolling on the floor.

John

Days later, I'm unsure whether I'm more nervous or scared as I sit in an armchair, facing Anne and James on their sofa. I'm suddenly regretting approaching them this evening.

"Can I get you another water?" Anne asks, her hands fidgeting in her lap.

My randomly asking to speak to them makes them as uncomfortable as I am. I need to put us all out of our misery.

"So…" I start. "I'm not sure how much Kendall shares with you, but we spend several evenings together each week. I really like your daughter, and I have a question for you."

While I thought my words would relax them, they seem to worry them more. I quickly replay what I said, realizing it sounds as if I plan to ask permission to marry their daughter.

"Kendall has shared portions of the trauma she experienced," I blurt, hoping to rest their worries.

"Really?" James draws out, surprised.

Anne's wide smile informs me she likes the idea of her daughter opening up to me.

"While she's not told me everything, I know most of it. I've tried to remain patient, but I can't wait for her to answer one looming question. It's my hope that you'll tell me the name of the guy. I can't press her for it. She alluded to the fact that he's from a prominent family of power, but that's all I know."

Anne looks to her husband, placing her hand upon his, which is resting on his thigh. They share a look for several quiet moments.

My heart beats violently in my chest as molten blood pulses loudly through my veins, and I'm sweating like a turkey on a farm the day before Thanksgiving.

James clears his throat, nervously adjusting himself on the sofa cushion.

"I'm not sure," he says before clearing his throat again. "It's her story to share. If she's shared everything but that fact, then she has her reasons."

Anne interrupts her husband's explanation. "She's made great progress in the past year. If she shared her tragedy with you…"

"She's never shared with us," James states. "And we've tried not to push for details. It's been our hope that her therapists help her open up and work through it."

"And she shared with you. That's huge!" Anne smiles widely. "She trusts you."

"The one thing we do know is his name. I hope you understand that we can't break what little trust she has in us by sharing a name," James explains.

"It's killing me not to ask you to share what you know," Anne confesses. "It's like we each hold a piece of a puzzle that needs her to connect us."

I don't understand her analogy, but I guess I understand why they won't betray Kendall. There's no way I'd divulge the secrets she's bestowed upon me.

"So, we wait," I state.

"I'm afraid so," James agrees. "I can't tell you how nice it is to meet you. She shares very little, and like we said, we try not to pry."

"She's told me a lot about you," I inform, happy to share this bit of good news.

"She may not be happy that you stopped by." Anne tells me something I'm very aware of.

"I'm toying with the idea of telling her I reached out and introduced myself to you," I confess. "She won't like it, but I don't think I can keep that from her. Who knows? She may be happy this awkwardness is over." I chuckle hollowly.

James chuckles, too. "I don't even want to be a fly on the wall when you tell her."

"That bad?" I wonder out loud.

"It won't be any worse than getting her to let you into her apartment was," Anne assures me.

"Maybe I'll find her in an exceptionally good mood," I hope.

"I haven't witnessed that for…" Anne trails off as we all know it to be prior to the kidnapping.

A heavy silence falls upon the living room. Not wanting to take up more of their time, I excuse myself, thanking them for talking with me.

Unsuccessful in my quest, I wonder if I'll ever learn the name of the evil guy that tore apart the lives of four people. I carry rage for a man I don't know. Even in the shell of a woman I've come to know as Kendall, I see hints of the vibrant, beautiful girl she was before. He stripped her of her future and happiness. He planted an all-consuming fear within her. For this, I need to know his name. I need to know who he is, and I long to get justice for Kristen, Kendall, Anne, and James. Now, more than ever, I need to support her and be patient with her. She's worth the wait; I feel it in my bones.

For now, I need to focus on protecting her from this unknown man that I see everywhere I look. She lives in a prison of her own making while he roams free. I long to place him in a cage and let her loose to fly.

"I have a confession," I announce while dumping our to-go containers into the trash.

"Do tell," she urges.

"You're not gonna like it," I divulge, giving her a moment to prepare herself. "I met James and Anne."

She doesn't react the way I anticipated. Her head tilts to the right, and a smile creeps upon her lips. I can't take her silent reaction.

"I thought since you've spoke with my Mom on video calls that it was time I met your parents, so I reached out to them."

Her smile, still present, worries me.

"I teasingly told them you might be relieved that the awkwardness was over," I continue. "So, that's done." I brush my hands together to add a visual to my words.

"Did James interrogate you?" she asks, still smiling.

I shake my head. "They were kind and didn't ask many questions."

"And you survived," she teases.

Still standing in the kitchen, I place my hands upon her shoulders. "Now, you're scaring me. I can't believe you aren't upset with me."

"I'm actually relieved," she confesses. "I've been trying to work up the courage to invite them over for dinner to meet you."

My eyes scan her face, finding I believe she's telling the truth.

"I'm surprised Anne hasn't texted me, fawning all over you," she says, tugging my hand, leading me to the sofa. "She's asked for details ever since I posted your business card on my fridge."

"Perhaps she's giving me time to confess before she calls. I told them I planned to share that I met them," I offer. "So, now that we've met, will you invite them over while I'm here?"

She bites her lips in contemplation. "We haven't strayed from our usual Monday night dinners. Maybe it's time I invite them over for drinks or to play cards. What would you think about that?"

I smile widely, loving that she opens up more and more each week. Although trips outside the apartment are still rare, she's making strides toward returning to a life outside these four walls.

"I'm game for anything," I quip, causing her to chuckle.

KiKi

Wanting to express my gratitude and overwhelming affection for the man sitting beside me, I straddle his lap, placing his beer bottle on the table to free his hands.

"I love you," I whisper, freezing in horror at my proclamation.

It's too soon. I've pressed him to take things slow, and then I go and blurt that out. I'm such a freak.

John's hand on the back of my neck draws my lips to his. A mere hairsbreadth between us, he murmurs, "I love you, too."

27

KENDALL

Meets Riley/meets Dawn first time on phone

A week later, I open my door for John. "Who's this?" I ask, motioning for him to enter with the little girl on his shoulder.

"Kendall, meet Riley, my cousin. She's the niece I mentioned Mom is raising after her sister passed. Mom's at a function tonight, so I'm babysitting." He places Riley on the floor, unloading a toy from his backpack. "I thought I'd bring her by to meet you," he explains.

Does he plan on me babysitting for him? My head tilts when he plops on the floor beside her.

"Wanna play?" he asks, patting the floor beside him.

I guess I'm gonna play.

"How often do you babysit for your mom?" I inquire.

"I try to at least twice each month," he answers, rolling the wooden car across the floor to Riley. "I wish I could make it once a week. Mom's got her hands full."

"That's kind of you," I state, rolling the car on my turn.

"Riley's a good girl, aren't you?" he baby talks.

When Riley smiles, her plump cheeks swell, and her eyes light up. Clearly, she loves her cousin, John.

"Does your brother help?" I ask.

He chuckles. "No. He tried it once. Riley was teething and put him through the ringer. He doesn't have the patience."

Interesting. Nelson sounds very different from John.

Riley places her chubby hand on my knee, her brown eyes gazing up to me. After a long, silent moment, her hand upon my knee pats me.

"Hi." She smiles.

My heart melts; she's so darn cute.

"Hi," I say in return.

She looks to John then back to me. Placing her palms on the floor, she clumsily pushes up to stand. Proud of her accomplishment, she claps, smiling again. Toddling two steps, she stands in front of me, still clapping. When I clap, she cheers.

"She likes you," John states.

"Of course, she does," I quip. "What's not to like?"

"I haven't found anything," John states.

I peek around Riley to find him smiling.

"Wanna stay for dinner?" I suggest.

He nods, his smile widening.

"I'm not cooking," I announce.

"Duh," he laughs. "I'm buying. What are you in the mood for?"

"You choose," I answer. "You know what Riley can eat."

"Num, num," Riley cheers, clapping.

"I'll get right on it," John states, pulling out his cell phone. Then he looks to his cousin. "Should we eat with Kendall?"

"KiKi," Riley cheers, clapping in my direction.

"Am I KiKi?" I ask her.

She nods her little head.

"I love it!" I cheer.

"May I call you KiKi, too?" John asks.

I nod, a wide smile upon my face.

Riley is adorable. She's so cute, and John is wrapped around her little finger. He caught me off guard, standing at my door, Riley in hand, but it was a nice surprise.

"She's almost asleep," I say, closing the story book.

"Let me pack up her stuff, and we will get out of your hair," he offers.

"Don't go," I blurt.

Where did that come from?

John's gaze assesses my sincerity.

"I'm... I don't..." I stammer. "I don't want you to go. Not yet."

John's eyes warm. I fidget slightly under his gaze, not wanting to disturb Riley as she lies beside me.

"It's still early."

I hate to beg. I've enjoyed their company. I find it harder and harder to be alone after spending time with him.

"I'll need to grab her portable crib from the truck," he informs.

My heart skips a beat. *He brought a crib; they can stay.* It might be selfish of me, but I'll take it.

"Okay," I prompt.

John

"Watch a movie?" I suggest after I place Riley in her crib.

"Start our Marvel movie marathon?" she offers.

"I'm game if you are," I challenge. At her nod, I login and pull up our first movie, loving the opportunity to be together several more times to see them all.

She heads into her bedroom, returning with two pillows as the title sequence of *Captain America: The First Avenger* displays on her television.

We start out sitting side-by-side; by the end of the movie, I'm horizontal against the back of the sofa with her back to me, my arm resting on her hip.

"Stay the night," she pleads, peering over her shoulder at me.

How can I refuse her? She's working through something, she's opening up to me, and she's taking a risk. Her asking me to spend the night is a gift I won't refuse.

"I guess we could," I murmur into her ear.

Happy with my answer, she tugs my arm tightly around her. I squeeze her in a one-arm hug.

"Should we watch another movie?" she suggests.

I tap a few buttons, starting *Captain Marvel.*

Our second movie over, I think back on how this evening unfolded. *Perfect. What a perfect night.* Riley brought many smiles to Kendall's face. *No. Not Kendall. She's KiKi.* I love the name Riley bestowed upon her. My new goal is to place many smiles upon KiKi's face as often as I can. She came alive playing with little Riley tonight.

I place a kiss to the crown of KiKi's head as it lays in front of me. She turns, looking up through her lashes. My breath catches when she moves slowly toward me.

My cell phone vibrates loudly on the table in front of us, interrupting the moment. Seeing my mom's name on the screen, I reach for it, answering the video call and grabbing KiKi's hand when she attempts to leave my side.

"Hi, Mom," I greet, answering her FaceTime call.

She's going to explode when she sees I'm still here.

"Hi, sweetie," she coos, her camera pointed toward the kitchen as she places her purse and car keys on the counter. "I just got home from the gala and wanted to check in. How'd Riley get along?"

"All's good here." I pan the camera lens to include the person sitting at my side. I anxiously wait for her to take in my surroundings as I watch her lens change to facing her.

"Oh, my!" she gasps then giggles loudly. "Hello, honey." Mom waves, still beaming.

KiKi smiles uncomfortably.

Oops. I guess I just introduced my girlfriend to my mother. I hold my finger up, halting her reply.

"Mom, I'd like you to meet Kendall." I hurry to make the introduction I should have made upon answering the phone. I smile towards the woman sitting beside me. "Kendall, this is my mom, Dawn."

"Hello, Ms. Hoover," Kendall greets.

"Oh, call me Dawn, sweetheart," Mom corrects, beaming.

I clearly see Mom's ecstatic I'm still here.

"Riley's a sweetie," Kendall states. "We had so much fun tonight."

"She even gave Kendall a new nickname," I share proudly. "Her name is now KiKi." I smile.

"Ah. I'm so glad Riley liked you," Mom beams.

"I keep forgetting to call you KiKi," I chuckle and place a peck on KiKi's cheek. Her cheeks turn crimson.

"How was the gala?" I return my attention to Mom, moving the conversation forward.

"We raised a ton of money, but I'm so glad it's over," she shares.

"Until you start planning next year's," I tease.

Mom points her index finger at me. "Don't even bring up next year's gala for at least three months."

We all chuckle.

"My parents were at the JDRF Gala tonight," KiKi informs Mom. "James and Anne..."

"Ward?" Mom finishes for her. "Your parents attend every year. It's a small world. Wait until you see what they..." She suspiciously trails off. "Well, I should let you go," Mom offers. "It's almost midnight, and you know what happened to Cinderella at midnight." She disconnects while KiKi and I laugh.

"Your Mom's a hoot," she chuckles, a large smile gracing her beautiful face.

I tilt my head. "I've been telling you that for weeks."

She nods.

28

KIKI (PREVIOUSLY KENDALL, REALLY KRISTEN)

"What should we watch now?" John asks after our movie.

I smile and suggest, "Wanna watch an episode of *The Orville* with me? I mean, I know you've already seen it..."

"*The Orville* it is," he agrees, remote in hand.

Two episodes later, I turn to face him, a smile upon my face. "Watch one more?" I offer, hoping he hesitates. I swipe my tongue slowly across my lower lip; eyes locked on his. I really want to...

I'm unable to finish my thought. All thoughts vanish as I lose myself in thoughts that he's about to kiss me. John closes the distance between us, pressing my chest to his, his mouth opening upon mine. My hormones explode in reaction, heating my body.

I press myself into his hard muscles, loving the delicious friction our contact causes. His tongue swipes across his lips before his strong tongue plunders. My heart threatens to beat through the walls of my chest. Our tongues and limbs tangle. I don't think; I feel. I allow my body to take the lead, shutting my brain down for the night.

My fingers release their grip on John's brown hair, my hands trailing down his shoulders and along his ribs to fist in the hem of his t-shirt. One of his hands upon the back of my neck softly holds my mouth to his, ensuring our kiss will not be broken.

I playfully suck his lower lip. Opening my eyes, I find his sparkling playfully. I raise my hands inch by inch, lifting his shirt between us. Less than an inch from him, I feel the friction of his shirt against my belly, my ribs... I halt, my hands just below my breasts.

I'm ready. I can do this.

My sessions with my therapist over the past couple of weeks swim through my brain. *John is not Zane; he's nothing like Zane. I want more; I want John—all of John.*

I pull in a long deep breath. *I've been working up to this for weeks. I. Want. This.*

John

Her eyes sparkle playfully, and she draws her lower lip into her mouth, her hands holding the hem of my shirt to my chest.

Why did she pause? Her eyes and mouth signal she wants more. *I wonder what the hesitation means.*

I choose to follow the desire I see in her eyes and mouth. I cross my arms in front of me, grasp my shirt, and lift it over my head. My eyes emerge from behind my shirt, finding her eyes devouring my chest, her lower lip between her teeth. Clearly, she likes what she sees. I fight the smirk threatening to emerge on my lips as she eye-fucks me.

I'm not a gym rat or a protein shake fanatic. I play sports, enjoy an occasional run, and plank every day. *Finally, my planking pays off.*

I clear my throat, chuckling at her embarrassment at being caught ogling me. I plant my hands on her hips, tug her toward me, and murmur low near her ear, "Like what you see?"

I laugh loudly when she swats my shoulder, scolding me. She pretends to be angry at my reaction, but I will have none of it. I pull her over me, urging her to straddle my lap, her folded legs on either side of me.

I nearly groan when the heat of her core collides with my swollen cock. Eyes locked on hers, I tuck her hair behind her ears. I silently will her to communicate her desire to continue, as I need to let her set the pace.

"That was easy," the red button on her counter proclaims into the silent apartment.

I look over my shoulder, finding what I already know. The kitchen is empty.

She laughs on my lap, her hands on my shoulders. My furrowed brow urges her to explain.

"It's Kendall." She giggles hard, wiping tears which have formed in her eyes.

I quirk my head. When she shared the story of Kendall leaving messages for her and giving her signs, I could tell she really believed it. She told me about the red button from Staples going off at random times, signaling and prompting her forward. While I believe in ghosts, I will be taking that button apart later to investigate.

"She's happy we're..." Her voice barely a whisper, she motions, pointing down to our connected laps.

My erect cock pleads for me to continue while my brain wonders if the ghost's interruption means we should stop for the night. I have no time to decide between my warring cock and brain; warm, wet lips trail kisses on my neck, over my shoulder, and to my pectoral. My hands fist in her hair, raising her mouth to mine.

KiKi

I freeze when John's hands fist in my hair. My eyes squeeze tightly shut. Sensing my reaction, John immediately unlaces his fingers, allowing his hands to fall to my shoulders. His mouth moves to place a peck upon my forehead.

"I'm sorry," he whispers, lips feathering my skin.

I press my forehead to his lips, needing his touch. "I need a minute," I murmur, my voice raspy.

"I rushed..." he begins to apologize.

I press the pads of two fingers upon his lips, my eyes meeting his concerned ones. I allow myself a moment to assess my feelings. I feel safe. I crave his attention and touch. I *want* this. His fingers fisting in my hair caused me pause but didn't trigger fear. I'm okay. I smile. *I'm okay.* I lace my fingers in John's, tugging him to follow me as I glance over my shoulder on our way to my bedroom.

John

I'm in shock. I don't argue as I allow KiKi to lead me into her bedroom. This is huge; it's huge for her. I'm not sure she's 100 percent ready, but I'm allowing her to be in charge. After her trauma, she needs control; she needs the power. I'm patient. I've been patient, and I'll remain patient; she's worth it.

Uncaged

The faint light from the other room casts shadows in KiKi's dark bedroom. At the end of her bed, she spins to face me, planting her palms flat upon my pecs. Looking up through her dark lashes, she licks her lower lip in anticipation.

I bend down to her eye level, searching… I'm looking for many things: clues to her true feelings about our actions, for any red flags, for any hesitation, longing to see how she honestly feels at this very moment in time.

"I…" She places a sweet peck to the corner of my mouth. "Want…" She mimics the action on the other corner. "You…" she states, pulling away, hands grasping the hem of her shirt and quickly pulling it over her head before tossing it to the floor.

My lips part, a gasp escaping. I'm awestruck as the woman before me sheds her clothing piece by piece, baring herself to me. I must remind myself to breathe, gulping in an audible breath. My fingers tingle, longing to caress her; my mouth salivates, hoping to taste every inch of her. My cock throbs, needing to bury itself balls deep within her.

"John…" Her husky voice stirs me from my fantasies.

She rounds the corner of the bed—hand in mine—switches on a lamp on the bedside table, then crawls onto her bed. She's a lights-on kind of gal—how refreshing. I love that she's comfortable in her own skin. She should be; she's beautiful inside and out. Her soft, olive skin begs me to touch. I plant a knee on the bed, preparing to join her.

"Ah, ah, ah…" She shakes her finger at me before pointing it up and down my body. "I think you're forgetting something." Her eyes bright, she bites her lips between her teeth, hiding her smile while waggling her eyebrows.

I raise one eyebrow in question.

"You have on too many clothes," she giggles. "Strip. Then join me," she instructs.

I do as commanded, excited by her playfulness. My body's on fire for her. I'm still very aware she's been through a trauma, and although she's seeking pleasure now, at any moment, she may be triggered and slam us to a halt. While I'll enjoy every moment with her, I'll be alert for signs we need to stop. I will not push her for too much too fast.

I don't hide my smirk, eyes locked on her as I remove each item of clothing, slowly peeling off layers, revealing myself to her for the first time. I pause, my thumbs in the waistband of my boxer briefs, daring her to stop me before I remove the final layer. KiKi's tongue darts out, slowly swiping across her lower lip, craving more. I lower my thumbs two inches, revealing my lower abdomen. Her lips form a soft 'O' and her brown eyes dilate, marveling at the dark smattering of hair I keep along my devil's trail.

I've never stripped for a woman. Hell, I've never had more than a quickie with the lights on; it's heady, the reactions I elicit from her while standing a few feet away. I lower my waistband two more inches, feeling my erection straining against the fabric, aware the base of my cock is now visible to her. KiKi gulps, her eyes looking up to me through her dark lashes. I could get lost in those chocolate pools. I'm unsure how long I drift in thought. Her slender fingers, grazing my hips while sliding my briefs down my thighs, jolt me back into the present.

Eager for attention, my cock springs from beneath the fabric, reaching for her. Already rock hard, I feel it grow like a flower, stretching toward the sun. Every cell in me feels her gravitational pull; I don't fight it. Stepping from my boxers, I move closer. Her eager hands grab my hips, slide to my ass, and pull me to her. I tumble to the bed, bracing myself above her. Her laughter dies when our hungry eyes lock.

"KiKi…" I murmur.

"Shh…" she admonishes. "Kiss me."

I slowly lower my mouth to hers, our eyes remaining open, our souls finding comfort in one another. Our kiss morphs from slow and sensual to hard, teeth knocking, all consuming, with the biting of lips and needy groans. Her nails bite into my flesh while her heels dig into my backside. My lungs burn for oxygen; I pull inches away, peering down at her bee-stung lips and heavy-lidded eyes. Our jagged breaths are loud.

Crap! A condom. I lean to my left, preparing to slide off the bed for my wallet, but KiKi's feet cross, her legs a vice grip around my waist.

"I need a condom," I murmur huskily.

She shakes her head. "I'm on birth control, and I'm clean."

My eyes search hers.

"I've never not worn…"

Again, she presses two fingers to my mouth, silencing me. "We're safe, and I trust you," she whispers before replacing her fingers with her lips.

When she nips my lower lip gently between her teeth and holds it playfully, I groan. "You sure?"

KiKi releases my lip, places her palms upon my shoulders, and pushes, rolling me onto my back beside her. In the blink of an eye, she maneuvers, straddling me proudly. Her hot core sears my groin. She runs one index finger in a snake-like trail down my chest and over my abdomen. Her brown eyes glint wickedly as she caresses my groin on my right then left side of where I need to feel her most. She's a vixen; I love the confidence and strength she's displaying.

Her right hand grasps my shaft, and her tongue darts out, swiping her lip as her thumb swipes over my tip. Her eyes follow her hand as she pumps me. Up, across the tip, then down. Over and over, she works me into a frenzy. On her next downward stroke, her eyes return to mine. She lifts her pelvis, weight on her knees, her hand guiding me to her entrance. Inch by delicious inch, she lowers herself, enveloping me in her hot, wet heat.

Focus. Focus. I can't lose control too soon. Buried to the hilt, KiKi stills all movement, eyes closed and lips parted. She's struggling—with what, I'm unsure. I pray she's overwhelmed in a good way.

"Breathe," I remind her, rubbing small circles at her hips.

Her eyes find mine; she nods.

"Are you okay?" I inquire, worried this might be too much too fast.

She rolls her pelvis forward in answer. Back and forth she grinds, her head tipping backwards and her back arching. She knows what she needs; she uses my body to seek her release.

KiKi

I find my rhythm, grinding forward and back, forward and back. The sensations skyrocket my desire, my head falls back, and I explode. White lightning bolts fire behind my closed lids, every muscle flexes, and my nerve endings zing.

I'm barely aware that John's hands at my hips urge my hips against him, as he thrusts into me two more times. I collapse against his chest, our heavy breathing the only sound in the room. Several long minutes pass, before our breaths even out.

Wow! Did that really happen? Orgasm--I thought I'd never want one, let alone receive one.

John's my cure, my antidote, the answer to all that's been missing in my life this last year. He's patient, and he lets me take the lead. He doesn't see me as broken, rather as on the mend. He encourages me, silently at times, to attempt things I once took for granted.

29

KIKI

Riley's babbles pull us from sleep shortly after seven.

"Good morning," John's gruff morning voice greets from under me.

"Mornin'," I return, lifting my head from his chest.

I can't believe I slept all night. I never sleep through the night. And I slept cuddled tightly to him on my bed, his arms around me.

"I'm not sure I have stuff for breakfast," I warn, worried about Riley.

"I have food for Riley in my bag, and I'll be fine," John assures.

I need to find something for him to eat; I can't have him leave my house after our first night together hungry. Leaving my bedroom, I wave at Riley in her crib on my way to the kitchen.

"KiKi," she cheers, making grabby fingers at me.

I love my new name.

"I have cold cereal and leftover pizza," I offer. "I even have a full jug of milk."

He laughs, lifting Riley. "I knew you'd have cereal," he teases.

"Good morning," I say to a smiling Riley as she pats her palm against her cousin's cheek. "I can change her diaper while you get her breakfast ready," I offer.

His eyes narrow, assessing my sincerity. I clap my hands then reach for Riley. She immediately leans towards me.

"Let's go change," I coo, walking to my bedroom with the diaper John hands to me. "Get all pretty and eat some breakfast."

"Num, num," she babbles, looking at me to agree.

"Num, num," I parrot.

John

"Breakfast's ready," I call as they emerge from her bedroom. "You'll have to sit on my lap," I tell Riley, extending my arms in her direction.

KiKi's all smiles, eating her cereal, watching Riley eat her baby food along with nibbles of my cereal. Riley's chubby little hand dips into my bowl, chasing the cereal floating in the milk. Of course, she drips milk down her arm and on my lap with each handful, but I don't mind. KiKi's smile makes it all worth it.

"So, what are your plans for the day?" I ask.

She shrugs. "I may see if Anne wants to get lunch," she thinks out loud. "What about the two of you?"

"I need to get Riley home soon, or Mom will come looking for her," I chuckle. "I'll probably eat lunch with them before I go home."

I'd love to drop Riley off and hurry back here. Spending my day off with KiKi sounds perfect.

Pulling from Kendall's parking lot, Riley decides to yell at the top of her lungs. Unable to do much from the driver's seat, I pass her my cell phone. She loves playing with it, and she immediately quiets. About a block from Mom's house, I hear a familiar female voice from the back seat.

"Miss me?" KiKi asks in greeting. "Oh, hi, Riley." She laughs.

"Sorry." I raise my voice, hoping she can hear me. "I gave her my phone to play with. She's never unlocked it before. I have no idea how she video-called you."

"It's okay," KiKi assures. "She needed more girl time. Didn't you, Riley? You wanted to stay all day with me."

I agree with Riley when she babbles back to KiKi that she did want to spend the day together.

At Mom's, I extricate Riley from her seat, placing her beside me as I grab the backpack. Reaching down to take her hand, I find she's gone. I see her toddling towards Mom on the sidewalk, my cell phone in front of her.

Crap! She's still on the phone. If Mom…

"Oh, hi, Kendall," Mom greets, holding Riley in one arm, my cell in her other hand.

Of course, Mom carries on a conversation with her; I'll be lucky if I get my phone back by noon.

"Okay, dear. Tell your mother I said hello," Mom croons.

She hands my phone to me after KiKi says goodbye.

"Let me have it." I urge Mom to begin her inevitable interrogation.

"Did you have fun with John and Kendall?" Mom coos to Riley as we enter the kitchen.

"KiKi!" Riley cheers, clapping.

"Oh, that's right," Mom agrees. "You like KiKi, don't you?"

Mom lowers Riley to the floor then focuses her full attention on me. "So, how was your night?"

I can't decipher the meaning behind my mother's weird tone. "She was a perfect little angel as usual," I report.

Mom tilts her head and furrows her brow. "Kendall? I mean, KiKi?" she asks.

"What? No. Riley." I state the obvious.

"It was a big night with KiKi…" Mom says.

I raise an eyebrow.

"Forgive me," Mom begs. "After I showered, I ate a snack. Then, I worried about Riley and you, so…" She draws out the word. "I used the Life 360 App…"

I close my eyes. Now, I know where this is going.

"So, I know the two of you spent the night at KiKi's."

At least she acts ashamed of her prying into my life.

"Calm down," I warn, hearing excitement growing in her voice. "We watched movies and talked. That's all."

How is it possible that my mom's megawatt smile doubles in size?

"One step closer to grandbabies," she announces.

"It's not like that," I quickly correct. "Slow, remember? Very, very slow." I shake my head.

She looks like she's about to pop.

"And Riley's more than you can handle at times. You don't need grandbabies," I only half tease.

She points her finger at me. "Don't ruin this for me."

KiKi

A pleased sigh escapes, and I smile, leaning against the locked door. Last night and this morning couldn't have been any more perfect. Riley's a sweetheart, and John absolutely loves her. He's a tender family guy, and it's so dang adorable. I pull my cell from my pocket.

> ME
> Wanna take me to lunch?
>
> ANNE
> Of course! When?
>
> ME
> Now
>
> ANNE
> Will text when on my way
> You decide where we eat
>
> ME
> (heart emoji)

Heart emoji? I sent her a heart emoji. She'll probably think a stranger has my phone or I'm possessed. She's probably tripping all over herself, scurrying over here.

"So, it's KiKi now?" Anne asks, a proud smile upon her face.

"If that's okay; I really like it. And the fact that little Riley labeled me? I can't resist," I explain, in hopes my faux parents will go along with it.

"It's fun and playful," Anne states between bites of her flour taco. "Now, I want to meet Riley. I can't believe I've known Dawn all these years and never met her niece. She's been holding back on me."

I nod, taking my last mouthful of my taco. "I'll invite you over for the next playdate we have," I tease.

"I can't believe I ate both tacos," Anne states. "I haven't eaten Tasty Tacos since…"

Since… We both know how that statement ends. As it was Kendall's favorite place, I've avoided it until now. I chose it today in honor of my best friend. I'm slowly making changes, and she's my motivation.

"So, you enjoyed time with Riley," Anne confirms. "Did you find time to hang out with John?"

I nod, sipping from my water glass. "Riley went to bed by eight. We watched two movies then a couple of shows."

Doing the math, she raises an eyebrow.

"We talk a lot." I make light of the fact she knows we were together last night, at least until 2:00 a.m. "We've started our Marvel movie checklist."

"That's a long list," Anne acknowledges. "So, you watched movies. What else? You seem to like his company."

"We talk a lot, play video games, and we have a lot in common." I'm honest with her. "He's…"

"He's patient?" She seeks confirmation.

I nod, unable to hide my giddy smile.

"I like him," Anne states, placing her hand upon mine on the table. "Thank you for inviting me to lunch today."

Tears sting the back of my eyes. Unable to speak, I nod, forcing a smile.

"We have a surprise for you," Anne confesses. "We bought you something in the live auction last night. Your dad's gonna meet us back at your apartment."

Hmm… Not sure how I feel about this. Until recently, I've not allowed them to purchase items for my apartment. Now, I may never get them to stop; it's foreign.

"Any place you'd like to go, or are we ready to head back?" Anne asks, our meal complete.

All I can think about is their surprise. "Let's head back; I don't want Dad to wait long."

Anne's large smile causes me more concern about what they have planned.

30

KIKI

When James and Anne leave, I sit on my kitchen floor, watching my new puppy explore the apartment. Alone now, I'm unsure what to do.

"Perhaps I should give you a name," I say to him as he sniffs nearby.

I've never named a pet before. Heck, I've never owned an animal before. *What were they thinking, giving him to me?* I shake my head. I know exactly why they brought this breed of dog to me. They worry about my safety and believe a big guard dog will protect me. *Why couldn't they bring me a talisman or statue to do the same thing?*

Vishnu! It's perfect!

"Come here, boy," I call while patting my lap.

The oversized creature tries to climb in my lap.

"I'm going to call you Vishnu," I inform him as he licks my neck and cheeks. "You like that name? You do, don't you?" I giggle at his inability to stop kissing me. "Vishnu, stop," I laugh.

I heave his heavy body from my lap. Quickly rising to my feet while he follows my every step, I take my cell phone in hand.

"Smile," I urge, snapping several photos of him.

> ME
>
> (send pic of Vishnu)
>
> New friend wants to meet u

> Stop by after your mom's?

John

"Mom," I call, unable to take my eyes from the picture KiKi texted me.

"Hmm?" she inquires from the island in the kitchen.

I extend my phone, showing her the cute photo. "I think KiKi got a dog."

"I know," Mom beams proudly. "John and Anne won him in the live raffle last night."

When I close the dog photo, Mom rapidly reads KiKi's texts. She wipes her hands on a nearby kitchen towel, places her hands on my shoulders, and rushes me out the door. She can't contain her excitement for me to further bond with Kendall. All she sees is grandbabies in her future.

As I climb into my truck, I send a text to KiKi, letting her know I am on my way.

As is my habit, I alert KiKi of my arrival, so she's ready at the door and not alarmed when I knock.

> ME
> I'm here

I hesitate outside her apartment door, allowing her video doorbell to alert her. *Beep, beep, beep, beep,* then *click, click, click.* I listen as she clears the alarm and opens the locks.

Her beautiful smile greets me through the five-inch opening in the doorframe.

Uncaged

"Are you ready for this?" she asks. "He's a big ball of energy."

I nod, smiling widely. I place my hand on the edge of the open door, slipping through carefully to ensure the puppy remains inside.

"Whoa!" The little beast places his front paws on my waist. His picture didn't accurately show his size. "Down, boy," I order, my voice forceful.

Of course, the puppy doesn't obey. We'll have months of training ahead of us. We... I like thinking of us as "we."

"Down," I order again. This time, I place his front paws back on the floor. Placing my palm on his back, I urge his bottom to the floor. "Down," I state firmly. He tilts his puppy head at my words. I kneel in front of him. "Good boy." I scratch between his floppy ears. "You're a good boy. Yes, you are."

I chance a glance up, finding KiKi's warm, brown eyes and soft smile. I already love this dog; it's helping her smile. My girl needs more reasons to smile. *My girl. I think she finally sees herself as my girl.*

My brow furrows at the open drapes and blinds behind her. What used to be a wall of heavy black curtains is now floor to ceiling windows overlooking a rooftop patio, allowing sunlight to fill her apartment.

"What's this?" I inquire, moving toward it.

"Part of the apartment I've never used. James set it up for Vishnu," KiKi explains.

I quirk a brow.

She shrugs. "I named him Vishnu."

I nod, smirking.

"It's the..." She starts her explanation.

"Hindu god," I finish, surprising her.

I love her approving smirk.

"May I?" I jut my chin toward the patio, looking at her, hoping I'm not crossing any of her boundaries.

"Sure. Take Vishnu, too."

She watches through the windows as I explore, the puppy on my heels. After Vishnu relieves himself on the nearby faux grass pad, I toss a ball. He fetches but doesn't release when he returns with the ball.

"Release," I order, grabbing the ball, which is still in his mouth. "Release," I demand, pulling it from his mouth. Then, I toss it across the patio again.

KiKi slowly emerges, sitting on the edge of a nearby lounge chair.

"That thing work? I could grill tonight." I point to her grill under a cover.

"It's new. I've never used it," she informs, body tight.

She's uncomfortable in this space. I find myself worrying how Vishnu will disrupt her life. Dogs require walks. Time on this patio will not be enough for this large puppy. I get that, recently, KiKi's opened up a bit and left the apartment, but this may be too much too soon.

I take a seat beside her, pulling her tightly to my side. Her puppy explores the space, sniffing nearly every inch. Knowing we should stay here longer, I decide a distraction will be the best thing for her.

"When we go back inside, I'll run to the store to get food to grill," I suggest.

She nods, hyper alert to the sounds of the city near us.

"What breed is he?" I ask, distracting her more.

"He's a seven-week-old Beauceron," KiKi says, a hint of pride in her voice. "I looked him up on the internet. He could weigh about 100 pounds. They are powerful protectors, loyal to their owners."

"His markings…" I'm in awe.

"Gorgeous, right?" She smiles proudly.

"Yep," I concur. "You know, if we string up some lights and put a patio table with chairs over there, this place will be great to enjoy the warm weather."

As she scans the space, I can feel her thinking about my suggestions. She nods when she looks back at me.

"I could install a dog door, one that locks unless the sensor on his collar is close enough to allow it to open," I further prompt. "Vishnu could come and go out here, and it would save you tons of trips to open the door."

"Find me the dog door online, and I'll order one," KiKi states. "I could cook you a meal to pay you to install it."

"Umm… I should cook the meal, and you could find another way to thank me," I chuckle, nudging her shoulder playfully.

"I could cook, and you could keep an eye on me to make sure I don't mess up," she counters.

"So, I'd be installing a dog door while keeping a keen eye on you in the kitchen?" I purse my lips.

"Fine. I won't cook; I'll pay you back another way," she pouts.

I fight the growing smirk upon my face. Her relaxed muscles and smile mean I've distracted her from her fears, and she's enjoying time on her patio with Vishnu and me.

KiKi

John ran to the store for a couple of items for the grill. He returned with six shopping bags. As we unpack, I find he purchased way too many dog treats and toys along with at least three full meals to grill. I bite my lips, hiding my smile; I love that he plans to spend more time here. I've come to enjoy his company, finding I miss him more and more when he's away.

"Do you earn a commission on the amount you spend at the store since you work there?" I tease, wadding up the plastic bags and placing them in the trash bin.

"Ha ha," he scoffs.

Vishnu repeatedly nudges John's legs.

"I think I should take him for a walk," he suggests, scratching my puppy under his chin. "Want... Would you like to go with us?"

Several emotions flood over me at once. I've been out on the patio twice already today; I think I've spent enough time out of the apartment for the day. Then again, it's a beautiful, sunny day. Vishnu is my puppy. John shouldn't feel he has to walk my dog by himself every time he visits.

John

A myriad of emotions swim across KiKi's face. I shouldn't have suggested she walk with us. I must be careful how much I push her out of her comfort zone, or she'll stop letting me see her.

"The complex has a dog park," she shares, pulling her emotions in check. "I might be up for a quick walk around the block." I hear the reluctance in her voice.

"We can walk around the block," I agree. "Then, if you feel like it, we'll let him play at the dog park. If not, he'll play on the patio while I grill."

She nods, not fully committed to our outing. I wrap my arms around her waist, pulling her to my chest. My heart breaks when I feel her tremble against me.

"Baby steps," I murmur into her hair. "Let's visit the dog park for a bit. If he runs with other dogs, he'll burn off his excess energy." I gently run my hands up and down her back as I speak. "I'll be with you the entire time," I vow.

I feel her nod against my chest before she wraps her arms around me and squeezes.

"Thank you," she whispers, looking up at me when she pulls away. She turns, addressing Vishnu. "Let's do this."

Her playful puppy lopes over, craving her attention, not knowing the adventure we're about to embark upon.

31

KIKI

In my typical Monday fashion, I ignore Ashley by playing online games until she's finished giving the place a once over. Mom texts when they leave their house, so I scramble to change my clothes then set the table in preparation of their arrival.

I open the door, standing aside as they carry a slow cooker, dessert, and two grocery bags into my apartment. *What's with all of the food?* There is no way the three of us will eat half of it. As usual, Mom overdid it.

Dad begins putting away the groceries from the two bags while Mom moves the chicken tortilla soup from the slow cooker into a large serving bowl and places it on the table.

"We'll need soup bowls," she instructs, prompting me to place them on the table for the three of us.

Often at these dinners, I long to be a normal daughter—or as normal as I can be. I imagine we'd be less awkward around each other, carry on meaningful conversations, and not force a meal every Monday.

Mom places the dessert into my refrigerator, her hand frozen on the handle when she closes the door, spotting my new calendar.

Crap! Did I not learn anything from posting the Marvel movie list? My new dry erase calendar is a megawatt, neon sign, begging her to notice every little detail.

"Well," she murmurs, "this is nice."

She helps Dad fold one of the paper shopping bags, tucking them both under the sink. Then they take their seats with me at the table.

In my peripheral vision, I see her smile; however, she says nothing. This is not the typical Mom reaction. *What's going on? This could be bad. Very bad.*

I'm on high alert as we say grace, fill our bowls, and begin to enjoy our soup. I sneak a glance up to Dad and Mom between spoonfuls of her soup. The torture is killing me.

"Looks like you'll be busy this month," Mom states moments later.

There it is. Let the interrogation begin.

"Mm-hmm," I mumble in answer.

"It warms my heart to see movie nights." Her smile proves she knows those to be date nights.

Dad's confused expression causes me to spew soup through my nose.

"Kendall," Mom admonishes, using her napkin to soak up my mess.

"Honey," she points to my refrigerator, "Kendall has a calendar on her fridge."

"So?" He brushes it off, oblivious.

"It has John's work schedule, his softball schedule, movie nights, and Vishnu's training sessions on it," she brags.

Wow! How'd she have time to note all of those in the brief moment she gazed at it? She's Superwoman, and it's her superpower.

Maybe someday I'll learn not to fight her interference in my life.

KiKi

Where did this Saturday afternoon go? It seems as if, moments ago, it was noon; now, it's nearly four. I place my cell phone back into my pocket; when I look up, I find John taking a short break to play with Vishnu. I'm amazed the two find enough room on my patio to play a decent game of fetch. Vishnu is still learning to give the toy back to him, but John is ever as patient with my puppy as he is with me.

"Release," John orders firmly. "Release."

Eventually, Vishnu's jaws slacken, and the toy falls to the ground.

"Good boy," John praises, scratching his head between his ears before tossing the toy one more time.

"Our parents should be here anytime," he states, striding toward me.

My eyes widen as I stare at him.

Sensing my worry, he pulls me into his arms, my head flat to his chest. "We're ready," he vows, his hand rubbing up and down my back. "Everything will be fine. It doesn't need to be perfect."

I nod against his chest without conviction. Instead of looking forward to this meal, I mull over all of the ways tonight might go off the rails.

"Trust me." John kisses my temple, his lips hovering on my skin. "Our parents have been acquaintances for years."

"I can't help it." I state what he's already aware of.

"Let's wait inside so we can hear when they are at the door," he offers, taking my right hand in his left. "Vishnu, let's go."

At John's words, my large puppy clumsily enters the house through the dog door John installed for him. John opens the door, allowing me to slip inside and him to follow. We have perfect timing; the doorbell sounds upon our first steps in the apartment. Again, John kisses my temple then leaves my side to open the door.

"KiKi!" Riley's sweet little voice yells to me across the kitchen while her chubby little hand waves, and she wiggles in an attempt to get out of Dawn's arms.

"Riley, where's my kiss?" John asks, pretending to be affronted. "Riley, you always kiss me."

The moment Dawn allows her niece's feet to hit the floor, Riley makes a beeline, toddling to me. I crouch, opening my arms wide for her approach. Her tiny hands clutch tightly to my shoulders as I wrap my arms around her. Not wanting to miss out on any action, Vishnu licks both of our cheeks.

"Vishnu, come," John orders, and he obeys; he'd surely knock us over.

Dawn wraps her arms around her oldest son, making a loud smooching sound when she presses her lips to his cheek. "I won't miss my chance like Riley did," she teases.

"Looks like the gang is all here," Dad announces from my opened apartment door, Mom standing in front of him.

"Don't embarrass me," John chides his mom under his breath.

I blow raspberries into Riley's chubby neck rolls in an attempt to hide my snicker, eliciting an explosion of little girl giggles.

"Okay, you two," John interrupts. "Time to welcome all of our guests, not just the cute, little one."

"Wait," Dawn swats at her son playfully. "I'm cute, too."

"I said cute and little," John argues.

"Son," Dad grips John's shoulder, shaking his head, "you're making it worse; quit while you're ahead."

John's wide eyes meet mine; I smile, nodding as I pass Riley to him. She opens her arms wide for her cousin, eager to soak up his attention.

"Come on in," I urge my parents and Dawn, swinging my arm into the apartment, away from the door.

Dad turns to lock the door while the women step toward the patio.

"I can't wait to see what you kids plan to fix for us," Mom states, passing me.

"Oh, I'm not worried," Dawn tells Mom. "John's a fabulous cook. I made sure both of my boys learned to cook before they left the nest." She smiles proudly over her shoulder toward her son.

"Trust me, we have too much food," I inform our parents, further urging them onto my patio.

Vishnu senses our destination, slipping through his dog door ahead of us.

Dawn freezes mid-step, clapping excitedly, hands in front of her chest. I'm not sure how she does it, but she surprises me by smiling bigger and wider each time I see her. Her full cheeks puff out, her skin glows, and the corners of her mouth curve in a smile up to the corners of her eyes. Not only is her entire face a light, her entire body beams with her excitement.

"John told me he installed this dog door," she says cheerfully. "I just love that your puppy learned to use it quickly." She pauses at the closed door, inspecting John's handy work. She looks at her son. "Honey, it looks as if it came with the door. You did a wonderful job."

Impatient, Vishnu pops his head back through the slot. I imagine he's wondering why we didn't follow him outside.

"Vishnu, out," John directs, and my puppy scurries across the patio.

"Don't be rude," Dawn scolds, affronted by his tone.

"Mom, puppies need structure and firm tones to help them understand our expectations," John informs her.

"Pish posh," Dawn scoffs, waving her hands in the air between them. "Puppies need cuddles, puppy talk, and playtime."

"He gets plenty of that," I interject, moving to John's side. "Inside here, he's a softy," I tease, poking his chest.

I love the smile he wears at my words and touch. His nearness soothes my nerves about this evening.

"What can I help you with?" Dad asks from the kitchen area as the women shut the patio door behind them.

"The grill's hot," John shares. "Help me carry the steaks. I'll grab the veggies, and KiKi will grab the appetizers."

The three of us make quick work of gathering our food and joining the moms outside. I place the tortilla chips, salsa, and queso on the table before encouraging

Uncaged

Dawn and Mom to join me at the table. John places the diced red potatoes and fresh green beans on the shelf beside the grill before opening the cooler.

"Ladies," he calls to the four of us, "what would you like to drink?"

Riley slides from my mom's lap, toddling over to peek into the cooler at John's side. Her hand grabs an ice cube, quickly dropping it to the concrete where Vishnu eats it, making her giggle and clap animatedly.

"Beer? Pop? Wine? Water?" John further prompts us, eyebrows raised. "KiKi?"

Riley moves her attention from the large puppy to me. "KiKi!" she yells and claps.

"Beer for me," I inform him.

"I'd like wine," Mom states.

"Me, too," Dawn agrees, rising. "Shall I go grab a couple of glasses?"

John extends his hand, halting her progress. "We have everything we need out here." He demonstrates, pulling chilled, stemless wine tumblers and a corkscrew from the cooler and places them on the table for the women.

"Tonight, we'll be grilling KC strip steaks, new red potatoes with fresh green beans, and cupcakes for dessert," John announces proudly.

Mom smiles, impressed, eyes looking between John and me.

"I helped make the cupcakes," I brag.

At Mom's over-exaggeratedly raised brow, John defends me. "KiKi helped prep the veggies and frost the cupcakes. She learns a bit more every time I cook for her. Before long, she'll be able to make entire meals on her own." He slips his hand into mine; his fingers entwining with mine. He squeezes my hand, demonstrating his support.

"I'm impressed, and I never doubted she could cook," Mom hedges. "She needed the proper motivation. That's all." She doesn't try to hide her love of all things pertaining to John.

Riley's squeals interrupt the moment. At the cooler, Vishnu chomps on ice cube after ice cube from Riley's extended hand.

"Those two will cause us nothing but trouble." John shakes his head, grinning. "Perhaps we should keep them separated."

"You can't be serious." I chuckle. "We're not keeping them from playing together, and they act like any other toddler and puppy their age. Lighten up," I challenge.

Mom giggles, and Dawn joins her. The two laugh so hard they fan their cheeks. Dawn snorts, eliciting laughter from all of us.

"Oooh," Dawn cackles, her face turning beet red. "Ooooh... Ooooh."

I worry she might wet herself if she doesn't get a grip on her laughter. I mean, I'm about to pee my pants, so she has to be on the verge of losing it. Vishnu's deep bark interrupts our comedic moment. Riley startles, never having heard him bark. I move to scoop her up, worried she'll cry but find she doesn't. Instead, she pats Vishnu's back, doing her best to soothe him. Yet again, the night flows smoothly while I worry that every interaction will cause the evening to fail.

"Riley," John calls to her, kneeling next to the cooler. "Want a drink?" He pulls a sippy cup from the ice, having prepared water for her ahead of time.

She claps as she approaches him, assuring him she's glad he thought of her, too.

"Let's grill," John cheers, moving to Dad's side. "I steamed the veggies ahead of time, so they'll cook at the same time as the steak."

Dad nods, impressed. "What seasoning do you use?" He rubs his fingertips across the surface of one of the strip steaks.

"I sprinkled sea salt on both sides," John shares. "I keep it simple. I've prepared some butter, adding lemon juice, garlic, salt, and pepper to plop on it when it's done."

Again, Dad nods. "The boy knows what he's doing," he professes, beer in hand, taking a seat beside Mom. "He uses steak butter," Dad murmurs near her ear.

"I taught him that," Dawn proudly confesses. "Taught him everything he knows."

"Yeah. Right," John scoffs, tongs in hand.

"Well, maybe not everything," she chuckles.

"Steaks on," he announces. "We'll eat in 14 minutes."

Fourteen minutes? Is he serious? Not 15. Not 10. Why 14 minutes?

Sensing my confusion, John explains, "Five minutes for each side. Then they'll rest for four minutes before we eat." He massages my shoulders while standing behind my chair.

"Don Don." I hear Riley call from my side. Turning I find her arms raised in hopes he'll pick her up. Unable to refuse her anything, he scoops her up, placing a kiss upon her plump cheek.

"Did you call him John John when he was a boy?" Mom asks Dawn.

Dawn shakes her head. "I'm not sure where she picked that up; she's always referred to him as 'Don Don.'" She shrugs with a large smile. "Kind of how she calls Kendall 'KiKi,'" she adds.

"Num, num," Riley prompts.

"Somebody's hungry," I state, cluing my parents in on the baby talk I've picked up from Riley. "Where's her cereal?" I crane my neck, looking around the cooler and the tub beside it, which we prepared for tonight.

"Riley, want some cereal?" he asks, approaching the tub. He lowers her.

Nearly upside down, she giggles as her hands clutch a plastic bag of dry cereal. "Num, num," she announces, proudly upright in his arms again. "KiKi!"

I want to believe she's making the connection that the bag contains my favorite cereal. I mean, she's had it here before. It's probably nothing; she's just calling out my name as John returns her to the table beside me. I've enjoyed the times she's visited my apartment, finding myself looking forward to any chance John has to bring her by. She gives me hope that a happy life is possible for me.

"Mmm, mmm," Dad mumbles, satisfied, rubbing his dad-belly. "The boy can cook."

I fight the urge to roll my eyes. "The boy." He's not a boy; he's a man.

"I'll use your butter recipe on my steaks from now on," Dad declares.

On Dawn's lap, Riley rubs her eyes with her chubby fists.

"I think it's time to set up the portable crib," I prompt in John's direction.

He nods, rising. "I'll bring out the cupcakes when I come back."

"Oh, my," Mom chuckles; Dad joins in. "I can't eat another bite."

"I'll have to take my cupcake home with me," Dawn states. "This is why I tend to eat dessert before my meal, to make sure I have room for the sweet stuff."

Her words draw laughter from our group. Looking over my shoulder, I watch John hold the door open and Vishnu join him inside. John wastes no time striding to the apartment door to fetch the crib from his truck. I bite my lips between my teeth when Vishnu sits at the exterior door, whining. Figuring John won't return, he slips back through his dog door to join our group. My pup is as tired as Riley.

John

The sun's dipping behind the horizon when I exit KiKi's building. I make a beeline for my truck, cursing myself for not carrying it inside before our parents arrived. I wanted to be prepared. Movement on my right side catches my eye. A person, it looks like a man, ducks between two SUVs a few parking spots from my truck. It's a public lot, but something about his movements piqued my attention. I press the button on my key fob, unlocking the truck doors. I pull the crib from the back seat. Closing the door, I scan the lot, but the person I saw before is nowhere to be seen. I shake my head; I'm sure it is nothing but my overactive imagination. I return to KiKi's apartment, making quick work of setting up the portable crib in the bedroom for Riley.

"Hey." KiKi's soft voice announces her presence in her dark bedroom. "She's already out like a light."

I carefully slide Riley from KiKi's shoulder, lowering her into the crib. I wrap my arm around KiKi's back as we watch Riley stir for a moment before settling.

"She's so sweet," KiKi whispers, further pressing herself into my side.

I press a gentle kiss to her temple. "C'mon." I urge her toward the light just outside the bedroom door. "Want to play cards?"

She smiles up at me. "We'll need to…" She stops abruptly.

Our parents enter the kitchen, hauling everything back inside for us, Vishnu keeping a close eye on all they do.

"I guess I'll fetch the cards," KiKi murmurs.

On its own, my hand swings out to playfully swat her bottom; I stop myself in the nick of time. It wouldn't be polite for me…in front of her parents.

"Anyone up for cards?" I ask, approaching the counter, guiding the clean up.

"Phase 10 or I have a regular deck of playing cards," KiKi offers, standing at her table, two card boxes in front of her.

"I'd be up for a game of Phase 10," Anne states, and James nods in agreement.

"Phase 10 it is," Mom declares, drying her hands before finding a seat at the round table.

I join the group, assuming the empty chair beside KiKi and Mom. John deals the cards, and our game begins.

Over an hour flies by as we play two full games, and the conversation flows. It's been a great evening. I'm glad I encouraged KiKi to plan this get-together. Although she hesitated and worried, she trusted that I would be at her side through it all. I like giving her these moments. She gifts me a smile, assuring me she's enjoying her evening, too.

32

KIKI

"Roll the credits," I cheer, clapping at the end of our movie.

John stretches his arms above his head on the sofa beside me. "Want anything from the kitchen?" he asks, preparing to stand.

Does that mean he's leaving? Or is he getting himself a drink to stay? I'm not ready for him to leave. I'm never ready for him to leave.

I rise, following him into my kitchen. He's placing a check mark beside this movie and ready to put my rating beside it.

"I give this one four stars," I state, and he nods.

I point to the next movie on our list. "Maybe I can watch the next movie at your place."

John's wide eyes illustrate how I caught him off guard, and his growing smile announces he likes that idea.

"Yeah?" he asks, placing his hands on my hips.

I nod, chewing on my lower lip. "I'd like to try." My head tilts to the side, and I shrug.

His firm lips collide with mine, slow at first. His fingers dig into my hips, pulling me to him. At my gasp, his tongue takes advantage of the opening. Through my parted lips, he laves long strokes, which I return. Our tongues tangle as do my fingers in his hair. A blissful moan escapes, causing him to chuckle against my mouth and his chest to vibrate against mine.

"Follow me," I urge, tugging on his finger, striding toward my bedroom.

"Um..." he chuckles. "Some of us work in the morning."

"I'll make it quick then," I tease.

John

KiKi stops with her calves against the edge of her bed, tugging me tightly to her. I press my forehead to hers.

"What if I don't want a quickie?" I counter, loving this playful, confident side of her.

"Then I invite you to take as long as you want," she teases, lifting her shirt over her head before scooting across the comforter to the center of the mattress.

Then take my time I will. Distracted by the beauty of KiKi laid out before me, my fingers fumble while unbuttoning my shirt like a 16-year-old boy. I moan when she lifts her hips, shimmying her leggings down her thighs. Unable to fight it, I lunge onto the bed, planking my body above hers.

"You have no idea what you do to me," I growl.

She playfully brushes the tip of her nose lightly against mine. I flinch when her palm presses firmly against my erection. "I think I have some idea," she teases, eyes sparkling.

Taking her lead, I nip her jaw then down her slender neck. She arches, urging me to continue my playful exploration. I alternate licking, nipping, and sucking over her clavicle, along her shoulder, and to the swell of her breast beneath the cup of her gray bra.

"I need you," she murmurs huskily.

"Patience," I urge.

My fingers tug her bra, my tongue dipping below the fabric, grazing her nipple. Her breath hitches, and she arches her chest, longing for more. The playful minx that lured me to her boudoir is long gone; she lays pliant and moaning.

Wanting to push her further, I exhale a hot breath against her nipple through her bra then trail kisses toward her naval and beyond. Licking the edge of her gray boy shorts, matching her sporty bra, she mews and writhes in pleasure. I believe I could make her climax without removing her panties. Perhaps another time. I'm dying to feel her warm walls surround me.

I stand for a moment at the end of the bed, removing my shorts and boxers, enjoying the sight of KiKi removing her bra, displaying her breasts to me. It's refreshing being with a woman secure enough to leave the lights on during sex. The female form is a sight to behold in all its variations.

"John," KiKi whines, lying in front of me.

I prowl up the length of her, eyes locked on hers, with one goal in mind. I part her thighs with a nudge of my knee, rubbing my cock against her while my mouth entertains hers. I nip her bottom lip, my eyes opening to hers.

Propping myself up on one forearm, I position myself at her wet entrance, burying myself to the hilt, my heavy-lidded eyes holding on to hers. She lifts her pelvis, grinding herself down on me before I withdraw in order to plunge forward again and again.

She fists her hands in my hair, forcing my mouth to hers. Our kiss is frantic, wanton, and communicating each of our needs.

I won't fight it, not tonight. I allow my climax to build quickly, climbing higher and higher. Each hour of this perfect day filled me with more love and desire for her. I long to tell her exactly how I feel; instead, I show her. My body worships her, filling her with all of the love I have for her.

33

KIKI

"What are these?" he asks, flipping through my large sketches on the table.

Guess I was too excited to see him to remember to hide them.

"Nothing really." I make light of my comics.

"She's a sin eater," he states while looking at a third sheet.

How the hell did he figure that out that fast? The sin eater? That it is a female? My blurred-out superhero's nearly invisible to others. She goes unnoticed, hiding...

"You've heard of sin eaters?" I ask, stunned.

"I saw it in a movie once," he states then admits, "It sparked me to read a book and article I found on them."

"Nerd," I tease.

"Um..." He swipes his hand in the air above my sketches. "I'm not the only one." He chuckles.

"It's a hobby," I defend.

"You should publish these," he urges. "It's free on Amazon."

"How do you know?"

"I like to read." He shrugs. "I do research on random stuff all the time."

I smirk. I used to be the same way. Maybe I'll be that way again.

"May I?" John asks, motioning to my sketchpad on the table.

I push down the bitter taste of bile that rises with my fear. I pull my lips between my teeth then nod. To his credit, John senses my fear.

"Sure?"

Again, I nod.

He pinches the dark cover, slowly lifting it. Silently, slowly, he turns page after page. I'm frozen when his gaze moves to me. "These are…" He glances back to my sketchpad then to me.

"You're talented." He smiles, continuing to flip page after page.

My heart rate quickens in anticipation of him finding my most recent sketches.

"That's Riley!" he announces, his index finger tracing her cherub cheeks. "You captured her…"

"She's easy to draw. So vibrant… So damn cute." I chuckle.

He shakes his head. "I love it."

"Turn the page," I prompt.

"Wow!" He places fingers to mouth. "Mom would love this."

"Take it," I offer.

"Really?" he asks, astonished.

"Yeah," I assure him.

"I'm gonna frame it. Her birthday is next week. I'll say it's from both of us."

I shake my head. "That's not necessary."

"She's gonna ask who drew it. One way or the other, she'll know it's you."

I shrug uncomfortably.

"You've witnessed her on video calls. You know what she's like…" He urges me to understand. "You should be proud of your work."

He wraps his arms around my shoulders, pulling me into a hug. His mouth near my ear, he says, "So talented. So. Damn. Good. You're gifted."

I want to argue, but it feels too good in his arms. I choose to enjoy his scent, his warmth, and the safety he provides.

John

"Are you ready?" I ask KiKi during our video call. "They're pretty keyed up tonight."

"The way you describe them, they always are," she teases.

While she speaks, I assess her mood. I don't want to push her if she's not ready. She seems at ease, so I move on, flipping the camera view.

"Hey, guys," I call to my co-ed slow pitch softball team. "Kendall's on the phone. Say hi."

They greet her with hi, hello, and cat calls. I shake my head, not at all surprised.

"Hi, guys," she greets. "Gonna win tonight?"

"Of course," my pitcher responds.

"If John's bat is hot, we will," the first baseman states.

He's not wrong. I'm the cleanup hitter for our team. More often than not, my RBIs are the only points we score.

"We wish you were here to bring us luck," the pitcher says.

"Someday soon, I'll attend a game," she promises.

I hope she's really able to attend before the season ends. One part of our relationship that weighs heavily on me is how important my team and friends are and my hopes she'll merge well into that part of my life. It's hard keeping the two separate right now; that's the reason for tonight's video call. I want them to meet.

"I think we played high school softball against each other," the shortstop states, pulling the phone from my hand.

I stand, mortified by this little tidbit. She means Kendall played softball, but she's talking to Kristen.

"You pitched in the district game, knocking us out my senior year," the shortstop reminds her.

"Oh, yeah. That was my freshman year," KiKi answers.

"Time to warm up," our pitcher informs, rescuing KiKi and me from the trip down memory lane.

I take my phone back in hand. "Sorry. I didn't know…"

"No worries," KiKi promises, interrupting my apology. "Good luck."

34

JOHN

I'm smiling head to toe as the elevator door pings open in anticipation of seeing KiKi tonight. I can't get enough of her; I spend my days counting the minutes until I can be with her. Time away from her moves at a snail's pace while time with her speeds by.

I pause midstep, half on and half off the elevator. In KiKi's hallway, I find a person standing—a guy in a gray hoodie. My body goes on high alert, cataloging every detail. He's not ringing her doorbell, and he's not knocking; he's along the opposite wall of the hall down from her door.

"Hey," I call to him, my feet working again.

The hoodie-guy doesn't turn to me. Instead, he walks briskly to the stairs and disappears. I'm torn between chasing him and checking on KiKi. I worry he was leaving her apartment, hanging around in the hall. This creeps me out.

Standing in her hallway, I will myself to calm down. I don't want to scare KiKi if he hasn't set off the Ring doorbell. She might still be unaware of the hoodie-guy. I'm just overprotective and maybe could have been at the wrong door.

I take a calming breath as my index finger presses her doorbell.

"I'm so glad you're here," KiKi greets, a wide smile upon her face. "Vishnu needs some male bonding time. He's being naughty."

I release a breath I didn't know I was holding. She's not upset; she doesn't know a stranger stood in the hallway. I squeeze by her, immediately greeted by puppy paws jumping up, pressing on me.

"Vishnu, down," I order.

I bite my lips, quickly looking toward KiKi when he follows my directions and backs off. I've worked with him a few times on this command; he seems to learn right away.

I bend down, praising him with scratches between his ears and under his chin. "Such a smart boy, aren't you? Yes, you are," I say in puppy speak.

"See? He needed male bonding time," KiKi points out. "He acts differently around you. He doesn't jump on me."

"You love your mommy, don't you?" I draw out, my voice raised. "You're just excited when I come over. Yes, you are." I turn to address her now. "If you left and came back, he'd try to jump on you, too."

She stares at me skeptically.

"We played with the chew toys you brought him today, and he didn't chew on the furniture or my clothes," she brags.

"Such a good boy," I say in puppy talk, rubbing Vishnu's belly. "Should we take him potty?"

"He's used the grass pad on the balcony twice," she shares. "And I took him to the doggy area once."

My eyes widen at this news. She left the apartment without me. Vishnu's proving to be a positive influence already. I make a mental note to share that tidbit with Anne and James.

"Let's take him out before we eat and start our movie," I suggest, rising to my feet. "Wanna make it a short walk?" I ask her.

"We can try," she agrees noncommittally.

I'm okay with that. The more she takes Vishnu to the dog park area, the more likely it is that will lead to her becoming comfortable with walks.

I remove the leash from the hook by the door and realize I greeted Vishnu but not KiKi. I approach her with Vishnu at my side, sniffing his leash excitedly.

"Come here, you." I pull her to my chest. "I didn't properly…"

I'm interrupted by KiKi's lips pressed tightly to mine. Great minds think alike. Our potty walk with Vishnu is momentarily delayed.

KiKi

"I think I'm ready to turn back," I state, glancing up at John beside me.

"Sounds good," he agrees. "My stomach's starting to growl." John chuckles, placing his hand on his belly.

I want to remind him it was his idea to take Vishnu to the bathroom and walk before we eat and start our movie, but I don't.

"What shall we order?" I ask. "If we order now, it will arrive about the time we get back."

John shakes his head. "I'm cooking your dinner tonight," he announces proudly. "Remind me to get the groceries and cooler from my truck on our way back."

I nod, a wide smile upon my face. He's cooking for me. *I like it.*

"What are you making?" I ask, my stomach rumbling loudly.

"Sounds like you are hungry, too," he chuckles, picking up our pace. "It's nothing fancy." He shrugs. "I'm making mac and cheese."

"Sounds yummy." I don't tell him that's one of my favorite things.

John

Rounding the corner of KiKi's building, I spot someone in a gray hoodie beside my truck, his hand flat on top of the hood. Everything in me wants to yell while running after him, but I refrain, not wanting to spook KiKi.

"Here." I pass Vishnu's leash to her. "You two head inside. I'll grab the groceries from my truck."

"Okay," she agrees without being any the wiser.

I remain on the sidewalk until she enters her building then head towards my truck, my cell phone in hand. As my phone rings, calling my friend, teammate, and cop, Meyer, I scan the parking lot, trying to spot the hoodie guy again.

"Sup?" Meyer greets.

"A stranger in a hoodie seems to be following me and Kendall," I inform. "I think I need your cop expertise."

"I'm on duty now," he states. "Want to meet me at the station?"

"I'm fixing Kendall dinner. Can I meet you later tonight?"

"Yep. Until then, don't approach him," he warns. "Text when you want to meet, and I'll head back. I'm on duty until 11."

"Gotcha. Later." I disconnect, unlocking my truck.

I remain alert as I snag the two grocery sacks and the small cooler from the cab of my truck and head inside KiKi's building.

35

JOHN

What's that smell? I scan the station, trying to find the source of the offensive odor.

"John." Meyer draws my attention back to his desk. "This is my partner, Officer Grey."

I nod to the patrolman rolling in his office chair to Meyer's desk.

"Start from the beginning," Meyer prompts.

"I guess I'm on high alert because I'm dating someone that's had a bad experience with a stocker over a year ago," I begin, hoping I won't sound paranoid. "About 5:00 this afternoon, I stepped off the elevator, seeing a guy in a hoodie hanging around outside her door. He wasn't ringing her bell or knocking, and his hood was up despite it being summer."

"So, this happened today at 5:00?" Grey asks while Meyer takes notes.

"Yes," I answer and continue. "I called out to him as I moved toward her door, and he darted for the stairs. Wanting to make sure Kendall was safe, I stayed at her apartment and didn't follow him."

"What is Kendall's last name and address?" Officer Grey seeks more details for their report.

I share Kendall's full name and address before moving on with my complaint, "She has a video doorbell, but she didn't know he was outside the door, so I didn't alarm her by asking to see it. At this point, I thought perhaps the guy had the wrong apartment number." I run my hands through my hair and attempt to release some stress as I blow out a long breath. "For the next 45 minutes, we took her dog to the dog park area then walked a couple of blocks before returning.

When we got back, I needed to get stuff out of my truck, and that's when I saw the same hoodie-guy by my truck. I sent Kendall into the building with her dog. When I moved toward my truck, I couldn't see the guy anywhere."

"What time are we talking about here?" Meyer questions.

"I'd say about 6:00," I shrug. "I didn't really look at the time. I just looked around for the guy then called you." I lift my chin toward Meyer.

"Look at your call log to see what time you made the call," Grey instructs.

Meyer and I both check our phones, finding the call happened at 6:08 p.m. Meyer quickly makes note of this in his notebook.

"Please take a screenshot of your call log to further document the date and time of that phone call in case we need the information in the future," Grey urges, and I comply. "Why did you wait until now to come into the station?"

"I planned to cook dinner for Kendall and thought I was making a mountain out of a molehill." Again, I shrug, brushing off my reasoning. "We ate dinner and watched a movie. When I left her place, I texted Meyer and drove straight here."

"Did you mention the guy in the hoodie to Kendall after spotting him a second time?" Meyer asks, tapping the end of his ball point pen against the legal pad on his desk.

I shake my head. "She still hasn't told me everything about her stalker, and she's still dealing with her trauma. She's agoraphobic; until last week, she'd only left her apartment three times in the last year and a half. With her new puppy, she now steps outside to the apartment complex's dog park, and tonight was her first walk. She has four locks on her door and an alarm system. She keeps her blinds and curtains closed; I don't want to worry her until I know for sure we have an issue."

Meyer nods, understanding. As my best friend, I've shared details from time to time about Kendall.

"I'm not sure if there's anything you can do," I speculate, frustrated. "It feels weird, and I'd never forgive myself if this was her stalker and he got to her again because I ignored some signs."

"Filing this complaint tonight will allow us to investigate," Grey informs. "We'll talk to management at both of your apartments. Usually, they'll cooperate by sharing security camera footage with us. You've given us two exact times to look at footage at her building. We may get lucky and capture his face on camera. I'll have the rookies screen footage at both your places for the past week to see if any hoodies appear. It's warm enough that any hoods up will seem out of place."

"We'll need a couple days," Meyer tells me. "I'll keep you posted of any progress, and you contact me immediately if you spot him again or if anything else happens."

I nod, still wondering if I've imagined the danger.

"I understand you're not wanting to upset Kendall, but if this guy was outside her door, she needs to be aware there is a potential danger anytime she leaves her apartment," Meyer encourages.

"I just can't tell her until I have proof." I shake my head, closing my eyes for a moment. "She already has high anxiety and panic attacks stemming from her trauma. I fear mentioning this will send her on a downward spiral. I really want to wait until I have more details."

"What do you know about her stalker?" Grey inquires. "I mean, we'll be able to pull up the old police reports, but what has she shared with you?"

I sigh deeply. "She won't tell me his name. She claims he's from a prominent and powerful family. She went on two dates with him before breaking it off. I guess he didn't handle that well. She pressed charges for kidnapping, assault, and stalking, but his family succeeded in getting all charges dropped."

Grey and Meyer share a look.

"We'll look into that and see if that guy has a link to the hoodie-guy from outside her door," Grey states. "We may need to view her doorbell video, too."

"That can be arranged by her parents, or if we find there is a danger, we'll tell her. She'll share the footage," I promise.

"Okay. We have what we need. We're both on tomorrow and will start investigating," Meyer vows.

"Thank you. I hope I'm not wasting your time," I worry.

"This is our job. You have every right to be cautious," Grey says. "Meyer will be in touch."

I walk from the station into the hot summer night. My eyes scan the parking lot, nearby roads, and vehicles parked on the streets. I need to be hyper vigilant; I must protect KiKi.

36

JOHN

I'm two hours into my shift the next morning when I glance at my vibrating cell phone.

> MEYER
> Need to talk
> @ station ASAP

As I read, the grocery store becomes a vacuum. I can't breathe; there is no air. I bend at the waist, my hand pinching my aching side.

Breathe. Breathe. I need to breathe.

A nearby checker asks if I am okay. I stand up straight, nodding in her direction. "Call another manager to the front now," I order.

I walk toward the nearby customer service counter. The clerk finishes with her customer before I speak. "I'm leaving. Family emergency."

She doesn't ask questions, and I don't offer details. I do the same with the manager when she approaches, then sprint through the automatic doors to the side of the store and the employee parking lot.

My hands tremble at the steering wheel of my truck. I decide I need to gather myself before I drive anywhere. I open my cell phone, shooting a text.

> **ME**
> On break
>
> U and Vishnu having fun?

While I wait for a return text that will signal KiKi is safe inside her apartment, I text Meyer back.

> **ME**
> On my way now
>
> **KIKI**
> We're being lazy. Text when you head here tonight

My eyes close, and I breathe a bit easier. Lazy means they're inside with no plans to leave the safety of her apartment-turned-fortress.

I place my phone in the cup holder, put the truck in gear, and head to the police station.

I decline Grey's proffered water, sitting nervously in the chair beside Meyer's desk. My eyes track Meyer, who is returning from the restroom.

"Hey," he greets once he's within earshot.

I can't speak, so I lift my chin in his direction.

"We caught him on camera," Meyer states, his expression solemn. "At your apartment, at the grocery store while you worked, and at her apartment."

I gulp, forcing down bile. It's worse than I imagined. My skin aches, goosebumps grow on my neck and arms, and my mouth goes dry. An oppressive fear I've never felt before overtakes me. My head pounds, and my ears ring. I force myself to focus on Grey and Meyer, sitting mere feet away from me.

I vaguely notice Grey raise his arm, motioning for someone to approach us.

"Hi, John," Patterson greets, his hand briefly squeezing my shoulder.

Why is Meyer's dad here? That's weird.

"Is there somewhere we can talk?" Patterson asks Grey.

I look to my best friend, unsure what to make of this new development. They can't leave me here. I haven't heard about the security videos they found; I want to see them. They haven't told me anything about the guy in the hoodie. I can't just sit here in the dark while they go talk to Patterson. I open my mouth to argue, but Meyer speaks before I do.

"Follow us," Meyer directs. "We'll tell you everything and share the video with you."

He extends his arm in my direction, herding me to follow Grey and Patterson. In my confusion, he must place his hand on my shoulder to guide me forward.

Sitting in a small interrogation room, the door and shades pulled shut, Meyer slides a bottle of water in front of me. "You're pale." He pushes the water an inch closer and orders, "Drink it."

My body follows the command, my mind still reeling. The cold water soothes my dry mouth but does little to wash the taste of bile down my throat.

"John, I've been brought in on your case," Patterson states, and his deep, authoritative voice cuts the fog in my brain. "An ongoing investigation in the FBI crossed paths with your complaint, so the FBI is taking over."

"What did you find...?" My voice breaks.

"We only searched back seven days on the surveillance cameras," Grey shares. "The guy in the hoodie appears daily on at least one camera at the apartments, the parking lots, and your work."

He pauses, allowing the weight of his statement to sink in.

"We caught his face on camera from several angles and instantly recognized him," Grey states.

"Kendall was right," Grey informs. "We know him and his family..."

"Who is he?" I growl.

"Son," Patterson warns, "we need to share information with you, but you have to remain calm. We have to do this by the book, or he'll get off on a technicality."

My nostrils flair with my heavy breaths, and anger pulses in my every cell. I nod, agreeing to rein in my emotions.

"His name is Zane McGuire," Grey states, eyes watching closely for my reaction as if I'm a ticking time bomb.

"The Senator's son?" I ask, already knowing the answer.

"He appears 17 times on video in proximity to Kendall and you," Grey informs, tapping on the tablet in front of him before turning it to face me.

I watch in horror as Zane enters Kendall's building, lurks outside her apartment door, uses the stairwell in my building, checks out the temp of the hood of my truck in the parking lot at work and at home… I close my eyes, shaking my head. I can't look; I don't want to see more.

Pretty party boy Zane-fucking-McGuire.

My stomach roils. I lunge to the nearby wastepaper basket, retching violently. The muscles in my stomach clench painfully for several long minutes as I dry heave and cough over the can.

I wipe my mouth on the back of my hand, slowly returning to my metal folding chair. "Sorry," I croak.

Grey raises his palm toward me as Meyer shakes his head.

"Can we get you some crackers or chips?" Patterson offers in his fatherly tone.

I shake my head, gulping from my water bottle to rinse the taste from my mouth.

"Now what?" I rasp, ready to take action.

"We'd like you to file a restraining order," Patterson encourages. "It's our hope he'll become enraged and break the order of protection so we can take him into custody."

"Done." I nod, slapping my palm against the table. "Is there anything we can do about the charges Kendall filed against him?"

Grey and Meyer's eyes dart to Patterson, who rubs his forehead with his hand, his elbow bent on the table.

"We're having trouble finding…" Meyer starts.

"There's no record of Kendall's complaint or charges and investigation of Zane," Patterson informs, anger on his face. "Of course, we found the media coverage but nothing at the precinct. We're still digging, and Internal Affairs is investigating the incident as a similar case has come to light."

"So, if I file a restraining order, what happens next?" I seek further explanation. "For me and for Kendall?"

"When you file, we'll deliver a notice to Mr. McGuire. We'll monitor your movements, watching for any instance he might break the order. If he does, we'll arrest him on site," Grey states, a glimmer of excitement in his eyes.

Perhaps they want to get this motherfucker as much as I do.

"We'll keep units on you at all times," Patterson promises. "If you're with Kendall, then we'll be watching her, too."

"For how long?" I ask.

Patterson sighs audibly. "I'm head of a task force investigating Senator McGuire and his son. We have the resources to investigate as long as it takes."

"He's been at Kendall's when I wasn't there," I state.

Meyer nods.

"But if I'm not with her, there are no units on her?" I seek confirmation.

Meyer nods.

If I go to work, Kendall's vulnerable. If I stay with her, she's protected. Mentally, I work through my schedule for the week, my vacation time available, and possible coverage for my shifts at the store. *Fuck it.* It's a no-brainer. Kendall's and my safety are more important than work right now. The store will understand.

"For now, let's file the restraining order," Grey prompts, and I nod.

"Do I tell Kendall?" I think out loud.

"That's up to you," Patterson answers. "While he's more active around your truck, work, and apartment, we do have video of him at her apartment. Add to that Kendall's account and the media coverage from a year ago… It's easy to believe Zane might be trying to get to her through you."

I nod. I'm not committing to telling her, but I'll take it into consideration. Perhaps I should discuss this with her parents first. They know her better than me.

37

JOHN

Halfway through *Thor*, our fifth movie in the Marvel Universe, KiKi's head rests on my shoulder, her body tucked close to my side. Then my cell phone rings. As it rests on the arm of the sofa opposite from KiKi, I turn my head, finding Meyer's text on the screen. I hide it from her view, opening the phone to read.

> MEYER
> He's in custody

The three words tell me all I need to know. Zane's an idiot. He breached the order, they arrested him, and KiKi is safe. I inhale then exhale a long, deep breath. Her arm, resting over my stomach, squeezes me in reaction.

"Everything okay?" she asks, looking up to me through her lashes, head still on my shoulder.

I kiss her forehead. *It's more than okay.*

"Meyer's texting," I tell her.

"Hmm," she murmurs, returning her attention to the movie.

My phone vibrates again. This time, it's a Google alert. I set them up for Zane, wanting to be aware of everything after my meeting at the station. It's a post from a local news station, reporting the arrest of Zane McGuire. It's public knowledge. *Hmm. When should I tell KiKi?*

In the months we've been together, she hasn't watched the news or read posts on her phone. She'll need to know but not right now.

KiKi

"I think *Thor*'s my favorite so far," I inform John as the credits roll and we wait to view the teaser for another movie tucked minutes ahead.

"I think it's Hemsworth you like, not the movie," he teases.

"Ahh… His brother's hotter than him," I blurt before I can think better of it.

"Luke or Liam?" John asks, not missing a beat.

"Liam," I respond. "I'm not familiar with Luke."

"He's the oldest brother, and he's in the other two Thor movies," he states.

I quirk my head at him. "You really are a Marvel geek."

"I never said I wasn't. And I now know to keep you away from all things involving Liam Hemsworth," John chuckles.

"Whatever." I blow him off. Liam might be in my top 10 fantasy men, but he's not in the top 5.

John's cell phone vibrates again, causing me to wonder what's really going on. He excuses himself, stating he has to take this, further piquing my curiosity. It's rare that he allows his phone to distract him when we're together. I hope it's not something wrong with his mom or Riley.

I look over the back of the sofa. John stands on the farthest side of my kitchen, using hushed tones in his conversation. In keeping my interest on John, I miss the teaser I anxiously wait to view.

John returns, his head downcast as he tucks his cell in his back pocket.

"I'm sorry. I need to go," he informs me, crouching behind the sofa.

I turn further on my cushion, allowing us to look eye-level at each other over the back of the couch.

"Is everything okay?" I ask for the second time tonight.

"Yeah. It's Meyer. He needs me." I see the anguish written on his face. He doesn't want to go.

"He's your best friend," I remind him. "If he needs you, you have to go." I'd drop everything if Kendall were still alive and needed me. "You'll let me know if I can do anything?"

A small smile graces his sexy-as-hell lips; it's impossible for me to fight the gravity of them. I lightly meld my mouth to his, my hand reaching out, tangling in his hair. In my kiss, I tell him how much I need him, I want him, and look forward to his return.

His hand upon my wrist, he tugs my hand from his hair, pulling his mouth from mine. His eyes at half mast, he pulls his lower lip between his teeth.

"You're making it hard to go," he whispers.

"Simply reminding you to hurry back." I flirt with a confidence I didn't know I had.

John

I'm barely in the door when Patterson begins. "Have you told Kendall yet?"

"No. I wanted to protect her as long as I could."

Meyer looks at Grey. Then they both look at Patterson. I sense something's up; I wait for the next shoe to drop.

"We believe Zane's taken another woman, and we need Kendall's help to find her," Patterson explains, his tone authoritative and urgent.

FFUUCCKK! Another woman's life torn apart by this douche? I can't protect her any longer.

"Umm…" I struggle with the information I'm about to share, but she may be able to help more than they know. "Let me call her folks and ask them to meet us in her parking lot," I offer, assuming they might help her handle the news we're about to share.

"Okay. Let's go," Meyer states.

"About that…" I hedge. "I need to tell you something about Kendall that might help your investigation."

The three men freeze.

"I need you to give me your word that you will not punish her for what I'm about to tell you." I'm met with furrowed brows and assessing eyes.

"Kendall's not in any trouble," Patterson assures me.

"She could be prosecuted for what I'm about to tell you," I share.

"I promise you we're not looking to charge her. We need her help," Patterson pleads. His stare assures me she's safe and I'm wasting time.

I hold up one finger. "Let me text her parents."

> **ME**
> Urgent! KiKi is safe
> Meet me in her parking lot
> I'm on my way there with police
> We need to update her on Zane

> **JAMES**
> On our way

"She's Kristen, not Kendall," I blurt. There's no way to sugarcoat it. "Her jaw was wired shut, she was in and out of consciousness for days, and she feared for her life. So, she didn't correct her parents and the medical staff when they assumed she was Kendall. She still hasn't told Anne and James."

"Whoa!" Meyer verbalizes what the others are thinking.

I take in the stunned expressions surrounding me. I give them a few moments to process my statement, before adding, "She likes to be called Kiki now."

Meyer nods, having heard me call Kristen this before.

"We won't pursue charges on multiple counts of fraud, forgery, identity theft, insurance fraud—any of it. We only ask for her help," Patterson promises.

"Okay. Let's go." I motion to the door.

38

JOHN

"Ready?" James asks on the elevator ride.

"I'm ready for it to be over," Anne answers. "He's in jail. This time, we'll make it stick."

"John?" James looks to me from his side of the elevator car.

I shake my head. Nothing can prepare me for KiKi's reaction. A million scenarios play like movies in my mind. As much as Zane's stalking bothers me, I can't fathom living through her trauma then facing the danger of him again. She's worked so hard to regain a sense of control in her life, to let me in, to trust me, and to venture out of her apartment. I pray this will not set her back. I won't lose her.

"How exactly shall we handle this?" I ask.

"We will follow your lead," Patterson answers.

I'm not sure whose lead he means. I look from Meyer to Anne and then to James. His shrug is the only answer I get. I shake my head as the elevator pings and the doors open.

"I'll go in first," I announce, stepping into the hallway. Hearing no arguments, I approach KiKi's door, ringing her doorbell.

I hear Vishnu bark twice followed by KiKi's commands to stop. It seems like an eternity as I stand there, waiting on her to see it's me, disarm the alarm, and open the four locks then the door.

"You're back," she greets, smile upon her face and Vishnu at her side.

"May we come in?" I ask, my arm motioning to the five people following me.

"What's this?" she asks, worry in her voice.

She crosses her arms over her chest; I can see her retreating. I wrap my arms around her, hugging her tightly to my chest. My mouth by her ear, I whisper, "You're safe. I promise." I place a soft kiss on her ear. "I love you. You're gonna want to hear this."

Pulling away, I find tears in her eyes and her lower lip trembling. My heart shatters into a million pieces at the sight.

"I'm Special Agent Patterson with the FBI." He flashes his badge to her. "These men are Officer Grey and…"

"I know Meyer," KiKi interrupts, giving a tiny wave in his direction.

"Come take a seat," James urges, his hands on the back of a chair at her table.

She looks from him to me. When I nod, she sits, and Anne, Patterson, and I do the same. James stands behind Anne while Grey and Meyer lean against the nearby kitchen counter. KiKi nervously fidgets, her hands on the table in front of her.

"Just tell me already," she demands, voice shaky.

"Zane's been arrested," I inform. "He's in jail."

Her eyes dart from mine to Patterson to Meyer, then to Anne and James. When her eyes return to mine, I see a twinkle of hope through her unshed tears. Her mouth opens and closes, but no words escape.

Assuming she wants answers, I help to start the conversation. "He was arrested for violating a restraining order I brought against him. I noticed a stranger wearing a hoodie with the hood up, several times. When I noticed him everywhere I went, I sought Meyer's help."

She wipes away her tears on the back of her hand. I look at James and Anne; when they don't jump in, I nod toward Patterson to take over.

"We've been investigating the McGuire family for some time," Patterson informs. "When John filed his complaint and local law enforcement identified the guy in the hoodie as Zane McGuire, our agency began a joint effort with the Des Moines P.D."

Kiki forces herself to breathe in and out, in and out, as I share the details of my sightings of the "hoodie guy". I see the fear growing within her as she realizes she didn't pay attention to her surroundings.

I look over my shoulder, motioning toward the two local officers. "Our investigation took a turn when the news station broadcast the story." I look back to KiKi. "Parents of a missing girl, Penelope James, from Rock Island, Illinois, contacted local law enforcement, claiming their daughter was last seen with Zane McGuire."

While the agent speaks, KiKi pulls her feet into her chair, her knees to her chest, her arms wrapped tightly around them. She rests her forehead on her knees,

Uncaged

her face hidden. I reach my arm around her, slowly rubbing her back, unable to witness her pain at hearing all of this.

"We're here today because we need your help," Patterson continues, causing KiKi to lift her head. "John shared your secret with us and gave us permission to speak in front of your parents. Is that okay with you?" She nods, and he continues. "Let me start by saying this: we know you're Kristen and have no interest in pursuing the issue of your impersonation of Kendall."

39

KIKI

I stare in horror as James' eyes widen, and he takes two steps back; Anne's hand flies to her mouth, a high-pitched sob escaping, her eyes bulging, color draining from her face.

"I'm sss…" I plead. "I'm so, so sorry." I look in their direction, barely seeing them through the tears clouding my eyes. "I…I…" I stutter as I wipe my tears.

Anne rapidly blinks while many emotions sweep across her face. James remains speechless, his warm, tear-filled eyes on mine, nodding his head. I bite my lips, holding in more apologies. Based on his reaction, James suspected my true identity. He's stunned by Patterson's announcement, though not as surprised as Anne appears.

"I understand this revelation is shocking," Patterson states. "However, time is Penelope's enemy. I need us to move on and for you to deal with Kristen's identity later."

James returns to Anne's chair, placing his palms on her shoulders. She gazes up at him before looking at me. She forces a smile.

"Kristen," Anne's shaky voice, addresses me, "you *are* our daughter. We love you and always will." She extends her arm toward me. I allow her hand to grasp mine.

"I'll explain later," I attempt to apologize.

John

Patterson continues, "As we investigated the incident and the cover-up by law enforcement, we understood your need to assume the identity to protect yourself. We don't have time to dwell on it; a 17-year-old girl needs our help. We'd like for you to tell us everything you remember from your kidnapping and escape. It's our hope that it will help us in our search for Penelope James."

Meyer steps up to the table. "She was last seen on surveillance footage at a truck stop on I-80, climbing back into a vehicle with Zane McGuire then pulling onto west-bound I-80. He might have brought her all the way to Des Moines."

"Now, we need to hear your story," Patterson urges.

While she still hugs her knees, KiKi's eyes look at me. I take her hand in mine, hoping to support her while she drudges up the painful memories she's buried.

KiKi nods.

"John..." Her tiny voice is barely audible. "John, please go get the large box from under my bed," she commands.

I rise without hesitation, following her directions. My mind reels with the possible contents of this box. She keeps it hidden, tucked away beneath her as she sleeps each night. I shudder to think of her reasons for choosing this location. I pull out the box, noting no dust upon its top while I carry it to the table. As I approach, KiKi drops her feet to the floor and reaches for the box, flipping the flaps open, then proceeds to dump its contents onto the table.

I stare as sketch after sketch falls. From where I stand, I can't make out the subject of each. However, the dark shadows hint to the horror recorded on every one.

Patterson, Grey, and Meyer silently take sketch after sketch in hand. KiKi's eyes look up to me through her dark, wet lashes. I want to smile in support, but now is not the time for smiles. Instead, I nod. Her eyes remain locked on mine as she speaks. "Memories flash, and I sketch them. I'm not sure if they'll help."

Patterson nods. "They do. Can you tell us your story now?"

"It's not a story," KiKi bites. "I'm sorry." She runs her fingers through her long hair, holding it in a makeshift ponytail at the back of her head.

I snag a black hair tie from one of the kitchen cabinet knobs, handing it to her as I resume my seat at her side. I notice a warm thank you in her eyes.

Securing her hair with the elastic, she continues. "Kendall..." Her voice cracks, so she clears her throat. "We attended a party at the Tau Kappa Epsilon frat house on the Drake campus. Zane was there. We hid in the bathroom while some frat guys escorted him from the property."

She shakes her head, eyes looking at me again. I hope, in looking at me, she finds the strength she needs to get through this.

"Something about him didn't sit right with me," she shares. "I broke it off after two dates, and he didn't like that. After he left, we danced a bit with a frat guy Kendall liked. The party was crowded. I was hot and went out on the back porch to get some air. One minute, I saw Zane. The next, I woke in a strange room." She shivers, a chill creeping up her spine at the memory.

She reaches into the pile of papers, pulling three sketches to the top, displaying them for the officers. "The walls were wooden, not flat, like a cabin." She points to the drawings as she speaks. "It contained a bed, a desk, books, a bucket with a lid, a speaker, and a tanning bed. I found a door hidden in the wall with no handle.

"I didn't see him for the first couple of days. He spoke to me through a speaker and watched me with a small camera mounted in one corner near the ceiling. He left me water but no food. In order to earn food, I had to follow his instructions." She exhales a heavy breath, passing more sketches to Patterson. "I didn't comply until I couldn't take the hunger anymore. He expected me to tan every day for 10 minutes to keep what he called 'my healthy glow.'" She cringes at the memory.

While I continue to rub circles on her back, my free hand forms a fist at my side, my fingernails biting into my palm. It takes concentration to temper my rage. She needs my support and understanding, not for me to react in anger.

"He made me brush my hair for 10 minutes at a time, change into the sundresses and silk pajamas he furnished, and wash myself as he watched in order to earn meals." She picks at the cuticles of her left hand, not making eye contact. "I lost track of time. With no windows, I couldn't know if it was day or night. And the satellite radio he left on for me while he was away didn't tell me the time, have rush hour traffic reports, or news reports. It seemed he came only once per day for a couple of hours." She shrugs. "Or he only spoke to me for a couple of hours. For all I know, he watched me 24/7."

"When he spoke to you," Patterson interrupts, "did you hear anything in the background? When he gave you food, what could you see on the other side of the door?"

KiKi sighs then shakes her head. She balls her hands into fists, preparing to continue. "After a couple of meals, he started…" She bites her lips between her teeth, a steady stream of tears trailing down her cheeks.

"He made me drink juice in front of him with my meal. It made my head swim; I tried to fight it, but I couldn't stay awake." She shakes her head as this memory replays in her mind. "I have flashes of him on top..."

Anne gasps, hand flying to mouth.

James murmurs into her ear; she nods then fans her face.

My stomach is a concrete block, the bile in my throat burns, and Hulk-like rage threatens to escape me. He... He... She confirmed my worst fears about her trauma. He assaulted her repeatedly. The son-of-a-bitch had better hope I never get my hands on him.

"Let's move on to your escape," Patterson redirects.

I'm thankful he stopped her. My mind already manifests horrible scenarios. I don't need to hear more about how Zane raped her; those are details for her therapist.

"Hours after he left one night, I used a spoon to pop the pins out of the door hinges to escape." She points to sketches of her escape. "On the other side of the door, I ran up a long, narrow, wooden staircase. There were no lights, and it was cool; it was a basement or a cellar. I ran through a small old room with one window near the front door that led to outside. That door was heavy. I remember struggling to open it."

"Once outside, were there any lights, houses, buildings, or trees?" Patterson prompts.

Again, she shakes her head. "The only light was the moon—no houses and no trees. There wasn't even a road leading to it. It was more like a path, like the road hadn't been used for decades. I ran down the path. Oh, there were weeds all around—waist-high weeds."

Grey and Meyer continue to browse the sketches while Patterson takes notes. I follow KiKi's downcast eyes. She's wiggling her toes on the floor.

"The ground hurt my bare feet, but I had to run. I had to escape before he returned." She gulps audibly, still wriggling her toes. With her eyes closed tightly, she continues, "The path met a gravel road. I turned...left, running on the sharp rocks. There were no lights. I'm not sure how far I ran. My lungs and thighs burned, and my feet screamed for me to stop. The gravel road met a paved road. I saw a light, so I ran...right. After maybe a mile or two, I saw lights ahead. I thought I heard a vehicle, so I ran as fast as I could."

I cease caressing her back, choosing to hold her hand in mine. She opens her eyes, looking at me before continuing.

"At the edge of the little town was an old gas station. It wasn't opened, but it had outdoor lights on and sat right off the four-lane highway. I hid in the shadows until I saw headlights approaching. I ran onto the side of the road, waving my arms in front of an approaching truck." She squeezes my hand for a moment.

"An old man got out, and I begged to use his cell phone. He offered to give me a ride, but all I wanted was to talk to Kendall." Tears fill her eyes, and her breaths become shallow.

"I should have had him drive me to a police station. I should have dialed 911," she sobs, shaking her head. "I needed to hear Kendall's voice, though. I called her, begging her to pick me up. The old man told me I was at the gas station on the edge of Hartford; I relayed this information to Kendall, telling her I would hide, and I asked her to honk three times when she arrived. I was stupid…"

"You did what you had to in the moment to survive," Anne explains. "You called the person you trusted most in the world. You can't be blamed for that."

James' hands squeeze his wife's shoulders in support.

"The old guy gave me directions to his house; down the road he'd come from then two blocks to the left. He said the porch light was on, and a key was under the mat. I should have hidden at his house. I should have waited hours before I called Kendall…"

KiKi

I shake my head, squeezing my eyes tightly shut. *I knew of the danger when I called her and begged her to pick me up. Nothing I ever do can make up for the fallout from that night. She died not knowing. Because I didn't share, she didn't know how much danger I—we—were in. She died not knowing what she was rescuing me from.*

Patterson reaches his arm across the table, covering one of my hands with his. "There is no one right reaction in your situation. You couldn't control the outside factors. But by helping us, you may be able to help Penelope James. Zane's refusing to talk. She may be alone in that same room with no food or water unless we find her."

Through my tears, I nod, taking in a shuttering breath. "Kendall drove us back towards Des Moines." I look toward Kendall's parents. "She saw his lights approaching quickly in the rearview mirror. She tried to speed up, but there was nowhere to hide and nothing she could do."

James kneels between Anne and me, facing me. "It *was not* your fault. It was *all* Zane. We know that, and we don't blame you. Please don't blame yourself."

Uncaged

I wrap my arms over his shoulders, sobbing loudly during the embrace. The others look on uncomfortably for several long moments.

Finally, Patterson speaks. "This helps," he says, closing his notebook and tapping on his cell phone. "Would you be willing to ride with me to Hartford? As we localize our search from there, you may see something that jogs your memory. Even a little detail might help us find Penelope."

I look from James to John; tears fill my eyes. My heart pounds wildly, and fear pulses in every cell.

"We'll ride with you," John promises. "You're ready for this. You can do this." He squeezes my hand, passing his strength to me.

I nod infinitesimally.

"We need to move fast," Patterson instructs.

Tucking my anxiety meds into Anne's pocket, Anne and James assist me with shoes. John remains close, keeping in constant contact. He's scared of what tonight might bring; he can't imagine… No one can imagine the degree of fear I'm experiencing right now.

40

JOHN

KiKi's head leans heavily on my shoulder as we ride in the back seat of Patterson's vehicle on the way to Hartford.

I cradle her tightly against my side, while inside, I scream in rage—inside, I weep for her pain.

Hearing her traumatic story wasn't a surprise. I assumed he'd assaulted Kristen, yet the words still slapped me in the face. While I love the woman she's become, I mourn the woman she was.

"Hey," KiKi whispers.

I turn my gaze from the window beside me down to her.

"Are you okay?" she inquires.

Are you okay? Am I okay? Is she really worried about me right now?

"Kiki, I'm worried for you," I murmur, my lips brushing her forehead. "Please don't worry about me." I place a peck on her forehead. "I love you," I whisper, squeezing her.

"I'm okay," she lies.

"No, you're not, but you will be," I promise. "We're gonna make sure you get through tonight, then tomorrow, then the next day…"

She nods against my shoulder.

My heart bleeds for her while my love for her grows exponentially.

KiKi

It's a bone-chilling, eerie cold. It's night, just as it was the last time I stood at this gas station. However, it's a clear summer night, and the moon is bright. I wrap my arms over my chest, rubbing my arms for warmth.

"Cold?" John asks, wrapping his arms around me, tucking me tightly against his hard chest.

"It's this place," I murmur, my voice failing me.

"I'm astounded by you," John confesses, at a loss for words. "I understand this is hard; you're doing great. I love you so much."

My breath catches; I look up at him. His warm, brown eyes soothe my soul. He's a calming balm; he's the yin to my yang. I learn more each day, and I'm blessed that he rang my bell with my grocery delivery all those months ago. I have no doubt Kendall had something to do with it.

A car horn honks into the night, and all law enforcement eyes turn with mine, looking in the direction from which the sound emitted. It's a car, far away from all of the law enforcement gathered. A smile slips onto my face. It's Kendall; it's a sign. She's taking credit for John at my door.

"Windmill!" I shout.

John pulls his head back, trying to understand me.

"There's a windmill near the house!" Excitement floods my system as I believe this is a clue. "John, a windmill!"

"There's Patterson." John points to our right, grabbing my hand, pulling me towards him.

"There's a windmill by the house!" I shout within earshot of him.

Patterson takes notice, nods in our direction, then speaks into his handheld, sharing this information with all search parties. He takes three steps, closing the distance between us.

"Kiki," he says, eyes upon mine, "would you mind retracing your steps with me?"

Adrenaline pulsing through every part of me, I agree. I want to help Penelope. I want my pain to help another.

"I'm by your side," John states, taking my hand.

Over an hour passes as officers scurry around the pop-up tent we sit under in the faint light of a lantern. I hear a car engine start noisily. *That's familiar.* I turn my ear toward the engine's roar.

Standing from my chair, I crane my neck, looking for Patterson, Grey, or Meyer. John rises beside me, hand on the small of my back.

"What?" he asks.

"I think I remember a noisy engine on the ground beside the house when I ran away. It laid on the ground and smelled like oil," I share as more of the memory plays in my mind.

James brings nearby agents in FBI windbreakers over, and I repeat what I believe to be a memory.

"And at the road, there was a chain blocking the drive with a metal sign that said 'No Trespassing.' I had to crawl under it at the blacktop," I share, adrenaline pulsing within me.

These two clues should narrow down the properties to search. The sign and chain by the main road should be easy to see.

The agents excuse themselves, immediately relaying the information into their earpieces. When I turn to take my seat, Anne wraps me in a tight hug.

"We're proud of you," she murmurs near my ear. "After all you've been through, reliving it to save this girl... I'm amazed by your fortitude."

John

Walking our way, Patterson talks into his cell phone as he motions for Grey and Meyer to come over. Disconnecting his call, he prompts Grey to escort all of us back to Kristen's apartment. KiKi begins to argue, but Meyer promises he'll update us soon.

As Grey whisks us toward his SUV, I hear Patterson order everyone to follow him. They have GPS coordinates of the abandoned house.

We spend the next two hours entertaining Vishnu under the fairy lights on

KiKi's patio. This puppy plays hard right up to when he drops for sleep. Anne and KiKi share a bottle of white wine while James and I enjoy beer.

It doesn't escape me that KiKi keeps glancing at her apartment door. Having first-hand knowledge of the horrors of his victims, I'm sure she's anxious for news. I place my free hand on hers. She turns it, twining her fingers in mine, giving my hand a brief squeeze.

Startled, I pull my vibrating phone from my back pocket.

MEYER
On my way up

ME
I'll get door

"Meyer is on his way up in the elevator," I share with the group. When KiKi makes a move to rise, I place my hand upon her shoulder, holding her in place. "I'll get the door."

I greet Meyer, ushering him to follow me to the patio.

"Any news?" James wastes no time, cutting to what we all want to know.

Meyer's wide smile tells us he brings good news. "We found Penelope!" he announces, causing us all to cheer. "Kiki, your help made it happen."

KiKi opens and closes her mouth, attempting to speak. I wrap her in a hug, placing a kiss upon her forehead. She presses her palm against my chest, freeing herself and turning to face Meyer.

"Did he ra...rape her?" she asks, her voice breaking.

Meyer glances at me, uncomfortable, before responding. "No. She'd only been there three days. She described the beginning identical to what you described."

Happy tears trail down her cheeks. She's been through so much today—so much in the past two years. It's a true testament to her strength that she's standing before us.

Kiki

. . .

It's over. Over! An audible sigh escapes, and a heavy weight lifts from me. I breathe easier. This time Zane's father can't make the charges disappear, he can't buy off the officers, his money and power mean nothing now. Two kidnappings, the car accident, and Kendall's death…he's going away this time—I'll do everything in my power to see to it.

EPILOGUE

KiKi—One Year Later

"Riley's asleep," I announce emerging from the hallway, finding John loading the dishwasher, while visiting to his mother perched across the room in her recliner.

"Dawn, are you ready for your next pain pill?" I stand in the open area between the living room and the kitchen. "Looks like you need more water, too," I note.

Exhausted and in pain, Dawn nods. Her smile shines with only half its normal brightness. It has been two months since she tripped over Riley's toy, breaking her hip. I still believe her fall was a blessing. In the hospital for her hip surgery, her physicians found abnormalities which led them to diagnose her with Stage II Colon Cancer. She swears she was asymptomatic. Who knows how much it might have spread if she hadn't broken her hip.

She's a trooper; undergoing radiation treatments and demanding to spend most of her days in her recliner surrounded by her family and friends, instead of in bed.

When I extend her next dose of medication, Dawn grasps my hand in hers, eyes locking on mine. "Thank you for giving up everything to care for me," her voice cracks, heavy with emotion and exhaustion.

I squat at the side of her chair, keeping my eyes on hers. "I've told you before, I love it here. It was time I started living again, and I couldn't do it in the apartment

I wasted so much time hiding in." I place my free hand on her cheek. "I was ready. I needed to find a purpose. I love your family…"

"We're your family," she corrects.

I nod, tears welling. "I'm happy to help, I love playing with Riley." I chuckle. "Heck, even Vishnu loves your house and fenced in backyard."

"I can't wait for you to officially join the family," she smiles.

My eyes closed, I shake my head, smiling. "About that…"

Dawns tired eyes, brighten. Now, I have her full attention.

"I wanted to ask if maybe we could plan a small ceremony in your yard before the end of summer…"

"Yes!" she cheers, while she begins to sit her recliner upright.

"Shh!" I admonish. "I haven't brought it up to John yet."

Dawn mimes zipping her lips tight. I love the big smile and sparkles in her eyes. I knew finally planning our wedding would excite her.

"What are you two whispering about in here?" John asks, startling me as he draws near.

"Girl talk," Dawn informs her son. "Now, you go walk the dog. We need our privacy."

Always a good son, he follows her instruction.

"Do you have a date in mind?" She asks as soon as the front door closes.

I shake my head. "I wanted to chat with you first. Then I figured John and I could check his work schedule. After that, I'm not even sure where to begin," I confess.

"After my treatment tomorrow, let's sit down with our calendars," Dawn encourages. "I'll make a wedding list, and we will begin planning."

"There's no rush," I remind her. "We can wait until you feel better later in the week…"

"Nonsense," Dawn chides. "The two of you put your lives on hold for Riley and me. It's time we get back to planning your wedding. There's no reason I can't make a list and conduct some online research as I sit in this chair every day. I need something to look forward to."

I know she does; that's why I brought up this idea in the first place. Dawn was over the moon when John surprised me with an engagement ring for Christmas. In the first two months of the year, she held five wedding planning meetings with Anne and me. We were contacting wedding venues the end of March when she turned abruptly at the kitchen island, falling over Riley's riding toy.

While John saw to his mom at the hospital, Vishnu and I packed our bags, moving into John's old room to care for Riley, and I never moved back. It surprised me how at home I immediately felt in Dawn's home. After my time in seclusion, I never expected to feel safe or live anywhere else. With Zane in prison, Dawn's security system, complete with cameras, and her police officer neighbor are all I need to feel secure.

John and I put our wedding planning on hold, focusing on Riley and Dawn. I already feel a part of his family; I don't need a wedding to feel loved. Honestly, I'd much rather elope in front of the Justice of the Peace than wear a wedding gown, standing in front of a group of people exchanging our vows. I couldn't do that to Anne and Dawn; they can't wait to plan and hold the ceremony.

In the privacy of our room downstairs and sitting on the patio before bed, John and I talk about how lucky we are. We count our blessings nearly every day. Dawn's cancer diagnosis put everything in perspective. We enjoy the little, every day things in our life. We're thankful for the grocery error that brought him to my door and every moment we've shared since that day.

I still have my moments, and sometimes have bad days. With the continued help of my therapist, I enjoy my life beyond my apartment. I'm taking fewer medications and speak to my therapist once a month, instead of weekly. I'm in love with the most amazing man on the planet. He's patient and values his family. I can't wait to start a family of our own. My time with Riley each day, stirs my maternal side.

I'm giddy like a middle-school girl. I kept one secret from Dawn tonight. When I bring up the idea of planning a small wedding in the back yard a few months from now, I'm also going to suggest we stop using birth control and start creating our family. I'm ninety-nine-point-nine percent sure I know how John will respond, and that excites me more with each passing minute.

As I help Dawn to the bathroom and then to bed, I'm sure she sees my excitement is due to the wedding conversation we shared. There'd be no getting her into bed if she knew the rest. Her oncologists are encouraged by her treatments and progress. I look forward to her health improving with each passing day and the return of her million-watt smile and boisterous personality. Our wedding and potential children will ensure she resides on cloud nine.

Dawn and I exchange our good nights, and I tidy up Riley's play area while I anxiously wait for my man to return from walking my dog. My hand freezes in midair at the sound of footsteps draw near. Here we go…

The End

I hope you'll look for all 7 stories
in 7 Deadly Sins Series of stand-alone books available now.

Help other readers find this book and give me a giant author hug—
please consider leaving a review on Amazon, Goodreads, and BookBub—
a few words mean so much.

Check out my Pinterest Boards for my inspirations
for characters, settings, and recipes.
(Link on following pages.)

ALSO BY HALEY RHOADES

Ladies of the Links Series-

Ladies of Links #1 -- Gibson, Ladies of the Links #2 -- Christy, Ladies of the Links #3 – Brooks, Ladies of the Links #4 – Kirby, Ladies of the Links #5 -- Morgan

Boxers or Briefs

The Locals Series-

Tailgates & Truck Dates, Tailgates & Heartaches, Tailgates & First Dates, Tailgates & Twists of Fate

The 7 Deadly Sins Series-

Unbreakable, Unraveled, Unleashed,

Unexpected, Uncaged, Unmasked, Unhinged

Third Wheel

The Surrogate Series-

The Proposal, The Deed, The Confession

Trivia Page

1. The character Dawn is based on my best friend. During a car ride, I explained my next series of books and she suggested I have one random character that appears in each book. Thus, I named the character after her and awarded her Dawn's positive spirit. In 2015 she was diagnosed with stage IV colon cancer. They found it late and it had spread throughout her body. She had chemotherapy every two weeks for 8 years. With all of this she was still a ray of sunshine and lifted others, like me, up. Her strength and selflessness inspire me to try and improve myself. She was the most upbeat and positive woman I know. I absolutely loved her laugh.
2. **Envy:** The first and last names of *ALL* characters in Unbreakable, 7 Deadly Sins: Envy are the names of vice presidents of the United States. (Except Chinook the dog.)
3. **Sloth:** Character names in this book are those of famous authors like: Kristen Ashley, Suzanne Collins, Kendall Ryan, HM Ward, Jamie McGuire, Zane Grey, Jill Shalvis, Stephen King, Anne Rice, Penelope Ward, James Patterson, Stephenie Meyer, Colleen Hoover, and John Grisham.
4. **Gluttony:** All character first and last names in this book are those of NFL Quarterbacks. (Except Denali & Snoopy the dogs)
5. **Greed:** The first and last names of *ALL* characters in this book are the names of world leaders. (Except Hagrid & Bocephus the dog.) Condoleezza Rice, Christina Fernandez de Kirchner, Edith Cresson, Elizabeth Queen, Hanna Suchocka, Helen Clark, Madeleine Albright, Michelle Bachelet, Sylvie Kinigi, Daniel Ortega, Felipe Calderon, Fredrik Reinfeldt, Gordon Brown, Hugo Chavez, Nelson Mandela, Omar Bongo, Stephen Harper, Winston Churchill
6. **Sloth:** The dog's name, Vishnu, is a principal deity of Hinduism. Vishnu is the Preserver, the guardian of people, he protects the order of things, and he fights demons to maintain cosmic harmony.
7. What are the seven deadly sins? The 7 cardinal sins, also called 7 deadly sins, are transgressions that are fatal to spiritual progress within Christian teachings. They include envy, gluttony, greed, anger or wrath, sloth, and pride. They are the converse of the 7 heavenly virtues.
8. My pen name is a combination of 2 of my paternal great-grandmothers' maiden names. (Haley and Rhoades)

ABOUT THE AUTHOR

Haley Rhoades's writing is another bucket-list item coming to fruition, just like meeting Stephen Tyler, Ozzie Smith, and skydiving. As she continues to write contemporary romance, she also writes sweet romance and young adult books under the name Brooklyn Bailey, as well as children's books under the name Gretchen Stephens. She plans to complete her remaining bucket-list items, including ghost-hunting, storm-chasing, and bungee jumping. She is a Netflix-binging, Converse-wearing, avidly-reading, traveling geek.

A team player, Haley thrived as her spouse's career moved the family of four, fifteen times to three states. One move occurred eleven days after a C-section. Now living the retirement life, with two adult sons, Haley copes with her empty nest by writing and spoiling Nala, her Pomsky. A fly on the wall might laugh as she talks aloud to her fur-baby all day long.

Haley's under five-foot, fun-size stature houses a full-size attitude. Her uber-competitiveness in all things entertains, frustrates, and challenges family and friends. Not one to shy away from a dare, she faces the consequences of a lost bet no matter the humiliation. Her fierce loyalty extends from family, to friends, to sports teams.

Haley's guilty pleasures are Lifetime and Hallmark movies. Her other loves include all things peanut butter, *Star Wars*, mathematics, and travel. Past day jobs vary tremendously from a radio-station DJ, to an elementary special-education para-professional, to a YMCA sports director, to a retail store accounting department, and finally a high school mathematics teacher.

Haley resides with her husband and fur-baby in the Des Moines area. This Missouri-born girl enjoys the diversity the Midwest offers.

Reach out on Facebook, Twitter, Instagram, or her website...she would love to connect with her readers.

- amazon.com/author/haleyrhoades
- goodreads.com/haleyrhoadesauthor
- bookbub.com/authors/haley-rhoades
- tiktok.com/@haleyrhoadesauthor
- instagram.com/haleyrhoadesauthor
- facebook.com/AuthorHaleyRhoades
- twitter.com/HaleyRhoadesBks
- pinterest.com/haleyrhoadesaut
- linkedin.com/in/haleyrhoadesauthor
- youtube.com/@haleyrhoadesbrooklynbaileyauth
- patreon.com/ginghamfrog

Made in the USA
Monee, IL
05 February 2025

11649546R10423